KU-525-089

HAVISHAM

by the same author

Winter Journey
Watching Mrs Gordon
A Long Weekend with Marcel Proust
Sandmouth People
A Woman of Judah
Paris
Penelope's Hat
Bluette
Underwood and After
Walking my Mistress in Deauville
The Sun on the Wall
The Lantern Bearers
Permanent Violet
Time in Carnbeg
Unwritten Secrets

HAVISHAM

A Novel

RONALD FRAME

faber and faber

First published in this edition in 2012
by Faber and Faber Limited
Bloomsbury House
74–77 Great Russell Street
London WC1B 3DA

Typeset by Faber and Faber Ltd

Printed and bound by CPI Group (UK) Ltd, Croydon, CR0 4YY

A CIP record for this book
is available from the British Library

ISBN 978–0–571–28828–1

2 4 6 8 10 9 7 5 3 1

I.M.

Alexander Donaldson Frame

1922–2011

Love is in the one who loves,
not in the one who is loved.

PLATO

Prologue

Four loud blows on the front door.

I stood waiting at the foot of the staircase as the door was opened.

The light from the candles fell upon their faces. Mr Jaggers's, large and London-pale and mapped with a blue afternoon beard. A nursemaid's, pink with excitement after listening on the journey down to Mr Jaggers's discreet account of me – my wealth, my eccentric mode of life, my famous pride and prickliness.

And the third face. The child's. She was standing a few paces behind the nursemaid; she was keeping back, but leaned over sharply to see between the two adults. She looked forward, into the house, across the hall's black and white floor tiles.

When she was brought inside, I studied her, from my vantage-point on the second tread. Her complexion was a little tawny, as I had been led to expect. She had raven hair, which was more of the gypsy in her, but her eyes were blue, from the English father.

Blue, silvery-blue, and wide open, staring up at me. At where I stood, wearing the wedding dress I should have been married in.

I lifted my hand from the banister rail and moved to the step beneath.

Immediately the child turned away. She raised her shoulder as if to protect herself, and hid behind the nursemaid's skirts. The woman smiled a nervous apology.

I retreated, one step up, then another.

'Too much light,' I said. 'That's all.'

The child's eyes rested on my bride's slippers. White satin originally, but soiled after these many months of wear.

'The light dazzles her,' I said. 'She will adjust. She only needs to get her bearings.'

I

YOUNG CATHERINE

Chapter One

I killed my mother.

I had turned round in the womb, and the surgeon needed to cut her open to let me out. He couldn't staunch her, and by the end of that evening she had bled to death.

My father draped the public rooms of Satis House in dust sheets. The chandeliers were left in situ, but wrapped in calico bags. The shutters were closed completely across some windows, and part-drawn at others.

My first days were lived out in a hush of respectfully lowered voices as a procession of folk came to offer their condolences.

My eyes became accustomed to the half-light.

One evening several new candles were set in one of the chandeliers. My mother's clavecin was uncovered, and someone played it again – notwithstanding that it was out of tune – and that was the point at which the house stopped being a sepulchre and was slowly brought back to life.

❧

It was the first word I remember *seeing*.

HAVISHAM.

Painted in green letters on the sooty brick of the brewhouse wall.

Fat letters. Each one had its own character.

Comfortable spreading 'H'. Angular, proud 'A'. Welcoming, open 'V'. The unforthcoming sentinel 'I'. 'S', a show-off, not altogether to be trusted. The squat and briefly indecisive, then reassuring 'M'.

The name was up there even in the dark. In the morning it was the first thing I would look for from the house windows, to check that the wind hadn't made off with our identity in the night or the slanting estuary rain washed the brickwork clean.

ꟹ

Jehosophat Havisham, otherwise known as Joseph Havisham, son of Matthias.

Havisham's was the largest of several brewers in the town. Over the years we had bought out a number of smaller breweries and their outlets, but my father had preferred to concentrate production in our own (extended) works. He continued *his* father's programme of tying in the vending sites, acquiring ownership outright or making loans to the publicans who stocked our beer.

Everyone in North Kent knew who we were. Approaching the town on the London road, the eye was drawn first to the tower of the cathedral and then, some moments later, to the name HAVISHAM so boldly stated on the old brick.

We were to be found on Crow Lane.

The brewery was on one side of the big cobbled yard, and our home on the other.

Satis House was Elizabethan, and took the shape of an E, with later addings-on. The maids would play a game, counting in their heads the rooms they had to clean, and never agreeing on a total: between twenty-five and thirty.

Once the famous Pepys had strolled by, and ventured into the Cherry Garden. There he came upon a doltish shopkeeper and his pretty daughter, and the great man 'did kiss her'.

My father slept in the King's Room, which was the chamber provided for Charles II following his sojourn in France, in 1660.

The staircase had been made broader to accommodate the Merry Monarch as his manservants manoeuvred him upstairs and down. A second, steeper flight was built behind for the servants.

I grew up with the rich aroma of hops and the potent fumes from the fermenting rooms in my nostrils, filling my head until I failed to notice. I must have been in a state of perpetual mild intoxication.

I heard, but came not to hear, the din of the place. Casks being rolled across the cobbles, chaff-cutting, bottle-washing, racking, wood being tossed into the kiln fires. Carts rumbled in and out all day long.

The labourers had Herculean muscles. Unloading the sacks of malt and raising them on creaky pulleys; mashing the ground malt; slopping out the containers and vats; drawing into butts; pounding the extraneous yeast; always rolling those barrels from the brewhouse to the storehouse, and loading them on to the drays.

Heat, flames, steam, the dust clouds from the hops, the heady atmosphere of fermentation and money being made.

I was told by my father that the brewery was a parlous place for a little girl, and I should keep my distance. The hoists, the traps, those carts passing in and out; the horses were chosen for their strength, not their sensitivity, but every now and then one would be overcome with equine despair and make a bid for freedom, endangering itself and anyone in its path.

The brewhouse was only silent at night, and even then I heard the watchmen whistling to keep up their spirits in that gaunt and eerily echoing edifice, and the dogs for want of adventure barking at phantom intruders. The first brew-hands were there by five in the morning, sun-up, and the last left seventeen hours later, a couple of hours short of midnight.

I woke, and fell asleep, to the clopping of shod hooves, the whinnying of overworked carthorses.

'It's a dangerous place, miss,' my nursemaids would repeat.

My father insisted. 'Too many hazards for you to go running about.'

But should I ever complain about the noise, or the smell of hops or dropped dung, his response was immediate: this was our livelihood/if it was good enough for my grandfather/you'll simply have to put up with it, won't you, missy. So I learned not to comment, and if I was distracted from my lessons or my handiwork or my day-dreaming, I moved across to the garden side of the house. Out of doors, in the garden, the sounds would follow me, but there were flowers and trees to look at, and the wide Medway sky to traverse with my thoughts.

Sometimes I would see a man or a woman reeling drunk out of a pub, or I'd hear the singing and cursing of regulars deep in their cups.

That, too, was a part of who we Havishams were. But I would be hurried past by whoever was holding my hand, as if they had been issued with orders: the child isn't to linger thereabouts, d'you understand. So we negotiated those obstacles double-quick, taking to side alleys if need be, to remove ourselves to somewhere more salubrious, while the rollicking voices sounded after us – but not their owners, thankfully grounded in a stupor.

Chapter Two

At an upstairs window, in Toad Lane, a bald-headed doll craned forward. One eyelid was closed, so that the doll appeared to be winking. It knew a secret or two.

In Feathers Lane lived a man who pickled and preserved for a trade. In *his* window he displayed some of his wares.

There in one dusty jar a long-dead lizard floated, with its jaws open and the tiny serrations of teeth visible. In another, three frogs had been frozen eternally as they danced, legs trailing elegantly behind them. Next to that was a rolled bluish tongue of something or other.

In the largest jar a two-headed object with one body was suspended, and I somehow realised – before Ruth confirmed it for me – that these were the beginnings of people: two embryos that had grown into one.

The window horrified me, but – just as much – I was fascinated by it. On the occasions when I could persuade Ruth to take me into town or home again that way, I felt a mixture of cold shivers and impatience to reach the grimy bow-fronted window where I had to raise myself on tiptoe to see in.

I thought – was it possible? – that through the slightly bitter citrus fragrance of pomander I could smell further back, I could catch my mother's sweet perfume and powder on the clothes stored flat in the press, years after she had last worn them.

I didn't even know where my mother was buried.

'Far off,' my father said. 'In a village churchyard. Under shade.'

I asked if we might go.

'Your mother doesn't need us now.'

'Don't we need *her*?'

'Some things belong to the past.'

His face carried the pain it always did when I brought up the subject of my mother. His eyes became fixed, pebble-like, as if he were defying tears. I sometimes thought that in the process he was trying to convince himself he didn't like *me* very much.

But those occasions would be followed by shows of kindness, by the purchase of another expensive plaything for me. This, the gift of the toy would be announcing, is how we attempt to put the sad parts of the past out of our minds.

I wondered if he really had recovered from the loss, or wasn't still privately nursing his grief, battening it down inside himself.

I would hear the cathedral bells every morning and evening. On Sundays and High Days the air crumpled with the pealing of so many other bells, from our Saints, Gundulph and Margaret and Zachary and Jude. All that eloquent and silver-toned pressure to be devout, or at least to appear so.

On Sunday mornings we worshipped at ten.

We would walk to the cathedral. Across the brewery yard into Crow Lane. Across the open sward of the Vines, into the Precincts, past the end of Minor Canon Row, with the Old Palace on our left.

I would always keep two or three steps behind my father.

Along the approach of worn flagstones to the Great Porch.

The archdeacon would bend low, his urgent hand pushing into the gloved palm of mine, because a brewer comes next to county stock, his is the aristocrat of trades. Even the lawyers and doctors stood back, and their eyepainted wives and petticoated daughters too, because they knew their place.

Into the gloom, into the reek of leather-bound hymnals and candlewax and withering tomb-flowers, that dry stale odour of old time oozing out of the stone. Heads would turn while I kept my gaze fixed straight ahead.

My sight adjusted to the little light. On the floor, pools of ruby and indigo from the stained window glass. The furious shimmer of candles stuck on spikes.

The pew creaked, it always creaked, as if the planed wood were sounding a complaint, a lament for the forest where it had grown.

In winter Ruth – or Eliza, who replaced her – provided me with a rug, a wrap, a muff, a coal foot-brazier, a water bottle. I imagined I was in a troika, speeding across a snowfield, the drowned Iven Meadow iced over. The ice sparked beneath the metal runners. Rime stiffened the horse's mane, tail, my eyelashes. My breath streaked past me like thin blue smoke.

The noble families were customarily represented at the services, but individual members came and went, and seemed more often away, up in London or at a watering-place or visiting their circle at their grand homes, worshipping – if they did – in private chapels.

By comparison we Havishams were rooted to the spot. People expected to see us there, and I took their expectation as a kind of right, due acknowledgement of our importance in the local order.

I would sit looking at the painted stone effigies on their tombs. I fixed on this or that figure, kneeling or recumbent: on the ruff or cuffs, on the still folds of a dress or the smooth line of a hosed calf. I stared so hard that I passed into a kind of trance. I forced myself to keep staring, scarcely blinking my eyes, not moving a muscle, as if I was turned to stone myself. After three or four minutes of intense concentration I achieved my purpose, supposing I could catch faint signs of life: the twitch of a slipper, the flutter of an eyelid, the trembling of a finger where the hands were closed in zealous prayer.

The grand figures, dignitaries in their time, might be able to deceive the rest of the congregation, but they couldn't fool *me*.

My father had to cough sometimes, or even reach across and shake my arm, to rouse me. I came back, but not quite willingly. In some ways I preferred my fear, the fright of discovering what I wasn't meant to know, where the truth of a situation was turned inside out.

I breathed in, breathed out. I smelt the melting candlewax, the calf bindings of our hymn books, the stuffy air which was the same uncirculated air as last week's.

When I looked again, the figures on their tombs were utterly still. Petrified. Incontrovertibly dead. Sharp-chinned, razor-nosed, prim-lipped, hands ardently clasped in supplication, that their souls should be received into Heaven.

We returned through the park opposite Satis House, known as The Vines. Originally it was the Monks' Vineyard, when St Andrew's Priory stood close by.

The rooks cawed in their high scrappy nests.

'Come on, Catherine. Keep up.'

My father didn't care for the monkish spirits of the place. We attended the cathedral because he wouldn't have been treated with full seriousness in the town if we hadn't, but his devotion was restricted to eighty minutes once a week. That was quite enough.

I never did get to the bottom of his reluctance, but I sensed that it had something to do with my mother's shockingly sudden end: a death that had made no sense to him, then or now, for which nothing and no one – not even I – could console him.

But he didn't talk about that; and in the house of (opportune, always dependable) silences we shared, neither did I.

Chapter Three

I continued to be taken out for my constitutional every day, a walk lasting an hour or so.

Two hours of lessons in the morning, luncheon, and then some exercise.

Exercise for the body and – once I'd won the confidence of the looser-tongued maids – for my mind also.

ﻌ

I heard about the old man who sold death in bottles.

About Nurse Rooley, who took away the little unwanteds before the mother grew too swollen: a premature borning.

Florry Tonkin, who sold her affections by the hour.

Mr Yarker, who would model your enemies in wax, and puncture the spirit out of them.

Captain Breen – not really a captain at all – importer of oblivion from Shanghai, via Rotherhithe.

The Misses Ginger, who communed with the dead departed, and spoke in voices.

The Siamese twins in Love Lane, genies let out of the pickling jar, walking with three shoes and two hats; one happy and laughing, the other downcast and glowering.

Miss Greville, who fasted keenly, and scourged herself with a twig switch, and who walked to the cathedral at Easter in bare feet and at other times with pebbles in her shoes.

Another spinster, Miss Maxfield in dirty canary yellow, who stood on street corners fretting about crossing the road for half an hour at a stretch, stamping on the spot, pointing at imaginary obstacles with the Malacca cane of her yellow parasol.

Canon Arbuthnot, who would tell neighbours that a Frenchman or a German friend would shortly be calling; but those callers were never glimpsed, and it was said they too came out of a bottle, a French visitor from Burgundy country and a German from somewhere about the Rhône or Moselle.

The Ali Baba house, whose owner farmed sugar plantations abroad, where four gigantic vases stood in vaulted niches high on the street facade, exposed to everything the elements could throw at them.

Our venerable town.

ಹ

Children, hand-picked, continued to come to Satis House.

No more than one or two at a time. And my father arranged to have us continuously supervised.

Thinking ourselves too old for playing, we behaved (as we thought) like young adults. I showed them my sewing, my drawings; we attempted a little rudimentary music-making; we walked in the garden. And, in short, we were thoroughly bored. We didn't say anything that couldn't be overheard.

I wondered what on earth was the point of it, unless my father liked to have reported back to him their envy for how I lived, wanting for nothing.

No one pitied me – or dared to mock me – for not having a mother.

The effect was to isolate me further, and to make me feel prouder still of my position.

I used my mother's silver-backed hand mirror, given to her by my father. On the back was engraved a Gothic 'H'.

It was large and heavy to hold. Its weight conferred solemnity.

I would look into the oval of glass long and hard, hoping to find some trace of my mother in my own reflection. But I only ever saw a girl with a brow furrowed in concentration, a too straight line for a mouth, a nose which threatened towards the aquiline, and a look in her eyes which was articulating a fear of solitude.

My father ensured that I should lack for nothing material.

Clothes and shoes. Books, dolls. A wooden barrow for the garden, and a set of nurseryman's tools. A leather horse on which to ride side-saddle. A box dulcimer, a recorder. A brush and comb of tortoiseshell inlaid with mother-of-pearl. Two oriental cats, which I called Silver and Gold.

I forget everything, because there was so much.

My father must have supposed that no other child could have had a happier time of it than I did. He showered me with gifts, which he didn't consider treats but things I had a perfect right to enjoy. But even amplitude and generosity pall. When I was by myself, I had a finite amount of imagination to help me play; when another child was brought along, I became possessive, only because I was afraid of having to reveal my embarrassment at owning so much.

❧

Mrs Bundy was our cook. She had come to us when I was very small. Her repertoire was limited, but my father preferred it to the more rarefied fare my mother had favoured.

To look at, she was striking rather than attractive. Wide eyes, a small tilted nose, and a large mouth that reached up into her cheeks when my father made her smile about something. A mane of thick brown hair which she wore rolled up and pinned behind, and was forever re-pinning. Large breasts, so that her apron usually carried a dusting of flour or whatever her chest came into contact with. She also had the curious habit of stepping out of her shoes when the kitchen grew too hot for her and walking about in bare feet, as if she considered herself mistress of this domain.

Mrs Bundy spoke about me. She told my father things he couldn't have known otherwise: about my talking to the workers' children, about disposing of my lunch vegetables in the fire or out of the window.

It was none of her business. Angry with her, I told my father I knew who was telling him.

'It's *her*.'

'Catherine –'

'Isn't it?'

'I don't want to discuss –'

'She's just our cook.'

'Don't speak of Mrs Bundy so dismissively.'

'But she has no right –'

'D'you *hear* me, Catherine?'

He was taking her side – yet again.

Sometimes on my constitutional I passed where she lived.

She came from the other end of Crow Lane to ourselves, but not from the most deprived part of it as I might have expected. Being a cook in a rich man's house, she must have managed to feed herself at her employer's expense, certainly to look as wholesomely nourished as she did.

There was a boy too, a year or so younger than myself. I had glimpses of him, grown a little taller every time, but just as pale – he lacked his mother's robustness – and just as nosy as I went on my way, accompanied by my maid for that afternoon. On one occasion I made a face at him, and the boy pretended to be affronted; but I realised too late that my mistake was to acknowledge him and to show him what he made me feel, and so I'd handed *him* the advantage of that moment.

I always had lunch on Sunday with my father, following our return from the cathedral.

Mrs Bundy would linger in the dining room, after we'd been served, after my father had been asked if everything was to his satisfaction. It seemed to me that it wasn't her place. Several times I would notice my father's eyes moving off her, and Mrs Bundy's eyes narrowing as she looked at me, as if he was seeking a second opinion from her about me. And just as much as on the other account, it seemed to me that the woman exceeded herself.

Mrs Bundy had the task of supervising my other meals in my mother's old sewing room.

'My food's not to your liking, miss?'

'I'm not hungry.'

The fish stared up at me, its eye glazed with stupidity.

'You will be by suppertime.'

'How d'you know?'

'I'll take it away, shall I? My hard work.'

'Take it away.'

'Magic word, miss?'

'Take it away – *please*.'

Later, when she was having some shut-eye wherever it was she went to take it, I would return to the kitchen and raid the storage jars, making the girls swear to secrecy. But – I see now – she must have known about that too, because how else was it that the jars were always kept topped up with currants, dried fruit, peel, nuts?

Mrs Bundy stands in the steam while pans simmer on the range. Bread is baking in the old oven, chestnuts – placed on the oven floor – are bursting their skins among the cinders.

She wipes perspiration from her jaw with the back of her hand. Her cuffs are undone and the sleeves rolled back. Her forearms are fleshy and white. Last summer they were fleshy but tanned, from her work in the kitchen garden; another summer on, she is pale, as a proper lady is pale, as her son is pale.

Cooling in a bowl are a rabbit's guts, which she earlier pulled out whole and hot. All in the day's work.

She doesn't see me looking as she rests. Briefly she forgets herself, she stands stroking one arm slowly with the fingers of the other. Moments pass, she is rapt in her fancies.

'How proud you are!'

Why shouldn't I be?

'Little Miss High and Mighty.'

'I'll tell my father. What you've just said.'

'Tell him what? That you're proud?'

Tell him that she'd dared to criticise me. (In that accent which wavers between flat backwoods Kent and something better.) But I felt that if I said what I was thinking, that gave her act of criticism some sort of validity.

Better instead that I should ignore her.

I snatched up my petit point, and attacked the canvas with such violence that I missed my aim. I cried out.

'Thumb for a pincushion?' she said. She had a laugh in her voice that incensed me.

'Not pin! Needle, needle! Don't you even know *that*?'

'Don't take on, it's nothing –'

'There's blood.'

'A very little. Suck it and –'

'How common!'

She came closer, but I snatched my hand away and turned my back on her. I didn't know why I was so vexed and angry.

'It's your temper I'd be bothered about, if I were you.'

'But you're *not* me. How on earth *could* you be?'

I was aware, through my anger, that I was being goaded. I closed my eyes.

Her voice moved in front of me again.

'Close your eyes, that's right, and count to ten.'

I opened them again and ran, screaming inside my head, from the room.

❧

For as long as I could remember a woman with an emperor's nose had paid occasional visits to Satis House. She wore layers of black, and spoke English in a strangely accented way.

My grandmother: my mother's mother.

My father had the servants address her as 'Madame', as the French do.

She would sit very straight-backed in her high chair, and imposed her powdery presence on us all. I was required to stand in front of her reciting, or playing a tune on my dulcimer. Invariably something in my performance touched her, because I would be summoned forward to have my hair and cheek stroked; her rings were cold, and hard, but not sharp.

Her visits became more infrequent.

And then she stopped coming at all.

On what was to prove her final visit she was very critical of the food she was served, speaking in front of Mrs Bundy. My father started defending our cook. My grandmother sent the woman from the room, and then – while I sat between them – she berated my father for showing his partiality. She did *not* expect to be shown up in front of some kitchen cook.

'Not just any kitchen cook,' my father said.

'Certainly, I agree. A very poor cook.'

'You have no reason for saying so.'

'I have just tried to eat the food you put before me.'

'You think I can't choose a good cook, Madame?'

'Never mind "good". Simply a decent one would suffice.'

'What gives you the right, I should like to know, to –'

'In my daughter's place I –'

'We don't know what Antoinette would have thought –'

'She would *not* have given her approval to *that* woman's being in this house.'

They both turned and looked at me. My grandmother's face was now as sour as a cut lemon. My father, spinning the stem of his wine glass with his fingers, seemed anxious on my account.

Later, before our visitor left, I heard my father saying that he would appreciate it if she didn't speak to the servants without his approval. She denied knowing what he meant.

'You've not been asking the maids questions?'

'Whatever has put that idea into –'

'I'm cognisant of what goes on in my own house.'

'As the maids are.'

'You *have* been asking them –'

'Antoinette would never have stood for it.'

'Stood for what?'

'You know very well what. Don't taint young Catherine, do you hear me?'

'I should tell you, I do not appreciate being advised how –'

'I am not advising, Mr Havisham. I am *demanding*.'

She didn't ever return to Satis House.

Every now and then I would receive a note from her. I would reply, but my father insisted on seeing what I wrote to her, and having me rewrite – more concisely – if he judged so.

I heard one of the girls say Mrs Bundy was relieved anyhow, to see the back of her, no more fancy French stuff to dish up *there*.

And another girl laughing back, Oh Mrs Bundy's got her own ideas what she'll do to this place, what's going to go into folk's bellies.

I knew that my grandmother wouldn't be back, even though I wasn't told so. Mrs Bundy walked about more amply; she had the girls running everywhere on errands – I even saw her passing through our hall with flour on her arms or a whisk in her hand. My father wouldn't have risked offending her with another visit from my imperatorial grandmother, even if he was denying the mother of the woman he'd married and lost, and was depriving *me* of an acquaintanceship with my one surviving female blood relative.

⁂

I had chased my cats down to the orchard. I happened to look up and jumped when I saw someone, a boy, crouching splay-legged in the fork of a tree.

'What are *you* doing here?'

Then I recognised him. Mrs Bundy's son, in new finery.

He raised himself nonchalantly on one elbow and considered me.

'I could ask *you* the same,' he replied languidly. He spoke as boys do who have begun to receive an expensive education.

'I asked *you* first.'

He smiled.

'Oh, Catherine Havisham has first say in everything, doesn't she?'

I glared back at him.

'It's not *your* garden,' I said.

'It's not yours either.'

'More mine than yours.'

'*Is* it?'

'It's my father's.'

'"It's my father's",' he repeated, exactly imitating my tone of voice.

'Who else?'

'Indeed.'

'Come down from there.'

He did eventually – taking a long time about it, and making it seem that he only pleased himself.

He was tall, lanky, pallid, not filled-out like his mother. He still had his thin foxy face. I had never cared for the look of him, this craven interloper.

'Well . . . ?' I said. 'What are you waiting for?'

'I just wanted to get a good look at you.'

'What on earth for?'

'So you'll give me sweet dreams. When I dream of this place.'

'The garden? It's private, I told you. It's got nothing to do with you.'

'Says who?'

'*I* say.'

He laughed.

'So, you're the boss, are you?'

I snapped at him. 'Don't be insolent!'

'Or else what – ?'

He reached up his arm, and might have been going to swing from a low branch, but he either didn't trust his strength or didn't care to soil his white hands and clean cuffs.

'I'll call my father.'

'Very well, I'm going. Don't you mention this to him.'

'Why shouldn't I?'

'Tut-tut! Speaking to town lads? In *his* garden? Whatever would the old boy think?'

And then, quite suddenly, Mrs Bundy left us.

Oh, joy and jubilation!

She was said to be living now outside the town.

I had a sighting one day. She was dressed like a respectable tradesman's wife, with a fur collar and a fur muff and a hat replete with a quiver of feathers. She had her son in tow, still lanky and still sallow-faced and attired like last time in the garb of a young gentleman. Both mother and son shared something I couldn't account for: an air of self-confidence, eyes not ashamed to meet anyone else's on that busy main street of our town.

I mentioned to my father that I had seen Mrs Bundy.

'Indeed?'

How grand she was trying to make herself look, I said.

'That isn't her way.'

'She seemed so to me.'

'To *you*, Catherine. But you never approved of Mrs Bundy.'

'No.'

'You too question the wisdom of my having employed her? I can't pick my own staff well, is that it?'

I had bothered him, I could tell that. A tic was pulling in his cheek, throbbing away.

'I didn't mean . . .'

'I don't wish us to discuss Mrs Bundy. Not ever again.'

Whenever I saw her son I would look away quickly. He was always watching me, with an expression I found confusing. He was disapproving, and superior, but also frankly curious. He had no compunction about staring at me, which I found presumptuous. Of what concern should I, a Havisham, be to the son of our erstwhile kitchen cook?

Chapter Four

My father's office was in the house. Next to it, entered either from that room or through an outside door in the yard but otherwise quarantined from the domestic premises, was the Compting House, where two rows of clerks sat at high desks keeping their tallies.

Luckily for Havisham's purposes, our proximity to Chatham ensured a large ready market for our brews. A marines' barracks had been built twenty-five years after the army one, and the town was thronged with sailors and troops and their dependents. The dockyards employed thousands. Their thirst was insatiable, and – as did one or two of our competitors – we obliged . . .

Along the Medway the Havisham net was cast – so to speak – by my father, with clever aim. To Gravesend upstream, and to Sittingbourne, Sheerness and Queensborough in an easterly direction.

I knew in which inns, and where, the Havisham brew and porter were sold. My father would point them out to me one by one as we came upon them on our travels. He'd have me memorise the names, and each time I would recite an ever-lengthening litany, as completely as I could. He would listen to me, nodding with satisfaction, and then supply the names I had missed from the list.

The Tun & Lute, Shovel & Boot; Turkey Slave, Cock & Pye.

(I would proceed by an eccentric system of associated images.)

Leather Bottle, Hundred House, Parson & Clerk.

The Rose of Denmark, Goat & Compasses, Q in a Corner.

Trip to Jerusalem.

'And Good King Lud.'

'Good King Lud,' I would repeat.

'It's the one you always forget. But the only one.'

We didn't own all the inns, but we were suppliers to each of them, several dozen in total. This was the Havisham inheritance, and my father liked to hear it retold over and over by my young voice.

❦

I saw them at the cathedral on Sunday mornings, those spinsters who had dried on the vine. Some had cared too long for parents, and now housekept for siblings. Two or three had been in love perhaps, but hadn't been decisive enough, and so they had lost the opportunity.

The carers, worn thin, seemed to have surrendered some of their own personality. Those who had failed in love were left with a kind of purposeless animation: restless hands fidgeting with gloves and prayerbooks, tremulous mouths and little lambs' tongues, eyes that flitted about the congregation – as if vaguely searching out someone who was never present.

I tried not to walk too close to them. They were ubiquitous, though, pervasive presences. I held in my skirts, as if I might be in dread of some contagion. The skinny ones had nimble ankles, the plump ones stood sturdily where they impeded free passage to the porch.

Instead of a governess I now had instructors. They came to Satis House, and – when he was a man – a maid sat in the room with us, about her sewing or penning letters home.

If they'd listened, the girls could have acquired an education as I was doing. Latin, poetry, French, arithmetic, drawing, music on the keyboard, elocution.

I knew that my father listened at the door when he could. He replaced a couple of my tutors (one, Miss Boutflower, favoured poetry of a deep religious hue), and he had suspicions about an athletic-looking young man who tried to kindle in me an enthusiasm for the history of our Dark Ages.

My father took advice where he could, but it wasn't as straightforward as he might have envisaged, educating a daughter above her station.

I wasn't beautiful. My mouth was too straight, while my nose showed increasingly imperial tendencies. My eyes were hooded, and looked heavy. I saw what I owed to my doughty grandmother.

I didn't give an impression, so said one of the tutors (subsequently dismissed), of being a country brewer's daughter.

'That's because you're not,' my father told me. 'Your mother had fine features. And you've been brought up with nothing but the best.'

I had thick fair hair with a natural kink in it, and even though the colour darkened a little with time I didn't lose that air of impractical glamour which fairness gives. My complexion was clear and untroubled. I was reckoned to have 'good bone structure'.

My appearance was picked over by the girls in the house, by my instructors when I overheard them gossiping, by the women who made my clothes, by the effeminate old man who fitted me for shoes.

I had this, I didn't have that. I was more than averagely one thing, less than averagely something else.

It was me they were discussing. But it also wasn't me.

I had a claim on this person, but so did others.

And what went on *inside* me seemed to be a different matter entirely: what the others couldn't see, but which they presumed to comment on. There, I believed, lay all the clues to being myself – a truer and more real Catherine Havisham.

Chapter Five

I was in the house working at Latin gerunds one afternoon when I heard a crashing sound outside. It was immediately followed by a terrible cry to freeze the blood – and then a clamour of voices, men's and women's, shouting and screaming.

I ran to the side door of the house. A crowd had gathered beneath one of the brewhouse hoists. I looked up and saw a length of rope swinging loose. The rope must have snapped and sent its load hurling to the ground.

I smelt the spilt beer before I hurried across. I saw the pieces of smashed barrel. Someone lay writhing on the wet cobbles, roaring with the pain of his injuries. I was going to try to push my way through when a hand on my shoulder roughly pulled me back.

'Don't look, Catherine!'

My father turned me aside, then himself hastened through.

The barrel, I heard the house-girls say, had dropped straight on to the loader waiting beneath.

I couldn't sleep that night.

On succeeding nights I slept fitfully, never far from waking.

In the daylight my eyes were drawn back, time after time, to the hoist. The ropes had been replaced, and sacks and barrels were being passed up and down as before, as if nothing had happened.

I'd learned that tendons had been severed in the loader's left leg, leaving him lame. I couldn't stop hearing the man's eldritch wail, and the shouting and howling of the others. Over and over, I wasn't able to drive the sounds from my mind.

My father kept the man on, and would always remember to

speak to him, stooping a little as if he were harbouring some guilt.

I saw for myself that the injuries were worse than I had been told. The right arm had been crushed, and hung loose. He trailed one leg. He now helped out the ostlers, and did watch duty.

His daughter would bring him something to sup at in winter, a bowl wrapped in cloths. It must have been hard going, through the warren of muddy unlit lanes, seeing her way in the dark, and I felt very distant from her as I watched from one of the house windows, comfortably settled indoors for the night.

She was about my own age, a little taller than I; pretty, with thick copper hair, plaited. I could see her better in the mornings, when her father's watch was over and she stopped by on her way to the Dame's school, where she did housework in return for a little learning. Sally's mother was ambitious for her, and had earned a bad name for it, but the town's talk only toughened her resolve to give Sally a better start than other girls of her kind got. A tidy appearance was one lesson she had learned at home, how to show herself well.

I admired her, from my distance. Her quiet composure, her fearlessness in the face of those comments about her which people didn't bother to disguise. Even her frizzy copper hair. I was intrigued by the way she had of keeping her eyes cast down, as if she must be rather sorrowful, and then in an instant raising them; those eyes would be shining with intelligence, I judged, and a ready sort of humour, even with things as they were.

Seeing her father, she would straighten up and smile a welcome. If she was concerned, she also needed to be hopeful. She knew not to take her father's other, uninjured arm, since he needed to get his balance for himself. Her tactfulness seemed to me precocious, prodigious.

I had never been allowed to play with the brewery children, nor had I wanted to.

Sally turned out to be the exception.

My father was unsure. But he was still troubled by his conscience, about his liability for what had happened to his loader. So he raised no objection, although I later realised he had set a string of informers among the servants.

Because Sally wasn't allowed beyond the laundry room, I took what I had to show her down there.

I set up my model theatre, and from either side we pushed the wooden characters on sticks and spoke in pretend grown-up voices. She played the servants and hoi polloi, in a local accent broader than her own, while I took the parts of the better townsfolk and the clergy.

I'd had difficulty talking with the other children who came to Satis House. I had none with Sally. I knew so from what my voice *didn't* sound like – tense and squeaky and dried out.

She was less deferential than I had expected her to be, but never impolite. It was strange to me how often our opinions coincided; how, with our very different backgrounds, we regarded certain people or our town's traditions in the same (sceptical) way – and how it was, for instance, that I could gauge her thoughts so well in advance of her saying them, and she mine, that we might finish off each other's sentences and start the next.

I taught her some of what I knew.

Good table manners. How to hold herself. How to tone down the Kent in her vowels.

Simple French grammar, and then Latin declensions, which she didn't get from the Dame. Dates in history, from the Dark Ages on. Some verses of poetry, and some prose passages.

She was a solid learner who forgot nothing. She might even have surpassed me if we had been equals, but thankfully we were not, and so I didn't even have to regard the irony of that.

Once I took Sally into the tack room, so she could admire my father's new saddle. My action was reported back to my father, and he told me quite bluntly that I wasn't to take 'company' – as then and in the future he would refer to Sally – beyond the door at the end of the scullery passage.

She had a quick mind. Memory, I know now, is an asset of intelligence; though I also know that to live an easier life, one should have one's full health and a short memory.

Sally, I felt, would always be like this, wanting to make things just a bit more difficult for herself. Needing to know what was in the next lesson before we got there; asking me how long it had taken me to memorise a poem and then learning it in half that time; asking me, how can they be sure of this, what proof is there of that? – King Harold losing an eye, five colours showing in a rainbow, the earth's having a dark side, there being no final number to count to.

'I'm only telling you what the books say, Sally.'

'Don't you want to know if it's true?'

'It wouldn't be there in the books if it weren't, would it?' I answered in exasperation. Sally stared at me, with a pitying expression. Was I really as naive as that?

⁂

I had my arm hooked through Sally's as we walked back along Hound Street. There was the sound of a horse being ridden slowly behind us on the cobbles. I turned round. It was my father: suddenly not looking at us, as if he hadn't seen who we were.

He rode past. I held tighter to Sally's arm.

For the next few days I felt he was paying me closer attention; but silently, furtively, between any remarks he had for me. Whenever I looked up my father would avert his eyes, either to hold on the view outside the window or examine some object in the room behind me. He would place candles where I might be clearer to him. He appeared to have some project in his mind.

For a while I saw a little less of Sally. It wasn't by my choosing, but because her mother had been able to find a position for her, lowly and beneath stairs, but such impressive stairs, in the home of two elderly sisters on Bolley Hill. The ladies endlessly sparred, I'd heard, and fought over everything the other had, or might want, including the respect of each new member of their staff. Sister would struggle with sister to win and keep Sally.

'I used to think you were proud,' Sally told me. 'People said you were proud.'

'I'm not proud to *you*, am I?'

'No. No, you're not.'

'And that surprises you?'

'Just a little, yes.'

'I used to think I was expected to be that way. Partly I was – and partly I became it.'

'Not to disappoint them?'

'I suppose so.'

And later.

'I think you bring out someone better in me, Sally.'

I took her hand. She looked quite astonished. I smiled at that.

'Why shouldn't I take your hand if I want to?'

Sally managed to smile back, but in a puzzled way.

'Give me one good reason why not,' I said.

But she didn't, because she couldn't.

One winter's night I had her stay with me in the house, all night, to sleep in my warm bed by my side. I was defying my father, of course, and no one else was allowed in on our secret.

In the morning, though, it couldn't be a secret any longer. Sally's mother had gone looking for her when she didn't return home, accompanied by some of her neighbours. She had come to the brewery yard at dawn, and it chanced to be a day when my father was up early because indigestion was troubling him.

He was furious: but with Sally, not with me. I tried to explain it to him; I told him I was the one responsible.

He instructed our Mrs Venn to strip the sheets from the bed and – why on earth? – boil them. I couldn't understand what all the pudder was about, and why the big vat had to be heated especially for the sake of my sheets. I watched the blankets being beaten and then hung up on a line to air.

We had lain telling each other stories, as if we were five years old instead of ten (me) and eleven (Sally). I didn't even feel sleepy, not at first, because of my excitement at having her there. Later, however, I followed her example and dozed off, with my arm covering her waist. Whatever was the harm in that?

My father told me afterwards that he had ordered Sally not to come back.

Her first exile from Satis House was beginning.

I managed to meet her a few times, down by the river and away from prying eyes. We arranged that she should be in this or that location on a Sunday morning, so that we could have a sight of each other on my way to and from the cathedral service.

But it wasn't the same as before: it couldn't be, no matter how much I wished it.

'It's what my father says.'

'What do *you* say, though?'

I stared at her, wrong-footed by her question.

'Catherine Havisham sings her father's song, I think.'

It sounded like a remark she must have overheard adults making.

'I do no such thing,' I told her.

'But you have no time for me now.'

'It's different now.'

'How is it different now?'

Because. Because, because, because.

I turned away.

'Why – ?'

'We're growing up,' I answered. 'That's all.'

'No. That's not it.'

Then I felt impatient with her. Why couldn't she just accept that these things are visited on us? We don't have a choice, we truly don't. I was a Havisham; she was Limping Johnnie's daughter, never mind what airs her mother gave herself.

I felt watching eyes were following me down to the river. My flesh crept on the back of my neck.

It was Sally who said we should stop. *Must* stop.

I reluctantly, very sadly, agreed.

I saw how she grew after that. I saw how the coppery colour

of her hair deepened, and the hair itself – with ribbons wound through – lost none of its thickness but was restrained still more tightly.

I saw small but significant things: the bruises on her ankles from the distances she walked every day, a red mark on her arm like a kitchen burn which her other arm tried to cover, a downward turn to her mouth on one side when she thought no one was looking.

But *I* saw.

Chapter Six

There's blood on the rug where I've been standing. It has run down my legs from the place I know to keep hidden.

There's blood on the sheets when I go back to examine the bed. And on my nightdress.

How have I wounded myself? I don't feel *hurt*: just a little light-headed, a little muzzy.

A skivvy brings me what I call for from the scullery.

I get down on my knees, gingerly, and try washing the rug.

With water, cold and hot. Then with vinegar. Then with the juice of a lemon.

The stains won't wash out of the wool; or from the sheets either, or my nightdress.

I rub frantically, but the stains are defiant – they seem to have settled there, where I've bled them.

Afterwards it was explained to me by Mrs Venn.

I didn't doubt my father had been informed, if cryptically. He asked me how I was feeling: as if I should be indisposed, ailing.

'This warm weather,' he said, 'very unseasonal; it's best not to tax yourself.'

He didn't let his eyes rest on me, as he normally did when he lent advice. He was embarrassed, as I was. We weren't talking, he and I, about the same Catherine Havisham of two days ago.

Left in my room by myself I sat in front of the fire, preferring to watch the pictures in the flames to what I could see through my window, that view of the yard and rooftops and the drab riverland beyond.

When the flames died down and the pictures faded, I looked instead at the fireplace tiles – tiles from Delft, blue and white – and my imagination wandered among the scenes there.

By the banks of the canals, over the bridges, past the windmills, stopping as people always do at the locks until the barge has nudged its way through. On horseback, galloping bareback across a plain under high sea clouds. In pattens, picking a path over cobbles to reach a friend's door, while the air of the town fills with pealing bells, and with a commotion of birds like a squall.

Until I remembered where I was – because embers were falling with a little rush into the grate, and rooks circled over the cherry trees outside, and the cathedral bells summoned for vespers, and because the room had grown colder around me.

ஃ

I had been sent off for a few weeks over Christmastime, to a cousin of my father's, who lived a good way off in Berkshire.

While I was away, and during that one quiet time in the year for the brewery when work almost stopped, my father took ill. Vessels burst in his heart. That same evening he'd eaten and drunk too much at a festive dinner, and it was thought that his untypical indulgence and similarly untypical walk home in the cold air must have caused the attack.

However it came about, he fell down in the frosty street. The first to see was Sally's mother; she had my father taken into a cottage and best positioned to restore his circulation. She'd run off to fetch the doctor herself.

I wasn't to be told, but Sally wrote to me nevertheless. I left Windsor at once, pretending on my return that I'd been on my way back anyway. I found Sally's mother tending to the patient;

and Sally running errands for my father, whatever he requested her to do.

Sally's readmission to Satis House came about for all the wrong reasons. But I was glad: firstly that my father was mending, and secondly that I had my good friend to hand, to confide my worries to, and – after my shock and double relief – to let me cry, quite literally, on her steady shoulder.

My father was up on his feet a fortnight later. He was able to walk, if slowly for the moment, and to talk down what had taken place, telling everyone he would be back to work as usual before too long.

❧

With Sally, it was like old times; there might not have been that two-year hiatus.

I knew that she forgave my father, merely because she never rose to my bait and offered any criticisms of him.

She had cut that wilful plumery, her copper hair, and she showed fewer of those carefree sun-freckles on her face. Now she was under one of the redoubtable, granite-featured housekeepers who organised domestic life in Minor Canon Row, in this case in the residence of that oily archdeacon and his astringent mother and dry-as-dust wife. Sally was worked hard, because every penny spent in that household was required to offer its full value in time and labour.

But Sally kept cheerful. Her own mother was pleased for her, and so – I claimed – was I.

'But now,' I said, 'you have to be my confidante as well. That's two jobs of work, I reckon.'

'Certainly,' she said. 'Whenever I can.'

'I'll be very disappointed if you're ever not able.'

I wondered if it could be quite the same as it used to be. We each had rules and responsibilities that were becoming clearer to us. We had little say in those; but we could surely try to stake other claims for ourselves, obeying our instincts only, about whom we called our *consœurs* and best friends.

Chapter Seven

For my thirteenth birthday and those following, my father gave me a painted porcelain Easter egg. Each egg was valuable in itself, but the surprise lay inside. There I would find, cushioned by a velvet lining, an item of jewellery: a fire-opal pendant, a bracelet of amethysts, a pearl halter, a gold rope necklace hung with rubies, white and pink diamond earrings, a rare yellow diamond on a ring.

In addition he passed over to me, item by item, my mother's jewels. Those had older-fashioned settings than my birthday presents. He arranged to have a topaz necklace reset, because I had taken such a fancy to the blue markings of the stones, like tiger stripes. The rest showed good taste, and I was happy to wear them.

My mother had inherited some of the pieces, and I was aware of the quiet dignity of their age. They weighed me to my chair, they slowed me slightly when I walked – not because they were heavy, but because they came to me complicated by their history – and it wasn't at all an oppressive sensation. I felt that I'd been granted an intimate contact with my mother. We were sharing this occasion of my wearing a necklace or a bracelet, and somehow my increased pleasure was being transmitted to her, through time and space. This experience was being recreated in another dimension; by wearing the necklace or bracelet, I was helping to close a circle.

My father grew sad and despondent for a while.

He had only just got back to regular work. His illness might have been to blame, still tiring him these eighteen or twenty months on, but I sensed – I had a premonition – that there was some other reason.

Several times he seemed to be on the point of telling me something.

Whenever he ventured beyond the brewery gates, he wore his darkest and most sombre outdoor clothes.

'I married again, Catherine.'

I thought I had misheard.

'Who married again?'

'Me. *I* married again.'

Pause.

'When?'

'A few years after your mother died.'

'Married whom?'

'The woman I wished to marry.'

'Who?'

'The woman I wished to care for.'

Pause.

'But she died. Just recently.'

'Who – who was she? Do I know her?'

'You know – you *knew* her, yes.'

'One of our friends?'

'It was Mrs Bundy. As she used to be.'

I stared at him. I felt I was falling through a hole in the floor. I was without mass; I'd left the sac of my stomach behind.

'And then of course she became Mrs Havisham.'

'No.' I shook my head at him. 'No, that's *our* name.'

At that my father's face sagged. His mouth hung slack.

'And . . .'

He stopped. He stared at the surface of the table.

'There's – something else?'

My head was still spinning, like a top.

'We had a son.'

'A son?'

'You have a half-brother.'

The boy I used to see her with, about the town, who was sent away to be educated.

As he briefly explained, my father wouldn't look at me, however hard I stared and challenged him to raise his eyes.

'I'm sorry I have to tell you like this –'

The boy's age was close to mine. And yet my father had said he married a few years after my mother's death. I knew what that meant.

'I should like something, Catherine.'

I let a few seconds lapse.

'What – what's that?'

'I should like Arthur – that is his name – I should like Arthur to come and stay here.'

'*Here?*'

'Yes.'

'How long for?'

'Satis House will be his home.'

'What?'

'It will call for one or two adjustments to our routine. But nothing we can't –'

'You want him to come and stay here with *us*?'

'He *will* be coming. To be one of the family.'

I didn't speak.

'I've told him. We've discussed it.'

'It's been decided?' I said.

'Yes.'

'Why are you asking me, then?'

I fixed my eyes on that gulch of loose skin on his neck, his throat, which had only appeared since his accident.

'I should appreciate – if you could help to make Arthur feel comfortable. In his new home.'

'"Home"? Satis House?'

'Yes. Home now for all of us.'

❧

Arthur was still thin. The Havishams had always had padding, so he was already marked out as being something less than ourselves.

He had thin wrists, a thin neck, but it wasn't the fine sort of inbred aristocratic leanness. I could see the sharp edge of his shoulder bones under his shirt. When he breathed out, or laughed – which meant rolling about at some small witticism from my father, or sneering at me – his ribs poked out of his chest. He had large thin grasping hands; obliged to shake hands with him, I was anticipating a stronger grip, as narrow wrists often produce – but his greedy fawning mitt was turned inside mine like some cornered, half-dead weasel.

Arthur didn't discuss *then* with me.

'That's my business.'

He wouldn't tell me where he and his mother had lived latterly, or how often they'd seen their provider.

It was information I couldn't ask my father for, because asking – expressing an interest – might appear to condone the marriage. (Why keep it a secret as he had unless he was ashamed?)

'Forthwith your brother will be known as Arthur Havisham.'

'But that's not his real name.'

'It will be now.'

I was shocked. How could he be either my 'brother' or a Havisham?

'In time Arthur will need to learn about the business. Receive a training.'

'He will?'

'Well, of course. That goes without saying, doesn't it?'

❧

He was attending a bona fide establishment for young gentlemen in the West of England, not that you would have deduced it from his conduct.

In the house he was late for meals. He dragged his heels on the floor. He entered rooms without knocking. If he took a book from a shelf he didn't replace it; if he dropped something he waited for a servant to pick it up. When my father wasn't there he spat fruit stones into the fireplace grate. One day some coins fell out of my father's pocket on to his chair, unnoticed by him, and I saw Arthur surreptitiously scoop them up and put them into his own pocket. He received his horse saddled from the stable, and left it sweating in the yard once he had ridden it hard, and showed no interest in the animal's well-being. Behind my father's back (and sometimes only just) he silently mimicked me, or he cocked a snook at my father, or pretended to be hacking up food into his hands. He aimed pebbles at small birds, then (as his confidence grew) bigger stones at my Silver and Gold.

After only months he was cocky enough to let his dislike of me stay expressed on his face, not now bothering to hide it from my father.

Our father, as he would have it.

'That sounds like God,' I reproved him.

'Thinks he *is* God too.'

I gawped.

'No one to tell him he isn't, I s'pose.'

And he talked of Satis House, with a leery smile, as his 'dear old chimney corner'.

'You're away at school,' I said.

'It's still my home.'

'I've always lived here.'

'And now *I* do too. High time I got to fit in with you lot.'

'What makes you think you ever will?'

'Oh, I'm adaptable.'

'Don't *I* have to be adaptable as well?' I asked him.

'You've no choice, have you?'

'No. No, I don't.'

'We're agreed on that, then.'

'That's the only thing we *do* –'

'Worry not, sister –'

'Half-sister.'

'– I'll make sure we're all quite cosy together.'

❧

I was surprised by Sally's continuing reluctance to condemn Arthur.

The son of the former and departed Mrs Bundy had forfeited the right to any sort of respect, I felt. I couldn't understand why she should try to think her way into the spiteful workings of his mind. Why should *he* merit anyone's special consideration?

'It's because I stand a little way back,' she said.

No. No, I didn't believe that.

And it wasn't because I hadn't strongly presented my case against Arthur. It might have been that she felt I argued *too* powerfully, but wasn't that a true Havisham's privilege?

❧

Arthur had no genuine interest in the brewery.

Between school terms he pretended that he wanted to learn, since he thought saying so would please my father: and he needed to be in my father's good books, to have a chance of his allowance being increased.

My father must have seen how things were; and heard, too. Whenever my father was absent, Arthur was curt and off-hand with the workers, thinking he was above having to deal with them directly; perhaps (I calculated for myself) because he understood that they were very suspicious of him, for having appeared from nowhere and displaying so little acumen for business.

It struck me that my father's brow was more deeply rivelled than it used to be. I could appreciate better now that he had only meant to be open and above board by owning to Arthur as his blood son. He believed he had finally done the right thing: while circumstances seemed intent, rather, on loosening and undermining the soft ground beneath his feet.

Arthur, I thought, must have taught himself to be this person from books, or – more probably – from watching plays in the theatre.

He ought to have been seen in the light from candles along the front of a stage. His entrances and exits should have been accompanied by the din of shaken tin for thunder rolls. Why wasn't he wearing make-up? (Or just conceivably he was?)

And I still thought that Sally too often failed to recognise what damned Arthur in my eyes.

He was uncouth, inconsiderate, a bully. Ignorant, and very smug about being so. Bitter, and possibly vengeful.

I read him like a book.

But Sally wouldn't condemn him outright. She told me, hadn't his position always been awkward, knowing he'd been born a Havisham ('half a Havisham', I corrected her), but unable to acknowledge his birth (his bastard birth, as I knew for myself)? Could we either of us, she asked, imagine how uncertain his future life must have seemed to him?

I nearly lost patience with her. I told her, we must agree to disagree; I was *not* to be converted to his cause.

'I don't mean to plead for him. I only tell you what I think.'

Sally was quite composed, and not fired or indignant. Perhaps one reason for my own discomposure was feeling that she could take a clearer and less partisan view, whereas I had the onus – the millstone – of Havisham dignity to defend.

II

DURLEY CHASE

Chapter Eight

The dining room one evening, suppertime.

My father on one side of the table, I on the other, and Arthur mercifully off at school.

'I've arranged for you to have an education, Catherine.'

I thought he was referring to my lessons in the house. I nodded.

'I mean, to share your studies. And to live with some grander types than you're used to here.'

'Who?'

'The Chadwycks. Spelt with a "y".'

'"Live with" them?'

'An acquaintance – Lady Charlotte and her children.'

Acquaintance? I had never heard of the person, or her children.

'In Surrey.'

Surrey?

'Not so far from Redhill.'

Should the name 'Redhill' mean something to me? It didn't.

'I think it would be the best thing. You'll see how that sort live. You'll become one of them.'

'Why, though?'

'I've told you.'

'Why me? Why the Chadwycks?'

'Because I was talking to Lady Chadwyck about you. And we decided.'

'When am I to go?'

'Just as soon as you can get yourself ready and packed.'

'I've really got to stay with them?'

'Yes.'

'What about my lessons here?'

'Your tutors will find other employment. Tradesmen's daughters round about.'

Already I had been elected to a different league.

I wanted to take Sally with me.

But how? As my maid?

I felt the matter most delicate. She had always treated me as the master's daughter, but I had never – even at my most heedless – treated her as a servant.

I waited for my father to ask if I had anyone in mind, but he settled the matter without our discussing it. He selected one of the girls in the house.

'I shall tell you all about it, Sally. I'll write.'

'You'll have too much else on your mind.'

'Not be able to find time for *you*?'

I knew my own resolve.

'Never,' I said. 'Never.'

I twitch my mantle blue: *Tomorrow to fresh woods, and pastures new*.

A dome showed over the tops of the trees.

The view cleared along the driveway.

The house appeared. Slab-sided, octagonal. Raised on a knoll. Red creeper on the walls. French doors stood open.

They were waiting for me. Lady Chadwyck, well preserved and dressed at least fifteen years younger than the age I guessed her to be, and smiling sweetly.

She had two daughters and a son, lined up in the portico to meet me.

Isabella, the eldest at nineteen, was the more attractive girl, with a commanding manner. Her brother William, home from Cambridge, had heroic good looks. Marianna was darker, and smaller, and more reticent. A plain-featured and soberly dressed cousin from Northumberland, Frederick, was at the same Cambridge college as William, and lived with them at Durley Chase in the vacations.

The memory of Arthur that had accompanied me on the journey fell away as I succumbed to the warm words of welcome, their easy smiles and their fine manners. After only a few minutes I felt I was giving myself to them: like some flower that's had a dark time growing, opening at last to the sun.

They had retained their childhood nicknames. Isabella was Sheba, as in 'Arrival of the Queen of', with a talent for making dramatic entrances. Marianna was Mouse, because that was her way. William was contracted to an amiable mumble, W'm (I was less sure why; he spoke quite clearly, and had an open, confident manner).

Frederick wasn't called that, but instead Moses, after Moses Primrose in *The Vicar of Wakefield*. Goldsmith's Moses was the second son, not very bright, and yet a pedant; sent to the fair to buy a horse, he was talked into spending the money on a gross of green spectacles. Cousin Frederick (a third son) was the cleverest of our group, by their say-so, and even if he was inclined to be pedantic, the name didn't seem to fit at all.

'That's the point,' Isabella said. 'Moses Primrose wouldn't have complained. And neither does Frederick, ever. So, that's the connection, you see.'

Quite frankly, I didn't see. I could tell why modest, restrained Marianna was Mouse; Moses in the Bible was a figure of some passion and vehemence, while *this* Moses in clerical black seemed forbiddingly introverted, certainly compared to either Sheba or W'm.

But I felt I wasn't entitled yet to question the Chadwyck family lore.

I would wake in a golden glow, early sunshine through the new yellow damask of my bedroom curtains. I felt the soft dense mass of duck feathers in the pillow beneath my head and inside the new coverlet.

Comfort and refinement. (This one room had been refurbished for my coming, Sheba told me. I couldn't fail to notice the signs of hard usage elsewhere in the house, but that was as charming to me as the freshness of my bedroom.)

A housemaid came in to stir the fire and bank it up, and then – when I'd given my consent – to open the curtains. She returned with bubbling hot water for my ablutions, and a service of tea presented on a tray.

Might she lay out my clothes?

Yes, of course.

She worked very quietly, but it wasn't a petulant silence as Biddy's sometimes was at home. It was as if she were trying to shade into my surroundings, and often I did forget she was there, and was startled when she took her leave of me, as if one of the pieces of furniture had mysteriously come to life.

Once she'd gone I sat for a while by the window.

There was dew on the grass, and fox trails. Swifts swooped low, criss-crossing. The trees gathered serenity into themselves.

At home I would already have been hearing the first bustle out in the yard. There I could never be quite alone with my thoughts. Here stillness reigned, with only the rustle of coals in the grate and the tiny scrabbling of a mouse behind the wainscot to momentarily interfere, and hardly even that.

⁂

Out of term time Moses helped me with my Virgil translation.

We were tackling Book IV. Dido, Queen of Carthage, is consumed with love for the adventurer Aeneas, but he rejects her.

I didn't look for assistance, but Moses was always ready with it.

How simple *he* could make it seem.

> 'Dido, fetter'd in the chains of love,
> Hot with the venom which her veins inflam'd,
> And by no sense of shame to be restrain'd . . .'

He had me read aloud the original first, before I construed. Then he would demonstrate how.

> 'Dido shall come in a black sulph'ry flame,
> When death has once dissolv'd her mortal frame.'

He put me right about my pronunciation, and the stress I placed on words, and helped me correct my errors; then we moved on.

I didn't know why he gave up his time to me. Sometimes I thought I caught a smile on his lips, especially when the back of his hand was raised to his mouth, as if to conceal it.

'Are you mocking me?'

His face was all shock.

'Well,' I said, 'weren't you smiling?'

'Was I?'

'I'm amusing to you? Or my inability is?'

'Not at all. If I was smiling, then it was involuntary.'

'So you may have been smiling after all?'

'At your achievement,' he said. 'To hear you conquer the text.'

'Oh, Dido! I wish we could be done with her.'

'She fascinates me, though.'

His craggy face, which put me in mind of his Northumberland provenance, lightened. His I found a stilted, rather saturnine kind of levity – as if the features of his face were a little too stiff for ready smiles, even at *my* expense.

'Because she's weak?' I said.

'Not at all. Quite the reverse. All that guilt she has.'

'Doesn't a clergyman-to-be regard guilt as a failing?'

'It can be an inspiration too.'

'Isn't Dido mad? "*I rave, I rave!*"'

'She sees that everything will be a falling away, inevitably. So she consecrates herself to a greater cause – the happiness she knew with Aeneas – she refuses to let *that* die.'

'But she has to die herself.'

'A minor detail.'

'Throwing herself on to a pyre?'

He was smiling again.

'You care for empresses and queens?' I asked him.

'No. For tragic heroines.'

'Why them?'

'Suffering and courageous women who deserve their own immortality.'

❧

We were all talking about the beauty of music. Mozart, Bach. And Purcell, who was their favourite.

Moses said, 'It's *almost* perfect.'

'You could write better?' W'm ribbed him.

'I mean . . . It intimates the perfect, the ideal. It takes us to just a hair's breadth away.'

At that Sheba groaned and W'm winked at Mouse. But I found myself listening more attentively.

'It's never absolutely perfect,' Moses continued. 'Because then we would have heard everything. The apotheosis.'

'Heaven on earth?' Sheba said.

'That's impossible.'

'"*The music of the morning stars –*"' Mouse sang the words softly. '"*– Here in their hearts did sound.*"'

'The utterly sublime is impossible,' Moses said. 'Until we reach the Godhead. Only God, and our absorption, is immaculately perfect.'

General hilarity. Moses caught me sober-faced, and because I didn't want him beholden to me I smiled quickly, then widened the smile unapologetically.

❧

I had a way with the reels, particularly when I was dancing with W'm.

He would often choose me in preference to the other candidates in a crowded room. I guessed they were just as worthy, and I sensed his mother's impatience sometimes, that he ignored the choice she was making with a discreetly indicating closed fan.

Handsome, lively W'm – how could he not inspire me to my best?

My feet would turn the nimblest little skip-step of them all.

In the dance I felt impossibly light. Cotillion or quadrille or double-time galop. I had air beneath my feet.

The Chadwycks had friends who had ballrooms in their homes. And public spaces that linked together, a succession of galleries allowing you to admire the company and price it. Outside, there might be a knot-garden or a temple.

Those friends would have a farm to supply them with milk and whey and cheese; they reared and killed and cured their own meat. Provisions would be sent up to London, to their residence there.

Those friends had friends who had a ballroom in each or all of their homes, who could make a party last across several counties, when a moon was clear to journey by. Their farms vied with one another to supply the best foods; every farm was separated from the next by a forest. So vast were the estates, I heard, that they contained space to erect alternative fantasy worlds: a jousting field, a galleon (or two) on a lake, a private version of old Rome, or St Petersburg, or Nile Egypt, to whatever scale the owners' ingenuity and means could take it.

ꕥ

The thoughtless day, the easy night,
The spirits pure, the slumbers light,
That fly th' approach of morn.

ꕥ

I accompany them across the fields to the chapel. The mist is still lifting. Further off it hangs like tattered banners, like dreams of glory fading. The cattle are like the ghosts of cattle. The grass is silvered with dew.

We follow a path of dried, hard mud. Sheba walks, as always, with an exquisite grace I cannot match; she is an example to us all.

The church bells carry, a soft peal. I hear them inviting us, not admonishing us.

‘I think’, Moses said one Sunday, walking closer beside me on our return, ‘everyone is two individuals.’

‘Ah.’

‘There’s the person here and now, the local person. And there’s the self that watches, from outside, looking down. The transcendental person.’

Why was he telling me this? Was Moses quite right in the head?

‘The local person works towards the other.’

‘“The other”?’

‘Towards conscience, I believe.’

I smiled, vaguely. Was there anything else I could do?

‘We’re lagging behind,’ I said, nodding to the others ahead.

‘Are we?’

I moved away from him, and without looking round I started running to catch up.

I realised it had been a ruse of sorts. The beasts of the field – *that* field – didn’t appreciate it was a Sunday, and Moses had wanted me not to notice they were at their rutting. A transcendental topic, and all to preserve my maidenly modesty.

Chapter Nine

Five miles away from home, I could start to smell the marshes. Mud, weed, iodine, salt. Sour and nippy. Watery, then vegetal. I was being sucked back to the place.

The mudbanks. The drowned fields of spargrass. The fast secret tides running beneath the old slow river-water on top. The calls of the godwits and plovers, 'tu-li', 'wicka-wicka', the different cries, of the birds flying free and those caught in snares.

Chimes blown from church towers further down the estuary. The hellish shudder of a frigate being unmasted at the dockyards. The sombre boom of cannon fire from the hulks sited downstream.

Was I returning to the spot? Or was it reaching out its tentacles on the salty breezes to envelop me?

'So, the reek of hops is not to your fancy, Miss Havisham?'

My father said it with a smile. But the smile, lopsided, was pulled back over a top incisor, so I knew to be careful.

'It is a strong odour,' I told him.

'Hops are a serious business.'

'But the smell gets everywhere.'

'Surely that is a small inconvenience to you. Given the benefits they bring this residence of ours.'

He waved his hand to indicate the many silent rooms of Satis House. The volume and shadowy grandeur of our surroundings, as he believed.

Even with the temporary absence of Arthur, Satis House wasn't Durley Chase, though. My father seemed to see what I was thinking.

'Hops have fed and clothed you these seventeen years.'

I turned my head, glanced away into a corner, fixed on a little framed view of a people-less street in some trim unvisited town.

I could hear my father catch his breath.

'The Havisham name isn't good enough for you, is that it?'

Why was he so irritable, unless he was also trying to justify his life to himself? Had I touched a bared nerve?

'What would you be known as?'

'The Havisham name suits me very well,' I heard myself telling him.

I was acquiring the honed vowels and clipped delivery which he did not have; I could be brittle and sharp and speak as if the remark was only an aside. It kept the colour from rising to my face. I was a little in awe of my own composure.

And so, I realised, was my father. But he had cause for satisfaction too, of an ambivalent sort, because this was what he was paying good money for, to raise me from hops, in elegant company.

⁂

The carriage bowled out of Durley village, and when we'd swung round the last corner the water-meads came into view. The purple haze of the wych elms; the blue flash of a kingfisher's wings; the statuesque *rightness* of the milch cows in that green place chomping on the rich flood-grass.

'*Un gentilhomme*,' Lady Chadwyck said of my father, after enquiring of his health.

She fluttered some pastry crumbs from her fingers. The tea party was in my honour, to welcome me back.

I smiled politely, but sat straighter in my chair, bearing my grandmother in mind, not wanting to let any of them suppose I was a complete ingenue.

Lady Chadwyck had had me sit beside her. She had invited neighbours, in the men's absence, and was in a mood for gaiety. Her face shone. She had that girlish, slightly simpering sort of prettiness which has a degree of pathos to it, because it comes dangerously close to being comic.

I had previously observed a girlish enthusiasm also; she would decide on a course of action in a moment, rising quite suddenly from her chair, dragooning us into a party to go off to . . . The obverse was – something she preferred us not to see – an equally impromptu retreat from high spirits, which her children were used to; this torpor confined her to her own quarters and left her merely watching us from a window.

All was well today, however.

'And now we have you back with us, Catherine!'

There was a new mint silver service, reflecting us where we sat in our chairs. The silver gleamed, and all the more so against the fine but sun-faded furniture, the once expensive but threadbare rugs.

'I am very glad to *be* back,' I told her, in all honesty.

Glad and relieved.

ꝏ

I had brought my box of books back with me, and my sketching pads which I'd been working on in the Cherry Garden at home, and my dancing pumps, in which I'd been practising in my bedroom above my father's office, and half a dozen new dresses. And two hatboxes.

They were the tools, the *emblems*, of an education, although I couldn't yet judge for what end – other than a veneer of accomplishment – I was being prepared.

ꝏ

We dressed three times a day. For morning; for riding; and for dinner.

In the mornings, where I used to have cotton or linen for my gowns, my negligees now were tabby, dimity, Canterbury muslin. Away from Durley, our promenades called for pattens and parasols, a new Camperdown bonnet.

For riding, to match the others, a habit of pompadour broadcloth (a shameless guinea per yard); white dimity waistcoat (with lapels, like the habit); a habit skirt of long lawn; habit gloves; a hat with a trailing feather. I acquired a vast greatcoat, and knotted a white handkerchief round my throat. We resembled strolling Gypsies.

In the evenings, after most of an hour's dishbill (Sheba's favourite neologism from *Fanny Burney*), we emerged like butterflies from our chrysalides. A clouded French satin gown, or rich-toned taffety. An otter-fur tippet for walking out, and a brown silk pelisse, which was the newest thing in greatcoats.

Is it me, that person?

My father dutifully settled all accounts. (£7 4s 0d for a riding habit? Very well.) He didn't demur whenever I felt I had to be in a smarter fashion, because we would be bound to meet even more exalted types soon: that black beaver hat with purple cockade and band. And I had been given the name of a simply divine mantua-maker, a Miss Williams of Tonbridge; everyone – absolutely everyone – swore by her.

❧

I'm not beautiful, not by a long chalk.

I'm not plain either.

My appearance is . . . distinctive. People suppose they can read my character from it.

My eyelids are the heavy Arab sort, and that makes my hazel eyes seem secretive, and possibly supercilious.

My mouth is straight, and is judged to indicate personal severity.

My nose is Roman, but that is *not* a hook.

I have clear facial bones, and a tidy oval chin.

My face is narrow; so is my forehead, but I also have a high brow, so I'm said to have more intelligence than I care to admit to. (I don't quibble with that, although I wish it were true.)

But I'm not just a face, or a body. I'm a Havisham. My appearance is wrapped around with an aura of wealth (provincial, not metropolitan; but money is money) and high living (vulgar rather than sophisticated; but time, between one generation and the next, is the best civiliser).

I don't *need* to be a beauty. Yet no one, except some person ignorant of my name, would consider me less than handsome.

W'm and Moses returned at the term's end.

Other than my father, I had never been as close physically to a man as I found I now was to W'm.

At his own instigation, I felt sure.

Sharing the table in the small study where I did my preparations and he his. Seated next to him at the dining table. Passing him in the corridors. Having my hand taken by him on the inclines of lawn, or at a stile. Letting him place my walking cloak around my shoulders.

Whenever Moses stepped in to do any of these things, it wasn't the same. He was self-conscious where W'm seemed natural and unaffected. I felt that Moses was looking at me every time so that I would register my approval of the deed; which was the reason for my feigning inadvertence.

I asked W'm questions about my schoolroom work. I asked him to explain, several times, Plato's theory of the 'idea' of things: a reality that doesn't alter despite the changing appearance, which – beyond mere sensations' reach – reason alone proves.

All the while I feasted my eyes on him: his sweep of fair hair, and white teeth, and golden eyes, and Greek profile.

I remembered to nod my head, as if I were really capable of understanding.

Moses would tell W'm to slow down a bit, to explain more clearly, and I was irritated. It was as if he assumed I was too stupid. But he had also seen that I truly made very little sense of it all. What right did he think he had to expose me like this?

I ignored Moses as much as I could, and gave my attention – I made a show of giving my attention – to W'm. But W'm wasn't always aware of it, and that was my true vexation.

They had two passions: performing *tableaux vivants* and attending masquerades. They read up about masques in the newspapers. Sheba kept illustrations: the Duchess of Bolton in a man's domino, and then wearing the costume she'd had on underneath, 'the most brilliant Sultana that ever was seen, covered with pearls and diamonds'.

Lady Chadwyck had opened an account at Jackson's Habit-Warehouse in Covent Garden, so I knew that it was a serious pursuit. For the first masque we went as 'Bohemians & Tziganes', in brown stuff jackets and blue stuff petticoats, with straw hats fastened beneath the chin; and red cloaks, in silk instead of rustic wool. Sheba had equipped herself with a crook and live lambs. Our hostess was in peasant wear, as she understood it; a fine pink-

and-white dress in her wardrobe had been cut down, but it was judged a sacrifice worth making.

The theme of the second *bal masqué* was 'Van Dyck'. We didn't have time to seek novel inspiration in the paintings, but had to take what was left in stock that was ruffed and lacy. Once we were decked out, as Charles I or Henrietta Maria or Stuart notables, we had to try to appear – aided or hindered by a hired monkey or spaniel or greyhound – as if we had just walked out of our frames.

Dressing up and acting out was one aspect of my Durley life – the theatrical one. The other was the academic: studying my text books, completing exercises, memorising high-minded and high-flown verse. Somewhere between was the business of singing, playing the keyboard, and drawing and painting: all of which, it seemed to me, involved not just *doing* the task in hand but taking up such a pose and attitude that it was incontrovertibly clear that that was what you were about – delivering a Purcell song with an Amazonian bearing, using the arms like pistons while playing my keyboard preludes and sonatas, musing with crayon or camelhair brush held hovering over the drawing pad or easel.

We learned to be nymphs and goddesses, Gothic abbesses and devout pilgrims, Persian empresses and desert potentates. We plundered the legends of Greece and Rome.

When we went to *bals masqués*, we also had to unmask, at one certain point in the proceedings. Then we were ourselves again: but not entirely so. It was stranger than the masks, seeing familiar faces in unfamiliar guises, aspiring to be somehow larger than life, with grander emotions to dispose of.

I was still being paired with W'm: on walks or at meals, over cards or playing music or at the dance. I wasn't sure how to deal with him.

There was the matter of our proximity; he was taller than my father or Arthur, taller than Moses, with an actor's archetypal good looks, and an actor's way of both positioning himself in profile and – in company – declaiming rather than speaking, yet doing neither with any hint of awkwardness.

More than this physical closeness, though, I felt uncertain about his way of thinking. He didn't seem aware of things like the weather, or atmospherics, as I and his sisters were, which made me think *our* concerns must be trivial in comparison. His had a broader sweep – classical history, his colleagues' reputations (or lack thereof), politics, the cost of property, philosophy, ketching, the price of a Smollett translation of *Don Quixote* he'd seen for sale in Cambridge market.

He never put me down. He assumed that my learning would cease once I was married, but in the meantime he knew not to discourage me. He wasn't adversely critical, as I felt Moses was, and he left me to get on with my own studies; it didn't occur to him that I might need the sort of help which Moses, in his clumsy way, offered me.

The trick was to shift my eyes away before he could catch me looking at him, which was difficult.

If we danced together, I held a fan or handkerchief to my chest, so that he shouldn't see the colour he brought to the surface.

I hadn't come across anyone who comported himself *de profil* like that, and who simultaneously scanned a room so exhaustively. I thought that it must be done for effect – until I discovered, firstly that he was quite short-sighted but wouldn't consider spectacles or a lens, and subsequently that it galled him if he failed to acknowledge someone whom his mother had warned him deserved to be recognised.

❧

If we were ever *alone* together, I immediately sensed his unease.

It was a simple matter of etiquette, of course. But without others around us, it was as if he started to lose his nerve.

At breakfast. In the book-lined passageway that constituted the house's library. Or in the summerhouse.

'Oh, Miss Havisham . . . ' (No conversable, free-and-easy 'Catherine' now.) '. . . have I disturbed you? If I'm disturbing you . . .'

'Not at all,' I would say.

In extremis he made an immediate getaway. 'Actually, I've just remembered . . . you must excuse me if I . . .'

And then he was gone.

Sheba and Mouse were loyal admirers. 'You *do* like him, Catherine?' they were eager to know.

'Oh yes.'

'Not as much as *we* do, of course!'

'But almost,' I said.

'Really?'

'Really.'

'We've noticed, naturally. We've been watching.'

'Oh.'

'And he likes *you*.'

'Yes?'

'Very much. We're both quite sure of that.'

❧

I could tell my father was impressed by my progress. I had snatches of Italian and (less confidently) German to complement my French. I could quote lines from Horace and Sallust. Even when he couldn't understand, he was very taken by the sounds, by the false conviction of my delivery. He could already put a value on returns from his investment.

'Another six months and you'll be up to the best hereabouts. The best, and no mistaking.'

Satis House smelt old and stale to me, as if history had been stacked up in the rooms behind the closed doors. At Durley Chase sunlight swilled about the rooms, and they sweetly smelt of beeswax polish and the scented bulbs and flowers distributed in bowls. My home oppressed me with its sombre fumed-oak panelling and the shadows of the glass-leading on the windows which barred and squared the dark uneven floors.

Arthur would brush against me, shoulder against shoulder, and push ahead of me leaving a room. It exasperated me.

'What do they teach you at that school of yours?'

'Not to go about with our noses stuck up in the air.'

'Not good manners, anyhow.'

'*You* know all about those, do you? Living with that rout.'

'Don't call them that.'

'I don't know why you bother yourself with them.'

Because I have a brother like you. Because he says things like that. Because he's not able to work it out for himself.

'Well . . . ?'

'It doesn't matter.'

'It matters, or you wouldn't go chasing after them like you do.'

'It doesn't matter, about having to explain anything to *you*.'

'Because you can't.'

'Because I'm tired of listening to you.'

'Can't you move all your stuff there?'

'And leave you with the run of this place? That's what you want, of course.'

'What do *you* know about what I want?'

'Precious little. Or care to.'

❧

I gave Sally some of the clothes I no longer wore. They had to be lengthened a little; but since she was thinner in proportion to her height than I was, they didn't need taking out. The fashions had dated slightly, but Sally wore them with such panache that it didn't matter.

'They might have been made for you.'

'I suppose they were. Now that I'm wearing them!'

She had a natural grace, which I envied, because I'd had to concentrate on choreographing my movements with the Chadwycks'; I worked hard to look so languorous. Sally was unaffected and simple, and never gauche. How was it done? I could have taken her into, say, an Assembly Room and passed her off as my cousin – my red-haired cousin – and no one would have suspected. I suggested it once or twice, but Sally declined, politely but quite firmly.

'Then what use will the dresses be?' I asked her.

'I do wear them. I promise you.'

'*When?* Tell me.'

She didn't say.

'You *don't* wear them,' I teased her.

'I do.'

'Promise me.'

'I promise.'

'When, then?'

'When I wish to do my passable imitation of Miss Catherine Havisham.'

'I haven't seen that.'

'No, of course not. We never recognise ourselves.'

We ended up laughing.

'This is silliness, Sally.'

'*You* started it.'

I reached out for her wrists. As I held them, her arms stiffened.

'But you'll take more dresses?'

'Any dress you want to give me.'

'Let me think.'

I continued to hold her wrists. She smiled again, but over her shoulder at the window, out into the yard. My captive.

Chapter Ten

The Cam River had frozen over.

The life beneath was trapped under frosted glass: a wintry half-life. Slow-motion fish and the solidified tendrils of river-weed. A pike, caught by its iced tail, fitfully thrashing; other pike gnawing at it.

A punt was boxed in beside a wall. The funnel of a green bottle stood upright, in magical suspension.

We sat on by the fire. The men talked. Or rather, they *debated*, symposium fashion.

On one side, by the fire-irons, W'm was arguing for rational, scientific thought: pure reason, the Greeks' crystalline *dianoia*. Everything in the universe could be explained.

'Except people's behaviour,' another student said.

'That too. Cause and effect.'

Moses, perched on the fender, was warming to the subject. He took the opposite tack, claiming that the world was quite unreasonable. Think of what lies beyond where the stars end; *do* they end? (I felt light-headed suddenly, just trying to imagine.) Life is an enigma. We have to approach it not scientifically but poetically.

'Piffle!' W'm said.

'Why have we been given souls? To elevate us above substance.'

I sat between the two of them. I inclined first one way and then the other, and back again. To and fro.

Outside, dusk drew on. A red blush rose in the sky, outlining towers and spires and cupolas. A red glow fell on to one wall of the room, and we all seemed to turn instinctively towards it.

'There's a perfectly cogent explanation', W'm said, 'for what we see.'

'We're not looking to understand *why*,' Moses responded. 'We're thinking of God. Or of a memory of some other time, a place. Or it's like life before we were born; swimming in the womb.'

W'm shook his head.

'Light and how it falls is a sequence of connected circumstances. Nothing more.'

'There's always something behind what we see,' retorted Moses. 'An image. A renaissance, or an ideal. Reality has a fourth dimension.'

W'm tapped his head. Sheba, who had said little, gave vent to some good-humoured laughter. Mouse sighed at the conundrum.

And for myself, I jumped when a coal in the hearth split, and sparks went whistling up the chimney into the dark.

Wine, heated and honeyed, was served to us from a silver chafing-dish embossed with the college's coat of arms.

Sitting there I had a sense of completeness, even though the argument hadn't been won by either party. There was a fitness, an appropriateness, about everything: whether conspiring to this end, or accidentally achieved. I felt I belonged here, in this set of rooms at the top of a flight of old worn wooden stairs, with these people, on this particular evening with the redness in the sky flaring to indigo and the sweet marsala wine in my old fluted glass sparkling against the firelight.

A door was unlocked, a bolt drawn back, and then we were admitted to a long colonnaded gallery furnished with stone heads, torsos, dislodged limbs. There were several dozen fragments of

Greek and Roman statues, each of them many times larger than life. Our footsteps echoed in the skylit gloom – as did our exclamations of astonishment.

Muscular shoulders. The spine's runnel on a goddess's back. Smooth buttocks, inviting a hand's touch. Assorted *parties intimes*, with or without sculpted vegetation for cover.

I didn't want to catch anyone's eye, so I stood behind the others to glean their reactions. Mouse contriving to be studious; Sheba, slowing by the goddesses and naiads to take note of the classical dimensions of beauty; W'm, with a reminiscent air, fascinated by first a hand and then a foot; and Moses, poor Moses, so horribly embarrassed, and making one believe – because he looked the opposite way – that the intimate parts on display were far below his high-minded regard.

It was Moses who later rounded up the other four of us and our two companions, older women friends of Sheba, and urged us to leave.

'Aren't you cold? I feel I'm turning to marble myself –'

I waited a while longer, to prove that I wouldn't be rushed, but I felt my eyes were out of my control, either swivelling about or waterily staring.

It *was* cold in here. More than that, though, it was airless, quite airless. I fanned myself with a pamphlet, as I might have done in the heat of high summer, and when I became a little dizzy I had to lean against a pillar. I closed my eyes. I felt a strong grip on my arm, my elbow, someone was holding me up. My eyes, still closed, saw W'm's face, but when I opened them he was at the door, and protecting me was Moses. I took back my arm.

'Thank you. I – I'll be fine.'

That long face of angles, with all its sensibleness intact, the redoubtable decency.

I hurried away. I didn't know why he had this effect on me, or why I was making so light of his kindness, even punishing him for it.

Chapter Eleven

Lady Elizabeth Gray was a favourite subject for tableaux. We took our inspiration from a couple of engravings. Valentine Green's for 'Lady Elizabeth Gray at the Feet of Edward the Fourth, Soliciting the Restoration of her late Husband's forfeited lands, 1465'. John Downman's later work caused us to enact 'Edward the Fourth on a visit to the Duchess of Bedford is Enamoured of Lady Elizabeth Gray'.

We portrayed the death of Lady Jane Grey, as Green devised it in our essential text, *Acta Historica Reginarum Anglia*. There was the Marriage of King Henry VIII with Ann Bullen. And – marking my preferment to the centre of stage, where I had expected to be a grieving lady-in-waiting – Mary Queen of Scots, about to be executed.

Look at me!

I'm dressed in black satin and velvet, with a high white ruff. I wear two crucifixes and a rosary. I have walked, quite composed, into the great hall of Fotheringhay Castle. I have instructed my trusty servant, Melville, to take word to my son James, the King of Scotland, that I have always sought the unification of the two kingdoms, Scotland and England. I have listened as the execution warrant was read aloud to me, telling me I am about to be put to death like some ordinary felon. I have prayed in a voice that might carry to the nearly two hundred spectators gathered here, for blessings on the English Church, for my son James and for the agent of my doom, Elizabeth of England. I have given solace to my sorrowing attendants, I have – strangely – spoken with no little wit to the men who will put me to death, my killers. I have stretched out on the floor and laid my neck on the block, placing myself in the hands of God. My ladies weep. The axe is raised. I am on the point of speaking those words which will be my last. 'Sweet Jesus.' Secreted beneath my gown but visible is the little Skye terrier, true now as ever to his mistress, offering me my final comfort.

The tableau has been given the motto Mary embroidered herself on her cloth of state, which is placed beside the block. 'In my end is my beginning.'

Look at me!

Awaiting the death blow.

I have laid my head sideways, so that the audience can see my face and I can see theirs. Just out of my sight – I'm thankful about it – is the executioner's blade, which has to be held quite still for the two minutes it takes as the commentary is delivered from the side of the stage.

Only the wee terrier moves, but even he might be conscious of the solemnity of the grand event being depicted.

Some in the audience take handkerchiefs to their eyes. There's a good deal of troubled wriggling in chairs. I feel chastened myself, and sad.

But this is Catherine Havisham's dignification, even though I'm wearing a red wig – hair as red as Sally's – and have my face heavily powdered. (There's a little drift of the stuff on the block, on the black velvet of my gown.)

I feel I'm at the centre of everyone's attention: or at any rate, the figure I represent is the focus of every pair of eyes in the room (the dog's apart). I shall never feel more essential to the Chadwycks and their friends and their friends' friends than I do at this supreme moment – actually two, extending to nearly three minutes – until the blade starts to wobble, and the dog (snuffling) wanders off, and the most pious in the audience need to excuse themselves for air, and one of my genteel ladies threatens to faint, and the dog barks.

Curtains are drawn across our stage. The actors all relax, and make for the side tormentors. For some reason no one thinks of assisting me to my feet. But what of it, I am only a pretend queen, and a queen done to death, as if the ritual of human sacrifice was still being practised in the year of grace, *anno domini* 1587.

❧

We were also attending Assemblies, in the towns of fashion in the South. We accompanied Lady Charlotte to Cheltenham. And thence to Bath, where we bathed with her in our caps and shifts. There too we were drawn to the lights and music, like moths.

A personable stranger's face meeting mine. The same pair of hands crossing with mine several dances apart, then for a couple in succession.

'You don't recall?'

'"Recall" . . . Should I?'

'The theatricals. At Chartridge. I saw your Mary Stuart. Splendid. I shed a tear or two.'

I was carrying my fan and a woollen shawl Mouse had lent me, since she knew about the Bath draughts.

In my embarrassment I let go of the fan. My interlocutor picked it up for me.

'A famous trick, that one.'

'I beg your pardon?'

'A lady dropping her fan.'

He laughed. I was puzzling how to respond when I felt a hand on the small of my back and I was very swiftly propelled from the spot. I hadn't time to do more than look over my shoulder, not even apologetically.

'It was someone who . . .'

'What, Catherine? Did I interrupt you?'

Sheba turned and looked back, in the wrong direction.

'No,' I said. 'Over there.'

But he had gone: and perhaps – quite possibly – Sheba hadn't even meant to look towards where he had been standing.

We repeated our success with the Queen of Scots. As I lay with my head on the block, I could see him. My fan-recoverer. I hadn't meant to notice anyone, but . . .

He was in one of the front seats, not at all secretive about his presence. I tried not to notice him after that. I concentrated on Mary instead, on her struggle to see nothing of what was happening to her, not to feel, not to think back or to think forward either, in case she screamed out with terror, but to give up her Catholic soul gladly to her Maker.

He found me.

He left the people he was talking to. Someone called after him, 'Mr Compeyson!', but he ignored the request. He congratulated me. The voices were so loud, he had to lean closer.

'Didn't they let you go on wearing your show-clothes, your friends?'

'Our costumes?'

'Not that I'm objecting to what you've got on, you understand. You could teach most of them here a thing or two.'

'I think not.'

'I beg to differ. Why so little confidence, Miss Havisham?'

'You know my name?'

He held out his programme. He had marked a red cross against my name.

Lady Charlotte was approaching, and I backed away from him. She was raising her glass to her eye. I swept past him, muttering an apology. I fixed my gaze on Lady Charlotte, and smiled boldly, feeling . . . feeling that an aviary of tiny panicking birds was suddenly let loose inside my head.

❧

'It's always been understood,' Mouse said, 'that's all. We've always known.'

'And W'm knows too?'

'Yes. He will make a good match, and assure the future of Durley.'

Why was I being told this?

'When?' I asked.

'When he finds whoever she is.'

Mouse smiled, looking out the window, across the small park to where our neighbours' began.

Why did she smile?

'"She"?'

'The one who's destined to be the mistress of the Chase one day.'

I waited.

What else was I supposed to think? W'm was honour bound to act, wasn't he? But I was aware that now there often wasn't a vacant seat next to mine which he could fill. Or a fourth was required for cards at the next table, and would I *or* W'm care to oblige?

He had caught a cold somewhere, and wasn't able to sing, although I didn't see why that should prevent him from turning my pages as I played the Broadwood. He was lent some gun dogs, and when we all went walking it was necessary for him to keep them in order, going off to whistle after them. Even in the dining room: Lady Chadwyck had had draughts on the brain since

Bath, and her son exchanged places with her, while experiments continued with rolled sausages of felt under the doors and putty in the window frames. All, so far as I could tell, quite legitimate, but no less frustrating, because no apology was ever offered to me.

My mind wandered off. I found myself thinking of someone else: the stranger. The mysterious Mr Compeyson. (Christian name unknown.)

His ready attention. His unsubscribing spirit as he'd mocked our dancing partners with his eyes. His amusing contrariness as he exchanged politesse with people he knew no better than I but pretended he did.

The sense that we were engaged, just briefly, in some mutual conspiracy.

The way his voice had dropped, warmly, into my ear.

The aviary birds inside my head, and the muffled commotion he'd set up in the pit of my stomach, another little whorl of excitation.

I had to lay the canvas on my lap, set out my colours on the little folding table, and paint the view.

'Paint what is *there*,' Signor Scarpelli had instructed me. 'Only what you see.'

What I saw, was that what was present? How similar was it to what Sheba saw, or Mouse?

Signor Scarpelli had demonstrated the grid; the boxes; he had told us about meet proportions, about 'pair-spect-eev'. But it didn't make the job of representing, of turning a presence into its image, any easier.

Chapter Twelve

I pulled my skirts in as I passed Arthur. I could smell the drink on his breath again.

'What? I offend you, do I?'

I didn't reply.

'You're too grand now to speak? And I'm not worth an answer?'

He grabbed my arm.

'Sister Catherine –'

'Let go of me!'

He was tall, nearly six feet already, but he didn't have the strength of mind to resist me. I shook him off.

A sum of money was missing from my father's quarters. He summoned the staff, one by one. They left the room looking more shocked by the questioning than indignant, as I felt they had a right to be.

'It was bound to happen,' I told my father.

'Why so?'

'It's not something that's ever happened before.'

'Exactly. What's changed, then?'

Then we didn't have Arthur living under the same roof as ourselves. I didn't need to say it. My father's eyelids dropped with the realisation, he made a little funnel for air with his mouth.

Arthur seemed to have no compunction about helping himself. He ordered clothes without telling my father, but expected him to pay for them. He took my father's horse one evening when we had guests to dine in the house. At three o'clock one morning he was found feeding his friends from the larder. He was revenging himself for the obscurity he'd had to suffer while living with his mother.

Other thefts were taking place, from coffers and sideboard drawers and the backs of presses, and we only discovered because a colleague of my father came across for sale in Canterbury a small silver dish engraved with a style of 'H' he recognised. I didn't know how many addictions he was having to finance: tobacco (his fingers were yellowing at the tips), snuff (his nostrils had a raw red look), wine (he only drank vintage Bordeaux). A pokerwork box containing ivory dice and several decks of playing cards was missing, a minor loss, but I thought it significant. He goaded the guard dogs, and I wondered if that was because he watched dogs turned against each other for amusement.

A curfew was set.

'In my own home?' Arthur objected. 'That's ridiculous.'

'You've got an answer for everything,' my father said.

'And if I forget?'

'I shall regard forgetfulness as disobedience.'

Arthur's response was to emit through his teeth a long, dying whistle.

Bolts were attached to the doors, to enforce the rules. Arthur tried climbing in through the windows, until the shutters were fastened by bars. He attempted to bribe the more gullible of the housemaids to let him in, but on the second occasion he was sick in the hall before falling heavily on the staircase; he was too drunk to get up, and my father found him there in the morning, in a sot's thick sleep.

'Say something to him, sister.'

'Say what to whom?'

'"Oh father of ours, forgive Arthur. It's just high spirits. Don't keep him short."'

'I'll do no such thing.'

'No, I didn't think you would. Selfish bitch.'

'You disgust me.'

'Always taking his side. What else should I expect?'

'Don't blame *me*.'

'Dead against me, aren't you?'

'You're an enemy to yourself. No one could do it better.'

'*You* told him. "No more cash." It was *you*.'

'My father can make his own mind up.'

'Whisper-whisper in his ear.'

'You're revolting.'

'You've put him up to this.'

'I don't know what you're –'

'"Make Arthur a pauper." As if I don't deserve the ready. Every bloody farthing.'

'You're a savage.'

'And you're a liar. A creeping Judas.'

'I'm a Havisham.'

'But so am I.'

'How do I know that?'

His face darkened. His features set to the hardness of mica.

'Well, I don't, do I?' I looked away. 'Your father could be any Tom, Dick or –'

I didn't see until it was too late, his hand taking aim, then swinging out at me.

Where did that strength come from?

He caught me full across the face. I felt – I distinctly felt – the sharp edge of his signet ring, tearing my skin. The stinging pain.

I doubled over with the hurt. A gash on my cheek was oozing sticky blood.

White flares dropped in front of my eyes; the floor ran away from me. I thought I was on the point of passing out. I closed my eyes and concentrated on not fainting, not fainting.

I was left slumped over the banister. I had a presentiment he was gone, and wouldn't be back for a while.

When I'd found a mirror I saw my face burning red, I had a cut on my cheek, and the first bruises were already spreading.

ℒ

My father had the brutal evidence in front of him.

'This is your brother's doing?'

'Not my brother,' I told him.

My mouth was swollen. I had to slowly shape words to come out, woolly approximations to words.

But I didn't need to tell him, anyway, that a real brother would not have done such a thing.

I had to wait until my face started to heal before I could leave.

My father had collected an inventory of complaints. I anticipated the trouble there would be once I was safely away.

Sally comforted me. She listened to my tales about Arthur, and didn't defend him; she was careful about criticising him directly, out of her own mouth, as if she felt she might be speaking out of turn. She sat with me in the garden. I described goings-on at Durley Chase, and I regaled her with it all. The tableaux, the masques. The sights of Bath and Cheltenham. W'm's mysterious preoccupations. My encounters with the stranger, Mr Compeyson.

'He sounds quite a familiar stranger.'

'It's a small world,' I said.

'Of course it is!'

I laughed with her, and even though it hurt my face, I couldn't stop laughing.

ℒ

My carriage bowled out of Durley Tye. When we'd swung round the last corner, the water-meads came into view. I was never so relieved to see them.

The thirsty willows, the cattle wading to their knees in the flood-grass, the sheep idly grazing on the drier pasture beyond.

And drowsy tinklings lull the distant folds.

❧

Another theatrical evening.

We were rehearsing our contribution, a *tableau vivant* of 'The Flight of the Duke of Northumberland, on the Entrance in Triumph of Queen Mary to London'.

The house was called Wix Grange. The owners were called Merriweather.

In an interlude I walked off to clear my head. I found myself in a walled garden, then in a second.

Suddenly – urgent footsteps, scattering gravel. Rounding a corner, W'm appeared. His face lit up when he saw me.

'The very person!'

He accompanied me, at a more seemly pace, to a temple standing by a pool. Or so I thought it was, until we came closer, and I realised it was only a windowless facade. On a pediment, in freshly gilded lettering, the name THESPIS. Twilight was falling on us.

We seated ourselves in the little temple, on a scroll-ended stone bench. As we sat there, bats we had disturbed flitted in and out above our heads, scratching about in the rafters. Swifts came darting low to drink at the pool, taking up water as they dipped, setting off tiny ripples on the dark surface of water, a hypnotic pattern of circles.

And all the air a solemn stillness holds.

The air itself smelt of lilac and magnolia, thickly sweet, and of sharper-tanged rosemary from the walkways where an occasional rabbit frisked along the brickwork. Rosemary for rue.

The temple was a folly. Somehow I forgot that it wasn't genuine, and it was a fact easily overlooked in the welter of other sensations.

We are led to Believe a Lie
When we see not Thro' the Eye,
Which was Born in a Night to perish in a Night.

What did we talk about, sitting there? Trivia maybe. I only remember that I was trying to read a different meaning into everything W'm said, which became the primary meaning.

How long did we talk for? A quarter-hour? Or was it half an hour?

I recall a man's figure twice, three times appearing in the outer garden, visible through an archway. He stopped to watch us. The third time he was there W'm drew closer to me, pointed to the closing eyes of the water lilies in the pool, and I thought it must be to distract me from the silver-haired observer in the dusk, to exclude him from this intimate ambience – scented by the shrubs, with its inaudible serenading of bats, written to the frantic crotchet runs of the swifts flashing past in the inky air.

I was chattering. I asked him, did he agree with Aaron Hill? In his book.

Agree about what?

Well, about there being – how many was it? – ten emotions to play out on the stage. Ten humours. I tried to remember what they were.

Joy. Sorrow. Anger. Envy. Love. Hate.

W'm didn't make any suggestions for the list. Four remained. I thought at first that he couldn't have been listening. But surely not. He came close enough for me to feel the heat of his breath. And then to catch traces of his perspiration: a dark musky fragrance, which had the effect of deliciously knotting my stomach.

We were still being watched. The man was dressed as David Garrick, after Gainsborough. I had seen him earlier, with a young woman in the guise of one of the painter's feathered and pearl-draped sitters; they had been laughing together in the comfortable way of people who haven't just newly met, who weren't aware that W'm was anxiously scrutinising them. (Could it have been to her that W'm had directed his letter, at the afternoon's end? I'd noticed him slip a sealed item of correspondence to a footman and tip the fellow a generous minding.)

I watched our watcher walking off. Diverted for those moments, I failed to register that W'm had lost whatever interest he'd had in talking to me. He jumped to his feet and told me, he must be off now. He didn't offer to walk me back to the house.

'Remember, half past eight.'

'Yes,' I said. 'I'm remembering.'

He didn't go out by the archway, which I supposed was the only egress. I heard a crackle of undergrowth, disappearing footsteps.

Making my own way back to the house, I felt a chill through my costume. From nowhere I had gained a companion. Moses. That absurd, juvenile name.

'Frederick –'

'Nobody calls me that, you know.'

'You frightened me. Why won't you announce yourself?'

I hadn't asked any such thing of W'm, but I wasn't comparing like with like.

'Are you feeling quite well?'

'Of course I am,' I said. 'Why shouldn't I be?'

'You look . . . downcast.'

'What?'

'Melancholic.'

'Why on earth –'

'A little pale. Don't be nervous.'

'What about?'

'The tableau.'

He offered me his arm, crooking it so that I might insert my own. I drew back.

His long face and outsized jaw. The large eyes, the bulbous nose. The hesitant and eternally patient smile.

'I can walk, thank you. I'm not as weak and vapid as you like to think I am.'

'I would never presume such a thing.'

'Someone else might require your propping up instead of me.'

He was mumbling, and I didn't catch all that he said. 'Moral support,' I heard. And '. . . no more than . . .'

He followed a few steps behind me, trailing me, a shadow to my shadow. The faster I walked, the faster he did. I dashed up the side steps, but somehow he reached the door before me, and was able to hold it open. I walked indoors, and felt the searing reprimand of my conscience – a necklace of hot coals round my neck – as I declined to offer him any thanks. I had tears in my eyes, and I didn't want him to see. Tears of frustration and disappointment, which blurred the interior of the green marble hall and transformed the staircase to a water cascade.

In the carriage at our departure Sheba was on the look-out for someone among the throng on the main steps of the house. She spotted the young woman who had earlier been the Gainsborough imitation, and she clasped Mouse's arm to have her look too. The sisters exchanged words out of the corners of their mouths.

Suddenly the woman turned to observe our carriage, as if she had known all along we were there, in the queue of transport waiting to leave. Her eyes had drawn me earlier as we passed in a corridor. They were half-closed, and yet I could have believed they were more alert than all the others, so wide and shiny and artificially sparkling, in the throng around us.

W'm was mounted immediately behind us. I couldn't see him, but I did notice a smile pass for the briefest instant across the woman's face as she turned away. The silver-haired man from the garden was descending the steps; clearly he considered himself the woman's proprietor as he alighted on her – as keenly, I felt sure, as any bird of prey on its quarry.

ℒ

The look of love alarms
Because 'tis fill'd with fire;
But the look of soft deceit
Shall win the lover's hire.

ℒ

I mentioned to W'm the Temple of Thespis three or four days later.

'Eh?' He gave me a charming, unremembering smile.

'By the pool,' I said. 'With the swifts.'

'Oh yes. Of course. The Temple. Of Thespis. Very good!' He laughed.

I couldn't break his spell, even if I were to try. His fall of fine hair. The firm, straight nose. The high cheekbones. The elegant, baroque mouth. Golden eyes. Couldn't those eyes see the truth in front of him – that I had been smitten from the moment of first seeing him? Nothing had changed. Yes, W'm played his little games, and he would carry on playing them. But I forgave him, as we all did. He allowed us no choice about that. Charmed by him, we could do nothing else.

Chapter Thirteen

Thereafter, we proceeded – advanced – to the Discourses.

W'm expressed his purpose: to unify Grecian grace and Etruscan simplicity.

Sheba stood on steps, right arm on her hip, to resemble a statue we knew from engravings, the Mattei Ceres in Rome; she wore a sea-green mantle, and in her left hand she held a blood-red rose.

I was Hebe, and a different challenge. I wasn't called upon to dance, but to stand – my torso slightly twisted – beside a plinth, one arm wrapped round a jar. A gold strophion plaited about my pink dress held my breasts high, in the antique way. My hair was piled and knotted, as the ancients would have appreciated.

I was the handmaiden of the gods, a creature of heavenly favour. I was about to pour out nectar from the vessel. I represented perpetual youth.

I tried to convey, as Milton had described, 'the Nods and Becks and wreath'd Smiles, such as hang on Hebe's cheek'.

Above me, supported from the side of the stage, was one vast, cleverly painted, outstretched wing of golden feathers: the wing of the mighty eagle which Jupiter had taken as his disguise. It overarched me, threatening to overwhelm and devour me – a menace every bit as much as a guard. But I continued to smile, not too broadly, to convey (so W'm had directed me) something of the unsuspecting, trustful joy of youth.

❧

The others were with various of their friends, who had descended on them at the same juncture, which meant he could find me quite straightforwardly. I was aware of his approach. I busied myself with a pot of black and yellow tulips.

'Miss Havisham –'

'Mr Compeyson –'

He drew me into conversation. He was unsure about the legends; he confused them – or pretended to – and told me he'd had a misspent youth. But he spoke so well, so eloquently, and was so much the picture of a gentleman, and wouldn't say how he'd misspent his time, that I happily gave *that* admission – his purported admission – no credence at all.

He was good-looking, if in a more predictable way than W'm. Summer-blue eyes. A straight but short nose. Brown hair that curled. Top lip a little thinner than the lower one, which had a sensual amplitude, as if, I fancied whenever I took advantage of his distracted eyes to look at his mouth, head had been set against heart.

He set out to persuade me I should tell him about myself. He wanted to hear.

'What about?'

'Anything you like.'

'You're so eager to hear for some reason – I could tell you anything, and you'd believe me?'

'I'd believe Catherine Havisham.'

I fussed with the petals of some of the black tulips in the jardiniere. He stroked the stem of a yellow.

'You wouldn't *know* if it was about me or not.'

'Who else *could* it be about?'

'Sally,' I said, and laughed.

'Who on earth's Sally?'

'She might be more interesting to hear about than me.'

'I think not.'

'You can't say most definitely. You'd need to contrast and compare.'

'Well, about this Sally first. And then, please, all about *you*.'

❦

Sally. In my old loose chintz sack. In my blue satin pumps with the yellow bows. With my copy of *The Sorrows of Young Werther*, and a list of quotations from the text which she has copied out in the neat script which I taught her.

'I tell him about you, Sally.'

'About *me*? Gracious, what for?'

'He likes to hear.'

'But what d'you say to him? There's nothing *to* tell.'

It was an innocent enough pastime. I tried to draw him out, on the sort of looks he preferred.

'Sally has green eyes.'

'Nothing so nice as tawny.'

'Thick hair.'

'What colour?'

'Copper.'

'Fair for *me*. Like yours.'

'A long neck.'

'That's fine for swans.'

'Quite dainty feet, considering.'

'Tire too easily.'

'Well, you won't believe me. But she's a very attractive girl, I assure you.'

'Good for her, then.'

'She's wasted. She should be set up as – some merchandiser's wife. At least.'

'Maybe she will be.'

'She doesn't rate herself highly enough for that. She needs someone to tell her.'

'And do *you*?'

'Oh no! I don't want her to go and desert me, do I now?'

❧

I was avoiding Arthur, but he followed me into the garden one evening. I didn't look at him.

'He used to play with me. Gave me things.'

'Who did?'

'My father. He told me I'd be rich one day. And my mother would be proud of me.'

'I know nothing about that.'

'He's setting *you* up very nicely, isn't he?'

'And he's sent *you* to school. You don't look poor to me. Those clothes and boots –'

'What are you saying to him?'

'It's none of your business what happens at Satis House.'

'I should have an equal share of it with you. When he croaks.'

'I'll tell him *that*, shall I?'

'Go rot in hell.'

I couldn't forget the strain of work on my father's heart, and I longed to ease the burden, however I could. Enlightening him as to the truth of Arthur's character wasn't the way.

❧

I showed Sally what had been delivered to the house. A small pot containing miniature black and yellow tulips.

'Don't you wish you were me, Sally? But you'll share the pleasure of looking at them with me.'

She admired them, but guardedly.

'Can you guess who they're from? Of course you can.' Of course she could.

Mrs Venn informed me later that it was Sally who had brought them to the house.

'*You* did, Sally?'

'Well, I was walking by. A horse with a pannier drew up and the rider asked me where I might find Satis House.'

'Was it him?'

'I hardly saw.'

I had her describe him to me.

'Brown hair? And curly?'

'Yes.'

'His face?'

'The details have gone.'

'Why didn't you say?'

'All I had to do was take the pot from him.'

'So, it wasn't a surprise? When I showed you?'

'I'd only glanced at them.'

'You sly-boots!'

Not that I minded at all. It brought Sally closer in to the delightful confusion of my afternoon.

'How shall I acknowledge it?'

'He'll know you've received it.'

'But I must thank him,' I said.

'D'you have an address for him?'

'No.'

'Then he can't mean you to thank him.'

'Until I see him again. Oh, what if I *don't* see him again?'

'I don't doubt you will.'

'Here, in the town. Whatever was he doing here? Did he come especially?'

'He meant you to have a souvenir. The tulips.'

'Yes,' I said. 'He must have.'

A few moments later it occurred to me: I hadn't supplied that particular – the arrangement of tulips – when I'd described the evening of the Discourses to her.

She had divined it somehow, that the choice of flower and colours wasn't accidental. I put my arm round Sally's waist.

'How lucky I am,' I said.

'To have met your Mr Compeyson?'

'No!' I laughed. 'To have met you first.'

Chapter Fourteen

I wrote to my father from Durley Chase. And then, when he'd granted his permission, I wrote to Sally. I had been invited to a Carnaval Masque (spelling thus). It promised to be one of the highlights of the season. Would she like to see it for herself? She wouldn't, needless to say, be my *maid*, not as such, but for purposes of form and protocol, we would have to agree she be called that for the evening.

Sally didn't reply immediately, and I thought I might have to write again. When I did hear from her, she sounded less effusive than I'd been expecting. Nevertheless, 'if my situation permits', she was willing to accept my proposal. She didn't mention anything about her duties, having to attend on me, and I was grateful that she spared us both that embarrassment.

At Durley Mouse explained to Lady Chadwyck, and the housekeeper was instructed to treat Sally more favourably than was usual for the two nights she would be under their roof.

Sally carried herself with a suitable dignity, and the housekeeper was impressed, supposing this was the calibre of staff we insisted on in Kent. To me, though, she seemed to be abstracted about something.

'You're not going to be in any trouble with the archdeacon, are you, coming away like this?'

She said, no, it had all been attended to quite amicably.

I asked after her widowed mother, was she well?

'Oh yes. She'll live to be a hundred.'

'Nothing else is bothering you?'

'No.'

'Nothing about the Carnaval? What you have to –'

'No.'

She smiled and put some cheer back into her face, but I wished I could feel more convinced. I hoped *I* wasn't responsible, guilty – inadvertently, through decent intentions gone awry – of compromising her good nature.

Even the Chadwycks, I sensed, were taken aback by the extravagance of the occasion.

The rooms had been hung with panels painted with scenes of Venice. Even though I had never been, I recognised the locations at once, the palazzi and bridges and receding canals, the grand salons – even grander than ours this evening – glimpsed through arched windows.

The footmen were dressed as they might have been in the Doge's Palace, while the waiters were imitation gondoliers. The food was prepared as spectacularly as if for a Venetian feast-day, piled high on stepped salvers. The goblets were of blue Venetian glass.

The company moved about in their masks – gold, silver, scarlet, multi-coloured, or stark black or white – and sweeping their trains and long cloaks. I could recognise almost no one.

Our hosts were in elaborate disguise. Lord Villiers carried a long staff surmounted by a large circular medallion trailing gold tassels. Lady Villiers's dress was in several sculpted sections, like the queen on a suit of playing cards.

We glided about the rooms obscured by our masks, the ladies further protected by our spread fans. We were serenaded with the music of Vivaldi and Uccellini, played on flutes, theorbos, violas da gamba. The musicians wore lace jabots and two-foot-high white wigs.

Red and silver roses were growing from Sheba's head. Her face was striped like a cheetah's. Her mouth was barely open at all, and she seemed to be taking her last earthly breaths of air. The mask-maker had provided me with a harlequin style, with lozenges of blue and yellow. The high, exaggerated lines of the cheekbones and the sharpness of the nose allowed a little vital air to circulate under the close-fitting shell.

Moses had excused himself from the evening, denying it was because he disapproved of the theme. Mouse might have taken him at his word, but W'm told her that Moses wouldn't have said it if he hadn't been feeling morally superior. Anyway, W'm added, Moses had another, very good reason for not joining in: leaving his preparations too late, in the little time left he'd failed to find a costume that would fit him. (Prosaic, I thought, but quite probable.)

At either end of one of the reception rooms two figures were suspended from the ceiling on platforms. On one, surrounded by aureate rays, the sun – androgynously dressed in gold-coloured material and skin painted in gold. On the other, a silver figure – similarly sexless, astride a crescent moon.

A plague doctor. Black-faced, with a fall of scarlet ribbons on his chest; a long beaked nose, cruel and pointed like a razorbill. A three-cornered hat, as black as the cape, with a plumage of black ostrich feathers. A white cane, tap-tapping on the polished floors.

But who was this?

A silver mask floating past mine. Or, when I turned my head, it would be only a couple of feet away over my shoulder.

'You really don't recognise me?'

I stared into the almond-shaped eyeholes. I couldn't tell the colour of those irises, even by the shine from the chandeliers in the atrium. His voice, it was only affecting the aristocratic drawl –

His hand reached out and lifted mine by the fingers, gently holding it in mid-air.

'Signorina –'

It was the rush of heat to my neck which told me. I pulled back my hand, even though it wasn't my true choice.

'Mr Compeyson? *You* were invited?'

'No, no. Certainly not.'

'What did you do – ?'

'Filched an invitation.'

'How?'

'There are ways.'

'But the Villierses . . .'

'. . . wouldn't be bothered with the likes of me?'

'No. I didn't mean . . . Why – why have you come?'

'Can't you guess?'

At least he couldn't see my full discomposure.

'What if they ask you to leave?'

'They won't.'

I noticed Mouse watching me through her eyeholes. From another direction I saw Sheba's rose garden moving towards us.

'We'll meet here again,' I said, 'in half an hour's time.'

He didn't ask, where's 'here'; like me, his instincts would lead him back to the spot.

There was always someone to interrupt us. I felt that the lagoon tides themselves were at work, allowing us to approach and collide and then, just as inevitably, sweeping each of us away again, on the night's irresistible flow. Because we had to speak in snatches, we let ourselves be more outspoken about our surroundings and the company, and I didn't interrupt, and by not stopping him I felt I was colluding with him, right at the hub, and I didn't care; it was a release to me, a brewer's daughter who found herself here by some nonsensical but (so far) undetected accident.

Some costumes were fabulously coloured, trimmed with stones and pearls that might be precious or not, they glittered in front of your eyes for an instant and then they were gone. All the unknown colours of Africa and India. Voluptuous silks, the softest furs. Immaculately impassive faces, perhaps studded with jewels, or glass. A movement of an eye inside a hollow socket, a glimpse of teeth in the shadow behind the parted lips, and that was all to serve as a clue to identity.

'The jungle cat's face –'

'That's Sheba.'

'Who?'

'Isabella.'

'I wondered why she was always prowling about.'

'She means well, I expect.'

'Yes?'

'She's protecting me.'

'From what? Or from whom?'

'I – don't know. I didn't ask her to –'

'Better to be safe.'

'I don't feel I'm in danger.'

'Big cats could do you more harm than anything.'

'Not Sheba.'

'You could trust your life to her?'

'I think I'm wanted. You'll have to excuse –'

'Fifteen minutes?'

'Let's say twenty.'

'The lady decides. Twenty it is.'

The rooms echoed with laughter, with shrieks and exclamations, with the sounds of frivolity. Yet eyes looking out from behind the gouged sockets might seem strangely old and tired, while the faces bore no blemishes and were infallible symbols of youth.

And always there was the plague doctor, with his long snout hanging down in front. He had the knack of materialising a few feet away from me, even fleeter than Sheba, and brazenly coasting past. He left a chill behind him; stirred in with the funereal perfume of the luxuriant white lilies forced for months under hothouse glass to offer just moments of diversion during the hours of this long night.

By the time the masks came off – there would unfailingly be an unmasking at some point in any evening – I couldn't find him. My eyes roamed around the rooms. I slipped away from the others, having shed my own disguise, but feeling that somehow the music that continued to serenade us would be a discreet cover.

Was he hiding from me? I was quite determined to find him. I knew that he couldn't escape me if he was still here.

Why leave without telling me?

Was it to save me embarrassment?

Or – or because he knew better the hold he had over me, and he meant to keep me in thrall? I went looking for Sally. Our maids and servants, milling about the back quarters, spoilt the illusion for us, not being in Venetian dress.

I discovered Sally by herself in a requisitioned laundry room, head down, sewing the hem of her dress. She jumped when she saw me.

'Oh, it's *you*!'

'Don't tell me you forgot about me?'

She forced a smile.

'I had a mishap, I caught my foot in the hem –'

I wanted to tell her who was here, but I didn't dare risk a disclosure at the moment, not even to Sally. She looked tired. Her eyes were a little puffy. Venice had had its back rooms of servants too, serving the formal ceremony – the pomp and circumstance – of the salons.

'Have you seen it, Sally?'

'A little.'

'You've been outside, at the fireworks? You have mud on your shoes.'

She looked down at her feet.

'Aren't you glad you came?' I asked her. 'Imagine having missed this!'

We left the house at three in the morning, in a drizzle. The candles in the outdoor lanterns fizzed and sputtered. Sally had my cape ready. I sat in the Chadwycks' carriage watching the departing guests. One with his silver face back in place proffered his three-cornered hat and bowed deep as we rolled past. My heart thumped in my chest.

He remained bowed, and I hoped Sally would see from the carriage behind.

I forgot all the other masks of the evening, remembered that peerless silver one, the smooth and featureless visage. Later, starting to doze a little, I opened my eyes and saw, here and there on the burgundy wool of my cape, tiny flecks of . . . silver leaf. I stared at them.

Astonished, I picked them up on the tip of my finger. I was puzzling on the silver motes when I noticed some mud trails on the front outside of the cape, at hem level along the bottom. Not quite fresh mud, but not dried either: a few hours old.

I reminded myself, I should check Sally about wearing my clothes without asking me. Politely, almost casually, because she was my friend. But the speckles of silver leaf were what fascinated me. As if I must have started to dream about him already, and there – in a light scattering – amazingly was the actual evidence of my mind's fancy.

Chapter Fifteen

As soon as I walked into Satis House I knew something had changed. No riding cloak, no boots, no crop, none of Arthur's discarded effects. No stink of tobacco, or snuff. Arthur was living out.

'There's been a parting of the ways,' my father said.

The lawyer Mr Snee was involved, because my father had decided he must change his will.

'He's not disinherited outright. There's something for him. But only a minding.'

There had been terrible tantrums from Arthur, and those had put my father into a rage.

'I had no alternative. "You'll drain us dry," I said. His spending was much worse than I thought.'

'Is he coming back?'

'I have no way of telling.'

'It'll be like old times.'

Not really, I realised, a moment after I'd said it. In times past, I hadn't known my father was remarried, nor that I had a half-brother.

'He knows where to go to receive his keep.'

My father picked up items of correspondence which awaited his reply. He coughed his chest clear. Then he fixed his spectacles on his nose to read with, and reached out for his pen. Back to business.

Along the Backs. The willows drooped down to the water and skimmed the surface. Dragonflies hovered in the blue air. The grazing cattle lowed in King's meadow. Laughter, a woman's and a man's, trailed down from Clare Bridge. The bridge was beautiful but slightly askew, which made me think – as we drifted beneath it, through the small but suddenly dank tunnel of arch – that Moses had been right: beauty does always leave itself something short of perfection.

But my brief sobriety lifted as we re-emerged into sunshine. I felt I wanted to do no more than glance, dance, along the placid surface of this present time.

❦

When we sat down to the play, on benches set out on duckboards in the college lea, the evening sun was still shining.

> 'Built for your Ease and Pleasure, Sirs, behold,
> This Night, our little Stage its Scenes unfold.
> Here, to the Muse, your fav'ring Smiles afford:
> Bid Genius flourish, and on Fancy's wing
> Mounted aloft, hear sweetest SHAKESPEAR sing!'

Time flew past. A wood near Athens. Another part of the Wood. Theseus's Palace. A room in Quince's House. I liked the Immortals best – Oberon, Titania, Puck, and the fairies – wearing their elfin green. I laughed as the love potion was sprinkled on sleeping eyelids, a juice to 'make man or woman madly dote upon the next live creature that it sees'.

Later, a chill started to seep up from the pasture-grass. A shiver passed through the trees. Act V. The conclusion was in sight, but all would not be resolved to every character's satisfaction.

Some of the players had to clear their throats, cough out croaks. Dampness must have got into the scenery, because corrugations were appearing on the painted backdrop of Theseus's

Palace. After the last lines one of the actors – Bottom unmasked – came forward to speak, to send us on our way.

> 'Precepts from hence with ten-fold Vigour dart,
> And seize thro' Eyes, and Ears, the captive Heart.
> Be VICE abash'd then, and be VIRTUE bold;
> Be honour ever free, and never sold!
> Protect the Stage on this determin'd Plan,
> And prove that Reason is the Test of Man.'

We started to make our way back to W'm's rooms, across the lawns. My feet felt wet through my shoes. A bright moon shone. The air was filled with our banter, our laughter, someone's philosophical exegesis. At one point I was walking beside W'm, but he seemed oblivious. Now I felt nothing either, and I wondered at that person I had been. He was busy talking to someone, not about Plato or Tibullus, but about one of his Surrey neighbours, Lucinda Osborne, teasing out information as adeptly as if he were playing a fish.

We followed the river. On the opposite bank, boldly illuminated by moonlight, I noticed a young woman stand listening to us. She twisted her head on one side to hear. Then she started walking. Down the embankment, to a small sliver of strand.

She continued to walk, and I kept looking, wondering why she didn't stop.

Into the river.

The water rose to her knees, then to her waist.

She kept on taking steps. A stumble on the stones at the bottom, but she stayed upright.

Now the water came up to the level of her chest.

(And the oddest thing, the detail I noted in these moments that seemed so slowed out of true, suspended from the rules of ordinary time: the young woman was wearing a hat.)

Moses was shouting down at her, then the others. Mouse screamed at her to stop, stop. Moses was first to go running down the bank, followed by two or three of the men. W'm held Sheba and Mouse close beside him.The woman had water up to her neck. Her face had a curiously seraphic and peaceful expression, she seemed to be smiling – smiling quite inconsequentially – over at us.

I was still supposing she was playing some queer game when her face disappeared beneath the water. (The hat on her head became detached: it was left floating while her face blurred palely beneath the surface. A straw hat with a scarlet ribbon and a white wax flower, adrift by moonlight.)

Moses had thrown off his coat and waistcoat and dived in. A hole exploded in the river. He swam out.

It was at the widest part of the river. By the time he reached the spot, the woman had disappeared from view. Moses reached down, tried grabbing, wrestled with the woman's limbs, which were becoming caught in weed.

From the bank it was all quite clear and candid to us. Huge events occupied only a very few seconds. Time stuttered.

Another two had gone swimming out, arms thrashing. They helped Moses haul the woman back ashore. The shore watchers were afraid to touch her. Her eyes were open, staring up at the moon in the sky. She still wore the expression of beatific certainty.

But the person she'd been was now a corpse. The skin seemed to be turning blue, like rich ripe cheese.

Moses, in sodden clothes, was praying for her soul. Something about the gesture, Moses's fervent bravery in the face of a terrible fact – or maybe the passion being wrung from a hopeless situation – moved me deeply. I was crying before I realised it. Sheba stared, transferring some of her horror at the night's tragedy on to me.

Next day we discussed it endlessly among ourselves.

While the others talked, I watched from the window. Suddenly Cambridge appeared very small to me. A collection of beautiful tended gardens, enclosed by high excluding walls. Beneath a high, vaulting, indifferent fenland sky.

> But yet the more we search, the less we know,
> Because we find our work doth endless grow.
> For who doth know, but stars we see by night
> Are suns which to some other worlds give light?

Moses was saying even less than I was. It was as if a part of him were temporarily absent, attending the dead woman's spirit.

I looked up at one point. He was staring across at me. Curiously, after his athletic heroism of the day before, his face now showed fear.

We avoided each other for the rest of that day and evening. By the *next* day he was coughing and sneezing, speaking through a blocked nose. I fetched him handkerchiefs and concocted a hot toddy for him to drink.

'Why d'you think she did it?'

I told him I had no idea. He seemed disappointed that I shouldn't know.

'A broken heart,' I suggested.

'Do people suffer so much?'

'For love? Oh, I imagine so.'

'To drown herself?'

'Why does that astonish you? Dido threw herself on the flames.'

'In legend.'

'And real life's different?' I asked.

'Cursed creature.'

'Hmm.'

'Bedlam Bess.'

'Aren't you meant to pity her?'

He was staring at me again, how he had done earlier.

More sneezes.

A knock at the door. Another friend's younger sister, asking if she could be of any help.

All this uncritical devotion to Moses. Even the memory of his vain dash to try to save the woman couldn't temper my impatience.

I thought of that seraphic face, prepared for death, and I made mine the opposite. I pursed my lips drily, crinkled my nose.

Moses was watching me, deeply confused.

I felt it must be magnetic repulsion, this failure of mine – which shamed me a little – to wreathe him with honour as his devotees did.

Chapter Sixteen

'*And* again!'

Sheba pointed.

'Your Mr Compeyson. Well, well!'

When it was time for us to pass each other, he was ready with a smile. He nodded at my fan.

'Hold on to that.'

Mouse whisked me away, with a vigour that surprised me.

'You haven't met all W'm's friends, have you, Catherine? Here're some more . . .'

There was an opportunity for a dance. I couldn't locate my partner on my card, and he came up to me shortly after the music started, telling me he had been let down by his, would I please do him the honour?

It was a fast gavotte. We managed to keep up. I was out of breath by the end, though; I felt that normally I wouldn't have been.

It was Moses's turn next, for a more sedate old-fashioned minuet, and I wished it wasn't. He tried too earnestly hard, treating it as another abstruse subject he should master. But dancing takes a certain lightness, a spring in the step, an elasticity in the calves; a kind of *joie de vivre*, or alternatively a leavening element of self-proclaiming stupidity in one's make-up. It wasn't Moses's forte.

'*You* show me,' he mouthed at me.

I simulated incomprehension. He was trying to uncover my true talents, the few there might be, and buoyed up by the music and by my previous dance I didn't intend to be patronised. I made my steps so deft and elegant, so sylph-like, but so deceptively simple, that I knew he would appear all the more of a clod.

⁂

After that 'my Mr Compeyson' was at the majority of the Assemblies and house-parties I went to with the Chadwycks. I could see the pleasure he took from my companions' irritation, to find, hell and damnation, here was somewhere else *he*'d managed to get himself invited to. It was an entertainment for him, to see if the Chadwycks could ignore his presence for an entire evening. It was a divertissement for me, and literally, to continue acknowledging his presence, so that only he should be aware – furtive glances, and holding myself side on, and allowing a smile for someone else to become (over their shoulders) a smile intended really for him.

⁂

He wasn't au fait with Virgil, or *The Sorrows of Young Werther*, or Clementi's keyboard sonatas. But he had an incomparable mastery of racecourse runners and their riders. He had an infallible recall of their past showings, and on that he based his predictions of future form.

John Pond's daughter, Miss Pond. Captain Shafto. Hugo Meynell, 'Hunting Jupiter'. Lord Clermont in scarlet, Mr Panton in buff. Bunbury, pink and white stripes, the Dundas white with scarlet spots. Brown Queensberry, crimson Grafton, straw silk for Devonshire.

'I'm the memory man.'

I couldn't judge his tone of voice. I was a little flustered.

'Of course,' I said, obeying no logic, 'Dido, *she* couldn't forget.'

He smiled blankly.

'The queen,' I said. 'Of Carthage.'

'Poor old biddy. What couldn't she forget?'

'Oh . . .' I shrugged, embarrassed. 'It doesn't matter. It's just a myth.'

'Best left to the artists, then. Painters, sculptors, that sort.'

'Purcell.'

The name so revered at Durley Chase became entangled with nearby laughter. He was saved from having to reply, and I thought I caught a flicker of relief pass across his smoothly, evenly handsome face.

ﾠ

'Coincidences happen,' Sheba said. 'But not *that* often.'

'Sometimes,' Moses began, 'we're too close to something, it's really out of focus, it gets distorted –'

'Nothing's distorted,' I snapped back.

'It's all right, Catherine,' Mouse put in.

'*Something*'s got under your skin,' Sheba said.

W'm laughed.

'That's what friends are for,' Sheba said.

'I don't know *what* they're for,' I told her.

'So that we don't get out of our depth,' Mouse said.

'So they'll let us know –' Sheba leaned closer, '– if we're likely to make a tiny little fool of ourselves. Warn us if it looks as though we might be heading for a fall.'

I wouldn't have tolerated a remark of that kind from anyone except Sheba: and even then, scarcely from her. I was furious with them all. I could either let them see that, or convince them of the opposite.

I knew what they were thinking. 'My Mr Compeyson' wasn't *our* sort of person. Too forward, too familiar, and who had ever heard of a tribe with *that* name? I found myself smiling at them, but it was done with a cold heart.

Mouse slipped her arm under mine, then Sheba. W'm raised one eyebrow (as eyebrows always are raised) quizzically. Moses looked as unhappy as I felt; he was still thinking of the drowned girl.

❧

But they couldn't stop me; they wouldn't keep me from him. There were always opportunities in an evening, and I was as adept as him at seeking them out.

A father who'd been a doctor at sea. A mother who didn't keep well. Several siblings.

A harsh school somewhere in the West, attended by sons of mainly naval and military families.

An anticipated inheritance from a Scottish relative reneged upon.

Introductions from old school friends. Other people's parties, in all the fashionable towns: Exeter, Salisbury, Nottingham, Chester, York, Tunbridge.

'I'm obliged to do a little work too, I'm afraid. Norfolk way. To earn a living for myself.'

'You shouldn't apologise. Work is honest and true.'

'That's your father's philosophy?'

'No. It's my own experience. I now realise that it is.'

And – before I could think to stop – I found myself telling him how it would give me no little pleasure at Durley Chase, but a private satisfaction I didn't declare to *them*, to consider how back home I saw wealth make itself: how I smelt it in the rooms of Satis House when the windows were open on the yard side and I could hear the men at their unremitting labour.

When I was physically close to him – as I used to be with W'm, only more so now – I was aware of an energy that was transmitted from him.

I felt like adamant, impelled by a magnet; the hardness of my substance no longer signified, against the power of that attraction.

ℒ

He remembered whatever I told him. He had complete recall. It was uncanny. The memory man. He could anticipate what I was going to say next. He seemed to have read the libretto of my thoughts beforehand.

He knew things, as if I must have told him but had forgotten that I'd told him. Only Sally previously had been granted such a degree of intimacy as I realised – without quite intending it – *he* enjoyed now, with the most elusive details of my life: my most personal past, my feelings, my dreams.

No Latin, no Dido and Aeneas.

('Why learn to speak like people who've been dead for a thousand years?'

'Nearly two,' I said.)

No Purcell.

(He whistled tunes he heard at the theatre, or which he heard the travellers at the racecourses playing on their fiddles and squeezeboxes.)

Again it was a reprieve for me, from too much sheer mental drudgery – not to have to come up with bons mots, or to weave the maxims of great men into my conversation.

'On the 20th, you see, Escape was at two to one. Field of four, over two miles. Coriander, Skylark, Pipator, they all beat him. On the 21st, field of six, over six miles. Escape was four to one and five to one. Chifney had twenty guineas on the second race, not the first. Both were his rides. Escape raced past the favourite, Chanticleer, came home well to the front.'

Now – and I was to tell him honestly – what did I think of *that*?

ꙮ

'But if he has all these friends . . .' I objected.

'Well, it's an art,' Mouse said, 'I grant you.'

'What is?'

'Collecting friends. Only, I should say, they're not.'

'Not what, Mouse?'

'Not friends, not properly. He drops their names, and they're too well-mannered – most of them – to show Charles Compeyson the door. They suffer him –'

'No, Mouse. That can't be –'

'– suffer him, because it seems everyone else does too, and we all *hate* to be different.'

'Don't they like him?'

'He just isn't one of them. He doesn't belong to the past.'

'*You* don't like him either.'

'I prefer to trust people.'

'And you don't trust him?'

'I need to *know* people to do that.'

'You know *me*?' I asked her.

'You're a friend.'

'But I've come too late. Remember – real friendships go back into the past. You said so yourself.'

'You're an exception, Catherine.'

'Why?'

'Oh . . .'

'Because I'm so foolish? Because I need your protection?'

'"No" to the first. But "yes" to the second.'

'Let's stop,' I said, 'please.'

'Only if you'll promise not to desert us. Your friends.'

'Nor you me.'

⁂

He didn't always tell me where he went between these re-encounters.

In a racing phaeton, I heard it said, a young fellow could put himself about over a weekend, travelling anywhere within a hundred-mile radius drawn from the capital.

He didn't have anything so fast at his disposal, that I was aware of. But he did have the healthy colour of a man who might well cover a lot of distance; and he certainly had the charm to assure himself of transportation, whether offering to drive a party or being given the use of a carriage for one or two days with an agreed time and place for its return.

He'd had his own life before I met him. Why should I expect him to account for the time when he was required to earn his own keep and was out of my ken?

I convinced myself that I *enjoyed* knowing as little about him as I did. I felt I was freer to fill in details from my imagination, when the picture was so sketchy; it gave me a bigger, not lesser, stake in his life, because I had to think myself into it more. And it occurred to me that he must be fully aware of this.

⁂

I told Sally things which, as soon as they had tumbled out of me, I realised I shouldn't have said.

(*Ah! how sweet it is to love.*)

About the jolts of excitement my body received from him; about waking up thinking of him.

(*Ah! how gay is young desire.*)

About dressing to please *him*, first and foremost. About finding him waiting for me in my dreams.

It was Sally who would remind me of what I'd said before, quoting my discrepancies back at me.

I laughed them all away.

(*And what pleasing pain we prove,/ When first we feel a lover's fire.*)

All the while Sally would be sewing or winding wool, even setting to some item of silverware she'd noticed hadn't been polished well enough.

(*Pains of love are sweeter far,/ Than all other pleasures are.*)

She was never still now, which made me wonder if she was losing interest a little – or was at the very least guilty, about the time I took up with my stories of Durley and elsewhere, my running narrative about a man I hadn't even mentioned to my father. But busy as she was, she must have been paying me very close attention, to be able to remember so much the next time about the Chadwycks and – especially – the fugitive figure of 'my' Charles Compeyson.

Chapter Seventeen

The Osbornes had the neighbouring estate, Thurston Park. Lady Chadwyck and the second Lady Osborne weren't on the best terms, but their children were of an age and quite content with one another's company. The Osbornes had the loftier pedigree, but were never tempted to condescend.

There was an amount of come and go.

But we hadn't set eyes on *him* before . . .

A hooded figure was just visible under the trees. A man with a collection of books tucked beneath one arm. As soon as he saw *us*, he immediately turned his back and hurried away.

'Who's that?' we asked.

'Our new hermit.'

He called himself Nemo, 'No One', because he wanted to shed the manner of life he'd had.

He lived in a grotto, beyond the ha-ha's sunken fence. It was built like a two-thirds-scale gate-tower to a castle. The slit windows had been glazed, and a flue and fireplace put in, but apart from those the man lived with few creature comforts.

'Candles. A cooking pot. He draws water from the well; a well we dowsed to find for him. It's terribly quaint, don't you think?'

We concurred.

'My father has him write down what he wants – well, what he needs, since he tells us he doesn't have "wants" any more. And also there's a resume of his activities for the past twelve months he has to supply in return for his keep. Which takes about ten lines.'

So, this was what wealth allowed: the luxury of supporting other people's eccentricities?

We stood watching for a glimpse of him, taking care not to snag our finery in the cultivated wilderness of rough grass and nettles. When we spotted him, on the other side of the ha-ha, where the deer came to crop, *he* was watching us from the cover of the arboretum. Probably he was wondering at our own quirks: this show of sartorial vanity, and the herding impulse, our uniform fascination as we stared back stupidly with the white faces of showground sheep.

ℒ

Charles told me that, following the report I'd given him, he'd come to an arrangement with Nemo.

'You've what? "An arrangement"?'

'That he'll make himself scarce every so often, and we can avail ourselves of his hospitality. He's quite well set up, you know. I thought it would be all sackcloth and ashes.'

'You've seen where he lives?'

'And so will you, very shortly.'

I couldn't stop myself from laughing, at the sheer effrontery. That eclipsed, for the moment, the question of propriety. He'd thought of that too.

'I've got the loan of a lad. He can serve us tea. If he's ever made the stuff.'

'Why shouldn't he know how to make tea?'

'Just wait and see.'

Boodle was a Negro, fourteen or fifteen years old, dressed in blue velveteen and gold buttons. (A snug fit, and the velveteen was worn, and the buttons tarnished, but the effect was all.) He had a smile of sharp white teeth, and wanted to show willing.

The lad's tea was inexpert, but I'd had a thirsty walk over and any refreshment was welcome.

The folly's interior was a little cramped, to be sure, with low ceilings. But it was decently furnished, with a fireplace where pine cones sparked in the grate; the fragrance of pine helped smother the underlying whiff of damp.

'Well, it's better than nothing, I thought.'

'Oh yes,' I said. 'Yes indeed.'

The shelves on the walls sagged with books. Some framed prints showed the grassy ruins of Rome.

From the (glazed) window I could see Nemo pacing about reading.

('I think he gets a bit lost if he strays too far. Don't let the house out of your sight, I told him.'

Was this another attempt not to offend the delicacies of *bienséance*, I wondered.)

And there we would go, to the hermitage, once every ten days or so over half a year, whenever he could get away and I could make the excuse of a long walk *sola* from Durley Chase. We were waited upon by the black boy while, outside, Nemo strode back and forth in view of us.

We took tea. And we talked. I told him about life with the Chadwycks, and he discussed none too respectfully the august company they kept. I was a little bothered that we kept Nemo out of his house, but I was assured that he was being adequately recompensed for the inconvenience.

'Some cash won't go amiss, I dare say. Of course those hermits always come from decent families who can provide for their own. But who knows what the Osbornes have taken from *him*?'

'Surely never,' I said.

'Never ones to miss out on a decent rental, the Osbornes.'

'I thought a hermit was –'

'A kind of decoration?'

'– to prove their intellectual qualifications.'

'Families like the Osbornes don't profit by their intellectual qualifications.'

'By what, then?'

'Their mercenary instincts.'

'No.'

'Oh yes. Come on, Catherine, that's the way of the world.'

The light playful tone of his voice puzzled me. If that was so, I said, then it was a harsh truth.

'A brewer's daughter like yourself too!'

'I'm meant to know all about the world?'

'*Don't* you?'

'This and that. But what it adds up to . . .'

'Well, you can just sit tight. In your cosy nest.'

'I can have aspirations, though.'

'Oh, heiresses don't need those!'

'Whose side are you on?'

He laughed, and I smiled, not because I agreed or even understood, but so that I wouldn't – if only for the sake of five brief seconds – be left behind and start to lose him.

❧

The things he knew about me. Trivial, unimportant things. It seemed to me those must be the most difficult facts of all to discover. That I preferred fish to meat, and grayling to mackerel, and sole to grayling. That I slept with my window slightly ajar, and never on two pillows. That I wore away the left inside of my right heel before any other part of either shoe. That I carried a sachet of orange blossom in my portmanteau. That I wrote letters wearing a clip-on cotton frill over my cuff. That I gargled with salt water three – and always three – times a day. And let down my hair and brushed it with fifty strokes – or as near as – every night before bed. That my favourite poet used to be Gray, but now it was Cowper. That I had the knack of cracking a Brazil nut lengthwise, and splitting an apple with just my two thumbs. That I preferred damsons, even bruised windfall, to a handful of sweet cherries. That I woke around seven o'clock every morning, whatever the season, however dark my bedroom was. That I always ran cream over the back of my spoon.

As if he'd been prying on me through the windows of the Chase.

His discoveries about me occurred in several quite different conversations.

I made a fuss about not wanting to hear any more, although I was fascinated to learn how he knew what he did.

'I can't betray my source. Or sources.'

'I'm under surveillance by someone? Who?'

He shook his head.

'*You* can't know by yourself,' I said.

'Whyever not?'

'You'd need to be invisible.'

'A ghost?'

'No, ghosts are people who're dead to us. Over and done with.'

'Then I'm the spirit of curiosity. A locked door is no impediment.'

'Well, if you won't tell me . . .'

I was bemused, but not alarmed. He might have been guessing sometimes, he might have had good hearing for eavesdropping; the Durley staff were as liable to blab as any – and Satis House had employed several loose-tongued girls in recent years. I wasn't bothered enough to think about it much, let alone worry. It might have been telepathy that was responsible, his kindred soul exactly in sympathy – in imaginative conjunction – with my own.

We were perfectly decorous together. It took the will of both of us to be so. I trusted him with me, and myself with him. The blackamoor shuffled about just outside the doorway, his ears tuned and the whites of his eyes shining in the darkness of the corridor, all his native skills of the hunt reapplied to protecting our staunch English etiquette.

Maybe, a little bit, I didn't want to trust myself so implicitly. But then I would try that much harder, fastening down hard on myself, to drive mischief of that sort right out of my mind.

Dallying, once, while he was outside with the boy, I took down a copy of the *Aeneid* from the shelves.

I found a passage I already knew, from Book IV.

> But anxious cares already seiz'd the queen;
> She fed within her veins a flame unseen;
> The hero's valour, acts, and birth inspire
> Her soul with love, and fan the secret fire.

At his approach I closed the book and quickly replaced it among the others before he should see. Virgil, I felt, didn't fit in with this modus vivendi on our secret afternoons.

He seemed to sense the touch of damp or cold on my skin as soon as I did myself.

'You're a little chilly?'

'A little.'

'Here –'

'No, I couldn't possib—'

'Come on.'

He would remove his coat and drape it round my shoulders.

'I should wear warmer clothes,' I said.

So, when I knew that I should, why didn't I?

ண

W'm's engagement had been announced. Sheba and Mouse were still recovering from the shock.

'We never thought . . .'

It wasn't to the young woman I thought I'd lost him to, but to one of her circle. The eldest Osborne daughter, and the plainest.

'Of course it's a very *good* match . . .'

Even Mouse had shown impatience with slow-spoken, slow-thinking Lucinda in the past; Sheba had neglected her, in favour of the younger three by the second Lady Osborne.

'I wish them well,' I said, not really caring if I did or not.

So much for a Cambridge education. All those people and places who were doomed to become my past . . .

ண

'Catherine, meet my friend –'

'"Your friend"?'

'The Red Spaniard.'

I looked about me. He laughed, and clicked his fingers. Clicked them again. The black boy came into the room at a run, bearing a bottle.

'Like Canon Arbuthnot,' I said.

'Who's he?'

'In our town. Entertaining his friend from Bordeaux.'

'And glasses, Boodle. Glasses, please.'

So we spent that afternoon, untypically, drinking red wine. I wondered if he had some cause, either for celebration or on the contrary to cheer himself, but he wouldn't say. I grew a little silly, imagining I was dispensing wit.

'"In the shadow of the gods",' I heard myself saying, '"I approach opulent altars".'

'What's that?'

'What's what?'

'That nonsense you were speaking.'

'You're right. Quite right. You were never righter. It makes *no* sense at all.'

On my way home I stumbled into a puddle, but that was all part of the afternoon's charm.

Mouse saw me first.

Was I all right?

Here – She helped me upstairs.

What on earth?

I'm all right, I'm fine, really.

Your breath.

It's nothing, I stopped by a farm.

It's cider?

Yes, yes.

Which farm?

It doesn't matter, I forget.

Oh, *Catherine*!

I didn't make the same mistake twice.

Mouse and I exchanged private looks, but they weren't as knowing as *she* wanted them to be. Something was afoot, she realised. But I was too complacent, or too fearful perhaps, to take her into my confidence.

If I had – if I had explained to her where I went and who it was I met there, might the course of future events have been quite different?

❧

Between my returns to Satis House I continued writing to Sally. Only she knew about the hermitage.

What I might have recorded in a diary, Sally received from me.

We play at cards! Stops mostly – Comet is v. fast – And Mariage. They're games of bluff, he says – there's a game inside the game, you have to get yr. opponent to declare – what you feel you never show, never.

Sally wrote back. There was still no news of Arthur. She saw my father about the town; he was improved, but he knew to work a little less and to conserve his energies. Her mother spoke of sending her somewhere further off, to London maybe. But it hadn't happened yet.

Some matters, though, I didn't confide even to Sally. I couldn't have.

❧

Whenever we accidentally touched at the gate-legged tea table or in the narrow doorway – fingers, back of the hand, wrist – it was like contact with sulphur. I felt that my skin was scorched for a minute or two afterwards. When he'd gone I would stare at the point of contact, as if there ought to have been a burn. Nothing worse resulted than some bright burnishing on my face, my neck.

I wanted to plunge into cooling water, immerse myself.

. . . and Joy shall overtake us as a flood.

He only had to reach forward, from where he was sitting, or to pause a moment as we risked a stroll at dusk. And he set up those nervous tremors again, spasms of excitement connected to feelings I couldn't fully articulate to myself.

It was cruelty: I should have seen it was that. But I was the very last person who would have.

He had me on a chain. No: on a silken halter.

Chapter Eighteen

'And my mother thinks it will be good for me.'

'Oh, Sally – How could it be good?'

'The opportunity . . .'

'You'll have others.'

'Not just a lady's maid, though. I'm to have some housekeeping duties. The kitchen garden –'

'In Hertfordshire? Why Hertfordshire?'

'Why not Hertfordshire? It has to be somewhere.'

'Only if you want to go.'

'I have to think of the future.'

She didn't sound convinced. I told her so. She sighed.

'And what shall *I* do?'

'Your life is so busy, it can't matter to you –'

'Oh, *Sally*!'

It must have had to do with her mother always wanting more and better for her. Did Satis House have too lowly a status now?

'*You* must decide, Sally.'

'I have.'

'Won't you think again?'

'I'm sorry. Truly. But this is what I mean to do.'

I asked where I could write to her.

It would be best, she said, if I wrote to a female cousin of hers in London. She wasn't sure that her employer would welcome correspondence.

'How ridiculous. What right has your Miss Stackpole –'

'Until I establish myself, that's all. My cousin can send letters on –'

'From London?'

'Yes. When I know how I'm placed.'

'I'm off to the Hot Wells at Llanirfon with the Chadwycks. I'll want to tell you all about that.'

'You will.'

'And the important news.'

'Yes?'

'About when I next see Charles, of course!'

❧

A primeval swamp. Sunlight sifting down through high, dense trees. The rush and swirl of hot water, clouds of steam.

A great water buffalo slowly submerges herself, covering her wrinkled hide. Heads without bodies float past me. The mineral vapour unpeels in curls off the surface of the bathing pool.

A crone stands beside a table of towels, to assist when you climb the old smoothed stone steps, green from the spa's chemicals. For a small rendering at the end of the week, she wraps you in towels, in front of a small cabin she has prepared for you. You lie back and look up at the oblong of open Welsh sky above the colonnade.

The Wells' was a strange geography to me, but not to the others.

In one of the steam rooms I lay on a cushioned chaise, anonymous in my brown linen petticoat and wrapped in towels apart from my face, which was probably too red to offer much clue to my identity.

I dozed off. Their voices somewhere behind me woke me: speaking not any louder than usual, but nudging me out of slumber simply because I recognised them.

'She *is* a funny little thing,' Mouse began. 'Catherine.'

'Well, hardly "little",' Sheba said.

'That's a term of speech. "Funny little" –'

'It would have to be. She's been filling out of late, have you noticed?'

'Moses doesn't agree, but she amuses *me*,' Mouse said. 'With those quaint country ways of hers.'

'That's what we're supposed to be getting rid of. Grooming her for a husband.'

'Every girl we know is being groomed –'

'That's *our* sort of girl, Mouse.'

'Maybe we won't be able to tell the difference, once she's finished.'

❧

I told Charles why I was now less comfortable with them than I used to be.

I thought halfway through my account of Llanirfon Wells that he might find it something to laugh about, and he'd say I was making too much of it, how terribly sensitive I must be.

He listened to me until I'd finished, and then he said *he* thought they hadn't behaved like proper friends, and I had a right to be aggrieved. I should try to make my peace, certainly, but I wasn't to build bridges and suppose it was worth *any* cost.

'You have to think of yourself too. Your pride.'

'Oh, my pride!' I said.

'Well, think of the friendship *you*'ve given. And the amount of returns from them.'

'That all sounds very mercantile.'

'It's as much as I know about. Just like your father.'

❧

I was treated at Durley exactly as I had been before.

But I knew now that there was less spontaneity in their actions.

They had rehearsed their affability very well, which was why they were so good at it and why earlier I had been fooled.

The situation was also a test of my own powers of dissimulation: not to reveal any clues as to my degree of understanding. This was the other education, in expediency, which they were helping to equip me with.

❧

Charles told me he'd been turning over in his mind the account I'd given him.

'And . . . ?'

'I think you should stick it out, Catherine.'

'With people who don't approve of me?'

'They could be useful to you. And anyway, they're good camouflage.'

'I suppose so.'

'Mark my word.'

'Very well, then.'

'Trust me.'

'Yes. I do.'

❧

Moses was reading 'Jean-Jacques'.

'Rousseau,' he explained. 'His "Reveries".'

'And what are those about?'

'To me, Rousseau is about sentience. Feeling.'

'Like Goethe?'

'That is about wallowing in feelings.'

'I found *Young Werther* affecting.'

'Because the wily old dog meant you to find it so.'

'And Jean-Jacques wouldn't do such a thing?'

'I think not.'

Like two figures in a watercolour, we were seated on a fallen bole. Over in Thurston Park the hermit was back in his picturesque grotto, the chimney was smoking lavishly.

'Isn't it preferable', I persisted, 'to feel better for having read a book?'

'What about thinking?'

'But didn't you say Jean-Jacques was about feeling?'

'Feeling what it is like to be solitary.'

'Like Young Werther?'

'Solitude is natural. There's no surer means of perceiving one's humanity.'

'With no one to compare oneself *to*?'

'The brain has the company of all the books it's ever read.'

'Werther suffers too,' I said.

'And how he suffers. Delectably, exquisitely. It's just another appetite for him.'

Our conversation on solitude and the two authors got no further. I wouldn't allow any more.

He asked me, 'You think I'm too solemn?'

I was in a charitable mood.

'Too *young* perhaps. Don't we have to live a little first? And read later?'

'How are we to know to avoid the pitfalls?'

'Only by realising later. That they *were* pitfalls.'

'Don't you mind the prospect of suffering?'

'I don't intend to suffer. My suffering will be – thinking that I held back from life.'

Chapter Nineteen

I would sit beside my father and, while I listened, he would address certain business matters, clearly enough for me to follow.

It had begun by my going to fetch the leather-bound records for him – tan or green or red – and finding the place he wanted.

I knew how beers were made, and something about the differences between them. But it was the arithmetic which he was quite ready and willing (to my surprise) to share with me, how the commodity purchases and the sales were calculated, how the profits and losses were worked out.

I attended, because I wished to, and more to the point because *he* wished me to.

There was a pleasing harmony to be found in the sums and subtractions, in ordering the balance of surpluses and deficits. I realised how intently my father was watching me, and I worried that I might have involved him in too much close work, in returning him too soon to what he ought to be taking a longer rest from. As it was, he was under doctor's orders not to be at his desk for longer than two hours at a stretch.

'No, no, Catherine –'

He put a hand to his mouth, before a sudden fit of coughing.

'If you're quite sure . . .'

'I need to tell a Havisham.'

'Then tell me, father, please.'

He took me into the brewhouse and led me through the stages of the brewing process. Grinding. Mashing. Boiling. Cooling. Fermenting. Racking. I listened carefully, I asked him questions about what I was seeing. Step by step, while he fought to curb his coughing.

Cleaning the malt, grinding it, diluting the grist with hot water in a mash tun, leaving the malt's sugars to dissolve. Draining the liquid wort; extracting final sugars with more hot water (sparging), then boiling the wort in copper vats, adding hops to sour the sweetness. Draining the hopped wort over used hops, and cooling it, before channelling it into fermenting vats and adding yeast. Leaving fermentation for five or six days, so that the yeast will convert sugar to alcohol and carbonic acid gas; skimming the film of yeast from the wort, once the sediment has sunk. After fermentation, diverting the green beer into tanks for several more days, while the yeast left further mellows the beer's taste. Conditioning: adding some caramel to darken the colour, adding finings (derived from sturgeon's bladder) to thin the brew's appearance. Storing the resulting beer in casks, introducing some extra sugar to aid supplementary fermentation, scattering dried hops for aromatic purposes.

After that I became interested to learn some of the tricks of the trade, and what might go wrong between one brew and the next.

Initially my father was uncertain: should he show me or not? But I wasn't afraid to know how we Havishams justified ourselves; and I had lived all my life within sight and sound and smell of the beer's manufacture, the source of our standing.

It seemed from her letters that Sally was also spending some time in London with her employer, and so she could simply pick up from her cousin any correspondence delivered for her.

I asked if there wasn't another address in London where Miss Stackpole put up, where I could write to. But Sally replied that she thought the arrangement was working well enough as it was, and if I was still quite agreeable –

Her letters, I felt, were a little vague in content. It couldn't be the case that they were being read by Miss Stackpole. But perhaps Sally didn't like to dwell too much on her new duties, if she wasn't finding them altogether congenial; and she might have thought it would be disloyal to say so.

I realised I must simply put up with the situation for the while.

❧

In my father's office one day I noticed an unsealed envelope on his desk. Even upside-down the handwriting was recognisable, and confirmed by the signature.

Charlotte Chadwyck.

He saw me looking, and pushed the letter beneath some other items of correspondence. He frowned.

I thought he looked grey and careworn.

'Some man will count himself lucky. When he first sets eyes on you.'

We had finished supper and taken ourselves through to the fire in the little sitting room. I was sewing; my father was sitting opposite, watching me.

'Yes?'

'Certainly,' he said.

'So . . . that is what my education's for.'

'It's the prospect for every young woman. To be married. Her responsibility even.'

'Or . . . ?'

'There *is* no "or". In your case.'

'Oh.'

He paused to cough some obstruction out of his chest.

'With all your advantages. Those you have and those you *will* have.'

'I see. I see.'

I consulted the racing news in the newspaper, and guessed where he would be. I walked to Durley Conquest Farm and asked, opting at the last minute for imperiousness instead of sweetness, to borrow their trap.

'Lady Chadwyck knows,' I lied.

'In that case, miss . . .'

They couldn't give me the mare. Solomon was properly too big for the task, and I'd heard he was grudging, but I only wanted to get away. I whispered in Solomon's ear as the trap was being wheeled out.

'We have to find him, we have to find him . . .'

I had heard reports about the place, its hazards. The horses racing pell-mell through the crowd, and the spectators galloping along behind. Cock-fighting, dog-matching. Thimble-rigging, crooked roulette.

But it was a quiet day. The dangers were largely out of sight. The sun was shining. I was dusty after my journey from Durley, a little light-headed on an empty stomach, but exhilarated just to be here.

An enchanted day, in my future memories of it, when no harm was meant to come to me.

The Epsom regulars pointed him out to me. I didn't even have to go searching for him.

I hailed him from the trap. (A humble farm trap negotiating parked gigs, chaises, cabriolets.)

The 12.30 race was over. A table had been spread for half a dozen, with mismatching chairs fetched from wherever they could be found.

When I saw that Charles had seen me, his face made me think of a mask, another mask: features frozen in a smile, with only the eyes registering his perturbation. But his voice was remarkably steady and assured.

'Another chair for our lady guest, Spencer.'

A space was made for me. One woman now among six men.

I surprised myself by saying thank you, I would, and then sitting down.

(An umbrella was opened and placed above me in the tree, to provide extra shade.)

A plate was handed to me; on it were several slices of rich red beef and a plump duck's leg. The sturdy fare men enjoy. I didn't send it back, and started to eat. I was hungry. And I was intensely relieved to have found him again, so grateful just to be sitting feet away from him.

The company was jovial, and increasingly raucous. I didn't mind any of it, the loud abrupt laughter and the boozy imprecations to enjoy myself. (As a contrast and not a comparison I was thinking of Arthur and his roving gang of scapegraces, with whom I would *not* have been at my ease.)

'You're sure you're all right, Catherine?'

'I'm sure I'm sure, thank you.'

Charles would cover the tops of his wine glasses with his hand when the bottles were passed round. He was keeping himself sober. It might have been that he didn't want to be shown up, or to forget himself.

Later.

'I'll accompany you back.'

'Really, there's no need.'

'You *are* going back? You haven't abandoned them?'

'The Chadwycks? Not yet.'

'You won't, though?'

'One day I shall have to.'

He didn't come to Durley itself, or even to the farm. We parted on a back road.

'I've ruined your day,' I said.

'You've *made* my day.'

I smiled uncontrollably. I thought I was going to cry with gratitude.

'Every time I see you,' he said, 'it's the same.'

'I have to go now.'

He leaned across.

'Catherine, please –'

What was he going to say, or do, next?

Flustered, I picked up my reins before I could find out.

'Goodbye,' I called back at him.

I hoped driving off that I'd dazzled him with my last quick-silver smile. *He*, I felt, had spun my head around.

At least that allowed me to handle the Chadwycks, because in my mind I wasn't *with* them. I was only conscious of where I was at Durley when I fell behind at mealtimes, or dropped something, or had to be asked a question three times.

'Catherine, please –'

He'd leaned across from his saddle and on an instinct I had picked up the reins. Remembering, I stared down at my hands in my lap, saw how clammy they were, and I buried them into the upholstery so no one else would notice.

A long accumulating knot of some pleasurable pain corkscrewed through my stomach. I was corseted, to maintain my poise, but my breath was coming in shorter and shorter and more difficult bird-like sips.

Chapter Twenty

I stopped hearing regularly from Sally.

I continued to write, supposing that there was only some delay in the delivery of *her* letters to me.

Finally one did arrive, but it was no more than a brief note. An acknowledgement of my last letters, and little else.

I wondered what reason there could be for her not being more forthcoming.

Was she dissatisfied in her post? Was she unwell?

Had my own letters sounded to her too much like exulting in my good fortune? To Sally of all people I'd thought I could confess these things. It might have been that distance and some little more experience had worked to change her.

I examined her note for signs of the former closeness, but there was too little in it to offer me any. Even her handwriting seemed more laboured, that script which she had – inevitably – had to base on mine; as if she had sat and written very slowly, very formally, only meaning to disguise what her true feelings were.

❧

'It was extraordinary,' Mouse said as we went walking. 'Just this morning I saw a black boy running across that field.'

I stared at her.

'In a blue suit with gold buttons.'

She laughed.

I continued to stare. Boodle's return to Thurston Park was news to me.

'D'you think I've become too secluded from life, or something?' she asked.

I guessed that she didn't know who the boy was, or – more to the point – who hired him to chaperone at our snatched rendezvous.

She and I saw the hermit approaching in our direction, but this time he made no attempt to avoid us.

He waited for us at a stile. He held out his hand for Mouse's as she negotiated the steps. While I was climbing over and having *my* hand held, he dropped the book he'd been carrying under his arm. I took pity, and bent down at the same time as he did. I saw Mouse smile, then turn away. The hermit retrieved the book first. From between the pages he extracted a small folded sheet of paper and – once he'd checked my companion wasn't looking at me – he presented it to me.

ᘛ

The little hermitage had been got ready. There was tea, and a selection of small fancy cakes to eat. Boodle fussed with my cushions, unrolled a linen napkin.

'I would light a candle,' Charles said, 'but we might be seen.'

I agreed that it might not be the best idea. And so we sat on while the light faded across the park, across that assiduous reconstruction of Arcady.

I asked him what was wrong.

'Nothing, nothing.'

I asked again. And again. He wouldn't tell me. I let a few minutes pass. His mood didn't improve. For the fourth time I asked him if anything was wrong.

'You don't want to know that.'

But I persisted.

Another inheritance he'd been depending on wasn't going to come to him after all. His cousins were disputing the old man's will.

(In *Young Werther* the very same situation had occurred. Goethe described the wear and tear on the soul, and because my head was still full of the book I wasn't surprised by what he told me. Goethe's art was to take perfectly from the life.)

He said he had accounts to settle.

I told him off the top of my head, I would lend him some money. I could do it without my father discovering.

'No, Catherine –'

'Whyever not?'

'I couldn't take it.'

'I insist.'

I asked him how much he needed.

'Won't you want a little more?'

I suggested I double the amount.

He stared at me.

'At last,' I said, 'Charles Compeyson is lost for words.'

⁂

Out of the others' hearing, Moses asked me, 'How did Sir Thomas put it?'

'"Sir Thomas"?'

'Browne.'

'Oh.'

'"Love is the foolishest act. Which dejects the wise man's cooled imagination".'

'You'll have to explain.'

'Ah . . . You're joking, I see.'

He started to laugh. I shook my head.

'No, I *don't* understand.'

After he had put his argument, I offered mine.

Love, I said, took no account of any rules or ordinances.

'Your wretched Werther again?'

But really I was thinking of inflamed Dido.

'The more foolish,' I tagged on, 'the more instinctive, the more natural . . . Then the better. Surely?'

It was hard for me to tell just what Moses thought of my response. He was going to reach into his pocket for his portable copy of Browne, but decided to leave it there. I had a feeling I'd lodged a stick very firmly in the spokes of his poetic wheel.

Our hermit, it transpired, was being obdurate. The not-so-saintly Nemo.

> *Thought he wanted a bit more cash, made him an offer, but he said it wasnt going to be enough. 'Name your Price, then.' He couldnt. I dont know what the reason is, but he's not so green, our friend Mr N.*

I set off to call at the hermitage. But when I had it in my sights, its occupant came into view, talking with W'm. Why W'm? I dodged behind a tree, not to be seen.

Afterwards I thought that W'm must have seen me, he was watching me so closely at the dinner table, just as he used to do.

We spoke about inconsequences.

Wasn't there, though, an ironic curl to his lips? – as if he knew something about me I wouldn't have wanted to be more widely known?

At Durley we had unexpected visitors, a party en route to the coast from London. Among them was the silver-haired man, Garrick's double, who had hovered as silent witness outside the

Temple of Thespis – called Calvert. And, with him, the woman I had once passed in a corridor who had seemed only half awake and yet, from under those heavy eyelids, had seemed to miss nothing. The two were now married.

Congratulations were offered to W'm, and Lucinda Osborne was put on display, to general disappointment and a deal of *Schadenfreude*.

I thought I would take advantage of their social activities to tackle the hermit again. Only steps away from his fastness I heard voices. Cries. The door was ajar. I went forward on tiptoe and looked in.

Two dishevelled bodies lay writhing on the floor.

His trousers were undone and his bare buttocks exposed.

Her dress and undergarments were hoisted high on her waist, and her legs were wide apart to admit him.

The pair gasped and moaned while he rode her like a wild thing. His buttocks thrashed and juddered as he plunged in and out of her.

It was W'm – and Mrs Calvert.

She let out a pained, ecstatic moan.

I stumbled back and fell against the door, which creaked. I rolled out over the threshold.

Outside I kept in motion. I started to run; I didn't stop, didn't look back, I ran on legs that seemed not to belong to me.

I continued running, back to Durley Chase, as fast as those legs would carry me.

Chapter Twenty-one

That evening I was invincible.

I chattered with our augmented company, I laughed, I argued for and I argued against, I continued to laugh, I regaled the troupe with Rochester tales, I ate my veal escalope heartily and diluted my wine with very little water, I charmed and I cajoled, I sent my laughter shooting up into the top left-hand corner of the frieze in the dining room, I devoured all the fragrance in the bowl of roses, I made faces at myself in the table silver, I imagined myself a beauty for our extended party and for a moment or two perhaps I deceived them as well, I couldn't decide between syllabub and strawberry fritters and took both, I laughed as we ladies got to our feet and then I carelessly drifted from the room, I played a jaunty sarabande on the Broadwood and my fingers flew, I won a hand of vingt-et-un and a second of loo as I knew I must, I laughed as easily at my wit as all the others did, and all this time I betrayed nothing of myself. I let W'm see just what he had let go by him. I was even prevailed upon to sing.

'You have such a pleasing voice, Catherine.'

'Thank you, Lady Chadwyck.'

I sang while Mouse accompanied me, keeping me in tune. The song excused me.

'I'll sail upon the dog-star and then pursue the morning;
I'll chase the moon till it be noon but I'll make her leave her horning.'

My voice had never been more supple, or my pitch surer.

'I'll climb the frosty mountain, and there I'll coin the weather;
I'll tear the rainbow from the sky and tie both ends together.'

Afterwards, alas, came the fall. I didn't appear next morning. I couldn't move from my bed. I lay quite still, staring at the ceiling, like an effigy on a tomb.

Lost all my tender endeavours
To touch an insensible heart.

A maid tiptoed in and out. The housekeeper came and stood over me, and departed.

Sheba, then Mouse, asked if I was ill; answer came there none. I was lamenting my innocence, grieving for my naivety. W'm had caught me first.

Did you not see my love as he past by you?
His two flaming eyes, if he come nigh you,
They will scorch up your hearts.

I had allowed myself to be educated, so that I could be close to him. Any learning I acquired had been for his sake, to try to impress him. How little I had really known about the world's ways.

Ladies, beware ye,
Lest he should dart a glance that may ensnare ye!

A tall, hawk-nosed man introduced himself as the family's physician. He placed his hand on my brow and against my neck, before testing my pulse. He stood against the wall for a good while, and I sensed that all he did was watch me. Moses came to the door, asking after me.

'My estimate would be, this is an upset of the spirits. Where the distracted mind goes, the body will soon follow suit.'

'I shall tell the others. Lady Chadwyck is very anxious to know. I have a letter from her son addressed to you – *with* enclosure.'

'Please thank him. Few deal with the practicalities in such brisk fashion.'

'My cousin is quick, you're quite right, and methodical when he wishes to be.'

W'm must have felt he had good reason to sweeten the physician.

I'll lay me down –

How easy it was for me like this.

– and die within some hollow tree.

I lay meanwhile on white feathers, layer upon layer, renouncing my folly.

> The rav'n and cat,
> The owl and bat
> Shall warble forth my elegy.

I had flattered him with my attention, and perhaps because of it W'm had thought to ply his charms elsewhere.

Did I really think I might have been half in love with him? He and his friends were too sophisticated and too worldly for love. They sneered at it. I'd had to be rejected to know to look for love elsewhere, and to find it with another. The thing I had seen, at the hermitage, had been a hideous travesty. It had repelled me, but it fascinated me too. Now I couldn't put the obscene picture out of my mind.

I reached for the bell pull, tugged on the cord. The maid came running. I told her to bring me water. I needed to be up, moving about, keeping occupied, busying myself. Or – or should I feel sorry for poor W'm, I wondered as the girl helped dress me:

oughtn't I to be pitying him for his ignorance of love?

In the mirror, I found myself again. Concentrating on my face, I worked on its colour. In front of me was someone who realised that this time at Durley Chase must draw to an end. The conclusion would come as it must, but the process had been accelerated within the past twenty-four hours.

At some point the name came up. We were sitting by ourselves, Sheba and Mouse and their mother, and Moses. Lady Chadwyck was talking about the London Set, who seemed to think that the county entertainments were laid on for *their* diversion. Now it was supposed that no event was complete without some representation from them. The Londoners in turn felt they could afford to be choosy about which events they attended.

'Mr Calvert's wife' was mentioned as one of the habitual offenders. I looked up from my book. Sheba turned towards her mother, while all the time darting her needle into her tapestry canvas.

'W'm isn't here to speak up,' Mouse said, blithely unaware. 'I'm sure he would want to defend her.'

'Your brother is a mere provincial to that grandee,' Moses told her.

'He says she has a false reputation.'

'Reputation for what, Marianna?' Lady Chadwyck asked. 'Or –' She hesitated. 'Ought I not enquire?'

'Who has *not* enquired!' Mouse laughed, dealing the last of the cards for a game of piquet with me. 'If that is how she wishes to spend her husband's money, gadding about –'

'She certainly keeps his name in circulation,' Moses said. 'That is one way of viewing her activities.'

At that very moment, at the word 'activities', Sheba caught my eye. I didn't look away in time, and felt the skin on my face heating. I stared at the spread of twelve cards in my hand.

'What is the matter, Isabella?' Lady Chadwyck asked.

'Nothing at all, mother,' Sheba said.

'Have you pricked your finger? Let me see what you've –'

'Don't concern yourself, please.'

It was clear to me now, as I prepared to exchange first on the baize, that I wasn't the only one to know this family's private shame. It felt not like a secret shared, however, but a secret twice hidden.

III

ROCHESTER

Chapter Twenty-two

My father was found lying insensible across the desk in his office. He had collapsed.

A new doctor came and pumped out green bile. He told me as soon as I got back home, his heart had suffered, like last time, on account of his diseased lungs.

'His lungs?'

'I gather your father had no knowledge.'

'He had a winter cough. And couldn't shift it.'

'You've been away, Miss Havisham?'

'What can be done about it?'

'You both must exercise forbearance.'

What did the man mean, 'forbearance'?

'He'll recover?'

'I . . .'

I begged him to tell me. Quite frankly.

'His disease will kill him. Later I can give him opium, to dull his pain.'

My father aged quickly after that. Years in only weeks.

Those were his final weeks. I hated what I was witnessing.

Until this point I had seen him not just as he was but as a man who included all his younger selves which I remembered. A composite. Now I couldn't mistake him for anyone except this grey and ashen invalid (when he was in bed) or this stooping and sullen man with whom I shared a house (when he was up on his feet, but shakily), who forgot not to break wind when I was there, who was preoccupied still with the brewery but who looked as if he longed for nothing more than to be done with it.

I would try to remind him that he shouldn't exert himself. Clearly he thought it was extraneous advice; there was work to be done. Born a Havisham and reared a brewer, he had no choice in the matter, and who else to do his job if he didn't?

Arthur returned, with a jackal's timing.

My father asked to see him. Arthur alone.

'If you might leave us for a little while, Catherine. Please.'

I stood guard outside the room. It wasn't such a little while.

I went outdoors, into the garden to cool my cheeks.

When I came back in, Arthur passed me in the hall. No engineered collision this time. He was staring in front of him, he didn't seem to notice me at all. His face was quite white, but he was wearing the widest grin I'd ever seen.

I discovered soon enough that my father had repented.

Mr Snee was summoned from London. The will was going to be altered.

My father wouldn't discuss anything with me until the deed was done, until the new papers were signed and Mr Snee had gone on his way again.

Unequal shares, but Arthur's restored inheritance would be a fortune enough.

My father had woken.

I was sitting by the bedside.

'I don't know why you did it, father.'

He didn't reproach me for saying so; he didn't even sigh.

'One day,' he said, 'you may understand.'

'I want to understand *now*.'

'That's my Catherine. Still proud, eh?'

I drew myself straighter in the chair.

He asked me, 'Is it about the money?'

'Of course not.'

'You'll still be a rich woman.'

'I'm not interested in that.'

'You think *you* have first entitlement?'

'Arthur . . .'

'He's had a difficult start in life.'

'He didn't need to.'

'You'd have preferred I was open about my marriage?'

'I'd have preferred . . .'

That my father hadn't married the woman. I stopped myself saying it, but he could finish the remark for himself.

'It's about repairing divisions,' he said, speaking slowly. 'Before it's too late. It's about trying to complete my life – benignly. Benevolently. Making the past and the present consistent. Match up.'

I didn't speak.

'Come on, Catherine. Don't let anything come between us now.'

I placed my hand on the counterpane. He placed his on top of mine. I stared at the marks on the skin that are called the brown flowers of death.

I felt the terrible strength in his hand. I realised he was quitting this life fast.

'I wanted to do what is – truest.'

Through the window I could see Arthur down in the brewery yard, tightening the bit on his horse as a punishment for some misdemeanour.

'I know the truth about Arthur,' I said.

'What's that?'

I had spoken softly so that he might not hear, if he chose not to.

'Nothing, father.'

'I only wanted to do the right thing.'

ℒ

I wished that I could hear from Sally again.

In her last letter to me she had said she thought Miss Stackpole would set off on her travels soon, with staff in tow.

I didn't see why that precluded Sally from writing letters, unless Miss Stackpole was such a tyrant that she didn't permit her servants enough time even to pen a brief note. What was the desirability of the job in that case?

But at least Sally must be having a taste of new places, and didn't she deserve to? It was what her mother had wished for, and I supposed – very reluctantly, though – that I must concede the point.

ℒ

In the last fortnight my father just shrank away.

He curled up in bed like a starved bird, with his face to the wall. He lay without moving, quite still.

If I touched his hand, he didn't register the contact with as much as a shiver. He continued to keep his back turned on us all and his face staring into the plaster on the wall: here was a complete geography in its cracks and pittings, rivers and lakes and coastlines, an entire continent to quieten him.

Even the brewery, when I spoke of it by his bedside, that couldn't draw him back. He'd had his fill.

Chapter Twenty-three

They wouldn't grant a resting-place inside the cathedral, let alone a brass commemorative plate.

While my father was alive they had taken his money; but now they didn't consider he justified any preferential treatment.

Born a commoner, he also died a commoner.

❧

The modiste advised twenty yards of bombazine for a mourning gown (with long sleeves) and petticoat. (A father's death called for nothing less.) Plus, nine yards of wildbore, for a black stuff German greatcoat. (Please bear in mind, Mademoiselle Havisham, the gown must have complete front fastening, and not a glimpse of petticoat.)

She suggested, since it was the done thing for first mourning, a black paper fan. And black calamanco shoes, even though it mightn't be the latest fashion; but, Madame Morgan said, I wasn't in London, and the choice was dignified.

❧

I had requisitioned a tame priest, a man with little faith who suited very well.

Carriages collected in front of the church. The building was respectably filled. Starting to walk to my pew, with Arthur behind me, I caught a glimpse of a small commotion in the porch, a figure in mourning removing stirrups from his boots.

Who else?

I mouthed his name. 'Charles, Charles.'

My spirits revived in an instant.

I glanced round. Arthur was watching the arrival too; I couldn't determine his expression – suspicion, alarm. I tugged at his sleeve, it was time to begin.

Somehow the service passed, and as soon as I had reached the porch I had already forgotten whatever easy words the priest had spoken.

By the graveside I was aware only of not raising my eyes in the direction of the straggling ilex tree, because that was the one *he* was standing beside. I glanced round again at Arthur, who was watching the pallbearers' efforts with disdain. (He hadn't offered to be one of them; his past was quite enough of a burden to him, without making an example of himself to all and sundry.)

It was only then that I forgot not to look over at the shiny jagged ilex tree, and when I did I found Charles quietly smiling: to encourage me, I told myself, to assure me he understood the very charybdis of violent emotions this day was putting me through.

He had arrived wearing deep second mourning. A black silk hat with crepe about the crown and a knotted bow. Black buckles.

I had no reason to be surprised. Perhaps it was the sight of him in so much black that moved me to tears: living and breathing and intensely alive inside his impeccable sartorial restraints.

'It was the death he would have wanted,' someone had the effrontery to say in my hearing, between noisy mouthfuls of tea, as I walked about the room.

People's faces were distorted as they tried to cram chicken legs and portions of pie and cake into their mouths. They drank quickly, before anyone else could drain the decanters.

They disgusted me. They had nothing to do with me.

I had *one* friend here, the truest, but where were the others who had called themselves my friends?

❧

A letter of condolence arrived from Lady Chadwyck. But, it occurred to me on re-reading for the fifth or sixth time, the condolences might have been due to the sender.

> – *I feel this to be as great a Loss to myself. The Acquaintanceship of Mr Havisham occurred most propitiously for me, when my Trust in my fellow Mortals was deserting me. Your father had an undue Sensitivity – for a Man, I mean – as to the Wants of a Noblewoman (the which he insisted on calling me!) left prematurely widowed.*

The letter rambled on – written beyond midnight, surely – and skirted round the precise nature of the relationship with the departed. Lady Chadwyck was still shocked by the news, and trying to put her own thoughts regarding the future into some (cryptic) order.

No letter arrived from any of the others. They would have heard, wouldn't they? Or had Lady Chadwyck preferred to conceal the news from them for a while – until the mist of uncertainty obscuring, so to speak, the lawns and topiary of Durley Chase had cleared a little.

❧

After the will had been read, my father's lawyer took me outside into the Cherry Garden.

'No surprises there, I dare say.'

'If you wish to put it like that, Mr Snee. No, there weren't.'

'Mr Arthur doesn't appear too pleased.'

He had just discovered that his inheritance was to be paid in annual instalments over ten years.

'It may teach him virtues of economy,' I said. But I doubted that very much.

Mr Snee was a small man, smaller than myself, with a face that might have been sharpened with a knife – and then treated with preserving vinegar. When my father first became acquainted with him, the lawyer was thought well of, but lean and hungry for success. Success soon came to him, and those clients he chose to retain were similarly equipped to do well.

My father had always been a little in awe of him; any meeting was preceded by an unusual degree of nervousness, even tension, in his manner.

'So you knew what to expect, Miss Havisham?'

'My father did explain to me.'

'To you both?'

'To us both, yes.'

His nose, when I inclined my head to the right and glanced a little down, looked sharp enough to cut my hand on. Then I realised that, without needing to turn *his* head, his eyes were swivelled sideways in their sockets, watching me.

I was embarrassed, and jumped in.

'But it's just *me*, is it, you want to speak to, Mr Snee?'

'Since it concerns yourself, yes, I judged it best.'

And he explained. (Before, he said, I should hear about it some other way.)

My father, he began, had been lending money for several years to a certain beneficiary.

'"Lending money"?'

'On such favourable terms, some might have judged the exercise foolhardy.'

'To whom?'

'That is the nub.'

'Someone connected with my stepmother?'

'There is no connection.'

'To whom, then?'

'You can't guess?'

'Not at all.'

'Really and truly?'

'I *can't* guess. Please, Mr Snee, tell me.'

Should I have been able to deduce the answer for myself?

'Your patroness, no less.'

'I *beg* your pardon –'

'The good Lady Chadwyck herself.'

I knew immediately how often I would return in my mind to these moments, how my memories of Durley Chase would be endlessly complicated by the item of information I had just been given.

What it had amounted to was this: my father, for his own reasons which *he* judged best, had gained the amity of the Chadwycks for me by the only means he knew. By buying it with his tradesman's ready money.

'Why, though?'

'You are a wealthy young woman, Miss Havisham.'

'I can't deny it.'

'I expect you'll have a wider circle now.'

'Very probably. But –'

'More friends than you ever knew you had.'

'What does this –'

'Your father craved – that isn't too strong a word – he craved you should have an introduction to that world. He wished doors to open for you. You needed to receive a training first.'

And the Chadwycks had obliged. My father had made it

worth their while to oblige. His association with Lady Charlotte had been mercenary from the outset.

'And the understanding with her ladyship? You'd like that to continue? Or . . . ?'

Why *not* continue with the arrangement? I could afford to do so. I wanted to prove to the Chadwycks, and also to myself, that I wasn't petty. (And maybe I wanted to savour too a little of my own glory.)

'Yes,' I said. 'Thank you, Mr Snee.'

'Have you seen any of them since?'

'No.'

'Or corresponded?'

I shrugged.

'We need discuss it no further. And my discretion in the business is naturally guaranteed.'

I nodded my appreciation.

Such attentiveness, from one whose erstwhile reputation for quick thinking and lawyerly subtlety had always been so considerable. I was bound to be paying for it, and heavily, but I was a rich woman now.

I concluded that money was capable of doing good and also terrible things.

It had brought comfort to Lady Chadwyck, but it had perverted relationships, making them seem what they weren't – and what they had no right to be.

I saw now, normally *they* would never have had the need to consort with the likes of me. Only my father's money had persuaded the children, at their mother's bidding, to entertain what must always have seemed to them an improbable friendship.

Chapter Twenty-four

Sally, Sally.

Maybe she had other interests now, and other loyalties? I presumed her cousin *had* received and sent on my own letters. Could it be that Sally had left Miss Stackpole's employment, or even been dismissed? If the latter, she would have felt embarrassed to write straight away; and time has a way of turning small procrastinations into habits. She might have felt it had got awkward, to take up where she'd left off, without the need of some explanation.

I was doing all I could to excuse Sally. Couldn't she get just an inkling of it, and respond with the briefest of notes, merely to keep in touch with me? Whatever her reasons for not communicating, I was only too ready and willing to forgive her.

❧

Arthur was coming in at all hours. He had meals prepared in the middle of the night. He let his dogs have the run of the house, his boots left the floors in a mess. Things had gone missing.

'So, what is this? A house, or some private museum?'

'You treat it like a staging-inn. And sometimes like a farmyard.'

I heard myself raising my voice at him. Which only set him smiling.

'Don't go upsetting yourself on my account –'

'I'm not . . .'

'Save yourself for someone who deserves you.'

His smile turned to rude, knowing laughter.

⁂

I received a letter from him.

'Most obediently, Charles.'

It carried no address except '*London*'.

My Dear Catherine,

I'm afraid that my Affairs are likely to detain me awhile. As you know I travel up to Norwich and whatnot, & things are at a head at the moment wh. makes it difficult to get away. You need all yr. wits for Business, as you will appreciate, & there is the possibility I shall have to venture further afield, wh. will be unplanned if & when. But I do assure you of my continuing concern, if I might presume so, & my best regards for your Success & Welfare.

Even allowing for his stylistic lapses, I concluded that the letter had been hastily written. He was telling me as much as he wanted me to know.

I read the letter over dozens of times. I wished I could reply.

Like Goethe's Werther, '*Today I put your letter to my lips and the contact of paper had me gritting my teeth.*'

⁂

I went into my father's office and sat down. I leaned back in the chair, and felt too small for it. The proportions of my back to the chair back and my legs to the shank of the seat were wrong.

He had sat here for twenty-five or thirty years, since he had inherited the private room – next to the general Compting House – from his father. This had offered him his outlook on the world. The desk, the shelves of past ledgers, the view of the brewhouse, the roofs of the outhouses, a few trees, a church tower. With the window sash pushed up, he would have been able to hear snatches of gossip and tittle-tattle from downstairs, when the domestic staff had recourse to pass the brewery workers or the delivery men.

And yet I wondered just how much I had really known with any degree of certainty about him.

I opened a ledger at the final completed page. 'Purchases'. I read down the figures on the list, entered in his tidy hand.

Tears welled up. Hot spicy tears that nipped my eyes. They sped down the runnels on my cheeks, dropped from my chin on to the page, and instantly blotted the ink. My own mark of proprietorship.

❧

Rates assessment:

£50 – Brew house
£70 – 4 malthouses
£26 10s 0d – 8 storehouses
£15 – 2 warehouses
£2 – cellar
£3 – cinder ovens
£10 – stock valued at £200

Twenty-four public houses had an average rateable value of £6 16s 5d.

I had to acquaint myself with the alternative accounting methods in the Compting House – and the twain didn't necessarily match, or were meant to.

Victuallers' Book, to register sales in butts to public houses.

A book to record country trade.

A Petty Ledger, detailing private dealings with favoured (personal) clients.

A Yeast Book.

A Grain Book, both specifying sales.

Additionally there were:

Brewing Books, noting every aspect of production, including each successive brew.

Letters Book.

Loan Ledger.

Bond Ledger.

Interest Ledger.

Rent Ledger.

Inventory Ledger.

Stock Ledger.

My father's office contained two other sets of records. First, the Rest Books: the yearly balance drawn up in early June, referring to debts and liabilities, and placing a value on the combined stock and trade. (Because my father was sole proprietor, answerable only to himself, he was under no obligation to keep these Rest Books. But since he had done, I deduced that he may have intended bringing in partners, or effecting an alliance with another sort of business than a brewer.) Secondly, the Private Ledgers: a register of every loan accepted and made that concerned the firm. These were kept in a separate locked drawer, intended for no one's eyes but my father's.

I had my clerks to assist me: the home clerks in the Compting House, and the abroad-clerks, who collected the monthly payments from publicans. Mr Tice was the brewery manager, whom I inherited. I promoted Mr Ambrose to be my chief clerk, which didn't please some of the others, not least Mr Tice.

I privately and confidentially asked Mr Ambrose if he would be a separate conduit to me of the brewers' and coopers' affairs, since – he might have guessed, although I didn't state it so to him

– I wasn't confident that I was receiving all the information I needed via the regular, formal channels.

❧

Another letter arrived from Charles, from London, forwarded through a third party. He told me he was obliged to leave the country for a while – on a matter relating to business, he said, which had arisen quite unexpectedly. It wasn't clear to him how long it would be until he returned: not before there was a satisfactory outcome, at any rate. But he assured me of his most sincere best wishes in the interim, and every success in dealing with the affairs of the brewery, as a little bird told him I was doing.

I re-read this letter, as I had done the previous one, dozens of times. I imagined where he might be. If not the British Isles – France, or Holland, or further afield than either? How thoughtful of him to dwell on my own struggles here to make sense of the brewery finances when he had his own equally pressing concerns.

I was to hear from him four more times over the next seven months. Every communication was one to be treasured. It surprised me a little to think of someone so fond of the excitement of chance games – cards, racing – currently having to subjugate himself to whatever those 'business matters' were.

But now we had this new and unanticipated bond between us.

❧

I wrote to Lady Chadwyck, thanking her for her commiserations, and those of the children that had eventually followed. I explained that I was necessarily detained at Satis House, that it wasn't at all clear to me when I might get away. I phrased my next remark with care: hoping that their own lives 'continued as before'. (Meaning – continued without any financial disturbance or upset.)

Once Durley Chase had seemed to me a fine and even perfect place. The octagonal domed house on its airy knoll; the french doors standing open. Family portraits, Greek maidens and their suitors gambolling round the ceiling friezes. The lawns, the peripheries of long grass; the picturesquely convenient fallen boles, the designed vistas.

Now . . . I felt now that I had outgrown it. That gracious but stultifying existence, the proper – oh, always *so* proper – narrowness of its scope. I was bored with it, the decorous routines, the never too indiscreet gossip, even the theatricals where we pretended at nobility and legend we fell so far short of.

Everything, finally, had been play, which seemed to me not enough for a life.

ೃ

I found a forgotten garter halfway up the second flight of stairs, kicked into the corner of one of the treads. I extracted it with the toe of my shoe. A frilled, flesh-pink garter.

The scene inside the hermitage on that last day flashed into my mind.

'Arthur! *Arthur!*'

'What in hell's all this noise about?'

'You recognise this?'

'I know what a garter looks like.'

'And its wearer?'

He shrugged.

'D'you forget so easily?' I asked him.

He raised his eyes. They were pink-rimmed, short-sighted, weak.

'*Not* wearing it, of course,' I said. 'That is the point.'

'Since when have I been accountable to you?'

I tried to field his question with a dismissive stare. A scowl. But it didn't silence him.

'Why should I listen to what a frustrated virgin tells me?'

That was too much for me.

'I won't have your harlots in this house. My father's house.'

'*Our* house.'

'I'll wear you down, I promise you. If *they* don't first. I'll prey on you, Arthur, until this is the last place you ever want to come again.'

I couldn't bear to have his company under the same roof after that. So, without consulting him but issuing my directive (as a command), I ensured that by partitioning the building into my territory and his, technically under *two* roofs, we shouldn't have to encounter one another more than once or twice in a week.

His friends were informed by him – with more accuracy than error – that I had planted spies among the household staff, and that he was treated as something of a criminal himself. Those same cronies of his were unsettled to be here, and came about much less often in this colder climate that prevailed.

I took solace in my work. It didn't bother me that Arthur remained uninvolved. Not in the least. The office wouldn't have been a refuge to me otherwise. An *active* refuge. I put in enough hours for the two of us.

Weeks passed. I hardly noticed. Just as I no longer noticed the smell of brewery hops in the air. Facts and figures, only those. A game of holding my nerve, when everyone else (except Mr Ambrose) thought I was bound to buckle at last.

The name HAVISHAM was repainted on the brewhouse wall. It had taken the weather; the paint blistered by the sun, the brick-work nibbled at by storms.

The letters remained green, and the same shape, but now they had a thin gilt strip on one side while, on the other, they dropped a small black shadow.

We were even more prominent now from the London road. We looked prosperous, singing our own praises.

Chapter Twenty-five

The brewery had its own malthouses. We bought our hops from four farms in a long valley near Ashford, at Burwell. My father would pay an annual visit, a few weeks ahead of harvesting time, to inspect the crop on its bines and to agree a price for however many hundredweight. Now the journey fell to me. I gave responsibility for the hop-buying to myself, but acting on sage advice from two of the firm's old hands.

It was arranged that they would ride there, and I would make my way in the curricle. We stopped to water the horses midway, at the inn where my father had always halted. The driver reminded me that my father had once brought Arthur, at the time when it seemed he would be working alongside him.

The owner of the inn presented himself. Would I do him the pleasure, the great pleasure, of resting in his best private room?

I thanked him, but told him we were late already, that I didn't –

'I venture to ask, ma'am, on behalf of another.'

'On behalf of whom?'

I discovered when I was shown into the room.

'Catherine –'

The blood rushed to my face.

'Charles!'

'Surprised?'

'How on earth did you know –'

'– you'd be here? Oh, I have ways and means.'

'But . . .'

'Never mind that now.'

He was dressed for a horse, but in dashing style. A waisted cut-away coat and tight breeches. What a handsome figure he –

I reached out for the support of the high mantelpiece.

'I'm not here,' he said. 'I'm far away. Officially.'

'"Officially"?'

'If anyone should ask.'

'Why should – ?'

He put his index finger to his lips.

'There's been a bit of confusion, that's all. Or there *might* be. It'll get sorted out, though.'

'Can I help?'

'You've been help enough.'

'That was nothing.'

'This is *my* doing,' he said, '*my* fault.'

'Your "fault"? What is?'

'No, Catherine. Remember what I said – ?'

I nodded my head.

Coffee and chocolate were brought into the room. He drank quickly.

'I'm so glad I was able to intercept you.'

'You could've called at the house,' I said.

'I think not.'

'No. No, I . . .'

My face heated again.

'I was waiting for the first sound of your carriage's wheels . . .'

He was gone before I was quite ready, taking a back staircase down. I had the touch of his hand on mine; I could still feel where he had brushed his lips against the skin on the back: speedily, but with great gentleness.

. . . and Joy shall overtake us as a flood.

The final moments were left so sweetly in my memory. I stood swaying slightly with emotion at the top of the staircase. I listened as his footfalls grew fainter, as the jangle of his stirrups faded; I heard the clatter of shod hooves on the courtyard cobbles, and five seconds later I could hear nothing of him at all.

It had been a decent year for the hops, I was told, with less disease about and less mould than last.

At Burwell we inspected the bines still to be picked. We compared the Flemish variety with the Kent. I was told the very best pickers were on two shillings a day, which seemed to me excessive, and I said so, but I didn't argue the point.

I was shown figures. Sixty-two hundredweight on ten acres last year, and a profit of £5 15s 0d.

'You're not complaining?' I asked them.

'Things could always be better.'

'These are hard times, Mr Foxton.'

'Indeed, Miss Havisham. But . . .'

'I shall look at my own ledgers. I can't make any promises, however.'

'That's most civil of you.'

Suddenly I was exhausted.

'Are you feeling all right, Miss Hav—?'

I saw again that scene inside the hermitage, the two bodies writhing at their pleasure on the floor.

My head was spinning.

'You've come over very pale, if I might –'

I was taken out of the sun, into the oast house. A chair was found for me. The hops were drying, and the air was hot and stifling from the wood fire. I could only manage a few minutes there, but that was sufficient.

Briefly I'd thought I was going to cry – I felt a sudden terrible sense of desolation – but just in time I pulled myself together, bundling my litter of wanton feelings back under cover.

An apprentice lawyer called Jaggers – in Mr Snee's practice – wrote to me, requesting the favour of my time on an issue – as he judged – of no little importance. He begged that I did not inform his employer of his communication.

I was intrigued.

I received a swarthy, sturdily built, bullet-headed young man. His wrinkled shirt collar strained to hold his muscular neck. Samson, I thought of, with the hair on his head cropped close to stubble.

He was far from disempowered, though, despite his subordinate position.

For a few seconds I was alarmed by this sizeable presence. He was tongue-tied at first, but I sensed the confidence he had in his own mission.

'We have something to discuss, Mr Jaggers?'

Indeed we did.

My visitor had discovered that Snee was an embezzler. He was defrauding me of this and that, but principally of the monies due to Lady Chadwyck. She had received nothing since before my father's death, since the time of his collapse.

'You're quite sure of your facts, Mr Jaggers?'

'I waited until there could be no possible doubt.'

'I see. I see.'

He had retreated to the other side of the fireplace. He stood chewing one index finger, clearly forgetful of everything except the gravity of his news. I liked that air of abstraction which was testimony of his diligence surely. His breath filled his bullock's chest, I could imagine the shirt buttons were ready to burst off.

'And you mean to gain nothing for yourself?'

The question appeared to shock him. I had asked it chiefly in play, in order to lighten the dark mood.

'Only to escape the infectious atmosphere of self-interest I'm forced to endure.'

'It really won't affect you too?'

'I'm young.'

'As Mr Snee was once.'

'You think the same is bound to happen to me, Miss Havisham?'

'Not necessarily.'

'It might, though?'

'Then I hope you'll prove yourself to me. As you have started to recommend yourself already.'

I confronted Snee myself. He denied my accusations more strongly than I anticipated. I called in my informant. Snee understood at once; there and then he wrote out a money order.

'To deal with this embarrassment, my dear lady –'

'"Embarrassment"? And how dare you "dear lady" me!'

I demanded that Mr Jaggers be allowed to gain his articles elsewhere. I would leave my affairs with Snee meantime. Thereafter, when he was fully qualified, Mr Jaggers would take over, representing my interests. If the transference was handled cleanly, I would *presume* that no earlier dishonesty had occurred, and forgo the pleasure of pressing criminal charges, as the older man must know very well he merited. With that I made the first of my enemies in business – Snee – and my first and trustiest ally – Jeremiah Jaggers.

However recompense might be offered, I would be admitting to the Chadwycks that I knew now about the financial arrangements that had pertained.

I could see no way around that problem.

No pretence of innocence was possible. Experience can never be undone, or knowledge unlearned.

Following my father's death, I had acted with the best intentions – not that they were ever likely to discover. Either I must simply let matters be, and hope other means were at the family's disposal, or I should pay them what was due.

The latter, I decided.

I wanted not to damage the past, even though I was acknowledging to myself that *that* part of the past was over.

War against France was pushing up taxation, and every brewer in the land had headaches.

Duty on hops was increased from fifteen shillings to 23s 4d per hundredweight. Duty on strong beer went up from eight to ten shillings a barrel. Malt duty was raised from 1s 4d a barrel to 2s 5d, then shortly afterwards to 4s 5d. The price of materials for pale malt almost doubled, from forty-four shillings a quarter to 81s 6d.

I got wind that some of the pubs were adulterating the brews, and I heard the idea being put about for ourselves too. (Substituting molasses for some of the malt. Mixing strong and light table beers, and marketing the result as 'strong'.) It would cut production costs certainly, but I felt it would be unfaithful to my father's memory to tamper with the recipes that had made us successful.

I tried to trim the labour costs, exchanging a few full-time for part-time jobs. I would have preferred to replace the voices that advocated watering down, but I was afraid of tangling with working practices at that level, at any rate before I had gained more expertise.

There's a silver lining to every dark cloud, however, and when it became too expensive for small house brewers and publicans to continue brewing, they turned to the common houses for their supplies. When one door closes, as they say, another one will open.

ھ

'How d'you know that?'

'Know what, sister?'

'About the Carnaval Ball.'

'Aa-*haa*!'

'Who told you?'

'Doesn't matter to you.'

'*Who*, Arthur?'

'Good God, I can't remember.'

'"Can't remember"?'

'No problems with your hearing, Catherine.'

'Or you *won't* remember?'

'What're you asking me for? I don't stuff my head with all that nonsense. Once something's happened, it's over. Gone.'

He was proud, like me. He took advice from no one, and would be obliged to no one. He thought he had his entitlements.

He selected what he wanted to take from the past: the past of his Havisham forebears.

He was aware that he had a role to play, and doubted that he had the talent for it.

He was afraid of revealing too much of himself.

For all that was different between us, we two had just as much in common, and this was my stumbling block, the point I could never think beyond.

Chapter Twenty-six

One morning it happened: Charles was standing in the yard.

I had to look twice. Suddenly my heart was up in my throat, I was swallowing on it.

He was back!

... and Joy shall overtake us as a flood.

The blood was pounding inside my head.

I turned in different directions before I decided which. I wanted to change my dress first. Reset my hair.

A knock on the drawing-room door.

'You have a gentleman visitor, miss. He said he's come back from abroad. And you'll be able to guess who he is.'

He had been in Holland.

'Do you mean to absent yourself again?'

'It's not my intention. But life throws up surprises.'

He was complimentary about his surroundings. He noticed little details of the architecture and the decor, and I congratulated him for it.

'*Shouldn't* I notice? Have I forgotten my English manners?'

'No, no. But – it's more than I was ... I'm glad, though.'

'Then I'm glad *you're* glad, Catherine.'

He didn't tell me what had detained him for all those weeks in Amsterdam.

'So, what's it like? Being a woman in a man's world?'

'I've had my honeymoon. After this ... well, I don't know.'

'So much has changed for you.'

'In some respects, yes. But –' I lifted my eyes, '– in other respects, I haven't. Not at all. I'm exactly the same.'

ꝭ

I suggested that we should meet in London. Charles sighed.

'I'm not "tired of life", Catherine. But I do get tired of London. London belongs to everyone. Somewhere else. Somewhere that's just our own.'

It was always somewhere else.

Wherever we wouldn't be likely to cross paths with the Chadwycks, although of course we could never be sure about that.

On the Downs. In Tunbridge Wells. The Weald way.

I would take along a maid, for form's sake, but send her and the driver off for an hour or two.

Charles and I would walk. Sit before a view. Talk.

Happy days! I knew they were happy as we were living them.

Standing looking over the parapet of a bridge, down into a slow weedy river. Strolling through the fragrant shadows of a wood. Climbing, once, up the staircase of a windmill with its great sails revolving and cracking in the wind.

He saw how content I was. He told me he wished he could draw me well enough to take a sketch, but anyway he would always remember me like this. (Did he, very fleetingly, look a little troubled? Or am I mentally painting myself an idealised portrait of the man?)

I said to him, I could better appreciate this time we spent together because it was so precious, stolen from the timetable I had set myself at the brewery.

What a pity, he said in his turn, that we *had* to steal it.

'What d'you mean?'

'If we couldn't organise ourselves that this *was* our life.'

'No guilt?'

He smiled at the question. And pointedly didn't reply.

I thought quickly.

'I could give other people my work to do,' I said. 'Some of it.'

'I wasn't quite thinking of that. In the short term, yes.'

'"Short term"? You have a long-term stratagem too?'

'It's taking shape up here.' He pointed to the site of his brain.

'Can you tell me?' I asked.

'Might be unlucky.'

We were having our conversation on a river, in a scull. A faster river than the Cam. I sat looking up at the trees rushing past against blue.

'You'll tell me when you can?'

'I promise.'

'Then that will do me *very* well.'

But there was also Arthur. To begin with, he had been pestering me for small amounts: just until he could lay his hands on the next whack of cash from his inheritance.

'It's nothing to *you*,' he would say. 'You've got pots of the stuff. Don't humiliate me.'

'What happened to the last lot?'

'Got all used up.'

'Aren't I supposed to be *lending* it?'

'Oh, you'll get it back.'

'When?'

'This is to make sure I *do* get the money.'

'The money to pay me back?'

'Naturally to pay you back.'

But I knew better than to believe him.

He kept asking. I would put up a fight, and he never received what he wanted, or even half of it sometimes. But I did give in to him.

'There's no more, though.'

'It's not enough.'

'It's all you're getting.'

'*You* can afford it.'

'Did I miss "thank you"?'

'Would you like me to prostrate myself too?'

'That really would be stretching all credulity.'

'*You* call the shots, all-infallible one!'

Shortly afterwards something occurred to make me nervous, on that reprobate's behalf.

Loud insistent knocks rained down on the front door.

My visitors were looking for Mr Arthur Havisham. They had some business to discuss with him, urgently.

(Arthur had removed himself that morning – by no mere accident, I now realised.)

They frightened me, the trio, with their undertakers' black clothes and faux-solemnity and their grave-robber faces.

I performed at my most imperious. I thought of Dido and of Carthage. From a window I watched them leave the yard. Arthur returned late in the evening, when darkness had come down.

'I think you owe me an explanation,' I said.

'They go dunning. They demand money with menaces.'

'Is the money due them?'

'I would give it to them if I had it. All the interest adds up.'

'What's it for?'

'Past pleasures, let's just say.'

'For which you are duly contrite?'

'If I knew what being "duly contrite" entailed –'

'Those men put the fear of God into me.'

'And me too.'

'Something truthful from you at last. All is not in vain.'

'Please. For our father's sake –'

I sighed out my soul.

'Just – just tell me how much . . .'

When Charles wasn't there, I sagged. (Did the trees droop by nature's will, or because I told them what my feelings were?)

I should have been walking tall – and, doubtless, proud. But I was afraid every time he left me, not just unhappy. Fear cut me right down to size, and then it slammed an iron bar against my stomach.

My panic was that he wasn't coming back, or that I wouldn't see him again. My imagination threw a caul of gentle thoughts around him, to protect him, but all the time I was having to cope with my demons.

Wherever Charles might be, he would know that he wasn't alone.

Where *did* he go?

There was a cousin in Suffolk, a farmer of some sort. Up in Norwich a friend sold land and stock. He visited this or that hospitable relative, or else he looked up a (temporarily, he hoped) ailing schoolfriend.

Here and there, hither and thither.

He had a sister in London, but he could only call at her home when her husband wasn't there. The man had heard false stories, put about by someone with a grievance. Charles claimed to be unperturbed.

'Doesn't worry me. I won't allow it to.' But he had to time his visits there carefully.

At last I received an address from him, in Blackheath.

'I've got some people staying.'

'Kin?'

'So they say.'

'Aren't they?'

'It's difficult to prove. Or disprove.'

We laughed at that.

'You don't pick your family,' he said. 'Unfortunately.'

'I wish, I wish.'

'But that's where my correspondence goes to.'

'That's all I need to know,' I told him.

'Is it so easy to please you?'

'You'd be surprised' – I spoke through my smile – 'just how little it takes.'

⁂

I would wake in the night, convinced at once that he was close to me, and naked, that he was a blaze on the sheets of my bed.

I reached out my hand and touched . . . only a very little warmth where I had been lying over on my flank.

And immediately I was ashamed of myself, and I wondered where these thoughts could have come from, how I was capable of bringing them to feverish mind.

I would settle back down. I was alone – of course I was.

I felt the tide of desire receding.

I closed my eyes and set about finding cool thoughts to think instead, safely stranding myself – as that troublesome tide ebbed and ebbed – on the drily ordinary and contingent, brewery matters and the soon-to-be needs of the housekeeping.

⁂

'Mr Compeyson will be passing through.'

('Tell your brother I'll be passing through.')

'I think you should meet him.'

('Say, you think he should meet me.')

'It's nothing to me,' Arthur said. 'But am I allowed to criticise the company you keep? As you criticise mine?'

'I thought you might want to see him.'

'Anyone who's taken with you, that *would* be worth –'

'He's not "taken".'

'Why's he here, then?'

'He's passing through. D'you listen to nothing I say?'

⁂

Arthur stood by the fire, with his boot up on the fender, eating cherries and spitting the stones into the hearth. He meant to leave our visitor in no doubt as to his own status in the house. He addressed him in his gruffest voice, calling him 'Compeyson'.

His purpose was as much to offend me, however, as to put Charles Compeyson in his place. (See, sister dearest, *this* is what I think of your choice of confidant.)

When he couldn't bear to look at me any longer, he kicked the coals back into the grate and stared into the flames.

I apologised afterwards. 'I'm very sorry about Arthur.'

'Not at all.'

'I've looked for redeeming virtues. I just can't find any.'

'Somewhere there must be.'

He shrugged Arthur off. What interested him, he said, was being allowed to see the brewery.

I asked Tice if he would show my guest round.

'*If* you'd be so good,' Charles said to him.

Tice drew himself fully upright. But of course, I told myself, he'll stand to attention for a man.

I waited until they'd finished.

'Don't pretend *that* was a pleasure!'

'But it was. You've known this place all your life, remember. It's an adventure to me.'

'Really?'

We had tea outside in the garden. I was a little nervous, in case Arthur appeared again. I chattered away, I spoke too much.

Arthur only appeared as we were saying our goodbyes. He might have timed it for that moment.

Another sneer.

But the two went off into the stable together, where Charles's mount was waiting.

I heard them talking. Arthur wasn't being openly insulting, I hoped.

I waited.

Something was said: ' . . . a licence to print money, isn't it?'

It must have been Arthur speaking. Denigrating Havisham's, as ever.

Charles came out, leading his roan stepper which I had helped him to buy.

'I'm sorry about that,' I said.

'He's all right.'

'You don't have to say anything nice about him. On *my* account.'

'He's not so bad.'

'I don't understand him at all.'

'It's easier for a man, maybe.'

'That's what I value about you,' I said.

'What's that?'

'Oh . . . your optimism.'

'Is that how you see me?'

'Looking on the bright side.'

'In lieu of all the other trappings?'

'It's a spiritual gift.'

His eyes widened momentarily, as if my observation alarmed him.

'Money alone can't buy it,' I said. 'Or privilege either.'

Chapter Twenty-seven

A few weeks later.

'I hear', I said, 'that your knowledge is very impressive, Mr Compeyson.'

'Met a brewer once. Things've stuck in my head.'

'I'll teach you what I know,' I heard myself telling him. 'If that's any use.'

'"Use"? You're schooling me?'

I felt I was in danger of blushing.

'Well,' I said, 'I'll need your advice. I mean, I would appreciate if you –'

'I'd be honoured. Couldn't be taught by better, could I?'

ꝏ

Before my father's physical decline, production of strong beer was running at over twelve thousand barrels per annum. I made that my own target.

I was buying another five public houses, at prices between £230 and £480 each. Including another thirty-six tied premises, the number of publics we supplied had risen to eighty-six.

ꝏ

On his visits to the town Charles put up at the Blue Boar. He ate there, unless I had invited others to dinner at Satis House, when I would persuade him to join us. But in Cinderella fashion, he was the first to leave. All this punctilious formality, this terrible fear of committing an improper deed. All this intense frustration he let build up inside me. I asked him to stay on awhile in the house, so that we might walk in the garden or sit by the fire, talking, dreaming of life.

But no, he must be getting back.

'If you really have to.'

'We can't always do as we want.'

'No?'

'There are rules. Precepts.'

'You're right.'

But I said it sadly.

❧

It occurred to me that perhaps they hadn't been what they'd seemed to me, those three men who appeared at the front door in their threatening poses, asking for Arthur.

I had no trust in anything Arthur said. All I could take as honest was his determination to embarrass me, to provoke my conscience, because it was I and not he who had inherited the greater part of the Havisham wealth.

Organising a few stage stooges to appear on the doorstep of Satis House, that would have been nothing at all to someone of Arthur's deviousness.

'It's only fifty.'

'*Another* fifty pounds you're asking me for. Added to the hundred.'

'I got my sums wrong.'

Here's yet another scene.

'How long d'you imagine this is going to go on?'

'It's just to tide me over.'

'You never tell me. What these "expenses" are.'

'That's because you don't want to know. Tell me you do.'

'Your life doesn't interest me, Arthur.'

'Maybe I'm keeping another household.' He laughed. 'I've got a nice little wife. And we're planning a brood of children.'

He continued laughing.

'That *is* a joke,' I said.

'What is?'

'You married. And a father.'

'And you see *yourself* married, I suppose?'

I looked away.

'All nicely set up?' (How bitter his voice sounded.) 'With the man of your dreams?'

ꝏ

First, Charles told me the house in Blackheath was shedding masonry. Then, that the building was being pinned up. For weeks the air had been thick with dust; the mortar wouldn't dry. The floorboards would have to be replaced. An elderly uncle was about to descend, needing to convalesce.

'From Norfolk?' I asked.

'Norfolk?'

'Your relatives. In Norfolk. Or Suffolk.'

'Yes, Norfolk. That's where he's from. From Norfolk. He needs looking after, so I've got someone in.'

'Oh.'

'Just a nurse. Sort of nurse.'

I nodded.

'He can get up to the river?' I asked.

'Who can?'

'Your uncle. You're close to the river in Blackheath?'

'He's a cussed so-and-so. I don't want to inflict him on you.'

'He's improving?'

'His health is. Not his temper, though.'

'He'll go back to Norfolk?'

'To Norfolk? Yes. Eventually.'

'Poor you.'

His spirits seemed to sink a little at that. His smile was wan. He shook his head.

'I don't deserve sympathy,' he said.

❧

I found I was trying now to excuse Arthur to Charles. I didn't want anything to come between the two of us, even that wretch.

'But you told me he wasn't up to it – didn't you?'

'He lacks experience,' I said.

'He'd ruin the business, though. Given a chance.'

'His mind's on other things. He's younger than –'

'Catherine, it's useless. You can't go on defending him.'

'Couldn't he learn?'

'No. He'd be useless in a situation like this.'

'So, what can I do about it?'

'Look – Arthur needs money. Access to money.'

'Certainly he does,' I said. 'I can't tell for what –'

'Let's not enquire.'

'That's his argument, "you wouldn't want to know".'

'Take your pick.'

'Gambling?' I suggested.

'Very probably. But our concern is to get him off your hands.'

'Indeed.'

'So – so you have to pay him more.'

'No. No, I thought you said –'

'Wait a minute, Catherine. Pay him, in return *for* something. Something that you want.'

'What's that? What do I want?'

'His share in the business.'

'I beg your pard—'

'You heard me.'

'Yes, but . . .'

'If you pay – if you pay for his holding in the company . . . You see the advantages, don't you?'

'I'm trying to.'

'Then you wouldn't have the worry of his involvement!'

'How would –'

'It can be done in stages.'

'But the cost of it!' I said.

'It would cost you a lot. But think of the rise in profits.'

'It would mean – I'd have to take over all the running, wouldn't I?'

'Not necessarily.'

'"Not necessarily"?'

Might I not, he asked, think of engaging some assistance?

'What kind of assistance?'

'Sharing the responsibilities.'

'How?' I asked.

'Turning it over to a new senior manager.'

'I don't know who . . .'

He was smiling. He started to laugh.

'*Who?*' I said.

'Who do you think?'

It took me three or four seconds to realise.

'*You?*'

'Don't sound so aghast!'

'But I hadn't . . .'

'Why not? I know what I know. And I'll learn. Quickly. I promise you.'

I stood staring at him.

'Your father didn't have you mixing with the Chadwycks so that you'd come back to run a brewery.'

I nodded at that.

'*And*,' he said, 'it'll give us a chance to be together more often. Won't it?'

He reached forward and took my hand. His was warm. I felt the surge of energy in the fingers.

He raised my hand. Lightly, tenderly, he touched the back with his lips. How – how could I have thought to refuse?

'But,' he said as he straightened, as he gently let go of my hand, 'I shall ever be discreet.'

How could I have told him that I didn't care if he was not; that I secretly wished he wouldn't be – that he'd be anything but.

❧

I wrote to Arthur in the fleshpot resort where he had taken up residence. I set out my proposals, the financial terms.

At first he refused me.

'Well, let *me* try dinning some sense into him.'

Whatever Charles must have said, Arthur was persuaded, and he agreed to my buying an initial portion of his interest.

The next time he was asked, the price of his remaining interest was doubled.

Charles reported back to me.

'That's just business, Catherine, I'm afraid.'

I sat down to complete another banker's order. I had never seen, let alone written, such a large figure before.

'You're hesitating . . .'

'It was my father's wish. For his son. His atonement.'

'Courage, Catherine.'

'If my father could've seen how much . . .'

'That's Arthur's asking price. He won't give an inch.'

'You're quite sure?'

'*Quite* sure.'

'Very well.'

'You'll recover it. And more. Much more.'

'It will take a while.'

'But if you don't act, if you don't do this – Arthur will be disagreeing with you about everything. He'll be saying you can't do this or that, you've no warranty, no authorisation –'

Charles unfolded a letter from Arthur's lawyer.

'This is *our* authorisation.'

'True,' I said. 'True.'

I started with a bold flying flourish to the first numeral of the total amount.

Charles was coming down from London each week, putting up at the Boar. He had asked me to appoint a works manager beneath him.

'For the hard graft,' he laughed.

'You work hard too,' I said.

'They'll think I'm pushing my way in. A cuckoo in the nest.'

'*I* appointed you.'

'You're the chief. I tell them that.'

'I know what they feel about having a woman in charge. Not that I am,' I added quickly. 'That's why I'm so grateful. Having you here. To deal with the men.'

'Man to man.'

'Yes.'

'Perhaps they're talking behind *my* back too.'

'Why?' I asked.

'They'll say – I don't know – that you have me on a leash or something.'

'Then show them you know your own mind.'

He came a step or two nearer. Very close to me.

'No,' I said, 'remember the hermitage –'

He stopped just in time. I had a memory flash of the two bodies locked together on the floor, passion sweeping all before it. A ferocious longing had welled up inside me, but now it collapsed in on itself again.

ఖ

'I hear you've had a visitor,' Charles said.

'Yes. Yes, I have. Mr Jaggers.'

'At your request?'

'No. Not at all.'

'A social call?'

'Not exactly.'

'About the Chadwycks?'

'He was just – taking stock.'

'A general sort of taking stock, was it?'

'He'd been aware I was drawing on my personal funds.'

'He misses little, our friend.'

'That's what I'm paying him for.'

'To be your lawyer?'

'Everything tidily within the law. "Nothing to upset the King". As he puts it.'

'And is there?'

'No. Naturally.'

'Naturally. He confirmed that, I hope.'

'I explained about Arthur.'

'If that's any of his business.'

'I don't mind. I have a soft spot for the formidable Mr Jaggers.'

I paused.

'But you're not "soft" on him?'

'Good heavens, no!'

I had an item of information to impart, gleaned from my visitor.

'The lawyer Arthur asked us to use –'

'Yes. Crabbit.'

'Apparently he's a crony of Snee's.'

'Who's Snee?'

'Someone I once crossed.'

'Is this significant?'

'The coincidence is peculiar.'

'Coincidences always are. That's their nature.'

'Yes,' I said, inattentively.

Snee wished to do me no favours. If he was involved, it was to exact some revenge – blatant or, more troublingly, covert – on his former castigator, Catherine Havisham.

I came back one day to learn that Arthur had cleared out the rest of his belongings from the house. A few small *objets* were also missing from the downstairs rooms – a silver box, a silver tankard engraved with our 'H' emblem – but I wasn't bothered: it only mattered to me to be shot of ***him***.

A note left for me announced that, all being well, I had seen the very last of yours truly. Now the two of us, he said, could have the run of the place. He wasn't sorry that he wouldn't be setting eyes on god-forsaken Satis House or this privy-hole of a town ever again.

Chapter Twenty-eight

Charles should look like a man of parts. I made him buy a supply of banyans for himself; Indian nightgowns. Waistcoats came curved now, with a narrow tail, and so I said he ought to have those too. A selection, embroidered as well as plain. And the new round hats with uncocked brim. And large buckles on his shoes, just as the macaronis used to wear.

He needed a manservant to take care of his appearance, and one was duly hired.

The roan was a fine pacer. I kept a closed carriage and also a curricle, for two horses apiece. But I thought it befitted him, and the dashing figure he cut, to be seen in a smarter sort of phaeton.

We discussed it. He demurred at first. However, as we talked more, I could tell that he was warming to the subject. He knew a good deal about the types available, the lightness of the bodywork by this or that coachbuilder, the speed you could expect.

'With a decent pair of horses, I mean.'

'Yes,' I said, 'of course.'

I dealt with the expenses as a practicality. It didn't occur to me that I – or he – was being extravagant or profligate. It cost a certain amount to live well. He had the easy manner of someone born to such advantage, for whom it was no more than a right, his patrimony.

Once I'd bought the phaeton for him, I would listen from the street side of the house for the first trace in the air of the wheels. The response from the horses as he turned them first right, then left, and along the length of the brewhouse. The singing of the chassis springs. My heart would lift, soar. These were the most desirable sounds in the world now to me.

❧

It was all money, impersonal and soulless. The more of it I gave him, the more I was trying to show him that it counted for so little against love. The value of money is the spirit in which we use it; otherwise it amounts to just the crackling of greasy paper, the piddle-clink of dulled coins.

❧

Charles was too careful of my reputation, and of his own, to think of putting himself up overnight. It occurred to me that he could have one of the cottages at the back of the yard, but refurbished.

'You need more space.'

This would deal with the awkwardness of his presence in the house. I knew that the staff talked, and it irked me that they should suppose they deserved to have an opinion on the matter.

Charles saw the merits of having his own detached accommodation, but the cottage's occupant, Tice, was holding out.

'I can smell trouble with that fellow.'

'Oh, I've been having it for months,' I told him.

'There must be ways and means of satisfying all parties in this matter.'

'Which matter is that?'

'My home comforts, of course!'

A few days later Charles announced he'd found another cottage to let in Tap Street, suitable for the Tices, and he'd expertly beaten down the landlord on a price. He showed me the lease he'd had drawn up, awaiting my signature. I allowed him to persuade me that this was the best solution.

I was neglecting to include Tice in my calculations, however. I discovered that *he* felt he had been robbed not only of the cottage but also of status.

'Leave it to me, Catherine. I'll sugar him a bit. It'll be all right.'

Because I didn't hear any more about it, I presumed things were on a better footing. Tice habitually had a morose expression for me anyway, even though I would hear him laughing with his colleagues (*and*, apparently, with his new landlord in Tap Street): so wasn't it an innocent misapprehension on my part, supposing that order if not quite harmony had been restored?

Charles used the cottage less than I had foreseen, but it was a gesture: mine to him. I was also advertising to the workers just what the new system was, how Havisham's was being run now.

I was unaware of any complaints about my appointment of a new chief manager. That was either because there weren't any or because Mr Ambrose, being the sensitive man I judged him to be, was filtering them off (almost like one of the brewhouse processes) before I had a chance to hear.

He's on the other side of the yard from me, with his own housekeeper and a skivvy for that compact roosting box of his. He's so near, but the distance of seventy or eighty yards is crucial. I'm feeling something more strongly than I've ever felt it before – an urgency between my legs, but not to relieve myself of water.

An alarming, thrilling sensation.

When I clamp my thighs tightly together and concentrate hard on that hidden spot, the fear increases to terror. But my shameless pleasure increases too.

To exhilaration. Abandonment.

I roam beneath my shift. I lightly pass my hand over the fork, brushing the wiry hair there. I have a compulsion to dally. I press down with more force. I open my hand and let my fingers probe.

I part my thighs. My fingers reach their way in, not gently.

I move inside, towards my inner ache. My fingers explore deeper. Hot, wet, silky flesh. Untravelled, but knowing to yield.

I fight for breath.

From the crown of my head to my toes, I'm consumed by an unspeakable euphoria.

࿐

In the evenings we played cards. I learned the alphabet of Misère terms.

Alliance. Blaze. Cut-throat. Finesse. Ouvert. Pip. Renege. Ruff. Sans prendre. Skat / Widow.

Charles told me again, you have to play *against* the rules. Innocents to the game would think the cards were – literally – stacked against them, and that the outcome of a game was inevitable. He repeated, you needed courage, principally that: and the quality of clever, inspired bluff.

࿐

I wasn't expecting it. His first question came from nowhere.

'Are we going to continue like this?'

I was sitting at my father's desk. He was standing at the window. Above his right shoulder, across the yard, a signboard for strangers who still didn't know whose yard they were in, HAVISHAM.

'"Continue like" – what?'

'This arrangement.'

'I thought you wanted to know about –'

'No, not about the business. About ourselves.'

I frowned, quite caught out.

'I'm sorry, I –'

'The two of us.'

'Me in Satis House, you mean?' I tried again. 'And you over in . . . ?'

He shook his head slowly.

'No. No, not that.'

I saw him swallowing hard, so that the Adam's apple in his throat jumped.

'Shouldn't we be thinking of getting married, Catherine?'

It was as if I was in one of the Chadwycks' *tableaux vivants*, immobilised. At last, after a hiatus, I returned to my senses, in an approximate fashion.

'I'm sorry,' he said. 'I shouldn't have –'

I stared at him.

'What I said –' He began again. 'I ought to have asked someone –'

'Asked whom?'

'One of your relatives. Please – you mustn't –'

And then, did I panic? Because I thought he might be going to withdraw the question, undo the past moments, erase them –

'No. No, no.'

'Catherine –'

'I shall. I *shall* marry you.'

He didn't spring forward, didn't throw his arms around me. He wasn't even smiling. At first he just stood nodding his head, as if he had known I would consent.

'Charles – ?'

I felt that now I was having to pull *him* back from somewhere.

'Good! Good!' A smile broke out on his face at last. 'I'm so glad.'

'You've made me the happiest woman in the world. "Joy, joy shall overtake us –"'

'What's that?'

'"– as a flood".'

I told him how many times after that. On each occasion he would grow more thoughtful.

Self-deprecation, I felt, I couldn't allow in my fiancé.

'You should be proud of yourself,' I said.

'To be able to make a proud woman happy?'

'The most difficult sort to *make* happy,' I told him.

'All those beaks at school who thought I was a dunce.'

'Never!'

'Who was I to say they weren't right?'

'The more fool you.'

'Their point precisely.'

And somehow I would win him from his thoughts in the end, back to quiet laughter.

&

He would have kissed me. But I was terribly afraid of what I might have been allowing to happen next.

'Please,' I said. 'Not now.'

'Some time?'

'I want to wait.'

'D'you mean that?'

No. Of course I didn't.

'Yes,' I lied.

'It's important to you?'

'Oh yes.'

He didn't try to argue the point.

'I only thought –'

'It's all right,' I said.

'I know it's serious to you. If that's how you feel.'

Important, serious: yes, but not for the reasons he might be thinking.

I was melting between my legs, I could feel dampness on my underclothes, I was afraid the stains would show through.

'Later,' I said, forcing the word out. Nothing had ever been more difficult for me to say. 'Later.'

And he did the decent thing and concurred, nodding his head, oh quite agreeably enough, while I wept and wailed inside myself for want of him.

❧

'When we're married . . .'

'Yes,' I said. '"When we're married . . ."?'

'Then I can allow you to lead the life of a lady.'

'Meaning – ?'

'Meaning, I shall be able to take over the running of the whole brewery.'

'You'll run it on your own?'

'Why not?'

'Single-handed?'

'You trust me, don't you?'

'Of course I trust you.'

'And you can be wife, mother, grande dame, patroness, whatever you want to be.'

'And you'll have the grind of Havisham's every day?'

'Most days, let's say. It will be my job of work. You told me labour was honest and true.'

'Yes, but –'

'You don't think it's beyond my capacities?'

'No, no.'

'You don't think it's beneath me, either?'

'Not at all. But I *shall* get to see enough of you, won't I?'

'As much as you saw of your father.'

'My father wasn't always here.'

'Off on business? I should have to go too.'

'Yes, I've neglected that side of things.'

'Your father wouldn't have been disappointed?'

'About what?'

'About us.'

'Why on earth – ? No, I'm sure it's a great solace to him. If he's able to hear us. To know the brewery will be in reliable hands.'

'Then, that's settled?'

I nodded.

'Yes, that's settled. For when the time comes. Once we're man and wife.'

⁂

The engagement banns were read.

I surrendered myself to everything, and became –

that cherry tree throwing its branches

the flame leaping on the new wick

the water tumbling joyfully over the weir

the fragrant spring wind seeping through the window cracks

the yellow cart rolling down the street

the vigorous hyacinths sprouting from their bulbs, after a dark cupboard-growing

the old Roman bricks stuck into the flint wall at the bottom of the garden, when I would sit in the mild sun staring and staring in front of me.

I was still trying to believe my luck.

⁂

My only regret was that Sally couldn't be here to share my joy and to play *her* part.

I hadn't known where to write to her, to pass on my news, to tell her about the preparations. At one time she had been the person closest to me. It had seemed so curious to lose her, an inexplicable thing, but never more so than now.

Letters of congratulation arrived from the town. My Havisham cousins and second cousins queued up in the hall on a certain Wednesday afternoon to offer me, one by one, their compliments and felicitations. (Implicit was their presumption that now my spirit must be a more generous one.)

I woke in the mornings with an immodest delight at life, raptured back *into* life, realising what a deliverance from my past this was, to feel every surge of joy that I was feeling. I floated through the day, never so light or carefree, hopeful to the very tips of my fingers and toes.

We were to be married at St Barnabas's.

'You don't mind if it's nowhere grander?' I asked him.

'Whatever pleases *you*.' (He would have agreed to anything.)

'The cathedral, you see . . . I used to go there under duress. And when my father died –'

'No. No, that's fine. Really. Truly.'

'It'll be my birthday too,' I added.

He was about to look away, but turned back, did a double-take. He must have forgotten; he had known so much about me, the minutiae, but this greater event ahead of us had thrown a mantle over all the lesser.

'Now it will be a special day for a much better reason. Because every year on my birthday I shall share our wedding anniversary with you.'

I asked him another time – other times, plural – what about our honeymoon?

Would it be France, or Switzerland, or Italy?

'The choice is yours,' he said.

The sun, I told him. Please. But not too much sun. And antiquity. Beautiful antiquity.

It must have come into both our heads at the very same instant.

'Venice?' he was saying.

'Venice!' I spoke over him.

Where else?

We didn't discuss the expenses, because I didn't want to embarrass him. The bills perforce would be *my* responsibility. (This was the whole point of having money: recognising what it was destined for.)

And my trousseau? I asked.

That's *your* prerogative, he said. Surprise me.

(Sheba would have been the one to ask. But . . .

I'd manage by myself, though.

Mine would be the trousseau of trousseaux. My initials would be sewn into every article as finely, as meticulously as if enchanted fairy needles had worked the stitches.)

Chapter Twenty-nine

Charles was talking about the trade there might be in setting up friendly societies at our tied houses. Those would hold the funds of whoever might want to place them with us, Havisham's being a fully reputable local firm always running a healthy profit. Government stock was unreliable; we could offer five per cent, and do very nicely out of it – expand our own interests, bind our customers tighter to us, encourage others to come in.

'Just like a bank?'

'Offering credit. Money-merchanting.'

'*You're* ambitious.'

'I'm being ambitious on your behalf, Catherine. Havisham's has the prestige.'

'I'll think about it.'

'We should discuss it.'

I. We. It wasn't so simple any more, was it?

'Later,' I said. 'Yes.'

❧

'I shall invite Arthur, though,' I said.

'You will?'

'Shouldn't I?'

'I hadn't thought about it.'

He had agreed to the list of guests I had drawn up, raising only a couple of queries.

'I'd do it for my father's sake. For no other reason.'

'Very well.'

'He mightn't come, I suppose. That'd be easiest.'

'Damn!' I watched him lean forward to inspect a stain on his boot.

'I won't if you'd rather not,' I said.

'It's all the same to me.'

I couldn't help wishing he would voice a sentiment, one way or the other. I didn't like to think of Arthur attending, too much drink in him, leering at us. But without him, much as it went against my better instincts, I felt I would be dishonouring the man who'd been father to both of us.

I had decided that the young Chadwycks – and cousin Moses – should be there at the wedding, notwithstanding all the reservations they'd declared about Charles. (They had misunderstood him, giving credence to stupid slanders; but I should be ready to forgive them, with my bride's magnanimity.)

I issued the four of them with separate invitations. I wrote four letters, as cover, expressing myself in much the same way to each of them. My life was about to change, and very *very* happy I was about it too, etc.

W'm replied from Devon. '. . . *quod bonum faustum felix fortunatumque sit* . . .' He made no mention of the state of his own engagement; there was no reference to Lucinda Osborne. However, he did say that 'personal reasons' (Mrs Calvert, by any chance?) must detain him where he was, in the West, and that therefore, '*tristissime* . . .'

Less promptly, Sheba and Mouse replied, in tandem, and sounding a little parsimonious in their congratulations. They very much hoped I *would* be happy . . . Unfortunately at the time of the wedding they were required to be in Llanirfon Wells with their mother, who was hobbling now with swollen joints, and therefore . . .

'See, Miss Havisham. What do you think, for the trousseau?'

'A la Turque', that's *the* style.

Muslin, gold India. Sashed and buckled. Gauze, ribbons.

We wear *this* over a light single petticoat. Very graceful, don't you agree? Capricious, even, I'd venture.

'Miss Havisham, you will feel you're walking a-float, inches off the ground.'

ꝯ

Charles had mentioned adulterants. One of the tricks of the trade, as others practised it. Or *mal*practised it. Using vitriol and copperas, to speed up the brew's maturing. Adding liquorice, quassia, wormwood, to give a hop flavouring; upping the beer's strength with cocculus indicus and opium.

'The law allows isinglass,' I reminded him. 'Nothing else.'

'The law's also clobbering us. Putting folk out of business.'

'Yes, I know.'

'The law doesn't *care*.'

'The law can take you to court. Fine you. The law could close this place down only too easily, and then everyone would be out of a job. And where does that get us?'

This was the most determinedly I had ever spoken to him. I knew what he was suggesting; the dissenters in the brewhouse had got to him. I had already been warned about this by Mr Ambrose.

'I'm just considering all the possibilities.'

'It's a solemn onus placed on us,' I said, repeating words my father had used. 'Supporting those men who come to work here every day. And their families.'

'It's not a charity we're running.'

'Yes, I know that.'

And, I wanted to add but didn't, it's *I* who still have charge of Havisham's. After we're married, then we shall attend to the transfer, but slowly, in good time, once I have assured myself.

Perhaps he could read from my face just what I was thinking. So be it. I had the name to think of, as always the name, because without it where was I, and where would he be?

I smiled at him, and waited – I kept smiling – until he finally responded in kind, with an easing back of his lips. We had never ended a conversation on a grumbling tone, and my mind was made up that we never would.

Love to faults is always blind,
Always is to joy inclin'd.
Lawless, wing'd, and unconfin'd,
And breaks all chains from every mind.

I didn't hear from Moses until ten days before the wedding. His letter was direct to the point of abject rudeness. I was incensed.

He had seen the notice of the engagement, and told the others. He hadn't written to me because he didn't know how he might be honest with me. Engagements don't always lead to marriage, do they? But now, in reply to *my* letter (for which many thanks), his profuse apologies, only it was going to be very difficult to alter his plans, when he had an extra parish in his charge at present. He did understand that my heart was set. He and his sister-helpmate Louisa were of an identical persuasion; yet they both sent me their best wishes, and wanted me to know that I should be in their thoughts. He would pray for me –

I tore up the letter. How dare he? How *dare* he?

All his sort amounted to were licensed meddlers; the loveless and unloved who cross themselves at the thought of other people's happiness; who couldn't in a lifetime of Sundays put themselves in the position of the beloved.

I tossed the letter into the fire's flames.

❧

I attempted to exorcise the incident by having dinner served to us that evening before the same fireplace.

'Should we try to woo back dear Boodle?' I wondered.

'Boodle priced himself a little too high for my pocket.'

'"Dear" indeed!' I said.

'Must've been talking to whatsisname.'

'Nemo.'

At that instant a memory flash . . .

'He could be my present to you,' I said.

'You're dreaming!'

'I'm sorry –'

'Not Nemo anyway.'

'No. Boodle.'

It had been a silly, misplaced remark, I said. I apologised for it, and I drew my chair closer to his.

It was usually he, I felt, who was dreaming. How far away he got from me sometimes. Eleventh-hour nerves, was it? About marriage? Or about his duties at work? I couldn't always wait for his mind to clear, and I would tug at his arm to shake him out of his brown study.

'It'll be all right,' I told him. 'Everything will be fine.'

He would stare at me for a few seconds, as if he didn't understand what I meant. I would pull at his arm again.

'I promise you,' I said.

At that a shadow of sadness passed across his face: only for another moment or two, until he was finally released from his doubts and was returned to me.

&

'What I have will be yours,' I said. 'And what you have will become mine as well.'

'I have the better of that arrangement.'

'And I shall honour you and obey you. As I must swear to do.'

He would be in charge of the brewery. I should have the running of the house. When he had to be away, I would leave brewery matters until he got back, and I would learn to forget that once I had done what he was doing.

Anything. He might ask anything of me, and I'd surely do it. All for love.

Chapter Thirty

I woke early, and it was the first thought in my head.

I marry this morning.

I lay for a while in bed. This would be the last time I took my rest like this, as a single woman. I felt a wonderful pleasurable confusion of anxiety, excitement and the comfort of my hopes achieved.

I bathed in my dressing room, in front of a fire, looking out at the blue May sky, at the martins' giddy zigzaggings. My helpers came and went. My bouquet arrived, not yet dried of its dew, tied with white and yellow satin ribbons.

I drank some tea and ate a coddled egg and a piece of toasted bread spread with cherry jam. The slices of cheese and ham I left untouched.

I felt just a little, gently dazed.

They dressed my hair first, which took half an hour, pomading and setting with silver combs and netting.

Then they powdered my body from head to foot.

Once I'd been wrapped in a peignoir, they went to work on my face.

My eyebrows were plucked to fine arcs. I was whitened again. They painted my lips, and ringed my eyes lightly with kohl, turning them up slightly at the outer corners. My fingernails were buffed and glazed, and my hands were creamed.

She was a woman I scarcely recognised, the one in the mirror, looking out at me with increasing incredulity and fascination.

It was a carnaval mask.

Sophisticated, experienced, worldly, a little arch, a little ironic: all the things Catherine Havisham hadn't been.

And then, finally, the dress, without its train, which was to fall twelve feet behind me. French silk; but the silkworms had been brought from China.

Sprig embroidery on the bodice and along the edges of the sleeves. The neck and cuffs were trimmed with Bath lace. There was a delicate tracery of gold foil on the back of the dress. The miniature buttons were each painstakingly worked in silk.

It fitted me exactly as it should have. I could move my arms, and breathe easily. There was no straining. I saw no gathers anywhere.

How strange, that such a consummately made garment should be worn for this one day only. But, as every girl growing up understood, her wedding day was the most significant she would know: a woman's crowning glory.

⁂

They left me.

It was just after half past eight. We had made good time. I was due to arrive at the church two or three minutes before ten o'clock.

I found myself thinking of my mother. I wished she could have seen me, and I could have seen her expression of wonderment. I thought of my father; I felt it unlikely he would have been disappointed, since the brewery – what he had cared most for – was going to be under the management of the man very shortly to take me as his wife.

As I was fitting my left foot into its satin slipper, there came a knock at the door.

A letter.

It was placed on the side-table.

If I hadn't had time to spare I should have left it there. But we were ahead of ourselves.

I put down the other slipper, laid it on top of the dressing table.

I leaned across for the envelope.

I recognised his handwriting at once. It must be his last word on my single state, I thought, a missive of love on this sweetest of mornings.

I split the seal with my thumb, drew out the sheet inside, unfolded it.

I had read only the first few words when I felt my heart leap up into my throat. I couldn't breathe.

'I cannot but expect that the Contents of this Letter must greatly aggrieve you –'

I stared at the sheet of paper, my eyes fixed. The lines of script swam in front of me; white spots flared over them.

'– because I do recognise how much your Heart was set on our Union.'

No.

No, no.

'What I must say will distress you, I am certain –'

I felt wetness on both legs, a stream of hot liquid starting to soak my stockings.

'– and I can think of no way of preparing you easily for it.

In short, Catherine, I cannot be your husband.'

I couldn't control myself; a rivulet of piss flowed out of me. Suddenly, in an instant, my life had turned to tragedy.

'I hope that with the passing of the months, you will find it within you to offer me some measure of forgiveness.'

He was having a last joke, wasn't he? It was meant to be a test for me.

'– to offer me some measure of forgiveness.'

I closed my eyes for several moments, then opened them again. The letter was still there.

'You will recover your Spirits and find some worthier Suitor for you than I could be.'

ﻌ

My cries brought the others to my room. I had fallen from the chair to the floor. I lay in my own urine. They helped me back on to the seat.

Someone fetched smelling salts, and held them under my nose.

'No. No, no, no, no, *no* . . . !'

I flailed at them, howling.

One of them had found the letter and read it; she was whispering as she passed it on.

'It's not true!' I shouted. 'It's not true . . .'

They held me to the chair. I tried to fight them off.

'None of it's true . . .'

The rug was mopped at with old towels.

'None of it's true . . .'

'It's all right, miss.'

I stared into the woman's face.

'What?'

It was all right, it would be all right.

Then she turned and I saw the look of utter dismay exchanged between her and the others. No. No, it wasn't going to be all right. She'd lied to me. I struck out at her with my arms, and she fell back. Her eyes widened in her face, staring and staring at the beast in its lair.

'Get away! Get away, all of you!'

Minutes passed, but I had no regard. Half an hour. An hour. Two hours.

People came and went all morning. Came and went.

Sometimes I screamed at them. Sometimes I said nothing. Sometimes I was unaware if anyone was there or not, I forgot . . .

All I knew, the only thing, was this: I had reached the end of the life I'd had. It was lost to me now.

⁂

They must have cleared the church, and the guests been dispersed. But they didn't ask me. I heard the whispers outside the door of my dressing room. Footsteps coming and going away. They knew they didn't dare disturb me again.

That was all I had. The letter. A sheet of paper. A message I couldn't comprehend.

Could he have thought that *my* love had dimmed?

Had he misunderstood something I'd said, or not said?

Had he allowed himself to be misled by what another person had told him?

'Lock the doors of the dining room, d'you hear me? Don't let them disturb the feast. The feast must be left, just as it is.'

> She last remains, when ev'ry guest is gone,
> Sit on the bed he press'd, and sighs alone;
> Absent, her absent hero sees and hears.

They tried to undress me, but I resisted them.

I felt . . . What?

I felt that if I was still wearing my dress, then the wedding would still take place. If I removed it, I would be denying myself the hope of a happy ending.

'I have to be ready, you see.'

They tried to persuade me, but I wasn't listening. I shook off their hands.

'When, miss?'

'Not yet, not yet.'

And shouldn't it have been 'Mrs Compeyson' by now? We ought to have set off on our travels, soon we would be enjoying each other's company in a strange foreign city, en route to the strangest of all, he and I intimately marooned together by its lagoon.

'Leave me as I am, will you? Just let me be.'

Frightened glances. Hands turned palms upwards, gesturing helplessness.

'Go now, go now!'

He needed more time, only more time, to prepare himself.

'He's taken cold feet, that's all. He's heard something, and it's quite untrue. There's been a dreadful misunderstanding. It's not serious.'

> Wilt thou have this man . . . obey and serve him . . . and, forsaking all other, keep thee only unto him, so long as ye both shall live.
>
> *The woman shall answer,*
>
> I will.

The next day I wore the wedding dress, and the next again. I became used to having that woman with me, framed in the looking-glasses. I would stare at her, and it was like watching one of those (nearly) stock-still tableaux. When she was seated, she scarcely made any movement at all, except to draw and exhale breath.

I instinctively held out my hands to warm them at the fire, while my eyes passed over the Delft tiles on the hearth's surround. There were canals there too. Windmills, barges, locks. Hump-backed bridges, skaters on an iced pond. A street of tall, narrow-shouldered houses. Tulips – no, chrysanthemums, growing in a garden pot.

. . . then the solemnisation must be deferred, until such time as the truth be tried

The canals grew colder and colder, and started to freeze; the ice islands sighed. A bird flew low, between the Dutchmen's high gabled houses, on the spruce scrubbed streets of Leiden and Arnhem, while the chrysanthemums – no, the tulips – shrivelled and died.

❧

'Tea, miss? Won't you try to drink some tea? Some toast? Here – You haven't eaten at all, miss.'

The wretched queen, pursued by cruel fate,
Begins at length the light of heav'n to hate,
And loathes to live.

'You need to eat, miss. Isn't there something? Whatever you tell me you want to . . . Miss Havisham?'

Try to remember. When it was you felt most alive.

Try to remember who she was.

One morning, rising to a blue May sky. Pink blossom on the cherry trees. The small flames of a new fire rustling in the grate, whispering excitedly.

Now,

– brooding Darkness spreads his jealous wings,
And the night-raven sings.

The cards. Play the cards.
Ouvert. Pip. Renege. Sans prendre. Cut-throat. Widow.

❧

'She won't speak to us. Well, nothing to make sense of. She only talks to herself. It sounds like gibberish. But it must mean something. Something to *her*.'

❧

I'll bark against the dog-star
I'll crack the poles asunder
I'll sail upon a millstone
And make the sea-gods wonder.

❧

If . . .
If . . .
If . . .
If I'd . . .
If I'd . . .
If I'd only . . .

If I'd only left the letter unopened / he might have been able to change his mind / somehow intuiting that I hadn't received his message / and returning to Satis House with me / he would have found a moment to remove the envelope / to slip it undetected into his pocket / and I should have been none the wiser / concerning those foolish, last-minute nerves / which is all they were.

'Tis folly
– where ignorance is bliss,
'Tis folly to be wise.

IV

CATHERINE REGNANT

Chapter Thirty-one

I felt I had a fire beneath me.

Poor Dido . . .

And that I was lying pinned, spread-eagled, on a pallet of live coals.

. . . with consuming love is fir'd . . .

Every pore of my body was dripping sweat. The coals hissed under me and grew hotter.

> Sick with desire . . .
> And seeking him – him she loves,
> From street to street
> The raving Dido roves . . .

I kept asking for my wedding dress.

'I need to be dressed. It will soon be time.'

Time to leave for the church, to begin my new life, to claim my happiness.

> So shall their loves be crown'd with due delights,
> And Hymen shall be present at the rites.

No. No, that wasn't how the verse ran, not now.

It ran quite differently, raving and roving.

> – for still – for still the fatal dart
> Sticks
> – sticks in her side, and –
> and rankles in her heart.

There were poultices and balms, steam and ice, all to try to bring my temperature down.

They seemed to realise now that I was back among them again, that I had good money to pay those doctors and nurses for their attention.

I was sleeping more regularly. Long deep sleeps, as if I hadn't slept for weeks and weeks. Sometimes I would sleep through the whole of a day, and that day was then gone from my memory; nothing of it remained.

I got up from my bed, feeling like a paper person, the figure of a woman who'd been cut out of paper and unrolled. I felt I had no substance.

Just now and then everything is in its proper place. Objects fit their shapes, and are their exact colours.

And there are other times when everything will have been knocked out of kilter. Objects grow fuzzy around their edges, as if they've been dislodged: they can't hold their colours, the colours percolate out. (Where – but no one ever tells me – where have they put the wedding gown?)

Some days dawn with the trees and the rooftops already in situ, settled. The cranes in the brewery yard are cranes, the furniture in my room is solid and neither warm nor cold when I touch it. Other days, I roll out of bed and I'm in a tilting room. The floor runs away from me, and yet somehow – what magic is this? – the furniture clings on. The trees are gowned and stooped dons, and the rooftops are the lecterns they lean against, and the cranes aren't cranes but arcane hieroglyphics, devilish script like the positioning of the windows and doorways in the brewhouse.

A crack is growing in my bedroom wall. It eats the old green silk paper, and now the fissure is wide enough in places to push a finger into. Plaster pulverises and trickles down inside the wall, for an age. The crack is a river traversing some vast deep, dark forest. I call into the gap and the sounds are scattered for miles; they snag on the topmost branches of trees too tiny to see.

How soon hath Time, the subtle thief of youth,
Stol'n on his wing my three-and-twentieth year!
My my . . .

A face rimous, crumbling, like the facade of an abandoned palace.

My hasting days fly on with full career,
But my late spring no bud or blossom showeth

Rain and wind have shaken the cherry trees to broken wire umbrellas.

And they haven't washed the powder off me.

It hangs in my hair, like a nest for rats.

The powder has gathered about my body in folds of skin, drifting, solidifying between my toes.

Perfumed and sweet has turned musky and sour. I smell of unassuaged longing, and of accumulated bitterness.

'If I'd worn green . . .'

'I'm sorry, I didn't catch –'

'Green. Like the Immortals. They wore green.'

'Who?'

Ignorance darkens the world, clouds of unknowing.

'Oberon. Titania. Puck. Living forever. If I'd worn green . . .'

'Rest now, miss –'

'Oh, there'll be time to rest afterwards.'

Decades of time. Centuries. Millennia.

⁂

I sit in the sun. The old walls trap the heat. Butterflies flit and flutter about the garden, scribbles of colour on the gassy air.

I sit in the sun watching the butterflies, and picking at a loose thread on my dressing-gown sleeve. The grass grows beneath my feet, and the earth sings.

A slow fly lands on the toe of my right shoe. I turn my foot in every direction, I stamp my shoe on the ground to shake off the fly, I shout at the interloper until it's finally dislodged.

A window sash is raised in the house. I angle my head to see. I can hear them talking about me, not what they're saying but the sibilant voices: droning, buzzing, cleverly drifting past my ear on the currents of air.

A ring of cathedral bells, carried over the wall.

I close my eyes. I command the bells to stop.

And lo, they stop.

The air clears of that complication. I open my eyes.

Butterflies are flitting and fluttering about the garden, like pastel scribblings. The air trembles. A slow fly lands on the toe of my left shoe, I turn my shoe in every direction, I stamp my foot on the ground, I shout at the fly . . .

⁂

I didn't want to think that the Chadwycks might have known better than I.

I didn't want to think at all.

But of course I would wake and catch him slipping out of my mind, with a backward glance and what might have been a smile on his face.

I asked if there had been any word of him.

'Of who, miss?'

'"Of *whom*",' I corrected them. 'Who else d'you suppose I'd be talking about?'

There was no message from him, no communication from any third party, no clue as to his whereabouts.

The trail had gone cold.

Nothing.

A man in a golden mask. He turns round. On the reverse of his head, which might be the back or the front, is another face, in silver.

'Eat, Miss Havisham. Can't I tempt you to a tasty morsel? No? Miss Havisham – ?'

'It's been a beautiful day.'

'I'm sorry – ?'

'Oh, so am I. My trap among the gigs. But now, gentlemen, I think I've had an ample sufficiency.'

'Please sit still –'

'I really have to go now.'

'– Miss Havisham –'

'They'll be expecting me.'

'Who will? Who is expecting you?'

'I . . . I can't . . .'

'No one, Miss Havisham.'

'But . . .'

Later.

They feed me *sorbet de crème*. Because it is considered strengthening for the digestive system. Eating cream ices will help me to live to a ripe old age. (Six egg yolks to two pints of double cream: can this be true?)

There's one flavoured with orange blossoms, and another with cherry kernel, and a third type with greengage.

The Italians stay clear of contagion this way. It's a delicious conceit, and almost worth getting better for. Almost.

Sitting in the cafes of Paris, which I've read about: the Dubuisson by the Comédie, or the Caveau in the Palais Royal, or its neighbour the Foy, where I perch on a chair in the palace gardens. Picking genteelly at my pyramid of ice while I wait, wait for someone who never comes.

'But leave the breakfast. Leave the breakfast.'

I must have had such fury in my voice, they knew not to disobey me.

The wedding feast remained where it was, set out on the extended dining table. If I were to lose that, I would be abandoning all hope.

In those first twenty-four hours, half of my hair had turned white with shock. I was left with a thick streak of white, which raced through the fair like a wave, roared like a flame. I had turned middle-aged overnight.

Nobody would have wanted to marry me. It was as if time had speeded up without mercy, and shown me the person who'd been hidden inside all along. I would have caught up with her, but not for another twenty or thirty years.

She was so cruelly different from me. The white bolt in her hair gave her eyes a hunted, obsessive look, as if the visible mattered much less than the mind's dark fancies. She terrified me, because I also knew (in a clearer part of my brain) that she had no separate existence behind the mirror's plane of wintry glass.

Chapter Thirty-two

I ambled about the house, for hours on end, wearing only a loose sack gown and shawls. I waited for night, until I saw the watchmen's brazier lit, and then trod circuits of the brewery yard. From the garden I watched dawn come up over the rooftops of the town. I walked for many miles without leaving the policies. Ceaselessly I was turning matters over in my mind, the how and why and what to do next.

The news must have travelled far and wide by now.

About the Havisham girl down in Kent. Queerest thing. Left standing at the altar.

It would be talked about for weeks, months. Remembered from years away. A very rum to-do there was, once upon a time, a brewery heiress in a Medway town, jilted on her wedding day she was.

They wouldn't know *exactly*, but somehow they would never have forgotten.

I'd had my wedding dress hung on the hessian mannequin. The veil was draped over three chairs. Nobody had been allowed to touch the dressing table. My powders and combs were where I'd left them. The lid was still raised on the jewellery casket, and all the items to hand as they'd been that morning. Beside it was the other white satin slipper I'd been on the point of fitting on to my right foot.

Only the letter was missing. How it had been lost I didn't know, and wasn't going to enquire.

I had the dressing room locked. I removed myself to a bedroom on the other side of the house. I had no dressing room there, but all I meant to do with my life was work at brewery business. What time would I have now for the vanities of dressing up?

❧

Once I was installed again in my father's office I put on a sober dress and a very little jewellery, to appear my most purposeful.

But I noticed straight away the change in Tice.

For one thing, the smirk as he sauntered into the room. He sat down without being requested to do so; I stared at him until my displeasure was fully plain to him, and he got to his feet.

In that conversation and the ones to follow he didn't allow me to forget that he'd taken on himself proctorship of the brewhouse in my absence.

He seemed to believe that we met now on altered terms: that he was privy to Havisham business as never before. (I realised he would have been able to acquaint himself with the contents of the ledger books in the Compting House.)

I attempted to put him right about that, without directly putting the man down. I couldn't decide if he was being deliberately obtuse, or truly didn't perceive my point. The former, I concluded, given that sly canny look of his.

I was obliged to be less subtle.

'I fear you may be under a misapprehension . . .'

He bit his lip, otherwise he might have spoken his mind. As it was, his remarks became terser, without the encumbrance of grammar: single-word responses sometimes, or a 'yes' or a 'no'. Not even a 'miss' to acknowledge my authority. Whenever I dismissed him, after informing him of my wishes, he would hold back for a few moments before turning to leave, as if he was awaiting some change of heart in me. I didn't care for his expression: a wily reminder to me, *I*-know-a-thing-or-two.

The men, I heard through Mr Ambrose, were wanting to be 'consulted'.

'Who's put that notion in their heads? Tice, let me guess.'

Mr Ambrose nodded.

'Did my father allow "consultations"? We'll have a revolution on our hands before we know where we are.'

I shook my head. It was the spirit of the times, but I was damned if I was going to entertain it here in Crow Lane.

'Quite out of the question. You might intimate as much to them, Mr Ambrose. However you judge best.'

'Very well, Miss Havisham.'

'*Someone* respects the name! Thank God for that.'

The ordinary labourers – the semi-skilled men (and a few women) – were the most docile. The cooperage foreman was a calming influence, and probably the chief storehouse clerk. They had too much to do perhaps, those stokers and yeastmen, the sparemen and drawers-off. (The draymen and horsekeepers were mostly loyal, but several wavered.)

However, our esteemed superintendent of the brewers, Tice, was winning over some of the clerks in the Compting House, including the abroad-men I used to patrol my empire.

I had books from the Compting House brought in to my office, and I pored over them, believing them less and less as I scoured the entry columns for signs of tampering. I scrupulously examined every blot, every repeated stroke of the pen. I compared single numerals for consistency. I checked and double-checked for errors in the sums and subtractions, which involved hours more of that close work.

They presumed I'd lost the knack, if I'd ever had it. I wasn't just a woman, I was a madwoman.

But the figures didn't add up, the entries on one page failed to tally with those on the next – and *they* imagined I wouldn't notice. The emendations appeared to have been made in various hands, so there must have been a more complex conspiracy afoot.

I might have banged the table and watched them jump out of their skins. Instead, when I was asking questions I dropped my voice and addressed my enquiry little louder than a whisper, and I hoped it made their flesh creep.

Who was responsible I couldn't tell. Maybe it didn't matter who. If I were to replace them all, I should have had to test the loyalty of their successors. But the brewery couldn't prosper on mismanaged figures, with a proportion of the profits being siphoned out by whoever was clever enough to get away with it. Now I was appreciating for the first time the magnitude of this endeavour I had taken on, which had the makings of a moral crusade.

༄

I didn't immediately understand what he was meaning.

'I don't follow you, Mr Ambrose –'

When I did, I couldn't curb my temper.

'You *dare* to suggest such a thing?'

'But only Mr Compeyson was permitted to –'

'That's a slander.'

Why on earth was I defending the man? What possible reason could I have?

'Take back that accusation. At once.'

'I would if I could, Miss Hav—'

'At once, d'you hear me?'

'I can't. I'm sorry.'

'You *will* be sorry.'

'It's my considered opinion.'

Whatever else Charles Compeyson had been, and done, I hadn't doubted that he'd supported me here.

I told Mr Ambrose, with just a brief quaver in my voice, in that case – if he was refusing to resile – I must inform him that I, and Havisham's, had no further need of his services.

A notice in the newspaper. The engagement was announced between the Honourable William Chadwyck and Lady Frances Tresidder.

I enquired about the name 'Tresidder'.They were a Cornish family, owners of tin mines. For two generations they had lived in a mansion built by one of Queen Bess's favourites.

Satis House had once entertained Elizabeth. It was she who had given rise to the name, after thanking her host for his abundant hospitality. That Cornish mansion must have been grander than Thurston Park, and tin mines an even better prospect than brews of ale.

Had I seen W'm's fiancée-to-be when I was still accounted one of them, the Durley Set? Had she been persuaded to visit the hermitage with him? No, probably not; that was by very special invitation only.

Thespis had turned everyone into practised actors, all of us except myself perhaps: so adept at not betraying our private purposes and designs.

I wore the darkest clothes I had, short of mourning. I felt that *light* didn't involve me for the present, either entering me or being expelled. I was a woman of business and nothing else. I left off powder and my other applications. I dressed my hair plainly. I chose a few older items of jewellery, those passed on to me. Havisham heirlooms. Others might have judged that time had taken the shine of desirability off them. But their value to me now was as tokens of my lineage, unshowy symbols of the legacy I embraced.

I spoke for *les fondateurs venerables*, those original Havishams no longer with us.

The ledgers continued to divulge secrets from the time of the Compeyson stewardship, so called.

I requested that Mr Jaggers send someone to help me go through the books: he confirmed that, yes, there had been consistent meddling. An attempt had been made to disguise handwriting, but *he* would wager it was by the same person.

At first I told myself it must have been the work of an unknown, intended to reflect badly on the man I had elected to be in charge, my fiancé. But it took this Londoner, interpreting the evidence for me as he viewed it with outsider's eyes, to convince me finally of the unwelcome truth of the matter.

I had kept to the old method whereby surplus grains and the residue in the tuns were sold off, for cattle-fodder and as fertiliser. *He* – whose name I couldn't bring myself to speak – had terminated the existing and long-established arrangements and made his own, presumably more profitable, ones (although the figures were deliberately obfuscated in the accounts).

He might have attempted to affect the means of production – by cutting costs, by altering temperatures and quantities and durations, mixing brews – but I would have been bound to hear about that. (Using wild yeast, say, would have foxed the beer and caused infection.) Instead he had confined himself to petty frauds on the housekeeping: reselling returned (stale) beer, buying an amount of used oak casks in any batch of new, even – I had trouble believing it – having the draymen collect the horses' dung on their rounds and taking a two-thirds cut for himself on what was sold.

It was pathetic.

Worse, though. Mr Ambrose had suspected he was holding up on credit, and may have been dealing with individual publicans who had the misfortune of bad debts. That was the next matter I must investigate.

Meanwhile . . .

They wanted me to restore the full-time jobs. They also wanted the average of working hours reduced.

I told them we were fighting for custom with our competitors. Everyone was looking for ways to trim costs. If I reduced general working hours, there would need to be pay cuts.

Tice appeared with a delegation.

'We know what price the barrels are being sold at.'

'I can't think who's told you. But the manufacturing costs have risen, doubled.'

'Brewers are like farmers. They never run at a loss.'

'Who says? Look, beer duties up twenty-five per cent. Malt tax, three hundred per cent more.'

'But is there a loss – ?'

'Quart pot of ale. It's been fourpence for how many years. Now suddenly it's sixpence. There are breweries up for sale all over the country.'

'Not this one, though.'

'Because I'm looking for fresh suppliers all the time.'

'That's what *he* was trying to do. Mr Compeyson.'

'I'm in charge now.'

'Isn't he coming back?'

'No. No, he's not. *I'm* master.'

Tice spoke. 'Don't you mean . . .' He paused for full effect. ' . . . "mistress"?'

All their eyes crossed tracks. Smiles, but no actual laughter. They will repeat the remark all evening long, and with each new mention the tone of voice will become more caustic.

'Whichever,' I said, 'there can only be one of them.'

They seemed disinclined to believe me.

ஃ

I had written Mr Ambrose three letters. The third brought him back to the Compting House. I led him through to my office.

'Thank you for coming, Mr Ambrose.'

'You wished to speak to me, Miss Havisham?'

'Please sit down, won't you?'

He waited for me to speak.

'Mr Ambrose, I think I owe you an apology.'

I was as modest as a nun. My manner was my best statement of contrition. Seated where he'd sat in my father's time, he was persuaded by ghostly presences to give me another chance. I took his hand and shook it, while he stared in mild shock at the boldness of our two hands' behaviour.

ஃ

I had another visit from Tice and his cronies among the workmen brewers. They wanted their salaries to match the clerks'.

'I'll think about it.'

But they were already getting their perks and gratuities. £750 for a second brewer, with a wife. Sixpence per hogshead commission.

'I don't see what you've got to complain about.'

'Mr Havisham, he wouldn't let us put money in.'

'You wish to invest? Although you say you don't receive enough?'

'It'd be a stake, though.'

And a means of applying stronger pressure on me. My father's original decision had been the correct one.

I could have increased the workers' wages a little. The additional price of their labour would have been quite insignificant set against the totals for purchases of materials and casks. I could have conceded something. But I was too angry to allow myself. They put a much lesser value on me, a Havisham born and bred, than they did on him, who had only ever been my appointee, and – strictly – a nobody.

To comfort myself, I asked Mr Ambrose to please make discreet enquiries about the rates of remuneration among our competitors. Just as I'd surmised, we were keeping pace very favourably.

'I've given this very careful and extended thought,' I told Tice.

'The pay?'

'Yes.'

'And the investing?'

'Both.'

'And . . . ?'

'I don't see any justification, I'm afraid, for what you're asking me. None at all.'

I had to let my ire with Tice and company cool. I consoled myself with the reflection that I'd remained guarded about the economic facts. We claimed seven or eight per cent return, after deducting interest charges on capital; really it was nearer fifteen per cent.

I had Mr Ambrose out interviewing those publicans who were closing their home mashers, and also calling by at some of the big farms and poorhouses where he'd learned ale was no longer being produced.

I needed two faces for this job. Perhaps I might have been left feeling guilty afterwards, if *they* – those bullyrags – hadn't insisted on bringing up his name still. The mention of 'Compeyson' wasn't spontaneous or accidental, but quite carefully calculated beforehand.

I would give just as good as I got.

Chapter Thirty-three

I took myself off to Norwich.

'Where would I go if I wanted to buy land hereabouts?'

Wherever I asked in Norwich I was provided with a list of the same names. Two were sited in the centre. One, in Madder Market, was owned by a man in his eighties and managed by his son and grandsons. I couldn't envisage any 'friend' being given a worthwhile job of work here, in these amply staffed premises. The other I found at Charing Cross, in the lee of the Strangers' Hall. A brass plate by the door announced CALLOWAY & CALLOWAY. I waited in the parlour of an inn across the street to see who entered and left. I interrupted my watch to speak with the proprietor.

'I'm thinking of buying a little land,' I said.

'Across the way?'

'I've seen a young woman. One of the Calloway children, I suppose?'

She had been a little older than I. Well dressed, with rather severe features, as if she had undergone some strain of late in her life.

'But I've not seen any *Mr* Calloway,' I said.

'He's dead, Mr Calloway is.'

'Oh. Just one? It's in other hands now?'

'Her you've seen, that's Miss Jane. *She's* the Calloway now.'

'She has charge of the firm?'

'Does not a bad job of it neither, by all accounts.'

I enquired of a few customers about Miss Calloway. 'Plain Jane', one called her. Another said she must be worth a good deal. 'Drives a hard bargain' was another verdict.

'Doesn't put the men off, though. Not short of suitors, that one. I'd like to see him that gets anywhere, mind.'

One, I heard, had persevered and got further than the others. A couple of years back, after her father died, there had been talk of a secret engagement. But a pair of her friends had got to hear, and managed to talk her out of it, just in the nick of time.

'Those clever types, like she is, clever at her job anyhow – don't seem to see the danger – anyone could've told her *he* wasn't the one for her.'

A smooth talker, bit of a popinjay to look at. Father had been a doctor at sea, mother kept ill . . . He'd hung about racecourses apparently, made a bit of money for himself that way. Back he would come, though, to the Calloway house out on the King's Lynn road. At the last minute she saw sense, and sent the fellow packing.

Name like 'Cumberstone', 'Compston'. She had kept him from everyone except those two friends who got to find out. Maybe she'd guessed for herself it was just a forlorn fancy. One of those crazy notions that threatens to get the better of us. She wriggled free of him, though. And now look at her, running the business as well as her father ever did.

ﻌ

The church lay low in the fields. Fields of ripe corn, swaying voluptuously.

A parish of rich spinsters. It was ideal territory for him; it might not serve his ambition so well (although, on second thoughts, spinsters' word-of-mouth could work a wonder or two), but he would certainly be well fed and dined.

He had a voice to fill the space. It would dip and then theatrically rise.

'"Suddenly there came a sound from heaven as of a rushing

mighty wind, and it filled all the house where they were sitting."'

The dowagers, warming themselves with their pugs and tiny terriers, lapped it up.

'"And there appeared unto them cloven tongues like as of fire, and it sat upon each of them."'

If they could have applauded him, they would have.

'"And they were all filled with the Holy Ghost, and began to speak with other tongues, as the Spirit gave them utterance."'

Anything he might have asked of them . . .

He raised both arms aloft, in inspired supplication.

God helps those who help themselves.

'Cold heaven, I've heard it called. Is the chill of your church a taste of it?'

'I beg your . . .'

'Good morning, Mr Chadwyck. Or it's just turned afternoon, if I'm to believe your bells.'

'It *is* Catherine? Catherine Havisham?'

'A little blue in the face. But it is.'

What was I doing here? Talking to Moses Chadwyck. (I still couldn't think of him as 'Frederick'.) Eating lunch with him, or trying to.

'We're delighted you've come. Thought to visit us. Aren't we, Aurelia?'

His sister glanced up from her plate, and when she couldn't catch his eye she smiled across the table at me. They had heard months ago that I wasn't to be 'Mrs Compeyson'; it wasn't being spoken of by any of us, but I sensed that at the time the news had come as a relief to him.

I dropped my knife, it clattered to the floor, and the maid darted over to pick it up. The housekeeper had been hovering outside, and she walked in, making straight for the canteen of cutlery to fetch a replacement.

They all doted on him, his women. What was his gift? Not physical attractiveness.

Those large hands, his big square cleft jaw, his premature stoop, his balding dome with its fringe of sandy baby-hair. An unbuttoned cuff; his necktie unravelling.

But his eyes, behind their rimless close-to lenses, were gentle, sympathetic, confidential: with a vision that saw beyond windows and pretty vistas, beyond self and immediacies.

'You were in the vicinity?'

'No. No, I wasn't.'

'You searched us out?'

'I was thinking back. To Durley Chase.'

'Well . . . My sister and I are very honoured.' It was said quite unironically.

I nodded an acknowledgement.

'You've changed, Catherine.'

'We all have.'

'Some fruit, Miss Havisham?' his sister asked. 'These are our own peaches.'

'No. No, thank you. I've had – an ample sufficiency.'

Petals shivered from an arrangement, falling to the table beneath.

'How have I changed exactly?'

'You seem – to live a little more inside yourself.'

'I don't see how – I'm running a brewery, aren't I?'

Aurelia looked with alarm between the two of us.

'*You've* changed too,' I said to him.

'How so?'

'You seem – to live *not* so much inside yourself.'

'Is that a good thing?'

'You're settled, I can see. Your sermons. The ladies and their lapdogs.'

'Oh, those dogs!'

'Do you still read your books?'

'Yes. But not so much perhaps.'

'And is *that* a good thing?'

'Maybe it isn't.'

'How well set up you are here. How comfortable.'

I felt unable to stop myself. I didn't know why I was repaying their hospitality so badly. I had drunk too much gooseberry cordial. But something about the house oppressed me: the regular mealtimes – no stranger to be turned away – when worthy tomes (if not as worthy as they once were; they had gaudier bindings) were laid aside with the bookmarks in place, and could be picked up again after a hearty feed and a doze in the high-backed armchair, positioned within reach of its footstool.

He played his role well, turning in a sterling performance in church and then retiring here to the semi-privacy of home. And yet . . . and yet the Cambridge books were still within his arm's reach, and the piles of papers, *those* weren't merely stage props, were they? His signet ring was engraved with a squared cross, + .

God, I felt, had managed to creep into the details. The white arum lilies. The demure chastity of Aurelia. The fruit remaining in the compotiers, strawberries for righteousness and pomegranates for resurrection. How the sun hit a green-and-blue glass bowl, spilling a holy potage of chapel-light on the rug.

We stood at the gate, he and I.

'What about the others?' I asked.

'I hear less of them now. The girls are married.'

'And their brother? With the tin lady.'

'Not yet. The engagement lasts and lasts.'

'None of you', I said, 'accepted my invitation to see *me* wed.'

'That is so. I do regret that.'

'Was it a conspiracy?'

'Not as such.'

'"Not as such". You're a Jesuit now!'

'I believe Lady Charlotte may have exerted a little influence.'

'Ah.'

'They're obedient children.'

'Adults, surely. Competent to think for themselves.'

'You were obedient to your father's wishes, weren't you? Aren't you obedient now to his memory?'

He surmised correctly. I nodded. The Chadwycks had been both wrong and right.

I heard skittering flints, and then the spinsters' voices as they approached. A lapdog yapped, sniffing a stranger. He looked away from them, directly at me. His eyes were filled with something more intense than tenderness. At the same moment I realised what it was I had never seen in another's eyes over all that time, up to my engagement and beyond. The vital absence: love.

'Catherine, I want to say what a pleasure, what a joy it's been –'

'Yahoo! Your reverendship!' a spinster called across to him. 'What a fugitive fellow you are! No more hiding from us *now*!'

I looked down at the dried mud surface of the lane, the flints' sharpness. God in the details.

At last I located my copy of the *Aeneid* on my shelves. I searched through the tracery of tiny ink cribs I'd marked in the margins. One passage was annotated in another hand. It must have been Moses's doing.

> The fated pile they rear,
> Within the secret court, expos'd in air.
> The cloven holms and pines are heap'd on high,
> And garlands on the hollow spaces lie.

> Sad cypress, vervain, yew, compose the wreath,
> And ev'ry baleful green denoting death.

I couldn't bear to read any further. I closed the book.

I was alone; there was no one else to hear. But I could only ask Moses for his forgiveness under my breath, confessing my misjudgements of the past in a penitent's whisper.

❦

Then, later, came talk of having to contribute workers to the defence forces, if the French should invade. Mr Ambrose informed me that now some other big brewery-owners wanted to move in. They knew all about the state of morale here, or the lack of it. They smelt my blood.

An offer was put forward, to take over Havisham's, which was increased before I could respond. Then a second offer came from another source. I didn't want to hear what worth they put on the firm. I was indignant. I was ashamed of myself, that I had somehow permitted this dire state of affairs to come about. The brewhouse men sent in yet another delegation to argue their points, to try to harry me.

I'd had more than enough of it, too much, much too much. I was exhausted. I was at the end of my fraying tether. It simply *couldn't* be allowed to happen, that frail rope snapping for a second time.

❦

I'd had an address – the one in Blackheath – where I could write to him in London. When I went there and asked, one of the tenants told me he was gone. The man gave me another address, at the Lewisham end. At that second house, the new occupants of the rooms made clear their distaste for the previous tenant, Mr Compeyson.

'We'd no idea the fellow *had* any friends. How his wife put up with him, God only knows.'

'His wife?'

'*She* seemed better. But all the more fool for choosing *him*.'

'You don't know where he is?'

'Nor care, frankly.'

I got out at the costume hirers in Covent Garden, and looked in through the windows.

There was a wall of masks, and a selection of period garments on hangers. A customer was leafing through a catalogue of items while an assistant on a stepladder was checking among drawers to see which were available. That life of pretence – that dream life – carried on just as before.

I went back to the second house, where the tenants of the apartment had been so candid. This was the closest I had come to him. But it still wasn't close enough.

I walked the pavement on the other side of the street. It was drizzling lightly. A woman with a child approached, keeping a careful watch on me. They stopped a few feet away. I ventured a smile, as much as to apologise for my presence.

Our umbrellas, it occurred to me, were going to collide. I stepped to one side.

'I was hoping it would hold off,' the woman said.

'No such luck.'

'It could be worse.'

'It might,' I concurred.

Now the woman was studying my umbrella.

'I knew someone with a blue umbrella just like yours,' she said.

'Yes?'

'Quite envious I was.'

He had bought it for me, when I once expressed a fancy.

'Is it so unusual?' I asked.

'I'd never seen one. Not that shade. What would you call it, a greeny blue?'

'I suppose it is.'

'She had one just the same. The lady across the way, I mean.'

I looked across to where the hand was pointing, the very house I'd had in my sights.

'Who used to be there, I should say. Mrs Compeyson.'

'You knew her?' I asked.

'Oh yes. We were neighbours.'

'D'you know where they've gone?'

'The Compeysons? Yes. Only, I wasn't to tell anyone.'

'You can tell me,' I said.

'I can?'

'We – we were well acquainted, he and I.'

'Not from Kent?'

'Yes.' I was startled. 'Why d'you ask?'

'His wife was from there. And he had something to do with a brewery in those parts. Only it didn't work out for him.'

'No. No, it didn't.'

'You know something about it?'

'I'm just – an observer. Now. But I would like to find out.'

The little girl was pulling on her mother's arm.

'I would like to find out very much,' I repeated, not certain whether I did or not. I thought the woman's eyes were kindly, for this cold and uncompassionate city.

'How to get hold of him,' I said. 'Can you help me? Please.'

They live in a tall house of flaking stucco, in a not insalubrious or inelegant quarter. Milborne Street in Wandsworth is hanging on to the coat-tails of genteel respectability that graces Putney to the west. The Compeysons are trying to move on and up in the world.

I stand beneath a dripping ash tree to watch, with my blue umbrella raised.

Drops of rain run down the back of my neck. I can feel dampness through the soles of my boots. My bones ache with exposure.

It's all for just a sight of him. He knows the quick ways home, and – I can guess how it is – he's able to make an exit from the house so furtively that he seems to be no more than some temporary readjustment of the light falling on a wall, or the momentary disturbance of vegetation at the side of the path.

She doesn't appear, either. Maids come and go, but not their mistress. Meanwhile I'm Lot's wife, a pillar of bitter salt. The cold brings tears to my eyes; my eyes sting with them. The house blurs, as our watercolour sketches for Signor Scarpelli used to do when a drizzle came on.

What am I doing here? It's an elderly woman who's asking me, her voice stretched long and taut with social pretension. That clears my eyes. I stare at her with the full eviscerating steeliness I can muster from my predicament. She takes several steps back, staring at me as if I am an unnatural sight.

The rain has passed when the front door of the house, once a more imposing residence, opens.

A figure begins to descend the flight of steps.

There's something familiar about her. And then I recognise just what it is.

Of course. The cape: a travelling habit. Broadcloth, donkey-brown.

It's identical to one that I had, a few years ago.

The coincidence interrupts my train of thought. Now she's at the foot of the steps, starting to walk on the path. She pauses, turns to look back, then sideways, down into the submerged area.

Perhaps it's to check if their maid's at her work. She stands still for several seconds, offering a profile to me.

No. No, it can't be. But it is, surely. How could I have forgotten? Her nose, brow, chin. The thickness, the copperiness of her hair. More than that, though. The walk. The clothes: the cloak I gave her. The air of aloofness, even a disdain for the ordinary. Everything that I taught her. My apprentice, only – now – more convincing than the original.

Chapter Thirty-four

I followed her along the drying street. She walked straight-backed, with her head set square on her neck, gaze directed in front of her. Her heels pecked busily at the paving stones. From that street, round the corner, on to the next.

Suddenly she stepped off the pavement and crossed over on a diagonal, negotiating the cobbles, to the other side. I did exactly likewise. She rounded another corner, with me in pursuit. She started to walk more quickly, and so did I.

She wasn't carrying herself with such confidence. She had lost a little height; her head craned forward – she might have had a stoop. Her heels were scraping now. She was proceeding at an untidy scuttle. She was less and less myself.

'Sally!'

I didn't mean to call out. But the word flew out of my mouth before I could stop myself. Hearing her name she slowed, stopped. She hesitated before turning round. Her eyes widened. Her mouth opened, but she didn't speak.

We stood staring at each other.

'It *is* you, Sally?'

She shook her head, as if she would deny me. Then she must have thought better of it.

'Why, Sally?'

I couldn't think what else to say. It was the only question I had in mind to ask her, because the answer would have to explain everything. I took a few steps closer.

'Why?' I said more softly, to tease the truth from her.

She stood in silence, coiled, sprung. She was holding her ground. Apprehensive she might be, but she wasn't afraid. I couldn't match her. It was I who was faltering. I had to reach out my hand to the wall, to steady myself.

She still hadn't answered me. I was none the wiser. On the edge of my vision, a cart passed along the street. A hawker cried out somewhere; a dog barked. Other lives were being lived: workaday, unsuspecting, uncaring.

I took my hand away from the wall, and wobbled slightly. I was so weary now – exhausted. I would have sat down if I could, on the pavement's edge. Only the dim consciousness of who I was kept me from doing so. ('Imagine! Old Havisham's daughter, slumped over a gutter!') I stayed up on my two legs, but barely upright. She was no more stooped than I was. I was curling like a leaf.

I tried to read her expression. Disdain? No. Pity? No. Fear? Embarrassment? No. Had I taught her this too – to give nothing of herself away? If I had, then the teacher had forgotten the lesson. Disdain or pity I would have tolerated. What I couldn't suffer was her silence, and her refusal to show me any feelings at all.

A leaf. A husk.

'*Why, Sally?*' My voice cracked on the words.

Her voice when she spoke was quiet, collected, to the point.

'No reason. Things just happened as they did. I wasn't meaning anything.'

She spoke without any emotion.

'There was no scheme, no plan. That's just how it is sometimes. One thing led to another.'

My eyes began to lose their focus on her face.

'Believe me,' she said, in the same flat tone.

It didn't matter to her, I knew, if I believed her or not. This was what *she* had come to believe. She might tell me there was no malice aforethought, but surely there must have been some guilt, some remorse, even some shame?

She was able to speak to me in the unimpassioned tones of one who is the victor. Her life was settled, so she could spare me her condescension.

It was I who turned away first: I wouldn't have her see my tears. I didn't wipe my eyes until I had turned the corner. What had possessed me to go after her? I had gained no satisfactory explanation, no knowledge of what had really taken place between the two of them.

I saw her in my mind's eye as I continued walking, with the street liquid in front of me. I'd had this last sight of her: turned into a very passable imitation of myself. An imitation or a parody? Cruel and heartless as she seemed to me, she would have considered herself without blame.

I returned by the river.

She would have told me that she had merely followed the current, gone with its flow. That was no excuse. I had the prerogative, surely, to feel betrayed.

I couldn't take my eyes off the river. My feet were being drawn towards it, across the bank's sward of green. The water ahead ran fast and dark and deep.

Who would not sing for Lycidas?

I was held, transfixed.

The lines, memorised in the schoolroom at Durley Chase, recurred as my own epitaph.

> He must not float upon his wat'ry bier
> Unwept.

I could even pity Sally now, not envy her, for feeling so little. At interludes I had dwelt among legends, in the knowledge of mythical beings. They are the archetypes, the bearers of their own fates and larger than life. In her complacency, safe and snug for the moment until that man grew tired of her one day, Sally would experience none of the surfeits. To taste the absolute joys, you also have to suffer absolutely for them.

I took a step forward.

> So Lycidas sunk low, but mounted high
> Through the dear might of him that walk'd the waves.

Another step and the bank would start to crumble beneath my feet, one further step and I would tip forward through crumbling air –

'Catherine!'

A hand had grabbed hold of my arm. It was drawing me back.

Two hands, one clamped on each elbow, guiding me gently but firmly up the grass banking.

I was shaking. I turned and looked into Sally's face. She didn't speak, and neither did I.

This was us even, she was letting me know; we were quits.

She waited, as quietly and dutifully as she used to be with me, until I had composed myself. I felt again the hardness of paving stones through my soles.

We parted.

'Goodbye,' Sally said.

'Goodbye,' I replied.

One simple word apiece, and then we turned in our different directions.

I didn't look back. (Is she watching *me*, I wondered.) I carried on walking, getting my strength back slowly. Already I knew that we should never meet again. I went on my way with gathering determination, trying not to think about what had nearly happened at the river's edge – how it was that, for once, my pride had failed me. Later I passed a building topped by a pediment. There carved figures, classical deities too high to distinguish, lolled and disported. No one noticed them on that busy street except myself. They were beyond time and the earthly, beyond chance and the accidental.

The Immortals. The Hesperides, the Furies –

I smiled with recognition. I matched my fate to theirs. By the triumph of the will, I should become just like them.

Chapter Thirty-five

Goose & Cabbage, Blade Bone, Noah's Ark, Bull & Butcher, King Lud.

('Things could always be better.')

Lion & Adder, Plow & Sail, Half Penny House, Cocoa Tree, Bombay Grab.

('These are hard times.')

Swan & Maidenhead, Swan with Two Necks, Swan & Sugar-loaf, Swan & Hoop.

('Sixty-odd hundredweight on, was it, ten acres, profit five pounds something.')

Whistling Oyster, Three Nuns & Hare, Copenhagen, Two Chairmen, Mother Redcap.

('You've come over all pale, miss –'

'Still? Not still pale?'

What about my mastery of my untidy emotions, my self-command? My pride?)

Foul Anchor, Ship Aground. World Upside Down, World's End.

⁂

I knew what they wanted, which was to have a man in charge, however they could effect it. Either I should appoint a man to manage Havisham's, or – their alternative wish – I should sell the business. (Did I detect the hand of Snee behind one of the hostile bids?) They all misjudged me gravely.

I defied the brewhouse, which was where all the trouble had begun. They could go hang. I accepted no new orders. When we had exhausted the stock, I ordered the brewing to be halted. I dismissed the workmen.

I heard the rappings at the front door, and then the door being opened a crack from inside and the person sent away. Another worker's wife thinking she could appeal to my humanity, my womanliness.

But I waited. I held my nerve.

I had the gates to the yard chained.

No capitulation.

I had been paying for the upkeep of the horses, and the services of an ostler or two, but I sold the horses and told the stablemen to search elsewhere for work.

I boarded up every window in the brewery that could be broken from the street.

'So . . .'

I watched from the room which had been my father's office and then my own. The ledgers were piled up on shelves behind me, gathering dust.

'. . . so, they haven't the courage of this poor paltry woman?'

I smiled at that.

They had forgotten the stock I came from: that I wasn't just any woman, but a Kent Havisham: proof and tempered, through and through.

Intrepid Fox. Fetterlock. Marrowbone & Cleaver. Tom o' Bedlam.

That scream.

Mr Calvert's wife lying beneath, and those thrusting buttocks as her lover drives up into her.

The woman was transported beyond her pain, enthralled into a fourth dimension.

Run aground, stuck fast as I was, how could I not be riven by envy of that outrageous metaphysical adventure?

⁂

They burned me on Iden Meadow.

My effigy was hoisted on top of a bonfire they'd built. A straw woman, wearing a wedding dress made of newspaper.

Put together from dry kindling, I went up – so I heard – magnificently.

Cheers, catcalls. Flames ten feet high. I exploded in a reveille of sparks.

> Wild through the woods I'll fly,
> Robes, locks shall thus be tore.
> A thousand deaths I'll die,
> Ere thus in vain adore.

I shall defy you again.

I shall hold out against you all.

He isn't coming now.

He will never come.

I can do whatever I like.

I might put on a wedding dress if I choose to, just to laugh at all those innocent virgins. Hear how I'm laughing at them, cruelly and without pity. How it *matters* to them, much too much, and yet they see nothing of how the world contrives to delude them.

Giving yourself in love, you give yourself as a hostage to fate. The less you think to think of yourself, the more easily you'll be betrayed.

Wearing white silk and a veil and satin slippers for a day will change nothing, and couldn't make a false man true.

You break a superstition only by challenging it.

There *is* no sorcerer's charm for happiness. You won't find it in the Book of Common Prayer. It's only a dress, and they're only slippers, sweated over in some dingy workshop.

Look at me, in my train and veil. Tell me what magic you see. This is the awful damage that men do. And still the foolish, forlorn virgins go on believing.

Look at me. Let your blood run cold at the sight.

Take heed. Beware.

Or you will suffer just as I have suffered.

Love, devotion, married bliss.

They're dizzards' dreams, that vanish with the dawn.

❧

I returned to the bedroom and dressing room that used to be mine: I reclaimed them.

'Fetch me my wedding dress.'

The veil disguised my hair. From a distance, seen from across the room, no one would have known my age; they would have presumed me young.

'Fetch my slippers. The spare pair.'

They hadn't been worn. When I put them on, they took the shape of my feet.

'Leave me now, will you. Go.'

I seated myself before the glass. I pulled back the veil. With my face scrubbed clean, the true ravages were revealed. I had to conceal them again. It was the face that held everything together.

So . . .

Paint it white.

Powder it, and sweeten it with perfume.

A slash of colour on my lips, a rim of black kohl round each eye, and a tiny upturned hook etched on the outer corners.

I did this twice over, to make sure, applying a second layer of everything.

From this point forward, Satis House would be a memorial to the real Catherine Havisham; a repository of holy relics.

❧

Fresh air invades and destroys.

Keep it out.

Keep it out; then everything can be preserved. The contents will be encased exactly as they are. We shall be impervious to change.

I issued my instructions.

Doors should remain closed, except for immediate ingress and egress. When leaving or entering the house, the doors must not – must *not* – stand open for a moment longer than required.

Window sashes have to be kept lowered. Sunshine, another destroyer, comes falsely smiling; and so the curtains and shutters should be drawn at all times in those apartments I mean to use.

('The sun was now Inned at the Goat –'

'Miss – ?')

For light, candles will be lit in the candle sconces.

Fires might be kindled, but not allowed to roar, which would agitate the stillness of the air. The servants stared at me. But it was only sound common sense.

> Where there is neither sense of life nor joys,
> But the vast shipwreck of my life's esteems.

I also had the clocks stopped. At twenty minutes to nine, when it was the fatal blow had been delivered. Those metal hearts would never beat again. A mausoleum demanded the solemnity of silence.

I was merely the one who tended the altar. I would perform the rituals of devotion, in order to disprove devotion. I wore my ostentatious wedding dress in order to become a shadow; I was nothing more.

Chapter Thirty-six

Day for night. Night for day. In this sepulchre there were to be no distinctions.

I did as was done on that morning. I powdered myself, applied colour to my cheeks, highlighted my eyes, teased a stubborn hair from the plucked arcs of my brows.

On the dressing table I had two candelabras, one on either side of the triptych of mirrors, with five candles apiece. By the bright light they cast I saw what I saw.

Not the woman sitting here, but the young woman who sat here one morning long ago, a bright May morning, making the final preparations before exchanging her old life for the new.

❦

I had described him to Sally with so much awe and admiration in my voice, she must have doubted the reality of the man. The only recourse I'd given her was to see him for herself, to discover just how much of what I'd said could be true.

❦

In the colder months – the *mois noirs* – water was stored in a lead sarcophagus, so that it didn't ice over. In winter and early spring my hair acquired a greenish-yellow tinge, and the shock of white was less shocking.

I still had my hair, the flyaway sort and only fair for half the year, a reckless aureole around my head. It unwound from the back like a plaited rope; then I hoisted it back up again, pinned it haphazardly into place with old silver and diamond clips.

The dress had needed to be taken in. Even with that, the seamstress had been too optimistic, and the dress ended up hanging. The silk better suited curves, and that fleshiness which used to be considered a sign of good breeding. But that woman was no more. Now the bones of my rib cage showed through.

The girl banked the fire high.

'Sawn ilex?'

'Please, miss – ?'

'It's of no consequence . . .'

She built a fire to last me a couple of hours, which would allow her to slip off to meet her young man. She would pretend that she hadn't heard me when I rang for her, or (her usual alibi) that she'd looked round the corner of the door, but I was napping.

When the coal heated and the flames deepened, I sat looking at the golden palaces of the moon. Soaring domes and minarets, invincible ramparts. Shining seas running beneath them.

Out there, beyond the closed shutters, everything changed and nothing changed. Sacristy Gate, Prior's Gate, Chertsey's Gate. Pilgrims' Passage, Minor Canon Row.

The Corn Exchange, the Butchers' Market.

The Theatre Royal, at the foot of Star Hill.

Chalk Church.

And the publics. The Leather Bottle, Crispin & Crispianus.

The shoals by the bridge.

Day for night. Night for day. There were to be no distinctions.

I wore the dress – except when I bathed (I did bathe) or when the dress required freshening (I still recalled the delicacies of that pampered child who used to live here).

When the powder thinned, I made my face up again: I ringed my eyes, rubbed rouge on to my cheeks and coloured my lips.

I should always look the same.

I couldn't go back; to be the woman I had been before the letter reached me, on the morning of what should have been my wedding. Now I lived in the present, where an event happens repeatedly and eternally. I couldn't get any younger: why should I need to grow any older?

Chapter Thirty-seven

Town rowdies had thrown mud at the name on the brewhouse wall, and pockmarked the 'V' and the second 'H' and the final 'M'. (The same youths who once climbed on to the house roof and tried to block up a smoking chimney, until Mr Jaggers – by good chance, he was visiting – kicked away their ladder and gave them a verbal thrashing they'd clearly never forgotten.) Lazy swallows picked at the mud to help make their nests, and so time and nature did their work, and life went on, and on.

And, I didn't know why, I failed to die.

ﻌ

Just as before, I told the modiste, it will be very fine work. A second dress. An identical dress. Silk from the same source, and the style copied exactly. Sprigged and trimmed with Bath lace, as it was; and embroidery of gold foil on the back. Repairs to the twelve feet of train. Another Honiton veil. A headband of entwined silk roses. Two new pairs of ivory slippers, with silver lacing, ten eyelets on each.

ﻌ

I was still inhabiting those places, the ones where my feelings were keenest. It was as if my feelings had imprinted themselves on the air there.

For animals, everything happens in the present.

Again and again I replayed my life, on a long continuum of time, where my future was nothing other than the past. I was living through events once more, with the same intensity they'd had for me then: it was the first time, and it always would be, over and over again.

ﻍ

Nine faces, which seemed to have materialised through the fabric of the wall. My dressing-room wall. Carnaval masks from Venice, which I'd had bought for me in London. Several were pensive, one (shaped out of a sickle moon) smiled enigmatically. Some wept, so that the black kohl ran from their eyes, streaking the white faces. My wailing wall.

> exiled from light, To live a life
> half-dead, a living death, And buried; but O
> yet more miserable!
> Myself my sepulchre, a moving grave;
> Buried, yet not exempt,
> By privilege of death and burial,
> From worst of other evils, pains, and wrongs.

ﻍ

They were living in accommodation which *my* money, Havisham money, had provided them with. He had married on an income donated by me, and what he scavenged. I had set them up, and in no little style.

How droll it must have seemed to him. Was *she* now sharing his laughter? No, I preferred to believe he'd kept her in the dark: that Sally still believed he was a man of business who had earned the wherewithal by his honest toil.

The way he had of pressing back on his heels before he walked forward. A habit of stretching his neck and straightening his head before he said anything meant to be of greater consequence.

How he smelt. The oil of bergamot on his hair, and the tar soap he was diligent about washing his hands with. The spicy tobacco in his snuffbox. The saddle-soap rubbed into his boots.

> T'was dead of night . . .
> Unhappy Dido was alone awake.
> Nor sleep nor ease the furious queen can find;
> Sleep fled her eyes, as quiet fled her mind.
> Despair, and rage, and love divide her heart;
> Despair and rage had some, but love the greater part.

❧

After Gold and Silver, I had continued to keep a pair of cats, pedigrees, about the house. Now I was told that the tom, Mace, a replacement for Gold's successor, had been found nailed by his paws to a tree. Thankfully he died a few days after he was taken down. I kept the tabby indoors after that. She seemed quite lost not to have her companion, and grew thin.

But later in the year there was a very curious development. The tabby, Saffron, spayed – or supposedly spayed – at an early age, gave birth to a litter of kittens. She was too weak to provide the survivors with the milk they needed, and I told one of the girls to look after them.

Saffron regained some weight. Her spirits revived. She took a critical interest in the four kittens left, and was gentle or sharp with them just as they deserved.

Had you deferred, at least, your hasty flight,
  And
And left behind some pledge of
Our delight,
Some babe to bless the mother's mournful sight,
Some young Aeneas,
  To supply your place,
Whose features might express his father's face,
I should not then
Complain to live bereft

I found the image of Mace crucified on the cherry tree with rusty nails was starting to fade. Instead I was distracted by the rivalry of the kittens for their mother's attention, scrapping with one another and rolling themselves into a large amorphous fur ball with at least a dozen legs.

I understood that, mysteriously, life will assert itself even out of despondency and despair.

'In my end,' Mary Stuart said of herself, lying on the executioner's block, 'in my end is my beginning.'

V

ESTELLA

Chapter Thirty-eight

The little girl stared at me.

She would always remember this occasion.

Seeing me for the first time, she was also entering what was to become her normality.

The rooms where it was neither day nor night. My attire, in celebration of an event that hadn't happened. The mouldering breakfast feast spread out on the table, and the high-backed chairs standing to attention, as if at any moment . . . The flames licking at the grate, the slivers of white light balanced on the candle wicks suddenly jumping in a draught, shadows flaring up the walls.

'Don't cry,' I said. 'Don't cry, please.'

I stretched out my arm, but the child turned away quickly, raised one shoulder to protect herself.

Her mother was a Romany, a felon defended by Mr Jaggers on a murder charge; it was claimed she'd strangled a rival for a man's affections. The father was native-born, with a misapplied intelligence, fallen into bad ways and transported.

'Not the most auspicious start, Miss Havisham.'

'The child cannot be responsible for their sins.'

'But she is their child.'

'She will be *my* child, Mr Jaggers.'

'And you can be sure to set her to rights? When the rest of the world would condemn her?'

'She and I will live apart from the world.'

She was to have come the next day, a Tuesday. Then she would have been 'full of grace'. By default she was a Monday child. 'Fair of face'. That was enough for me.

I chose her name.

Estelle. Estella.
Or sometimes Estelle for Esther.
Esther, Hester fem., *poss. Persian 'star';*
or der. *Babylonian, Ishtar, the goddess Astarte*
Dims. *Essie, Hetty.*

Estella she would be.

I tried again to touch her, but I fared little better. She was astonished that I should want to, and she would shy away. It was as if any contact at all caused her physical pain.

If I then smiled, I did so out of embarrassment; not because I felt any pleasure at her confusion – but she may not have understood this. A wild look would flicker in her eyes; she seemed to be searching for an escape.

And it was because I was afraid of losing her that I had Mrs Mallows take her – resisting, crying at the woman to let go – to her room and lock her there for the next hour or two hours. I always unlocked it myself, and brought her in a little treat, either something sweet to eat or some coloured paper scraps for her to paste into her album. Usually this brought her round, because she liked sugary flavours and the gaudy colours of the paper angels and grandees.

I watched how she would grab at things, and hoard them. That was the gypsy in her.

'No one is going to take them from you, child. Now put them back. You will have much more given to you than you ever dreamed.'

She would keep a fierce hold on the object until I could prise her fingers apart.

'Who is going to deny you, you little fool?'

She still recoiled from me, afraid I was going to strike her. She would drop whatever it was, on to the floor, at my feet.

'No. *You* pick it up. Estella, do as I say.'

On the third or fourth time of asking she would pick it up and hand it back to me.

'*Now* we trust one another. Thank you.'

She would run off and hide; she was the one embarrassed now, and ashamed. That was good – it meant she was starting to see that the deepest feelings are the ones we do our learning from.

I had her taken out into the open air. I instructed her to run about. She must grow healthy and strong.

I supervised her diet. I arranged the buying of clothes, extra warm for winter and light and cool for summer.

I ensured that *her* rooms were daylit and ventilated well, that it shouldn't ever grow too hot and her skin dry out, or the temperature drop too low and slow the blood. I wanted her to have a perfect second start in life.

I required that she play in front of me.

'Play, child. Amuse yourself. Go on!'

She brought me flowers from the garden. And, later, chatter overheard from downstairs but not comprehended.

'Show me how you play. Let me see, Estella. Play away, *now*...'

❧

There were always petitioners. My cousins and second cousins. Every Wednesday afternoon. They sat in the hall until I was ready to receive them. If I wasn't in the mood for an audience, they went away even more disappointed than if – as was normal – I'd refused their request, but they would return with the same promptitude the following Wednesday, ready for more of the humiliating ritual.

If I mocked them, they said nothing by way of complaint. I might be as rude as I liked, and they wouldn't raise a single objection. So, there was no pleasure to be had from them. It was no more than a tedious necessity: a rich woman being supplicated to.

They were dismissed, and even if I had been agreeably disposed that afternoon no one ever believed that I'd been as generous as I might have been. ('Her belfry's chock-full of bats, that one.') I thought they would actually *despise* me if I didn't offer them, so infinitely remote as it was, the hope of seeing me throw gold at their feet.

Estella knew that I was not her mother. I told her that I didn't want her to call me her mother. If she must call me anything, then why not . . . why not 'Nana'?

She should look on me as her provider in all things else.

'But I had a mother?'

'She gave you birth.'

'Do you know about her?'

'What I know is that I shall take care of you. *This* is your home.'

'But you're not my – the thing I mustn't call you – ?'

'I'm better than a mother. Mothers can vanish. You're here in this house because I wish you to be. I mean no harm to come to you so long as we're living under this one roof together.'

I ensured that my growing Estella should want for nothing.

Clothes and shoes. Books. Dolls. A wooden barrow for the garden, and a set of tools. A leather horse on which to perch side-saddle.

I would have bought her a model theatre, or looked out the one I used to play with so long ago, but she expressed no interest in that idea. Instead I gave her some jointed shadow puppets on sticks, which she articulated – indifferently – against a lighted wall. She didn't much like the little carriage for her dolls, but she asked me (coyly, prettily) if she might have a parasol for herself – and some cups and saucers, such as adults use for entertaining, so that she could play host to those invisible friends she preferred to the flesh-and-blood young companions I now and then asked to Satis House.

She was oddly casual with her possessions. She would leave the barrow out in the rain, or her dolls. She didn't fold the parasol as I showed her, and the china cups and saucers acquired cracks and chips. Sometimes she eyed the things quite hostilely: resenting the demands they made on her, to play dutifully.

I didn't chide her about her negligence, her indifference. I had a fear of provoking her. In time I came to see that I was wrong, and guilty of neglecting my duty to *her* by not remonstrating. But by then we were settled into our routines, in the perpetually shuttered and candlelit reception rooms, and it seemed too late to jeopardise this slender harmony.

⁂

She had been sitting at my dressing table, hadn't she?

There was a trace of powder under her jaw line, and by her left ear. She smelt sweet.

Even though she'd had the guile to be careful, I knew from looking at the dressing table – shifting the candelabra about to see better – which items had tempted her. There was a place for everything, and the tiny disturbances to the dust told me just how she had proceeded.

'Well, Mr Jaggers . . . ?'

I'd had a single shutter inched back in his honour. I stood close to him, shading my eyes, as he watched Estella through the grimy window glass.

'. . . what do you say?'

He liked a little silence to expand after any question I asked him. Perhaps it was a courtroom trick, compromising a witness into thinking she had to speak and letting her say too much.

I wasn't going to be put on trial in my own drawing room, though. I waited for his reply.

'Coming on. Coming on.'

'Is she recognisable?'

Pause. He put his head on one side.

'To ourselves.'

'And not to anyone else?'

Pause. He considered the flattened tip of his index finger.

'Surely not.'

'I'm glad to hear it.'

Pause.

'You've quite remade her.'

As he chewed at the fingernail his eyes didn't move off Estella; they grew smaller in their sockets with the keenness of his concentration.

'It's a beginning –' I had started to say when he interrupted me.

'That woman would have killed her. She wanted to. With her bare hands.'

I shuddered involuntarily at the thought of it. But Mr Jaggers was smiling as he unrolled his white handkerchief.

'What would she have deprived us of?' he said. 'Thanks be to God.'

I corrected him. 'Thanks be to Havisham money.'

The children I invited to Satis House had to come singly. I selected those with parents or guardians who would regard it as an honour of sorts to be asked, who wouldn't dare to refuse me. The idiots delivered their offspring, blinking, all of them, at the candlelight and shadows. I left the rest to Estella.

'Speak, Estella – why don't you?'

Estella would be sitting with whichever child I had chosen for her. In the drawing room like this her manner became quite stately.

'Say something, Estella. Tell me, is our visitor today your favourite of the ones who've come to see us?'

It was hard for me to keep the laughter out of my voice.

'Tell me, visitor,' she asked, 'do you play at dominoes?'

The answer was invariably 'No'.

'Then I must show you.'

At which point she would rise.

'Come along –'

Already her voice had a ring of majestic impatience.

'– what are you waiting for? Follow me.'

To your doom, you poor noodle born of nincompoops.

The Misses Wilcox had their great-nephew staying with them: Master Drummle, a lumbering boy a little older than Estella.

With the two women he was charm personified, keeping a couple of paces behind them except when he jumped forward to open a door or a gate. But once his great-aunts took up talking – gabbling – again, his face would fall, and two deep and prematurely adult lines fixed on either side of his mouth, advertising his discontent and boredom.

I said to the Wilcoxes that they might take a turn about the garden: I would sit with the children for a while. It was spoken as a directive, not as a suggestion. The two women didn't want to risk offending me, and went waddling off, into daylight.

I sat down to spectate.

'Tell me, visitor –' Estella emptied the box, '– do you play at dominoes?'

'Dominoes? Why on earth should *I* play at dominoes?' Even if he had a lagging gait, the boy's wits were quick enough. Estella stared at him.

'"*Why*"?' she repeated, and sounded mystified.

'That's a game for publics. Not for well-born types.'

Quite flummoxed, Estella swept the pieces back into the box, scarcely looking at what she did.

'If *you've* got a better idea . . .'

'It's too stuffy in here.'

I had a timely hunch I should pretend to be asleep. Eyes closed, I let my head tilt to one side.

'It's a rum place, this.'

The boy had dropped his voice, but Estella was shushing him.

'Why does she wear her wedding clothes?'

Estella whispered, 'That's just what she wears.'

'Is something wrong with her?'

'"Wrong"?'

'Don't tell me you haven't noticed.'

'Noticed what?'

'C'mon. I'm going outside.'

'Outside?'

'D'you have to repeat *everything* I say?'

'Why on earth – ?'

'Look, are you coming or not?'

'Where to?'

'Anywhere'll do.'

Estella told me afterwards how he had teased and baited

whatever he could find out of doors. Two of the cats, a dog, a squirrel, a horse standing in its harness.

There was no tone of disapproval in her voice as she told me. At nine years old she merely stated matters of fact. One visit from young Drummle, I felt, had been quite sufficient.

⁂

She was looking at me queerly.

'What is it, Estella? Why the big eyes?'

'Didn't you ever want to wear your old clothes again?'

'Instead of . . . ?'

'Instead of your wedding clothes.'

(It was the end of something. Her naivety. Her uncritical acceptance. And what was I to say to her? Because – because everything is symbols and gestures. I knew that now. Because we only play and declare at life. Because true life is too awesome and terrifying to bear.)

'Were you going to be married?'

'I thought I was.'

'But you didn't *get* married?'

'The man who was meant to be my husband . . . he decided . . .'

'It was *his* fault?'

I started to nod. Then I stopped myself.

'It wasn't to be. That's all.'

'Were you sad?'

'Oh, I was too angry to be sad.'

She continued to stare at me. At my wedding dress, at my greying hair shot through with white. She was staring in the same way I used to stare, myself, at the strange sights I saw when I was being walked about the town. The poor souls, people would say of them, they'd lost their minds.

I wouldn't have anything changed, even though my dimensions were bound to have altered.

Just as before, I told the modiste's niece, it will be very fine work.

A third wedding dress.

Silk, Lyons silk, in that same old-fashioned style. Sprigged and trimmed with Bath lace, as used to be favoured; and – on the back, as delicately done as gossamer – gold foil, which was the taste at that time too.

Repairs to repairs on the train. A Honiton veil. A headband of silk roses. Three more pairs of ivory slippers with silver lacing, ten eyelets apiece.

Chapter Thirty-nine

The blacksmith Joe Gargery had brought up his wife's little brother, and I requested that he deliver the boy to Satis House.

Pip Pirrip kept apart from other children, I'd heard, which was to the good. The children from the better homes knew that Estella was my ward, and brought their parents' prejudices with them. *This* boy had no such expectations.

'Play,' I told them. 'Play together.'

Estella treated him roughly.

'Why do you keep staring at me? Are you slow-brained?'

I laughed. Estella so trenchant, and the boy – dressed up in his starched best – so out of sorts. They played with marbles, and then Estella showed him her articulated wall puppets, but the boy tangled the limbs of his and Estella snatched the puppet from him and flung them all back in the box.

'They're ruined now.'

'Take yourselves off into the yard,' I said. 'Or the garden.'

I heard them from my window.

'*I* don't know why she dresses like that. Why do you dress like *that*, boy?'

They returned, and played Beggar My Neighbour.

It's called a game of chance, but I knew my Estella would win.

'Hear him! He calls the knaves "jacks", this boy.'

I watched him. How his face crumpled whenever she said something to hurt him. Then, between times, how he got a little of his confidence back, and tried to recommend himself to her. And how cleverly and instinctively my Estella would put him down again.

Even a blacksmith's stepchild may have some little pride, and

Estella was set on puncturing it. But a cat will kill its mouse, and so I had to ring the bell and summon Mrs Mallows, before my entertainment was ruined. I had to prolong the pleasure.

'You will come to us another day, Master Pirrip,' I said – I commanded.

At that he looked quite shocked. But I knew it was also exactly what he'd been hoping against hope to hear.

❧

For a while Estella had been aware of her attractiveness.

It was precocious in a child, but her associations with other children had been of a kind – brief, and to the point – that enabled her to sum them up quickly. She could read their opinions of her from their faces.

She felt as isolated on that score, I guessed – because she carried the stigmata of beauty – as she did because I kept her to myself. Later she must want to let more people see her, a different sort from the ones who saw her performing her piety in the cathedral on Sunday mornings; that was bound to make my task easier when the time came. She might become haughtier than she currently was, but that would be her strength and her safeguard.

❧

The Pirrip lad had returned to us, for more of the same.

Further visits – in response to my summonses – followed.

He was quite willing, and Estella didn't object. And I was curious to see what would happen.

He had clever eyes. He'd been born, as some are, out of their proper locus in life. His manners were still crude, he had all a country boy's gaucheness. He would *learn* manners, though, that was the easy part; natural intelligence will take anyone far.

'So, Pip, what do they say about me?'

He told me, eventually, when I had worried at him and worn him down.

That I was crazed in the head. I didn't ever bathe, ate as little as a sparrow, and drank only French champagne. I could sleep standing on my feet. My belfry bats were allowed to fly about the house.

> The loud report thro' Libyan cities goes.
> Fame, the great ill, from small beginnings grows:
> Swift from the first . . .
> Soon grows the pigmy to gigantic size . . .

'Well, Pip, you've certainly been keeping your ears open.'

'I didn't mean to hear.'

'And you've got a good memory, I'm thinking too.'

'Yes?'

> Talk is her business, and her chief delight
> To tell of prodigies and cause affright . . .
> Things done relates, not done she feigns, and
> Mingles truth with lies.

'And what do they say about the fair Estella?'

They said that she was an angel for looks, but as conceited by nature as I was. She was inclined to society ('Aa-*ha*!'), but not sociable. They wondered what she was doing in such a town as this one, when it was clearly her destiny to dazzle on a larger stage.

'And she's still only a child!' I said.

Some folk, the boy added, foresaw an unhappy end for her.

'Then we must prove them wrong, mustn't we?'

'Must we?'

I laughed.

The door opened, and Estella walked in. She didn't look at our guest, but her question was directed at him.

'I suppose you bring the local scandal about me.'

I looked at Pip, and he looked between me and Estella.

'No,' he said. 'No, I haven't.'

An inspired fibber, even if not one by forethought. I smiled at him. I'd been hoping to find some complications in him, some density, and now – thank God – I had. With some *esprit*, but also with some mental ballast in reserve, he might be able to put up a challenge to Estella, to test her as any weak reed would never do.

He expected to see my hands like claws. But my hands had always been judged one of my better features – a lady's hands and not a brewer's daughter's, pale and etiolated (a word Moses taught me), elongated and tapering. They had a way of arranging themselves, hanging loosely over the end of a seat arm, like the gently winnowing fronds of some sea plant.

How he stared at the flashing stones of my rings.

'Play, boy, will you? Play!'

I watched the two of them, the forgeman's charge and my Estella. Her behaviour with him was natural at one moment and then artificial the next. She ran skidding on the gravel like a girl, threw her doll to him like a girl, but she spoke to him – proudly, dismissively – and flounced past him like someone twice her age.

The boy was losing his bearings with her. How he stood with his shoulders hunched and his arms gawkily loose and limp by his sides, and his eyes not so clever that they could disguise his dejection as he stared after her.

He could write his letters very neatly. He multiplied and divided quickly in his head.

'Would you like to learn Latin?'

'I don't know if I should have need of it, Miss Havisham.'

'That depends on what you want to do in life.'

'I'm bound to be something in Mr Gargery's line, I think.'

'*He* is . . .'

The boy looked awkward, ashamed to admit it.

'. . . the blacksmith, isn't he? Out Lower Higham way?'

'Yes, Miss Havisham.'

'And what do you *want* to do?'

(Those good hands, not made for the anvil. His clear skin would coarsen in the forge-fire.)

'I haven't thought, Miss Havisham. Not really.'

'A doctor? A lawyer?'

'*Me*, Miss?'

'Or a teacher? A scholar?'

'I don't know – Mr Pumblechook, in the High Street –'

'A shopkeeper, you mean?'

'No. He's a corn factor, Miss Havisham.'

I nodded.

'Yes,' I said, 'you're quite right to correct me. I was wrong.'

He shifted from foot to foot, raising his eyes and then, whenever he caught mine, lowering them again.

In the dragon's den!

He laid temptation before me, to give my leading-lady performance – to act Sarah Siddons off the stage and into the wings. He was my perfect audience.

He was remembering this, all of it. One day he would attempt to make sense of the experience, meaning to tell himself that Estella couldn't have been as unbenign as she appeared – so implacably hard on him.

The boy with the absurd name and the clever eyes. Pip Pirrip.

Estella liked to search through the clothes presses in my dressing room.

'And this?'

'A *chemise de la reine*,' I explained. 'I wore it in the mornings.

There's a sash for it somewhere. Blue Persian, that was the fashion.'

A history lesson.

'And my riding habit.'

'I've seen that.'

'My summer one. Nankeen.'

How important it had been to be *comme il faut*. It must be stone-coloured, lined with green, and matching green for the waistcoat.

'"*Habillée en homme*". *Jolie comme un cœur*.'

And hats. The wide brims had buckled and creased, but Estella tried to uncurl them. I fitted her with the little cane undress hat, and straightened the festoon of ribbons which hung down at the back. The pink had faded; some of the strands in the weave were quite colourless now.

I thought of another straw hat with scarlet ribbons and a white flower, afloat on the Cam. In my memory it floated forever on that surface of darkening water, like a wreath.

'*You* wore this hat?'

'There are always rules,' I said. 'And those were the rules in the ancient of days.'

I watched her sleeping. I stood back, in case my shadow falling across her should wake her. Seen like this in profile, her peerless features cried out to be touched, but very very gently. The merest contact of a finger skimming over them might wake her; better the most evanescent shiver of a feather.

I dreaded disturbance, causing her to open her eyes, having her stare up at me not able to comprehend for the first few moments. Oh, Estella! You don't realise the reach of the power that lives in you. You mustn't let it be squandered through ignorance.

I woke once more in my bed, in the night or the day, convinced a man was close to me, lying naked, ablaze on the sheets alongside me.

I stretched out my hand and touched only a very little warmth where I had been lying over on my flank. I was alone. Of course I was.

It didn't happen again. I felt no shame, nor regret either. My life was now spared those fleshly embroilments. I rarely felt those surges between my legs which I used to, and the want was less urgent.

I lay back. The tide of desire was ebbing quickly, drying off to traces, and I was left safely stranded, among my reliable shadows and with the same tried and proven air I had been breathing in and breathing out for long months, for years.

'Hand me my stick, young Pip. I have an ache today.'

He did as he was bid.

I pointed ahead, across the passage, to the circuit of the dining room we followed.

'You know what comes next?'

'Yes, Miss Havisham.'

I held on to his shoulder.

'Very well. Walk me, walk me.'

We proceeded along both sides of the long table.

He stepped on a dead beetle. The husk crackled under the sole of his shoe.

Cobwebs covered everything, draped like spun sugar over the feast and the chairs. The disintegrating bottom layer of cake had started to subside, and the other three above leaned tipsily.

He stared at this rich woman's indulgence. But he must have known that the worst disgrace to befall a woman was not to be abandoned before she was married, but to be jilted while she was wearing her wedding dress. My shame excused my capricious ways: my lunatic ways, if you will.

How he stared.

'Come along! Walk me, walk me!'

We had bewitched him.

But he had fallen under our spell, I could believe, before he ever set eyes on us. Out at the forge he would have heard all about us, and been set wondering. I pictured him walking past the high walls and looking up at the shuttered windows. He had imagined the secret garden that must grow behind the house. He had envisaged the rooms ill-lit by candles, rooms as vast as sea caves.

And now – it was his original enchantment he was trying to recall. The reality, or what we offered him, couldn't ever match the pictures of us he'd carried in his head. He used his politeness – his unctuousness – to try to conceal the disappointment, but I saw right through his cover.

'This is my birthday, Pip.'

'Happy –'

'No, I don't suffer it to be spoken of.'

I stared at the mouldering food which lay strewn with spider silk and dust.

'And on this same day my wedding breakfast was set out. The mice have gnawed at it. And sharper teeth – fangs – have feasted on me too.'

His shoulder had stiffened under my hand as he concentrated harder.

'Maybe my death day will be on this day also?'

I didn't mean it as a question, but he answered me very earnestly.

'Oh, I should hope *not*.'

I meant to smile at that, but for some reason my lips wouldn't oblige. As he looked round at me in the gloom, he must have thought I was grimacing. I made out the expression of disquiet on his face.

'But I have much to see achieved before then, Pip – you've no idea. I have my curses to lay first.'

'"Curses"?' he asked, right on cue.

❦

It was always twenty minutes to nine in Satis House. The passage of the weeks was marked for me instead by the Wednesday afternoon arrival and departure of the cousins, on their petitioning business that was never satisfied.

I was annoyed by their myopic clock-watching regularity, even though I insisted on it: presenting themselves, I presumed, at the same minute of the same hour every week, staying not a moment longer than I had demanded of them. I was relieved that they were so compliant, but I felt the differences between us were exemplified by their servitude to time: time as it was measured out to the artificial dictates of a pendulum swinging (as is the clockmaker's tradition) on a length of gut, the tube that carries semen from a bull's testicles.

❦

'And now, madam –'

Estella jiggled forward in her chair with joy decipherable on her face. I heard it in the sudden breathlessness of her voice.

'– for the first time –'

She threw down her last card, the Queen of Spades.

'– I have beggared *you*!'

I sat back. I couldn't withhold a smile.

She wasn't expecting me to smile. Her own pleasure faded from her face. Those petulant furrows reappeared in the middle of her brow, drawing in her eyebrows. They were the only blemish she had, but they bothered me. (How was I going to eradicate them? Not by my smiling.) It seemed I had ruined her moment of victory: the 'daughter', as through the whole of human history, managing at last to trump the 'mother'.

'You've trounced me, Estella.'

She pushed her chair back.

'It's only a stupid game of cards!'

It was always when the game excited her that she took colour to her face. Now her anger was burning her, from the inside out. But that, poor child, only aided her beauty, like refiner's fire.

Chapter Forty

The passing years had done no favours to the fabric of the house. Thieves attempted to break in several times, at the back, and once they succeeded. I had bars put up at the windows.

I couldn't take myself into my father's office now, nor the Compting House. It pained me too much to remember . . . I had those windows bricked up. Inside I locked the doors, and placed the keys somewhere for safe keeping, and later I wasn't able to recollect where. The maids occasionally spoke of hearing noises from behind the office door: surely not ledgers being opened and shut or papers sorted through, as they liked to frighten themselves by thinking, but whatever had happened to fall down the chimney, maybe a bird with a broken neck beating its wings on the hearth stone.

A carriage had stopped across the street, and its two passengers had stepped out.

They were watching the house closely.

The woman was dark and compact. My contemporary for age. The girl who accompanied her was dark also, and a little shorter than Estella.

The woman was speaking. The girl listened, following the direction of the other's eyes.

Was it really her? Marianna Chadwyck? Mouse?

With – whom? – her daughter?

Mouse's appearance was now of the sort (kindly) called quaint. She was wearing a melange of mismatched pelts and feathers, lacking Sheba's ready advice.

We entwined our arms, and she failed to do the obvious, by *not* commenting on how I was living, by candlelight, in unaired rooms, and dressed as I was for a wedding.

I saw tears in her eyes, but I couldn't tell if it was with pleasure or sorrow: with both perhaps. I was introduced to her daughter, who had to be prompted forward, and who offered me a hand tense with misapprehension.

I heard Mouse lightly gasp when Estella entered the drawing room. Her daughter, alarmed, drew closer to her side.

Estella was intrigued, I could see, because these were grander visitors than our usual, as the lit chandeliers announced. Only I would have been able to gauge her reaction, from my experience, because as ever her looks were triumphantly unmarred by the evidence of superfluous feeling.

Mouse and Eveline admired in silence. Estella had lost that original dusky tincture, but the passage of time had enhanced the colour of her eyes: violet eyes, which added to her strong presence in a room. Hers were the ideal proportions of my youth, the high narrow waist and long arms, with a deep bosom to come. For the last two or three years she'd been able to fix her own braid of hair, and to roll and pin it on top of her head in increasingly complex arrangements, as if the touch of others offended her for its clumsiness.

Estella and Eveline went off together, into the garden.

I didn't ask Mouse why she'd come, but at one point she mentioned the name 'Jaggers', and I wondered if she had picked up something about the true circumstances concerning the payments to her mother.

Lady Charlotte had gout, and she had become short of memory.

'Her forgetfulness was amusing, to begin with. Then a little irritating. Until now . . .'

Mouse expressed sympathy for my own past 'predicament', using a tactful choice of words which I pictured her rehearsing to herself on the journey over.

W'm was finally married, she said, although it had been touch and go. Sheba up in London never had an evening unaccounted for in her social diary; and few mornings or afternoons were left spare either. Mouse herself had another three children, and sometimes took in Sheba's two, when she felt particular pity for them.

I mentioned the name of Mrs Calvert (last seen by me on the floor of the hermitage).

'Oh, her husband's become someone terribly important, and I expect she'd look down her nose at us now. I always thought she did that anyway.'

(I didn't remark.)

Lucinda Osborne shared Thurston Park with a fearsome female companion, and gave generously of her time to the church.

And what of Moses? He was where I'd left him, eleven or twelve years ago, only busier than ever now.

'He's kept his faith?'

'I think so. Why do you –'

'It must've been truer to him than his inheritance.'

'His inheritance?'

'Not that there is,' I said. 'For the youngest son.'

'Oh no, Moses isn't the youngest. He'll get a title from a favourite uncle. And what comes with it, lucky man.'

'This is a recent development?'

'No, no. He's known since he was a boy.'

'But I thought . . .'

It had always been there in my mind: the notion of his (comparative) poverty. I'd thought that God's ministry had to be worn like a badge, signifying one's humbler status.

'Oh no, Catherine. You have that quite wrong.'

And so, on the flimsiest of social pretexts, I had been content to judge him. I avoided Mouse's eyes for a little while.

'I used to feel you didn't believe me,' she said. 'But Moses is a fine man. I have no doubts about that at all.'

'I see so now. Only, it's taken me too long.'

'Better late than never.'

I smiled, but not as confidently as I wanted to.

We didn't speak about my father's payments to Lady Charlotte, and Snee's malversation. I knew that she knew. At another mention of Mr Jaggers's name she took my hands in hers.

'Has it been very hard for you, Catherine?'

'Round about here, they used to think I was a girl who had everything. That has been the hard part: realising that I didn't.'

'I thought you might have left. Taken yourself off somewhere new.'

'Twitch'd my mantle blue?'

'I'm sorry – ?'

'I felt I could hold on to more by staying here. If I'd gone off . . . I'm not sure I would have known who I was. I would have come apart perhaps.'

How reasoned I made my behaviour sound, when I couldn't remember it having been so. I had surely depended on something much closer to raw instinct.

'Perhaps,' Mouse said.

'But I made my choice.'

Or did I really mean the opposite – that events had chosen for me? And because I'd needed to be practical, what had been more necessary for me than to try to save as much sanity as I could?

We parted. I promised Mouse that I would keep in touch.

'For Estella's sake, Catherine.'

'For Estella's sake, yes. She has become my life now.'

By coincidence, shortly after Mouse's visit, past matters came to be spoken of again. I'd had no word of the subsequent life and career of Charles Compeyson, following my visit to Blackheath. When I was finally enlightened, my source was Mr Jaggers.

As ever, he was circumspect, enquiring merely as to whether or not I wished to be apprised of certain reports on 'not incontiguous matters' that had come his way.

I indicated that he should go ahead for the nonce.

'You will understand to whom I refer but shan't name?'

I nodded. Mr Jaggers paused only to ease the tightness of straining shirt collar round his wide neck.

'To be brief . . .'

Following three 'iniquitous offences' (forgery of documents, falsely claiming on a charity, passing of stolen banknotes), where the wronged parties had elected not to prosecute, the (nameless) man's luck had run out. He was charged and found guilty of a fourth – a sustained programme of embezzlement – and sentenced to a couple of years in jail. Or rather, on board a prison ship.

'Moored not so far from a shore you will be familiar with.'

(Why did I feel *that* was Mr Jaggers's true condemnation of the man: the fact that he'd been fool enough to get caught.)

'I can supply a few more salient details, should you wish.'

'I would rather *not* hear, thank you.'

I didn't feel it was either a release or a vindication to me to know this, the man now touched me so little. Along the way he had become abstracted, as he fully deserved to be. I hadn't forgotten a single one of my own humiliations; but I had turned my ire since then on men – all of the genus who conceitedly, smugly supposed that they were indispensable to a woman's personal completeness, her felicity.

Mr Jaggers's news – as scant as I wished it to be – confirmed my own thoughts, but also consolidated, *hardened* them in the following few nights of insomnia.

A woman can only satisfy and fulfil herself, I understood, when she establishes her own authority, and sees beyond equality, realising how terrible and damaging her own power – if unleashed – might be.

But there was more. Something to do with Arthur, I gathered.

I was confused. All these pronouns, 'he', 'him', 'his'. I begged that we revert to names. I needed to get this sorted out in my head.

'It seems that they've all been living together,' Mr Jaggers told me. 'Arthur. And the . . .'

'Let names be named.'

'Arthur and the Compeysons.'

'"Living together", you say?'

'Off and on.'

'No!'

'Indeed.'

'Arthur couldn't stand the man.'

Pause.

'So your half-brother claimed.'

Mr Jaggers stood holding his unfolded handkerchief, but he didn't apply it to his nose.

'Arthur got bought out, though,' I said.

Pause.

'Exactly.'

'I'm sorry, I don't . . .'

'Would Compeyson – would it have occurred to him to buy Arthur out if he hadn't known that was what Arthur wanted too?'

'What?' I found myself thinking aloud. 'They – they'd discussed it first?'

'In quite a detailed way, I should think.'

'Before it was suggested to *me*?'

'It was important that you should be the last to know.'

'A plot, you mean? Between the two of them?'

I stared between the unused handkerchief in Mr Jaggers's hand and the unblown nose.

'I think you'll find it makes a kind of sense, Miss Havisham. Criminally speaking.'

ᘛ

A name, 'Charles Compeyson', and so little else. The years had rubbed away at the physical features. If the facial details had surrendered themselves so easily, it must have been that they had lacked some definiteness to begin with.

If the set of a face can give clues to the firmness of a personality, I had to doubt that I'd read him properly.

It had been enough that he was a man who attended upon me, and who lightened the mental load I was carrying at that time. *Who* he was had mattered less to me than the fact that he was there, and so often.

I renewed my concentration, and then details did return to me.

The exact hue of his eyes, their cerulean blueness. The precise degree of brownness of his hair, the evenness (too much evenness?) of that brown, and how it had curled around his head. How one eyebrow would rise and arch higher than the other. His chin had shown a small cleft, almost apologetically small; that had saved it from being a wholly anonymous chin.

But his nose, his mouth, those eluded me. Likewise his teeth.

His hands had a sweep of brown hairs on the backs, and neat clusters on his knuckles, but I couldn't bring to mind the shape of his fingers.

He evaded me now because, I realised, he always had. I had been in love with someone I had half imagined to life, half invented for myself.

Chapter Forty-one

Mrs Mallows sketched in what had happened. Blood stains on the rug in Estella's room. On her sheets. On her nightdress.

Estella looked pale and strained; she was getting through the small actions of the day by rote, without thinking. Her replies to my questions, which were harmless enough, were all delayed, and sounded irritable. I stopped saying what was unnecessary; Estella relaxed in the longer silences; she even allowed herself to smile faintly, as if aware that she wasn't any more the child who'd been brought to this house.

❧

Because Estella was filling out, and my old clothes didn't seem so oversized, I had a seamstress tack a few items with pins and take them in.

Estella asked if I wouldn't be wanting them again.

'I have nowhere to go in them,' I said.

'And where shall *I* go?'

'You will have your own toilette made when we send you out into society. As it calls itself. Polite or otherwise.'

'When will that be?'

'Oh. Soon enough. Once we're ready.'

'Are you coming with me?'

'In spirit,' I said. 'In spirit.'

❧

She could read and write well, and count less well, but ably. Her history was only so-so. She could point to no more than half the countries I asked her to find on the turning globe. She muddled poems she had to memorise, splicing lines from one into another, and then forgot them quickly. Academically she was *not* going to prove exceptional.

It occurred to me to have her speech worked upon, to remove the local giveaways she had picked up from the servants. An elocution teacher was hired. Mr Jaggers helped find me a good instructor in French, also fluent in other languages, who came to the house three times a week.

Pianoforte.

Singing.

Sketching.

Needlework.

Deportment.

Dancing.

All that she might need.

⁂

Before too long I was observing new aspects of behaviour in my Estella in the presence of visitors. A way she had of being coquettish without ever forgetting herself. A facility for listening to an interlocutor, so that all her attention appeared to be given to that one person, out of all the persons whose opinions she might have been receiving in that room. Taking leave with one long backward glance, which spoke eloquently (or appeared to) of caring and loss, and so imprinting her image on the person's recollections. The trick of rounding off a conversation with a concluding *trait d'esprit* so that all the previous wit in the repartee seemed to accumulate to her, like gamblers' money. She was learning how to sparkle and how to cast an allure, and how to make the business look nothing at all like the machination it really was. I wish I had known such tricks when I was young.

She was also a creature of moods, especially with her peers. I could spot the dangers, for them but perhaps for her also.

She teased Pip shamelessly. If he was discouraged, he struggled not to betray it. I admired his pluck. I forgave him his folly. How entertaining it was.

'What do you think, Pip? Does she grow prettier and prettier?'

'Yes. Oh yes.'

Estella devoured his praise, but she was a mistress of disguise. Such adeptness at subterfuge! Obscurantist supreme! She would have her rewards.

'Does she suit diamonds better, Pip? Or rubies?'

I would hold the stones against her.

'Or fire opals?'

Estella's eyes would catch the gleam of my jewels.

I watched them play cards. She still beggared him. He was learning, but he wasn't fast enough yet. He imagined that it was only a matter of time, and so he supposed he could be more beneficent in defeat.

(And he thought, did he, he was going to get away with his precious heart intact?)

❧

I lamented now my fine hands. They had never been *delicate* hands. Strong hands, which I also used to communicate with. I would see how approvingly Lady Chadwyck watched them ply knife and fork and, in the saloon, shape the air to help express the meaning of some remark I was making.

I had stopped the clocks of Satis House, but I hadn't stopped time, and this was its handiwork: these thickened (sometimes bloated) fingers that were starting to point in different directions. Here and there on the back, a first trace of the marks that will grow to become those same brown flowers of death that danced across my father's hands.

I'd had the rings widened; the rich deep lustre from the stones distracted the eye a little, their radiance reminded whoever saw them of the Havisham money that had bought them, and the respect formerly owing to us.

❧

Estella continued her Sunday morning appearances in the cathedral. On her return she had difficulty telling me which anthems and psalms had been sung, or which Books the readings were taken from. It wasn't because she was devout that she carried on going, I knew that.

When I asked her about the gathering there, she was better able to answer. But I judged that there were evasions too, and she wasn't disclosing all that she might. Her colour some Sundays was a little high, as much before she left Satis House to walk there as afterwards. (She always took care that it should be the dullest girl in the house who accompanied her, both as a screen and against whom she was seen to even more startling effect.)

My Estella, I realised, was acquiring depths: shadowy places where I was not allowed to follow. But I also understood how it had come about, because a similar need used to occur to me, and I'd had to stake those secret corners just as she was doing.

❧

Pip had a sixth sense as to just where Estella was in the house at any moment. He sensed her presence, above us or below us, or out in the garden.

Even if she was about the town somewhere, and she kept us waiting, he was with her there – wherever she might be – in his thoughts.

If Estella was cognisant of the hold she had over him, she didn't acknowledge it. That was her craft.

Pip looked pained: still a youth, but somehow understanding more, and at his wit's end wondering how he was ever going to win her approval.

I pitied him standing there. I suffered to watch him, because I was remembering . . . But it also filled me with anger, to see someone – this lad, or myself as I used to be – so unprepared, so unprotected.

Equip yourself! Get sword and shield and helmet! Or you will have no means of defence.

Quick – go arm yourself, boy!

Gradually my bones had grown stiffer and stiffer. It hurt me to move about. Some days I felt I had hot wires pulling inside my legs, my ankles, my feet. I was off-balance. I had to be assisted in and out of bed.

My money bought me labour, whenever in the day or night – it was all one to me – I required it. The maids took no pleasure in their work, but they were paid well enough to show willing.

I tried not to be a burden to Estella. I wanted her to remember who I'd been, when I could stretch straight and stand tall and move freely. This wasn't who I wanted to be, so I made sure that at least she stayed out of my bedroom and didn't have to witness me at my very worst. She had the tact – or was it only distaste? – not to look at me when she might have done, sneaking covert glances instead. When we were together, talking and eating, I hoped she was seeing me in the plural, a synthesis of her recollections, someone I preferred should be half a fiction of her past to this sorry extant fact.

Chapter Forty-two

Have I o'ercome all real foes,
And shall this phantom me oppose?

Estella didn't care for Purcell. Too morbid. Give her Lockwood's or Renshaw's jolly tunes. She sang those prettily enough, but their music was too sweet and too flowery for my ear.

'I sing to enjoy myself,' she said. 'Not to have gloomy thoughts.'

'Purcell can be joyful too. When I was your age we –'

'Oh, he's just a curmudgeon. I can't think he ever wasn't old.'

❧

Attached to a piece of correspondence on another matter, Mr Jaggers begged to inform me that a youthful acquaintance of ours – he named names this time; it was none other than young Pip Pirrip (estranged, as my correspondent would have it, between the states of 'Master' and 'Esquire') – had recently come into a sizeable and unforeseen legacy. Mr Jaggers was representing the benefactor, who wished to remain anonymous. The fortunate but still callow recipient was to be educated rigorously to the standards of a gentleman.

'*I see myself playing the role of a physician, engaged in a surgical experiment on a living being that cannot be undone.*'

Mr Jaggers had been requested, by the aforementioned (name-naming lapsed for the interim), to communicate his sense of honour and gratitude . . .

The boy's feelings on his situation were of no concern to me. Or – or did he suppose *I* was the one responsible, and so Mr Jaggers was only fulfilling an instruction he knew to be quite mistaken?

At least Pip's recent absence from Satis House was now accounted for. Yet the nuisance was twofold. He had been a gauge to me of the changes affecting Estella; and I should want for exercise, without him to lead me round the dining table. Once he was educated – Mr Jaggers mentioned that the benefactor ('the fountainhead') was in favour of Pip's 'prolonged sequestration' – he would judge he was above and beyond us.

I should need to make alternative arrangements.

ꕥ

I showed Estella a necklace, a heavy gold chain with an opal pendant. It had been one of my father's gifts to me. Her eyes lit up with interest.

'Put it on.'

She did so. The necklace complemented her beauty, perfectly served it.

I passed her a hand mirror, so that she could see.

It was hers to keep, I told her.

She took my hand and grazed my wrist with her lips, an awkward gesture which embarrassed us both.

'But we must give you places to visit,' I said. 'So that you can wear it and be seen.'

'In the town?'

'No, not in the town.'

ꕥ

I had been musing on Pip's rise to good fortune, which didn't so much cast the seed of an idea in my mind as affirm other thoughts already germinating there.

I wrote to Mouse. I told her, 'in confidence', that I meant to give Estella some extra polish, and then to introduce her about.

Mouse replied at once. She was shortly sending her own daughters to an establishment on the coast, by Eastbourne. Might Estella, she asked, benefit from the same?

Estella wasn't effusive at first, that was not her way. But I could tell from the manner in which she returned to the topic, and the frequency of her enquiries, that she was very curious, and that she would eventually agree.

'My friend writes that you will receive invitations,' I explained to her. 'You must take advantage of those. It is a responsibility now. To let others "in refined circles" – which is her term – to let *them* see Estella Havisham.'

I organised a new wardrobe for her, to her taste rather than my own. I had the carriage refurbished, so that she might arrive in some style and not be ashamed.

And so . . . Away!

One nervous wave of her gloved hand as the carriage lurched forward, then – for myself – ne'er a backward look.

⁂

Without her there in the house, I sat in a great deep well of silence.

I sat and I thought.

I schemed. I plotted. I manufactured the future.

Each time she came back home, she was somehow *more* Estella-ish.

Hands closer to her sides, she walked taller and straighter. Yet she was even more feline, with a cat's ability not to make contact with any object she was passing, to leave the stale air undisturbed.

What if Pip were to see her now? But he'd been taken off, by altered circumstances, and was only a memory – if that – to his persecutor. She had discovered the world since then, and the world could count itself very fortunate to have discovered *her*, a paragon, my darling Estella, the Havisham girl.

We would sit by the fire, she and I, long into what she told me was her night.

I asked her to describe the people and places she'd just seen. I built pictures in my mind.

(I knew who the families were she spoke of, with whom she mixed now on equal terms. I had their recent genealogies mapped out in my head, from the talk at Durley Chase or on the Chadwycks' circuit. A mention to Mr Jaggers, or to Mrs Bradley in Richmond – a sister of one of my father's early colleagues in trade, and a devotee of Debrett's *New Peerage* – and I received confirmation by return.)

Sometimes it seemed to me that those mental scenes remained clearer for me than for her. Because I had to put them together for myself, the effort ensured that they stayed fixed, whereas Estella gave her characteristic indications of casualness, forgetting from one telling a few days back to the current one.

Every little chip was fitted into the mosaic, and maybe she thought I was too fastidious about it, but this was my method, to repeat her words – to turn them over, scrutinise, test them – and then to refashion them into the images I saw with my mind's eye.

When she'd retired to bed at last and I was left alone, to sit on until the dawn chorus sounded outside, I worked on the scenes, to put a glaze – a lacquer – of familiarity on them, so that they would stay vivid to me and not dim. I transformed them into my memories, and the process left my brain hurting, as if I'd literally embedded them there.

My life was bound up in Estella's. When she was at home with me, I planned where she should go next, and whom she should meet there. If she showed any signs of resisting, I threatened to cancel her next dress fitting or postpone the next purchase of shoes, since she didn't have the same need of them. That always brought her round.

When she'd gone off, I spent the time envisaging what she was doing now, and now, writing notes to her and awaiting her replies, reading her scratchy despatches.

She fleshed out her accounts on her returns.

Details, details: I needed to hear the minutiae. About their clothes, of course, and their equipage. But also about how many dances she managed with A or B, and how many people B or C had introduced her to, and to which events C or D had invited her, and meanwhile what was happening to A and B.

'I forget, I forget,' she would claim sometimes. 'Does it matter?'

Oh yes, it did. Indeed it did.

I would sit up long after she'd left me for bed, and I would have to remind myself – when a coal fell in the fire and the other coals shifted – that she'd been gone for an hour, or perhaps two hours, and that the last expression I'd seen on her face, turned on me from the door, was petulance or boredom or grudging pity: or, on good nights, the wry humour – that puckish and conniving air of irony – which convinced me she was reading my mind very well.

I received a letter one day.

The handwriting of my name and address was familiar to me: *a*s and *d*s and *m*s as I wrote them myself.

I had a baleful premonition before I picked up a fruit knife and split the seal on the back.

Dear Catherine,

It is a cause of regret to me that I must be the bear of Sad Tidings.

YOUR BROTHER ARTHUR HAS PASSED AWAY.

Relations between you were never quite favourable, and I have to confess that I often found the demands he made on my Patience very great. But he fell a victim of his own Weaknesses, and latterly he was able to see this for himself. He was an impressionable fellow, susceptible to Persuasion, and frankly unable to resist Strong Temptations. The opiates he took were the worst of it, and an Infernal Sentence.

I should offer my Condolences, if I felt they were appropriate. But, as you used to tell me, Arthur had forfeited the Right to your Respect. He had his Virtues also – he might be cheerful company when unbefuddled, and his Prodigality hinted at a Generous Spirit unfortunately gone awry.

Arthur, I shall merely say, was well cared for during his Final Days, and his Dying Pains eased as much as we could dispose.

It is my Earnest Hope that this should, notwithstanding, find you in Good Health and Settled Spirits.

Obediently,

Sally C.

I sent no reply. What could I have said?

Oh Sally, Sally, why did you do it?

You don't speak of the other man, of *him*. How often has he betrayed you? Have you received any joy at all?

Was marrying him worth the loss of my friendship?

Like the 'I' of the name once painted in green on the brewhouse wall, it's I who have been the sentinel, the one who kept my senses (whatever they've put out about me to the contrary), to sound the dire warning.

– Give a man your love, and he'll abuse you for it.

– Promise him everything, and he'll leave you with nothing.

– Sleepwalk into marriage, and you'll wake in purgatory. Then he'll steal your heart, and let you rot in hell.

The house leaked, but no puddles on the landing floors yet. Loose drainpipes banged against outside walls. Indoors, dampness was a louring presence on several walls, and had warped some of the woodwork. But more than the substance of the house was damaged.

Pain collected at my joints, then shot into my hands or along my arms and legs. My fingers were knobbly and twisted, like vegetable roots.

I moved in response to my pain, jerkily, like a doll, like a puppet on ravelled strings. I was like a woman who couldn't make up her mind. So I broke my own rule in trying to lessen the pain: shouting at the servants to remind them who was their mistress. Sometimes I talked too briskly to Estella, and she took (silent) umbrage, removing herself to another room.

If I couldn't walk, I perambulated in a moving chair with wheels, rather than sit grounded to the spot.

My head was like a bulb of intelligence, pure mentality, trying to float free of the rest of me: this soon-to-be cadaver, with its misshapen joints, a knee that was swollen to twice its size, the unremitting and grubbing pain.

'Well, the place is no dustier than it was.'

Estella's voice had the pure pristine chime of the best crystal.

'Is *that* how you've remembered it?'

'Satis House is many things in my mind.'

'Yes? Sit by me, Estella.'

I indicated which chair she should take, but she took another, beyond it and four or five feet further from the fire.

'Aren't you cold – ?'

I couldn't call her 'child' now, a young woman gifted with such graces.

'A little.'

'Draw closer, then.'

'A fire is no friend to the complexion.'

'Ah.'

The Greenwoods and the Welbys were off to France, Estella told me another day. They were to be 'finished'.

'"Finished"?'

She let out a long sigh. I was meant to hear it as an exclamation of her envy.

She came over and lowered herself on to a stool beside me. She even allowed me to trace the outline of her cheek with the tip of a tuberous finger.

'And would *you* like to see France, my darling?'

She replied without a moment's hesitation.

'More than anything in the world.'

Chapter Forty-three

'And now,' I said, when France had 'finished' her, 'you are to be my ambassadress.'

'What must I do?'

'You will represent the Havisham name.'

'But what must I do?'

'Impress them with your beauty, your *savoir faire*.'

'How?'

'Captivate them however you can. Talking with them, dancing with them, laughing, staring into their eyes.'

'Who are "they"?'

'Those you meet. But the ones who will appreciate your talents best.'

'Who, though?'

'The young men, of course.'

'Which young men?'

'Haven't I said? The ones you see eager to respond.'

'And what is the point of it all?'

'The point?'

'Of being an ambassadress? Representing the Havisham name?'

'To win their hearts, my darling. To make them unable to forget you.'

They were hardly older than boys, the first ones, wet behind the ears.

Then, as they aged by a couple of years, they learned more seriously what it was to be hurt: expecting more from someone – my precious Estella – than they were due, and watching her reject them, humiliate them.

Names, I always wanted names. Parents or guardians, grandparents, great-aunts and uncles. I liked to know with whom we were dealing.

'And . . . ?'

'And he looks at me with his big doleful eyes!'

'What is that like, tell me –'

'Like being trailed by a spaniel!'

Or, 'He is so arrogant and superior.'

'Isn't Estella Havisham his match? Then give him the proof. He is only a fondling, a cosset who has never known what it's like not to get his own way.'

'What proof? How do I . . . ?'

'That is the amusing part. Answer him back. Question what he means, everything he says to you. Laugh at *him* and not at his jokes.'

'What if I scare him?'

'Arrogance never runs away. It stays, it'll put up a fight.'

'And if he wins?'

'He thinks he wins if he has your approval. *Almost* give it to him, and then trump him – beggar him – when you snatch it away.'

Estella would take her hostages – I trusted her to do it – and, by some instinct, by the contriving genius of my laboratory, she would know how to treat them quite unmercifully.

A Mr Pirrip was waiting in the hall.

'Who did you say, girl?'

'Mr Pirrip, miss.'

'The boy from the forge,' Estella called over. 'Who had the good fortune.'

'And now – and now he threatens it.'

'Threatens it how?'

'Send him up,' I said to the maid. 'Send him up to us.'

A couple of raps upon the door.

'Come in, Pip.'

Enter – a young gentleman. Most presentable, and prosperous-looking.

I told him at once, before he would mention it, that I was aware of his altered circumstances.

He kissed my hand.

'I'm a queen, am I?'

(He still considered *me* the unnamed person responsible, did he?)

Estella was seated on a stool at my feet. He stared at her, almost as if he was having difficulty recognising who she was.

Estella at last held out her hand. He bowed low to kiss that too.

'Do you find her much changed, Pip?'

His mouth fell open.

'She hurt you with her pride,' I said. 'She insulted you.'

'That was long ago.'

'Do you see much change in Pip?' I asked Estella.

'A good deal of it.'

'Not the blacksmith's boy any more?'

Estella laughed.

I sent them both outside, to take a turn about the garden.

When they came back in, I had Pip to myself for a few minutes.

I thought he looked hot, and agitated.

I asked him to please push my mobile chair.

'Now explain about yourself –'

He told me he was being educated, an education to set him up for life, and he was *most* grateful for the opportunity. Whoever his benefactor – or benefac*tress* – might be, craving anonymity . . .

Anonymous benefactions, blah-blah, gift horses be damned.

'Enough!'

'I do beg your pardon. I've been at fault, I apolog—'

'Well, is she not beautiful, Pip?'

He comprehended straight away.

'Miss Estella? She is indeed, Miss Havish—'

'Do you not admire her?'

'I do.'

'Tell me, how does she use you?'

He didn't reply. I repeated my question.

'How does she use you? How?'

Before he could speak, I had another question for him.

'Could you love her? Whatever she does to try you and test you – are you the man to love her?'

He nodded at me.

'Tell me, Pip. Say it.'

'Yes. Yes, I would.' How dry his voice sounded. 'I do.'

'Would *what*? You do *what*?'

'Love her.'

'And you know what love is?'

'I *think* so.'

'I shall enlighten you. It's devotion. It's submission. It's giving up your whole heart. It's sacrifice.'

'You – you know this, Miss Havisham?'

'It was so with me once. And to what purpose – ?'

My voice broke. Pip, pushing my chair, stopped quite still, drew sharply on his breath, as if he'd heard a banshee cry.

I listened to a falling echo of Estella's voice in my own. And then I realised she was speaking to us from the doorway.

'What's this, what's this . . . ?'

She was smiling brightly: too brightly, as if she also was on edge.

'. . . Is this how we welcome back Sir Hotspur?'

ꙮ

'One day, he told me, he wants to write a novel.'

Estella paused to laugh.

'Imagine – once a blacksmith's boy!'

But she was giving him her time. If he were just a blacksmith's boy, what would be the sense of that? It was because he could talk of such things, of writing a book, that she was exercised by the possibilities: just what he might make of himself in the future.

'A novel, you say?'

'*He* says. Yes.'

'He's got all that going on inside his head?'

'Well, I expect he would base it on something.'

'Such as?'

'Something real. A place. The people he encounters. That academy he attends. If he ends up at university, or becomes a lawyer. *Us*.'

And so Estella helped me put my finger on it: why at another level I had instinctively distrusted Philip Pirrip. He had the ready charm of one who would betray you.

I'd been able to tell straight away that the forge was no more than an accident of birth. He was clever, he was one of that sort who can think themselves out of their initial lot in life, he learned quickly from watching others.

Our lives are fictions. How others interpret us. What we allow others to do with us. What we make of ourselves. What we fancy, make believe, we *might* do.

ꙮ

Now Estella wouldn't automatically launch into an account of her travels. I was required to ask her questions, and she would reply. Some answers were quite full; others came slowly and were incomplete, I had to try wheedling them out of her.

She made me wait, playing on my curiosity, baiting me. She did it with a semblance of inattention she had been cultivating in the Assembly Rooms of southern England and northern France, all the while smoothing out the travel creases on her dress and twisting the ringlets of her hair round one finger.

In France she'd come of age, and the party had gone on long into the night; I was dealing now with someone, a bona fide adult, who considered me – not warmly – across a metaphorical channel, from the other far shore.

Why did she wound me like this?

All that I had given her, and the little that I looked to her to give me in return . . .

Where was the justice?

But who ought to have known better than I the uselessness of such reasoning? There was no fairness, there never is, so I shouldn't seek to find it.

⁂

She mentioned a name I recognised. 'Drummle'. It jarred with me. A few sentences further on, I took her back to that earlier point in the conversation.

'Drummle?' she repeated. 'Yes, that's right. Why?'

'The Somersetshire Drummles?'

'I've no idea. He didn't mention anything about –'

'You didn't enquire? Afterwards?'

'No. Should I have?'

'Not if it wasn't important to you.'

'It's important to *you*?'

'Whatever concerns yourself, Estella . . .'

'You know of him?'

'It's only the name.'

'Am I to pay him attention in the future? Is that what you mean?'

'I didn't mean anything –'

'I dropped my fan, and he picked it up for me. There.'

Fans, gloves. Oh Estella, don't you realise, that's the very oldest trick in the book.

'He once came here,' I said at dinner.

'Who did?'

'The Drummle boy.'

'Are we still on about *him*?'

'I merely point it out to you.'

I watched her push the food around on her plate. Doubtless we didn't provide fine enough fare now.

'He came with his great-aunts, the Wilcoxes.'

'Why?'

'Why what?'

'Why did he come?'

'He was brought here. To play with you.'

'I can't remember it.'

'You were very young at the time.'

'He didn't say.'

She turned away.

'Didn't he?' I asked her.

'No.'

'I wonder why.'

'Because he must've forgotten.'

'Surely not. Surely not.'

'I don't see why –'

'How would that be possible?' I said.

'What be possible?'

'That he could ever have forgotten meeting *you*? Not Estella Havisham.'

⁂

Pip assisted me to my feet. I could feel the vigour of youth in him, it passed along his arm. He smelled of soap. He scrubbed his skin, until it shone. He washed his hair before he came. Brushed under his fingernails.

He was a picture of cleanliness and good health. I watched him, smelt him, felt his vitality. He was no taller than average, carried no excess weight, but he was robust, foursquare. If I leaned more heavily against him, he didn't waver. He volunteered every time, proffering me his arm, and we would set off, around the dining room. Round and round.

The table was a tempest sea of cobwebs, rising like waves over crystal jugs and plate-stands, all breaking around that great lopsided scar, the centrepiece, the cake which would have been kept until last at the feast.

The cobwebs tugged over skerries, layers of cobwebs, tides and riptides. I clung on to my pilot, and he steered me. We would discuss Estella. He thought she was ridiculing him, pillorying him. But he was taking her abuse manfully, or he pretended he was. I could tell that he had already forgotten what his existence had been like without Estella. She was an exquisite addiction, one that was slowly poisoning him.

⁂

I said the name to Estella. 'Drummle'. But she immediately started talking about something else, a family quite unconnected, as if she hadn't heard me.

When I repeated the name, she couldn't ignore me.

'Have you encountered the Drummle fellow again?'

She hesitated, and looked away.

'Which fellow is that?'

'His name was Drummle, you told me.'

'Did I?'

'You haven't crossed paths with him again?'

'I can't have.'

She was looking past me, at the tubs and phials on my dressing table. Everything was in its customary place. She knew that the powder was replenished, and the fragrances in the bottles replaced. The presentation on my dressing table was a *symbol.* It would be twenty minutes to nine for ever, but – in order to be symbolic – the moment had to be reconstructed, and that meant replenishing and replacing but taking care that the containers weren't moved, that the unworn slipper remained where it always was. It wasn't a lie, what she saw: it was an artful illusion.

She had learned from my example. Her insouciance was what she intended me to see at this juncture, but she was having to work hard to maintain it. Perhaps she *did* resort to blatant untruths, but youth will always lack the subtlety which experience can bring to its cunning.

'It's Mr Pirrip again, miss, downstairs. Says he begs your indulgence.'

He came because he adored her. His eyes followed her everywhere, they didn't let her alone for a moment: unless I knocked my cane on the floor, and spoke so loudly that he couldn't fail to hear.

'I'm sorry, Miss Havisham – ?'

You will be, sir, you will be.

A navy was launched for the sake of one woman's face. So why shouldn't a facsimile gent risen from a blacksmith's forge be turned head over heels?

I sometimes thought that I disappointed him. He would have

liked me to be more of a 'Miss Havisham' than I was. Had he been directing me in a play, he would have heightened the effects. I should have laid the whole house waste, and not just the dining room. There wouldn't have been any retainers coming and going. He would have had chains on the front doors. Every room in the building would have been shuttered. I would have treated Estella as my prisoner, had her permanently under lock and key.

❧

Not all was left to the imagination, though. A sapling protruded from a window in the old brewhouse. Birds flew in and out of the building. The debris of smashed rooftiles from many storms lay in the yard.

The lettering on the wall had worn away; the green had washed out. The name was on the point of disappearing; it seemed to be doubting its own existence, or its ever *having* existed.

❧

At first I hinted, but Estella was clearly being obtuse, and then I had to address the issue more directly. The Drummle men had never been known for considerateness to their women. They didn't look after their money. They had hearty appetites.

'Appetites?' she repeated.

'For life,' I said.

She looked at me for a few seconds, puzzled. Something occurred to her, and her brow corrugated in folds. Then, just as suddenly, the folds vanished as she sent those moody thoughts packing; her face lightened because she had already – so soon – forgotten the need of my minding.

❧

To Pip, *I* was his benefactress. Who else could it have been? I was the only wealthy person of his acquaintance, and he supposed he must *know* whoever had chosen to fund the lush mode of living he enjoyed.

He came back, to be humiliated again and again at Estella's hands. Did he think this was the penance to be paid for his progress in the world?

ꕥ

I was on the street side of the house, by a shuttered window, when I heard the high-stepping trot of a brace of harness horses. For several moments I was returned to the brewery days, when I would stand by an open window waiting to hear the first footfalls of *his* sleek horses, and the singing springs of the phaeton's suspension. My heart would be wound tight like clockwork, so tight that it hurt.

The horses this day stopped outside the gates. The bell on the wall was rung, impatiently, three, four times. A pair of feet in outdoor clogs hurried across the yard to open the gate.

I heard Estella's voice, clipped and peremptory, before she turned to whoever had delivered her to me in their fast carriage. Perhaps she was explaining that I was a recluse, or was ill, and apologising for me, and all the time hoping her driver wouldn't persist in wanting to meet me. She must have been persuasive on this occasion, and in my mind's eye I saw her enter the yard alone behind her luggage, snapping her orders.

The carriage was being turned in the street. The horses whinnied on their close reins. A blasphemous cry, 'Jesus wept!', not in any coachman's accent. Then the man made off, at the same brisk trot and, past the first narrow corner, whip-cracked the horses into a young blood's madcap canter.

Her charioteer had brought her all this way.

Could his name be Drummle, by any chance?

She must have made an impression on him. With anyone else I would have been glad; in this case I was more troubled, to dwell on the risks I ran in sending out such an accomplished and desirable young woman to do my old witch's sorcery for me.

In Estella my love lived on. But I imagined it as a love grown wise in its own dark way.

She knew not to make the mistakes that I'd made. She knew now to keep her love pure and – because no man was deserving of it – her own secret.

She would play at love, like the actress she was. She would convince her admirers, but it would only be a performance, a charade.

Take them as far as you can, Estella – and then, beautifully, abandon them.

Use your will to, finally, deny them.

Make them endure agonies.

Rule their hearts, and savour your sovereign victory.

You will only ever know your own strength through the spectacle of others' weakness.

I was greedy for whatever news she might give me. I snatched at it, I wolfed it down.

My ambassadress, with her irrefutable credentials. Furred and bejewelled, and on her face an expression of the most professional inscrutability.

The cruel warrior that she also was laid out her scalps before me.

The names were all recognisable to me from Durley talk. She had no compunction about who they were, her admirers, how high she reached: no family was ineligible by their lofty rank.

But who, in all honesty, could have resisted her?

This was what the Havisham fortune was *for*. Estella was its creation. Every penny clawed in from each of those drinking-holes stinking of beer-slop and the huddle of poor folk, their piss runs on the alley walls. All of it was done in *your* name, Estella Havisham, so that you will never have to know a future like my past.

Pip's voice was thick and croaky; his throat sounded parched. His eyes burned with the sight of her, but he couldn't tear them away.

He stood stock still while Estella serenely catpawed around him. She aimed her laughter at his face, and he didn't think to turn away, or to stop her. A certain blue vein appeared again on his temple, resembling a submerged forked twiglet; it throbbed, alarmingly, and I had no doubt that he was hers body and soul.

Whatever she did to him, he would accept his punishment, only to prove his undying fealty to her.

I asked Estella about him.

'You've asked me before.'

'You didn't reply.'

'What on earth have I got to tell you about Pip Pirrip? Nothing.'

'Well, think.'

'He hasn't mentioned writing his novel again, anyhow.'

'He may have changed his mind.'

'He doesn't want to work in some dingy chambers, pen-scratching, I'm sure.'

'You sound', I said, 'as if you approve. Of his literary ambitions.'

'I'm quite indifferent to what he chooses to do.'

'Unless what he chooses to do – or plans to do – unless that involves *you*.'

'How could it?'

'He's beneath your regard, I see.'

'With the start *he* had in life?'

'He's quite the young milord now, isn't he? With prospects.'

'There are hundreds of those.'

'Very well,' I said. 'We shan't invite him any more.'

'I didn't say that.'

'Give me one good reason why we should.'

'He makes me laugh.'

'Not because he means to,' I said.

'Don't *you* find him entertaining?'

'What about the hundred others?' I asked.

'We've trained him up to be our jester. Even if *he* doesn't know that.'

'Are you sure that's the only reason, Estella?'

She picked up her needlework.

'Well –' She spoke without raising her head, and more curtly than before, '– what other reason could there possibly be?'

Chapter Forty-four

Mr Jaggers always carried the weather on his clothes. He wore a gold repeater watch on a heavy gold chain; it chimed the quarter-hours in his breast pocket, by which means he calculated the cost to his clients of his time.

'What news do you bring me of the world?' I asked him.

'That's a very wide field, I fear.'

'There are few fields in London, Mr Jaggers.'

He put his head on one side.

'So we narrow the news to London news? Let me think.'

I knew that he took a deep interest in the more disreputable sorts of crime, and their perpetrators. He was often about his business in Newgate. He was greatly respected but also greatly feared: no one read the criminal psyche better, and he was famous for his ruthlessness in court. But a good few felons who ought to have been convicted – including the low-born; he was no respecter of degree – owed their freedom to his slippery reasoning and silver tongue.

This wasn't the news I had in mind to hear. But his house in Gerrard Street wasn't on the social calling lists, even though so many knew his name. His view of life – from the offices in Little Britain – had a very particular bias.

Which was why the conversation took its strange turn merely by my making that simple, incidental first enquiry.

'You appreciate my mind's bent, Miss Havisham?'

'Certainly,' I answered.

He continued to favour the pause in our exchanges: as if to load what he said with some tangential significance, with an ironic allusion.

'Certain matters, Miss Havisham, we have preferred to deal with in circumlocutory fashion.'

'That is so.'

Pause.

'In order for us to deal with them at all.'

'Names', I said, 'don't always need to be named.'

'And it might be unwise to alter our tactics now.'

'I trust your judgement on that, Mr Jaggers.'

Pause.

'Our lives take us all in different directions. Even though we might presume a sympathy with particular individuals, to be disproved by later events.'

He was wanting *not* to tell me something. And yet he felt that he should put me on my guard.

'Subsequent elucidation,' he said, 'however illuminating it is, might not prove to tell the whole story, though.'

There was more to know about that man than we had allowed for?

'The disposition of a misdemeanant –' He studied the tip of his index finger, polishing the nail with his handkerchief. '– It seldom improves. A fascination develops, to discover the excesses of which he – or she – might be capable.'

'Even', I asked, playing this elaborate verbal game along with him, 'if he – or she – is under legal restraint?'

'Impoundment limits company to one sort. And a thoroughly unsentimental education it generally turns out to be.'

Mr Jaggers stood fingering the exaggeratedly thick gold chain of his repeater, which straddled his broad barrel chest.

'Once that period of detention is at an end, the same company may be unwilling to permit this one of their number to sever his – or her – ties. And if he – or she – should suggest that these ties *are* dispensable, then the prior company may conclude that certain constraints should continue to be exerted.'

I was losing track.

'"Constraints"?'

'Theirs is a violent society. Conscience and pity have no part. Rather, those qualities are despised. Life itself is valued at very little.'

I shuddered, and felt myself blench beneath the coating of white powder on my face.

Mr Jaggers looked troubled, as much by my reaction as by what he knew but was unwilling to tell me. But I didn't want him to misunderstand.

'I have lived in seclusion all this time,' I said. 'The old life is long ago and far away.'

Pause.

'Doesn't the mind continue to dwell on the past, though?' he asked me.

'Less and less on the details. Not on who and what and when and where.'

I remembered what I'd felt, but not *who* had made me feel those things. I remembered what the experience of knowing Charles Compeyson had done to the young woman called 'Catherine Havisham', so much less worldly than she'd liked to think she was.

Now I couldn't even bring the face of her betrayer to mind. Over years it had faded away, into the furniture, into the walls.

'I can see the desirability of that,' my informant said.

His watch started to chime the second quarter. An imposed mechanical pause, while we both listened.

Just what was I being warned about? Firstly, that Mr Jaggers had underestimated this one criminal's degeneration, his viciousness? And secondly, what the man might do to wrest himself free of the 'constraints' which that erstwhile prison company intended to put on him?

'The human mind, Miss Havisham!'

His final words. To remind me of what my seclusion had needed to save me from.

'How low it can reach! And sunk at the very bottom of human nature – take my word – is a terrible, lightless lair of wickedness.'

❧

One night a storm blew up. Estella couldn't sleep through it. She came to find me, folding her dressing gown decorously about her. We listened to the wind howling through the empty brewhouse.

A branch torn from one of the venerable cherry trees smashed through the roof of the old ice-room behind the kitchen.

Estella perched on the fireside fender. Her eyes widened as Satis House with its two centuries of history quaked around us. Fresh blasts of wind buffeted the walls and rattled the glass in the window frames. Unearthly moans issued from the brewhouse.

The flames leaped in the grate, then cowered. There was a mess of soot on the floor.

Out of doors – as we were to discover – birds' nests and uprooted shrubs from the garden flew past. A thunder roll was a dislodged rain barrel being tossed across the cobbles in the yard.

Estella kept close to me, but closer still to the fire. Every new squall had her retying the sash of her dressing gown tighter and glancing over at me for comfort.

'It will pass,' I told her.

'When?'

'Once it's done with. Blown itself out.'

My reply disappointed her. Shouldn't I have known 'when'? Formerly perhaps I might have done; or she would have believed whatever I might have told her, and taken it for a likely fact.

She turned back to the sputtering fire. I saw she was shaking, and that she retied the sash so often to try to disguise how afraid she was.

If I had just leaned across then, stretched out my arm at that moment to touch hers . . . if I'd only . . . if . . .

❧

The next time he came, Pip seemed out of sorts. He was almost off-hand with me, which he had never been before. And then I realised he was being off-hand to himself. His smiles were somehow bitter, but they weren't intended for me. They were being directed back at himself, I felt: at the person he used to be, who had once put his trust in what had turned out subsequently to be false.

He looked around, and shook his head, not meaning me to notice. He caught sight of himself in a mirror, and stopped. In the mirror he belonged to this room. Step out of the frame, and he didn't.

Since he'd last attended us, he had learned something about himself: perhaps the true source of his material prosperity. And he'd been sorely vexed at the discovery.

I had never enquired on the subject. I wouldn't ever do so.

'Estella will be coming,' I told him. 'Look about the garden, if you like. It's wrack and ruin, I know –'

'I never saw a better.'

'A better garden?' I smiled at that. 'Whatever d'you mean?'

'It's just as I imagined it would be,' he said.

'Thistles and cabbages?'

'I can see what it must have been like.'

'You will have Estella to show you.'

What was I setting him up for? The garden had run to riot, run to rot, and –

'*When* she comes,' he said.

'Just be patient.'

❧

Estella sighed.

'But *one* day I must marry.'

'Where does that remark come from?'

'What?'

'About . . .'

'About marrying?'

I stared at her.

She stared back at me. At my yellowing wedding dress. At the two ragged slippers on my feet.

'I meant all this to be an example to you,' I said. 'A caveat.'

'Telling me what?'

'Not to believe what *I* was foolish enough – gullible enough – to believe.'

'But not that I shouldn't ever get married?'

'I – I don't know. I didn't . . .'

Estella as a wife?

I had planned, of course, that she should be supremely eligible. As her provider I had given her everything which I judged from my own experience she might want. Now she asked for the very thing I hadn't had myself. A wedding.

A gold band on her finger, next to an engagement ring. A honeymoon. A married woman's establishment.

She would be Mrs This. Or, even, Lady That.

How was it possible I had failed to anticipate her question?

I had required my Estella to sparkle and entice. Men would fall for her. She should promise much, and be promised more in return. She should lead them to think she was a prize, their booty, for the simple taking. And then – majestically, devastatingly – she should disappoint them.

Which was as far as my design had reached. I hadn't planned for anything beyond. That was the future lying ahead of the future, but Estella was already rattling at its door.

Pip told me he knew someone – a fellow tutee at Pocket's seminary in Hammersmith – who talked of Estella.

'And who might that be?'

'His name's Drummle.'

'Ah.'

Later: 'This Drummle specimen – is he a friend of yours, Pip?'

'I can't say he is.'

The world shrinks and shrinks, but nothing should have astonished me . . .

'Aren't you compatible?'

'No. Not really.'

'Why not?'

'I don't know if I should say.'

'Do.'

'But seeing that he knows Estella –'

'All the more reason.'

Reading between the lines, Drummle was a boor. Tactless, lazy, surly, prone to despondency. His irresponsible behaviour would have seemed refreshing to Estella, a release. When he wasn't despondent, he was likely to be the obverse, the very life and soul, and in those circumstances, fifty miles away from Satis House might as well have been a thousand to Estella. She would return to me with his laughter ringing in her ears, seeing his eyes still smiling into the carriage at her: *my* carriage, which I insisted she travel in now. (Oh I know, Estella, I know just what it is you're going through. I see far better than you, but there's nothing I can do to stop you.)

'Propel me round the room if you will, sir.'

'Certainly, Miss Havisham.'

'But this time we shan't talk.'

'Whatever you wish.'

'Oh, wishes and dreams!'

It was when we set out to make those come true that they deceived us, they became the sure-fire means of our undoing.

❧

Estella was tired of her life with me, just as *I* had grown weary of my life at home. She longed to make her escape, just as I had longed to make mine. I should have had perfect sympathy for her, therefore. But I didn't.

Her mother was a murderess, her father a transported convict. Without me she would have grown up in an orphanage, then a poorhouse. I had taken her in, I'd fed her and warmed her, I'd given her a second chance at life. She had everything to thank me for, and yet I received back little or no gratitude.

When I told her she was heartless, all that she could reply was, well, who was it who'd made her like that?

❧

Perhaps Bentley Drummle was the one man she couldn't keep down. Was he presenting her with her greatest challenge? Did he even have the semblance of a heart for her to grind away at?

Why couldn't I put him out of my mind?

The grandeur of the Drummles' social habits, like their self-opinion, had always been in inverse proportion to their means. Other families kept their wealth or got richer (or, like the Chadwycks, entered into 'arrangements'); while the Drummles, losing money by slothful inattention, insisted all the more on their dignity, elevating it to noblesse. (All those elderly spinster aunts and bachelor uncles were the problem. Never mind that they didn't have proper blue blood, the Drummle blood simply wasn't mixing enough: it was thickening instead; coagulating.)

This Drummle wanted Havisham money. He wasn't too proud to come after us.

Estella was no greenhorn. She had the measure of him, but there was something about him which affected her differently. He resisted the worst she could deal him. Any other man would have succumbed and gone under by now.

Pip was hurting, and Estella saw that, and she had ceased to be interested. She played with Pip and had ruthless sport.

Drummle didn't hurt. By dint of stupidity and insensitivity, he had held out. He filled her thoughts, because she couldn't dispose of him. He wouldn't honour her as the others did; she hadn't worked out yet how he was to be broken, or even if he could be.

I could see it all in my mind's eye. He was impertinent back to her, he showed his temper, he neglected her for a while, then he was generous in a belittling way. He covered his ears when she came after him – before he lurched, lunged at her, pinned her to the wall, pressed himself intimately against her, laughed at her until she started laughing too.

Estella Havisham had met her match.

Everything was confused. Water lapping against mossy Venetian steps. Dido, *ghastly she gazed . . . red were her rolling eyes*. Faded green lettering on a brick wall. A Negro boy wearing a blue velveteen coat with gilt buttons. A bald-headed doll in a window, who winks one eye. Windmill sails cracking in a stiff breeze, Dutch clouds as plump as eiderdowns. Along a Zealand canal a gondola nudging its way, beneath willows, passing a woman's straw hat that floats on the cold dark water and trails scarlet ribbons. A straw woman, roped to a chair, crowning a bonfire, who explodes in sparks. The black boy announcing, a man is making love to a woman on the Bokhara rug. A perspective grid laid over a blank sheet of sketching paper.

I opened my eyes. I couldn't tell if it was night or day, autumn or spring. I couldn't be sure if I had woken up or if this was me falling back into a familiar dream.

Estella twisted her mouth at me, as if she had some bad taste in it. How had we got to this?

'Have you ever thought of *me*? When I was bringing all this credit to you –'

'What am I hearing? "Me"? "*Me*"?'

'That I was a person. Not some – some marionette.'

'Oh, spare me, Estella. Don't weep for yourself.'

'*Someone* has to.'

'Why?'

'The idiocy of it. The *tragedy*.'

'It can't be both,' I said, 'whatever you're talking about.'

'You know quite well.'

'Do I?'

'Deceitful too?'

'I have never deceived you, Estella. Never.'

'Well, when you haven't allowed me a breathing life like other people –'

'What nonsense you're –'

'– then truths and lies don't matter, there're no such things. Whether you've deceived me or not –'

'Ha! You're retracting –'

'Certainly not. You've *used* me. To do your perverse will. But not so I'll know why I'm doing it.'

She was in tears.

'Marionettes don't cry, Estella.'

I took two or three steps towards her. Then I stopped.

'Hush, hush!'

She kept on crying. More tears than I thought were possible: unless they had been collecting for these weeks, months.

If I'd been able to stretch out my arms, to hold her . . . But I couldn't bring myself to.

I couldn't manage it. And everything which was to follow – from that one solemn and foreboding moment it had been determined.

ـ

He repeated the name. 'Drummle, you say?'

'The same, Pip.'

'*Drummle?* He's the very last – Tell me this is some joke, Miss Havisham.'

'It isn't. I wish it were. How I wish it were.'

'Where's Estella? Let me speak to her.'

'She's gone off for the aftern—'

'Didn't she know I was coming?'

'Yes, Pip.'

'Then she won't get her play with me. Will she?'

He quietened. But he also grew gloomy. 'You should see how the oaf drives.'

'And how is that?' I asked.

'So fast round corners in the brougham, he scrapes the body on the lamp-posts.'

'He sounds . . . high-spirited,' I said, not concealing my own dejection.

'Reckless. A hot-head. Hell-bent.'

My worst fears were being confirmed.

'And the horses are all on edge. He'll run someone down soon, I've no doubt about it. Only he'll be going so fast, it won't matter to him.'

'Because he hasn't seen?'

'Because he cares not a damn.'

Estella was coming and going exactly as she pleased. She wouldn't tell me what her arrangements were. She only dropped a word or two, of the barest necessity, in passing.

I could have disinherited her, as my father had done to Arthur.

But the Havisham money was the essential component in her allure. Without it she would have been much like any other of a multitude of girls. What else was to be done with her bounty anyway? The wealth was inseparable from the name. The name was inseparable from the fact of our wealth. It was the identity which we had in common, we two last Havisham women.

She was telling me nothing. Of where she went, whom she saw. She thought she could do without me. She was twenty-one, her own woman, with ample funds as it was. She thought she should be able to forget me.

But I was in the air. I was in the bloodstream, I was in the bone.

I was there in the mirror. I was there in front of your face, so you tried – *tried*, Estella – to wave me away.

I'm the tread on the staircase behind you. I'm that little gulp of air in your throat after you've taken a swallow of food or drink, whatever you need to nourish you. I'm the small plaintive scratching of a branch at the window, I'm also the cold north wind rumbling low in the belly of the chimney. I'm the heat of your bedroom in summer, I'm the frost which patterns those extravagant ice ferns on your window. I'm the dampness of autumn oozing out of the stonework, I'm the wearisome predictability of spring budding, which is only the continuance into another year, and into the next, of your neglect of me and your unhappiness for yourself.

But didn't she deserve to forget me?

I had shrunk the love inside her to such a tiny thing, a thing that she realised could not sustain her.

I couldn't condemn her for ingratitude to me, because she didn't know – I hadn't trained her – to have any warmer feelings.

Chapter Forty-five

Estella went off to Richmond, to stay with Mrs Bradley, by the Green. In the silence – the utter dearth of communication – that followed, I had to set the scene for myself.

She was being paid court to, as ever. She was behaving (I hoped) like an icy empress. But I suspected that covertly – in well-bred Richmond – an axe was being ground; Estella was making contingency plans, in order not to continue her life as a second 'Miss Havisham'.

I told Pip she had gone to the opposite end of the country. He was ready to set off after her. I told him I needed him here.

But *he* was turning too.

'I begin to see what you've done.'

'"Done"? What have I –'

'Will you now play the innocent, madam?'

'What's this?'

'I was some kind of experiment, was I?'

He was indignant, and yet his voice didn't quite lose its tone of urbane politeness.

'What precisely was I intended to prove to you, Miss Havisham?'

I could have feigned not to understand. But I had my answer instantly ready.

'When you praised Estella, that confirmed my success with her. And when I persuaded you to stand up to her, then – you were testing *Estella's* resolve.'

'An experiment. Anyone could have been in my place, it just happened to be me?'

'You – you needed to be intelligent. Someone who – who didn't quite fit, so to speak –'

'But I was expendable?'

'Then why should I have persisted with you – only you – if you were?'

'You can't soften me with your blandishments. You're not answering my question. "Why *me*?"'

'You're too clever to let this –'

'That's just where you're wrong. If you'll excuse my directness.'

Mannerly to the last, even when his criticism of me was harshest.

He slumped down into a chair. It was as if the stiffening had been pulled out of him. He was bearing some immense loss he couldn't confess to.

He saw me looking. 'The other aspect of intelligence', he said, 'is susceptibility. Although it's unmanly to admit as much.'

I watched him. I remembered what it had been like with the backbone filleted out of *me*. That terrible vast helplessness. The waste ranged behind, and the nothingness extending in front. A frantic lethargy. Despair lodged deep, deep in the gut.

I hauled myself out of the wheelchair and blundered past him, out of the room. I could feel my bladder about to burst.

I was caught halfway along the landing. My God, my God –

A warm trickle spurted down one leg, down both legs.

I slowed, tried to tighten loose and strained muscles, and then I continued towards my dressing room. The stockings, sodden on my thighs, rubbed together. The liquid warmth was cooling away by the second.

❧

It must have been the middle of the night. *Their* night. I couldn't bear to be seated, but I didn't have the strength to walk either, so I went down on all fours and I crawled.

. . . as ye will answer at the dreadful day of judgement, when the secrets of all hearts shall be disclosed . . .

And then it came to me, as I was pushing myself forward, how the animals walk – slowly, slowly, and the pain of my motion quite excruciating – it came to me then with exemplary clarity, just what it was I had done.

I was no better than *he* had been, so long ago. This was the irony of my history: by trying to deny him subsequently, I had turned myself into an imitation of him. Our vices were the same.

'Is it too late, Pip? Is it?'

He stared at me. Once I'd been a giantess to him, and now he had to adjust his eyes downwards.

'Don't say, don't say!'

'I have to go, Miss Havisham. I can't come here any more –'

I held his arm tighter.

'– I can't stay. Please, let me go.'

I fastened myself to him, closer than ivy, around the strength and forcefulness of a living man.

'Just once more, Pip.'

I had dispensed with the wheelchair. We started to walk, haltingly, round the room.

Firelight, candleshine.

We followed the same unvarying circuit. About the cobweb-festooned table and the chairs awaiting the wedding guests, past the fireplace on one side and the double doors on the other.

Then a second turn of the room.

A circus track. No – no, a coliseum.

I had to turn myself away from the sight of his face, so deeply etched with pain was it. His voice bore all his desolation.

A third time.

The sombre tread of our feet. The tremor of my silk. His squeaky boot-leather.

A perpetually uncompleted son et lumière.

Alas,
What good are shrines and vows to maddened lovers?
The inward fire eats the soft marrow away,
And the internal wound bleeds on in silence.

ꕥ

A letter came one morning. I opened it at the dressing table.

To Dear Nana,

How long is it since I called you that?

And now you must learn to think of me not as Estella Havisham but as . . .

This is the first time I've written my new name.

MRS BENTLEY DRUMMLE.

There!

It is not exactly a Secret, that we were married, but we chose not to advertise it in the Newspapers, & in truth my Husband's Parents think he has been a little – underhand, sh. I say. His Sister attempted to dissuade me, wh. provoked B.'s anger with her. I had Mrs Bradley swear not to speak of it.

So, we are not quite under-a-cloud, but nor are we in high-favour.

Yet this may not be News to surprise YOU, I wonder? You have always had a Skill for seeing thru my Dissembling.

For the nonce we remain here in Richmond.

And remain yours truly, both of us, in the hope of yr. Approval & Esteem.

Estella

I crumpled up the note and tossed it into the fire.

It missed the grate.

Later I fetched it out, and unrolled it again.

Over the succeeding days I memorised the words. Phrase by phrase, sentence by sentence.

As if I had to convince myself, only this way, that it could possibly be true.

⁂

The next year. One noon-time. A carriage was waiting in Crow Lane.

A young woman in a cloak and feathered hat was shown in.

'Mother –'

Or did I imagine that was the word she spoke, those two syllable-movements of her lips?

She stood removing first one glove, but she hesitated before she peeled off the other.

I saw the fine ring she wore: a cluster of rubies inside diamonds.

'How – how are you?' she asked.

'Oh . . . I'm alive – just. And you?'

'Quite well, thank –'

'Come closer, Estella.'

'What for?'

'So that I can see you better, of course. You won't begrudge me this little? When you have denied me so much else.'

'Oh, that. My wedding.'

'As if it were nothing.'

She looked away. She adjusted the rake of her fashionable hat, straightening the plumes.

'If it didn't signify – *that's* why you didn't want to tell me?'

'I haven't come to quarrel with you.'

'But you *have* come.'

'Yes.'

'Then let me see you. Come closer.'

But still she resisted. I had just the fragrance of her rich woman's perfume, too much of it perhaps.

I leaned forward and grabbed at her arm. She squealed, and tried twisting it away. But I held on tight.

'You're hurting me!'

'I would never hurt you, my darling.'

'Please leave me alone –'

I let go of her. She rubbed at her forearm through her satin sleeve, where I'd been holding her.

'*Assieds-toi, mon enfant.*'

She shot me a glance. She forgot about her arm, it dropped by her side.

She averted her eyes to the window.

'. . . *mon enfant*.'

She knew that I knew: she was carrying a child, *his* child.

'I've a way to go,' she said. 'I just wanted to see you for myself.'

To have the proof for yourself, that what they'd told you was true, I was still alive?

'And now you have,' I said.

'Yes.'

(While I should be worrying about myself, Estella Drummle, that expression of determined pity was really saying. I can forget about *her*, she'll survive.)

After we'd said our goodbyes I prised back a shutter and, shading both eyes against daylight, I watched her leave.

She stopped at the gate and looked round, fastened her gaze on the window and raised her hand. She didn't wave; it was a gesture of recognition – of all that I had done, sometimes harming her when I had meant the very opposite.

The greys stamped their hooves. Fine beasts they were too. He had provided her with them in anticipation of a legacy which he could be as profligate with as he liked, being answerable to no one. All he was waiting for was my demise.

⁂

'I've been to Richmond,' Pip said. 'You didn't tell me she was there.'

'No, I didn't.'

'Why not?'

'What good would it have done?'

'Good? You can use that word?'

'Did you speak to her?'

'How could I? When he had her on his arm. I watched them. That was enough.'

'How – how do they look together?'

'Not ecstatically happy.'

I leaped on the remark.

'*Not* happy?'

Relief vied in me with grief.

'Scarcely filled with the joys of married life,' he said.

He stood for a while in silence, recalling what he'd seen. His hands were clenched by his sides, knuckles flaring white.

⁂

My relief passed. I was ashamed of it. I waited for Estella to write, but I heard nothing. I learned only – from Mrs Bradley – that they'd moved away.

Estella would have written, I felt, if she'd had the confidence. But now she couldn't even pretend. She might still wear fashionable hats, but they were a disguise, they deflected people's scrutinising eyes. She dressed for a masquerade.

I couldn't sleep. I spoke to her instead, under my breath; I tried to calm her, to bring her just a little cheer, I tried to offer my darling the only gift she needed now – hope.

⁂

Pip wrote to me. He had heard about the birth. He had heard other stories too, that Estella was quickly losing the man's affection, if she'd ever truly had it. There were rumours of drinking sprees, and women up in London.

'*His neglect is bad enough, but they say it's done with violence, and behind closed and locked doors. There he takes out his disgust of himself on his wife, the mother of his child.*'

What kind of devil was she closeted with? To what depravities would this blackguard not stoop in order to impose his will?

Only one certitude awaited her: it was my abominable bequest to her.

Everything was revealed to me in a freak instant, and left me wringing my hands, pulling the combs from my hair.

There was no future beyond the future. Estella's fate would be this. To suffer, and to know nothing else.

To suffer; and, when she thought she'd reached the limits of endurance, to suffer some more.

⁂

'It's Mr Pirrip here to see you, miss –'

He didn't wait to be shown up, but strode into the room.

I had been anticipating a visit. I hadn't envisaged so much anger.

His anger had turned to rage. I asked the girl to leave us.

'Miss, are you quite sure – ?'

A storm whirled around him. Here was my nemesis, come to

me in my own drawing room: my reckoning, and my doom.

He had found out more; he wouldn't tell me what, except to say he judged Drummle bestial.

'If there's justice in an afterlife – unless justice really can be brought upon him here on this earth . . .'

'Try to calm yourself,' I said.

'Not while Estella is in that villain's clutches.'

There was no consoling him. I couldn't say anything to him.

'What can she be going through? What's going on inside her mind – ?'

I shook my head.

'Have you seen her?' he asked me.

'No.'

'Or heard from her? Tell me truthfully.'

'Since the birth, not a word.'

'Why doesn't she want to say?'

Because I trained her not to speak. Because I taught her to keep her unhappiness a secret to herself. Because I equipped her only with the knowledge of how to suffer.

'Oh, Pip . . .'

'It's too late. Much too late.'

'What have I done?'

She was supping on horrors, I sensed it.

'Everything that's happened –'

'This damned house!' he called out.

'I only meant . . .'

It was useless, I couldn't justify myself.

'This infernal house!'

I watched him walk over to one of the windows. He started to unbolt the shutters.

I cried out to him to stop, but he wouldn't. He pulled back one shutter, which rasped on its hinges. Daylight broke into the room, like a dam burst. I covered my face with my arms.

I heard him flinging open the other shutter, as I was begging him not to. I buried my face in my hands. I couldn't bear to see the damage being done, the grey English light reclaiming the room.

The light seeped between my fingers. My eyes stung with it, even tight shut, through the pink of the lids.

'Close the shutters! Close the shutters!'

The shutters on the other window screeched as they were unloosed.

Daylight continued to pour in. I felt it swilling into every corner. It was drowning the room.

'Please! What are you trying to – ?'

'It should never have been like this.'

Closing my eyes even tighter, I jammed my hands to my ears, so I wouldn't have to hear any more. But he only raised his voice, to *make* me hear.

'It couldn't change anything. What difference was it going to make, living walled up here?'

His good manners of the past were all forgotten.

'Incarcerating Estella in this dungeon!'

I couldn't muffle his fury.

I got up, and my stick clattered to the floor. I left it there.

I dragged myself across the room, risking all that light. His voice followed me. I held on to the furniture, with my eyes screwed up in my face, every movement an agony to me.

I opened the door, lurching for the familiar gloom of the corridor. I crossed to the other side of the passage, turned the handle of the dining-room door, and pushed as hard as I could with my shoulder. I stumbled forward; I just stopped myself from falling by clutching on to the back of a chair.

'Leave me in peace.'

'Why did you go on inviting me here? Why did you let me come?'

'You repay me like this? This is brutal persecution of –'

'It's your conscience that torments you, Miss Havisham, not I. *That's* why you have me here, isn't it? So I'll help reprieve you from just a little of your guilt –'

'Keep the room dark!'

'It *is* too late for that.'

My Sisyphus boulder of guilt – how right you are – and the pain searing in my shoulder from the burden of it.

'Just leave me!'

'Not like this, Miss Havisham.'

'Please!'

'I'm concerned.'

I heard laughter from somewhere. Then I realised it had come from myself. A wild yelp that only sounded like laughter, which had no mirth in it.

'Are you unwell, Miss Hav—'

'Why should *you* be concerned?'

'Because I think you might do yourself an injury.'

'The injury is all done,' I said. 'All done.'

Guilt was ravaging me. He understood that. Everything was collapsing in on me again. Guilt was punishing me with a vengeance, sparing me nothing. I was dying of it.

I stared into the flames of the fire.

'Forgive me.'

'Miss Havisham –'

'Say you forgive me, Pip. Tell me, please, pl—'

I reached out for him. He was behind me. I turned round. Somehow, though – I lost my bearings, or I was distracted – something else was happening –

'The fire! The log! Miss Havish—'

Great wings were flapping at me, like a bird's, an eagle's, then they became wings of flame, a phoenix's, and I heard that ragged laugh rising again.

As he snatched at the table cloth, the wedding breakfast flew into the air, the top layer was sliding off the cake, I saw mice and moths escaping, worms and maggots, the cake caved in on itself.

'Dear Jesus!'

He was dancing round me with the remnants of the cloth, trying to cover me.

Flames passed along my arms, I saw them and felt just a gentle warmth. Flames were sprouting from my head.

He was shouting at me.

'Christ Jesus!'

I'm watching it happen, the fire's consuming greed, its ardour and passion. I dip my hands in the liquid gold of the flames – scarlet and orange and gold, with flickers of blue – I clasp them against my cheeks, my tinder-dry hair.

A tunnel of draught spirits me high, and the next second my dress roars into a ball of fire.

Now I shall go soaring above rooftops and steeples, into the ether. My lungs are melting. A long tongue of flame darts out of my mouth, uncurls, it'll lick a way through . . .

I want to laugh again, but he's spinning me round.

I'm aware just briefly of a numbing heat, which might be ice. Suddenly I have no feeling in any part of me.

He envelops me. Blackness. I lose my balance. I'm on the floor, he's rolling on top of me, I can't breathe.

This blackness.

The heat no longer hurts. Or it cauterises me so intensely, so icily, that I'm submerged in it.

I *am* the fire.

Chapter Forty-six

> My fatal course is finished; and I go,
> A glorious name, among the ghosts below.

But wait . . .

'She has damaged her heart.'

(It's always the heart.)

'If she were a younger woman –'

(Instead of this old hag. But *inside*, gentlemen –)

'Her burns can be treated, they're only disfigurements. Skin-deep, that is. But the harm done to her heart, that weakens everything.'

They're figures against the white light, coming and going.

Suddenly there's so much light. Brilliant daylight. Everywhere.

And fresh air. It cools my skin, even through the muslin compresses. A briny breeze, salting my lips and blowing their words away again.

'Good sea air, Mr Jaggers.'

'If you say so.'

The breeze has carried to our wooded escarpment across the Channel, from France.

Boats fill their sails. In the cold northern countries, witches sell wind to sailors, they knot it with thread into bags.

'Do they really? Fancy!'

'That's one thing I expect you *didn't* know, Mr Jaggers.'

A meek smile is in order, sir. Turn your hand, declare. Like this.

Only my fingers are unbandaged, they obtrude from beneath the travelling rug. The old Havisham diamonds wink slyly in the sea light.

I have to wear a shift. A simple shift of white cotton.

When I try to take it off, the girl calls out, 'For pity's sake, madam . . .'

White. As my wedding gown once was.

There are no mirrors here, except conscience.

I disprove their expectations. ('Any day now surely, it can't be for much longer . . .')

One doctor or the other shuffles in, he examines me, shuffles out again.

They've doused my burns. Either the burns ache and keep me awake, or – mysteriously – I have no sense of them at all.

Sometimes I suppose that this business concerns me. And at other times it isn't of the least significance to me; I'm flying above it, trailing my white shift like a proper angel.

'If I'd worn green . . .'

'I'm sorry,' the girl says, 'I didn't catch –'

'Green. Like the Immortals. They wore green.'

'Who . . . ?'

(Ignorance darkens the world.)

'Oberon. Titania. Puck. Living forever. If I'd worn green . . .'

'Rest now, Miss Havisham –'

'Oh, there'll be time to rest.'

Decades. Centuries. Millennia.

Estella places her hand on the counterpane.

I place my swaddled hand on top of hers.

She looks at it, and seems surprised. Or is she surprised to be feeling, in my exposed fingers, the ungentle, primitive grip of a dying woman?

'I saw Mr Pirrip leaving.'

'I've been asleep.'

'He sat beside you for a while.'

I hold her hand captive, and she allows me.

'In his novel,' I say to her, 'he will want me to die earlier. He will be evasive on the point. But *you* will know how it was.'

Mr Jaggers's hand reaches inside his jacket. From a pocket he extracts a folded sheet of newspaper.

'You have something you wish to show me, sir?'

He unfolds as much of the page as is relevant and lays it flat on the table top.

He steps back.

'I shall leave it there, Miss Havisham. You can peruse it when I'm gone. Or have it read to you, by someone who has no inkling.'

'Today you're a delivery boy?'

He withholds his smile.

'Won't you explain?' I ask him.

He puts his head on one side.

'It is a private business, I think. What is recorded there.'

'I see.'

My voice is baked. I force a smile, and it seems to me that he sorrows to see it.

'I beg your pardon,' he says. 'If you judge I've done wrong.'

I nod.

'Surely granted, my old friend.'

He smiles gratefully at that, looking not at me but at his famously peremptory index finger.

'Some madeira, sir? Sherry wine and biscuits? Nothing better for the spirits on a frosty autumn afternoon.'

'The afternoon is fine, Miss Havisham. And warm. We're still in summer.'

The watch strikes in his pocket, and I'm back in the garden of Satis House hearing the cathedral bells in our ancient town fall across the vanished grey mornings of my life long ago.

Found drowned, the newspaper report tells me. Downstream on the Thames.

The deceased, one by the name 'Compeyson', with a long criminal record.

Not magniloquently, not romantically drowned. Not in a barque called *Ariel*, not capsizing in a summer storm.

Not like that.

But following a brawl with an escaped convict who bore a deep grudge, and churned beneath the paddles of the Rotterdam steamer, the life thrashed out of him.

Blood frothing the spume. A flotsam of soft swollen pulpy matter, muscle tissue and brain jelly . . .

His face has vanished completely from my recollection. I have no tears for him. I can't cry, even for myself. A destroyer such as he, who is destroyed in his turn, he's owed no grief.

Drowned. The location ought to have been that majestic and most serene city, at Carnaval time. He would have been wearing a mask. Its features are smooth and settled, untroubled. His youth is gilded. There isn't a single defect on the face: if you disregard the eyes, that is, where the horror lives on, gelled into place, but only until the fish start nibbling for their supper.

These dear-bought pleasures had I never known,
Had I continued free, and still my own;
Avoiding love, I had not found despair,
But shar'd with savage beasts the common air.
Like them a lonely life I might have led,
Not mourn'd the living, nor disturb'd the dead.

❧

After that, I suppose I – I too – must have died. It was a slow, tranquil drift. I lost the use of my legs, my feet, my arms, my hands, my fingers.

The struggling soul was loos'd, and life dissolv'd in air.

I continued to think, though.

Thought carried me over. From the bed, through the glass of the window, into the branches of the tree. Not literally, or the thrush would have flown; how I had lain in bed placing myself there for the past few days, but now I had nothing to bring me back. No pain, no drag of old bones, no thunder of blood in my temples.

I was somehow myself, or the disembodied essence afloat in the tree's greenery. The thrush still sang, undisturbed.

VI

VALEDICTION

Chapter Forty-seven

Estella – in half-mourning – sits by candlelight four or five feet away from the cheval glass in her bedroom. She sits straight-backed, just as she was taught. She stares at her reflection, turning her head this way, that way.

The candles illuminate the damage, all down the left side of her face. Swollen patches of yellow, purple, and – on her jaw line – black. Her husband has hit her repeatedly, and hard.

Delicately she presses the tips of her fingers on the skin, as if she might shape it back into its correct contours. She winces, but she carries on, fascinated by the gruesome spectacle and by the pain of it. Rather than look away, she confronts her battered self with tears in her eyes.

'Are you satisfied?' she asks, although there is no woman in a wedding dress to answer her now.

What her upbringing in Satis House amounted to was the bleakest, most accidental kind of self-knowledge.

She somehow *knows*, by an intuition developed in Satis House, that for her guardian the terrifying awareness of what she had caused to happen came too late to alter anything. Catherine Havisham, even as she looked helplessly on at this marriage, was spared learning the worst.

Three years later.

Estella puts on one of the necklaces. Pink diamonds and fire rubies. This was one of Antoinette Havisham's favourites. She picks up the hand mirror, engraved on the back with a baroque

'H', outsized for the taste of the day.

The necklace's heavy gold filigree is likewise rather too fussy, but (she wonders to herself) the stones could be reset, couldn't they, into a simpler arrangement? And what about the South Sea pearls?

She checks that the pearls are there, in the box where she placed them last time. It has come to her attention that several items have gone missing. Her husband is surely responsible, but naturally he blamed a maid, who was dismissed – and when the pilfering continued, of the same swanky types of trinket and bauble as before, another maid was accused and given her marching orders.

Either the bijoux have been passed on to some trollop, or he sells the pieces and uses the proceeds as petty cash for his gambling.

She should be angrier; she should at least – to his face – implicate him in the thefts, if not accuse him of doing the light-fingered deed himself. But the business of removing the gee-gaws keeps him occupied, and the female company and the habitués of the gaming tables distract him in other ways, possibly relieving her of more frequent roughings-up.

It's six months since Drummle roared into death, after flogging the life out of his horse.

Dressed in the same half-mourning she wore for her guardian, Estella picks up a newspaper. She knows, even before she finds the words in the first paragraph, what it will say: *which* London bank it is that has failed.

She drops the newspaper, the room is turning turtle. Rising from her chair she loses her balance, she grabs hold of the curtain. The curtain pulls away from its rail and time slows as she falls forward, goes crashing down to meet the floor.

Ask for Mr Pirrip in the Crispin & Crispianus and they would point to that man with thinning hair and a Cairo complexion. But no one does ask for him. He keeps to himself, on a settle at the back of the pub.

He has lost his boyish looks. There's an old burn mark from a fire on his neck. His brow carries the deep creases of someone who dwells too much in his thoughts. From his manner you would gather that he lives alone; he wears a wedding band, but the gold is lustreless and the ring is sunk into the flesh of his finger. He makes a drink last. It's to eavesdrop that he comes in, to hear tales of the town as it used to be, two or three generations ago.

No one recognises him from his childhood. They could tell from his smooth, surprisingly plump hands that he hasn't had to earn his living by manual labour. His hands show their real skill whenever he uses a pencil to dash down his observations or an overheard remark into the notebook he tucks back into his pocket.

He stares into the flames. What he sees is what he remembers, or what he thinks he remembers. He has the shape of a story in his head, and trims his details to fit.

There are different versions of the story, though. One story, with – he believes – three viewpoints.

Estella's. His. The madwoman's.

Ten years on from her lowest point, when she lost her home, Estella stands on a terrace. Supported by a walking cane, she watches her children and their friends on the lawn beneath.

Her hair shows grey. The paving on the terrace is crumbling, but there isn't enough money on a doctor's salary to make any repairs that aren't essential. She is conscious of how reluctant she is to give herself to this moment, or to *any* moment. Her husband is a very nonpareil of patience; he treats her more kindly, she thinks, than she deserves.

She turns one of the rings on her fingers. A Havisham ring. Some of the remaining jewellery from Rochester days has had to be sold, discreetly. She hopes they might land a small windfall somehow or other, to tide them over.

They've lived in Shropshire since they were married. She doesn't move in the same county circles as she would have done once. Her former friends – no, 'acquaintances' is what they were – deserted her gradually when news of her first husband's violence got about. People started to think she was unlucky.

Maybe she was. Maybe she *is*.

Henry stridently, nobly, believes the best of her.

But – but she can feel her face going slack when, as now, there is nobody about to see, when the children are too far and making too much noise to notice.

She thinks often of that woman, and of her childhood in that big gaunt house. She feels bitterness towards her, and she feels pity too, and she becomes exhausted trying to balance her feelings. It's as if the woman is still around, even on a mild late summer's afternoon like this one: using the cover of the children's voices to come closer, to creep up on her, to listen to the thoughts in her head.

She can shut her eyes and clasp her hands to her head to shut her out, but it doesn't do: her visitor won't go. So she stands there, swaying on her feet – unsteady on the uneven paving stones, until she feels she's ready to swoon – and she knows she isn't alone. Her past is just a shadow's length behind her.

She spent long enough under that cursed roof, inside Satis House, to be able now to speak Catherine Havisham's words for her. Death might have stolen the breath from old Havisham's daughter, but he hadn't concluded her narrative.

'I only ever wanted to protect you, Estella mine, nothing else; I didn't wish anyone to harm you. *This* is love: forget hearts and flowers and billets-doux. Love proclaims truest in adversity.'

In after years the contents of Satis House were scattered about several counties, sold at auctions or already in the hands of pawnbrokers or debt-collectors.

Furniture and effects continued to change hands. They were displayed in shop windows, with coded price tags attached: an ebonised cabinet; a marquetry commode; a canteen of engraved cutlery.

Showy stuff, it was called. Little featured in the text books on Georgian style. It was considered second-generation, semi-arriviste taste of its time.

The objects may have been less inanimate, however, than on first appearance.

A sideboard door creaking open – the secret drawer in a writing desk shooting out – the chime of a fish-tailed cartel clock which had once been stopped at twenty minutes to nine – reflections moving across the back of a silver spoon – the rasp as the frame of misted mirror in a triptych tilted upwards.

They were restless, and some supposed that the objects were trying to summon back their grander past. To others, it was as if a ghostly spirit haunted them. To others still, the items might have been trying to pass on a lesson: that the former owners of these things had suffered for them, and had also loved and laughed, and here – in a window display, or at the back of an auctioneers' dusty sale-room – was the result.

In the branches of the tree, while the thrush sings its solitary song, Catherine Havisham has her final thought.

It all passes in the world, at least.

This is her summons to leave.

To fresh woods now, in Elysium.

The moment has come as it will, for her as for everyone, at its due time.

If I had a mantle blue, I would twitch it.

And so – away!

Acknowledgements

I owe an enormous debt of gratitude to the following:

To Adrian Searle, for restoring my faith in literary agents and being an all-round good egg.

To Lee Brackstone, for valiantly championing Catherine Havisham and bringing me back into the Faber fold.

To Mary Morris, for proving to be the most diligent and sympathetic (and polite) of editors, *and* – to my delight – a jazz bird to boot.

To everyone at Great Russell Street, for working so enthusiastically and so hard on my behalf.

To Matthew Bates, at Sayle Screen, for sticking by me, for his sage advice and cool-headedness.

Havisham was a drama, broadcast on BBC Radio 3.

Chambers Concise Dictionary provided information on the name 'Estella'.

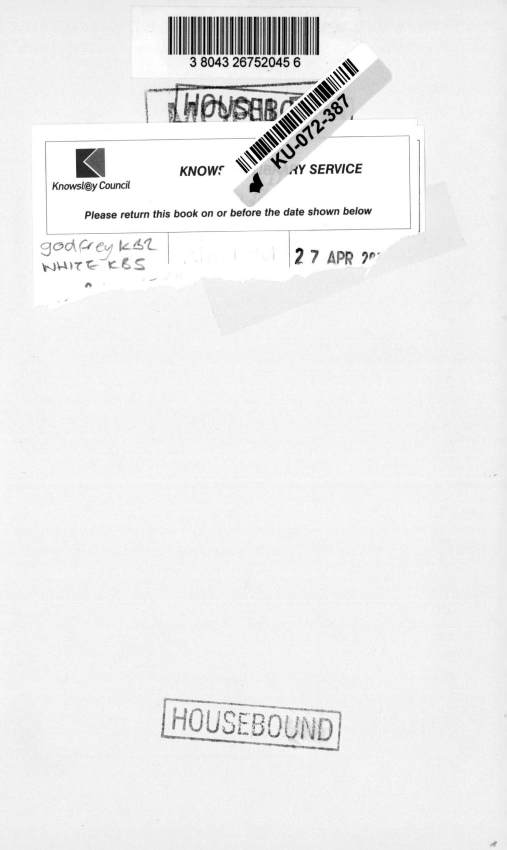

SPECIAL MESSAGE TO READERS

This book is published under the auspices of

THE ULVERSCROFT FOUNDATION

(registered charity No. 264873 UK)

Established in 1972 to provide funds for research, diagnosis and treatment of eye diseases. Examples of contributions made are: —

A Children's Assessment Unit at Moorfield's Hospital, London.

•

Twin operating theatres at the Western Ophthalmic Hospital, London.

•

A Chair of Ophthalmology at the Royal Australian College of Ophthalmologists.

•

The Ulverscroft Children's Eye Unit at the Great Ormond Street Hospital For Sick Children, London.

You can help further the work of the Foundation by making a donation or leaving a legacy. Every contribution, no matter how small, is received with gratitude. Please write for details to:

THE ULVERSCROFT FOUNDATION,
The Green, Bradgate Road, Anstey,
Leicester LE7 7FU, England.
Telephone: (0116) 236 4325

In Australia write to:
THE ULVERSCROFT FOUNDATION,
c/o The Royal Australian and New Zealand College of Ophthalmologists,
94-98 Chalmers Street, Surry Hills,
N.S.W. 2010, Australia

Robert Goddard was born in Hampshire, where he and his wife now live. He read history at Peterhouse, Cambridge and worked as an educational administrator in Devon before becoming a full-time writer. Other titles by the same author include: *Take No Farewell, Hand in Glove, Closed Circle* and *Into the Blue* (winner of the 1992 WH Smith Thumping Good Read Award and dramatized for TV in 1997, starring John Thaw)

PLAY TO THE END

When actor Toby Flood arrives in Brighton whilst on tour with a Joe Orton play, he is visited by his estranged wife, Jenny, now living with wealthy entrepreneur Roger Colborn. Jenny is worried about a strange man who has taken to hanging around outside her shop in the Lanes. Roger has dismissed her concerns and she hopes instead that Toby will be willing to get to the bottom of the man's behaviour. Next day, Toby confronts the man. Derek Oswin blames Colborn for his father's death from cancer, on account of dangerous practices at the defunct plastics factory run by Roger and his late father. Before he fully understands the risks he is running, Flood finds himself entangled in the mysterious — and dangerous — relationship between the Oswins and the Colborns . . .

Books by Robert Goddard
Published by The House of Ulverscroft:

IN PALE BATTALIONS
TAKE NO FAREWELL
HAND IN GLOVE
CLOSED CIRCLE
BORROWED TIME
OUT OF THE SUN
BEYOND RECALL
SET IN STONE
SEA CHANGE
DYING TO TELL
PAST CARING
DAYS WITHOUT NUMBER
SIGHT UNSEEN

ROBERT GODDARD

PLAY TO THE END

Complete and Unabridged

CHARNWOOD
Leicester

First published in Great Britain in 2004 by
Bantam Press, a division of
Transworld Publishers
London

First Charnwood Edition
published 2006
by arrangement with
Transworld Publishers, a division of
The Random House Group Limited
London

The moral right of the author has been asserted

All characters in this book are fictitious and any resemblance to actual persons, living or dead, is purely coincidental.

British Library CIP Data

Goddard, Robert
Play to the end.—Large print ed.—
Charnwood library series
1. Suspense fiction
2. Large type books
I. Title
823.9′14 [F]

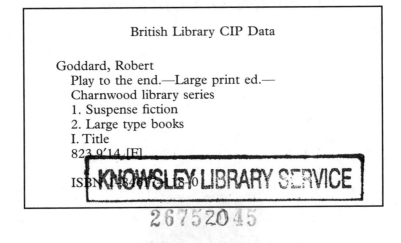

ISBN 1–84[illegible]–0

Published by
F. A. Thorpe (Publishing)
Anstey, Leicestershire

Set by Words & Graphics Ltd.
Anstey, Leicestershire
Printed and bound in Great Britain by
T. J. International Ltd., Padstow, Cornwall

This book is printed on acid-free paper

For
Marcus Palliser
1949–2002
Sailor, writer, debater, debunker
and much missed friend

A transcription of tape recordings made in Brighton during the first week of December 2002

SUNDAY

What I felt as I got off the train this afternoon wasn't what I'd expected to feel. The journey had been as grim and tardy as I suppose it was bound to be on a December Sunday. Most of the others have chosen to go via London and they won't be coming down here until tomorrow. I could have joined them. Instead I volunteered for the slow South Central shuffle along the coast. I had plenty of opportunity to analyse my state of mind as a seamless succession of drab back gardens drifted past the grimy train window. I knew why I hadn't gone up to London, of course. I knew exactly why bright lights and brash company weren't what the doctor had ordered. The truth is that if I *had* fled to the big city, I might never have made it to Brighton at all. I might have opted out of the last week of this ever more desperate tour and let Gauntlett sue me if he could be bothered to. So, I came the only way I could be sure would get me here. Which it did. Late, cold and depressed. But *here*. And then, as I stepped out onto the platform . . .

⋆ ⋆ ⋆

That feeling is why I'm talking into this machine. I can't quite describe it. Not foreboding, exactly.

Not excitement. Not even anticipation. Something slipping between all three. I suppose. A thrill; a shiver; a prickling of the hairs on the back of the neck; a ghost tiptoeing across my grave. There wasn't supposed to be anything but a protraction of a big disappointment waiting for me in Brighton. But already, before I'd even cleared the ticket barrier, I sensed strongly enough for certainty that there was more than that preparing a welcome for me. More that might be better or worse, but, either way, was preferable.

I didn't trust the sensation, of course. Why would I? I do now, though. Because it's already started to happen. Maybe I should have realized sooner that the tour was a journey. And this is journey's end.

The tapes were my agent's idea. Well, a diary was what she actually suggested, back in those bright summer days when this donkey of a play looked like a stallion that could run and run and the mere prospect merited a lunch at the River Café. A chronicle of how actors refine their roles and discover the deeper profundities of a script before they reach the West End is what Moira had in mind. She reckoned there might be a newspaper serialization in it to supplement the two thou a week Gauntlett is ever more reluctantly paying me. It sounded good. (A lot of what Moira says does.) I bought this pocket audio doodah on the strength of it, while the Cloudy Bay was still swirling around my thought processes. I'm glad I did now.

But it's more or less the first time I have been.

I abandoned the diary before I'd even started it, up in Guildford, where the Yvonne Arnaud Theatre hosted the world première of our proud production. Is it only nine weeks ago? It feels more like nine months, the span of a difficult pregnancy, with a stillbirth the foregone conclusion since we had word from Gauntlett that there was to be no West End transfer. I thank God for the panto season, without which he might have been tempted to keep us on the road in the hopes of some magical improvement. As it is, the curtain comes down next Saturday and seems likely to stay there.

It shouldn't have turned out this way. When it was announced last year that a previously unknown play by the late and lauded Joe Orton had been discovered, it was widely assumed to be a masterpiece on no other basis than its authorship. What greater proof was needed, after all? This was the man who gave us *Entertaining Mr Sloane, Loot* and *What the Butler Saw*. This was also the man who sealed his reputation as an anarchic genius by dying young, murdered by his lover, Kenneth Halliwell, at their flat in Islington in August 1967. I have all the facts of his extraordinary life at my fingertips thanks to carting his biography and an edition of his diaries around with me. I thought they might inspire me. I thought lots of things. None of them have quite worked out.

The script of *Lodger in the Throat* was found by a plumber under some floorboards in the flat where Orton and Halliwell used to live. I imagine Orton would have been amused by the circumstances of its discovery. Maybe he actually planted it there as a joke. Or maybe — my preferred theory — Halliwell hid it during the final phase of his mental disintegration, not long before he bashed Orton's brains out with a hammer and then killed himself by swallowing a fatal quantity of Nembutal tablets. The Orton experts date the play to the winter of 1965/66 and reason he gave up on it when *Loot* was revived after a disastrous initial tour. Now I come to think about it, that tour bore eerie similarities to the experiences of the cast I've been trying to lead this autumn. *Loot* worked second time around, of course, because Orton was alive and well and willing to revise it. The irony is that he's not available to salvage *Lodger in the Throat*, the play he consigned to a bottom drawer (or maybe the floor-space) in order to return to *Loot*. We're on our own. And, boy, does it feel like it.

Enough about the play. We've analysed its potential and its problems, my fellow performers and I, till we're sick of the subject. Sick *and* tired. It was supposed to put my career back on the rails, or at any rate haul it out of the siding into which it was unaccountably shunted a few years ago. I'm the man who was in with a chance of being the new James Bond when Roger Moore packed it in, something I now find hard to believe, even though I know it's true. What's also true is that you don't realize you've stopped going up until you start going down.

There are plenty of signs if you're smart enough to spot them, of course, or if you're willing to let yourself spot them. My name tops the bill, but Martin Donohue, who plays the part of my younger brother, has somehow managed to emerge from our dismal run with enough credit to make my primacy look shaky if we were ever cast together again — which, naturally, I'd move heaven and earth to prevent. Time was when Mandy Pringle, our ambitious deputy stage manager, would have set her sights on me, not Donohue. But that time is past. Not long past, but past none the less. Maybe they're looking forward to a week in Brighton. What they certainly won't be thinking is that I'm looking forward to our week in Sussex-by-the-sea. But I am. At least, I am now.

* * *

It rained all last night in Poole and was still raining when I got on the train this morning. Brighton must have caught the deluge too, but it was dry when I left the station and trudged south along Queen's Road through the mild grey dusk towards the darker grey slab of the sea. I'd already written off my weird presentiment. I'd accepted the exact and unappetizing character of the next six days. And the idea of making any kind of a record of them was about as remote as it could be.

I turned east along Church Street, a fair enough route to take to my destination, but one that also permitted a detour along New Road, past the familiar period frontage of the Theatre Royal. This will be my fourth professional engagement on its antique boards and I'd happily swap any one of the others for the eight renderings of *Lodger in the Throat* that the near future holds.

I stopped and examined the poster, wondering whether I'd visibly aged since the photograph was taken three months ago. It was hard to tell, not least because I haven't been taking any lingering looks at myself in the mirror lately. But it was me all right. And there was my name, listed with the others, to prove it. *Leo S. Gauntlett presents Lodger in the Throat, by Joe Orton, starring Toby Flood, Jocasta Haysman, Martin Donohue, Elsa Houghton and Frederick Durrance, Monday 2 to Saturday 7 December. Evenings at 7.45 p.m. Thursday and Saturday matinées at 2.30 p.m*. Part of me longed to see a CANCELLED sticker across the poster, but it wasn't there and it isn't going to be. We're on. There's no way out. Until the end of the week.

I didn't linger, cutting round by the Royal Pavilion to the Old Steine, then heading east along St James's Street. The Sea Air Hotel is neither the chicest nor the cheapest B & B establishment in Madeira Place, one of the guesthouse-filled streets running down to Marine Parade, but Eunice is as actor-friendly a landlady as they come, willing to suspend her winter closure just for me. As the tour's gone from bad to worse and the play's immediate future has shrunk, I've started economizing on accommodation in order to have some dosh to show for my efforts even if kudos is out of the question. I'd probably have opted to stay with

Eunice anyway, but just now the Sea Air has a number of crucial advantages apart from the tariff, principal among them being the fact that none of the others will be staying here. I have Eunice's word on it. 'I couldn't cope with a party, Toby. All that coming and going. All that bathwater. I reckon you'll do for me.'

I've only ever been here out of season, to share the dining room with the ghosts of summer holidaymakers. It's a peaceful house, thanks to Eunice's serene temperament and aversion to noise of all kinds. Even Binky, her cat, has learned not to purr loudly. Eunice is *Mrs* Rowlandson, complete with wedding and engagement rings, but Mr Rowlandson is a subject never touched upon, sometime existence presumed but fate unspecified. It's true to say, mind you, that Eunice might not be able to discard the rings even if she wanted to. A thin woman she is not. And less thin than ever. An aroma of baking wafted up from her basement flat as she ushered me into the speckless, flock-papered hall and up the Axminster-carpeted stairs to the first-floor front bedroom, furnished like an Art Deco museum and with a bay-windowed view of its shabby twin on the other side of the street.

'Do you want some tea?' Eunice asked, watching me from the doorway as I dumped my bag and returned the room's silent welcome.

'That'd be great,' I replied.

'And some cake? You look as if you need building up.'

She was right there. She was indeed spot-on. I smiled. 'Cake would be great too. Oh, and do you have yesterday's *Argus*, Eunice?'

'I dare say I could put my hand on it. You'll not find much in it to interest you, though.'

'I only want the cinema schedules. I thought I might catch a film tonight.'

'Mmm.' She looked seriously doubtful.

'What's wrong?'

'I wouldn't make any definite plans if I were you.'

'Why not?'

'There was a phone call for you earlier.'

I was puzzled by that. Those who knew where I was staying were more likely to have rung me on my mobile. 'Who from?' I asked at once.

'Your wife.'

'My *wife*?'

The puzzle instantly became a mystery. Jenny and I *are* technically still married, but only because the decree nisi is a month or so short of becoming absolute. Given that her husband-to-be's country estate (well, that's what Wickhurst Manor sounds like to me) is only a few miles north of Brighton, I'd caught myself wondering on the train whether Jenny was thinking of coming along to one of the performances. I'd reckoned not. She'd keep her distance. She'd put my presence in the city out of her mind. But it seemed she hadn't.

'Jenny phoned here?'

'Yes.' Eunice nodded. 'She wants to see you, Toby.'

* * *

It's time to own up. It's time to say what I've long since known. I love my wife. My soon-to-be-ex-wife, that is. I always have. I just haven't always acknowledged the fact, or behaved accordingly. Actors' marriages are notoriously unstable, like actors themselves, I suppose. We sometimes forget where the part ends and we begin. Sometimes, in the absence of a part, we invent one. Usually, because we perform rather than create, it's a character from stock: the hard-drinking, fast-driving womanizer, forever on a spree of one kind or another. It's easier to keep a mask in place for fear of what peeling it off would reveal.

That's only one of the problems between Jenny and me. And, ironically, it's a problem the last few years have abundantly solved. I know myself now, perhaps too well. But self-knowledge has come a little late. You're not supposed to wait until the brink of your half-century to understand the workings of your own mind. Better than never at all, I suppose, although some might disagree.

We'd still have made it, I reckon, despite the infidelities and indiscretions, the lost weekends and broken promises, but for something else neither of us could have anticipated. To have a son. And then to lose him. There. I've said that too. His name was Peter. He was born. He lived for four and a half years. And then he died. Drowned in the oversized swimming pool that went with the oversized house that went with the lifestyle we thought we were supposed to enjoy.

We blamed each other. We were right to. But

the blame should have been shared, not contested. You can't alter the past. And maybe you can't alter the future either. But you can wreck the present. Oh yes. You can lay that thoroughly to waste.

When Jenny left me, I told myself it was for the best. Platitudes like 'Time for us both to move on' fell regularly from my lips. I think I may even have believed them. For a while.

Not any more, though. I should never have let her go. I should have done things differently. Very differently. Hindsight is the sharpest sight of all. It lays bare the truth.

And the bleak truth is that there's nothing I can do to repair the damage I've done. There's no way back. At least, that's what I would have said. Until tonight.

* * *

Jenny had left a mobile number with Eunice. When I rang it, she answered instantly. And all I could manage by way of greeting was, 'It's me.'

'I expect you were surprised to hear from me,' she said after a long pause.

'You could say that, yes.'

'Can we meet?'

'When have I ever objected to the idea?'

I heard her sigh before she answered. 'Can we?'

'Yes. Of course.'

'This evening?'

'All right.'

'You're not busy?'

'What do you think?'

Another sigh. 'There's no point to this if you're going to be — '

'I'll be whatever you need me to be, Jenny. OK?' I could, perhaps I should, have asked why she wanted to see me. But I didn't dare to. 'Where and when?'

* * *

The Palace Pier at six o'clock was about as quiet as it ever gets. Most of the bars and attractions were closed, although the Palace of Fun was open for the benefit of anyone determined to pump money into its fruit machines. The sea sucked sluggishly at the beach below, while a couple speaking what sounded like Hungarian huddled in one of the shelters, sharing a bag of chips. All in all, the venue struck me as improbably distant from Jenny's natural habitat.

Then, as I reached the end of the pier, where the helter-skelter and merry-go-rounds were shrouded in wintry darkness, another thought struck me. Perhaps Jenny had chosen to meet me there just because of the shortage of witnesses, especially witnesses likely to know her. She didn't want to be seen with me. That was the point. The pier was somewhere she could be confident of a very private word.

She was leaning against the railings halfway back along the other side, dressed in a long dark coat and boots, gazing vacantly down at the beach, her face obscured by the brim of a fur-trimmed hat. If I hadn't been looking out for her, I might not even have noticed her. Though she, presumably, would have noticed me.

'Great night for a promenade,' I said stupidly as I approached. 'How about a barbecue later?'

'Hello, Toby.' She turned and looked at me, a tight half-smile flicking across her face. 'Thanks for coming.'

'You look well.' (This was something of an understatement. Separation from me had evidently agreed with her. Either that or she's found a good beautician in Brighton. I prefer to believe the latter.)

'Shall we sit down?' she asked.

'If we can find a seat.' This didn't raise even half a smile.

The bench in the nearest shelter was dappled with droplets of rainwater, shimmering in the lamplight. I thought I caught a few words of Hungarian drifting over from the other side of the structure as I brushed some of the water away. We sat down.

'The chippy's open,' I said, nodding over my shoulder towards the kiosk I'd passed earlier. 'Fancy sharing fifty penn'orth?'

'No, thank you.'

'When was the last time we shared a bag of chips on a draughty sea front, would you say?'

'Have we ever?'

This wasn't going well. Jenny didn't seem remotely pleased to see me. Which was odd, since we were meeting at her request.

'How's the play going?' she asked suddenly.

'Do you really want to know?'

'I read about Jimmy Maidment.'

Well, that was no surprise. The apparent suicide of a famous comic actor, albeit one not as famous as he once was, makes plenty of headlines. Throwing himself under a Tube train the day before he was due to open in *Lodger in the Throat* may have been Jimmy's characteristically pithy way of telling the rest of the cast that he doubted the play would resurrect his career, or anyone else's. Alternatively, maybe he was just drunk and missed his footing. The coroner will say his piece in due course. Either way, though, it wasn't a good omen. I miss him. And so does the play.

'It must have been a shock,' said Jenny. 'Was he depressed?'

'Perpetually, I expect.'

'The reviewers seem to think . . . '

'That we're lost without him. I know. And it's true. Fred Durrance isn't in Jimmy's class. But that's not the only problem. And I'm sure you didn't suggest meeting so we could analyse where it's all gone wrong, so — '

'Sorry,' she interrupted, her voice softening.

A brief silence fell. The sea hissed soothingly beneath the pier. 'Me too,' I murmured.

'Will it go to London?' she asked.

'Not a chance.'

'So, this is the end.'

'Apparently.'

'I *am* sorry, you know.'

'Sorry enough to have me back?' I smiled thinly at her in the lamplight. 'Just joking.'

'I'm very happy with Roger,' she said, apparently assuming I doubted it, which actually

I didn't. 'We've set a date for the wedding.'

'Pity I left my diary at the Sea Air.'

Jenny sighed. I was trying her patience, an art I unintentionally perfected a long time ago. 'Let's walk,' she said, rising before the words were properly out, and striding off towards the shore, boot heels clacking on the planks of the pier.

'Where are we going?' I asked as I fell in beside her.

'Nowhere,' she replied. 'We're just walking.'

'Look, Jenny, can I just say . . . I'm glad you're happy. Strange as it may seem, I've always hoped you would be. If there's anything I can — '

'There is.' Her voice was firm but far from hostile. That's when I guessed what was really making her so edgy. She had a favour to ask of me. Since the last favour she'd asked of me was to get out of her life and stay out, it was, however you cut it, a delicate situation. 'Will you do something for me, Toby?'

'Gladly.'

'You haven't heard what it is yet.'

'You wouldn't ask me to do it if it wasn't the right thing to do.'

She might have smiled at that. I can't be sure. 'I have a problem.'

'Go on.'

But she didn't go on until we'd turned off the pier and started west along the promenade, the empty beach to our left, the thinly trafficked sea front to our right. A full minute of silence must in fact have passed before she started to explain, which she did with the bewildering question,

'Have I told you about Brimmers?'

'No,' was the best answer I could give, sensing this wasn't the time to point out that she hadn't told me anything at all in a good long while.

'It's a hat shop I own in the Lanes. I've really enjoyed making a go of it. It's quite successful, actually.'

'You always wanted your own business.'

'Yes. And now I've got it.'

'That's great.'

'Roger's fine about it.'

'Good. And what line of business is Roger in?'

'Corporate investment.' I was still puzzling over what precisely that meant when she briskly continued: 'Look, this has nothing to do with Roger. The thing is, some weird bloke's been hanging around the shop. There's a café opposite where he sits in the window, sipping endless cups of tea and staring across at Brimmers. I find him standing around outside when I open or close up. I've seen him out at Wickhurst too. There's a footpath that runs close to the house. I can't walk along it without bumping into him.'

'Who is he?'

'I don't know.'

'Haven't you asked him?'

'I've spoken to him a couple of times, but he doesn't respond. He answers 'Can I help you?' with 'No', then stares some more and wanders off. He's beginning to prey on my nerves. I think he's harmless, but he just won't go away.'

'Have you spoken to the police?'

'To complain of what? A man patronizing a café and walking along a public footpath? They'd think *I* was persecuting *him*.'

'Is he persecuting you?'

'It feels like it.'

'Sure you don't know him?'

'Positive.'

'What's he like?'

'Creepy.'

'You can do better than that.'

'All right. He's . . . middle-aged, I suppose, but a bit childlike at the same time. There's something of the overgrown schoolboy about him. The nerdy, socially dysfunctional kind of schoolboy. Wears a duffel-coat, with all sorts of . . . badges on it.'

'Obviously dangerous, then.'

'If you're not going to take this seriously . . . ' She tossed her head in a well-remembered gesture.

'What does Roger say?'

'I haven't told him.' It was an admission she seemed reluctant to make, even though she must have known she'd have to.

'Really?'

'Yes. Really.'

I can confess now to deriving some small but twisted pleasure from the discovery that Jenny had a secret from her affluent and no doubt handsome fiancé — and was sharing it with me. The pleasure distracted me to some degree from the mystery. Why hadn't she told Roger? She supplied an answer swiftly enough.

'Roger travels a lot on business. I don't want him worrying about me or staying home on my account.'

But it didn't ring true. Jenny should have known better than to feed me such a line. I know her too well. Whatever she said, I had Roger down as the protective, not to say possessive, type. Her real concern is that her independence is at stake if she asks the new man in her life to save her from the stalking nerd of the Lanes. And Jenny values her independence. Very highly.

'Besides,' she added, 'what could he do?'

Several possibilities sprang to mind, but I didn't put the more extreme of them into words. After all, by the same token, what could *I* do? 'He might recognize the bloke.'

'He doesn't.'

'How can you be sure?'

'We were together when chummy walked past us recently. On the footpath I mentioned. I asked Roger if he knew him. He said no. Definitely not.'

'But you didn't explain the significance of the question.'

'Obviously I didn't. Besides . . . '

'What?'

'I think I might know what chummy's connection with me is. And it isn't Roger.'

'What, then?'

'You mean *who*.'

'OK, who?'

'You, Toby.'

'What?'

We both stopped and turned to look at each other. I couldn't make out Jenny's expression clearly in the shadow of her hat. But I dare say she could read me like a book. She's always been able to. And what she must have read was disbelief.

'Me?'

'That's right.'

'But it can't be. I mean . . . that doesn't make sense.'

'Nevertheless . . .'

'How can you be sure?'

'I just am.'

'OK.' I relented. 'What made you think it?'

Jenny glanced over her shoulder. She'd noticed before I had that a group of youngsters was approaching. With a touch on my arm, she steered me to the side of the promenade. The precaution turned out to be unnecessary, because the youngsters promptly dashed across the road towards the Odeon Cinema. But still she lowered her voice as she spoke. 'Sophie, my assistant at Brimmers, often goes to the café where chummy hangs about. She's noticed him too. Well, last week, she spotted a video he'd bought lying by his elbow. He'd taken it out of the bag to look at. Guess what it was.'

I turned the puzzle over in my mind for a moment, my gaze drifting towards the carcass of the West Pier, a hump of black against the blue-black sky. '*Dead Against*,' I murmured.

'How did you know?' Jenny sounded genuinely surprised. *Dead Against* was the last of my all too few Hollywood engagements, released to vinegary reviews and absentee audiences all of eleven years ago. A sub-Hitchcockian thriller in which I play an English private detective pursuing a glamorous hit-woman in Los Angeles,

Dead Against turned out aptly to have nothing going for it. My co-star, however, Nina Bronsky, has gone on to better things, which is why, according to Moira, some of her earlier films are suddenly making it to the video-store shelves. Perhaps a royalties cheque eighteen months from now will quell my resentment. Then again, perhaps not.

'There aren't that many videos out there in any way connected with me, Jenny. *Dead Against* it had to be. But it could mean nothing. Maybe chummy's a Nina Bronsky fan. He sounds her type.'

'Be serious, Toby. Please. I'm worried about this man.'

'Well, if he's a fan of mine . . . ' I shrugged. 'I guess that makes me in some way responsible for him.'

'I'm not blaming you, for God's sake. I just want this weirdo off my back.'

'How can I accomplish that for you?'

'Go to the café tomorrow morning. See if you recognize him. Or if *he* recognizes *you*.'

'I haven't changed that much in eleven years. He *should* recognize me.'

'Then speak to him. Find out who he is; what he wants. See if you can't . . . '

'Get rid of him?'

'All I want him to do is lay off, Toby.'

'Plus tell me why he's on your case. *If* he's on your case.'

'It's something to do with you. It must be. The video proves that. He's found out we used to be married and — '

'We still are, actually. Married, I mean.'

Jenny addressed the quibble with a seaward glance and a brief silence. Then she said, 'Will you do it?'

'Of course.' I smiled. 'Anything for you, Jenny.'

I meant it. I still do. But there's more to it than that, as I suspect Jenny's well aware. The video alone proves nothing. If our duffel-coated friend is interested in me, he could also be interested in Roger. Jenny says she doesn't want to worry Roger. But maybe she doesn't quite *trust* Roger. Maybe she wants to find out on her own terms what this is really all about — if it's about anything beyond the daily habits of a millinery fetishist. And maybe she knows she can rely on me to dig out the truth, because I still love her and haven't given up hope of making *her* love *me* all over again. She's playing a dangerous game, my once and future Jenny.

'What time should I show up?' I asked.

'He'll be there by ten. Without fail.'

'I'd better get an early night.'

'Don't come to the shop. Don't let him think I've sent you.'

'I'll do my best. Ad libbing's always been my forte.'

'Thanks, Toby.' There was genuine relief in her voice and maybe fondness too, although there I admit I could be kidding myself. 'I'm more grateful than I can say.'

'Shall I phone you . . . afterwards?'

'Yes, please.'

'But you'd rather I didn't pop round to report?'

'It's not that. I . . . '

'Perhaps Roger wouldn't be pleased. If he got to hear about it.'

'This has nothing to do with Roger.'

Jenny brushed a strand of hair back beneath the brim of her hat, exploiting the action to avoid my gaze. 'As it happens,' she said, 'Roger's away on business at the moment.'

'Is that so?'

'Yes,' she replied coolly.

'So, this is just between us.'

'I'd like to keep it that way.'

'I understand.' So I did. And so I do. We have an understanding all right. But it depends on not being made explicit. Neither of us is being entirely honest.

'I'd better be going,' said Jenny, with a sudden conclusive motion of the head. 'I'm meeting friends for dinner.'

Jenny's always been good at making friends. I didn't realize how good until she left me, taking most of them with her.

'Goodnight, Toby.'

I watched her cross the road and head up West Street past the cinema. Then I started back along the promenade, towards the Palace Pier and the Sea Air beyond.

* * *

Eunice said I was looking cheerier when I got back than I had been earlier. She'd probably have said that whether it was true or not, harbouring as she does a romantic Burton and

Taylor vision of me and Jenny. But a glance in the hall mirror told me she was right. I saw reflected there what I haven't glimpsed so much as once during our long weeks on the road: a faintly optimistic sparkle in the eye.

* * *

After tackling Eunice's steak-and-kidney pud, I needed a walk. Time spent in reconnaissance being seldom wasted, as my old dad used to say, I made my way to the Lanes and prowled around, until, after several double-backs, I found Brimmers.

Jenny's good taste is pretty obvious just from the stylish window display and candy-stripe colour scheme. I couldn't see much of the interior and, if I'm to obey Jenny's orders, I'm not about to. But who knows? Not me. I'm just hoping.

The Rendezvous café was also closed, as you'd expect. The sign promises morning coffee, light lunches and afternoon teas. There's a counter at the rear, tables and chairs in the centre and a broad ledge along the glazed frontage, with stools, where customers can perch and watch the world of the Lanes go by as they sip their beverage of choice. You can easily keep Brimmers under observation from there, of course, though not without being observed yourself, which may or may not be the object of the exercise for my alleged fan. We'll see about that. Tomorrow, as promised.

Reconnaissance done. I ambled off to a pub I

generally end up in at some point during Brighton runs — the Cricketers in Black Lion Street, allegedly Graham Greene's favourite — and downed a reflective pint. Sunday in Brighton had already exceeded my expectations, which admittedly wasn't difficult, but little did I realize that it still had a surprise in store for me.

I was at a table in the corner of the bar not visible from the door, idly watching a middle-aged married man and a woman who clearly wasn't his wife getting slowly sloshed. Sunday night can induce more than its fair share of morbidity. It's my only free night of the week at present, so I should know. Tonight, however, I was feeling just fine.

That's probably why my heart didn't sink when a bloke sidled over from the bar, said, 'Mind if I join you?' and plonked himself down next to me.

He struck me at first sight as your typical garrulous pub bore. Short and stout, with moist blue eyes, veinous nose and cheeks, thin sandy-grey hair and a tongue that seemed too large for his mouth, he was dressed in a crested blazer that could surely never fasten round his paunch, off-white shirt and stained cavalry twills. In one hand he held a glass of red wine, in the other a flier advertising *Lodger in the Throat*.

'You're Toby Flood or I'm a Dutchman,' he announced.

'And you're not a Dutchman,' I replied.

'Can I buy you a drink?'

'I'm fine for the moment, thanks.'

'It's a relief to see you, to be honest.'

'A relief?'

'I've got a ticket for Tuesday night.' He held up the flier. 'So, it's good to know you've made it down. Syd Porteous. Pleased to meet you.' He extended a large, saveloy-fingered hand, which I had little choice but to shake.

'You a regular theatregoer, Syd?' I ventured.

'No, no. Leastways, I didn't used to be. But I've been trying to . . . broaden my horizons . . . since I've had more time on my hands.'

'Just retired, have you?'

'Not exactly. More . . . downsized. You've got to duck and dive in this town. Well, *city* they call it now. Nice for the councillors, that, but bugger all use to those of us who keep them in expenses. Anyway, I can't claim to have been to the theatre' (or thee-eight-er, as he pronounced it) 'more than the gee-gees this year, but maybe next, hey? It'll soon be New Year resolution time and I've turned over more new leaves than the average rabbit's eaten, so . . . '

The way he'd started gave me the impression I could be on the receiving end of a stream-of-consciousness monologue till last orders. I was just beginning, in fact, to devise an excuse to leave him to it when I became aware that there was a small, still point to the turning world of his rambling thoughts. And I was it.

'Any chance of a new series of *Long Odds*, Toby?' Syd suddenly asked. 'I used to be glued to that.'

Sad to say, Syd was in a small minority there. My 1987 TV series about a compulsive gambler who dabbles in private investigations on the side (or was it the other way round?) is about as likely to be revived as Empire Day. 'No chance, I'm afraid.'

'Don't seem to have seen you much on the box lately.'

'I'm concentrating on the theatre. Live performance is more challenging.'

'Yeah, well, there's that to it, I suppose. Your fans get to see you in the flesh.'

'Exactly.'

'This play must be getting you a lot of attention. I'm looking forward to it.'

'Good.'

'I met him, you know.'

'Who?'

'Orton.'

Against my better instincts, my curiosity was aroused. 'Really?'

'Oh yes.' Syd lowered his voice melodramatically 'Here. In Brighton. Just a couple of weeks before he died. Summer of 'sixty-seven.'

I'm familiar enough with the diaries Orton kept from December 1966 until his death in August 1967 for Syd's reference to have struck me as at least superficially authentic. Orton and Halliwell came to Brighton in late July, 1967, to spend a long weekend with Oscar Lewenstein, co-producer of *Loot*. Orton was bored out of his brain by the visit. I didn't recall a younger version of Sydney Porteous lurching onto the scene, however.

'How did you come to meet him?' I casually enquired. A public lavatory sprang to mind as the venue, given Orton's sexual habits, but Syd's answer was rather more disconcerting.

'Bumped into him in this very pub. A Sunday night, it was — like now. We chatted about nothing much. He didn't say who he was, though the name wouldn't have meant a thing to me if he had. I was an ignorant young shaver. Clocked his face in the papers a fortnight or so later, though. A bit of a shaker, that was. Looking back, I think he was trying to pick me up. Weird, isn't it?'

'What is, in particular?'

'Well, him and now you, in the Cricketers on a Sunday night. What would you call that if it isn't weird?'

'I'd call it coincidental.' (If it was true, which I rather doubted.) 'Faintly coincidental.'

'Even so, you want to be careful. I'm not the superstitious type myself, but you actors are supposed to be. The Scottish play. The Superman curse. All that sort of malarkey.'

'I'll try not to let it worry me.'

'Look, I'm an old Brighton hand. My ma had a bit part in *Brighton Rock*. And I'm in a crowd scene in *Oh What a Lovely War!* So, I almost feel like an honorary member of the acting profession. Anything I can do for you while you're here — anything at all — just say the word. I'll give you my mobile number.' He scrawled the number on a beer mat and thrust it into my palm. 'Not much I can't lay hands on or find out in this town. Know what I mean?' He winked.

Unsure whether I really wanted to know what he meant, I smiled weakly and pocketed the beer mat. 'I'll bear the offer in mind.'

'You do that, Toby.' He gave me a second, more exaggerated wink. 'I wouldn't like to think of you getting into trouble for the lack of a word to the wise.'

* * *

Shaking Syd off wasn't easy. He was all for 'going on somewhere'. I had to dredge up considerable reserves of charm to avoid offending him. Somehow, though, I doubt he takes offence easily. He can't afford to with his personality.

Back here at the Sea Air I've had the opportunity to check Orton's diaries for late July, 1967, which have raised more questions than they've answered. He and Halliwell arrived in Brighton on Thursday 27th and spent three days cooped up discontentedly at the Lewenstein house in Shoreham, leaving on Monday 31st. Just about the only time Orton was alone, oddly enough, was Sunday evening. He had gone with Halliwell and the Lewenstein family to see the new Bond film, *You Only Live Twice*, at the Odeon Cinema, but it was sold out. The others opted to see *In Like Flint* instead, but Orton preferred to cruise off in search of casual sex. He succeeded in getting himself sucked off by a dwarf in a public convenience. (Orton seems to have given the word 'convenience' a very liberal interpretation.) Then he had a cup of tea at the railway station and walked back to Shoreham.

No mention of the Cricketers, then, nor of

anyone who could be Sydney Porteous as an ignorant young shaver. Orton wasn't much of a pub-goer by his own and others' accounts. The incident doesn't ring true. Syd, I conclude, was spinning a yarn.

Or was he? No Orton scholar for sure and certain, how did he manage to get as many facts right as he did? As it happens, Sunday, 30 July 1967 was the only evening when he *could* have met the great and soon to be late Joe Orton in a Brighton boozer.

Besides, I can't deny that there's something slightly disturbing about Porteous's story. Orton's weekend by the sea wasn't wholly lacking in superstitious significance. His agent, the legendary Peggy Ramsay, had a house in Brighton. She met up with the party on Saturday night and they dropped by her place on the way out to dinner. There Orton made some characteristically scornful remarks about a horus she showed him — an Egyptian wood carving in the likeness of a bird, traditionally placed on graves to escort the souls of the departed to heaven. Peggy thought such disrespect was tempting fate. Sure enough — if you're that way inclined — Orton was dead within a couple of weeks.

I'm not, of course, that way inclined. At least. I try not to be. But Eunice brought yesterday's *Argus* up to me earlier, as I'd asked her to, and I see the Odeon is showing the latest Bond film. Just as it was in July 1967. I haven't been to see it. I might have done, if only to glare in envy at Pierce Brosnan. But circumstances conspired to prevent me. Just as they prevented Orton.

And now I find myself keeping a diary of sorts. Just like Orton.

* * *

Thinking, drinking and talking. I've done too much of all three. I should get that early night I promised myself. But my body clock's geared to the rest of the week, when I'll be up till the small hours. I can't seem to relax. I can stop talking, though. That at least is in my control. Besides, there really is nothing else to say. For now.

MONDAY

The alarm clock roused me at half past eight this morning, *hora incognita* as far as I've been concerned recently. Novelty did not lend enchantment to the experience. A squint through the window revealed a grey sky and a wind-driven burger carton bowling up the street. The man whose face I met in the shaving mirror didn't look to be at his best.

He still wasn't after breakfast and a walk down to the sea front. But I had a promise to keep. And it wasn't going to wait until my biorhythms were in synch. I headed for the Lanes.

* * *

It was gone ten by the time I reached the Rendezvous, but not long gone. I spotted chummy as I moved at a practised amble towards the door, but didn't look at him, any more than I glanced into Brimmers. A duffel-coated shape in the window seen from the corner of the eye was enough to justify the witheringly early start. Whether the proprietress of Brimmers was watching I didn't know, though I hoped Jenny would have the good sense to lie low. This was one show that didn't need an audience.

The Rendezvous was in a lull between workers looking for a caffeine fix and shoppers resting their feet. It aims for a Continental ambience, with lots of dark wood and sepia photographs of Third Republic Paris, but doesn't quite hit the mark, thanks to the bright and breezy staff and manifestly *un*Continental customers. Chummy was a case in point. The duffel-coat, jeans and desert boots were more Aldermaston March than Champs-Elysées. From where I parked myself with a double *espresso* and a complimentary *Indie*, I couldn't make out what the badges were, but there had to be at least half a dozen of them on his coat, dimly reflected in the window through which he was gazing across the lane towards Brimmers. He had a book open in front of him, but it wasn't getting much of his attention.

Nor was I, come to that, which called into question Jenny's contention that I was the key to his interest in her. It also raised the issue of how I should best approach him, an issue I hadn't really thought about beforehand. He didn't have the video of *Dead Against* with him and had displayed no interest whatsoever in my arrival on the premises. He hadn't so much as twitched a toggle in my direction.

My impression, based on a three-quarters profile view, was that Jenny had him about right. A middle-aged mummy's boy, whether his mummy was still around or not. There was an obviously home-knitted sweater visible beneath his coat. His hair was a pudding-basin mop of brown and grey. The glasses perched halfway down his nose were about fifteen years out of fashion. When he drank from his cup, he used both hands to raise it cautiously to his lips. He wouldn't have been out of place standing at the end of the platform, notebook in paw, as my train drew into Brighton station yesterday afternoon.

But stereotyping, as every actor knows, is a treacherous business, as miserable to experience as it can be misleading to apply. I needed to handle this sensitively. I followed up the *espresso* with a *latte* and cobbled together the least worst cover story I could contrive. Then I moseyed over to join him.

'Excuse me,' I said, 'are you local?'

'Yes,' he replied, turning his head slowly to look at me. 'I am.' He spoke as slowly as he moved, with a slight lisp. Recognition failed to flicker in his eyes.

'I'm a stranger to Brighton. I wonder if you could help me with some directions.'

'Maybe I could.'

The badges, I now realized, were actually painted enamel brooches, depicting characters from Hergé's Tintin books: Captain Haddock, Snowy, Professor Calculus, the Thomson twins and, naturally, the legendary quiffed one himself. 'I'm looking for the public library,' I pressed on. (Pretty lame, I know, but there it is.)

'It can be . . . difficult to find.' He smiled wanly. 'They moved it, you see.'

'Did they?'

'It's in New England Street.'

'Right. And that is . . . ' My gaze drifted down to the book he'd been reading, which ironically had the yellowed margins and cellophaned cover of a library book. Then I noticed the title at the top of the page. *The Orton Diaries*. I said nothing, though my eyes must have widened in surprise.

And at that moment — of all the hellishly inconvenient ones — my mobile rang. 'Someone's after you,' said chummy, as I wrestled it out of my pocket.

'Sorry,' I blurted out. 'Excuse me.' I had the blasted thing in my hand now. I turned and moved back to the table where I'd been sitting to answer. '*Yes?*' I snapped.

'Toby, it's Brian. Not too early for you, I hope.'

If Brian Sallis, our indefatigable company stage manager, had woken me from a well-deserved lie-in, I'd have felt less irritated than I did. What in God's name could he want? The question was swiftly, though to my mind far from adequately, answered.

'I just wanted to check you had a smooth journey yesterday.'

'I made it, yes.'

'Good.'

'Look, Brian — '

'You haven't forgotten our press call this afternoon, have you?' So that was really why he'd phoned: to ensure I wasn't likely to cop out of our meet-the-media session. 'Two thirty, at the theatre.'

'I'll be there.'

'With the technical to follow at four.'

Every Monday afternoon of the tour had been the same: press call at 2.30; technical rehearsal, to get the feel of a new stage, at 4.00. Brian could hardly have thought I'd forgotten the schedule. My state of mind was probably his more immediate concern and it was actually none too good, though for reasons he could have no inkling of. 'I'll be there,' I repeated. 'OK?'

'Splendid. I just — '

'I've got to go now.'

'You are all right, aren't you, Toby?'

'Fine. See you later. 'Bye.'

I ended the call before Brian had a chance to say his own goodbye and turned round to re-engage chummy.

But he wasn't there. His stool was empty, his coffee-cup drained and abandoned. Chummy, complete with *Orton Diaries* and Tintin badges, had vanished.

Cursing Brian Sallis, I grabbed my coat and rushed out. There was no sign of chummy, but in the narrow, dog-legging Lanes that was no surprise. Choice of direction boiled down to a fifty-fifty guess.

I looked in through the window of Brimmers as much in hope as apprehension. Jenny had either seen nothing, in which case she couldn't help me, or she'd spectated at a pretty comprehensive balls-up, in which case . . .

Elegantly trouser-suited and severely unsmiling, brow furrowed in the only gesture of exasperation she could allow herself with customers present, she stared out at me along a narrow line of sight through the windowful of hats. I grimaced. And she inclined her head to the right.

I turned left, hurried round the next corner and headed on, scanning the shops and side turnings as I went. No glimpse of duffel rewarded my efforts and within a few minutes I was out in North Street, amidst traffic and noise and bustling passers-by.

Then, incredibly, I saw him, pacing up and down at a crowded bus stop on the other side of the road. He pushed his glasses up to the bridge of his nose with a stab of his middle finger and squinted expectantly in the direction from which a bus would come. A gathering of bags and folding of buggies amongst his companions at the stop signalled its imminent arrival even as I watched. I glanced to my left and saw a double-decker bearing down on them.

The bus had stopped and was loading by the time I managed to dodge across the road. I saw chummy stepping aboard and, peering through the window, spotted his desert boots as he took the stairs to the top deck. 'Where's this bus going?' I asked the harassed mother ahead of me and relayed her answer to the driver when I made it to the front of the queue. 'Patcham, please.' But there turned out to be a flat fare of a pound. My destination was entirely up to me.

Actually, of course, it was up to chummy. I sat about halfway back downstairs and awaited his descent. The bus lumbered round by the Royal Pavilion, took on more passengers and headed north.

Ten minutes slow going took us up London Road to within sight of the Duke of York's Cinema. Several people got up as we approached a stop. Then the desert boots appeared round the corner of the stairs. Chummy was on the move. I rose discreetly behind a broad-backed youth and was last but one off the bus.

Chummy was walking north by then, towards the traffic lights at the junction ahead. I followed at what I judged to be a safe distance, lingering in a shop doorway as he reached the lights and waited for them to change, then hurrying after him as he crossed.

He was heading east now, along Viaduct Road, where heavy traffic roared past dingy Victorian terraces. He plodded along, head bowed, displaying not the slightest interest in his surroundings, nor any inclination to glance over his shoulder. It seemed to me that if he'd left the Rendezvous so abruptly because I'd aroused his suspicion, he should have been warier. I concluded that he'd more probably left because he was ready to; as simple as that — I was irrelevant.

I saw him dig a bunch of keys out of his pocket a few seconds before he stopped by the door of a house dingier even than most of its neighbours and let himself in. I heard the door clunk shut as I approached. I carried on walking, noting the number as I passed: 77. Then I stopped and doubled back at a slower pace for a second, more lingering look.

Number 77 was a standard two-up, two-down Victorian working-class dwelling, rendered in a shade of blue darkened by grime and neglect. Paint was peeling from the sash window frames. The front door was not original, being plain and unpanelled, but it wasn't in much better condition than the rest of the house.

I'd slowed nearly to a halt, my brain struggling with the problem of what to do next. I'd discovered where he lived. It was something. But it was a long way short of enough. Perhaps I should try the knocker, though if he answered I'd only have another problem to grapple with: how to explain myself.

Then the door suddenly opened. And chummy stared out at me. 'Do you want to come in, Mr Flood?' he asked.

'Well, I . . . '

'You may as well, seeing as you've come this far.'

There was logic in that. There was also a hint of menace. But that could merely have been a symptom of guilt on my part. I felt more than a little foolish. 'You know who I am?'

'Yes.'

'You have me at a disadvantage, in that case.'

'My name's Derek Oswin.' He pushed his glasses up on his nose again. 'Are you coming in?'

'All right. Thanks.'

I stepped past him into a cramped hallway. Steep, narrow stairs straight ahead led to the upper floor. To my right was a sitting room, with a kitchen at the end of the hall. The sitting room looked to be anciently furnished, but tidy. The condition of the exterior had prepared me for a scene of squalor, but what met my eyes was the complete reverse.

The front door closed behind me. 'Can I take

your coat?' Oswin asked.

'Er . . . Thanks.' I took it off and he hung it next to his duffel-coat on one of three wall-mounted hooks. The hall wallpaper was some kind of anaglypta, in a pattern I seemed vaguely to recognize. It's the sort of thing one of my great aunts would have chosen and very possibly did.

'Would you like a cup of tea?' Oswin enquired.

'OK. Thanks.'

'I'll turn the kettle on. Go through.' He flapped a hand towards the open door behind me. I turned and stepped into the sitting room while he padded off to the kitchen.

The room was small and spotlessly clean, dominated by a sage-green three-piece suite. There was a television and video player in one corner and a bookcase in another, either side of a tiny tile-flanked fireplace. The walls were papered in the same pattern of anaglypta as the hall. Derek Oswin's parents — or maybe his grandparents — had obviously decided to keep it simple.

'I'm afraid I've run out of biscuits,' my host announced, reappearing in the doorway.

'Don't worry about it.'

'I expect you're wondering . . . how I know who you are.'

'And why you pretended not to back at the Rendezvous.'

'Yes.' He grinned nervously. 'Quite.' Then the kettle began to whistle. 'Excuse me.'

He vanished again and I took another look around the room, spotting the video of *Dead*

Against lying on top of the bookcase. It turned out to be just the plastic cover, however. The video itself had been removed. The picture on the front of the cover showed Nina Bronsky in her black leather hit-woman's gear. I'd only been given a head-and-shoulders shot on the back.

'Here we are,' said Oswin, reappearing once more, this time with a teapot, two mugs and a bottle of milk on a tray. He set the tray down on the small coffee-table next to the sofa. 'I hope you don't want sugar. I . . . never touch it.'

'Just milk is fine.' I held up the video. 'One of my questions is answered.'

'Not really.'

'No?'

'I didn't need that to recognize you, Mr Flood. I remember you as Hereward the Wake.'

This was a genuine surprise. My TV début a quarter of a century ago in a studio-bound series about the legendary leader of resistance to the Norman Conquest is a vague memory even for me.

'I've always been a fan of yours.' Oswin broke off to pour the tea. 'Won't you sit down?' He lowered himself into an armchair. I took one end of the sofa and added some milk to my mug. It was a Charles and Di wedding souvenir mug, I noticed, as was Oswin's. 'I bought a dozen,' he explained, seeming to sense that he needed to. 'As an investment.'

'You shouldn't use them, in that case.'

'Don't worry. It was a very poor investment.'

I sipped some tea. 'What's this all about, Mr Oswin?'

'Call me Derek. Please.'

'OK. Derek. Why are you bothering my wife?' It seemed pointless now to pretend Jenny hadn't put me onto him. It seemed indeed that 'Derek' had foreseen everything that had happened.

'Are you two still married, then? I thought, with her living in Mr Colborn's house . . . '

'Our divorce hasn't been finalized yet,' I said through gritted teeth.

'Oh, I see.' Derek eyed me over the rim of his mug. 'That's interesting.' He pronounced 'interesting' as four distinct syllables. He was, I realized, a strange mixture of maladroitness and precision, insecurity and perceptiveness.

'Interesting in what sense, Derek?'

'I'm sorry about the . . . charade . . . earlier. I suppose I . . . enjoyed stringing you along. Besides, I thought we could . . . speak more freely here.'

'So, speak.'

'I didn't mean to worry' — he smiled — 'Mrs Flood.'

'She seems to feel you've gone out of your way to worry her.'

'I can see how she might think that. But it isn't true. I just couldn't come up with any other way of engineering a meeting with you.'

'You've been harassing her in the hope that I'd come and ask you to lay off?'

'Yes.' He grimaced sheepishly. 'I suppose I have. Sorry.'

I should have felt angrier than I did. But Oswin's meek air of vulnerability somehow drained all hostility out of me. Besides, I was perversely grateful to him for another meeting he'd engineered, albeit indirectly. 'That wasn't a very clever thing to do, Derek.'

'Not very nice, I admit. I really am sorry if I've worried Mrs Flood. But clever? Well, I think it *was* that, as a matter of fact. Because it worked, didn't it? As soon as the Theatre Royal announced you were coming, I knew I'd have to try and meet you. But how could I be sure you'd *agree* to meet me? That was the problem.'

'Your solution seems to have been pretty hit and miss to me.'

'True. But I have time on my hands, Mr Flood. Lots of it. So it was worth trying.'

'How did you know my wife owns Brimmers?'

'She gave an interview to the *Argus* when the shop opened. There was only one tiny reference to you. But I spotted it.'

I bet he did. Derek Oswin was some kind of nutter, that was clear. Eccentric, if you wanted to be generous. Obsessive and possibly manic, if you didn't. But was he dangerous? I sensed not. Still, the acid test was yet to come. 'Why were you so anxious to meet me, Derek?'

'Because I've always wanted to. Ever since you played Hereward. You're my hero, Mr Flood. I've seen everything you've ever done. Even *Lodger in the Throat*. I travelled up to Guildford for a matinée in its opening week.'

'What did you think of it?'

'Marvellous. Absolutely marvellous.'

'That's not been the general reaction, I'm afraid.'

'No, well, it wouldn't be, would it? Most

people are too stupid to get the point. The plot's wasted on them. They just laugh at the jokes.'

'If only they did.'

'Orton pretended to be crude and cruel, but actually he was sensitive and soft-hearted. I've been reading his *Diaries* and that's what I've come to understand. Look at the way he couldn't bring himself to abandon Halliwell, even when Halliwell started to become violent. He paid for that with his life.'

'I'm glad you enjoyed the play, Derek.'

'Oh, I did, Mr Flood, I did. You know, the set reminded me of . . . well, of this house.'

Glancing around, I saw what he meant. The set for *Lodger in the Throat* is the shabby sitting room of a small and neglected lower-middle-class family dwelling in an unnamed Midlands town. When the play opens, the three Elliott siblings, along with the wife of one of them, have gathered there following their mother's funeral. I play James Elliott, the oldest of the three. Jocasta Haysman is my wife, Fiona. Martin Donohue plays Tom, my resentful younger brother. And Elsa Houghton is our sister, Maureen. Mother's death, following Father's disappearance fifteen years previously, has freed us to sell the house and share the proceeds, which we're eager to do as soon as we can rid ourselves of Mother's disagreeable lodger and suspected lover, Stanley Kedge, the part Jimmy Maidment was ideal for but Fred Durrance somehow isn't. The property boom should have given this aspect of the plot added piquancy, but that's been lost along with a lot else during the tour. 'Actually,' I said, 'this is all far too spick-and-span to be mistaken for the set.'

'Thank you.'

'How long have you lived here?'

'All my life.'

'Your parents?'

'Both dead.'

'Any brothers or sisters?'

'No. I was an only child.'

'So, no resemblance to the Elliotts.'

'No. None at all.' He laughed — a soft, whinnying sound. 'I really like Orton's depiction of the family, though. And the way you play it. You think you can get shot of Kedge very easily, but then he starts to undermine you, one by one, to expose your guilty secrets. The state of your and Fiona's marriage. Tom's redundancy. Maureen's lesbianism. I was sorry, in a way, that Orton introduced so much farce into the plot rather than just letting Kedge pick you apart, a step at a time.'

'That would be more Chekhov than Orton.' I didn't care for the way Derek had referred to me in the second person when talking about James Elliott. The identification was — and is — a little too close for comfort. Still, I couldn't deny his analysis of the play was acute. After needling away at the Elliotts to no great effect, Kedge plays his decidedly un-Chekhovian trump halfway through the first act. Father did not just disappear fifteen years ago. Mother murdered him. '*Stuck him with the carving knife like an underdone Sunday joint*', as Kedge puts it. He shows them the bloodstains on the floorboards under the carpet and recounts how he buried the body in the garden. They can't sell now, can they, for fear that the new owner will discover the corpse and the police conclude that they knew all about it? But maybe they can, if they're desperate enough to take the risk. Except that at the end of the first act a Water Board official, Morrison, turns up to report that a leak in the locality has been traced to the stretch of main beneath their garden. It's going to have to be dug up. '*But don't worry*,' says Morrison. '*We'll put everything back as we found it*.'

'I saw you once in Chekhov,' said Derek. '*Uncle Vanya*. At Chichester.'

'You think I should play James Elliott as more of a tortured soul than a greedy prig?'

'Perhaps. I mean . . . none of you seem to miss your mother . . . or your father. There's no . . . love.'

'Do you miss your mother and father, Derek?'

'Oh yes.' He looked away. 'All the time.'

'Sorry. I didn't mean to — '

'It's all right.' He gave a crumpled smile. 'It's nice of you . . . to ask.'

'You'll have to blame Orton for the lack of love in the play.' And us for failing to draw any out, I reflected. At the beginning of the second act, James stumbles into the sitting room at dawn the following day and wakes Tom, who has spent the night there on a Z-bed. It suddenly occurred to me that I could delay waking him and look round the room at the pictures and ornaments, at all the reminders of our childhood, that I could, in a few telling moments, inject some real feeling — some love — into the part, before the farce resumes. Derek Oswin had somehow succeeded in making me want to improve my performance. Even though, by any logical analysis, it wasn't worth the effort.

'I suppose so. Although you could argue . . . that it ends on a loving note.'

'You could, yes.' Panic mounts among the Elliotts as the second act unfolds. It's Saturday and the Water Board are due in with their digger on Monday. There is an argument about whether to attempt to remove the body in the interim, assuming Kedge can be persuaded to reveal exactly where it's buried. But Kedge has an alternative to propose. He has a hold of some kind over Morrison — by implication, sexual. If the Elliotts let him stay on, he will ensure that the garden remains unexcavated. To this they reluctantly agree. Then, just as they're about to leave, an old man turns up, claiming to be a long-lost relative, as indeed he is — their father. His return from the supposed dead exposes Kedge's fraud, to which Morrison was party, and the tables seem utterly turned, until Father points out that the house is now his and he has no intention of selling, or evicting Kedge. They are, it seems, former lovers, free to admit as much and live together now Mother is no longer able to come between them.

'But Mr Durrance doesn't carry it off very well, does he?'

'No, Derek. He doesn't.'

'Was Mr Maidment better?'

'A lot.'

'I thought so.'

'He was one of the reasons I took the part.'

'And then he died.'

'Yes.'

'Which changed everything.'

'Well, death does, doesn't it?'

'You're thinking about your son?'

I stared at Derek in amazement. It was true. Peter had come into my mind, as he often does, peering uncertainly round the corner of a door my thoughts have nudged ajar. I should have realized Derek Oswin would know about him. But somehow I'd failed to.

'Now it's my turn to apologize.'

'No need.' I drained my mug. 'I must be going anyway.'

'You have a busy afternoon ahead of you.'

'Quite busy, yes.' I stood up. 'I'd like to be able to tell my wife you'll stop hanging around the shop.'

'I will. I promise. There'd be no point. Now we've met.'

'Thank you.'

'I hope the play goes well this week.'

'Are you coming to see it?'

'I wasn't . . . planning to. I haven't got a ticket.'

'I could get you one.'

'Well . . . that's very generous. Thank you.'

'What night would suit you best?'

Derek thought for a moment. 'Wednesday?'

'Wednesday it is. The ticket will be waiting for you at the box office.'

'OK. I'll look forward to that.' He rose and

extended his hand. 'It's been an honour meeting you, Mr Flood.' We shook.

'Next time, approach me direct.'

'Will there be a next time?'

'I don't see why not.' He wore such a look of puppy-dog eagerness that I added, before I could stop myself, 'You could join us after the show on Wednesday. We'll make up a little party and have a meal somewhere.'

'Are you serious?'

I smiled to reassure him. 'Yes.'

'Gosh. That really is generous. Thanks a lot.'

'Until Wednesday, then.'

'Until Wednesday. Meanwhile' — he grinned — 'I'll try out some other cafés.'

'You do that.'

'Apologize to Mrs Flood for me, will you?'

I nodded. 'I'll be sure to.'

* * *

For a man as thoroughly duped as I'd initially been by Derek Oswin, I felt surprisingly pleased with myself as I headed south down London Road. I'd solved Jenny's problem for her and reckoned I could capitalize on her gratitude. Roger Colborn's absence on unspecified business I counted as a distinct advantage. True, I hadn't turned up anything to his discredit, as I'd hoped I might, but there was still every reason to suppose I could manoeuvre Jenny into seeing me again. I cut through the Open Market to reach The Level, buying a juicy Cox's Orange Pippin on the way, which I munched sitting on a bench near the playground. Then I rang her.

'Hi.'

'Jenny, it's me.'

'I hope you've got better news than I think you have.'

'As a matter of fact, I have.'

'Really?'

'I've spoken to him, Jenny. His name's Derek Oswin. He's harmless. A bit weird, like you said, but basically OK. And he's going to stop bothering you. I have his word on that.'

'What's that worth?'

'You won't have any more trouble with him. You have my word as well as his.'

'Are you sure?'

'Positive.'

'Well . . . ' Her tone softened. 'Thanks, Toby. Thanks a lot.'

'My pleasure.'

'Derek Oswin, you say? I don't know the name.'

'You wouldn't.'

'Why's he been doing this?'

'It's a long story. Which I'd be happy to share with you. We could go into it over lunch.'

'Lunch?'

'Why not? You still eat, don't you?'

There was a lengthy pause. Then she said, 'I'm not sure meeting again is a good idea.'

'When does Roger get back from his business trip?'

'Tomorrow night. But — '

'Let's have lunch tomorrow, then. While you've time on your hands. I'd suggest today, but

I'm due to meet the press at two thirty and it would be a rush.'

'Oh God.' The tone of her voice suggested exasperation, but there was a faint, residual fondness thrumbling away beneath it. She wasn't going to turn me down. She didn't have the heart to. Besides, lunch was the least she owed me. 'I suppose . . . '

'Just an hour or so, Jenny. There's no hidden agenda. A friendly little lunch. That's all.'

She sighed. 'All right.'

'Great.'

'I'll pick you up from the Sea Air at twelve thirty.'

'I'll be waiting.'

'OK. I'll see you then. But, Toby — '

'Yes?'

'Don't try to make something of this, will you?'

'No,' I lied. 'Of course I won't.'

* * *

I snatched a pub lunch on my way to the theatre, but nobly refrained from alcohol. Upon arrival, I was looking, it seemed to me, a good deal brighter than either Jocasta or Fred, the other two cast members regularly wheeled out to meet the press. (I'd taken steps early in the tour to block Donohue appearing on such occasions.) It was the last time we'd have to do this, but no end-of-term jollity crept into our exchanges with the less than dynamic representatives of the local media whom Brian

Sallis shepherded into the auditorium.

Fred cracked his usual jokes. This he does more or less on autopilot, dreaming the while, no doubt, of a TV sitcom contract. Jocasta put on a brave face — and there are none braver — to describe what a pleasure it was to return to Brighton. I recall her saying much the same about Guildford, Plymouth, Bath, Malvern, Nottingham, Norwich, Sheffield, Newcastle and Poole. They were evidently both a little surprised when I embarked on an unprecedented consideration of whether the Elliotts' fractured relationships were a reflection of Orton's own family history. I have my doubts whether any of it will make it into print, but what the hell? Strangely, I felt it needed saying.

'Popped in to see your shrink yesterday, did you, Toby?' Fred enquired afterwards over a cup of tea. 'It's a bit late to come over all Freudian.'

'Just trying to ring the changes,' I replied.

'Ringing tills are the only thing that would have stopped Leo closing us down. And they didn't happen. So there's no point arty-farting round the script now.'

'I can't help myself,' I said with a shrug. 'I'm an artist.' To which Fred's only response was a peal of laughter.

* * *

While I was trading insults with Fred, a note was pressed into my hand. I didn't bother to read it until I popped into my dressing room to use the loo before the technical rehearsal got under way. The contents of the note were, to say the least, a surprise. *Please phone Jenny. Urgent*. I rang her straight away.

'Hi.' Even in that one minute monosyllable there was detectable tension.

'Jenny, it's me.'

'What in God's name are you playing at, Toby?'

'What do you mean?'

'You said you'd got . . . Oswin, or whatever he calls himself . . . off my back.'

'So I have.'

'No. You haven't. He's still there. Still monopolizing a stool at the Rendezvous and staring across at us. At *me*.'

'He can't be.'

'But he is. He's been there all afternoon.'

'That's impossible. He assured me — '

'He's *there*, Toby. Take my word for it. Like I took yours. For all the good it did me.'

For a moment, I was dumbstruck. What was Derek Oswin's game? In promising me that he'd leave Jenny alone, he'd sounded utterly sincere. And breaking his promise so swiftly was doubly perverse.

'What do I do now?' Jenny snapped.

'Leave it with me. I'll — '

'*Leave it with you?*'

'The technical starts in a quarter of an hour. I can't get away until after that. I'll go back to his house. Find out what the problem is.'

'I thought you already had.'

'Obviously not. But he won't pull the wool

over my eyes a second time. You can count on that.'

'Can I?'

'Yes, Jenny, you can.' I grimaced at myself in the mirror above the dressing table. 'I won't let you down.'

* * *

The technical rehearsal is a blurred memory. My thoughts were vainly devoted to unravelling Derek Oswin's devious motives. Staging practicalities suddenly counted for nothing. Martin Donohue made some crack about me having late improvements to suggest, Fred having presumably tipped him off about my comments to the press, but they were far from my mind. I had nothing whatsoever to suggest, except that we finish as soon as possible. And for that there was no lack of consensus. We were done in less than an hour.

I headed straight for the stage door afterwards, debating whether I should check the Rendezvous before trying Oswin's house. But the debate was resolved before it had properly begun. A letter had been left for me with the doorman during the rehearsal. 'By some bloke in a duffel-coat.' Oswin was still at least one step ahead of me.

I stepped out into Bond Street, tore the envelope open and read the note inside, written in ballpoint in a small, precise hand.

Dear Mr Flood,

I am sorry I misled you earlier. I did not

expect you to contact me so soon. I was not properly prepared. I did not tell you the whole truth. I think now I should. It concerns Mr Colborn. So, if you want to know what it is, meet me by the Hollingdean Road railway bridge at 8 o'clock this evening. I realize that is a very inconvenient time for you, but I think I must ask a small sacrifice of you as an earnest of your good intentions. I will be there. I hope you will be too. It would be best if you were. I will not give you another chance of learning what this is all about. And you will regret spurning that chance, believe me. I shall look forward to seeing you later.

Respectfully,
Derek Oswin

Yesterday afternoon, I knew nothing of Derek Oswin. This morning, I was still unaware of his name. Now, within six hours of our first meeting, he had me dangling on a string. I cursed him roundly under my breath as I walked through the crowds along North Street in the approximate direction of the Sea Air, wrestling in my mind with the conundrum of how to respond to his message.

He wouldn't be at the Rendezvous, of course, even if it was still open. He wouldn't be at home either. He'd make sure I had no chance of speaking to him until the time he'd chosen: 8 p.m. And to speak to him then, with curtain up at 7.45, I'd have to pull out of the evening's show. Such, in his own quaint phraseology, was the earnest of my good intentions he'd decided upon. Common sense said I should scorn his summons. Pride in my own professionalism rammed the point home. But there was the definite hint of a threat in his closing sentences. There'd be a penalty to pay for standing him up. That was certain. And only he knew what it was.

⋆ ⋆ ⋆

I didn't get as far as the Sea Air after all. I doubled back to Bond Street and skulked about on the opposite side from the stage door. When I'd left, Brian had been putting the understudies through their paces, but I didn't reckon that would take long. The last week of a Londonless run is no time for doing more than the minimum. Sure enough, I'd not been there above ten minutes when Denis Maple and Glenys Williams emerged into the lamplight.

I dashed across the road and caught up with them before they'd reached the corner. They looked understandably surprised to see me.

'Hello, Toby,' said Glenys. 'What's wrong?'

'Nothing,' I replied. 'Could we have a word, Denis?'

'Sure,' said Denis, frowning at me.

'I can take a hint,' said Glenys. 'See you both later.'

She beetled obligingly off, leaving Denis with the frown still fixed on his face. 'Shall we go back in?' he asked, nodding towards the stage door.

'No. What about a quick drink somewhere?'

'Do you think that's a good idea?'

'Oh yes.' In ordinary circumstances, drinking

so close to a performance would have been a very bad idea. But the circumstances weren't ordinary. Not by a long way. 'Definitely.'

⋆ ⋆ ⋆

I piloted a bemused Denis to a youth-oriented pub in the North Laine, where anonymity for a pair of middle-aged actors was virtually guaranteed. Denis is easing his way back into the theatre after heart trouble and I was well aware he didn't need the stress I was about to inflict on him. The least I could do was give him a chance to get used to the idea that tonight wasn't going to be quite like every other night on tour.

I ordered a scotch and persuaded him to join me, then we plonked ourselves down as far as possible — which wasn't very — from the nearest rock-blaring loudspeaker.

'Something on your mind, Toby?' Denis prompted.

'Yes.' I took a swallow of whisky and came straight to the point. 'You'll be playing James Elliott this evening.'

'What?'

'You'll be standing in for me, Denis.'

'What do you mean?'

'Just what I say. I won't be there.'

'But . . . there's nothing wrong with you.'

'I have to be somewhere else.' I would have lowered my voice as I ploughed on, but the wall of sound meant our conversation had to be conducted at a bellow. 'It can't be helped.'

'You're baling out?'

'Just for tonight. Normal service resumes tomorrow.'

'You're joking.'

'No. I'm serious, Denis. You're on.'

He stared at me for a moment, then said, 'Bloody hell,' and gulped down most of his whisky.

'Want another?'

'Better not, if I'm performing tonight.' He thought about the prospect, then added, 'On reflection, perhaps I better *had*,' and held out his glass.

By the time I'd fetched our refills, his shock had lessened enough for puzzlement to show through. 'Not like you to let the side down, Toby.'

'No choice.'

'Care to elaborate?'

'Can't.'

'Are you planning to phone in sick?'

'No. Brian would be round to the Sea Air quicker than you can pour a Lemsip. And I wouldn't be there. So, I wondered if . . . '

'You want *me* to tell them?'

'Would you?'

'Bloody hell.' Denis made a pained face. 'What am I supposed to say?'

'Exactly what's happened.'

'It won't go down well.'

'I imagine not.'

'Leo will get to hear.'

'Of course.'

'It'll be a black mark against you.'

'Not the first.'

'Even so . . . ' Denis worked with me on several episodes of *Long Odds*. We know each other well enough for much to be left unsaid. The consequences of my no-show were sure to be uncomfortable, but, given the severely limited future of *Lodger in the Throat*, no worse than that. A little local difficulty was all either of us had cause to anticipate. 'You do know what you're doing, don't you, Toby?'

'I think so. Besides . . . ' I smiled. 'You'll wow them, Denis.'

* * *

There was well over an hour to go till I was due to meet Derek Oswin when Denis and I parted. I walked down to the front and stared out to sea. I could still have changed my mind then. In fact, I *did* change my mind, several times, as I contemplated the fall-out from what I was about to do. Leo would play the heavy producer with a will. And I could hardly complain. Walking out on the show, albeit for one night only, was gross dereliction of an actor's duty. Part of me was appalled that I was even considering it.

But, in the final analysis, what did it really matter? They can say what they like. They can even dock my salary if they want to. The play's going nowhere. We all know that. Whereas my rendezvous with Derek Oswin . . .

I suddenly decided that maybe I didn't have to choose after all. I ran most of the way up to the taxi-rank in East Street and jumped breathlessly into a cab. We were in Viaduct Road ten minutes later. Telling the driver to wait, I dashed to the door of number 77 and hammered at it with the knocker.

No response, of course, and no light showing. That was as I'd expected, really, but it had been worth a try in case I caught Oswin on the premises. My guess was that he was already lying in wait for me at the meeting-place he'd nominated. I leapt back into the cab and named it as our next port of call.

⋆ ⋆ ⋆

Hollingdean Road is one of the limbs of the 'Vogue Gyratory', as the driver called the confused meeting-point of thoroughfares near the Sainsbury's superstore out on the Lewes Road. He stopped just short of the railway bridge, in the gateway of a used-car pound, where I told him to wait again. The cuboid roofline of a modern industrial estate loomed above me as I got out, next to the older brick ramparts of the bridge. You think Brighton is all pier and theatricals and in my game you don't have to question the thought, but Oswin was drawing me into a duller, grimmer Brighton altogether. I just had to hope I could draw myself out again in double quick time.

I hurried under the bridge, checking my watch as I went. It was gone seven now. The point of no return was approaching more rapidly than I'd allowed for. The road curved sharply right on the other side, while an access lane led straight on into a dimly lit sprawl of depots and factories.

Two stark blocks of flats reared above them to the west. I looked around. There was no sign of Oswin.

A minute passed. And part of another. Then I knew. Oswin wasn't going to show up early. I wasn't going to catch him out. The terms he'd set were all or nothing. I started back to the cab.

'Where now?' the driver asked, as I opened the door and slumped into the passenger seat.

I looked at my watch again. It was 7.05. I could still be at the theatre by 7.10, the latest acceptable arrival time for the cast, or at least very shortly after. It was what I should do, professionally, prudentially. It was crazy to let Oswin mess me around. I didn't need to. I simply wasn't willing to. And yet . . . '*I will not give you another chance of learning what this is all about.*'

'Back into the centre?' the driver prompted.

'Yes,' I answered in an undertone. 'Back into the centre.'

He pulled out into the road, then reversed into the gateway, preparatory to heading back the way we'd come. I thought of Jenny and the true nature of the chance Oswin might be offering me.

'No,' I said suddenly. 'I've changed my mind. I'm staying here.'

* * *

By 7.20, Denis must have broken the news. Jocasta and Elsa would probably be worried about me. Fred's reaction would veer more towards the sarcastic, Brian's the disbelievingly dumbstruck. But he *would* have to believe it. As for what Donohue might say . . .

By 7.40, after fruitless attempts to raise me on my mobile as well as at the Sea Air, Brian would authorize the announcement to the audience. '*In this evening's performance, the part of James Elliott will be played by Denis Maple*.'

At 7.45, as the curtain went up, I was standing under the Hollingdean Road railway bridge, watching and waiting. I silently wished Denis luck — and myself some too.

* * *

'Mr Flood?' I heard Oswin's call before I saw him, slipping out of the shadows along the access lane. 'I'm over here.' It had just turned eight o'clock.

I moved forward to meet him. His face was a sallow mask in the sodium lamplight. I didn't have much doubt in that instant that I was dealing with a madman. But I already knew his was a very strange kind of madness. Almost more of an alternative sanity.

'Thanks for coming,' he said.

'You didn't leave me much choice.'

'You could have honoured your contract with Leo S. Gauntlett Productions. Just as I could have honoured my promise to leave Mrs Flood alone.'

'So, why the bloody hell didn't you?'

'I explained in the letter. You took me by surprise. I . . . panicked.'

'Still feeling panicky?'

'A little. I thought you might be . . . angry.'

'I will be.' I stepped closer and stared straight at him. 'If you don't tell me now what this is really all about.'

'Oh, I will. Of course, Mr Flood. Everything.'

'For a start, what are we doing here?'

'I used to work round here. Like my father. And his father before him. We all worked for the Colborns in our time.'

'Doing what?'

'What we were told. I'll show you the site.' He led the way up the gently sloping land and I fell in beside him. 'That's the wholesale meat market,' he said, indicating the long, low building to our right, above which we were steadily rising. 'And this is the City Council's technical services depot.' He pointed to the drab, straggling structure to our left. 'Up here used to be the entrance to Colbonite Limited.'

What in God's name, I wondered, was the point of all this? We'd reached a padlocked wire-mesh gate, blocking access to a compound of slant-roofed shacks, decrepit workshops and debris-strewn yards. I gazed past Oswin into the dark and dismal middle distance, perceiving nothing of the slightest significance.

'It covered the whole area between here and the railway line,' he went on. 'There used to be a siding serving one of the warehouses. It was disused by the time I started, in nineteen seventy-six, straight from school. My A levels weren't much use at Colbonite, but Dad reckoned I should be . . . contributing.'

'What did Colbonite do?'

'Made things, Mr Flood. Anything and everything in plastic. Kitchenware. Garden furniture. Radio and television casings. And boxes. Lots and lots of boxes. Mr Colborn's great-grandfather founded the business in eighteen eighty-three. And his father wound it up one hundred and six years later. I haven't had a steady job since. Thirteen years there. And thirteen years away.'

'Well, I . . . '

'Not much to look at, is it?'

'No, but — '

'Why should it be? That's what you're thinking. Companies come and companies go. Livelihoods with them. So what? Who cares?'

'Apparently you do, Derek.'

He looked round at me in the darkness. I couldn't tell what sort of an expression he had on his face, couldn't tell if there was any expression at all. The traffic rumbled under the bridge behind us. A dog barked somewhere. The wind rattled a corrugated roof on the other side of what had once been the premises of Colbonite Ltd.

'How about coming to the point?' I said, trying to squeeze the impatience out of my voice.

'Yes. Sorry. Of course. Mind if we walk on?'

'Where are we going now?'

'Back towards Viaduct Road. My route home every working day for thirteen years.'

The lane curved sharply to the left ahead of us and climbed between a high wall to one side and the Colbonite site to the other. There wasn't a soul to be seen. What exactly did I think I was doing prowling around such an area with a borderline head case for company, when I was supposed to be on stage at the Theatre Royal? So far, I'd gained nothing but unsought and unwanted information about Derek Oswin's one and only spell of regular employment. He'd worked for the Colborns. He no longer did. As he himself had said: so what?

'Since my parents died,' he went on, 'I've had a lot of time to myself. Too much, I expect. Living on your own, you get . . . set in your ways.'

That was undeniable. But there are ways . . . and then there are Derek Oswin's ways. 'You said you were going to come to the point.'

'I am, Mr Flood, I am. Colbonite *is* the point. I've studied its history, you see. I've become an expert on it.'

'Have you really?'

'I probably know more about it than Mr Colborn does himself. Do you want me to tell you about Mr Colborn? Young Mr Colborn, I mean. I imagine you do. Is he worthy of Mrs Flood? The question must have crossed your mind.'

'What would you say?'

'I'd say not. He has . . . a treacherous character.'

'But it was his father who closed down the business.'

'Under pressure from his son. Roger Colborn wanted to close us down from the moment he first became involved. Colbonite held a valuable patent on a dyeing technique. He reckoned it was more profitable to sell that than keep us going. He was probably right.'

'You call that treacherous?'

'I do, yes. The workforce didn't get a slice of what the Colborns sold the patent for. All they got . . . was redundancy.'

'Even so — '

'And there was more to it than that. A lot more. So, I decided to put my excess of spare time to some use. I compiled a detailed history of Colbonite. I wrote the whole story. From start . . . to finish.'

The lane had turned another bend by now and brought us out onto a busy road leading down into the city. A brightly lit tanker was visible in the far distance, cruising across a wedge of darkness that was the sea. We started down the hill towards it.

'This is Ditchling Road,' said Derek. 'It's a straight line of sight from here down to St Peter's Church and out to the Palace Pier. It always was a lovely view to walk home with.'

'I'm sure it was, but — '

'I want the history to be published, Mr Flood. That's the thing. I can't bear to think I've gone to all that trouble for nothing. I asked Mr Colborn for help. He'd know the right people to approach. Or he could finance publication himself. He can well afford to. But he refused even to consider the idea. Of course, not everything in it is . . . to his credit . . . but it *is* the truth. Isn't that what matters?'

'It should be, Derek.'

'Not the whole truth, of course. I can't claim that. There are things I know — things Mr Colborn knows — that aren't in it. He'd realize that if he read it.'

'But he hasn't read it?'

'I don't think so. I've sent him a copy. More than one, actually. I thought the first might have gone astray. He doesn't respond to my messages. That's why I've been trying other ways to get his attention.'

I'd found Roger Colborn out in a lie. He knows Derek Oswin. I suspect he knows him only too well. It's not much of a lie, of course. Why trouble your fiancée with such a tale? A half-cracked ex-employee with a no doubt unreadable company history he wants you to usher into the literary world is someone any of us could be forgiven for airbrushing out of our acquaintance. As for closing down Colbonite and flogging off a patent, some would construe that as good business practice. Hard-headed, yes, but not especially hard-hearted.

'It's become clear to me that I'm wasting my efforts where Mr Colborn is concerned,' said Derek.

'You may well be.'

'I have higher hopes of you, Mr Flood.'

'Really?'

'Your agent, Moira Jennings, represents writers as well as actors.'

'How do you know who my agent is?'

'It wasn't difficult to find out. It's not difficult to find out lots of things, if you have the time.'

'You want me to get your history of Colbonite published?'

'It's called *The Plastic Men*. What do you think of the title?'

'Not bad. But — '

'Anyway, I don't expect you to work miracles, Mr Flood. I just want the book . . . seriously considered. If it's not deemed marketable, I shall accept that.'

'You will?' Derek's sudden ascent into realism had taken me aback.

'I'll have to.'

'Well, er, yes, you — '

'Would you be willing to ask Miss Jennings to take a look at it?'

'I might.' I pulled up. Derek carried on for a few steps, then turned to look at me. 'On one condition.'

'I promise to stop bothering Mrs Flood.'

'You promised before.'

'Yes. I'm sorry. I won't break my word again.'

'How can I be sure?'

'Because I broke my promise — and obliged you to miss tonight's performance — for a very specific reason. It was to help you.'

'Help *me*?'

'Certainly.'

'How in God's name do you reckon you've done that?'

'Can't you guess?'

'No, Derek. I can't.'

'I'd better explain, then.'

'Yes. You had.'

'It's a little . . . delicate.'

'I'm sure I can cope.'

'What I mean is . . . why don't we go back to my house and discuss it? I could . . . make some cocoa.'

* * *

Some offers are too good to refuse. Cocoa with Derek Oswin isn't one of them. But soon enough there we were, in his neat, tidy sitting room, two mugs of steaming unsugared cocoa and a plate of digestive biscuits between us. He'd obviously stocked up since my earlier visit. I eyed him expectantly across the coffee-table.

'This had better be good, Derek.'

'Don't worry, Mr Flood. It's Cadbury's cocoa. Not some supermarket brand.'

The man makes jokes. Not good jokes. And not often. But any humour's better than none, I suppose. Mine was veering towards the rueful, given that they'd be into the interval at the Theatre Royal by now.

'I didn't time our appointment to test your seriousness,' he continued through a taut smile. 'I didn't doubt that you meant to do all you could to help your wife.'

'Why, then?'

'Well, what happened when I put in an appearance at the Rendezvous this afternoon?'

'She called me.'

'And what will happen now we've met again?'

'That remains to be seen.'

'You'll surely let her know the outcome, though?'

'Yes,' I cautiously agreed.

'To achieve which you'll have let down your fellow actors and aroused the ire of Mr Leo S. Gauntlett.'

'I'm glad you appreciate that.'

'I do. And so will Mrs Flood, won't she?' His smile relaxed. 'Don't you see? I've increased her obligation to you. I've put her further in your debt. I've made it easier for you to . . . win her back.'

'I don't believe it,' I said. But I did believe it. Derek Oswin, Brighton's least likely match-maker, had decided to punish Roger Colborn for scorning his manuscript — punish him in every way that he could devise.

'I mean your wife no harm, Mr Flood. None at all. But . . . if you want to let her think I might . . . in the interests of spending more time with her . . . ' He pursed his lips and gazed benignly at me. 'That's fine by me.'

I sighed and took a sip of cocoa. It was easy to get angry with this man, but hard to stay that way. 'Broken marriages aren't so easy to put back together, Derek. They really aren't.'

'You don't know till you try.'

'OK. But look — ' I pointed a finger at him. 'From now on, you let me try — or not — as I see fit. Understood?'

'Absolutely.'

'You do *not* interfere.'

'Mrs Flood won't see me again unless we pass by chance in the street. I won't go to the Rendezvous. I won't even walk past Brimmers.'

'I'll hold you to that.'

'Of course.'

'I can get my agent to consider your book. I can also get her to *un*consider it.'

'I do understand, Mr Flood.'

'All right. You'd better hand it over.'

He jumped up, suddenly eager. 'I ran off a copy for you this afternoon. Hold on while I fetch it.'

He went out and up the stairs. I took another sip of cocoa, then turned round in my chair to inspect the contents of the bookcase, which was just behind me. I recognized my host's Tintin books by their phalanx of narrow red spines. He looked to have the full set. I pulled one out at random — *The Calculus Affair* — and opened it at the title page, where, next to a picture of the aforesaid professor pottering down a country lane, a fountain-penned inscription read, *To our darling Derek, from Mummy and Daddy, Christmas 1967*.

'Are you a Tintin fan?' The question came from the doorway. I turned to find Derek, photocopied manuscript in hand, staring quizzically at me.

'No. Just . . . ' I closed *The Calculus Affair* and slid it back amongst the others. 'Looking.'

'That's all right.' But it didn't sound all right. There was a tightness in his voice. He was still staring, past me now, at the row of books. He plonked the manuscript down on the table, circled round behind my chair and carefully removed *The Calculus Affair* from the shelf. Then, his tongue protruding through his teeth in concentration, he fingered aside two other books and pushed it into the space between them. 'You put it back out of sequence, Mr Flood,' he explained. '*The Calculus Affair* is number eighteen.'

'Right. I see.'

'Order matters, don't you think?'

'Yes. I suppose so. Up to a point.'

'But where does the point properly lie? That's the question.'

'And what's the answer?'

'We must each find it for ourselves.' He stood upright and retraced his steps. 'And then we must preserve it. Or, if endangered, defend it.'

'So, this is *The Plastic Men*,' I said, leaning forward to inspect the manuscript, happy indeed to change the subject, given how hard I'd have found it to say what the previous subject really was.

'Yes. That's it.'

The manuscript didn't look as bulky as I'd feared it might. No thousand-page epic, then, for which I was grateful, if only on Moira's behalf. But handwritten, to judge by the top sheet, which bore the words, *THE PLASTIC MEN, a History of Colbonite Ltd and its Workforce, by Derek Oswin*. There were traces of line markings in a rectangle in the centre of the page. As I leafed through the sheets, I saw each one was the same. Derek had written his book on feint-line A5, so that photocopying it onto A4 had isolated the words within wide, white margins. Not exactly conventional presentation.

'Will you read it yourself, Mr Flood, or just send it straight off to your agent?'

'I imagine you'd like a swift response.'

'Well, I would, yes.'

'Best send it straight off, then.' Neatly handled, I reckoned. Let Moira get somebody to flog through it. She's paid to do that sort of thing. 'This way, you'll probably hear something before Christmas.'

'Oh, good. That would be nice.'

'I can only ask her to give you an honest opinion, Derek. You know what that means, don't you?'

'She may turn it down. Oh yes. That's clear enough. And fair enough. It's all I'm asking for.'

'If she says no, I don't want to hear that you've reappeared at the Rendezvous.'

'You won't.'

'I'd better not, Derek. Believe me.'

'I do, Mr Flood. I do.' He looked so contrite that my heart went out to him, sentimental fool that I am.

'I know you thought you were acting for the best this afternoon and I'm grateful for your concern. It was still a stupid thing to do, though. Nothing of the kind must happen again.'

'It won't.' He smiled, presumably in an attempt to reassure me. 'I guarantee.'

'Good.'

'Although . . . '

'What?'

'I just wondered . . . '

'*Yes?*'

'Well, when do you next intend . . . to speak to your wife?'

'That's none of your business.'

'No. Of course not. But if I can help . . . ' His wobbly smile reshaped itself. 'Mr Colborn's away at the moment, you know.'

'I do know. But how do *you* know?' Stupid question, really. How does he come by any of his copious store of information?

'I, er, keep my ear to the ground. Anyway, it occurred to me . . . you might want to . . . visit Wickhurst Manor. While Mr Colborn's not in residence.'

'That doesn't sound like a very good idea.'

'No? Well, it's up to you, Mr Flood, entirely up to you.'

'So it is.'

'Marlinspike Hall, I call it.' There came a snatch of his whinnying laugh. 'Of course, if you're not a Tintin fan . . . '

'It's where Tintin lives in the books. I know that much, Derek.'

'Yes. Well done. Actually, Captain Haddock owns the house and Tintin and Professor Calculus also live there. But they didn't always. It originally belonged to Max Bird, the corrupt antiques dealer. In *The Secret of the Unicorn* — ' He broke off and blushed. 'Sorry. You're not interested in all that. Though there's an odd coincidence. Mr Colborn runs his business from Wickhurst Manor. Just as Max Bird ran his from Marlinspike Hall. And they both have a habit of overlooking what's right under their noses.'

This struck me as no coincidence at all, even if it was all true, but I nobly refrained from saying so. I made to rise. 'Well, I think I'd better be — '

'Do you want to see a photograph of the house?'

'Of Wickhurst Manor?'

'Yes.'

I should have declined the offer. Instead, I heard myself saying, 'All right.'

'I won't be a tick.' he was off again, out through the door and up the stairs.

I gazed at Derek's treasured manuscript. A history of a defunct plastics company. Ye gods! I turned the title page over. Derek, to my surprise, had contrived an epigraph of sorts for his *magnum opus*, a skit on the start of T. S. Eliot's poem 'The Hollow Men'.

We are the plastic men
We are the moulded men
Leaning together
Headpiece filled with polymer.

Yes, I reckoned, Moira was really going to love this.

Then Derek was back, a wallet of photographs in his hand. He sat down and carefully laid the contents out on the table next to the manuscript. *A* photograph, he'd said, but he'd actually used an entire roll of 24 on assorted middle-distance views of Wickhurst Manor.

A red-brick neo-Georgian residence of considerable size and style, the place is, viewed from any angle, absurdly large for two people to live in. Two matching pedimented bays with tall sash windows flank the central block, which boasts a four-columned portico to the entrance reached across a paved and pot-planted terrace. There are wings to the rear, one connected to a single-storey extension that doubles back on itself to enclose what looks like a kitchen garden. There's a large lawn to the rear, bordered by trees, a smaller one to the front, bisected by a curving drive. At the opposite end of the house from the kitchen garden there's a car park, occupied in most of the pictures by ten or twelve vehicles.

The trees are in full leaf. Sunlight gleams on the car roofs and picks out the white curls of croquet hoops on the rear lawn. This was Wickhurst Manor in high summer. When the photographer, I reflected, would find camouflage easiest to come by.

'I took most of them from the public right of way,' said Derek. I noted his delicate use of the word 'most'. 'The house was built in nineteen twenty-eight by Mr Colborn's grandfather, on the ruins of the medieval manor. The family had lived in Brighton until then, in one of the villas along Preston Park Avenue. Business was obviously booming, though Colbonite's wage rates were still rock bottom at the time.'

'What business is Colborn in now?'

'General investment. Moving his money around to make the most out of it, day to day. And advising other people on how to do the same. Hence the staff. It's an intensive operation. Mr Colborn believes in capitalizing on any advantage, however slight.'

'Perhaps he needs to, to maintain this place.'

'Perhaps so.'

‘Handy for you, the right of way.’

‘Rights of way are meant to be handy. I believe in using them.’

‘I’m sure you do.’

‘The path leads down from Devil’s Dyke, crosses the Fulking road, cuts through the woods near Wickhurst and heads north-west towards Henfield.’

‘Sounds like you’re giving me directions, Derek.’

‘Well, if you need directions — ’

‘I’ll ask.’ I stood up. ‘Now, I’d better be going.’

‘Right.’ Derek gathered the photographs and replaced them in the wallet. ‘By the way . . . ’ He looked at me uncertainly. ‘Does your offer of a ticket for Wednesday night still stand?’

I smiled. ‘Of course. Unless the stunt you’ve pulled today goads the management into withdrawing my privileges.’

‘Gosh.’ His eyes widened in horror, causing his glasses to slide halfway down his nose. ‘Do you think it might?’

‘On balance . . . ’ I affected indifference. ‘Probably not.’

* * *

I left *chez* Oswin with *The Plastic Men* in a Sainsbury’s carrier bag and the dregs of the evening ahead of me. The theatre would be turning out shortly. Brian Sallis had probably left a dozen messages on my mobile, none of which I wanted to hear. Nor was I eager to return to the Sea Air — where doubtless more messages awaited me — any sooner than I had to. I dropped into a pub halfway down London Road and weighed my options over a scotch. '*When do you next intend to speak to your wife?*' Derek had asked. It was a good question, given that I knew she'd want to be told what I'd accomplished as soon as possible. And there was only one answer. I finished the scotch in one and headed for the taxi rank at the railway station.

* * *

Half an hour later, I was out in the colder, darker world beyond the downs, pressing a button next to an intercom grille set in one of the pillars supporting the high black-railed gates at the head of the drive leading to Wickhurst Manor.

There was a crackle. Then I heard Jenny's voice, nervously pitched. 'Yes?'

'It's me, Jenny.'

'Toby?'

'Yes.'

'What are you doing here?'

'Can I come in?'

'Why didn't you phone?'

'I thought you'd want to hear what I have to say in person.'

'Oh God.' There was a pause. Then she said, 'Well, since you're here now . . . ' Then there was a buzz. The gates began to swing open.

I stepped back to pay off the taxi driver, then hurried in through the gates and started along the drive.

The noise of the taxi's engine faded into the

distance. All I could hear after that was the hiss of the wind in the trees and my own footfalls on the tarmac of the drive. I rounded a screen of shrubs and saw light from the house spilling across the lawn. Then I saw the house itself. There was a figure standing in the brightly lit porch, waiting for me.

Jenny was dressed in jeans and a sweatshirt, a stark contrast with the outfit I'd glimpsed her in at Brimmers. But her expression, I realized as I drew closer, was much the same. She wasn't smiling. Then a dog barked and appeared at her side — a reassuringly placid-looking Labrador.

'Yours or Roger's?' I asked, nodding to the dog, who padded out across the terrace to meet me.

'Roger's father's originally,' said Jenny. 'Here, Chester.' Chester obediently retreated. 'You'd better come in.'

'Thanks.' I followed the pair of them into a wide hall, panelled in light wood and scattered with thick, vividly patterned rugs.

'You shouldn't have come here, Toby,' said Jenny, calmly but firmly. 'I asked you not to.'

'Did you?'

'It was understood between us.'

'But we haven't always understood one another properly, have we, Jenny?'

She sighed. 'Why did you come?'

'To tell you what's happened.' I held up the bag. 'This is part of the price I've paid for getting Derek Oswin off your back. For good, this time.'

'Are you sure I've seen the last of him?'

'Nothing's certain, I suppose. But I'm

confident. Because of this.'

'What's in the bag?'

'I'm not sure you'll believe it.'

'Try me.'

'Why don't we . . . go in and sit down?'

'This was just an excuse, wasn't it, to nose around here?'

'Not *just*, no.'

'All right. Come up.' She led the way up the elegantly curved staircase. 'Roger uses the reception rooms on the ground floor for his office. We do most of our living on the first floor.'

The stairway and the landing were decorated with tasteful lavishness, modern abstracts jostling for space on the mellow-papered walls with landscapes and portraits from a more distant era. We entered a drawing room where logs were crackling in a broad fireplace, in front of which Chester had already stationed himself. The furnishings were like a cover shot for an interior-design magazine — throws, rugs, urns; fat-spined books on the table; thin-stemmed candlesticks on the mantelpiece. Jenny favouring to my certain knowledge a plainer style, I categorized it as stuff Colborn had probably had shipped in for him by a lifestyle consultant. Disliking him was already proving to be simplicity itself.

'Do you want a drink?' Jenny asked. She held up a bottle of Laphroaig.

'Thanks.'

She poured me some and handed me the glass.

'I'd have had Roger down as a Glenfiddich man.'

'You've never met Roger.' *And you're never going to*, her eyes added.

'Derek Oswin's met him. Many times.'

Any reaction Jenny might have displayed she artfully hid in the motion of sitting down. She waved towards an armchair opposite her and I lowered myself into it. Then she said, 'Just tell me, Toby.'

'All right. Oswin used to work for Colbonite. You know about the company?'

'Of course. Roger's father closed it down . . . years ago.'

'*Thirteen* years ago.'

'There you are, then. Ancient history. Roger wouldn't remember one employee out of . . . however many there were.'

'He'd remember this one. Odd you should mention history, actually, because that's what's in the bag. Oswin's history of Colbonite. He's been trying to persuade Roger to help him get it published. Roger hasn't wanted to know. But Oswin's not one to take no for an answer, so, in his very own crackpot fashion, he's tried to pressurize Roger into reconsidering . . . by harassing you. The fact that he's a fan of mine . . . is purely coincidental.'

Jenny looked relieved to hear this explanation. She even smiled. 'I see. So, Roger pretended not to recognize Oswin in order not to worry me. While I didn't mention Oswin in order not to worry *him*.'

'Probably,' I grudgingly agreed.

'Why have *you* got the manuscript?'

'It's part of the deal I struck with Oswin. I'll have Moira give it the once over. In return, he'll lay off you.'

'But surely it's unpublishable.'

'For certain, I should think. But he'll be content as long as it's given serious consideration. I reckon that was Roger's mistake. Refusing even to look at it.'

'More likely he knows Oswin of old as a waste of space.'

We exchanged an eloquent glance. Jenny's sympathy for the flotsam and jetsam of society used sometimes to annoy me. None of it was on show now, though. Was this new hardness, I wondered, one of the consequences of her relationship with Roger Colborn, the plastic man turned arbitrageur and landed gent?

'Will Oswin honour your . . . deal . . . if Moira turns the book down?'

'He says so.'

'And you believe him?'

'Yes. He knows there's nothing more he can do.'

Jenny looked less than wholly convinced. 'Well, at the very least, I suppose it'll be a breathing space. And I'm grateful for that. How did you manage to accomplish this so quickly?'

'I missed this evening's performance.'

'You did *what*?'

'It was the only time Oswin was willing to see me.'

'Why on earth did you allow someone like that to — '

The telephone was ringing. I stared at it and so did Jenny. I think we were both certain who was on the other end. Jenny leaned across the arm of her chair and plucked the receiver out of its cradle.

'Hello?' She smiled. 'Hello, darling . . . Yes . . . Yes, very quiet.' She was on the move now, slipping out through a communicating door into an adjoining room. The door closed behind her and her voice receded to a muffled murmur. Chester opened an eye, registered her absence and sank back into a torpor.

I cast a jaundiced glance round the room, wondering if I'd recognize any of the items she kept when we separated. But there was nothing, not a single familiar object, only more of the same impeccably composed contents of an idyllic country-house life. 'Is this really what you want?' I muttered, refraining from supplying the obvious answer.

Then I spotted a framed photograph on top of the cherry-wood hi-fi cabinet. I rose and went across for a gander. There was Jenny, carefree and happy, grinning at the camera as she wrapped an arm round the new man in her life. Her companion had to be Roger Colborn. They were leaning together by the tiller of a yacht, a triangle of sail visible above them, a sparkling chunk of sea behind. Colborn looked lean, muscular and nauseatingly handsome, with thick dark hair greying at the temples, blue eyes, a firm jaw and assorted indicators of rugged machismo. To make matters worse, he and Jenny appeared to be very much in love. I sighed and turned away, only to confront a reflection of myself in the mirror above the mantelpiece. Hair thinner and greyer than Colborn's, waistline looser, musculature less evident, I could do no more than shrug.

The door clicked open and Jenny stepped back into the room. 'Sorry about that,' she said. 'Roger always calls around now when he's away.'

'Thoughtful of him.'

'Look, Toby — '

'At a guess' — I tilted the photograph towards her — 'I'd say he's about my age.'

'Yes.' Jenny compressed her lips. 'He is.'

'But wearing better.'

'I don't want to play this game, Toby. I'm grateful for what you've done about Derek Oswin. But — '

'Mention him to Roger, did you?'

'No. Of course not.'

'I should, if I were you. Secrets at this stage of a relationship . . . can prove tricky.'

'I probably will discuss it with him when he gets back.' I sensed she wanted to tell me to mind my own business. But the favour I'd done her meant she couldn't take such a stance. 'You can leave that to me.'

'Yes. Of course. Sorry.' I smiled, daring her to smile back. 'It's hard to get out of the habit of offering you advice.' The same, I could have added, went for several other habits. Touching her, for instance. That's something I badly want to do — now I'm not allowed to.

'I *am* grateful, Toby.'

'Least I could do.'

'I'm sorry it led to you missing the show. Won't that get you into quite a lot of trouble?'

'I'll survive.'

'I'm sure you will.'

'Are we still on for lunch tomorrow?'

'Actually, no.' She gave an embarrassed little smile. 'Roger's coming back earlier than he expected. He suggested . . . picking me up for lunch.'

I found myself wondering, for no rational reason, whether Roger had somehow got wind of my contact with Jenny and decided he'd better hurry home and spike my guns. It was an absurd idea, of course, but in that instant strangely credible. 'We could make up a threesome,' I suggested, using sarcasm to shield my disappointment.

Jenny looked at me for several silent seconds, then said, 'I'd better drive you back into Brighton.'

* * *

Jenny's bought one of the new fish-eyed Minis. She's always liked Minis. I remember the one she had when we first met. Travelling in the modern souped-up version tonight revived more than a few memories for both of us. But we didn't share them. My mind wrestled with a slippery tangle of things I wanted to say and needed to say — but didn't. Time was suddenly short. And all I could do was watch it pass.

Eventually, oppressed by the thought that we

may well not meet again before I leave Brighton and spotting the Duke of York's Cinema ahead as we approached Preston Circus, I said, 'Derek Oswin lives in Viaduct Road. Number seventy-seven.'

'Do I need to know that?' Jenny countered.

'You may do.'

'I hope not. If Oswin leaves me alone, I'll be happy to leave *him* alone.'

'When you mention him to Roger, will you also mention me?'

'What do you think, Toby?'

'I think not.'

'Really?'

'Yes. Really.'

'Well, there you are, then.'

'But am I right?'

Her answer took so long coming that I began to think it never would. She had to say something, though. 'I only asked you to approach Oswin because I genuinely believed you were the key to his interest in me. I'm grateful to you for proving that isn't the case. But now you have . . . '

'You want me to back off.'

Another wordless interval followed. We were past St Peter's Church by this time, heading south down Grand Parade. I watched Jenny clench and unclench her jaw muscles. Then she said, 'That's what separation means, Toby.' She glanced round at me. 'Let it go.'

* * *

Back here at the Sea Air, Eunice had gone to bed, leaving a note for me on the hall table.

> Brian Sallis called. Phone and in person. Seems you've been a naughty boy, Toby. I hope you know what you're doing. Well, there has to be a first time for everything, doesn't there?
>
> E.

Even in my less than joyous condition, I raised a chuckle at Eunice's characteristically perky perspective on events. I'll have to do some fence-mending tomorrow, no question about it.

I came up here to my room, broached my emergency whisky supply and pondered Jenny's parting plea to me. '*Let it go.*' Rich, that, I reckon. She came to me for help and I obliged. Now she wants me as well as Derek Oswin off her back. Life isn't quite as simple as that, Jen, however sweet and easy lover boy's made it feel lately. I'm not letting this go. Not just yet. Tomorrow, I'll post *The Plastic Men* to Moira. Then . . . we'll see.

* * *

And what *about The Plastic Men*? I need something unreadable to lull me off to sleep. Let's take a late-night look at the little man's *chef d'oeuvre*. Let's get past the title page and the epigraph and see what we find.

An *Introduction*, no less.

The Oxford English Dictionary defines plastic as 'any of a large and varied class of wholly or partly synthetic substances which are organic in composition and polymeric in structure and may be given a permanent shape by moulding, extrusion or other means during manufacture or use'.

Most of us know what the word means without needing to understand the chemistry of polymerization. Acrylic. Alkathene. Araldite. Bakelite. Bandalasta. Beetleware. Celluloid. Cellophane. Ebonite. Ivoride. Jaxonite. Lycra. Melamine. Mouldensite. Nylon. Parkesine. Perspex. Plasticine. Polythene. Polystyrene. PVC. Rayon. Styron. Terylene. Tufnol. Tupperware. UPVC. Vinyl. Viscose. Vulcanite. Xylonite. We are all familiar with at least some of these.

The first semi-synthetic plastic, based on cellulose nitrate, was invented by Alexander Parkes during the 1850s. He named the substance Parkesine and displayed it at the International Exhibition of 1862. In 1866 he launched the Parkesine Company to market products made using the material. Parkes was a brilliant inventor but a poor businessman. In 1869 he was forced to sell his patent rights to the Xylonite Company. He did not give up, however. When those patents expired, he set up in business again, launching the London Celluloid Company in partnership with his brother Henry in 1881. This venture also failed.

The Parkes' works manager, Daniel Colborn, decided to carry on alone. He returned to his native Brighton and built a workshop in Dog Kennel Road (the original name for Hollingdean Road), where he began trading in 1883 as Colbonite Ltd.

The Colbonite workforce was at first very small. It soon began to increase, however, as the company prospered. Labour was in plentiful local supply. A large area of artisans' dwellings (later categorized as slums) existed to the south. By the outbreak of the First World War, Colbonite's workforce stood close to a hundred. One of those hundred was my grandfather, George Oswin, who took a job working 55½ hours per week in the Colbonite acid shop in 1910, at the age of fourteen, on a wage of 1½d. per hour. His descriptions to me of his working life are one of the principal sources of information I have drawn on in the compilation of this history, especially where the early period is concerned.

Before I enter into an account of working conditions at Colbonite during this period and the industrial processes applied there to plastics manufacture, I should try to set the scene.

Colbonite's premises filled a roughly triangular plot bounded by the Brighton to Lewes railway line, the municipal slaughterhouse and the Jewish cemetery in Florence Place. The slaughterhouse opened in 1894, replacing the Union Hunt kennels which had given Hollingdean Road its original name.

To the south lay the small and largely middle-class parish of St Saviour's. The next parish to the south was St Bartholomew's, where most of the Colbonite workforce lived in densely packed terraces.

Most of these houses were demolished in the slum clearance programmes of 1955–66. Only photographs and memories can tell us what the area looked like before then. St Bartholomew's Church, which has the highest nave of any parish church in England, was built in 1872–4 at the instigation of Father Arthur Wagner as an inspiration for its poverty-stricken parishioners. It soared to what must have been awesome effect above the narrow streets, just as it still soars above the car parks and vacant lots that have succeeded them.

My grandparents began their married life literally in the shadow of the church, at a house in St Peter's Street. My grandfather walked past St Bart's every workday morning at about 6.30 *en route* to Colbonite, where he was due to clock on at 7.00. In London Road he could catch a tram that took him most of the way, but he only did this in severe weather. Usually, he crossed London Road, cut through via Oxford Street to Ditchling Road and walked north uphill to Hollingdean Lane, which led round to the Colbonite site.

I imagine him — as I want you to imagine him — in the final stage of that walk, dawn breaking over Brighton on a chill March morning *circa* 1930, as he approaches his destination. He is familiar with his surroundings. There is the railway line behind him, emerging from a cutting. A train may be chugging east along the track, belching steam as it accelerates away from London Road Station. To his left is the ivy-clad brick wall enclosing the Jewish cemetery. Ahead, on lower ground, is the slaughterhouse, where at that moment doomed creatures are very possibly being unloaded from a line of trucks shunted onto the siding that also serves Colbonite. Behind the slaughterhouse, smoke is rising from the chimney of the corporation's so-called dust destructor, where the collected refuse of Brighton is daily reduced to ashes. It is not a pleasing vista, though no doubt any vista is pleasing to a man such as my grandfather, who survived four years on the Western Front during the First World War — the Great War, as he always called it. (He remained grateful to old Mr Colborn for keeping his job open for him during the hostilities.)

He looks to his right as he rounds the bend in the lane and sees Colbonite's brick-built workshops, roofed in corrugated iron. He turns in past the company sign — COLBONITE LTD, PLASTICS MANUFACTURER, EST. 1883. He nods to the gateman and proceeds across the yard towards the shed where his clogs and leggings are stored. He has arrived.

The first chapter of this history will

> attempt to recreate in detail the kind of experience an average working day for an average employee of Colbonite such as my grandfather would have been at this time. Later chapters will consider the company's efforts to keep pace with changes in the plastics industry worldwide and how these affected the workforce. The closing chapters will analyse the circumstances leading to the closure of the company in 1989 and the fate of those who found themselves out of work as a result.

Mmm. An 'average working day' for an 'average employee' of a defunct plastics company more than seventy years ago. I'm not sure I want to know about that. I'm not sure anyone does. I'm even less sure that Moira will be willing to try and sell it. Sorry, Derek. I don't think we're onto a winner here.

I'm suddenly weary. Wearier than I would have been if I'd done my stuff at the theatre this evening. It's been a long day. And a strange one. It's time to call it a night.

TUESDAY

Tired as I may have been last night, I woke early this morning, roused as much as anything by queasy anticipation of the recriminations that were bound to flow from my no-show. A strategy of sorts evolved as I showered and shaved. It amounted to pre-emptive grovelling.

First, I wanted *The Plastic Men* off my conscience, though. I scrawled an explanatory note to Moira (that was naturally less than comprehensive in its coverage of recent events) and reached the St James's Street post office just after it had opened. I bought a large jiffy bag, stuffed the note and the manuscript inside and despatched the lot to my esteemed agent by recorded delivery. She'll receive it by noon tomorrow.

The morning was dry but drearily overcast. Brighton needs sunshine to look even close to its best. In its continued absence, I plodded down to the sea front and struck west towards the Belgrave Hotel, where I knew Brian Sallis to be staying. (Along, theoretically, with Mandy Pringle, although in practice she was almost certainly tucked up with Donohue at the Metropole.) My plan was to catch Brian early, perhaps over breakfast, before he'd properly remembered how angry he was with me.

But his day turned out to be further advanced than I'd expected. As I neared the Belgrave, I spotted him ahead of me on the promenade, dressed in jogging kit and using the railings above the beach for a hamstring-stretching routine prior to reeling off a brisk few miles along the front. I hailed him.

His first reaction was surprise. Then came puzzlement. Followed shortly by exasperation. 'Good morning, Toby,' he said through a mock smile. 'And fuck you.'

'I'm sorry about last night, Brian,' I responded.

He stared at me, then cupped a hand round one ear. 'Is that the end of the speech?'

'What else can I say?'

'You could try telling me your absence was something I just dreamt; that your unexplained, unannounced, utterly inexcusable failure to do what we pay you to do — and pay very generously at that — was merely a figment of my imagination.'

' 'Fraid not.'

'Alternatively, you could offer what I personally suspect you're not going to be able to concoct: a decent excuse for letting us all down. Or, failing that, maybe you could just try the truth, Toby. Yes. On balance, I'd favour that.'

'It was a personal matter, Brian. A critical situation. I had no choice but to be somewhere else.'

'Are you going to tell me what this critical situation was?'

'No. But it's over now. Permanently resolved. You have my word on that.'

'A word from you is what I'd have welcomed

yesterday afternoon, Toby. A word of warning that you were going to run out on us.'

'I warned Denis.'

'You don't work for Denis. You work for Leo. And as Leo's representative, I was entitled to an explanation.'

'Yes. Like I say, I'm sorry. I don't expect to be paid for last night's — '

'You won't be, believe me. In fact' — he tossed his head and gave the railing a thump with the heel of his hand — 'Leo was all for laying you off for the rest of the week. I talked him round in the end, not because I was anxious to go easy on you, quite the reverse, but — '

'Because you'd sell fewer tickets.'

'Yes,' Brian reluctantly agreed.

'Which Leo would have been quick enough to realize himself once he'd stopped spitting nails. I do understand. We're locked in a commercial embrace.' As grovelling went, this sounded defiant even to my own ears. I tried at once to soften the message. 'I'll give it a hundred per cent for the rest of the week.'

Brian sighed. 'That's something, I suppose.'

'It's the best I can do.'

'Just don't expect any offers from Leo in the near future.'

'I won't.'

Brian frowned at me. Good-hearted fellow that he basically is, he'd worked off his anger, leaving space in his mind for gentler thoughts. 'You're not in any kind of trouble, are you, Toby?'

'None you can help me with.'

'What's that supposed to mean?'

'I don't know.' I summoned a smile. 'Generalized mid-life crisis. Plus pending divorce from a woman I'd very much like to stay married to. Troubles enough, without pissing off one of the West End's leading impresarios for good measure.'

'You said it.' Brian pondered my litany of woes for a moment before continuing. 'Does this have anything to do with Jenny? I gather she lives in Brighton now.'

'So she does.'

'And?'

'And nothing. Tell me how the show went . . . without me.'

'Since you ask, Denis rose to the challenge magnificently. He turned in an excellent performance.'

'Maybe I did him a favour, then.'

'Maybe. But let's be clear. This was a one-off. Any repetition . . . and I couldn't answer for what Leo might do.'

'There'll be no repetition.'

'Officially, it was twenty-four-hour flu.'

'I've recovered ahead of schedule, then.'

'Just make sure there isn't a relapse. I'd like you at the theatre early tonight. Let's say six thirty.'

'Fair enough.'

'Until then . . . '

'Yes?'

'Stay out of critical situations.'

'I'll be sure to.'

'OK.' He began a tentative jog on the spot.

'You should take up running, Toby. It might help with those troubles.'

'I'll think about it.'

'See you later, then.' He turned and started off towards Hove.

'You will,' I shouted after him.

⋆ ⋆ ⋆

My evening performance as James Elliott was in truth the only certainty in the day that lay ahead of me. Last night, light-headed after whisky on an empty stomach and overtired to boot, I confidently asserted that I'd prise my way into Roger Colborn's secrets in the hope of finding some that would sour Jenny's relationship with him. Easier said than done, of course. Walking slowly in the direction Brian Sallis had run off in, I admitted to myself that I had no good reason to suppose such secrets existed, let alone any obvious method of penetrating them.

I stopped and leaned against the railings, staring out glumly at the grey, listless motion of the sea. It wasn't too late to talk Eunice into rustling up some breakfast. Nourishment might even prove inspiring. I decided to head back to the Sea Air.

My mobile rang before I could act on the decision. I guessed the call would be from Moira. I suspected word of my misdemeanour might already have reached her. But it wasn't from Moira. Nor from anyone else I'd have expected to hear from.

'Ah, Toby. Denis here.'

'Denis? What are you doing up? You should be sleeping the sleep of the just after standing in for me so valiantly — and so impressively, Brian tells me.'

'The play went all right, no question. It was good . . . being out there again.'

'Why do you sound so down in the mouth, then?'

'Could we meet . . . for a chat, Toby? Like . . . now?'

'All right. But . . . what's this about? I can assure you I'll make it on stage tonight.'

'It's nothing to do with the play.'

'What, then?'

'I'll tell you when we meet.'

* * *

I had to be satisfied with that and we agreed to meet at the Rendezvous in a quarter of an hour. Denis, of course, had no reason to think the choice of venue significant. I told myself it made sense to check that Derek Oswin really was laying off Jenny. But maybe the proximity to Jenny it offered was its real appeal.

I was the first to arrive and had guzzled a Danish by the time Denis put in an appearance. Happily, there was no sign of Derek. I stood Denis a coffee and we sat down at a corner table, where he lit up with ill-disguised urgency.

'I thought you'd given up,' I remarked with studied neutrality.

'So did I.'

'I hope this isn't a reaction to performing last

night. I never intended to put any undue — '

'Forget the play, Toby. This is about what happened afterwards.'

'Afterwards?'

'I've been in two minds about whether to tell you. But I think . . . you really had better know.'

'Know what?'

'I'm ashamed of myself, to be honest. I should never have allowed the situation to develop. But . . . the evening had gone so well. I just thought it was getting better and better.' He shook his head. 'Stupid. Bloody stupid.'

'What are you on about, Denis?'

'All right. I'll get to the point.' He lowered his voice and leaned forward confidentially. 'Several of us went into the Blue Parrot for a drink after the show. You know the place? Just along from the theatre. Anyway, I'd not been there above five minutes when this girl — a real looker, she was — sidled up to me and congratulated me on my performance. She called me Toby and said what an honour it was to meet me. I assumed she'd missed the announcement about me standing in for you and, I don't know why, but I didn't . . . point out her mistake. Well, I do know why, of course. I was afraid it might put her off. I mean, she was just gorgeous and . . . she was giving me the eye and . . . '

'You thought you were onto a good thing.'

'Yeah.' Denis nodded in dismal agreement. 'That's about the size of it. She didn't speak very good English. She clearly *wasn't* English. I reckoned that accounted for the misunderstanding. But I wasn't bothered. Why would I be? It's not often I get luscious young lovelies coming onto me. She suggested going to some club she knew. I was half-cut and . . . pretty pleased with myself. So, I left the others to it and Olga — that was her name — and I went to some basement jazz joint this side of North Street. We weren't there long. I mean, she was all over me, Toby. Starstruck and . . . randy with it.'

'Why do I have the feeling this ended badly?'

'Because I wouldn't be telling you about it otherwise. Next stop after the jazz club was her flat. She lives in Embassy Court. Well, that's where she took me. You know it? Art Deco block on the sea front. Seen better days. A lot better, let me tell you. Outside it's just dilapidated. Inside . . . it's a rathole. I should have turned round and walked straight out.'

'But you didn't.'

'No. We made it to her flat. I was . . . pretty high by then. I reckon she must have spiked my drinks. I was . . . up for anything. And so was Olga. Before I knew what was happening, she started taking her clothes off. Well, I gave her a helping hand. Who wouldn't in the circumstances? It seemed like my lucky night. Turned out to be anything but, I'd just got her down to her G-string when a door from an adjoining room burst open and this big bloke — I mean, seriously big — was suddenly pulling us apart. He was frighteningly strong. And angry. But angrier with Olga than with me. 'This is the wrong man,' he shouted at her. 'This isn't Toby Flood, you brainless tart.' Then he threw me out. Literally threw. I'm lucky not to have some broken ribs to add to the bruises. I remember bouncing — yeah, actually bouncing — off the wall on the other side of the corridor and seeing the door of the flat slam shut behind me. I heard Olga screaming inside. I think . . . he was hitting her.' Denis's head drooped. 'I got the hell out.'

I couldn't find anything to say at first. The implication was clear. Somebody had put up the girl to lure me back to a flat in Embassy Court. Why? What exactly were they planning to spring on me? And who were they? More to the point, who were they working for?

'Perhaps I should have tried to fetch help,' Denis went on. 'I feel responsible for whatever man mountain did to Olga after I'd slunk away. I *did* mislead her, after all.'

'You also think she spiked your drinks, Denis. Remember that.'

'Even so . . . '

'And where would this help have come from? The police?'

Denis rolled his eyes. 'Seemed wiser to crawl back to my B and B and pretend it had never happened.'

'I'm sure it did.'

'Thought I'd better fill you in on it, though. Somebody targeted you, Toby. No question about it. Maybe Olga's under age. I mean, you just can't tell these days, can you? Specially when you're not thinking straight to start with. It could have turned nasty. Very nasty.' He smiled grimly at me through his cigarette smoke. 'Except you'd probably have had the good sense to give her the brush-off at the Blue Parrot.'

'I'd like to think so.'

'Did you see something like this coming? Is that why you didn't do the show last night?'

'Absolutely not. Believe me, Denis. I had — I have — no reason to think I'm being . . . targeted.'

'But you are, old son. Take my word for it.'

'I don't suppose Olga gave you her surname?'

'No. Nor her national insurance number. She's probably an illegal. And, before you ask, I didn't think to note the flat number. I can't even be sure which floor we were on. I wasn't at my most observant. Even if I had been, it'd probably do you no good. As for man mountain, I'd go a long way to avoid meeting him, if I were you.'

'Yes, but — ' Interrupted by the trill of my mobile, I snatched it out of my pocket. Moira this time? Wrong again.

'Hello, Toby.'

'Jenny. Hi.'

'What are you doing over there?'

'Oh. You, er, spotted me, did you?' I craned for a view of Brimmers through the window, but could discern little beyond smoke, condensation and assorted passers-by. 'Well, I thought I ought to check that Derek Oswin's playing ball. And I'm glad to say he is.'

'So I see.'

'Don't worry. I'm not going to make a habit of it.'

'Is that Denis Maple with you?'

'Yes. Do you want a word?'

'No, no. But . . . give him my love.'

'OK.'

'Goodbye, Toby.'

The call ended. Denis raised an eyebrow at me. 'Jenny?'

'She lives in Brighton. Runs the hat shop opposite here, actually.'

'Really?' He peered towards Brimmers. 'Is that why you chose this place to meet?'

'In a sense. She sends her love, by the way.' A strange commodity, love, I thought. Ample to share among friends and acquaintances, yet it can't be dispensed, even on a token level, to an estranged spouse.

'You should never have let her go.'

'I'm well aware of that.'

'Is it too late to . . . repair the damage?'

'Probably.'

'But not definitely.'

'No. Not definitely.'

'You've got the rest of the week to work on it.'

'So I have.'

'Ah!' Denis seemed suddenly to have glimpsed the truth. 'Is that what you were up to last night?'

'Maybe.'

'Just as well Olga got the wrong man, then. Wouldn't have looked too good to Jen, would it, if the police had been after you for whatever was planned to happen in that flat?'

'No, Denis. I think we can safely say that it wouldn't.'

* * *

I left Denis to chill out as best he could after his experiences of the night before, walked back down to the front and made my way along to Embassy Court. I remembered it vaguely as a visually striking chunk of Thirties Art Deco: white-plastered balconies tiered like a sleek-lined wedding cake. But the only wedding cake it resembles now is Miss Havisham's. Lumps of plaster have fallen off. Some of the windows are boarded up. Rust is leaching through the balconies.

I stood by the Peace Statue on the seaward side of the road, looking up at the building, wondering if by any chance Olga was looking down at me. Perhaps it was just as well Denis couldn't remember which flat she took him to. There was no telling what might happen if I succeeded in tracking her down.

Someone had put her up to last night's mischief, though. That was obvious. Who stood to gain from blackening my name? I could only think of one candidate. But he wasn't supposed even to be in Brighton, let alone have any reason to believe I posed the slightest threat to him.

Then another thought struck me, as disturbing in its way as it was also weirdly comforting. Why had I missed the show? Because Derek Oswin had forced me to. As an earnest of my good intentions, so he'd said. But could he actually have lured me out to Hollingdean Road to ensure I came to no harm elsewhere? Was it possible that he'd appointed himself my guardian angel?

If so, it suggested he knew who was gunning for me. I hot-footed it up to Western Road and boarded the next number 5 bus to come along.

* * *

My mobile rang just as the bus was pulling away from the Royal Pavilion stop. At the third time of asking, it *was* Moira.

'A very good morning to you, Toby. How's the head?'

'Clear as a bell, Moira. Why shouldn't it be?'

'Not hung in shame, then? Nor topping off a spike outside the Theatre Royal?'

'Ah. Leo's been onto you, has he?'

'Yes. And I fully expect his lawyers to be onto me some time today as well.'

'No, no. He'll call off the dogs when he hears I'm back on board. The box office would take too big a hit without me. I'm in sackcloth and ashes. But I'm still in a job. You don't need to worry about your commission.'

'I'm actually more worried about you, darling. You've not previously been noted for an artistic temperament. What happened? Did everything get too much for you?'

'A personal crisis blew up. Now it's blown over. Simple as that.'

'Doesn't sound simple.'

'I'll tell you all about it next time we have lunch.'

'I'll hold you to that.'

'Meanwhile, I've, er, a favour to ask of you.'

'Apart from salvaging your professional reputation, you mean?'

'Yes, Moira. Apart from that.'

* * *

By the time I got off the bus near the top of London Road, Moira had agreed, albeit bemusedly, to have one of the agency's literary specialists give *The Plastic Men* prompt and serious attention as soon as she received it. She had also urged me to put in a *mea culpa* call verging on the obsequious to Leo Gauntlett, in the interests of papering over the cracks in his opinion of me. I reckoned I'd need a few stiff drinks before making such a call, which was one of several good reasons for postponing the task.

The chance of an illuminating chat with Derek Oswin was another. But no answer came the stern reply at 77 Viaduct Road. Whatever he was doing in lieu of camping out at the Rendezvous, it evidently didn't involve staying at home. Nor did I have a mobile number for him. In fact, I rather doubted he possessed a mobile. Even a land-line was touch and go. I'd not noticed a phone in the house. It would be entirely like him to be technologically incommunicado.

I found myself walking back into town along Ditchling Road, past the Open Market. Remembering Derek's account in his introduction to *The Plastic Men* of his grandfather's route to work, I cut through to London Road along Oxford Street. The vast, soaring flank of St Bartholomew's Church was dead ahead. I began trying to imagine the area in the old man's day. Trams, gas lamps and as many horse-drawn vehicles as petrol-driven. All the men in hats, all the women in skirts. It wasn't so very different. Not really.

Standing outside St Bart's, though, I realized

that wasn't true. Where had all the houses gone? Where were the rows upon rows of 'artisans' dwellings'? Vanished. Swept away. Erased. Such is the reach of municipal dictate. But its reach isn't limitless. It can't alter the past. It can only rewrite the present. And pay lip service to the future.

Suddenly, I remembered Syd Porteous. '*Anything I can do for you while you're here — anything at all — just say the word.*' And for him I did have a mobile number. Why not tap his allegedly compendious local knowledge? Why not indeed? I tugged the beer mat with his number on it out of my coat pocket and gave him a call.

'Hullo?'

'Syd Porteous?'

'Hole in one. That sounds like . . . hold on, hold on, let the grey matter work its magic . . . Toby Flood, the errant actor.'

'You're right.'

'But are *you* right, Tobe? That's the question. My contacts in the usheretting community tell me you let down the punters last night. I've got a ticket for tonight, you know. Should I be asking for my money back?'

'No, no. I'll be on tonight.'

'Great news. And I'm more than appreciative of this personal reassurance. Nice one, Tobe.'

'That's not . . . the only reason I rang.'

'No?'

'You said . . . if there was anything you could do for me . . . '

'Any assistance, small or large, a pleasure and

a privilege. You know that.'

'I wondered if we could . . . meet up again. Run over a few things.'

'Absolutely-dootly. When did you have in mind?'

'As soon as possible. This lunchtime, perhaps?'

'Fine by me. The Cricketers again?'

'Why not?'

'Okey-dokey. Noon suit you?'

'Well, I . . .'

'Grrreat.' Whether Syd was genuinely trying to impersonate Tony the Tiger of Frosties fame I wasn't sure, but it certainly sounded like it. 'See you there and then.'

* * *

I had just over an hour to concoct a cover story for the questions I planned to run past Syd. I went into the church in search not so much of inspiration as of a quiet place to think and found myself in a vast and curiously empty space more like a Byzantine ruin than an Anglican church. Father Wagner had cleverly supplied the parishioners with as complete a contrast to their domestic circumstances as could be imagined. I wondered if little Derek had come here of a Sunday with his parents and grandparents. I wondered if he'd gazed up at the distant roof and dreamt of touching the sky. I decided then to abandon the cover story before I'd invented it. I decided to ply Syd with an approximation of the truth.

* * *

His Tuesday lunchtime gear was the same as his Sunday evening kit, but he'd swapped wine for beer and put one in for me as well. 'Unless,' he said with a wink, 'you go Methodist on play days.'

'Beer is fine,' I responded, just about catching his drift.

We retired to a fireside table with two pints of Harvey's. 'It's a real bonus seeing you again so soon, Tobe,' he said after a swallow of best bitter. I winced more than somewhat at 'Tobe', realizing that I really hadn't misheard on the phone, but knew I'd have to go with it. 'To what do I owe it?'

'Well, it's, er . . . a delicate problem.'

'Delicacy is my speciality.'

'My wife and I split up a few years ago.'

'Sorry to hear that. Occupational hazard, so they say.'

'It's pretty common in the acting profession, that's for certain. Anyway, our divorce hasn't come through yet, but — '

'Are we talking last-minute reconciliation here?'

'No, no. Jenny lives with a man. They plan to marry as soon as they can. I . . . well, they live near Brighton, as a matter of fact. The point is that Jenny and I parted amicably. I'm still . . . concerned about her. So, I'm anxious to assure myself that this bloke's not . . . '

'A wrong 'un?'

'Yes. Exactly. And he's local. So, thinking

about what you said Sunday night, I wondered if . . . you might know anything about him.'

'Hoping to dig up some dirt, are you, Tobe? Something that would make Jenny think twice about marrying him?'

'If there's dirt to be dug, fine. If not, fine again.'

'Point taken.' Syd leaned as far across the table as his paunch allowed. 'Who is he?'

'Roger Colborn.'

Syd frowned thoughtfully. 'Colborn?'

'Know the name?'

'Maybe. What else have you got on him?'

'Some sort of businessman. Lives in a big house out near Fulking. Wickhurst Manor.'

'Thought so.' Syd grinned. 'Father in plastics.'

'Yes. Colbonite Limited.'

'That's it. Colbonite. Walter Colborn — Sir Walter, as he became — was Roger's old man. He had a younger brother, Roger's uncle, Gavin. Gav and I were in the same year at Brighton College.'

'You were?'

'No need to look so surprised. My dad had high hopes for me. His timing was spot-on, as it happens. He didn't go bust until the year after I left. But that's another story. Gav made senior prefect and went to Oxford, much good that it did him. Time's evened up the achievements score between us, I'd say. He's having to prop and cop these days, same as me, but he doesn't have the aptitude for it. Too old, too lazy and usually too drunk to make the effort. That about sums him up.'

'How well do you know him?'

'Middling to fair. We're not exactly close.'

'And the nephew?'

'I've met him a few times. Nothing more. Gav doesn't speak kindly of him. That I can tell you. Whether it damns the fellow . . . is trickier to say. Gav got nothing out of the family business, see. His father left it all to Wally, probably for a good reason. That's niggled away at Gav over the years. So, the nephew who inherited the lot isn't top of his pops.'

'I suppose that might make Gavin quite . . . forthcoming . . . where Roger's concerned.'

'Very possibly.'

'Any chance of . . . '

'Meeting for a chinwag? I think I might be able to arrange that, Tobe. Seeing as it's you who's asking.'

'It'd be great if you could.'

'Shouldn't be too difficult. Can I let him know scotching Roger's marriage plans could be a part of the equation?'

'If you think that'll make him happier to talk to me.'

'Sure to, I'd say.'

'I appreciate this, Syd. I really do.'

'Don't mention it. Leave *me* to mention it, when I need a favour in return.' Syd guffawed. 'Don't worry. I haven't got a starstruck niece trying to get into RADA by the back door. The odd complimentary ticket's about the most I'm likely to touch you for.'

'Any time.'

'Actually, though, now I come to think about

it . . . ' He looked almost sheepish as he turned an idea over in his mind.

'What?'

'Well, I, er, I'm . . . bringing a guest to the play tonight. A lady. To be as frank and open as you must already know I always am, Tobe, Audrey's not been that long widowed, so I'm treading carefully. Trying to register a few Brownie points. If you could see your way clear . . . to joining us for a bite of supper after the show . . . I reckon I might just zoom up in her estimation.'

In the circumstances, I could hardly refuse. Not for the first time, Syd had outmanoeuvred me, since it appeared that I'd be repaying a favour before it had actually been done. 'My pleasure, Syd.'

'Grrreat.' He beamed tigerishly at me. 'We're going on to the Latin in the Lane. Do you know it?'

'I think so, yes.'

'Maybe you could catch up with us there when you've got changed. You know, spring a surprise on her.'

'OK.'

'And by then . . . ' He winked. 'I might have news of my old school chum.'

* * *

Supper with Syd Porteous and Audrey the eligible widow wouldn't have been my choice of late-night entertainment, but at least it sounded safe, which, with Denis's misadventures in mind, was an undeniably good thing. I excused myself from a prolonged session at the Cricketers on the excellent grounds that Syd would want me to be at my actorly best come the evening and took myself off for a fish and chip lunch. Gavin Colborn promised to be a valuable contact, possibly *in*valuable: an embittered uncle to tell me the worst about his well-heeled, good-looking nephew. Or the best, depending on your point of view.

⋆ ⋆ ⋆

A couple of hours' zizz was what I needed to set me up for the evening. I headed for the Sea Air with that as my sole ambition for the afternoon. Halfway along Madeira Place, however, I was waylaid.

I noticed a sleekly glowing dark-blue Porsche parked on the other side of the road. One admiring glance was all I gave it. Then I heard the door slam and my name was called. 'Toby Flood?' I turned and looked.

And there was Roger Colborn in jeans, leather jacket and sweatshirt, leaning against the driver's door and gazing across at me. He smiled faintly, as if daring me to pretend I didn't know who he was.

'Can we have a chat?'

I crossed over to his side, elaborately checking for traffic to give my brain a chance to work out what he was up to. It failed. 'Roger Colborn,' I announced neutrally.

'Pleased to meet you, Toby.' He offered a

hand. We shook. 'I've just been having lunch with Jenny.'

'Oh yes?'

'She told me about the help you've been giving her . . . with this little shit, Oswin.'

I nodded. 'Right.'

'I'm ahead of my schedule today. So, I thought I'd come over and thank you. In person.'

'There was no need.'

'When someone goes out of their way for me, I like to acknowledge the fact.'

'But I didn't . . . go out of my way for you.'

'For me. For Jenny. Same difference.' His smile broadened. 'Busy this afternoon?'

'Not really, no.'

'Then come for a drive with me. I reckon we ought to . . . get to know each other.'

'You do?'

'It'll avoid any . . . future misunderstandings. Come on. This beauty's been cooped up while I've been away. I need to give her a run. Why not come along? We can talk on the way. And let's face it, Toby, we do need to talk.'

* * *

Colborn had a point. He also had an edge of steel beneath the thin, silky affability. I could have argued the case for declining his invitation. But the case for gleaning whatever there was to be gleaned from his company was a good deal stronger.

We started north, the Porsche dawdling throatily along the city streets, then struck east towards the racecourse. Colborn's priority seemed to be to explain why he and Jenny had kept each other in the dark where Derek Oswin was concerned, although he must have realized I'd place my own construction on that, whatever he said.

'There's been a communications failure, Toby, in this case for the best of reasons. Neither of us wanted to worry the other. I know Oswin of old, of course. I've been ignoring him in the hope that he'll go away. It never occurred to me that he'd bother Jenny. Seeing him with a video of one of your old films naturally made her think his interest in her had something to do with you. There you have it.'

'I quite understand.'

'I'm glad you do. And, like I say, I'm also grateful. To be honest, I think it's a good thing we've met like this. You and Jenny were together quite a while. There's no sense trying to pretend your relationship with her never happened. It's part of her. We're adults, you and me. We know how it works. We should be able to deal with it.'

'I agree.'

'Great. So, what have you got lined up after this play?'

'Oh, there are several possibilities.' I had no intention of discussing the state of my career with Colborn, however adult and rational we were supposed to be. A change of subject was in order. 'I'm curious about Oswin. What can you tell me about him?'

'He used to work for my father's firm, Colbonite. I did myself, for a while. On a different level from the likes of Oswin, obviously. Christ knows what he's been up to since it folded.'

'Nothing, as far as gainful employment's concerned.'

'No surprise there. The guy's a loser.'

'But he's been in touch with you?'

'Sadly, yes. He's bombarded me with letters and phone calls about this history of Colbonite he's written. He's even sent me copies of the bloody thing.'

'Read it?'

'I'm a busy man, Toby. Ploughing through the rambling reminiscences of Derek Oswin isn't something I have either the time or the inclination to get around to. My father wound Colbonite up thirteen years ago. It was just a two-bit middling plastics company. One obscure victim of the slow death of British manufacturing. Who the hell cares?'

'Oswin said something about a valuable patent.'

'Did he?' Colborn's brow furrowed briefly at that, then he concentrated on the mirror as we joined the A27, heading east. A surge of acceleration took the Porsche into its preferred cruising range. But its driver's discourse had stalled.

'Was it valuable?'

'Mmm?'

'The patent.'

'Oh, moderately. It was a formula to prevent discoloration by sunlight. One of the company's precious few assets. But selling it didn't make my father rich beyond the dreams of avarice, let me tell you.'

'Richer than the redundant workforce, though, I assume.'

'They were paid their dues. Oswin has nothing to complain about.'

'I'm not sure he *is* complaining. About that, anyway.'

'What will your agent do with the book?'

'Read and reject, I imagine.'

'Let's hope that satisfies Oswin.'

'I think it will.'

'And you think I should have arranged something similar before this got out of hand. Well, you think right.' Colborn glanced at me. 'Thanks for getting me out of a hole I dug for myself, Toby. You've done *me* a favour as well as Jenny. I won't forget that.'

⋆ ⋆ ⋆

How magnanimous of him. And of me. At this rate he'd soon have been inviting me to a round of golf at his club. We were two civilized men of the world, finessing our way round the compromises and contradictions of embodying both Jenny's past and her future.

Complete bullshit, of course. What Roger Colborn was really engaged in was risk assessment. Was I an irritant that would soon go away of its own accord? Or a challenge he had to face down?

Somewhere beyond Lewes, he turned off the main road and headed up a steep lane onto the downs. There was a parking area at the top and broad vistas in all directions: a quilt of fields and woodland to the north, a grey slab of sea to the south.

'Game for a walk, Toby?' he asked in the moment of silence after the engine had died. 'I find the open air helps clear my thoughts. And there's something I really do want to be clear about.'

I agreed, with little enthusiasm. We climbed out into a cold-edged wind. I gazed along the crest of the downs, where a couple of hikers were the only humans in sight. The going looked chill and muddy. I was persuaded to squeeze into a spare pair of wellingtons. We set off. And Colborn began to lay out his thoughts.

'Jenny's made me a better person, Toby. Maybe she did that for you as well. If so, losing her must have been a real blow. I certainly wouldn't want to go back to being what I was before I met her. It was the biggest stroke of luck in my life. I'll never do anything to hurt her. You have my word on that. I love her. I honestly believe I always will. And I know I'll always protect her. She's safe with me. It's important you should understand that. I may not be quite as good for her as she is for me. That would be impossible. But I'm good enough. Plenty good enough.'

'I'm sure you are,' I lied.

'But what about you, Toby? Where are you going? According to Jenny, things aren't looking too bright for you. Tell me to mind my own business if you like, but, as I understand it, this play you're in has been, to put it bluntly, a flop.'

'It hasn't gone as well as we'd hoped.'

'And film work's pretty much dried up for you.'

'I wouldn't — '

'There's no need to be defensive about it.' He held up a hand to silence me. 'The point is that I have contacts in the film world. Not Hollywood, it's true, but in Europe. Co-production's the name of the game. I have a stake in several projects.'

'What are you trying to say?'

We stopped. He turned to look at me, the wind ruffling his hair. 'I'm saying I could get you into something. Back on the screen. In the relatively big time. Where you belong.'

He meant it. That was obvious. And whether you regarded it as the repayment of a favour or the removal of a stone from his shoe, the effect was the same: a problem solved for both of us. This, I suddenly realized, was what being a businessman meant. The making of attractive offers. The doing of productive deals. Cost-effectiveness. The profit margin. The bottom line.

'We don't have to like each other, Toby. Mutual respect is all it takes.'

'Why be a loser when you can be a winner? Is that what you mean?'

'Something like it.'

'I'd be a fool to turn you down, then.'

'So you would. But I come across plenty of fools. I'm used to having win-win propositions thrown back in my face.'

'I'm a jobbing actor, Roger. I can't afford to say no.'

'In that case, we'd better make sure there's something lucrative on hand soon for you to say yes to.'

'It'd be music to my agent's ears.'

Colborn smiled 'Don't you just love being pragmatic?'

'It's something of a novelty for me,' I coolly replied.

'You'll get used to it.' His smile broadened. 'I promise.'

* * *

We returned to the car and started back towards Brighton. Colborn elaborated briefly and pointedly on the nature of his profitably pragmatic business.

'It's all about timing, Toby. When to get into something. When to get out. And the key to timing is the same as the condition upon which God hath given liberty to man: eternal vigilance. That's what my staff do for me. Observe vigilantly. Freeing me to take time off. And to open my mind. I've learned to reject nothing without considering it. And to be willing to reject everything. It's worked well for me.'

'Do you have any relatives or dependants to support?'

'Ex-wives and children, you mean? None. Which helps, of course. It's easier to take risks when there's no-one else to worry about. Meeting Jenny's made me a little more risk-averse, I admit, even though she's quite capable of supporting herself, as the success she's made of Brimmers demonstrates. To be honest, I'd always avoided long-term relationships, partly because I knew they might turn me into a more cautious operator. But I've got to the stage where I can indulge a little caution. And Jenny's well worth any adjustments I've had to make to my life.'

It was all plausible enough, this slickly packaged version of himself Colborn was serving up. But it didn't convince me. And not just because I didn't want to be convinced. I'd spotted a flaw in his logic. What exactly was the ratio between the profits he'd turned on his shrewdly timed investments and the pile of cash he'd no doubt inherited from his father — the residue of that 'two-bit middling plastics company'? It wasn't so much about timing as editing. And when you edit a story there's always a danger that you'll leave a few loose ends dangling. I decided to give one a tug.

'Where was your office before you inherited Wickhurst Manor, Roger?'

'I didn't . . . put the business on its current footing until after my father died, actually.' That was one up to me. And he knew it. His change of tack was swift and clumsy. Or maybe it was just meant to *seem* clumsy. 'I hope missing the play last night didn't get you into too much trouble, by the way.'

'I'm weathering it.'

'Good.' He judged a pause minutely before continuing. 'How did your stand-in cope?'

It was an unusual question to ask. Why should he care? Why should he even bother to enquire? The only answer that came to mind was a deeply disturbing one. It was bad enough to think Denis might have been the victim of a botched set-up meant for me and commissioned by the man who'd just made me an offer too good to refuse. But it was somehow worse, far worse, to suppose that the set-up hadn't been botched at all; that Denis's brush with calamity had been devised quite deliberately as a message to me: a demonstration of what might befall me if I were foolish enough to reject the offer.

'I trust he didn't do too good a job,' Colborn went on with a chuckle. 'You wouldn't want the idea to get around that you're . . . expendable.'

⋆ ⋆ ⋆

Soon enough we were back in Madeira Place. 'Thanks for the ride,' I said as I climbed out. 'My pleasure,' he responded. I closed the passenger door behind me and watched him pull away. The car sped the short distance to the end of the street. Its brake lights blinked. Then it swung onto Marine Parade and was gone.

I headed straight across the road, sleep out of the question now but some kind of rest definitely in order. A glance up at the ground-floor bay window of the Sea Air told me that too was to be denied me. The residents' lounge ought by rights to have been deserted, given that I'm the only resident. As a result, I thought for a fragment of a second that the face I saw peering down at me might be some kind of hallucination. But no. Melvyn Buckingham really was there, craning his neck round the wing-back of his chair for a view. Our celebrated director had paid me a call.

* * *

I encountered Eunice in the hall, bearing a tea-tray towards the lounge. She whispered an apology to me. 'I'm *really* sorry about this, Toby. I couldn't turn him away, could I? Not when he's come all this way.'

'You didn't have to bake him a cake,' I grumbled, catching the homemade aroma rising from a generous slice of Dundee.

'I baked it for *you*. Here.' She handed me the tray. 'Take it in while I get back to my chores.'

I scowled after her as she descended discontentedly to the basement, then took a deep breath and processed into the directorial presence.

* * *

Melvyn was kitted out in the squirely tweeds he favours despite his metropolitan lifestyle. His expression, which ranges swiftly from approving smirks to pained grimaces during rehearsals, was currently fixed in a frown that indicated either anger or perplexity.

I plonked the tray down and smiled at him. 'Brian didn't say you were thinking of coming down.'

'It was to be a surprise,' Melvyn responded. 'Ever since Leo told me he wasn't bringing the play in, I've been meaning to see for myself where you've gone wrong. I was in the Canaries last week, catching the sun, so this was the soonest I could manage. I mentioned the trip to Leo over lunch yesterday. As you can imagine, it's turned out to be rather more apposite than I'd anticipated. Leo called me at an ungodly hour this morning, asking — nay, insisting — that I read you the riot act on his behalf.'

'He's over-reacting. I missed one performance. That's all there is to it.'

'Very possibly. But he who overpays is entitled to overreact.'

'Do you want some tea?'

'I *want* a stiff gin, dear boy. But in its absence I suppose the soothing leaf will suffice.'

I poured and handed him his cup, adding, 'I recommend the cake,' in my most enticing tone.

'It does look good.' Melvyn's gluttony has always eclipsed his professional judgement. He was a goner. 'All right.'

I handed him that too and watched as he took a bite. He was still munching through a first mouthful to his evident satisfaction when Eunice flounced into the room, balanced a plate bearing another slice on the arm of my chair and flounced out again.

'Leo's anxious to ensure things don't go off the rails this week,' Melvyn spluttered through the sultanas.

'They won't.'

'Fortunately, the *Argus* didn't make a big thing of your . . . indisposition.' He nodded to a copy of the paper lying on the floor next to his chair. 'There's a lot of flu about.'

'But I'm over mine.'

'I certainly hope so.'

'There's nothing for Leo to worry about.'

'He doesn't seem to agree. I fear the letter spooked him.'

'What letter?'

'You didn't know about it?'

'I've no idea what you're referring to.'

'Oh.' He wiped some crumbs from his lips. 'You'd better take a look, then.' With an effort, he pulled a piece of paper from his jacket pocket and handed it over. 'It was delivered to Leo's office this morning.'

As soon as I unfolded the sheet, I recognized the handwriting. In one sense, the source was no surprise. In another . . .

77 Viaduct Road
Brighton
BN1 4ND

2nd December 2002

Dear Mr Gauntlett,
I do not want you to worry when you hear

that Mr Flood has missed this evening's performance of *Lodger in the Throat*. As you may be aware, Mr Flood's estranged wife lives here in Brighton. Since Mr Flood arrived yesterday, I have been assisting him as best I can in his endeavours to effect a reconciliation with Mrs Flood. I feel sure you would not want to stand in the way of such a development. After all, it would make Mr Flood a more contented man and therefore a more assured actor.

As it happens, it is necessary for Mr Flood to be somewhere other than the Theatre Royal this evening. He will probably decline to explain his absence, which is why I am writing to emphasize that it is quite simply unavoidable if his future wellbeing is to be secured. In the circumstances, I am confident that you will be tolerant of the inconvenience caused to your company.

Incidentally, perhaps I could take this opportunity of mentioning that the play's disappointing performance on tour is largely attributable in my opinion to the unsympathetic direction of Mr Buckingham, who has insisted upon treating it as some form of drawing-room comedy rather than the merciless satire on family life that it actually is.

Respectfully yours,
Derek Oswin

The name Edna Welthorpe popped into my thoughts as I finished the letter. She was the pseudonymous phantom Joe Orton invented for the purpose of writing teasing and tendentious missives to institutions whose pomposity needed pricking (in his opinion). Sometimes she'd even fire off a prudish complaint to a newspaper about one of Orton's own plays, all publicity being good publicity. I felt instantly and instinctively certain that Derek had written to Leo in the spirit of Edna Welthorpe, calculating that I would see the joke — but that neither Leo nor Melvyn would. But, though I saw the joke, I was also the victim of it. Derek really was mad, in the Ortonian sense. There was no telling what he might do next. If I'd thought I was in control of the situation, this letter showed me to be deluding myself.

I handed it back to Melvyn. 'I seem to have a prankster by the tail,' I said through a simulated smile. 'This is rather embarrassing, isn't it?'

'You *are* acquainted with Mr Oswin, dear boy?'

'Yes. But he isn't acting as my go-between, or — '

'Then why did you miss the play?'

My smile became a stiff grin. 'You've got me there.'

'Who is he?'

'Nobody you need to bother about. In fact, that's exactly what he is. Nobody.'

'I wish Leo agreed with you. He seemed to think the ghastly little pipsqueak had a point.' Melvyn reddened. 'About my direction.'

'Oswin's just trying to get a rise out of us.'

'But *why* did you miss the play?'

'All right.' I held up my hands in surrender. 'It

did have to do with Jenny . . . and my attempts to persuade her to . . . call off the divorce. But Oswin isn't . . . assisting me . . . in any way.'

'Then how does he know so much about it, pray?'

'Oh God.' I stood up and stared out through the window, a view of slowly falling dusk seeming preferable to holding Melvyn's gaze. 'There'll be no more Edna letters, I assure you.'

'Edna?'

'Never mind. Forget Derek Oswin. Please. Leave him to me.'

'I'd be glad to.'

'I'll sort him out.' I gave my dimly reflected self a confirmatory nod. 'Once and for all.'

* * *

I eventually persuaded Melvyn to leave on the grounds — to which he could hardly object — that I needed a rest before the performance. This was undoubtedly true. But lying on my bed, with the only light in the room a drizzle of amber from the nearest street lamp, I found rest hard to come by. What did Derek Oswin think he was playing at? The question would have been troubling enough to ponder without the added complication of Roger Colborn's brazen attempt to buy me off, backed up as it very possibly was by the threat of still cruder inducements. What in the name of sweet Jesus had I got myself into? And how, more to the point, was I to get myself out?

Not, I reasoned, by storming round to Viaduct Road and throttling the epistolarian of number

77, tempting though the idea was. Derek would probably claim he had written to Leo in the genuine hope of persuading him to go easy on me, just as he had supposedly manoeuvred me into missing the play in the first place solely for the purpose of making Jenny think well of me. It could even be true. I didn't know whether I was over- or under-estimating him. He'd sent the letter to Leo before knowing if I'd do his bidding, which suggested a supreme confidence in his tactics. But confidence and madness often go hand in hand.

Not in Roger Colborn's case, though. He's the ultimate rationalist. And confident to boot. It occurred to me that he and Derek are strangely alike, for all their apparent dissimilarity. They both think they have the measure of me. And they both might be right. *I* certainly don't have the measure of *them*. Yet.

* * *

Gavin Colborn may be my conduit to the truth. And I was relying on Syd Porteous to lead me to him. Until my post-show supper with Syd and his lady friend, therefore, I could make no headway. Derek would have to wait. Everything was on hold. Until I'd got back on stage and done my stuff. As some seemed to doubt I still could.

* * *

But I wasn't one of them. In fact, tonight's performance of *Lodger in the Throat* was a liberation for me. I could stop thinking about the complexities of the Jenny — Roger — Derek triangle and enjoy myself as James Elliott, the middle-aged middle-class man of repute who suddenly senses that his carefully managed life is falling apart around him. I stopped straining for effects and played it like I saw it was. For the first time, I found myself believing in the person I was supposed to be. Orton hadn't written a comedy with a serious undercurrent, I realized. He'd written a tragedy so bleak you had to laugh at it.

And *how* they laughed. A Brighton audience was bound to be at the sophisticated end of the spectrum of those we'd played to, but their responsiveness none the less took me by surprise. If it had been like this earlier in the tour, we'd all be looking forward to a New Year in the West End. We'd hit our stride too late.

That we'd found it at all was attributed by an over-excited and over-lubricated Melvyn Buckingham to my more assertive projection of the character of James Elliott. And this, he told anyone who was willing to listen as drinks and hangers-on circulated afterwards round the star's and co-star's dressing rooms, was the result of an intensive examination of the role we'd conducted earlier.

'It's strange,' I smilingly whispered to Jocasta. 'I don't seem to have any memory of that.'

'Something galvanized you, Toby,' she said. 'Even if it wasn't Melvyn.'

'More likely to have been the widespread reports of how well Denis did last night.'

'He did do well. But he's still not in the same

league as you, not when you're really on form, anyway. That bit at the start of act two, where you delayed waking Tom and took a sort of poignant tour of the set — where did that come from?'

'Not sure. It just . . . came.'

* * *

I was sure, of course. Derek Oswin of all unlikely people had turned me into a better James Elliott. I didn't know whether to welcome his influence or resent it. Either way, he was hardly a conventional source of artistic advice. In fact, however you looked at it, he was a thoroughly disturbing one.

Melvyn was evidently set on making his night in Brighton memorable. I extricated myself with some difficulty from the party he was getting together and headed for the Latin in the Lane.

* * *

The restaurant was three-quarters full, bubbling and bustling in best late-night Italian tradition. Judging by the numerous glances and murmurs I attracted on my way through, many of the diners had adjourned there from the Theatre Royal. Among those was Syd Porteous, who'd added a tie to his standard clobber. It looked worn and thin enough to be of the old-school variety. He greeted me as if we'd known each other for years (which in some strange way it felt as if we had) and introduced me to his suitably surprised companion.

'Sydney, you dark horse,' she exclaimed. 'You never said it was Mr Toby Flood we were meeting.'

'An evening with me is a venture into the unexpected,' Syd responded with a roll of the eyes. 'Tobe, this lovely lady is Audrey Spencer.'

Audrey *was* lovely, despite an outfit that might have flattered her fifteen years ago but now verged on the affectionately sarcastic. There was a lot of bosom and a lacy fringe of bra on display. And the pink trousers — I couldn't avoid noticing when she set off for the loo later — were stretched round a bottom that needed camouflage rather than emphasis. What age couldn't either wither or expand, though, was the sparkle in her eyes, her mischievously crooked grin and her effervescently winning personality.

'I haven't enjoyed myself at the theatre as much in I don't know how long,' she enthused. 'That Orton was a one, wasn't he? Not that the words would count for a lot if you didn't deliver them so well, Toby. Sydney tells me he actually met Orton once. Has he mentioned that to you?'

'He has, yes,' I replied, glancing at Syd.

'I had no idea he moved in such exalted circles, you know. I'm beginning to realize he's a man of mystery. Just as well I like a good mystery, isn't it?'

At which Syd fingered his tie and tried to give his self-satisfied smirk a mysterious edge.

* * *

Such banter continued as we ordered our meals and made steady inroads into the Piedmont end of the wine list. Syd wasn't one to stint ladies *or* actors. Feeling more than somewhat pleased with myself following what had to count as our best yet rendering of *Lodger in the Throat*, I was happy to indulge my host, especially in view of the pay-off I was hoping for.

This was delivered during the first of Audrey's nose-powdering expeditions. Syd lowered his voice to a hoarse growl, leaned towards me and announced, 'I've been in touch with Gav Colborn as promised, Tobe. He's happy to meet. The Cricketers at noon tomorrow suit you? Same time, same place, like? May as well keep it simple.'

'I'll be there.'

'Perfecto. Although, as it happens, you don't have to wait until then for some interesting gen on the Colborn clan.'

'I don't?'

'No. Wait till Aud gets back. She can spring it on you.'

'Audrey can?'

I had to be content with one of Syd's ludicrously choreographed winks by way of an answer. Within a few minutes, though, Audrey rejoined us, whereupon Syd asked her to tell me all about something they'd discussed earlier.

'Oh, *that*.' Audrey cast a sympathetic glance in my direction. 'Are you sure Toby wants to hear about it, Sydney? It's really not very exciting. Or jolly. And we're supposed to be having fun.'

'I hope you are, darling,' said Syd, using

'darling' for the first time I could recall. 'Tobe *will* be interested, I promise.'

'All right, then.' She turned towards me. 'Sydney asked me if I'd heard of a plastics company called Colbonite, though why he should think I might have done . . . '

'He that asketh receiveth,' murmured Syd.

'Well,' Audrey went on, 'it's a strange thing, but I do know the name. I'm secretary to one of the consultants at the Royal Sussex. He's a cancer specialist. Over the years, he's treated quite a lot of people who worked for Colbonite. The thing is — '

The trill of my mobile was a sound I didn't want to hear. With a gabbled apology, I plucked it out of my pocket, intending to dispose of the caller in short order. Melvyn in his cups was my bet, urging me to join the party. But it wasn't Melvyn.

'Toby, this is Denis. Where are you?'

'A restaurant in the Lanes.'

'Is there any chance . . . you could meet me . . . sort of right now?'

'I'm in the middle of a meal, Denis.'

'I wouldn't ask if I wasn't . . . pretty desperate.' And it was true to say he did sound desperate. There was a quiver of anxiety in his voice.

'What's wrong?'

'The man mountain who threw me out of Embassy Court has shown up at my digs. They're after me, Toby. Christ knows why. But I'm frightened, I don't mind admitting it. I don't know what to do.'

'Where are you now?'

'I'm at a bus stop in North Street, with a load of students waiting for a midnight run back to the University. I figure there's safety in numbers. But there won't be any numbers to be safe in when the bus turns up.'

I struggled to suppress my irritation, knowing that if Denis was in trouble, it was probably on my account. 'OK, OK,' I said. 'I'll be with you as soon as I can get there.'

I rang off and smiled ruefully at my bemused companions. 'I'm *really* sorry about this. A friend of mine is . . . in difficulties. I'm going to have to go and find out what the problem is.'

'You're leaving us, Tobe?' Syd looked positively distraught. 'Don't say that.'

'I've no choice, I'm afraid.'

'We understand, Toby,' said Audrey. 'What are friends for but to help out in an emergency?'

'True enough,' Syd reluctantly agreed.

'Do you have time for me to finish telling you about Colbonite?' Audrey asked. 'There isn't a lot to it, in all honesty.'

'Well . . . ' I glanced at my watch. It was approaching a quarter to midnight, which meant Denis was safe enough for the present. 'I can stay for a few minutes.' And I did want to hear about Colbonite. Oh yes. 'Your boss treated a lot of workers from Colbonite, you said. For cancer?'

'Yes. Of the bladder, mostly. I don't know about 'a lot', though. More like a steady trickle. Terminal cases, usually, I'm afraid.'

'And this has gone on . . . since the company closed?'

'Yes. Well, cancer often develops a long time after exposure . . . to whatever causes it.'

'And what does cause it . . . in these cases?'

'I don't know.'

'But Gav might,' put in Syd.

'Yes. I suppose he might.' I looked back at Audrey. 'How many cases are we talking about?'

'I couldn't say.'

'Go on. Just a guesstimate. I won't quote you on it.'

'Well . . . ' She thought for a moment, then said, 'Several dozen at least.' And then she thought for another moment. 'Maybe more.'

* * *

I must have left the Latin in the Lane later than I'd thought. By the time I reached North Street it was five past midnight. The city centre's main thoroughfare was cold and empty. There was no knot of raucous students waiting for transport back to the campus. And no sign of Denis.

I retrieved his mobile number from my phone and rang it. No answer. I tried again. Still no answer.

I stood at one of the deserted bus stops, wondering what to do next. Denis might have got on the student bus, I supposed, although a trip out to Falmer would only leave him with the problem of how to get back. Or he might have pulled himself together and returned to his lodgings. But there we came to a gaping lack of information. I didn't know where he was staying.

Unable to think of any other recourse, I rang

Brian Sallis. There was a slur to his voice when he answered and a blurred hubbub in the background. I imagined he was in a restaurant somewhere, with Melvyn and most of the cast. And I imagined they were having a good time — unlike me.

'Toby? Where are you?'

'A bus stop in North Street, since you ask.'

'*What*? Get yourself down here. We're at the King and I in Ship Street. Great squid, let me tell you.'

'Nice idea, Brian, but I have to find Denis Maple. Do you know where he's staying?'

'He's probably tucked up in bed by now.'

'I don't think so. And this is urgent. *Where is he staying?*'

'No need to shout, old chap. Anyway, I haven't got that info on me, Toby. Somewhere in Kemp Town, I think. Hold on. I'll ask.' But asking did no good. No-one's memory was working too well. I cut Brian off in the middle of further urgings for me to join them and rang Denis's mobile again.

Still there was no answer. 'Where are you, Denis?' I said aloud. 'Where in hell are you?'

Could he have headed for the Sea Air? It was one possibility I could check fairly easily. And it was in the same general direction as his lodgings, so there was some frail kind of logic to it. I started walking. Fast.

Within minutes, I'd reached the Old Steine. Traffic was thin and buses there were none. The stops to left and right were all empty. I started across towards St James's Street, redialling on my mobile as I went. Yet again, there was no answer.

But then, just as I was about to give up, I heard a bleeping, joining the ringing tone in a weird stereo. I was halfway along the pavement that runs past the northern side of the gardens around the Victoria Fountain. I stopped dead and listened for a second, hardly able to believe what I was hearing. The phone stopped ringing and the message service cut in. I cancelled the call and redialled. The phone started up again. I turned to my right, towards the fountain.

There was a figure lying on the ground near the base of the fountain, readily mistakable for one of the many deep shadows cast by shrubs, bench-ends and cast-iron dolphins. I knew it was Denis before I reached him. He was lying on his side, legs drawn up. As I stooped and rolled him over onto his back, his mobile fell out of his hand.

'Denis? Denis, are you all right?' But he was as far from all right as you can get. His mouth was open. But he wasn't breathing. His eyes stared sightlessly up at me, a shaft of lamplight catching the whites. I felt beneath his ear for a pulse, then at his wrist. Nothing. I jabbed at the 9 button on my mobile. A chasm of time opened around me in the darkness and the silence. At last, there was an answer. I demanded an ambulance. I gabbled out our location. 'He's not breathing,' I shouted. 'I think his heart's stopped. I need you here *now*.'

* * *

It's a straight run from the hospital. The streets were empty. The ambulance was probably there within five minutes. It felt infinitely longer, of course. I dredged some first-aid principles out of my memory and tried to kick-start Denis back to life with mouth-to-mouth and chest compressions. But it's more than likely my technique was too faulty for any good to have come of it. I felt stupid and helpless and desperate. And responsible. Yes. I felt that as well.

Death's the biggest absolute of all. Strange, then, that we can be so vague about the moment of its arrival. The heart stops beating. The body stops moving. Later, eventually and reluctantly, the brain closes down. When exactly that happened to Denis Maple — at what precise minute he finally blinked out of existence — is a matter for futile debate. Was it before I found him? Or while I was manhandling him to no effect? Or during the ambulance ride? Or later still, at the hospital? I don't know. I never will.

The pronouncement, though: I can be clear about that. A nurse came to me in the hospital waiting area. 'I'm afraid it was too late,' she said. 'We couldn't save him.' Denis was dead, a heart attack the preliminary verdict. I'd mentioned his heart trouble, so it must have seemed a straightforward case to the doctors. Something like this was always on the cards for a man in his fragile state of health. Alcohol; stress; overexertion: anything could have brought it on. He was just unlucky to be alone when it happened.

Unlucky? Yes, Denis was certainly that. Maybe his biggest misfortune was to be a friend of mine. I put him up for the understudy job. He needed something undemanding to ease his way back into acting. And he needed the money. So, I helped him out.

Of this world, it now transpires. The strain of performing last night. The strife he ran into afterwards. And the events of tonight, which I can never ask him to relate or explain. I brought those down on his head. And his heart.

I must have phoned Brian. Or else I must have asked the nurse to do it for me. I can't remember exactly how it happened. But at some point he was there at the hospital, along with Melvyn and Jocasta and Mandy. They were all there. And so was I.

But Denis wasn't. He was nowhere.

* * *

'What happened?' they asked me. And I tried to tell them. But I didn't really know. And what I did know can have made little sense. A garbled call. A search. A discovery. A death. You could squeeze the context and meaning out of it if you were so minded and all you'd be left with is a medical fact. Denis's heart stopped. And so did he.

* * *

They delivered me back to the Sea Air, concerned that I was in shock and shouldn't be left alone. I roused myself sufficiently to persuade them that I'd be all right. Eventually, they left.

In the morning, Brian will notify the rest of

the cast and company. Then he'll contact Denis's next of kin. 'A tragic misfortune' is probably how he'll describe it. Not like Jimmy Maidment's suicide. There's no cause to think this is a jinxed production. As for the rest of us . . . life goes on. And so must the play. Let's see it in proportion. Denis wasn't well. A game guy, but an ailing one. Even understudying was too much for him. It's sad it had to happen. What else is there to say?

* * *

I sit here in my room, with my whisky and my tape recorder, trying to piece together in my mind what must have happened. After the second act got under way, Denis probably went for a meal with Glenys. (I can check that with her in the morning.) Then what? A few drinks on his own somewhere? (Glenys is no night owl.) A film, maybe? If I'd looked, I might have found an Odeon ticket stub in his pocket. It's a trivial detail in itself, of course. The fact is that around eleven o'clock Denis must have got back to his lodgings and found the man mountain from Embassy Court waiting for him. Or spotted him waiting and beaten a retreat. Maybe he was followed. That would explain him taking refuge in a bus queue. Maybe he just *thought* he was followed. Same difference, really. So, he phoned me. The only one who'd take him seriously. But the bus arrived before I showed up. He didn't get on. He waited for me. Not for long, though. Maybe he saw man mountain again. Maybe he just panicked. Same difference again? I don't think so. I was only five minutes late. Surely he'd have hung on that long. My guess is that he left because he had to. He was followed. Or chased. Was he running when the pain hit him? He must have known what it was. He headed for the benches by the fountain to rest. Or to hide. He took out his phone to make a call. For an ambulance, maybe. Or to me. Whichever it was, he never got as far as dialling the number. He went down. And stayed there. His pursuer melted away into the night. Precious minutes slipped by. Too many minutes. Until I found him.

* * *

What do I do now? They were getting at Denis to warn me off, to show me what they were capable of. They can't have meant to kill him. They can't have known he had a weak heart. But he did. And now he's dead because of it. And because of *them*. And because of *me*. Somebody should pay for that. Yes. Somebody really should.

WEDNESDAY

I woke this morning to the fleeting delusion that Denis Maple's death was just a dream. Reality soon had me back in its grip, however. I'd slept for seven solid hours, but didn't feel more than superficially refreshed. It was gone ten o'clock. I was due to meet Gavin Colborn at noon. And there was someone else I needed to see first.

Already, my day was barely under control. My days on tour had previously been slow, short and empty. But that had changed now I'd come to Brighton.

I showered, shaved and dressed hurriedly. Then I called Jenny. She didn't sound pleased to hear from me. And she didn't want me to come round to Brimmers; I could say what I wanted over the phone. But I couldn't. In the end, I think she understood that. We settled on the Rendezvous at 11.15.

* * *

Heavy rain was falling from an ashen sky, the rain driven diagonally up Madeira Place by the wind beating in off the sea. The weather made the route I took to the Rendezvous, along the storm-lashed front and up Black Lion Street, a crazy choice. But I wasn't ready to cross the Steine yet and to pass the spot near the fountain where I'd found Denis. I wasn't just looking for answers. I was avoiding some as well.

* * *

I wondered if the staff of the Rendezvous had begun to notice Derek Oswin's absence, or to recognize me as a regular. They gave no sign of either as I bought a coffee and joined Jenny at her table.

She was looking stern and impatient. I think she'd been debating with herself whether I was in danger of becoming as much of a nuisance as Derek. Clearly, she had no idea what I was about to tell her.

'Denis Maple's dead.'

'Oh God.' Shock silenced her for a moment. Then she asked, 'What happened?'

'Heart attack.'

'That's dreadful. I'm sorry, Toby. You and he got on so well. It must be a blow. To the company as well. I mean, coming after Jimmy Maidment . . . When did this happen?'

'Just after midnight.'

'And when did you hear about it?'

'I was there when he died, Jenny. Or just after. He'd phoned me. He was worried, you see. Worried and frightened. Somebody was following him. *Chasing* him.'

'Surely not.'

'Surely yes. You know why he and I met here yesterday morning? Because Denis wanted to tell me something. Something he reckoned I *had* to be told about.'

'What?'

I studied Jenny's face as I related Denis's story and the events of last night. I blurred the context, of course. I said nothing about Syd Porteous or the meeting with her fiancé's uncle he was setting up for me. Nor did I mention said fiancé's virtual offer to me of a film part. The rain sluiced down the window behind me. Steam rose from the *espresso* machine. And skittering there, in the faintest twitches of Jenny's mouth and the flickers of her gaze, I read the beginnings of doubt. She wasn't sure — she wasn't absolutely certain — that all this amounted to nothing.

'I'm sorry Denis is dead,' she said, breaking the silence that fell after I'd finished. 'He was a lovely man.'

'Yes. Which would be tragic enough. But he didn't need to die. That makes it worse than a tragedy.'

'You don't know what happened after you spoke to him. You can't know. He may have . . . imagined the man at his lodgings.'

'No. Denis was as level-headed as they come.'

'He was also a sick man. For all you know, sicker than he was letting on.'

'I'll give you that. It's possible, entirely possible. But something more than his own imagination tipped him over the edge. And that something comes back to me.'

'What are you suggesting?'

'I'm *deducing* exactly what I'm supposed to deduce, Jenny: that paying attention to Derek Oswin isn't a good idea. That I should lay off.

That I should leave well alone.'

'Denis was drunk by his own admission on Monday night and probably drugged too. You can't draw any conclusions from what he *thought* happened to him at Embassy Court.'

'I think I can.'

'Well, you *can't*.' She glared at me. 'It's absurd.'

'Reckon I've got it all wrong, do you?'

'Yes. I do. Why in God's name should anyone want to stop you speaking to Derek Oswin?'

'Presumably they're afraid of what he might tell me.'

'What *can* he tell you, Toby? He worked for a plastics company, not MI5. For Christ's sake, pull yourself together.' She blushed and looked around, suddenly aware that she'd been speaking too loudly. She hunched forward and dropped her voice. 'Listen to me. You're upset about Denis. You're getting this out of proportion. There's no conspiracy going on. There's just . . . life . . . and death.'

'I suppose a heart attack's better than cancer.'

'What's that supposed to mean?'

'A lot of Colbonite's staff died of cancer. Did you know that?'

She didn't answer. Maybe she couldn't answer. She stared at me, blinking rapidly, struggling to decide there and then whether the things I'd said reflected any more than my desire to believe the worst of Roger Colborn. She wanted to believe the best of him, naturally. Neither of us was exactly unbiased. Which made the truth hard for us to come by — or to recognize when we did.

'I may have given Roger the impression yesterday that I could be bought off. Could you put him right on that for me, Jenny? There's no deal.'

Now she was angry. I'd taken a step too far. I'd lost her. 'Nobody's trying to buy you off, Toby.' She pushed her chair back, the feet squealing against the floor, and stood up. 'I'm not going to listen to any more of this. It's — ' She steadied herself, holding up both hands and closing her eyes as she took a deep breath. Then she opened them and looked down at me.

'Jenny, I — '

'*No*.' She looked at me a second longer. 'Not another word.' She turned and headed for the door.

Leaving me to stare into my coffee and begin the all too easy task of calculating how I could have handled our conversation so much better. The waitress came over to clear Jenny's cup. As she did so, the spoon fell out of the saucer and clattered down onto the table.

'Sorry,' she said.

'Me too,' I murmured.

* * *

I was still slumped over the dregs of my coffee some minutes later when my mobile rang.

'Toby, it's Brian Sallis. How are you feeling this morning?'

'Much the same as last night, Brian. How are you?'

'Rather shook up, actually. But I, er . . . just wanted to . . . check you were OK.'

'I'll be on stage tonight. You don't need to worry.'

'I didn't mean that. I meant . . . generally.'

'Generally? On the grim side of OK, I suppose.'

'This has knocked the wind out of everyone's sails, Toby. I've been . . . notifying people all morning. There's a lot of . . . distress.'

'Denis was a popular guy.'

'So he was. Look, on that subject, could you do me a favour?'

'Try me.'

'I spoke to Denis's brother earlier. Ian Maple. He's coming down here today. He wants to know what happened and, well, you know more than anyone.'

'You want me to talk to him?'

'I'm meeting him off the train and taking him round to the undertaker's. After that, I'm not sure what he'll want to do. Could I ring you this afternoon and fix something up?'

'Sure.'

'Thanks. I appreciate it. It's shaping up into a pretty bloody day, to be honest, with the press to handle and . . . everything else. Melvyn's gone back to London, by the way. I mean, that was the plan all along, but — '

'We wouldn't want Melvyn to have to change his plans.'

'No.' Ordinarily, Brian would have sprung to our director's defence, but he didn't seem disposed to make the effort this time. 'Thanks again, Toby. I'll be in touch later.'

* * *

It was close to noon when I left the Rendezvous, dashing from shelter to shelter through the rain to the Cricketers, where the foul weather had kept custom to a minimum.

Rain or shine made little difference to Syd Porteous, however. He was already installed with a pint and a crumpled newspaper. He greeted me with a frown of concern and a solicitous pat on the shoulder.

'Sorry to hear you've lost one of the company, Tobe. Bit of a facer, that.'

I looked at him in some dismay, unprepared as I was for the news to have spread so fast. 'How did you know?'

'It was on the local news this morning.'

'What did they say?'

'Nothing much. Denis Maple was his name, right? Understudy. Heart attack, apparently.'

I nodded. 'So it was.'

'The name rang a bell. Tell me to mind my own if you like, Tobe, but was it him you had to rush off and meet last night?'

'Yes.' I had no choice but to admit it.

'So . . . what happened?'

It was a fair question. I couldn't have supplied a complete answer even if I'd wanted to. Syd already knew more about my affairs than was good for him. Far more than I knew about his. Some judicious pruning of the facts was called for. 'Denis was obviously upset when I spoke to him. He was probably already feeling unwell. He'd keeled over by the time I got to him. There was nothing I could do.'

'He was the bookie in *Long Odds*, wasn't he?' Syd asked.

'You have a good memory.'

'Names and faces.' He tapped his forehead. 'They've always stuck. Aud and I were sorry you had to dash off like that. If we'd — ' He broke off as the door opened behind me. 'Watch out. Here's Gav.' Then he added, in a hasty whisper, 'Best not mention the untimely to him, hey? Might jangle his nerves.'

I was still puzzling over Syd's reasoning when he commenced a grinning introduction. Gavin Colborn failed to reciprocate with a grin of his own, my impression being that he'd need lessons before attempting one. His narrow, bony face was set in sombre lines beneath a jutting brow. He was as thin as a rail and slightly stooped, dressed in a frayed grey suit and black rollneck beneath the sort of raincoat Harold Wilson used to wear. He'd lost most of his hair and the only similarity to his nephew was to be found in the bizarrely beautiful sapphire blue of his deep-socketed eyes. The idea that we needed to worry about making him nervous seemed utterly absurd.

'Great to see you, Gav,' Syd enthused irrepressibly between the practicalities of ordering drinks. 'It's been too long. Far too long.'

'I don't get out so much these days,' said Colborn, a gust of sour whisky reaching me on his breath.

'You'll have seen Tobe's face on the poster at the Royal.'

'I've not passed that way recently. I'm no theatregoer, Mr Flood.'

'It's not everyone's cup of tea,' I responded, speculating idly on what Gavin Colborn's cup of tea could possibly be.

'I gather you want to discuss my nephew.'

'Small talk's never been Gav's speciality,' said Syd as we carried our drinks to the fireside table that was rapidly becoming our regular berth. 'I've told him it's the key to success with the ladies, but he takes no notice.'

'I assume you're a busy man, Mr Flood,' said Colborn, lighting up a cigarette. 'I don't want to bore you.'

If this remark was meant as a put-down, it signally failed. 'We're on first names here, Gav,' said Syd. 'Isn't that right, Tobe?'

'Yes, Syd,' I said with self-conscious emphasis.

'Well, then . . . *Toby*,' said Colborn, 'let me see if I understand the situation. Syd tells me you're seeking to assess my nephew Roger's suitability as a husband for your ex-wife, about whose welfare you're still . . . concerned.'

'That's right.'

'You've met him?'

'Yes.'

'How did he strike you?'

'They didn't come to blows, Gav,' put in Syd.

Colborn said nothing, letting his question hang in the air while Syd got a chortle out of his system. 'He's obviously intelligent,' I eventually replied. 'And charming. Attractive to women, as well, I imagine.'

'Yes,' said Colborn deliberatively. 'He's certainly all of those things.'

'But is he honest?'

'That's the essence of your inquiry, is it . . . Toby?' (He still didn't seem at ease with my Christian name.) 'Is Roger an honourable man?'

'Well, is he?'

'What do you think?'

'I'm . . . inclined to doubt it.'

'So you should.'

'Any . . . particular reason?'

'Several. But I must declare an interest. Or rather a grievance. I have Roger to thank for my present situation. Penury's a miserable experience and it grows more miserable with age. You can be poor, happy and young. So they tell me, anyway. But poor, happy and old? That you cannot be.'

'You should have backed more of my tips over the years, Gav,' said Syd. 'You've got to speculate to accumulate.'

'I wouldn't need to if Roger hadn't shafted me.' There was bitterness in Colborn's voice now. He was no doting uncle.

'How did he do that?'

'By manipulating his father — my elder brother, Walter — who took over the running of the family firm, Colbonite, when our father stepped down. He thought he could do a better job without me on board. I was . . . eased out.' A rough calculation suggested that Roger could only have been a child at the time Gavin was describing and in no position to manipulate anyone, but I didn't contest the point. Soon enough, I sensed, we'd come on to meatier stuff. 'I had some company shares, held in trust during our father's lifetime and subsequently mine to do with as I pleased. The same arrangement was made for our sister, Delia. They weren't worth a lot. Or so I thought. Roger went straight into Colbonite from university. In the mid-Eighties, he . . . persuaded me to sell him my shares. He chose his moment well. I was . . . going through a bad patch. I needed the money. I found out later he'd pulled the same trick with Delia. What neither of us knew was that he'd already started encouraging Walter to wind up the business. Closing Colbonite down freed them to sell the company's most valuable asset — a dyeing patent. That set Roger up very nicely. Having bought Delia's shares as well as mine, his slice of the pie was that much bigger. And Delia and I got no slice at all. Do you know what he said when I confronted him? 'It was nothing personal, Uncle,' he said. 'It was just a matter of business.' A matter of business? The bastard. It was a matter of *two and a half million pounds*.'

'Christ!' Syd choked on his beer. 'I never knew it was that much.'

'You know now.'

'No wonder you were seriously dischuffed.'

'I had no legal claim, you understand, Toby,' Colborn went on. 'I could only ask for what Roger described as a hand-out. I could only . . . beg. Which I did. To no avail. He wouldn't pay me a penny.'

'What about your brother?'

'Walter said it was up to Roger. After all, it was

Roger who'd bought my shares. So, Walter settled into a comfortable retirement at Wickhurst Manor, Roger slid off to Jersey to dodge the taxman and I . . . got by as best I could.'

'Delia too, presumably.'

'No. Delia got lucky. She met a rich man and married him. It was wine and roses for her too. I was the only one on bread and water. Still am.'

'Roger more or less admitted he hadn't been above a bit of sharp practice in the past,' I said. 'He claims to be a reformed character since meeting Jenny.'

'The love of a good woman can work miracles,' said Syd with a sickly smile.

'Believe that if you want to,' Gavin retorted. 'Roger will certainly want you to. He was an evil child. And he's grown into a devious, self-serving man.'

'We're into leopard-and-spots territory here, are we, Gav?' Syd enquired.

'Put it this way.' Gavin's voice dropped to a sandpapery rasp. 'If Roger's suddenly developed a soft centre, how come he's failed to put right any of the strokes he's pulled? A hand-out to his impecunious uncle wouldn't go amiss, considering how he ripped me off sixteen years ago, but there's been bugger-all sign of it. And what about all those poor sods who've had their lives shortened by working for Colbonite? What's he done for them, eh?' Gavin made a circle with his thumb and forefinger. 'That's what.'

'Are you talking about . . . the cancer victims, Gavin?' I tentatively asked.

'You're better informed than I thought,' he

replied, treating me to a meaningful stare.

'I mentioned them,' said Syd.

'I wasn't aware you knew either.' Gavin's stare swivelled round to his old school chum in a less than chummy fashion.

'I keep my ear to the ground and my nose to the wind. It's amazing what you pick up.' (Especially if your girlfriend's secretary to an oncology consultant, I reflected.)

'Is there a definite connection between these cancer cases and Colbonite?' I asked.

'Not as a scientifically proven certainty, no. Walter and Roger hired a chemistry boffin at the University to tie the argument up in knots. Most of the people affected are dead now anyway. There'd be their next of kin, of course. If they could make the case stick, they'd be entitled to compensation.'

'Stacking up to more than two and a half mill?' put in Syd.

'No doubt a lot more. As I understand it, the carcinogen was a curing agent used in a dyeing process. The patented method required its use in a dangerously unstable form. Inhalation of the fumes over a period of years . . . was a death sentence.'

'Did Roger and your brother know that?' I asked.

'I suspect so, yes. Not at the beginning. But before the end. They sold the patent and closed the company down not because it was unprofitable but because they were afraid the cancer scare would slash its value. Technically, Colbonite didn't go into liquidation. It was sold to a shell company that was wound up shortly afterwards. Roger's idea, I'm sure of it.'

'You're going to have to explain that ploy to us high-finance duds, Gav,' said Syd.

'It means that even if a case for compensation was made out, Roger couldn't be billed for it, because the responsible party, Colbonite, last belonged to somebody else.'

'So he's in the clear?' I asked.

'Not quite. If he knew about the risk and failed to disclose it to the purchaser of the patent, he's guilty of fraud.'

'And who was the purchaser?'

'A South Korean conglomerate.'

'Who'd be just as anxious to dodge compensation.'

'That's true.'

'So they're hardly likely to sue Roger.'

'No. But a criminal case could be brought against him in this country.'

'Theoretically.'

'I admit it's . . . improbable.'

'Looks like you'll just have to dream on, Gav,' said Syd.

'Indeed. But that's hardly the point you're interested in, is it . . . Toby? You wanted to know the moral calibre of the man. Now you do.'

'Think this'll put the missus off him, Tobe?' Syd asked.

'If she believes it, yes.'

'Then I hope you can convince her,' said Gavin.

I looked enquiringly at him. 'Some proof would help.' Then I remembered *The Plastic*

Men. And Roger's stubborn refusal to read it. Maybe there *was* proof, in the least expected quarter.

Gavin, of course, knew nothing of Derek Oswin and his painstaking history of Colbonite. But that didn't mean there weren't any pointers he could put my way. 'I don't know what kind of evidence is likely to sway your wife. Roger has a gift for deceiving people, as I've learned to my cost. She probably wouldn't believe anything I said. You could ask Delia to speak to her, I suppose. One woman to another. But Delia's grasp of the facts is . . . limited.'

'How could I contact her?'

'I'll give you her telephone number.' He reached for Syd's newspaper, tore an edge off the front page and wrote a name and number on it, then handed the scrap to me. 'If you do speak to her, send her . . . my regards.'

The Colborn family was clearly no warm and harmonious unit. Syd raised an eyebrow at me as I pocketed the note. A brief silence fell.

Then Gavin said, 'There's something else you could mention to your wife. Walter's death . . . left a lot of unanswered questions.'

'Car smash, wasn't it?' Syd asked with a frown.

'Walter was hit by a car while walking along a lane near Wickhurst Manor. The driver was charged with manslaughter.'

'I never knew that,' said Syd. 'I thought it was just . . . an accident. But . . . *manslaughter*?'

'The case never came to court. The driver died while awaiting trial.'

'How does that help me convince Jenny that Roger covered up the cancer connection?' I asked.

'The driver died of cancer,' Gavin replied. 'He was a former employee of Colbonite. And he was terminally ill when he drove Walter down. If you want my opinion, he held Walter responsible for his illness.'

'You mean . . . he murdered your brother?'

'In effect, yes.'

'Good God.'

'I can't say I blame him.'

'Maybe not. But . . . when did this happen?'

'November, nineteen ninety-five.'

'Was their . . . working relationship . . . reported at the time?'

'I don't recall. I knew of it. As did others. Whether it made the pages of the *Argus* . . . ' Gavin shrugged. 'Roger's a great puller of strings.'

'You could check that, though, Tobe,' said Syd. 'They'll have the *Argus* back to eighteen hundred and God-knows-when up at the Library.'

'Yes,' I mused. 'So they will.'

'I hope I've been of some help,' said Gavin.

'You have. Yes. Thanks.' My mind drifted to the contents of Derek's book. How had the introduction concluded? '*The closing chapters will analyse the circumstances leading to the closure of the company in 1989 and the fate of those who found themselves out of work as a result*.' The word 'fate' took on a sharper meaning in the light of Gavin's revelations.

Derek had to know about the cancer. He couldn't very well have avoided writing about it. His history of Colbonite amounted to a charge sheet against Sir Walter and Roger Colborn. No wonder Roger didn't want to help him get it published. I could only wish in that moment that I hadn't sent it off unread to Moira. I could get it back from her, of course. And even sooner I could speak to the author himself.

'Did Colbonite have a pension scheme?' Syd suddenly asked.

'I don't know,' Gavin replied brusquely. 'What does it matter?'

'I was just thinking it could have been a bargain operation for Sir Walt and Roger the compensation dodger. Half the staff claimed by the big C before they could make any inroads into the fund? Sounds like one long contributions holiday.'

'It has to be said, Gavin,' I remarked, 'that your brother doesn't seem to have been any more scrupulous than your nephew.'

'Walter didn't cheat me out of my shares.'

'No. But he cheated a lot of his workers out of a long and healthy retirement.'

'Under Roger's influence. He thought the boy could do no wrong. He never saw his true nature. Besides . . . ' Gavin took a long pull on his cigarette. 'Walter didn't have a long and healthy retirement himself, did he? He was made to pay for what he'd done.'

'Unlike Roger.'

'Yes. Unlike Roger.' Gavin stared morosely into his glass, then looked up at me. 'So far.'

* * *

Inventing an appointment at the theatre in order to extricate myself, I left Syd and Gavin to chew over old times if they had a mind to and headed for the taxi rank in East Street. A cab was soon speeding me north to a tower block beyond the station, a lower floor of which houses Brighton Central Library.

Where I discovered, to my chagrin, that my taxi driver wasn't a regular patron of the library service. Either that or he was singularly bloody-minded. Because, after paying him off and mounting the steps, I found the door firmly locked. Brighton Central Library is closed on Wednesdays.

I sheltered in the porch, cursing the bureaucrat responsible for such a stupefyingly inconvenient arrangement. Then I noticed the soaring roofline of St Bartholomew's Church to the south and realized just how close I was to Viaduct Road. Maybe, I thought, this wasn't a wasted journey after all.

* * *

There was no immediate response to my knock at the door of number 77. But the top sash of the ground-floor window was open by several inches. Derek surely wouldn't have gone out leaving it like that. I knocked again, more firmly.

I thought I heard Derek's voice from the other side of the door. But a lorry thundered by, drowning out every other sound for several seconds. I knocked once more. Then I *did* hear his voice, pitched at a panicky falsetto.

'Go away. Leave me alone.'

'Derek,' I shouted. 'It's me. Toby Flood.'

There was a silence. Then: 'Mr Flood?' Panic seemed to be subsiding.

'Please let me in, Derek. It's wet out here.'

'Are you . . . alone?'

'Just me and fifty cars a minute.'

The door opened and Derek peered out at me like a water vole apprehensively observing a river in spate. 'Sorry, Mr Flood,' he said. 'I didn't . . . well, I thought . . . he might have come back.'

'Who?'

Derek ushered me hurriedly in and closed the door. He pushed firmly against the latch to make sure it had fully engaged, then pointed me towards the sitting room, my question having apparently escaped his attention.

'Who did you think might have returned, Derek?'

'Mr . . . C-Colborn.'

'Roger Colborn's been here?'

'Y-yes.' The stress of a visit from his former boss had evidently introduced a stammer into Derek's already hesitant delivery.

'What did he want?'

'Please . . . go through.' He was still pointing to the sitting room.

I went in and nodded towards the lowered window. 'If you're worried about a return visit, shouldn't you close that?'

'Oh God, yes.' He moved past me, yanked the

window shut and turned to me with a wavering smile. 'Sorry. I'm a l-l-little . . . on edge.'

'So I see.'

'Mr Colborn shouted at me. I don't like . . . shouting.'

'I'm not going to shout.'

'No. Of course not. Please . . . sit down.' For the moment at least, the stammer had subsided. We sat down either side of the fireplace. Derek kneaded his hands together, frowning down at them. Then he looked across at me and said, 'Is it true . . . that Mr Maple's dead?'

The question was oddly phrased. He could either not know or be in no doubt on the point. 'Yes,' I replied cautiously.

'Oh. God. I am . . . sorry.'

'You say that as if it's your fault.'

'P-perhaps . . . it is.'

'He died of a heart attack, Derek. It was nobody's fault.'

'I'm not sure.'

'Why not?'

'The way . . . Mr Colborn talked about it.'

'What way was that?'

'He, er, mentioned it . . . and said . . . '

'What did he say, Derek?'

Derek took a deep breath to steady himself. Then he said, 'He came here and told me to stop causing trouble for him. To forget my history of Colbonite. To leave his . . . your wife . . . alone. And to leave you alone too. He said I should go away for a few days. Until *Lodger in the Throat* had finished its run. I told him I didn't want to go anywhere. That's when he mentioned Mr

Maple's . . . death. He said it was an example of what happened when people got out of their depth. He said . . . it should be a warning to me.'

'A warning?'

'Yes. How did . . . Mr Maple die, Mr Flood?'

'I'm not sure. I think he was being chased when his heart gave out. He wasn't a well man. After Monday night's show, he met someone who seemed to think he was actually me. They didn't realize he was the stand-in. I think they had something nasty planned for me. When they realized their mistake, they sent Denis packing. But last night, according to a phone call he made to me, they came after him again.'

'Do you think . . . they were working for Mr Colborn?'

'What do you think?'

'I don't know.'

'Tell me, Derek, did you manoeuvre me into missing Monday night's performance to save me from whatever was planned?'

He looked at me blankly and shook his head. 'No. I had no idea . . . *anything* was planned.'

'That letter you wrote to Leo Gauntlett . . . '

'Did it help?' he asked eagerly.

'Not exactly.'

'I wanted him to understand that you weren't being irresponsible.'

'Really? Wasn't it just a little . . . tongue-in-cheek?'

'Well . . . ' Derek flushed coyly. 'Maybe . . . '

'It reminded me of an Edna Welthorpe missive.'

At that he beamed. 'They're gems, Mr Flood.

Absolute gems. Do you remember her exchange of correspondence with Littlewoods?'

'You aren't going to write to any more of my associates, are you?' I'd have been sterner with him, but so fragile was the state Colborn had left him in that I felt I couldn't risk even hardening the tone of my voice. 'It's got to stop, Derek.'

'Yes. Of course.' He hung his head like a guilty schoolboy. 'I'm sorry.'

'No more tricks. No more stunts. Clear?'

'No more.' He gazed at me earnestly. 'I promise.'

'Good.'

'Is that why you came? Because of the letter?'

'Partly. I . . . found myself in the area.'

'Not on your way to the Library, were you?'

'What makes you ask?'

'It's just that . . . when we met at the Rendezvous on Monday, you asked me for directions to the public library.'

'So I did. And you told me it was in New England Street.'

'That's right. But actually . . . it's closed on Wednesdays.'

'I know. I've just come from there.'

'Oh dear. That must have been annoying for you. What were you trying to find out? If I can help . . . '

'I wanted to look at back copies of the *Argus*.'

'Ah. Actually, the *Argus* isn't archived at New England Street. You need the Local Studies Library in Church Street for that.'

'Also closed on Wednesdays?'

'I'm afraid so. You'll have to wait until tomorrow.'

'Not necessarily. You see, I think you *can* help, Derek. In fact, I'm sure of it. I wanted to read what the *Argus* had to say about the death of Sir Walter Colborn.'

'Oh. That.'

'Yes. *That*. I understand he was knocked down by a car, driven by a former employee of Colbonite, who was terminally ill with cancer at the time.'

'Sounds like . . . you already know all about it.'

'Is it true a lot of Colbonite workers contracted cancer of the bladder after handling a carcinogenic curing agent used in a dyeing process?'

'Yes.' Derek's reply was almost a whisper. 'One of the chloro-anilines. Nasty stuff.'

'No doubt you mention this in *The Plastic Men*.'

'Oh yes, Mr Flood. It's all there. Chapter and verse.' He smiled weakly. 'There was a sign on the door of the dyeing shop. Somebody spray-painted over the E in dyeing on one occasion. A pretty black sort of joke.'

'Did you work with this stuff?'

'Good Lord, no. I was a filing clerk.'

'But those who did are mostly dead now?'

'Yes. I checked on them all. They're listed in an appendix to *The Plastic Men*. Names. Ages. Cause of death.'

'Which one of them murdered Sir Walter?'

'He was only charged with manslaughter.'

'Who was he, Derek?'

'Kenneth Oswin.' Derek stared at me. 'My father.'

It was as obvious now as it should have been before. He didn't blame Roger Colborn for closing Colbonite down. At least, not only for that. There was something far worse to lay at his door. 'Why didn't you tell me?'

'I thought it might . . . put you off.'

'Because there's a feud between your families? Well, it certainly skews the perspective, that's for sure.'

'There's no . . . feud.'

'In your book, do you accuse the Colborns of knowing how dangerous the curing agent was?'

'I don't exactly . . . accuse them. But . . . '

'You lay it on the line.'

'I suppose I do. Yes.'

'That's libel.'

'He could sue me. I wouldn't mind.'

'You asked Colborn to help you get the book published. Why? You must have known he'd move heaven and earth to *stop it* being published.'

'I just wanted to . . . get a reaction.'

'Well, you got one, didn't you? More of one than you bargained for, if the state you were in when I arrived is anything to go by.'

Derek squirmed in his chair. 'I just don't see why he should get away with it.'

'Take after your father in that, do you? He obviously decided Sir Walter shouldn't get away with it either.'

'It wasn't like that.'

'What was it like?'

'Dad went out to Wickhurst that day to plead with Sir Walter to help out the families of the men who'd died and those, like him, who were already terminally ill. He'd gone down with cancer shortly after Colbonite closed, but he'd recovered. Then it came back. He'd been a shop steward in his day. He . . . felt responsible. He thought he could talk Sir Walter round. He'd only bought the car a few years previously, so Mum could drive him back and forth to the hospital. Anyway, he told me later what happened when he got to Wickhurst Manor. Sir Walter refused to discuss the matter. Ordered him off his property. Then stalked off to take his dog for a walk. Dad sat in his car for a while, fuming, then decided to go after Sir Walter and make a last effort to talk him round. He'd seen him set off along the lane that leads north from Wickhurst towards Stonestaples Wood, so that's the way he went. He was going too fast. And he was never a good driver, anyway. He was in a lot of pain by then as well. He went round a sharp bend and saw Sir Walter too late to stop or swerve aside. It was an accident, Mr Flood. That's what it was. Just an accident.'

'The police obviously didn't think so.'

'Well, Dad said some things . . . about his illness. He wanted them to charge him with manslaughter, you see, or better still murder. He wanted a high-profile trial. The chance to say what Sir Walter had done to his workers. The truth is, though, it *was* an accident.'

'Does Roger believe that?'

'I don't know what he believes. I'm sure he had the trial delayed, though. He has a lot of friends; a lot of influence. Thanks to him, Dad never had his day in court.'

'I'm sorry for your loss, Derek.'

'Thanks, Mr Flood.'

'When did your mother . . . '

'Not long after Dad. Looking after him put a huge strain on her. After he passed away, she just . . . faded.'

'Leaving you alone, to think about Roger Colborn and how to get back at him.'

'I'm not after revenge.'

'No? Well, he won't give you a day in court any more than he gave your father one, Derek. That's the truth. You've more or less admitted the book's libellous. No publisher will touch it. The only way you can get anywhere with this is to prove the case — scientifically. And even then . . . ' I hesitated. If Derek didn't know about the sale of Colbonite to a shell company and the consequences of the move, I wasn't sure I wanted to be the one to tell him.

'Mr Colborn has taken precautions against every contingency, I know. He's been very clever.'

'You're not the only one bearing a grudge against him, if it's any consolation. I met his uncle. Gavin Colborn. He told me all about Sir Walter's death. Except that he never mentioned your father was the car driver.'

'He's probably forgotten the name. There's no reason why he should remember it. We've never met. I saw him a few times, at Colbonite. But I was . . . beneath his notice.'

'You have something in common, though. A desire to put a spoke in Roger Colborn's wheel.'

'It would be nice . . . to do something.'

'Yes. And I'm the spoke, aren't I? If I could win Jenny back . . . '

'Mr Colborn would be seriously put out.'

'It's not exactly justice. But it's better than nothing. The only problem is, I'm not sure I can pull it off.'

'Surely, if Mrs Flood understands what Mr Colborn did to people like my father . . . '

'*If* she understands, Derek. Oh yes. She couldn't stomach that. But how do I prove it to her? How do I convince her I'm not levelling an unfounded accusation in order to split them up? Where's the hard, incontrovertible evidence?'

Derek pursed his lips, rocking back and forth slightly in his chair as he pondered our shared difficulty. Then he said, with a meek acceptance of the unalterable, 'There isn't any.'

'You see?'

Suddenly, Derek stopped rocking. He pondered a little longer, then said, 'No evidence as such. Only witnesses.'

'The tainted kind, if you mean the likes of you and Uncle Gavin. He suggested his sister, Delia, but seemed to doubt she knew enough to sway Jenny.'

'I feel he's almost certainly right there. As far as knowledge is concerned, I could only suggest Dr Kilner.'

'Who?'

'The biochemist Colbonite 'consulted' over

the risks posed by the curing agent. Dr Maurice Kilner. He was a head of department at the University of Sussex.'

'*Was?*'

'Since retired.'

'With a handsome pay-off from the Colborns, presumably.'

'I'm not sure. If Mr Colborn has a weakness, it's parsimony. I saw Dr Kilner in Waitrose a few months ago. He didn't look as if he was living in the lap of luxury.'

'No?'

Derek shook his head, smiling faintly at the notion he'd planted in my mind without needing to put it into words. 'No.'

'I'm surprised you haven't spoken to him about this.'

'I don't think he'd be willing to discuss anything with a former employee of Colbonite. He'd be fearful of the consequences.'

'What about somebody who'd never worked for Colbonite?'

'It might be different.'

'There's only one way to find out.'

'Yes, Mr Flood. There is.' Derek cleared his throat. 'Would you like to know where Dr Kilner lives?'

* * *

I left Derek in a much calmer state than I'd found him in. *The Plastic Men* was going nowhere. He understood and accepted that. But our campaign against Roger Colborn — if it *was* a campaign and if it *was* ours — *that* might yet have legs. It was agreed I'd try to contact Dr Kilner and would tell Derek what I'd accomplished, if anything, after tonight's show.

⋆ ⋆ ⋆

The rain had stopped. I walked down London Road through the drying grey early afternoon, wondering just what kind of an ally I'd saddled myself with in Derek Oswin. He can be relied on in some things, but not in others. And he's frightened of Roger Colborn — understandably. Perhaps I should be as well. But other imperatives have blanked out fear. I can't let Jenny marry this man, even if I fail to win her back. And I can't ignore what happened to Denis.

⋆ ⋆ ⋆

The Great Eastern in Trafalgar Street was still serving food. I sat in a cosily gloomy corner and worked my way through a late lunch while mulling over my next move. I had an address for Dr Kilner, but no telephone number. I borrowed a directory from behind the bar, but he wasn't listed, so there was no other way to approach him but on the doorstep. I swapped the directory for a Brighton *A — Z* and found Pennsylvania Court in Cromwell Road, Hove, just behind the county cricket ground. There was nothing to be gained by delay, unless I wanted to give myself the chance to change my mind. And that I didn't. Resisting the lure of a second drink, I headed for the taxi rank up at the station.

* * *

The cab was most of the way to my destination when fate intervened, in the form of Brian Sallis on my mobile.

'I'm with Ian Maple, Toby. We're at Denis's lodgings in Egremont Place. Can you join us here?'

Dr Kilner, it was apparent, would have to wait.

* * *

Thanks to already being in a taxi when Brian called, I was at Egremont Place in no more than ten minutes. Brian was waiting for me outside number 65, a narrow-fronted, bay-windowed house near the northern end. Ian Maple, he explained, was inside, sorting through his brother's possessions.

'He's pretty cut up, Toby, as you can imagine, and looking for answers.'

'Answers to what?'

'Questions raised by a message he had from Denis last night. Look, he knows you found Denis and that the two of you went back a long way. Can I leave you to . . . go through what happened?'

'You're not coming in?'

'I have to get back to the theatre. Just tell the poor chap as much as you can. Mrs Dunn will let you in. She's expecting you.'

* * *

As promised, Mrs Dunn *was* expecting me. She'd put Denis up more than once over the years and was clearly upset. 'It's a terrible thing, Mr Flood. He was too young to go and do this on me.'

'I know.'

'His brother's upstairs. Second floor, front. Will you tell him what we talked about earlier is fine by me?'

'Sure.'

* * *

I climbed the stairs and found the door to Denis's room ajar. A younger, balder, bulkier version of my late friend and colleague was sitting on the edge of the bed, staring into space. He was wearing blue jeans and a grey fleece over a sweatshirt. He looked like a tough guy who at the moment wasn't feeling very tough at all.

It took several seconds for my presence to register with him. Then he stood up slowly, the bed springs creakily extending themselves, and fixed me with a clear-eyed gaze.

'Toby Flood?'

'Yes. Pleased to meet you.' We shook hands, his grip large and powerful. 'Though sorry, of course, about the circumstances.'

'Yeah.'

'Mrs Dunn asked me to tell you . . . something you discussed earlier . . . is fine by her.'

'I asked if she could put me up for a couple of days.'

'You're stopping over?'

'Till I find out what Denis had got himself into. Brian Sallis reckoned you might know.'

Thanks, Brian, I thought; I owe you one. 'He said you'd had a message from Denis.'

'Yeah. On my answerphone.' He pulled a small tape recorder out of his pocket and stood it on the bedside cabinet. 'Want to hear it?'

'If you don't mind.'

He pressed the PLAY button. An electronic voice announced, '*Next new message. Received today at eleven fifty-three p.m.*' Then Denis was speaking to us, his voice hushed and fuzzy. '*Hi, Ian. Big brother here. Sorry not to have caught you. I've run into some trouble. Not sure how serious. Could be very. I might need some help. I have a bad feeling and . . . Send Mum and Dad my love, will you? It's too late to call them. Hope all's well with you. 'Bye.*'

Ian Maple rewound the tape, then switched the machine off. 'What's it all about, Toby?' he asked.

'Hard to say.' I sat down on the only chair in the room, playing for time to little purpose. My instincts told me not to involve this man I hardly knew in my dealings with Roger Colborn. Yet I couldn't simply deny all knowledge. I should have checked the events of the previous evening with Glenys. I should have prepared myself. I'd done neither. Playing a part without any kind of rehearsal is playing with fire. But it's what I had to do. 'Denis phoned me shortly before he left that message for you. He said someone was . . . chasing him. He wasn't very specific. He was at a bus stop in North Street. I agreed to meet him there at midnight. When I got there, he'd gone. I walked towards my lodgings, thinking he might have headed in that direction. That's how I came to find him, by the fountain on the Steine.'

'Already dead?'

'I'm afraid so.'

Ian sat back down on the bed, to another squeal from the springs. 'Do you think someone *was* after him?'

'He said so.'

'Did you believe him?'

'Yes.' I couldn't write Denis off as a fantasist, however evasive I was being. 'I believed him.'

'Who was it?'

'I don't know.' (True enough.)

'No idea at all?'

'None.' (Not true enough.)

'I mean to find out.'

'I wish you luck. It's going to be difficult.'

'I won't let that stop me. Having me as a kid brother wasn't always a cakewalk. I owe it to Denis to try.'

'How are your parents taking this?'

'It's knocked them for six. Me too, I don't mind admitting. Another heart attack was always on the cards. You just don't think it'll happen, though, do you?'

'No. You don't.'

'When did you last speak to Denis? Face to face, I mean.'

'We had coffee together yesterday morning.'

'How did he seem then?'

'Chirpy as ever.'

'Sallis said Denis stood in for you the night before.'

'Yes. I had flu.'

'That a fact?' There was a hint of scepticism in his tone. His gaze was disconcertingly direct. I was already certain that he suspected me of holding something back. 'If you remember anything, Toby, however minor, however . . . apparently trivial, that could help me . . . '

'I'll let you know straight away.'

'Denis said you fixed him up with this job.'

'I put a word in, nothing more. It was the least I could do. Denis was one of the best.'

'Yeah. He was. That's why it's such a crying bloody shame it had to end like this.'

* * *

I couldn't disagree with that last sentiment. But nor could I share everything I knew with Denis's brother and aspiring avenger. Derek was in a fragile enough state as it was without having Ian Maple cross-questioning him. As for Roger Colborn, I didn't rate Ian a match for him. And one favour I did owe Denis was to avoid dragging another member of his family into my troubles. If I could.

* * *

The light was already failing as I trailed back towards the Sea Air. I'd just about concluded that there wasn't enough time to have another go at Dr Kilner, when I reached St James's Street and spotted a bus bound for Hove bearing down on me. A sprint to the next stop got me aboard with just enough breath to ask the driver if he was going along Cromwell Road. And since he was . . . I paid my fare and sat down.

* * *

As soon as I'd got my breath back, I phoned Brian.

'How'd it go with Ian Maple, Toby?'

'As well as could be expected, given that you'd told him I knew what Denis was mixed up in.'

'I didn't have much choice once I'd listened to the tape. Besides, you do know, don't you? That's the vibe I'm getting.'

'Ian's going to get himself mixed up in it as well if he has his way. I'd like to prevent that.'

'Can't help you there, Toby. The guy's entitled to ask who he likes what he likes. This is really no legitimate concern of Leo S. Gauntlett Productions.'

'Great.'

'Sorry, but there it is.'

'Yeah. Of course. Look — ' I was going to ask him for Glenys's mobile number, but suddenly changed my mind. What was the point now of finding out what Denis did or didn't say to her last night? I could hardly expect her to keep Ian Maple in the dark on my account. The cards would simply have to lie as they fell. 'Never mind. See you later, Brian.'

* * *

The phone was hardly back in my pocket when it rang again. My first thought was that Brian was back on to check I hadn't taken umbrage on a disastrous scale. I had no stand-in now, after all. But it wasn't Brian.

'Hi-de-hi, Tobe. Syd squeaking. Anxious to confirm you got as much as you wanted out of my old school chum, Gav of the omnipresent smile.'

'Meeting him was a big help, Syd. Thanks for setting it up.'

'You thinking of paying his sister a call?'

'Maybe.'

'Only, if you are, I suspect the encounter might go more smoothly with me riding shotgun for you. Delia and I have what you might call history.'

'Do you really?'

'It's just a thought, Tobe. Could make all the difference.'

'I'll certainly bear it in mind.'

'Just give me a bell whenever.'

'Will do.' (Or, far more likely, will not do.)

'One other thing.'

'Yes.'

'Aud's suggestion, actually. But I'm all for it, natch. When are you planning to leave Brighton?'

'Sunday.'

'Fancy a spot of lunch before you go? Aud

roasts an awesome joint, let me tell you. I could motor you over to her place and deliver you to the station afterwards. Send you off well fed and watered. Know what I mean? Chance to catch up with how the week went.'

Sunday suddenly felt an impossibly long way off. How will the week have gone? For the moment, I couldn't have hazarded the remotest of guesses. There seemed, however, no point in arguing. I can easily pull out nearer the time. 'OK, Syd. You're on.'

'Grrreat.'

* * *

Pennsylvania Court: a bland red-brick five-floor apartment block on the cusp of well-to-do and down-at-heel. I rang the bell for flat 28 and put the odds on a response at eighty-twenty. Where else would a retired academic be on a winter's late afternoon but at home? I was right.

'Hello?'

'Dr Kilner?'

'Yes.'

'I wonder if we could have a word. My name's Flood.' How to talk my way in was a problem I'd failed to devise a cast-iron solution to. 'The thing is — '

'Toby Flood, the actor?'

'Well, yes. I — '

'Come on up.'

The door-lock release buzzed. Obediently, I pushed and entered.

* * *

Maurice Kilner was a short, stocky, beetle-browed man with greased hair and unfashionably thick-framed glasses. His rumpled cardigan and baggy trousers were hardly *homme à la mode* either. He ushered me in with a welcoming smile that never made it to his watery grey eyes. The flat was comfortable in a senior-common-room kind of way, but the furniture was generally as threadbare as its owner. There was presumably a good view of the cricket ground, though. And two shelves full of *Wisdens* in one of the several bookcases suggested that was a feature Kilner might well appreciate.

Much less apparent was why he'd so readily admitted me. A fan, perhaps? Somehow, I didn't think so.

'Roger Colborn warned me to expect a visit from you, Mr Flood.'

'Did he?' (Clever old Roger.)

'This is sooner than I anticipated, though. Do you want a drink? Scotch, perhaps?'

'No, thanks.'

'Keeping a clear head for this evening's performance? Very wise. You don't mind if I have one, do you?'

'Not at all.'

He poured himself a large Johnnie Walker. I wondered if he was bolstering his nerves, but reckoned it more likely to be a bachelor's early-evening habit. 'When do you have to be at the theatre?' He sat down and waved me into another chair.

'Shortly after seven.'

'I'd better not hold you up, then. You've obviously come to talk to me about Colbonite.'

'Yes. I have.'

'What have you heard?'

'That just about anyone who had the bad luck to work in their dyeing shop went down with bladder cancer on account of a carcinogenic curing agent. And that Roger Colborn and his father did nothing to prevent it.'

'I was merely engaged by Colbonite to do some research for them.'

'I know.'

'I'm glad you do. Because that's all it was. Research. Carried out rigorously and diligently.'

'Research into what?'

'The mechanics of carcinogenesis arising from exposure to aromatic amines, specifically methylated chloro-aniline — the infamous curing agent.'

'Which you gave a clean bill of heath?'

'Of course not. It was identified as a carcinogen nearly forty years ago.'

'Then why were Colbonite using it?'

'Because there are no ready substitutes. It's still in regular use today, Mr Flood. The issue is the scale of risk. Based on the quantities involved and the working practices put in place, my findings suggested that Colbonite were not exposing their staff to unacceptable levels.'

'How come they all wound up dead, then?'

''All' is an exaggeration. And a certain proportion of any cohort is bound to develop cancer. For the rest, I'd be inclined to suspect wilful disregard of safety procedures as the cause. People working in dangerous industries are often their own worst enemies, you know. You must have seen road menders operating pneumatic drills without bothering to wear ear defenders.'

'It was their own fault, then?'

'It's one possibility. Another is that Colbonite were routinely using larger quantities of the substance than they declared to me. But I think that unlikely. Sir Walter Colborn was an ethical and responsible employer.'

'What about his son?'

'I'd say the same of him.'

'Perhaps your research was flawed.'

'Even more unlikely.' Kilner smiled. 'Approximation may pass muster in your profession, Mr Flood. Not in mine.'

'Let me get this straight. Colbonite's workers weren't in any danger other than of their own making?'

'I didn't say that. I advanced their inattention to proper safety procedures as a hypothetical explanation for any disproportionate incidence of bladder cancer that medical practitioners may have detected. I say *may* because it's certainly never been brought officially to my attention. Mr Colborn has explained to me your interest in this matter. It can hardly be described as dispassionate, now can it?'

'Can yours?'

'By definition.'

'How much did they pay you? How much is Roger Colborn *still* paying you?'

'I was paid an appropriate fee at the time. That's all.'

'You don't expect me to believe that.'

'I can only state the facts as I know them to be.'

'Don't you care about the men who died?'

'They didn't die through any negligence on my part.'

'You have a clear conscience, then?'

'I do, yes.'

'Or maybe no conscience at all.'

Kilner sipped his whisky and smiled tolerantly at me, as if I were a student at a seminar making provocative remarks that he had no intention of being provoked by. 'Roger Colborn is a businessman, Mr Flood,' he said softly. 'I recommend you do business with him.'

* * *

I walked down to the sea front after leaving Pennsylvania Court, then headed east towards Brighton and the Sea Air. The evening was turning cold and I was grateful: I needed the chill and the darkness after my encounter with Maurice Kilner. What kind of a deal he'd done with Roger Colborn hardly mattered. He'd done one that suited him and he advised others to follow his example. Derek had suggested he might be a weak spot in Colborn's defences, but in reality he was rock solid. And all the more contemptible because of it. I wondered if Derek had known exactly what I would find, if he had chosen Kilner as an example to me of the moral bankruptcy to which a man could be led by bargaining with the ever-eager-to-bargain Roger Colborn. It seemed all too likely. Derek had promised to give up his trickery. But maybe he didn't regard this as trickery. Maybe this was just what came naturally.

⋆ ⋆ ⋆

The show must go on. Like so many clichés, it's horribly true. Denis was such an amiable and popular man that everybody involved with *Lodger in the Throat* was depressed this evening. Badinage was absent, leaving an empty space to be filled with doleful exchanges and soulful looks. Fred's supply of wry one-liners had dried up. Jocasta was puffy-eyed and virtually mute. Even Donohue's egotism had failed him. But we were present and correct. We were ready to perform.

⋆ ⋆ ⋆

Just after the quarter-hour call, I had a visitor to my dressing room: Glenys Williams.

'I'm really sorry to interrupt, Toby, but I feel I ought to let you know that Ian Maple wants to see me this evening, to discuss . . . Denis's state of mind last night.'

'Did you have supper with Denis?'

'Yes.'

'How was he?'

'Fine, I thought. But, looking back, I suppose he was rather on edge. He mentioned — well, implied, really — that standing in for you the night before had . . . got him into some trouble. He wouldn't elaborate. But he did say . . . you knew all about it.'

'I see.'

'Yet his brother said to me on the phone this afternoon that you'd been unable to help him. So, I'm guessing you'd prefer me not to mention Denis's remark to him.'

'I would, yes.'

'But doesn't Ian have a right to know?'

'Yes. And I'll make sure he does know eventually. I can't ask you to lie, Glenys, but . . . just for the moment . . . '

'You want me to cover for you.'

I nodded. 'How about it?'

She gave me a grim little smile. 'Denis always said you were hard to say no to.'

* * *

We performed, everyone agreed, very well, though without scaling last night's heights. I was often distracted and fractionally slow to respond. It wasn't so much that I couldn't concentrate as that my concentration was elsewhere. The audience was entertained without being entranced.

At the interval, some instinct, some impression I'd picked up, made me call the box office from my dressing room to check that Derek had collected his complimentary ticket. But no. He hadn't.

The second act was even more of a blur than

the first, as I tried and failed to stop myself wondering between other people's lines why he hadn't shown up. He'd said he would be there. He'd claimed to be looking forward to it. What could have prevented him?

The box office confirmed after I got off stage that his ticket was still lying unclaimed in its envelope. There were no messages for me. There was no word from Derek Oswin. He hadn't come. He wasn't going to.

I'd arranged to meet him at the stage door twenty minutes after the curtain fell. I waited there until half an hour was up, refusing repeated invitations to adjourn with the rest of the cast to a restaurant. Then I called a taxi and headed for Viaduct Road.

* * *

It was a quieter place late at night. The traffic still came in pulses, regulated by the lights at Preston Circus, but there was less of it. Most of the houses were in darkness. Pedestrians there were none.

To my surprise, a light was showing at number 77, in the hall. I could see the glimmer of it through the open curtains of the sitting room. The room itself looked to be empty. I knocked at the door and waited. There was no response. Then I put the knocker to longer, heavier duty use. If Derek was asleep in bed, I didn't mean him to stay that way.

Still no answer. I stooped and took a squint through the letterbox. It gave me a view of the hall, the lower half of the stairs and the doorway into the unlit kitchen. Then I noticed the bulky hem of Derek's duffel-coat hanging on its hook. He wouldn't have gone out without it. He had to be at home.

But then I noticed something else. Two of the balusters on the staircase were broken, their snapped halves protruding at forty-five degrees, as if they'd been kicked by somebody standing on the stairs. The same somebody, perhaps, who'd rucked up the hall rug. You couldn't have walked across it without tripping.

'*Derek!*' I shouted through the letterbox. But nothing stirred. I moved to the sitting-room window and peered in. Nothing appeared out of place, as far as I could tell, although the fact that the curtains, including the nets, were open was odd in itself. The nets had been open when Derek had slammed the window shut earlier, I remembered. Perhaps —

He hadn't flicked the snib back into place. I must have distracted him. And then he must have forgotten about it. The window was unlocked.

I glanced about. There was no-one within sight. I waited for a wave of traffic to pass, then pushed up the sash. The squeal of the wood sounded loud to me, but was probably nothing unusual. After another glance along the street, I hoisted one leg over the sill and scrambled in, then closed the window behind me.

The distinctive, indefinable scent of somebody else's home met me, in a general silence that amplified the ponderous tick of a clock in the kitchen. My eyes adjusted to the half-light as I stood there. Then I saw Derek's books, strewn on the floor beneath the bookcase. Nothing else in the room had been disturbed. But it didn't need to have been. I knew Derek wouldn't have done even that. He wouldn't have creased a single page of his Tintin collection, let alone have them lying higgledy-piggledy on the floor.

I went out into the hall and looked up the stairs. There were muddy shoe-prints on several of the treads. Derek's? I didn't think so. I climbed to the landing, where the light was also on. There was a bathroom and two bedrooms, the front one containing a double bed and dressing-table. I guessed it had been where Derek's parents slept, kept by him as they'd left it. His room was to the rear, the door half-closed, a light on within.

I pushed the door fully open. The bed hadn't been slept in. There was a desk by the window, an ink-spotted blotter neatly positioned dead centre, between an anglepoise lamp and a globe. The drawers of the desk had been pulled open. In the centre of the room a wooden chest lay on its back, the lid open on the floor, the contents spread across the rug in front of the fireplace: a photograph album, old children's annuals, an ancient much-loved teddy-bear and a slew of paper.

I stood in the room, staring down at Derek's scattered keepsakes, trying to reconstruct the events that had left these clues behind. I went back out onto the landing and looked down the stairs. The broken balusters; the rumpled rug:

what did they mean? I imagined Derek answering the door to threatening strangers, retreating up the stairs, being overhauled and dragged back down, struggling and kicking. Then I saw a glint of metal on the doormat below me. I padded down the stairs for a closer look.

It was one of Derek's Tintin brooches, lying face down. I turned it over and Captain Haddock grinned up at me through his bushy tar-black beard. I stood up with the brooch in my hand and noted the tear in Derek's duffel-coat where it had obviously been ripped free. The hall was narrow. It had probably happened without anyone noticing, not even Derek.

There'd been a brief but focused search. That was clear. The bookcase and the bedroom chest and desk had been the targets. Maybe they'd found what they'd been looking for in one of them. *The Plastic Men* was my guess. The manuscript — and any related documents. That had to be the answer. I looked back at one of the shoe-prints on the stairs. A small, muddy oak-leaf had been trodden into the carpet. Where, I wondered, was the nearest oak tree to Viaduct Road? I didn't know, of course. I hadn't a clue. But there were oaks out at Wickhurst. I was sure of that.

What had happened after they'd got what they came for? Why wasn't Derek here, traumatized and trembling? Because they'd taken him with them, that's why. They'd probably called a van round from wherever its driver was waiting, bundled Derek in and driven off. It wasn't just the book they'd come for. It was the author.

Would I see matching shoe-prints outside on the pavement, maybe skid marks where the van had sped away? I edged the front door open for a look.

The latch slipped from my grasp as the door was suddenly thrust wide open, striking me in the chest and throwing me back against the wall. A bulky figure moved in and past me, slamming the door shut behind him.

'Hi,' said Ian Maple, staring at me beadily from close quarters.

'You,' was all the response I could manage.

'Yeah. That's right. Me. I followed you from the theatre. Glenys Williams isn't a good liar. And you're not a much better one. So . . . how about telling me what the fuck's going on?'

⋆ ⋆ ⋆

It seemed I had no choice. We sat in Derek Oswin's armchairs, as the kitchen clock counted the continuing seconds and minutes and hours of his absence. And I told Ian Maple everything that had led to his brother's death. There was no point holding any of it back. Like Glenys had said, he had a right to know. And now he'd asserted that right.

⋆ ⋆ ⋆

'Denis was caught in the crossfire between you and Roger Colborn,' he accurately and bleakly concluded. 'There's no other way to look at it.'

'No,' I had to agree. 'There isn't.'

'And now Colborn's grabbed this Oswin guy.'

'Looks like it. Though not in person, I imagine.'

'No. His goons will have done that for him. The same goons who went after Denis.'

'Probably, yes.'

'Not a very nice man, Colborn, is he? Except in your wife's opinion.'

'She knows nothing about this.'

'Perhaps it's time she was told.'

'She won't believe me.'

'Maybe she'll believe *me*.'

'Maybe.'

'What do you want to do about Oswin?'

'I'm not sure. Call the police?'

Ian looked at me sceptically. 'You haven't a shred of evidence against Colborn. Even if the police believe Oswin's been abducted, they won't go looking for him at Wickhurst Manor. And they wouldn't find anything if they did. From what you tell me, Colborn will have been sure to cover his tracks. As things stand, the police would be more likely to arrest us than anyone else. Besides, my guess is that Colborn just wants to put the fear of God into Oswin. He'll have him back here by morning.' He shrugged. 'If not, I'll pay him a call. And find out just how tough he really is.'

* * *

And so it was agreed, however reluctantly on my part: we'd await Derek's return, find out what had happened to him and decide how to react then. Ian was confident he'd be back. I was less certain. Colborn's no fool, I told myself. Doing Derek serious harm would be asking for trouble. And yet . . .

I found a key to the front door in one of the kitchen drawers and pocketed it when we left. We walked south through the chill, star-spattered Brighton night. Little was said. We'd talked ourselves out back at Derek's house. And neither of us quite trusted the other.

We parted by the Law Courts in Edward Street. 'I'll go back to Viaduct Road mid-morning,' I said. 'I'll let you know whether Derek's there or not. And, if he is, what state he's in.'

'I'll be waiting on your call.'

My call, yes. But watching him walk briskly away along the street without a backward glance, his broad shoulders hunched against the cold, I had the distinct feeling that what happened next would be his call, not mine.

* * *

But that's been the way of it ever since I arrived on Sunday. First Jenny, then Derek, now Ian Maple. Plus Roger Colborn, of course. They've all dictated my agenda, in their different ways. They've all decreed what's best for me. Or worst, depending how you look at it.

There's a matinée tomorrow. From lunchtime onwards I should be thinking about nothing beyond the dramatic and comedic challenges of

Lodger in the Throat. As it is, acting is likely to be just about the last thing on my mind.

I'm so tired I can't sort the questions I should be asking myself into any logical order. Did I interpret the scene at 77 Viaduct Road correctly? Is Derek Oswin really being held somewhere against his will? Fraud and corruption you might expect of a certain ruthless type of businessman. But abduction and possibly worse? I thought Colborn was too clever for that, too subtle, too confident that less overt measures would always serve him better. Maybe I thought wrong.

If so, it's not just Derek I should be worried about. There's Jenny to consider as well. What kind of a man has she become involved with? She's normally a good judge of character. She must know what he's really like. He can't have deceived her so completely. Can he?

I don't know. I'm not sure. About that or anything else. I have a feeling akin to seeing something out of the corner of my eye that isn't there whenever I look directly at it. Something's going on, beyond Colborn's dirty tricks and dirtier dealings. I've been told so many different and conflicting stories that I can be certain of only one thing: I haven't come close to the truth; I haven't even glimpsed it.

But I will.

THURSDAY

It had to happen eventually. The sun was shining, low and cold in a cloudless sky, when I left the Sea Air this morning after one of Eunice's hearty breakfasts that somehow hadn't heartened me. I walked north up Grand Parade, chilled by a biting east wind and a gnawing anxiety about what I'd find.

Near the Open Market I fell in with the imagined footsteps of Derek Oswin's grandfather as he traced his daily route to work seventy or eighty years ago. But they kept on climbing the hill towards Colbonite, while I turned into Viaduct Road and made my way to the door of number 77.

There was no answer to my knock. It was as I'd feared, then. Derek had not returned. I let myself in and was met by the unaltered silence of last night; by Derek's duffel-coat hanging on its hook, the broken balusters sagging from the stair-rail, the books strewn across the sitting-room floor.

I glanced into the kitchen, then headed up to the bedroom. Nothing had changed there either. Nor, in Derek's continued absence, was it likely to. I sat down on the bed and rang Ian Maple.

'Yuh?' His answer was gruffly matter-of-fact.

'Toby Flood here, Ian. I've done as we agreed. There's no sign of him.'

'Understood.'

'What do you mean to do now?'

'Pay our friend a visit.'

'Be careful.'

'I'll call you later.' And with no assurance as to carefulness, he rang off.

* * *

Ian hadn't asked what my plans for the day were. I think he assumed I'd be busy at the theatre, leaving him free to probe the affairs of Roger Colborn in whatever way suited him best. But I had four hours at my disposal before I had to report for the matinée and I intended to put them to good use.

I picked up the photograph album from among the scattered contents of the chest and opened its stiff leather cover. The pages were black card, the captions beneath the photographs written in white ink in a copperplate hand. The Oswins' camera-caught memories kicked off with Kenneth and Valerie's wedding at St Bart's in July 1955. Kenneth was a thin, hollow-chested man with curly hair and a toothy grin, Valerie even thinner, fine-boned and graceful, surprisingly beautiful. (Why that surprised me I couldn't say, but it did.) The best man and bridesmaids were also snapped and identified and the best man cropped up in other pictures as I leafed on through. Burlier than Kenneth Oswin, with slicked-down hair and a stern gaze, Ray Braddock, or 'Uncle Ray' as later captions referred to him, was some sort of close family friend or relative to judge by the frequency of his appearances. He was to be seen standing by the pram when baby Derek made his début in front of the lens in the summer of 1958. Grandfather Oswin was a rarer subject, an older version of Kenneth who cropped up sporadically and never with Grandmother; she'd presumably died some time before 1955. Valerie's parents and siblings were rarer still. Perhaps they lived some distance away. Certainly the Oswins didn't travel far with their camera. Beachy Head was just about the most exotic locale. Brighton sea front, Preston Park and the back yard of 77 Viaduct Road were the commonest settings. Around 1972 the captions started being written in a different hand, which I recognized as Derek's. That was also when Grandfather Oswin died, if his abrupt disappearance from the album was anything to go by. But Uncle Ray was still on the scene and remained there until the photographs fizzled out in the early Eighties, with several pages still unused. Never the most prolific of snappers, the Oswins appeared to have given up altogether.

By then Kenneth, Valerie and Uncle Ray had moved from their twenties into stolid middle age and Derek had grown from infancy to a mop-haired young man of uncertain bearing. He'd changed little in the years since, while his parents had both died, leaving him alone in this house of his childhood, a family home become both his refuge and his prison. As for Uncle Ray . . .

I phoned directory enquiries and they confirmed that there was a Braddock, R., listed in the Brighton area. They even gave me his address: 9 Buttermere Avenue, Peacehaven. I tried the number. No reply. And no answerphone either. Well, I could easily try later.

Next I conducted a search of all the obvious places where Derek might have stored or hidden the original of *The Plastic Men*. On top of the wardrobe and behind it. Under the bed. Beneath the stairs. In the kitchen cupboards. I didn't expect to find it, of course. I was as certain as could be that it had left with him. Sure enough, I found nothing.

Then I put a call in to Moira, crossing my fingers that I'd catch her in an obliging mood.

'What can I do for you, Toby?' Her tone left the issue of her mood tantalizingly undecided.

'You received the manuscript yesterday?'

'Yes. But if you think I've already got a response to it for you, then — '

'No, no. It's not that. I have another favour to ask of you.'

'The news about Denis was dreadful,' she said, apparently failing to register my last remark. 'I'll really miss him, you know, even though I hardly ever saw him. He was always so chirpy.' It was only then that I remembered Denis had been a client of hers, albeit not one of her most famous. 'Brian Sallis said you found him. Is that right?'

'Yes. It is.'

'If there's anything I can do . . . '

'There is, actually. It concerns the manuscript.'

'What's that to do with Denis?'

'Long story, Moira, which I'll be happy to go into another time. The point is, I need it back.'

'The manuscript?'

'Yes.'

'But you've only just sent it to me.'

'I know. And now I need it back. Urgently.'

'Why?'

'It's too complicated to explain. But it's important, believe me.'

'You're not making any sense, Toby. First you send me this, this . . . what is it, plastic something? . . . demanding an instant evaluation, then you demand it back again.'

'I'm well aware that it must sound crazy. Moira. You'll just have to trust me when I say there's a very good reason.'

'I know you and Denis were friends from way back. You must be upset. But — '

'*I need to see the manuscript.*'

'All right. All right. Calm down. If you want it, you must have it, I suppose.'

'Thank you.'

'I'll have it posted to you this afternoon. What's your address in Brighton?'

'Actually, Moira . . . '

'What?'

'I was hoping someone could bring it down to me. Today.'

'Are you joking?'

'No. You have umpteen juniors at your beck and call. You wouldn't miss one of them for a few hours. I'd rather not rely on the post. And it really is *very* urgent.'

'May I remind you that the bloody thing's only up here because you sent it to me, Toby?'

'I realize that. But — '

'Can't you ask the author to run you off another copy?'

'Impossible.'

'Any point my asking why?'

'Not really. Just lump all my credit points together and offset this favour against them.'

'What credit points?'

'Be reasonable, Moira. I'm asking you to help me out of a deep hole here.'

'Of whose digging, may I ask?' She paused, though not long enough for me to devise an answer, then resumed, her voice suddenly gentler. 'Sorry. You've been under a lot of strain, I know. Probably *more* than I know. All right.' During the next pause I heard her take a long draw on her cigarette. 'Tell you what, Toby. I really can't spare anyone today. Tomorrow, though, I'm supposed to be working at home. I'll substitute a day trip to Brighton, manuscript in hand, and you can pour out your troubles to your aunty Moira over lunch. Good enough?'

* * *

Only *just* good enough, to be honest. I wanted *The Plastic Men* in my hands, there and then, to comb for clues to what had happened and evidence to use against Roger Colborn. Short of going up to London to get it, however, I was going to have to wait until Moira brought it to me. The matinée meant I couldn't leave Brighton. The consequences of another no-show by me, with no understudy on hand, didn't bear contemplation. I suspected Moira had volunteered to act as courier because she wanted to reassure herself as to my state of mind. She'd lost two clients in this run of *Lodger in the Throat* — Jimmy Maidment was one of hers as well — so maybe she was getting twitchy.

If so, it seemed she wasn't the only one. I let myself out of the house and headed round the corner into London Road to catch a bus back into the centre. While I was waiting at the stop, Brian Sallis rang me.

'Good morning, Toby. How are you?'

'You don't need to worry, Brian. I'll be at the theatre by two o'clock.'

'Oh, I didn't phone to check up on you. Please don't think that.'

'I'll try not to.'

'It's true. The thing is, well . . . '

'Spit it out, for God's sake.'

'All right. Sorry. Leo and Melvyn are coming down to see the matinée. I thought you ought to know.'

'The pair of them?'

'Yes.'

'Why?'

'Just to see how we're going, I suppose.'

'Don't give me that. We're two days from closure.'

'Ah, but are we?'

'What do you mean?'

'I have the impression Melvyn's report on Tuesday night's show may have made Leo think twice about taking us off.'

'You can't be serious.'

'I don't see any other way to read it. Play it this afternoon like you did Tuesday and . . . who knows? It could be very good news.'

* * *

Brian's definition of good news and mine were quite a way apart at that moment. I sat on the top deck of the number 5 as it rumbled south, bemused by the ironies of my situation. If Leo really was considering an eleventh-hour stay of execution for *Lodger in the Throat* and, by implication, a London transfer, I should be psyching myself up for a persuasive and possibly clinching star turn as James Elliott. The rest of the cast could be relied on to pull out all the stops. The chance was there to be seized.

But the chance was to me more of a burden. I couldn't spare much thought for acting as matters currently stood. In fact, I couldn't spare *any*. Reality doesn't often intrude into the life of an actor. Pretence is all, off stage as well as on. For me, though, that had changed. Utterly.

The only problem was explaining my predicament to other people in a way that would make sense to them. And I knew it was a problem I couldn't hope to solve.

As if to underline the point, Brian was back on to me before I'd even got off the bus.

'I've just spoken to Melvyn, Toby. I'm having lunch with him and Leo at the Hôtel du Vin. It's in Ship Street. You know, where Henekeys used to be.'

'I'm sure you'll have a wonderful time.'

'Ah, but Leo's suggested you join us, you see. That's why I called. Not for the whole meal, obviously. Wouldn't want to put you off your stroke.' His laugh was not contagious. 'One o'clock OK for you? It's only a ten-minute walk from there to the theatre.'

* * *

I agreed, of course. I only had to think how rejecting a lunch invitation from our esteemed producer would go down with my fellow cast members, whose salaries he paid, to realize I had no choice. Buttering up Leo and Melvyn was something I had neither the wish nor the leisure to engage in, but come one o'clock I was going to be doing it none the less.

* * *

I hopped off the bus at the Steine and doubled back at an Olympic-style walk to the Local Studies Library in Church Street. I glimpsed a representative sample of library-going folk poring over microfilm-readers as I entered, but fortunately there were several vacant places. I just had to hope none of those using the machines were consulting November 1995 editions of the *Argus*.

As I peeled round to the enquiries desk, however, I came face to face with someone extremely unlikely to have come there in search of anything else.

'Toby,' said Jenny, shuffling together a sheaf of

photocopied pages, conspicuous by their having been printed white on black. 'What are you doing here?'

'*I could ask you the same question*' was such an obvious retort that I didn't utter it. I just looked at her, then down at the sheets of paper in her hand, recognizing at a glance the headlines and columns of a newspaper page and deciphering a date at the top of one: *Friday, November 17, 1995*. Then I looked back up at her and said simply, 'Snap.'

* * *

A few minutes later, we were standing in the grounds of the Royal Pavilion, near the entrance to the Museum. It was cold enough to ensure we were in no danger of being overheard. A dusting of frost still clung to the grass where the sun hadn't reached. And Jenny's breath clouded faintly in the air as she spoke. Anger as well as a chill wind had reddened her cheeks.

'You set me up, didn't you? It was a test, to see which way I'd jump. Well, congratulations, Toby. You twitched the lead and I came running.'

'I don't know what you're talking about.'

'I should have realized you'd put Ian Maple up to it, of course.'

'Up to what?'

'Drop the pretence, Toby. It won't wash.'

'You've spoken to Ian Maple?'

'You know I have.'

'No. I don't. When was this?'

Jenny shifted her gaze and took a long, slow

breath. The white-on-black photocopies were clutched tightly in her hand. I reached out and tugged gently at them. She let go.

'The print's come off on your fingers,' I remarked, irrelevantly. She shivered, tempting me for a moment to put a warming arm round her shoulders. But of course I didn't. 'Why don't we grab a coffee somewhere?'

'Tell me the truth, Toby.' She looked me in the eye. 'Did you send Ian Maple to see me?'

'No.'

'He came to the shop just after we opened.' Which meant *before* I phoned him from Viaduct Road, I realized; nice of him to mention the visit. 'He was very . . . insistent. And the things he said about Roger . . . ' She shook her head. 'I don't believe any of it.'

'I told him you wouldn't.'

'So you did send him?'

'No.'

'But everything he knows . . . '

'He had from me, I admit.'

'Including this nonsense about Oswin being abducted?'

'Not nonsense, actually.'

'It must be.'

'If you're so sure, why did you look these up?' I fanned out the photocopies in my hand.

'To remind myself of the facts. Which Roger told me a long time ago, in case you're wondering.'

'And what *are* the facts, Jenny?'

She cocked an eyebrow at me. 'Perhaps you should read them for yourself.'

'Why don't you just tell me?'

'Because you might not believe me.'

'If we could agree on what the truth is, Jenny, we'd have no choice but to believe each other.'

Her mouth tightened. Her focus flicked cautiously around the middle distance. Then she said, 'All right. We'll talk. But you'll have to read the *Argus* reports first. Then we'll both know what we're talking *about*. There's a café in the Museum. I'll wait for you there.'

* * *

I sat down on a bench where the surrounding buildings screened me from the wind but not the sunshine and sorted the photocopied sheets into chronological order.

There were seven in all, the first five dating from November 1995. A short but prominent article, accompanied by an indistinct photograph of a car cordoned off behind police tape in a country lane, reported Sir Walter Colborn's death in the issue of 14 November. The headline reads, PROMINENT LOCAL BUSINESSMAN KILLED IN COLLISION WITH CAR. It goes on:

> Sir Walter Colborn, former chairman and managing director of Brighton-based plastics company Colbonite Ltd, died yesterday after being struck by a car while walking along a lane close to his home. Wickhurst Manor, near Fulking. The incident occurred shortly after 3 p.m.

> The driver of the car, a dark-blue Ford Fiesta, has not been named. He has been detained in custody and is assisting the police with their inquiries.

By the following day, the *Argus* was able to report SURPRISE MANSLAUGHTER CHARGE FOLLOWING DEATH OF SIR WALTER COLBORN:

> Police yesterday charged a man in connection with the death on Monday of prominent local businessman and politician Sir Walter Colborn. Kenneth George Oswin, 63, from Brighton, has been charged with manslaughter and will appear before Lewes magistrates tomorrow.

Another page of the same issue carried a fulsome obituary of the eminent departed.

> Walter Colborn was born in Brighton in 1921. He was the grandson of the founder of Colbonite Ltd, a plastics company based in Hollingdean Road, Brighton, which closed in 1989. Walter Colborn was educated at Brighton College and went up to Pembroke College, Oxford, after serving with distinction in the Army during the Second World War. He succeeded his father as chairman and managing director of Colbonite in 1955 and later served as a West Sussex County Councillor for many years, latterly as deputy leader of the Conservative

group. He was also energetically involved in a host of charitable causes and was a prominent member of the Brighton Society and an adviser to the West Pier Trust. He was knighted in 1987 in recognition of his distinguished record of public service. He married Ann Hopkinson in 1953. The couple had one son, Roger, who survives Sir Walter. Ann Colborn died in 1982.

Next day, Kenneth Oswin was remanded in custody by Lewes magistrates, according to a terse paragraph lodged obscurely near the bottom of a page. Someone had cottoned on to his connection with Colbonite by the day after, however, raising the profile of the case. MAN CHARGED WITH MANSLAUGHTER OF SIR WALTER COLBORN WAS FORMER EMPLOYEE ran the headline, above an article revealing how Roger Colborn had got in on the act.

Roger Colborn, son of the late Sir Walter Colborn, confirmed yesterday that Kenneth Oswin, the man charged with manslaughter following Sir Walter's death on Monday after he collided with a car being driven by Mr Oswin, was a former employee of Colbonite Ltd, the Brighton-based plastics company, founded by Sir Walter's grandfather, which closed in 1989. Mr Colborn, who assisted his father in the management of the company, said he knew of no reason why Mr Oswin should bear Sir Walter any ill will. Mr Oswin, he added, had been

> 'generously treated, like all the company's staff, at the time of its closure, a regrettable but unavoidable event brought about by increasingly intense foreign competition'.

How nice, how bland, how very reasonable Roger sounded. There was no mention of chloro-aniline or cancer or shell companies or deftly dodged compensation. The average uninformed reader probably concluded, if they concluded anything, that Kenneth Oswin was some kind of nutter with a grudge, the details of which would emerge at his trial.

But there was to be no trial, as a paragraph in the *Argus* for Wednesday, February 7, 1996, made clear.

> Kenneth George Oswin, 63, of Viaduct Road, Brighton, the man awaiting trial for the manslaughter of Sir Walter Colborn last November, died yesterday at the Royal Sussex County Hospital in Brighton, where he had recently been transferred from Lewes Prison. He had been suffering from cancer for some time.

That wasn't quite the end of the matter, however. An inquest followed two months later, skimming over the ground that a trial would doubtless have examined in depth. SIR WALTER COLBORN'S DEATH WAS UNLAWFUL KILLING, CORONER RULES, ran the *Argus* headline.

An inquest heard yesterday that the prosecution would have argued at the trial of Kenneth Oswin for the manslaughter of Sir Walter Colborn that Mr Oswin intended to do Sir Walter serious and probably fatal harm when he drove a Ford Fiesta car into him on a quiet country lane near Sir Walter's home north of Brighton on the afternoon of November 13 last year.

Detective Inspector Terence Moore of Sussex Police told the coroner that the collision occurred on a stretch of the lane with good visibility and that examination of the car showed that Mr Oswin had first struck Sir Walter a glancing blow, knocking him to the ground, then reversed over him. A charge of manslaughter was only preferred to murder because of doubts about Mr Oswin's state of mind, which might well have justified a plea of diminished responsibility. Mr Oswin was suffering at the time from cancer, of which he later died while awaiting trial. Detective Inspector Moore added that Mr Oswin consistently denied deliberately killing Sir Walter, but refused to give any account of what had occurred on the afternoon in question.

The coroner said in his summing-up that the outcome of Mr Oswin's trial could not and should not be taken for granted, but that a verdict of unlawful killing was clearly appropriate in the matter of Sir Walter's death. He added a personal tribute to the deceased, whom he described as a great loss to the community.

I went into the Museum and up to the café on the first floor. Jenny was waiting for me at a table overlooking the art gallery. She'd have been able to see me coming from there, though the intensity with which she was staring into the frothy remains of her *cappuccino* suggested she might easily have missed me. I bought a coffee for myself and joined her.

'OK. I'm up to speed on the facts,' I said quietly, laying the sheaf of photocopies on the table between us. 'Those the *Argus* printed, at any rate.'

'Kenneth Oswin murdered Roger's father,' said Jenny, leaning forward across the table and treating me to a lengthy, scrutinizing stare. 'You accept that?'

'Yes.' I had to. Derek's suggestion that the collision was accidental could only be wishful thinking at best. His version of the event was seriously at variance with the facts. 'But the question is: why?'

'Because he blamed Sir Walter for the cancer that was killing him.'

'With good cause.'

'Yes, Toby. With good cause.' She went on staring at me. 'You think Roger's answerable for his father's cavalier attitude to the health of the Colbonite workforce?'

'I think Roger aided and abetted his father in evading responsibility for the consequences, Jenny. By which I mean *financial* consequences. I also think Roger may have taken extreme steps to silence Derek Oswin on the point.'

'Rubbish. I don't believe for a moment Roger's even been to see Oswin.'

'Where's Derek gone, then?'

'How should I know?'

'You say Roger told you about all this a long time ago?'

'Yes.'

'How come you didn't recognize Derek's surname when I mentioned it to you, then?'

'Roger never actually told me the name of the man who killed his father, as far as I can remember. If he had, I might well have forgotten. I didn't think it mattered. I still don't.'

'What about the cancer cases, Jenny? Not a penny paid in compensation. How does Roger square that with his conscience? How do you?'

'Sir Walter resorted to undeniably shady tactics when he wound the company up. Roger makes no secret of that. He protested against them at the time and fell out with his father as a result.'

'We only have Roger's word for that, presumably.'

'I believe him.'

'Naturally. And let's suppose it's true. Just for the sake of argument. Suppose Roger really did advocate coming clean about the chloro-anilines but was overruled by his old man. Why didn't he do something about it when Sir Walter died and he inherited the wherewithal to pay out some long overdue compensation?'

'He considered the idea. He took advice.'

'Oh yeah?'

'To pay out in one case would mean paying out in all. It would have bankrupted him.'

'Well, we couldn't have that, could we?'

'As a matter of fact . . . '

'What?'

'He has . . . helped . . . in a few of the more desperate cases. With hospice fees and the like. He's had to be . . . discreet about it.'

'To avoid admitting general liability?'

'Yes. So, is that what you're accusing him of, Toby? Trying to repair some of the damage his father did without ruining himself in the process?'

'No. That's your gloss on what I suspect he's really been up to. And I'm not the only one who suspects it.'

'Ian Maple said you'd spoken to Roger's uncle.'

'Yes. Informative fellow, Gavin. See a lot of him, do you?'

'I've never met him. But I know his version of events can't be trusted.'

'And how do you know that? Because Roger told you so, perhaps?'

'His sister Delia says the same.'

'Does she?'

'Yes. And I can arrange for her to say it to you as well if that's what it'll take to make you call off this . . . ludicrous campaign.'

'Denis is dead, Jenny. And Derek Oswin is missing. I'm not making any of that up. I think Roger is a dangerous man to know.'

'Ah. So, you're trying to protect me.'

'Why wouldn't I?'

'Why indeed?' She sat back and shook her head at me. 'Surely you can see you're deluding yourself, Toby? Denis died of a heart attack. It's sad, but it could have happened at any time. As for Derek Oswin, so what if he's gone walkabout and left his house in a mess? You can't blame Roger for that.'

'Can't I?'

'You're not going to believe anything I tell you, are you?'

'Are you going to believe anything *I* tell *you*?'

Jenny sighed. 'For God's sake . . . '

'It cuts both ways, you know. You think I'm deluding myself. Well, that's exactly what I think you're doing.'

'Yes.' She almost smiled then, some of her old exasperated fondness for me bobbing briefly to the surface. 'I suppose you do.'

'Tell me what you'd accept as proof.'

'Proof?' She thought for a moment, then leaned forward again. 'All right. Delia has no axe to grind. Certainly not in Roger's favour, anyway. He bought her Colbonite shares as well as Gavin's and ultimately netted a substantial profit on them. So, she should resent him on that account. Agreed?'

'Yes,' I responded, suddenly cautious. Gavin had portrayed his sister as a fellow victim of Roger's machinations. He'd even suggested I ask her to corroborate his story. But Jenny seemed oddly confident Delia would back up Roger's version of events. If she did, I wouldn't have proved my case. In fact, I'd have gone a long way towards *dis*proving it.

'Come and see her with me. She knows the history of all of this. And she's an honest person. I can assure you of that. If she sides with you . . . I'll have to take it seriously.'

'And if not?'

'*You'll* have to take it seriously.'

'How do I know this isn't a set-up?'

'You have to trust me, Toby. That's how.'

I drank some coffee, studying Jenny's face over the rim of the cup. She was right, of course. I had to trust her. If I didn't, I was lost. But she'd misunderstood me, anyway. It wasn't her I suspected of setting me up. Not that it mattered, really. I'd left myself without an escape route. 'All right. Let's do it.'

'When?'

'You tell me. There's a matinée today, so I'm pushed for time, but I'll fit it in.'

'I'll have to give Delia some notice. How about this afternoon — between performances? She lives in Powis Villas. It's a short walk from the theatre.'

'I know where she lives. Gavin gave me her address.'

'All right. I'll phone her and explain.'

'Why not phone her right now?'

'Why not?' Jenny smiled at me defiantly, took out her mobile and dialled the number. A few moments passed; then she started speaking. But only to leave a message asking Delia to call her urgently. She rang off. 'I'll let you know what I fix up. It may have to be tomorrow, of course. I can't speak for Delia's availability. I'd better be going now. I've left Sophie in charge long enough.' She stood up and reached out for the photocopies, then changed her mind. 'You can keep those.'

'Thanks. It'll spare you the effort of hiding them from Roger.' I regretted the remark instantly. But there was no taking it back.

Jenny looked down at me with a kind of baffled pity. 'You really don't understand, Toby, do you?'

'Don't I?'

'No. And it seems, God help me, that I'm going to have to prove that to you.'

⋆ ⋆ ⋆

I tried Ray Braddock again after Jenny had gone. Still no answer. I had his address, of course, but there was no point going there if he wasn't in. I walked back out into the cold, clear, late-morning air, where the shadows were long, but sharply etched. I looked across at the minarets and onion domes of the Royal Pavilion and spared a sympathetic thought for sad old fat George IV. All he'd really wanted to do was enjoy some cosy domesticity with Mrs Fitzherbert, who happened, after all, by every seemly definition to be his wife. Yet they were forced to live apart. Their separation was in many ways George's own fault, just as losing Jenny was mine. But culpability doesn't make such miscarriages of life easier to bear. Quite the reverse, actually.

* * *

It was just gone noon and there was little I could usefully do before joining the three musketeers for lunch. Why I gravitated to the Cricketers I'm not sure, except that it had become something of a midday habit. What I hadn't realized was that it was also a midday habit for my self-appointed friend Sydney Porteous.

'Great to see you, Tobe. Couldn't keep away, hey?'

'Something like that.'

'Allow me the distinct pleasure of buying you a drink. Pint of Harvey's best?'

'I'll plump for tomato juice, thanks. There's a matinée this afternoon.'

'So there is. Very wise.' He ordered a Virgin Mary and a top-up for his own pint. 'Shall we huddle by the fire? It's brass monkeys out there today.'

Drinks in hand, we went and sat down. Syd smacked his lips at another swallow of beer, while I sipped my under-Worcestered tomato juice and glanced wincingly around at the ever tinselier auguries of Christmas.

'Wrecks the whole month, doesn't it?' said Syd, evidently reading my thoughts. 'Piped carols and office parties. Who needs them, hey? Not pagans with no office to go to, that's for sure.'

'Quite.'

'Still, my Christmas is shaping up to be a little less throat-slittingly depressing now Aud's on the scene. She's really looking forward to seeing you on Sunday, by the way.'

'Sunday?'

'She's cooking you lunch, remember?'

Now I did remember. Yes, of course. Sunday lunch with Syd and Aud. How had I ever agreed to that? It was a good question. But the rhetorical alternative I actually posed was, 'How could I forget?'

'You've got a lot on your mind, Tobe. A spot of forgetfulness is only to be expected.' He lowered his voice confidentially. 'How goes the campaign?'

It struck me as odd that he'd used the same word as Jenny to describe my activities. What made it odder still was how unlike a campaign they felt to me. 'I'm making steady progress.'

'Excellent. Decided yet whether you'll need me to ride shotgun for you when you drop in on the fragrant Delia?'

'I won't need to impose on you, Syd.'

'It'd be no imposition.'

'Even so . . . '

'Your call, Tobe. Entirely your call.'

'I appreciate the offer, but . . . '

'You'd rather go it alone. Understood. I suppose I was just angling for an excuse to renew our acquaintance.'

'How *were* you acquainted?'

'Oh, well, Gav invited me out to Wickhurst Manor a few times during our schooldays. Delia's a couple of years older than us. I remember her first as a Roedean sixth-former. Awesomely ladylike. She taught there for quite a few years, you know, after finishing school and

Oxford — or Cambridge, I can't honestly recall which. I always fancied her and there was a period in my late twenties and her early thirties when . . . ' He spread his hands. 'Well, I blew my chance, that's what it comes down to. But I don't reckon I ever had much of one. I wasn't really in her league. As I've not an itty-bitty doubt her sister-in-law made crystal clear to her. Ann Colborn was always down on me. And she and Delia were like that.' Syd wrapped his index and second fingers together.

'Ann Colborn died young, didn't she?'

'Fairly.'

I waited for Syd to expand on the remark, but he didn't. Such reticence was uncharacteristic. 'I looked up Sir Walter's obituary in the *Argus*, Syd,' I said by way of a prompt.

'Ah. So you know, then?'

'That his wife died in nineteen eighty-two, yes. When she can't have been much more than fifty, judging by Sir Walter's age.'

'Didn't it mention . . . how she died?'

'No.'

'So you *don't* know.'

'Know what?'

'Suicide, Tobe. Ann Colborn took her own life. Drove her car off Beachy Head. Nice car, too. Jaguar two point four.'

'She killed herself?'

'Well, it definitely wasn't murder.'

'Why did she do it?'

'Depression, I think they said. You know, 'while the balance of her mind was disturbed'.

Let's face it, it'd have to be disturbed for her to take the Jag with her. Mind you, it's a classier exit than going under the wheels of a Ford Fiesta.'

I've thought about that last comment of Syd's since. Yesterday, he claimed not to know that the driver of the car that killed Sir Walter was charged with manslaughter. Strange, then, that he should none the less remember the model of car involved. When he dropped it into our conversation at the Cricketers, I made nothing of it, still dismayed by the realization that Roger Colborn's mother had committed suicide. Looking back, however, I see it as proof of what I've begun to suspect: that Syd's garrulous manner conceals rather more than it reveals; that he knows rather more than he's so far chosen to disclose.

'I think Delia was still living at Wickhurst Manor then. Ann's death must have been a real blow to her. She's married since, of course. And married well, according to Gav. So, if reasons are what you're looking for, you could ask her, I suppose. She's had twenty years to get used to what happened.' Syd thought for a moment, then went on. 'Say, you don't think Ann Colborn topping herself is . . . connected with all this, do you?'

'No. Do you, Syd?'

He shrugged. 'No way to tell. Doesn't seem likely, does it? I certainly wouldn't put a lot of money on it. But, then again . . . ' He grinned. 'I might risk a fiver.'

* * *

I reached the Hôtel du Vin ten minutes late thanks to my brain-picking session with Syd. My mind was still focused on the distant mysteries of the Colborn family. I was in no mood and poor condition to make up a foursome with Brian Sallis, Melvyn Buckingham and the demigod of the West End himself, Leo Simmons Gauntlett.

They were already at their table in the large and busy restaurant when I arrived. Melvyn was all smiles and 'dear boys' after several pre-prandial gins, but Leo looked as if his ulcer was playing him up again. A man of notably untheatrical appearance — more accountant than impresario — he can charm and schmooze and fly kites with the best of them when he has to. His natural temperament veers more towards the plain and practical, however, and sometimes the downright pessimistic. It was immediately apparent to me that he hadn't arrived in Brighton with the highest of hopes. But, canny financier that he is, he doesn't like to give up on any investment unless he absolutely has to. This was my chance to persuade him that in this case he might not have to. Unfortunately, not only did I feel unequal to the challenge, I also felt signally indifferent to the outcome.

'Melvyn thought he saw something new in the show Tuesday night,' he said over his doctor's-orders salad after I'd ordered a starter and a mineral water to keep them company. 'Did it feel like there was something new in it to you, Toby?'

'Not sure.'

'Not sure's a bit bloody weak this late in the day.'

'It's the best I can do.'

'Denis's death has knocked us all sideways, Leo,' put in Brian.

'Ah yes,' said Melvyn, slurping some wine. 'Death — the great leveller.'

'I don't know about death,' said Leo. 'What concerns me is whether there's any life in *Lodger in the Throat*.'

'There always has been,' I said. 'We just haven't been very successful at finding it.'

'Hah. Sounds like you agree with your friend Unwin. It's all down to unsympathetic direction.'

Melvyn choked and spluttered on another mouthful of wine. 'Am I never to hear the last of that ghastly fellow and his impertinent letters?'

'Actually, Leo, his name's Oswin,' I pointed out. 'Not Unwin.' Then Melvyn's use of the plural registered in my mind. 'Did you say letters?'

'Oh yes,' Melvyn replied. 'Another one arrived this morning.'

'I suppose you get used to your fan mail containing a certain percentage of crackpot material,' said Leo. 'It's come as an eye-opener to me, though.'

'What did the letter say?'

'See for yourself.' Leo flourished a sheet of paper from inside his jacket and handed it to me. 'Keep it if you like.'

It was Derek's distinctive handwriting, no question about it. He'd sent a second letter, after promising me he wouldn't. Or had he? He probably posted it yesterday morning, *before* he undertook to end the correspondence. Technically, he hadn't broken his promise. But nor had he warned me that a second missive was already on its way. Not for the first time, he'd been economical with the facts. It seemed to be something of a local custom. Why, I wondered, had Derek seen fit to write to Leo again?

77 Viaduct Road
Brighton
BN1 4ND

4th December 2002

Dear Mr Gauntlett,
Further to my previous letter, I realize that I omitted to say something very important about Mr Flood. As someone to some degree responsible for the advancement of his career, you should be aware that it is not only for his considerable acting abilities that Mr Flood is to be cherished. He is also, you see, an honourable and generous man, as I know from my personal experience. He has tried to help me just as I have tried to help him. I find it hard to imagine that any other person of Mr Flood's eminence would spare me so much attention. It is a reflection of the nobility of his character and I wish to pay tribute to that. I only hope it does not redound to his disadvantage. Should it do so, however, I call upon you to do everything

you can to assist him. He would richly deserve any kindness you could render him, since there may come a time when he is not the best judge of his own interests.

Respectfully yours,

Derek Oswin

'You assured me he wouldn't write again, dear boy,' said Melvyn as I folded the letter and slid it into my pocket. 'Is it to become a regular event?'

'No. Definitely not.'

'First he questions Melvyn's direction,' said Leo. 'Now your judgement, Toby. A bit bloody presumptuous, isn't he?'

'I'm afraid he is, yes. But you've heard the last of him.'

'Really?'

'You reserved a ticket for him last night, Toby,' said Brian. 'It wasn't taken up.'

'I believe he's left town.'

'Good riddance,' mumbled Melvyn.

In some ways, I wanted to echo the sentiment. If Derek was in trouble, as I believed he was — big trouble — then it was of his own making. But I wasn't trying to get him out of it just in order to win Jenny back. I was also trying to help Derek for his own infuriating sake, as he in his oddly acute fashion seemed to understand. In the opinion of some, the time has already come when I'm not the best judge of my own interests. And in the opinion of others, I never have been. But, as it happens, I'm the only judge who counts.

Not as far as the future of *Lodger in the*

Throat is concerned, though. That's down to Leo S. Gauntlett.

'I hope I haven't had a wasted journey,' he grumbled, spearing a cherry tomato.

'Don't worry, Leo,' I said, dredging up some bravado and beaming at my companions like the versatile actor I am. 'I'll ensure you go back to London with a spring in your step and a song in your heart.'

Leo regarded me acidly for a moment, then said, 'You're not going to try and turn it into a bloody musical, are you?'

* * *

Brian and I left Leo and Melvyn to their coffees (and brandy, in Melvyn's case) in order to be at the theatre by two o'clock. We were threading through the crowds of Christmas shoppers in North Street when Jenny rang me.

'I've spoken to Delia, Toby. She can meet us late afternoon. When will you be free?'

'We'll finish about five fifteen. I could be at Powis Villas by . . . a quarter to six.'

'All right. I'll be there when you arrive. It's number fifteen.'

'I know. Fine. But look . . . ' I edged into a doorway, waving Brian to go on ahead, which he did, though only far enough to put himself out of earshot. 'Jenny, there's something that's bound to crop up when I speak to Delia and I'm not sure if you know . . . about it.'

'Oh yes. What's that?'

'Roger's mother. Ann Colborn.'

'Yes?'

'She killed herself, Jenny. She and Delia were pretty close, apparently. I . . . well, I didn't want . . . to spring it on you.'

There was the briefest of delays before Jenny responded, but it was a delay that told a tale of its own. 'Of course I know about Roger's mother, Toby. It's not a secret.'

'Good.' *I've just done you a big favour, Jenny,* I thought to myself. *Do you realize that? You can clear this up with Delia before I arrive now. Thanks to me*. 'I just . . . wanted to check.'

'Well, now you have.'

'Yeah, OK. See you later.'

* * *

I caught up with Brian and explained to him that I'd have to leave the theatre straight after the show. There'd be no time for a debriefing session with Leo and Melvyn. He was clearly put out by this, since they wouldn't be staying for the evening performance, but, as I said to him, 'Leo will decide what's best for business, Brian, you know that. With or without encouragement from me.'

* * *

I was glad to reach the haven of my dressing room and relieved, in some ways, to be about to go on stage. The adrenalin doesn't course through my system during live performances the way it used to, but I was confident there'd be enough of it pumping around to put the tangled complexities of my involvement with the Colborn and Oswin families past and present out of my mind for a couple of hours.

* * *

I changed into my costume, applied a little make-up and sat quietly, trying to will myself into the thoughts as well as the persona of James Elliott. The quarter-hour was called, then the five minutes. And then my mobile, which normally I'd have switched off, trilled into life. In the interests of my preparation routine, I should have ignored it. Naturally, I didn't.

'Yes?'

'Ian Maple here, Toby. We need to meet.'

'I'm due on stage in a few minutes.'

'Things have taken . . . an unexpected turn.'

'This will have to wait, Ian.'

'It can't.'

'But it has to.'

'When can we meet? It's got to be this afternoon.'

'All right. Come to the theatre an hour from now. Use the stage door. I'll leave word you're to be shown to my dressing room. We'll talk during the interval.'

'Understood.'

He rang off and I headed for the door.

* * *

My mind lost all focus during the first act. That's not as bad as it sounds. Sometimes I'm at my best when I just surrender control and let it happen. The down side is that I'm in no position to analyse such a performance. It is what it is, good *or* bad. The rest of the cast were probably on their mettle, knowing Leo and Melvyn were in the audience, but how they thought it went, or more importantly how they thought Leo thought it went, I have no idea.

* * *

Ian Maple was waiting in my dressing room, as agreed. He looked sombre, but, surprisingly, more relaxed than last night. He remained where he was on the couch when I entered. On the floor at his feet was a long, narrow object wrapped in a carrier bag bearing the name Dockerills, an ironmongery shop in Church Street I'd passed several times.

'Thanks for telling me you'd already dropped in on my wife when we spoke this morning,' I said by way of an opener, turning the dressing-table chair round and sitting down to face him.

'You've seen her?'

'Yes.'

'Ah.' He rubbed his unshaven chin. 'I didn't know you were planning to.'

'I wasn't.'

'But I was. I told you that.'

'All right. Let's not waste time.' It was true to say we couldn't afford to. And recriminations were clearly not going to make any impression on Ian. He meant business. 'What's happened since? Have you met Colborn?'

'Not exactly. I've seen him.'

'Seen as in 'observed'?'

'As in 'followed'. I hired a car and drove out to Wickhurst. Spotted Colborn leaving in his Porsche as I was cruising towards the entrance, so I just fell in behind and let him take me where he was going.'

'And where was that?'

'Car park up on Devil's Dyke. Where a bloke was waiting for him in a Ford Transit. A big bloke. Fucking huge.'

'Denis's man mountain.'

'That's what I figured. Colborn pulled in next to the van. They talked for a few minutes. Colborn handed him an envelope. Then they went their separate ways. I followed man mountain.'

'Are you sure they didn't spot you?'

'It's a nice day. There were quite a few cars up on the Dyke. Dog-walkers and such. I blended in. I'm good at doing that.'

'OK. So, where did man mountain take you?'

'Fishersgate. Part of the sprawl between here and Worthing. A mix of housing and factories. There's a small, down-at-heel industrial estate next to Fishersgate railway station. He drove in there and went into one of the units. There was no-one waiting for him that I saw. Unless they stayed inside, of course. The main shutter-door was down. He let himself in by a wicket-door. Came out about ten minutes later and drove away. I kept following. He headed into the centre of Brighton. Stowed the van in a lock-up garage in Little Western Street, then took off on foot. By the time I'd parked the car, I'd lost him. So, I went back to Fishersgate and took a closer look at the warehouse he'd gone into. No signs of life. No trace of ownership. Bloke in the welding outfit next door knew zilch.'

'What do you reckon, then?'

'I reckon it's where they're holding Oswin.'

'Based on what?'

'Based on man mountain going there to check on something after a confab with Colborn. And it's a guess I mean to back up.'

'How?'

'We're going in tonight.' He toed open the bag on the floor to reveal the jaws of a stout pair of bolt-cutters. 'These'll get us through the perimeter fence and the padlock on the wicket-door.'

'You're serious?'

'The best way to nail Colborn is to spring Oswin. There's no sense in holding off. But . . . '

'What?'

'I'll need you to watch my back and, maybe more importantly, explain to Oswin that I'm one of the good guys.'

'This sounds risky.'

'Of course it's risky. What did you expect? A stroll on the beach?'

'It's just . . . I'm an actor for God's sake. I'd be a liability.'

'I can't do it on my own. And there's no-one else I can ask to help. Now . . . are you in or out?' He stared at me levelly, defying me to pass up the chance I undeniably craved to pin something on Roger Colborn. Nor was that the only consideration, as Ian was well aware. 'Delaying won't help Oswin, you know. The longer someone like him is in the hands of man mountain's kind, the worse it'll be for him, believe me.'

'I do believe you.'

'Well, then?'

'All right. Let's do it.'

'I'll pick you up from the bottom of Madeira Place at midnight. OK?'

I nodded. 'OK.' There really was, it seemed, nothing else for it.

⋆ ⋆ ⋆

The second act sped past, my mind autopiloting me through to the close. The applause sounded less than wholeheartedly enthusiastic, but midweek matinées attract an undemonstrative lot. In a fragmentary conversation afterwards, Jocasta struck a hopeful note. 'I think we've given Leo something to think about.'

Well, she might have been right. But, even if she was, it was nothing like as much as I had to think about. Two performances of *Lodger in the Throat* and a spot of breaking and entering constituted a distinctly challenging workload.

'If I were you,' I said to my reflection in the dressing-room mirror as I changed out of my James Elliott kit, 'I wouldn't do it.'

⋆ ⋆ ⋆

Night had fallen by the time I left the theatre. Gift-laden shoppers were trailing along North Street. The air was cold and the spirit Christmassy, as a gust of piped 'Jingle Bells' from a shop near the stage door forcibly reminded me. I hurried along Church Street past the fuming crawl of traffic and cut across Dyke Road to Clifton Terrace, where a chill, quiet serenity prevailed, then round the corner into Powis Villas, a sloping street of semi-detached residences sporting stylish verandahs and expensive cars in the driveways.

* * *

Jenny answered the door at number 15 and showed me into a high-windowed drawing room furnished and decorated with tasteful restraint. A log fire blazed invitingly beneath a gilt-framed oil, the subject of which I instantly recognized as Wickhurst Manor.

Delia Sheringham rose from a fireside chair to greet me. Tall, slim and fine-boned, dressed plainly but elegantly, she was grey-haired yet younger in appearance than her probable age had prepared me for. Her eyes were a softer, more forget-me-not shade of blue than her brother's and nephew's. Her smile was softer too, her voice altogether gentler. But her self-control was palpable. There was no way to tell whether she had just been recounting the circumstances of her sister-in-law's suicide or the state of her preparations for Christmas.

'Would you like a drink, Mr Flood?' she

enquired. 'Jenny and I are having tea.'

'Tea would be fine, thanks.'

Jenny poured me a cup. We all sat down. I sipped some tea.

'My husband and I have tickets for your play on Saturday night,' said Delia. 'I'm sure we'll enjoy it.'

'We aim to please.' Whether Orton's scatological humour would appeal to her I privately doubted. The state of mind of the lead actor come Saturday night was also questionable. Delia was facing a less certain prospect than she knew.

'Jenny's explained your . . . difficulty, Toby. May I call you Toby? I dare say you find people tend towards overfamiliarity because of your profession. It must be a bore for you.'

'Not at all. And certainly not in your case.'

'Very well, Toby. You should understand that I'm not in the habit of discussing my family's affairs with outsiders. Indeed, I'm hardly in the habit of discussing them with other members of my family.' She smiled thinly. 'The Colborns do not wear their hearts on their sleeves. But that doesn't mean they don't have hearts. Or consciences. The illness that affected so many Colbonite employees has weighed on Roger's conscience, I know, as it should have. I believe Jenny has told you of his efforts to help some of them.'

'Yes.' I glanced across at Jenny. 'She's told me.'

'No doubt you think those efforts inadequate. Well, you may be right. He is constrained, however. You should be aware of that. I've done a little for some of them myself. Again, no doubt, too little. I played absolutely no part in the management of Colbonite, of course. I had no idea what . . . corners . . . Walter might have been cutting to sustain the business at a time when others were going to the wall in the face of foreign competition. They *were* Walter's decisions, however. No-one else's. Certainly not Roger's. I believe he did his best to improve safety practices after joining the company. As for his purchase of the shares Gavin and I held, I regarded that as an expression of his confidence that he could make a success of it. I was happy to sell. So was Gavin. Roger took a risk and profited from it. Why should I resent that? I know Gavin resents it, but I fear he's blaming Roger for his own mistakes. You've met Gavin. You know the kind of man he is.'

'He sends his regards.'

My remark drew a sharp look from Jenny, but Delia smiled tolerantly, as if she'd been the subject of a justified rebuke. 'Ours would be called a dysfunctional family in the current jargon. Gavin's character is flawed by self-indulgence. A refusal to accept responsibility for his own actions is the greatest self-indulgence of all.'

'He seems to think he was cheated out of his inheritance.'

'You can't be cheated out of something you haven't earned, Toby. Gavin has never understood that. But I don't want to be too hard on him. His elder brother was not without flaws himself. They were flaws of a rather different order, however. Walter wasn't a self-made man. How could he be as the third generation to run Colbonite? But he'd have liked to be, you see, and probably would have been in other circumstances. The company could easily have collapsed in the nineteen fifties. Walter sustained it virtually single-handedly. Father's contribution was negligible by then. Thanks to Walter, the Colbonite workforce probably had an extra twenty to thirty years of employment. He saw that as a genuine achievement.'

'But there was a price to pay, Delia, wasn't there?'

'Yes. It's clear now there was. Which brings me to Walter's greatest failing: his absolute inability to admit a mistake when he'd made one. Gavin's tactic is to blame others. Walter's was denial. I don't believe he went to such lengths to evade liability for the cancer cases simply because of the huge amount of money that might have been involved. I believe he did it because he couldn't convince himself that he *was* liable. It would have meant he was wrong to have done the things he did to keep Colbonite in profit, which, by his definition, he couldn't have been. There was his reputation to consider as well. He feared public disgrace far more than bankruptcy. He was a stubborn and dogmatic man. I say that though I loved him dearly. He could not, *would not*, admit to error, in large things or in small. He could be infuriating. Sometimes worse than infuriating.'

'Is that what drove his wife to suicide?'

Delia didn't flinch at the mention of her late

sister-in-law. She'd been prepared for it, after all. But her face did quiver slightly. It was a tender subject, even after twenty years. 'Ann wasn't a strong person. That wasn't Walter's fault, of course. But he ignored the warning signs. He didn't take enough care of her. He was too busy. With Colbonite. With his politics and good causes. It shouldn't have happened. But it did.' Delia diverted her gaze towards the fire and fell silent. It seemed she'd said as much as she could bear to about Ann Colborn's fatal plunge from Beachy Head.

'I'm sorry for putting you through this, Delia,' said Jenny, with a glare in my direction. 'Toby insisted on hearing the whole story.'

'With good reason, I've no doubt,' Delia responded. She looked across at me then, her expression fractionally but significantly altered from the placid earnestness of earlier. Jenny couldn't have seen the strange, fleeting hint of ambiguity in her eyes. It was reserved for me. There was more she could have said, it lightly implied, more she could have divulged. But not more of the same. I'd been given the authorized version. And I wasn't going to be given any other.

* * *

Jenny showed me to the door, transparently keen on a private word before I left.

'It wasn't easy for Delia to go into all that, you know,' she whispered to me as we stood in the porch, the front door half-open. 'I hope you're satisfied.'

'You think I should be?'

'Of course.'

'Well, that's settled, then.'

'I'd like you to say it as if you mean it.'

'And I will. When I do.'

'You have to give this up, Toby.'

'Tell you what, Jen. If I find Roger has nothing to do with Derek Oswin's disappearance and the poor bloke duly reappears unharmed . . . then I'll give it up.'

'You promised to abide by what Delia said.'

'No. I promised to take it seriously. And that's exactly what I'm going to do. What I want *you* to do is take care. I meant what I said earlier about Roger being dangerous. Hard as you may find it to believe, that's why I'm being such a pain.'

'Not hard to believe, Toby.' She opened the door wide. 'Just impossible. As you always are.'

* * *

When I left Powis Villas, I had barely half an hour at my disposal before I was due back at the theatre. Tomato juice and a bag of nuts in a nondescript pub halfway between the two made for a frugal pit stop. I turned my mobile back on to check for messages and found one waiting for me from Moira. Fearing she'd changed her mind about delivering *The Plastic Men* in person tomorrow and wondering how the bloody hell I was going to get hold of it in that case, I listened in.

'*Toby, this is Moira. What exactly is going on? I thought we'd agreed I'd bring this wretched manuscript down to you tomorrow. If that wasn't good enough, you should have said. Anyway, is lunch still on or not? Perhaps you'd be so kind as to let me know.'*

What in God's name was the woman on about? I called her at the office, but only got the answering machine. It was the same story on her home number. I left messages on both to the exasperated effect that as far as I was concerned our plans were unaltered and I'd be expecting to meet her off the 12.27 train, *The Plastic Men* wedged firmly under her arm. She's always adroitly managed to avoid giving me her mobile number and now I was left wondering why I can be contacted more easily by my agent than she can be by me.

* * *

The time for wondering was not long, however. I was soon on my way down Bond Street to the stage door of the Theatre Royal. Brian greeted me with the news that Leo and Melvyn had departed for London well pleased with what they'd seen. I fancied he was just trying to put me and the rest of the cast in a good mood, but others seemed wholly convinced that a West End transfer had been snatched from the jaws of a provincial fizzle-out. Donohue was looking even more pleased with himself than usual, for instance, though Fred suggested to me in passing that Mandy Pringle was more likely to be responsible for that than Leo S. Gauntlett.

‘That’s Brighton for you,’ he said with a wink. ‘So they tell me.’

* * *

This evening’s performance is an even hazier memory for me than this afternoon’s. I’ve been James Elliott for *Lodger in the Throat*’s two and a half hours of running time on seventy-seven occasions since we opened in Guildford ten weeks ago, so it’s hardly surprising that most of those are part of one vague and messily merged recollection. None of them faded faster into that *mélange* than tonight’s, however. It ended only a few hours ago, but it could as easily be several days, or even weeks. Those few hours have made sure of that.

* * *

The others must be getting used to me opting out of communal supper parties after the show. No-one made more than a desultory effort to talk me into joining them. Perhaps they realized I wasn’t likely to be good company.

I walked down to the pier after leaving the theatre, bought a portion of fish and chips and ate them in the biting cold night air, staring out across the sea that could be heard more than seen in the inky darkness, wondering with oddly detached curiosity whether I really was going to go through with what Ian Maple had planned. I still didn’t really know, when the time came, which way I’d jump.

* * *

I got back to the Sea Air just before 11.30. That was past Eunice's normal bedtime, so it was a surprise to see her light still on and even more of a surprise to be met by her in the hall, looking flustered and far from sleepy.

'Thank goodness,' she breathlessly greeted me. 'I was beginning to think you'd be out till the small hours.'

'Would it have mattered if I was?'

'Ordinarily, no. Of course not. But . . . after what's happened . . . '

'What *has* happened?' My first thought was that Binky had met with an accident. What else could disrupt Eunice's domestic routine as dramatically as something clearly had?

'I didn't like to phone you at the theatre. I knew you'd need to concentrate on your performance. But it's been such a worry for me, not knowing what to make of it.'

'Make of *what*, Eunice?' I piloted her into the residents' lounge, switching on the lights as we entered.

'It's been such a to-do. My nerves are all a-jangle.'

'Sit down and tell me all about it.'

'Yes. Of course. You must be wondering why I'm making such a fuss.' We settled in opposite armchairs in front of the gas fire. 'Turn that on, will you, Toby? It's as cold as the grave in here.'

'Sure.' I flicked the fire into life and returned to my chair. 'So, what, er . . . '

'It was while I was out shopping this

afternoon. You were at the theatre for the matinée, of course, which meant the house was empty. It's almost as if they knew it would be. The policeman who came reckoned it was what he called . . . an opportunist. Looking for money to buy drugs, like as not, and just gave up and went away when they couldn't find any. I'm not so sure though.'

'Are we talking about a burglary, Eunice?' (If so, the policeman sounded spot-on to me.)

'I suppose we would be if anything had been taken. But that's the point. Nothing was. They smashed a pane in one of my windows and forced the latch. The basement's out of sight unless you're right outside on the pavement, of course. Upset my Busy Lizzie, climbing in, they did. But nothing else was touched downstairs, as far as I can tell. If they were looking for money, they didn't look very hard. Walked straight past my Chivas Regal. There must be a good few quid in there all told. The policeman reckoned notes were what they had in mind, but, like I told him, if they're so desperate, why would they be so choosy?'

A dimly recalled glimpse in Eunice's kitchen of an old Chivas Regal bottle, used as a repository for small change, mostly of the copper variety, was all that enabled me to follow this account. Once again, I had to side with the policeman. But I sensed that wasn't what Eunice wanted to hear.

'Till the glazier's been tomorrow, I shan't feel safe. And there's you to consider, Toby. They'd have gone through the house, wouldn't they?

Stands to reason. Was there any money in your room? The policeman asked me to check with you. Nothing looked to have been disturbed up there, but how can I say for sure?'

'The only cash I've got is in my pocket, Eunice. Nothing to worry about there.' Then it struck me that maybe there *was* something to worry about. 'Hold on, though. There's my chequebook.'

'Oh, my.'

'I'd better go up and see if it's still there. You stay here. And relax. There's not much you can do with a chequebook these days without the plastic to back it up.'

* * *

When I reached my room, I saw at once that Eunice was right. It had a distinctly and reassuringly undisturbed look. I pulled open the drawer of the bedside cabinet and there was my chequebook, lying just where I'd left it. All was well.

Except that it wasn't. As I turned round from the cabinet, my glance fell on the small table next to the armchair. The dictaphone was also where I'd left it, on the table. But the hatch of the cassette compartment was open. As I moved towards it, I knew what I'd see. The cassette was missing. Trembling now, I went back to the cabinet and reopened the drawer, wider than before. The previous cassette was also missing.

* * *

Everything I disclosed to this machine, secretly and confidentially, yesterday and Tuesday and Monday and Sunday, had gone. Everything I said and guessed and hoped and suspected could be heard by another. How to put your enemy several steps ahead of you in one easy lesson: tell them what you've done and what you're going to do; then make them a gift of the whole lot.

The unused tapes in their plastic outers had been left behind, as if to assure me that the burglars had known exactly what they were doing. No-one could have known I was making these recordings. To that extent, their theft was opportunistic. The break-in was a fishing expedition. And the catch must have surpassed expectation.

It was five minutes to midnight by my alarm clock. Ian Maple might already be waiting for me at the end of the street. The risks he'd proposed to run were surely doubled now. Whoever had the tapes could listen to them and judge what we were likely to do. They didn't know Ian had trailed man mountain to the warehouse, it was true, but they knew we'd be looking for Derek. They knew we weren't going to stand idly by.

Time was nearly up. I headed downstairs.

* * *

Eunice had fallen asleep, her anxiety lessened, I supposed, now I was on the premises. I turned off the fire and nudged her awake.

'Oh. Toby. There you are. I must have . . . Is everything OK?'

'It's fine, Eunice. Nothing touched. Cheque-book intact.'

'Well, that's a blessing, though — '

'You should get to bed.'

'Yes. Yes, I should.' She rose stiffly from the chair and I saw her out into the hall. 'I'm glad you haven't lost anything, Toby. But to my mind that only makes it more mystifying.'

'These druggies don't necessarily do things that make sense. It could have turned out a whole lot worse.'

'Well, yes, that's true.'

'I'll say goodnight, then. Try not to worry. You need some sleep. We both do.'

That last point was undeniable. But I wasn't going to have the chance of any shut-eye for some time yet. I watched Eunice toddle off downstairs and waited for a minute or so after the basement door had closed behind her in case she came back. Then I headed out.

* * *

Ian Maple had parked his hire car at the end of the street. He flashed his headlights as I stepped out from the porch of the Sea Air. In the thirty yards or so of pavement I covered to reach him, I rehearsed the ways I could convince him that we shouldn't go ahead. The hardest thing of all to explain was how I'd failed to realize what a hostage to fortune the tapes represented. I should have taken better care of them, or better still never recorded my thoughts and experiences in the first place. That's what he'd say. It's certainly what he'd think. How could I have been so stupid? Just how big a liability was I?

But he never said or thought anything of the kind. Because, when I opened the door and slipped into the passenger seat. I knew, with the shock of sudden self-awareness, that I wasn't going to tell him. I wasn't going to breathe a word.

'All set?' he asked, glancing round at me.

'All set.'

* * *

We drove west along Kingsway through the chill and empty night. The Regency terraces of Hove gave way to the redbrick semis of Portslade. Ian kept assiduously to the speed limit. Nothing was said. The journey stretched into the darkness beyond the amber coronas of the street lamps.

Some time after the road veered away from the shore, he turned off into the drab hinterland of Fishersgate. We went under a railway bridge and turned west again along a residential side street, ending in the closed gates of a small industrial estate.

'Here we are,' he announced, pulling in some way short of the gates.

The jumble of brick-built warehouses and workshops within was deserted, the run-down look of most of them suggesting they contained no riches to make breaking in worthwhile. The close proximity of housing and the height of the fence were powerful deterrents as well.

'You're not going in here, are you?' I asked. 'It

only takes one insomniac to look out of the window . . .'

'Follow me,' said Ian, opening his door. 'You'll see.'

We set off on foot, Ian carrying on one shoulder an old rucksack, which I assumed held the bolt-cutters and any other tools he reckoned we might need. An ill-lit path led off beside the garden wall of the last house before the gates to a footbridge over the railway line, with steps down from the bridge onto the empty eastbound platform of Fishersgate station, a small unmanned halt. I lagged behind as Ian started down the steps from the bridge. The platform below us was fenced off from a strip of no-man's-land between it and the perimeter fence of the industrial estate. But there was nothing to prevent Ian scrambling over the railings near the bottom of the steps and dropping down into the strip. He signalled for me to follow, which I did, so much less adroitly that he had to give me a hand. We were trespassing now. And we'd soon be doing a lot worse than that.

The fence round the industrial estate was topped with razor-wire. There could be no question of climbing over it. We crouched at its base in deep shadow, listening and watching, just in case. But nothing stirred. There were no insomniacs, no late-night prowlers — other than us. Ian pointed to the warehouse whose side wall was facing us and whispered, 'That's it.' The shuttered entrance was no more than twenty rubbish-strewn yards away. He slid the bolt-cutters out of the rucksack.

That's when I heard the rumble of an approaching train. Ian heard it in the same moment and crouched lower, pulling me down with him. There was a spark from the conductor rail somewhere behind us, then the train was rushing past through the station, its thinly peopled carriages brightly lit. And then it was gone again, surging on towards Worthing.

'Don't worry,' said Ian as we cautiously raised our heads. 'No-one will have seen us. And even if they did . . . '

He left the thought unfinished and started at the fence with the bolt-cutters. The wire yielded easily and within a couple of minutes he'd cut a large semicircle in the mesh. He pulled it back and held it there for me to crawl through, then scrambled after me.

We picked our way between a rusting skip and a pile of old car tyres to the front of man mountain's warehouse. There we paused again, ears and eyes straining in the darkness. But there was nothing to hear or see. The premises around us hardly warranted guard-dog patrols. And we were out of sight of the nearby houses. I began to feel fractionally less anxious. There was clearly no-one about. Maybe man mountain hadn't thought we might try something like this. Or maybe, it occurred to me, the warehouse was a deliberate blind.

There was only one way to find out. Ian flicked on his torch and trained the beam on the padlocked hasp securing the wicket-door, then handed the torch to me and fastened the jaws of the bolt-cutters round the U-bar of the padlock. It put up stiffer resistance than the fence wire. Ian's forearms shook as he strained to pierce the steel, his breath steaming in the torchlight.

Suddenly, the steel gave. The U-bar snapped, the padlock fell to the ground and the hasp flopped forward. Ian shoved the bolt-cutters into his rucksack, flicked the hasp fully back and cautiously tried the handle below it. The door opened. He took the torch from me and stepped through. I followed, pushing the door shut behind me.

The torch beam moved around the interior. Quite what I'd expected I couldn't have said, but there was certainly no sign of Derek. The place looked like it had once been used for car repairs. I glimpsed an inspection ramp and a rack half-filled with tyres. Towards the rear was a small, partitioned-off office. But Derek's face did not pop into view at the window.

The torch beam moved back to the door. There was a panel of switches beside it. 'Try them,' said Ian. 'Let's see what we've got.'

I pushed one of the switches down. It controlled a fluorescent light fitted to one of the beams above us. The tube flickered and hummed into action. I pushed another switch, activating a second light. The shadows retreated.

But no secrets were revealed. The warehouse was bare and dusty, ancient car-repair equipment abandoned in its corners. We stood where we were for a moment, gazing about us in search of something, anything, that might suggest we were on the right track. But there was nothing to see. And nothing to hear either. If Derek was really being held there, even bound and gagged, he'd surely have made some noise. Yet there was none.

We moved past the office to an open door at the rear of the warehouse. Ian stepped through with the torch and almost immediately retreated, shaking his head to me. I went back to check the office, even though I could see through the window that it was empty, save for one broken-backed swivel chair. There was nothing else.

'Looks like we've drawn a blank,' I murmured to Ian as I joined him in the centre of the warehouse.

'I don't believe it.'

'You can see for yourself.'

'He's here. I know it.'

'There's no-one here except us.'

'There has to be.'

'But there isn't.'

'Hold on. What about those?' Ian pointed to a row of four steel plates, set in the concrete floor. 'Covers for an inspection pit, do you reckon?'

'Must be, I suppose.' I caught his gaze. 'What are you thinking?'

'I'm thinking we should take a look at what's under them.'

He moved to the rectangle covered by the plates and prised up the ring handle countersunk in the one farthest from the entrance. A gentle tug didn't achieve anything. The plate was evidently heavier than it looked. Ian braced himself and pulled harder.

For a shard of a second I thought some creature — a mouse maybe — had raced out from under the plate and sped towards the wall. Something certainly flew faster than my eye could follow in that direction, then straight up the wall. There was a loud cracking noise above us. I looked up and saw the descending shadow of something large and heavy. I opened my mouth to shout a warning to Ian, who was standing directly beneath it. But he'd already seen it coming and was throwing himself clear.

Too late. With a deafening crash, a pear-shaped lump of concrete large enough to be used as a wrecking ball slammed into the floor. Ian screamed and fell, his trailing leg caught beneath it. The rope that had held the ball aloft wound down after it into the cloud of dust raised by the impact. The ball wobbled and rolled clear of Ian, then threatened to roll back again. I rushed forward and held it off him, then looked down into his white and grimacing face.

'Jesus Christ,' he hissed through gritted teeth. 'Jesus fucking Christ.'

My gaze moved to his right leg. The curvature of the ball meant his foot and knee had escaped injury, but his ankle and lower shin were a bloody pulp. The angle of his foot and the jagged spike of bone protruding through a blood-darkened rent in his jeans told their own story. 'I can't hold this for long,' I shouted down to him. 'Can you move?'

'Not . . . ' He dragged himself a short distance

across the floor, shuddering with the effort. 'Not . . . far.'

But it was far enough. I let the ball roll back into position and knelt beside him. There was sweat beading on his forehead. He was shivering, his breaths coming fast and shallow.

'Some sort of trap,' he said, forcing the words out. 'Very . . . fucking clever.'

'Your leg's a mess. Broken . . . and then some.'

He nodded, absorbing the information. 'Is there . . . much bleeding?'

'Not so very much, no.'

'Let me see.' Pushing himself up on his elbows, he squinted down at his leg. 'Christ. That doesn't look good.' He slowly lowered his head to the floor. 'Raising the cover . . . released a rope. I saw it. But not . . . quickly enough.'

'Me too.'

'Safe . . . if you tie it off on the wall first. Otherwise . . . ' He shook his head, willing himself to concentrate. 'What's in the pit?'

For a moment, I'd forgotten that was what we were supposed to be finding out. I kicked the loosened cover aside and peered in. Neatly stacked plastic bags of white powder met my gaze. I pulled up the other covers to reveal more of the same. 'It's a drugs cache,' I said. 'There's a lot here.'

'Fuck,' was all Ian managed by way of reaction.

I knelt back down beside him. 'I'm going to call an ambulance,' I said, pulling out my mobile and glancing at the wound in his leg. 'There's nothing else for it.'

'Don't.' He grabbed my arm. 'We'll both be arrested.'

'We have no choice. You can't stand up, let alone walk out of here.'

'No. But . . . you can.'

'I'm not leaving you in this state.'

'You have to.' He coughed, wincing from the pain that must have been increasing all the time. '*I'll* call the ambulance.' He thrust his free hand into the pocket of his fleece and pulled out his own mobile. 'And I'll tell the police the truth. Except . . . I'll say I came here tonight . . . alone. I'll say . . . I didn't tell you . . . what I was planning to do.'

'You think they'll believe you?'

'I don't know. But . . . they're likelier to . . . than if they have us both down . . . as burglars . . . or worse . . . trying to talk our way out of trouble . . . aren't they?'

'I'm not sure. There has to be — '

'I don't have the strength to debate it. It's what we're going to do. You'll back up . . . my story . . . when the police . . . question you . . . won't you?'

'Of course. But — '

'That's good enough.' He pressed the button on his phone three times and stared up at me. 'You'd better get moving.'

* * *

The fact that leaving Ian to wait for the emergency services to show up made sense didn't make it easy to do. He was in a lot of pain and his condition wasn't going to improve until he got the medical attention he badly needed. But he was right. By staying, I'd only be asking for trouble. Whatever I could do to redeem the situation couldn't be done from a police cell.

The sirens were yowling closer through the still air when I scrambled back through the fence and hauled myself up onto the steps of the railway station footbridge. I stood at the top of the steps for several minutes as they drew closer still. The flashing lights of police car and ambulance began to strobe through the darkness beyond the rooftops of the nearby houses. They were almost there. I walked to the other end of the bridge and down the steps into the next street, dialling Ian's number on my mobile as I went.

'Yuh?' He sounded gruff and breathless, but alert.

'The cavalry's arrived.'

'So I hear.'

'How are you feeling?'

'I'll make it, Toby. Don't worry. And don't phone again . . . or do anything stupid . . . like contacting . . . the hospital. OK?'

'OK.'

'Be seeing you.' With that, he rang off. And I hurried on into the night.

* * *

It was a long, cold walk from Fishersgate station to the Sea Air. I had time to think, time to put what had happened into some kind of logical framework. Ian Maple would be all right, or as all right as somebody could be facing a long stay in hospital and interrogation by the police. Their first thought was bound to be that he was involved in drugs trafficking. I could talk them out of that, of course, as I intended to. But they only had our word for it that man mountain was associated with Roger Colborn. Drugs and prostitution could be seen as the beginning and the end of it. We hadn't found Derek Oswin, after all. We couldn't even prove he needed to be found. And we certainly couldn't prove Colborn was responsible for his disappearance. But we could put some pressure on him. We could oblige the police to ask him a few awkward questions. It wasn't much. But it was better than nothing. Colborn had been using man mountain to do his dirty work. That was clear to me, even if it wouldn't necessarily be clear to the police. What we'd stumbled on at the warehouse was likely to put man mountain behind bars, however, and therefore out of action. Colborn wouldn't be able to call on him any longer. He was going to be on his own. And I was betting he wouldn't like it.

* * *

I trudged up Madeira Place more than an hour after leaving Fishersgate station, chilled and weary, as barely able to put one foot in front of the other as I was to piece together the consequences of our bungled night's work. I slid my key into the door of the Sea Air and pushed it open, eager to reach the sanctuary of my room.

Then I stopped. There was an envelope lying on the doormat in front of me. It hadn't been there earlier. I picked it up, carried it to the hall table and switched on the light. There was no name or address on the plain brown manilla envelope, no clue as to who might have dropped it through the letterbox. The contents were bulky, sharp-edged and solid to the touch. I tore the flap open and slid them out.

Three dictaphone microcassettes, held together by a rubber band. Not two, the number stolen earlier, but *three*. I snapped the band off and looked at them. They were all the same brand. There was no way to tell which two were mine and which the odd one out. Except that two had been rewound to the start of the tape. I hadn't done that. It was as simple a message as could be devised. They'd been listened to and then discarded. Returned to me, almost scornfully.

The third had tape wound onto the right-hand spool. Not much, but some. This was another kind of message.

* * *

I hurried up to my room, slid the cassette into the machine and pressed the rewind button. Within seconds, the tape was back to the start. Then I pressed the play button. And heard Derek Oswin's voice.

'Hello, Mr Flood. Sorry . . . about all this. I've

got us both . . . into a l-lot of t-trouble. The thing is, well . . . I've been told . . . to say this to you. Drop it. Everything. S-s-stop asking questions. L-leave it alone.' He gulped audibly. 'If you d-do that . . . and go quietly back to London on Sunday . . . they'll let me go . . . unharmed. And there'll be no danger . . . to Mrs Flood. That's all you have to do, Mr Flood. Nothing . . . at all. Otherwise — '

* * *

I poured myself some whisky and listened to the tape again. Derek sounded strained and nervous, as well he might. I didn't feel too good myself. The glass trembled in my grasp and the whisky burned in my throat. Colborn was determined to stop me digging out the truth, because the truth had the power to destroy him. I was close to the answer, too close for his comfort. Listening to the tapes must have confirmed his worst fears, hence the change of tactics. Trying to buy me off hadn't worked, so now he meant to scare me off. And, just in case I didn't care what he did to Derek, there was an additional threat he could be certain I'd take seriously. To Jenny. So much for his claim to be genuinely in love with her, to be a better man because of her. Maybe he was bluffing. But he knew I'd never call his bluff. Because I *do* love her. I would never do anything to endanger her.

* * *

Some time tomorrow, the police will come to me and ask me to corroborate Ian Maple's story. How can I do that without effectively rejecting Colborn's ultimatum? Calling off the search for the truth is almost as difficult as going on with it. And judging what's best is more difficult again. But I'll go on making these recordings. That's one decision I have made. I'll have to take better care of them, of course. I'll have to carry them with me to make sure they don't fall into the wrong hands a second time. In one way, they're a liability. But they're also a true and accurate record of events. I may have need of that when this is all over. Colborn thinks he can force me to do his bidding. Maybe he's right. We'll see. But, even if he is, that may not be enough. We may have passed the point of no return. If so, doing nothing won't be an option. For either of us.

FRIDAY

I was roused this morning by Eunice knocking at the door of my room and calling my name. The sleep I came out of was so deep it left me confused and woolly-headed. Memories of the day and night before reassembled themselves scrappily in my mind. I'd lain awake till God knows when, debating with myself what I should and shouldn't have done. Then, at some point I couldn't recall, a trapdoor had opened, plunging me into oblivion.

'Toby, Toby,' came Eunice's voice. 'Are you awake?'

'I am now,' I muttered, scrabbling for a sight of the alarm clock. The time apparently, was eight minutes to ten. I felt like I could have slept till noon. 'What is it?' I shouted, gravel-throated.

'There's a couple of policemen downstairs. They want to speak to you. It's urgent, they say.'

They'd come, as I'd known they would, come with their battery of questions, to which I had no better or safer answers after sleepless hours of reflection than I had before. 'What's it about?' I asked, sitting up woozily and silently congratulating myself on my disingenuousness.

'They wouldn't tell me. Just insisted they had to speak to you.'

'All right. I'll come down. But . . . it'll take me ten minutes or so to wash and dress.'

'I'll tell them.'

* * *

My thoughts were only marginally clearer fifteen minutes later when I made a gingerly descent to the residents' lounge. I was unshaven and I'd strained a muscle in my thigh, probably while climbing up onto the footbridge at Fishersgate station. I was neither looking nor feeling at my best.

The same may have been true of Detective Inspector Addis and Detective Sergeant Spooner, as they introduced themselves. Their suits were rumpled, their faces set in glum folds. Both were paunchy, liverish-looking men, unhealthily accustomed to late nights and canteen fry-ups. Addis, the shorter and balder of the two, had distractingly exophthalmic eyes, a gum-chewing habit and a subdued Black Country accent. Spooner sounded local, but didn't seem any friendlier on account of it.

'Sorry to disturb you so early, Mr Flood,' said Addis, with light sarcasm.

'I don't generally get to bed till the small hours after a performance, Inspector,' I said, already sensing that I needed to be on the defensive.

'Late nights are an occupational hazard in our game as well as yours, sir,' said Spooner. 'We haven't had much sleep ourselves.'

'No? Well, I'm sorry to have kept you waiting. But I'm here now.'

'Your landlady kept us occupied, sir, with her colourful observations on the shortcomings of our uniform division.'

'Yeah,' said Addis. 'Gather you had a break-in here yesterday.'

'There was a break-in, yes. Eunice was very upset about it.'

'But nothing was taken.'

'Apparently not.'

'And not much of a mess made.'

'That's unusual,' put in Spooner, with an exaggerated nod of deliberation.

'But I don't suppose it's why you called.'

'No, sir, it isn't,' said Addis. 'Though what's brought us here is also . . . unusual.'

'Are you acquainted with a Mr Ian Maple, sir?' asked Spooner.

'Yes. He's the brother of a recently deceased fellow actor, Denis Maple. Denis died earlier this week of a heart attack. Ian came down here a couple of days ago to, er . . . '

'Find out what had happened,' said Addis. 'Yeah. So he tells us.'

'Look, Inspector, what exactly is this all about?' I tried to look genuinely mystified.

'Mr Maple's under arrest, sir. Well, he will be when he wakes up from the anaesthetic. They're operating on him now up at the Royal Sussex.'

'Operating?'

'Badly broken right leg, sir,' said Spooner. 'He was in a bit of a mess when we got to him. Any idea why he might have been breaking into a warehouse out at Fishersgate last night?'

'What?'

'The large quantity of hard drugs stored on the premises seems the obvious explanation,' said Addis; they were warming up their double act now, alternating their lines in a practised routine. 'But Mr Maple tells it differently.'

'When did you last see him, sir?' asked Spooner.

'Er . . . yesterday afternoon. He came to see me at the theatre during the matinée interval.'

'To discuss . . . what, sir?'

'Well, he'd, er, been trying to track down a man Denis said had . . . threatened him. It seemed likely . . . to both of us . . . that the encounter had put a lot of stress on Denis, leading to his attack.'

'Who is this man, sir?'

'I don't know. I never met him.'

'But Denis Maple mentioned him to you?'

'Yes.'

'And you mentioned him to Ian Maple?'

'Yes.'

'Did you also tell him you thought this guy had mistaken Denis Maple for you?'

'I said Denis thought that.'

'But you don't?'

'I've no reason to.'

'No reason, sir?' put in Addis.

'That's right, Inspector.'

'Really?'

'Look, I — '

'Are you acquainted with a Mr Derek Oswin, sir?' asked Spooner.

'Yes.'

'Also a Mr Roger Colborn?'

'Yes.'

'What about a Mr Michael Sobotka?'

'Who? No, I — '

'Big fellow,' said Addis. 'Very big. Polish extraction. Known to us. Suspected pimp, pusher, God knows what. Mr Maple's description of the man his brother had some sort of run-in with fits Sobotka to a T. Mr Maple claims the drugs in the warehouse belong to him.'

'Is that so?'

'We don't yet know, sir,' Spooner answered. 'We're still checking.'

'Well, I . . . wish you luck.'

'Do you know of a connection between Oswin, Colborn and Sobotka?' asked Addis, his tone suddenly hardening.

'No.' The lie was told. 'I don't.'

'Do you have any reason to believe Mr Oswin may have been abducted?'

'No.'

'Or that Sobotka may have carried out that abduction, acting on behalf of Mr Colborn?'

'No.'

'Do you know of any reason why Mr Colborn should wish to have Mr Oswin abducted?'

'No.'

'Or why Mr Maple should believe he had a reason?'

'No.'

'Strange.' Addis gave me a long, cold stare. 'Mr Maple seemed sure you would.'

'We called on Mr Oswin before coming here,' said Spooner. 'There was no-one at home.'

'Maybe he's gone away.'

'When did you last see Mr Oswin?' asked Addis.

'Er . . . Wednesday afternoon.'

'Did he say he was thinking of going away?' asked Spooner.

'Not that I recall. But . . . I wouldn't have expected him to. We're not exactly close.'

'How are you acquainted with him, sir?'

'He's a fan.'

'Really?' put in Addis.

'Yes.'

'Do you pay house calls on many of your fans?'

'They don't generally invite me.'

'But Mr Oswin did?'

'Yes.'

'What did you discuss with him?'

'My . . . career.'

'Your *career*?'

'Is it true that Mr Oswin's been bothering your ex-wife, sir?' asked Spooner. He consulted a notebook. 'Jennifer Flood, proprietress of a hat shop in the Lanes?'

God, the sheer mental agility required to carry off a lie is so exhausting. I could only hope by this stage that my acting technique was compensating for any obvious deficiencies in the logic of my account. 'She's not my ex-wife yet, Sergeant,' I said wearily. 'Technically, we're still married.'

'But separated?'

'Yes.'

'Mrs Flood is currently living with Mr Colborn, in fact?'

'Yes.'

'So, has Mr Oswin been bothering Mrs Flood?'

'He wanted her to arrange for him to meet me. I agreed . . . in order to get him off her back.'

'Sounds like the answer's yes,' commented Addis.

'Have you been to Mr Oswin's house since Wednesday afternoon, sir?' asked Spooner.

The key to successful lying is to avoid as many subsidiary lies as possible. It's a principle I clung to then, tempted though I was to abandon it. 'Yes,' I said. 'Yesterday morning. First thing. He wasn't in.'

'Snap,' said Addis. 'I can see why you think he may have gone away.'

'Anything strike you as amiss at the house, sir?' asked Spooner.

'No.'

'Didn't take a squinny through the letterbox, then?' Addis put in.

'No.' I was clearly meant to infer they had.

'Why did you go there?' asked Spooner.

'He didn't use a ticket for the Wednesday evening performance I'd had put back for him. I wanted to find out why. I suppose a spur-of-the-moment trip away is the likeliest explanation.'

'You're not worried about him?'

'No. Why should I be?'

'Why, indeed, sir?' Addis responded.

'About Mr Maple . . . '

'Yeah?'

'Are you really intending to charge him?'

'The circumstances don't leave us much choice. We've got him bang to rights. We'll be investigating every aspect of the case, of course.

Unless the Drugs Squad take it over. It was a big haul, I can tell you that. Unless you can back up Mr Maple's version of events . . . it looks bad for him.'

'I'm sure whatever he did last night was motivated by a genuine concern for his late brother. There'll have been no criminal intent.'

'That's your opinion, is it, sir?'

'Yes.'

'But you can't actually confirm this Oswin — Colborn — Sobotka connection?'

'No.'

'That's our problem, you see.' Addis interrupted his gum-chewing long enough for a fleeting smile. 'Well, it's more Mr Maple's problem, actually.'

* * *

After they'd gone, I cadged a mug of coffee off Eunice, assured her I wasn't about to be carted off to the police station and stumbled upstairs for a shower and a shave. I kept telling myself I'd done the only thing I could in the circumstances. Letting Ian Maple down was redeemable. Defying Roger Colborn might not be. But I wasn't sure it was true. Exonerating Ian would mean daring Colborn to do his worst, this week or next. And that threatened Jenny, who mattered far more to me than Ian Maple or Derek Oswin. Colborn's ultimatum was even more effective than he could have hoped.

* * *

My first thought when I heard Eunice's by now familiar knock at the bathroom door was that Addis and Spooner had come back, a sufficiently disturbing possibility for me to tighten my grasp on the razor and nick my chin as a result.

'I'm sorry to disturb you again, Toby,' Eunice called. 'There's someone else to see you.'

'Who the hell is it this time?' I shouted, wrenching off a length of loo paper to mop up the blood.

'A Mr Braddock. Elderly gentleman. Most insistent. He says he won't leave till he's spoken to you.'

Ray Braddock, come to my door, rather than me to his. I felt sick as I confronted my reflection in the mirror above the basin. This didn't sound good. 'All right,' I called back. 'I'll be right down.'

* * *

A few minutes later, I was back in the residents' lounge, struggling to assemble another and subtly different version of events for the benefit of my latest visitor.

Ray Braddock was a man of seventy or so, big-limbed and broad-shouldered, but bent and hollowed out by age and labour, white hair cut squaddy-short, as if to emphasize the hearing aid looped round one of his spectacularly large ears. His face was raw-boned and weather-worn. His rheumy eyes gazed out at me from beneath a hooded brow. The raincoat and flat cap I'd spotted hanging in the hall clearly belonged to him. They were of a piece with the baggy tweed jacket, patched jeans and slack-collared shirt. His solitary and taciturn nature was palpable. There was no Mrs Braddock waiting at home, nor had there ever been. He was a man reliant on his own devices.

He rose from his chair and shook my hand, his grip carrying with it a memory of faded strength. 'Good of you to see me, Mr Flood,' he said in a rumbling voice.

'You're a friend of the Oswin family, I believe, Mr Braddock. Derek mentioned your name.'

'He mentioned yours to me and all, Mr Flood. That's what brought me here.'

'Oh yes?'

'I'm worried about the boy, see.'

'Let's sit down.' I pulled up a chair for myself close to his, into which he stiffly lowered himself. 'Why are you worried?'

'The police were at the house in Viaduct Road this morning, seemingly. I had a call from the boy's neighbour, Mrs Lumb. They'd been asking her what she'd seen of Derek lately. Well, she's not had sight of him since Wednesday. And it was Wednesday afternoon he came to see me. He was in a . . . peculiar mood. That's when he mentioned you. You're helping him with his book, apparently.'

'Well, I . . . sent it to my agent, certainly. To see what she thinks of it.'

The frown permanently fixed to Braddock's face deepened at that. 'Read it, have you?'

'I glanced at the first few pages, nothing more. I . . . wasn't sure what to make of it.'

'I'll tell you what I make of it. A temptation to fate, that's what. Bloody Colbonite. Why can't he leave it alone?'

'I don't know.'

'No.' He stared at me in silence for a moment, then said, 'Reckon you wouldn't.'

'Did Mrs Lumb say why the police are looking for Derek?'

'They didn't let on. Now then, Mr Flood, have you seen Derek since Wednesday?'

'Not as it happens, no.'

'I was afraid you'd say that.'

'Perhaps he's gone away.'

'Where to?'

'I wouldn't know.'

'No. And you wouldn't suggest it if you knew the boy as well as I do. He'd not go far. Unless he was forced to. Mrs Lumb heard some sort of a commotion Wednesday night. She couldn't make out what was going on. Anyhow, she's not seen Derek since. She *thinks* she saw a strange man leaving the house yesterday morning, but she's not sure. He might have been just turning away from the door. She didn't catch a clear sight of him, worse luck.'

Au contraire, I thought to myself: it was *my* very good luck. 'We are sure he's not at home, are we? I mean, perhaps he's just . . . lying low.'

Braddock shook his head. 'I have a spare key, Mr Flood. I let myself in. I was afraid . . . well, you never know, do you, with someone like Derek? He hasn't the strongest of temperaments. Anyhow, he's not there, but there's been some damage done. Things turned over and such. I can't help but be worried about him. He's my godson, see. With his mother and father gone, I feel . . . responsible.'

'I wish I could help.'

'From what Derek told me, he'd made a nuisance of himself to you. Hanging around your wife's shop. To be honest, it occurred to me you might have set the police on him. I couldn't blame you. The boy's his own worst enemy.'

'But essentially good-natured. There's no harm in him. I made no complaint to the police, I assure you.'

'You felt sorry for him, I take it. Well, that's to your credit. A man in your position doesn't need to truck with Derek's sort. I know that. Mind, he did, er, mention your wife's . . . association . . . with Roger Colborn.'

'Ah. Did he?'

'None of my business, of course. None of Derek's either, if it comes to it. But Colborn's not to be trifled with, any more than his father was. I don't say that lightly, Mr Flood. If Colborn was seriously rattled by this blasted book of Derek's, he'd not be above . . . ' Braddock's jaw muscles champed away during the wordless interlude into which the thought drifted. Then he said, 'The boy's out of his depth. That's what it amounts to. If he'd only leave it alone . . . '

'I know all about Colbonite, Mr Braddock. And about the part Derek's father played in the death of Sir Walter Colborn. I do understand . . . your concern.'

'Do you, though?'

'I'm glad to see you looking so well.'

'For an old Colbonite hand, you mean?' Braddock grunted. 'I got out early. Soon as I started to notice my skin turning yellow. Oh yes. It was as bad as that. I took a lower-paid job with the Co-op. I tried to talk Ken into leaving as well, but he said he needed the money, with Val and Derek to support. He reckoned Colbonite was the only place he could find a job for the boy. Well, he was probably right, at that. And there were other reasons. I see that now. Ken played his cards close to his chest, even with me.'

'Derek seems to think Sir Walter's death was an accident,' I said, aware that I shouldn't in strict prudence be encouraging the old man's ruminations, but still eager, despite myself, to penetrate to the heart of the mystery.

'It was no accident,' said Braddock, compressing his lips.

'You and Kenneth Oswin were close friends.'

'We were. Since boyhood.'

'Were you surprised . . . when he took such drastic action?'

'I was. I'd not have said he was the vengeful sort. Mind, he denied to me later that he'd done it for revenge.'

'Why, then?'

'He wouldn't say. Except that it was for Val and Derek's sake.'

'How could that be?'

Braddock shrugged. 'He was a dying man. I've never been sure he knew himself why he'd done such a thing. There was no way Val and Derek could gain by it. He must have been . . . rambling.'

'Do you think Sir Walter got what was coming to him, though, whatever the motive?'

Braddock weighed the question in his mind, then nodded. 'You can't deny the natural justice of it. A lot of good men died young to line the Colborns' pockets. But that's the way of the world. You can't fight it.'

'Maybe Kenneth Oswin was determined to try.'

'Maybe. But that's for him to account for to the Almighty. What bothers me now is the thought that Derek might have tried his hand at the same game.'

'What do you mean to do about it?'

'Nothing I can do. If I go to the police, it might only make things worse for the boy.'

'Yes,' I said, affecting reluctant agreement. 'It might.' It might also alert Addis and Spooner to how economical I'd been with the facts during our discussion. All in all, I had a lot of compelling reasons to steer Braddock away from the forces of law and order, at least for the moment. 'But aren't they likely to come to you?'

'Only if someone points them in my direction. Mrs Lumb knows better than to do that. She and I don't make trouble for each other.' He cleared his throat. 'I'm hoping you might . . . agree to watch what you say . . . if they come a-calling on you.'

It was just as well, I reflected, that Braddock hadn't arrived an hour earlier — for both of us. 'You can rely on me,' I said. 'I'm sure Derek will turn up soon, with no harm done.'

'I wish I was sure.'

'If I hear from him, I'll let you know straight away.'

'I'd take that as a kindness, Mr Flood. My number's in the book.'

'Right.'

'Well, I've taken up enough of your time. I'd best be on my way.' He stood up, but made no move towards the door. It was apparent that he still had something to say. I rose and looked at him promptingly. Several seconds passed during which he seemed to ponder the wisdom of his words. Then, in a gruff undertone, he finally unburdened himself. 'Derek's the nearest to family I have left. I must do what I can for him.'

* * *

It was nearly noon by the time Ray Braddock made his plodding exit, leaving me with less than half an hour to get up to the station and meet Moira off the 12.27. I flung on a coat and hurried out into a cold, grey, mizzly midday. A glazier's van was parked outside and I could hear Eunice in conversation with its driver down in the basement area. He was one visitor to the Sea Air I didn't need to worry about.

On my way to the taxi rank in East Street, a thought suddenly came to me. It would have occurred to me sooner, but my own need to avoid the police was so well served by Braddock's similar reluctance that I hadn't bothered to question it. Yet the question was a good one. Why *was* the old man so leery of the boys in blue? What did he have to be frightened of? Like more or less everyone else mixed up in the misadventures of Derek Oswin, he was hiding something. But what? And why?

* * *

My brain was obviously suffering from anxiety overload, because it was only when I was halfway to the station in the back of a taxi that I remembered Moira's bizarre message of yesterday afternoon. I turned on my mobile and checked for further word from her, but there was none. My various tart responses had presumably dispelled the muddle she'd somehow got herself into. Ordinarily, I'd have looked forward to a boozy lunch with the gossipy guzzler herself, but, the circumstances being about as far from ordinary as conceivably possible, the prospect had lost its lustre. Even the opportunity to lay my hands on the manuscript of *The Plastic Men* had turned sour on me. If I couldn't use any ammunition it provided me with against Roger Colborn, maybe, I reflected, I was better off not knowing what that ammunition might be.

* * *

This reflection was about to recoil on me, however. The 12.27 arrived only a couple of minutes late and Moira was one of the first passengers through the barrier. Loud, red-haired and generously proportioned, she's never faded into any background I've ever seen. The *faux* leopard-skin coat and purple beret made sure the concourse of Brighton railway station on a dull December day hadn't a chance of being an exception. What I noticed, however, even before the mandatory hug and triple kiss, was that she was carrying nothing apart from her handbag.

'Where's the manuscript, Moira?' I asked, as soon as we'd disentangled ourselves.

'You don't have it, do you?' she responded bafflingly. 'I was afraid of that.'

'You were supposed to bring it with you.'

'I was hoping your messages didn't mean what they seemed to.'

'What the hell's going on?'

'That, Toby, is a very good question.'

* * *

It was a question I only got some sort of an answer to once we were installed in a taxi, heading for La Fourchette in Western Road, Moira's choice of lunch venue.

'I had to go out shortly after you called yesterday morning,' she began. 'I didn't get back to the office till after lunch. That's when I found out what had happened.'

'Which was?' I prompted impatiently.

'Well, I'd asked Lorraine to retrieve the manuscript from Ursula because you wanted it back in a hurry, but I hadn't told her I was planning to bring it down here today, so, when this guy showed up — '

'What guy?'

'He said you'd sent him to fetch the manuscript. Naturally, Lorraine thought you'd told me you'd send someone round for it and I'd forgotten to mention it to her. Simple as that. So — '

'She handed it over?'

'I'm afraid so.'

'Catch this guy's name, did she?'

'Er, no.'

'What did he look like?'

'Unremarkable. Medium height, medium build. She probably did no more than glance at him. After all — '

'Why should she bother to take reasonable care of something I'd entrusted to you? Good question, Moira. And I can't think of an answer. Mr Nobody swans in off the street, tickles Lorraine under the chin and walks out with a manuscript he had no claim to. Most natural thing in the world. Perfectly understandable. Happens every day.'

'Look, Toby, I'm sorry. It's very . . . unfortunate.'

'Unfortunate?'

'I shall have a serious word with Lorraine. You can be certain of that. But what's the big deal? Surely you can get another copy from the author as I suggested to you yesterday.'

'The original's gone missing.'

'What?'

'Along with the author, as a matter of fact.'

Moira stared at me in amazement. 'Missing?'

'As in 'vanished without trace'.'

'But that means . . . ' Her brow furrowed in

agently concern. 'What have you got yourself mixed up in, Toby?'

⋆ ⋆ ⋆

The answer was more than I had any intention of divulging to Moira. Colborn must have learned of the copy of *The Plastic Men* I'd sent to her from Derek. He'd had the original — along with any other copies — removed from 77 Viaduct Road. An artful sortie to the Soho offices of the Moira Jennings Agency had now completed the collection. There was no other way to read it. Roger Colborn's opportunistic instincts had prevailed yet again.

⋆ ⋆ ⋆

'You're not going to tell me what this is all about, are you, Toby?' Moira demanded after we'd ordered our lunch and started on a bottle of Montagny, her insistence that she had a right to know only enhanced by the embarrassment she felt at losing the manuscript. 'You're putting me in an impossible position.'

'Actually, I'm not. It's telling you that would do that.'

'Does this have something to do with Denis?'

'I can't discuss it, Moira. Sorry. My hands are tied.'

'But that bloke who tricked Lorraine was part of some . . . conspiracy. Is that what you're saying?'

'I'm saying I can't discuss it.'

'And Jenny. Is she involved? I know she lives down here. Brian Sallis implied your no-show on Monday night was on her account.'

'When did he imply that?'

'When I spoke to him yesterday afternoon, after trying to speak to you.'

'I see.'

'Do you? Do you *really*? As your agent, Toby, I have to look at the big picture, which at the moment isn't a very attractive one where you're concerned.'

'What's that supposed to mean?'

'It means you need to be careful. There's a chance Leo may decide to bring *Lodger in the Throat* into London after all.'

'Well, that's good news, isn't it?'

'It is . . . ' She paused, apparently unconvinced. Then she added, '*If* you're still in the cast.'

I bridled instantly. 'Why the bloody hell shouldn't I be?'

'Because, Toby,' she replied, lowering her voice, 'Leo may calculate that the only viable way of bringing it in is by economizing on the salaries. And thanks to my negotiating skills your salary's the biggest by quite a margin.'

'He wouldn't do that.'

'Wouldn't he?' Moira looked at me over the rim of her glass, one eyebrow cocked. 'I dare say Martin Donohue would be willing to take over your part at a cut-price rate just for the career leg-up it would give him.'

There was no denying that. In fact, the harder I thought about the possibility Moira had raised, the more horribly plausible it became. I'd seen little of my fellow actors off-stage in recent days. I'd opted out of all their post-show suppers. I'd made myself remote and semi-detached. If there were whispers going round, they were unlikely to have reached my ears.

'Leading the cast of an unsuccessful production is plain bad luck,' said Moira. 'Getting sacked from that role in a production just about to redeem itself, on the other hand . . . is something you can't afford to let happen, Toby. Trust your aunty Moira on this one. It's an absolute no-no.'

* * *

Our meals arrived. Moira tucked into hers with relish, while I picked listlessly at mine and reflected on the truly sickening prospect she'd conjured up for me. Martin Donohue replacing me as James Elliott? His name, *and not mine*, up in lights outside a West End theatre? The week was just getting worse and worse.

Perhaps my pitiful expression penetrated Moira's defences. Or perhaps sating her hunger allowed the sympathy in her soul to take flight. She ordered a second bottle of wine, which I'd refrained from suggesting for fear of being thought even more unprofessional than she already had me down as. She lit a cigarette and reached across the table to give my hand a consoling squeeze.

'It probably won't happen, Toby. I just want you to be aware of the vulnerability of your position. Besides, acting's only a job. There *are* more important things to think about. Your marriage to Jenny, for instance.'

'It ends next month, Moira. Decree absolute.'

'Does it have to?'

'I can't think of any way to stop it.'

'You could try telling her you still love her.'

'She knows that. The problem is that *she* no longer loves *me*.'

'I bet she does.'

'Your cheer-up act lacks subtlety, Moira. You haven't seen Jenny in over a year. How would you know what she feels?'

'You two belong together. It's as simple as that.' Our plates were removed. She leaned back and observed me with narrow-eyed acuity through a curl of cigarette smoke. 'If you hadn't lost Peter, you'd never have lost each other. You know that better than I do.'

My mouth dried. My self-control faltered. It's strange how, despite the passage of time, the grief I never properly shared with Jenny remains no more than a stray word away. 'There's nothing to be gained by dwelling on what can't be altered,' I said stiffly.

'Have you seen much of Jenny since you came to Brighton?'

'Not as much as I'd like. And not exactly in favourable circumstances, either.'

'But you *have* seen her?'

'Yes. Several times.'

'At whose instigation?'

'Well, initially . . . Jenny's.'

Moira smiled. 'Doesn't that tell you something?'

'She simply wanted me to do her a favour.'

'Really?'

'Yes. Really.'

'As your agent, friend and counsellor on female psychology, Toby, I have to say that sometimes you can be mind-numbingly obtuse. Don't you get it?'

'Get what?'

'The message.' Moira stubbed out her cigarette and leaned across the table again. 'No woman eagerly counting the days to the legal finalization of her divorce asks her soon-to-be-ex-husband for anything, however minor, however trivial, or contacts him for any reason whatsoever, unless, in some secret part of her mind, she's come to doubt whether she genuinely wants to lead the rest of her life without him. She's not going to admit that, of course. She's going to deny it vehemently, in fact, even to herself. But it's the truth. My experience of divorce is, let's face it, considerable, so you'll have to acknowledge me as an authority on the subject. Jenny *was* asking you to do her a favour. But it wasn't the one she spelt out. Forget the pretext, Toby. Concentrate on the subtext. Do *yourself* a favour.'

* * *

Men mismanaging their love lives was a subject that evidently appealed to Moira. When we left La Fourchette, well fed and altogether too well wined, she announced her intention to tour the Royal Pavilion before returning to London. 'High time I saw inside the old sot's lair.' I walked her through the Christmas shoppers to the Pavilion entrance, but declined to accompany her further. We parted outside, Moira fudging a climactic apology for losing the manuscript of *The Plastic Men* by advising me to forget whatever *l'affaire* Oswin amounted to and devote my remaining leisure time in Brighton to winning back Jenny. Then, in a tipsy swirl of leopard-skin, she was gone.

* * *

I walked down to the pier and out along it, remembering my meeting there with Jenny last Sunday. Could Moira be right? Was Jenny as reluctant in her own way to let go as I was in mine? The afternoon was cold and murky, the pier all but empty. The sea was a heaving, foam-flecked mass, greyer than the sky. A fine drizzle blurred the illuminated signs. I stopped and stared back towards the shore. Colborn had been too quick and too clever for me. He had me where he wanted me. He was in control. But not of Jenny. She was his weak spot. And my chink of light.

* * *

Ten minutes later, I pushed open the door of Brimmers and entered the shop for the first time. Two customers were debating the merits of a fluffy pink cloche with a thin, bright-eyed, blonde-haired young woman I took to be Jenny's assistant, Sophie. Of Jenny herself there was no sign. I headed towards the door at the rear marked PRIVATE. But Sophie cut me off.

'Excuse me, sir,' she said, starting with surprise as she either recognized me or deduced who I was. 'Oh,' she added, her mouth holding the shape of the word as she stared at me.

'I'm looking for Jenny.'

'She's . . . not here . . . at the moment.'

'When are you expecting her back?'

'I'm not, actually.' Sophie cast a nervous sidelong glance at the pair with the cloche and dropped her voice. 'Mr Flood, I — '

'Where is she?'

'I . . . don't know.' Reading the scepticism in my face, she lowered her voice still further, to the level of a whisper. 'She's gone away.'

'She said nothing about this yesterday.'

'It was arranged at short notice. She phoned me this morning. An urgent family matter, apparently. She won't be back until after the weekend.'

I'd done it again. I'd underestimated Colborn. Jenny was gone, whisked away, placed beyond my reach. I said no more. I couldn't bear to. I brushed past Sophie and hurried out of the shop.

* * *

From a window-seat in the Rendezvous, I rang Jenny's mobile. It didn't come as any great surprise to find it was switched off. I left no message. Sipping my *espresso*, I wondered if there really could have been a family crisis. It seemed wildly improbable. But a tactical retreat to her parents' house in Huntingdon or her sister's in Hemel Hempstead wasn't. I had both numbers back at the Sea Air, but ringing them was pointless. Either she hadn't gone to them or they'd be under instruction to tell me she hadn't. Besides, there was another possibility I *could* check, personally. And at that moment I badly wanted to do more than log up futile phone calls.

* * *

The taxi dropped me a hundred yards or so short of the entrance to Wickhurst Manor, at the end of the lane leading north towards Stone-staples Wood, the lane where Sir Walter Colborn met his end seven years ago and from which his killer's son, Derek Oswin, took those covert photographs of the house he'd shown me. I'd bought an Ordnance Survey map of the area before leaving Brighton, but the light was failing so fast it wasn't going to be useful for long. A chill, damp winter's evening was encroaching rapidly as the taxi pulled away and I started up the lane.

Derek had mentioned a right of way skirting Wickhurst Manor. The dotted green line shown on the map diverging from the lane about a quarter of a mile ahead had to be it. I stepped up my pace, racing against the twilight.

If the path hadn't been marked by a

fingerpost, I might easily have missed it. The route meandered off muddily through the trees flanking the lane. The going was slow and slippery, thorns dragging at my coat and trousers as I diverted round the deeper puddles. But I pressed on, confident that the boundary of the manor couldn't be far.

Nor was it. Through the tangled undergrowth I spotted the perimeter wall ahead, creeper-hung flint patched in places with brick. It was no more than five feet high and I could see the trunk of a fallen tree propped against it that looked the likeliest means of climbing over.

The theory was fine, its execution clumsy. The tree trunk was slimy and soft with decay. I scrambled up onto it and immediately slipped straight off, further jarring my already twanging thigh muscle, an unwelcome reminder that I was neither young nor fit enough for such antics. But needs must. I scrambled up again, stretched precariously to a foothold on top of the wall and crouched there, squinting for a view of the ground on the other side.

The shadows were too deep, however. It was a question of trusting to luck. I lowered myself cautiously down, clutching onto a flint-edge and a branch of the tree, and ended up knee-deep in a patch of nettles. Blundering clear, I found myself on the fern- and thorn-strewn fringe of a plantation of fir trees. Their serried ranks opened up tunnels of sight through the deepening dusk to open ground beyond. Wincing from sundry nettle stings and thorn slashes, I headed along one of the diagonals, the going easy under the conifers through rustling drifts of needles.

I caught my first sight of the house as I emerged from the plantation on its far side. A barbed-wire fence separated me from a hummocked stretch of parkland. Beyond, the chimneys and roof of Wickhurst Manor were silhouetted, black against the grey-black sky. There were lights on in several of the ground-floor windows and a couple on the first floor as well. As I watched, a car came into view, moving down the drive away from the house, its headlamps tracking round the leafless branches of the trees as it followed the curving route to the gates.

I snagged my coat on a barb as I squeezed between two wires of the fence, but tugged it clear and set off across the park. Fifty yards or so took me to another fence. Beyond this and a narrow lawn lay the single-storey wing of the house enclosing the kitchen garden. I was on the opposite side of the house to Colborn's office quarters. It was quiet here. There was no-one about. But, then, why would there be? It was nearly dark and growing colder by the minute. The drizzle was thickening into rain.

I crawled under the bottom wire of the fence, crossed the lawn and took a squint through the nearest window. This wing had originally been the servants' domain, I supposed. It looked now to be used for the storage of gardening equipment. I headed round the angle of the building in search of a door.

The first one I came to was locked. I went on, down to the rear lawn, moving away from the house so that I could see into the room at the far end, from which light was spilling onto shrubbery, without being seen.

It was one of the offices. A young woman in a regulation black trouser suit sat at a desk, talking on the telephone as she tapped at a computer keyboard. I stood where I was, watching and waiting. Two or three minutes passed. The telephone call ended. She continued to sit at her desk. Then the door of her office opened and Roger Colborn walked in. He was more casually dressed, in open-necked shirt, jacket and jeans. They exchanged smiles and a few words. Then he was gone again.

Another minute later, so was I, back across the lawn to the unlit part of the house. Logic and architectural tradition suggested there should be a rear entrance about halfway along the wall, facing the lawn. Its outlines clarified themselves as I approached. With the building occupied, it wasn't likely to be locked. But I braced myself none the less, half-expecting to trigger some dazzling security light with every step.

Nothing happened. I reached the door, sheltered by a porch. I tried the handle. The door opened, without so much as a creak. I stepped inside, closing it carefully behind me.

What to do now? The question imposed itself upon me as I stood in the shadow-filled hallway, listening to the distant sounds of office life. A telephone rang. A printer whirred. A filing-cabinet drawer clunked shut. I was trespassing on Roger Colborn's private property — playing into his hands, for all I knew. My first and only thought since hearing that Jenny had gone away was that she hadn't really gone away at all; that Roger was either holding her here against her will or had, more probably, persuaded her to lie low until I left Brighton. But what if I was wrong? What if she'd lost patience with both of us and gone away to think? If so, the most I could accomplish by coming here was to make a fool of myself.

Yet there are worse things to be than a fool, I reflected. I'd come too far to turn back. I tiptoed along the hall to the corner, where it opened out between the stairs and the front door. The lights were on here and, glancing up the stairs, I could see lights on above as well. The double doors leading to the office quarters could open at any minute, of course. I couldn't afford to linger. I swung round the newel post and started up the stairs two at a time, treading lightly.

About halfway up, I remembered the dog. Where was Chester? Docile or not, he was quite capable of barking. But he was Roger's dog, not Jenny's. With any luck, he had a basket in the office and was dozing in it right now. I pressed on.

There were lamps on in the drawing room and the door was open. I stepped into the room half-expecting to see Jenny sitting by the fire, reading a magazine and sipping tea, perhaps with Chester flaked out on the hearthrug. But the grate was empty. Jenny wasn't there. And nor was Chester.

The door into the adjoining room, where Jenny had gone to speak to Roger on the telephone during my previous visit, was ajar, a light shining within. I took a look inside. There was no-one there. I doubled back to the landing and tried one of the other doors at random. It led to a darkened bedroom. I retreated, my confidence in my own reasoning ebbing with each blank I drew.

Then I heard a noise above me — the creak of a floorboard. I stood stock still, my ears straining. There it was again, quite distinctly. Someone was up there.

The main stairs ended at the first-floor landing. There had to be a set of back stairs leading to the second floor. I hurried along the passage to the door at its far end and opened it. Sure enough, a narrow staircase led up from here as well as down — the servants' route, in times gone by. I started climbing.

A door at the top led to a passage running the width of the house, its ceiling angled to accommodate the slope of the roof. A couple of dormer windows admitted enough light from the lamps round the main entrance below them for me to see by. There were doors off to the right at intervals, but none was open. Nor was a glimmer of light visible beneath any of them. I walked stealthily past, pausing by each to listen. There was no sound either. Yet there *had* been a sound. Floorboards don't creak of their own accord.

I was nearly at the end of the passage when the lights came on. I heard the flick of the switch behind me. A split-second later I was blinking and flinching in a sudden flood of brilliance.

'Turn round.' It was Roger Colborn's voice,

raised and peremptory.

I obeyed, but slowly, playing for the time my eyes needed to adjust.

He was standing at the other end of the passage, having either followed me up the stairs or, more likely, stepped silently out of the first room I'd passed. The creaking floorboard had been a calculated effect, designed to lure me up there. That was obvious to me as soon as I saw what he was holding in his hand.

'It's a gun, Toby,' he said. 'As an actor, you should be used to handling some pretty good imitations of the real thing. But this *is* the real thing. And I know how to use it. I'm not a bad target-shooter, if I say so myself. And you're quite a tempting target, believe me.'

It occurred to me that he might really intend to shoot. Fear coursed through me, followed almost immediately by a strange, calming fatalism. Then logic kicked in. 'Murder, with a house full of witnesses?' My voice was quavering slightly. I could only hope it wasn't apparent. 'Is that a good idea, Roger?'

'The odds are I'd get away with it.' Roger smiled. 'We're two floors up from the offices. Nobody down there would hear the shot. I'd make sure your body was found many miles from here, of course. I can arrange that. And I will, if I have to. I don't want to kill you, Toby. But if you force my hand, I won't hesitate. Is that clear?'

'Crystal.' A little bravado goes a long way, I reasoned. I had to show I was afraid of the gun, not of him.

'Why did you come here?'

'I was looking for Jenny.'

'She's gone away.'

'So the girl at Brimmers said. But — '

'You thought she might be hiding from you here. Or that *I* might be hiding her?'

I shrugged. 'Something like that.'

'And you thought you could just walk in and rescue her? You're a bigger fool than I took you for. She isn't here. She really has gone away. As for walking in, you ought to know that a security camera was tracking you from the moment you got within twenty yards of the house. I saw you coming, Toby. Actually as well as metaphorically.'

'Where's Jenny gone?'

'That's none of your business.'

'And why has she gone?'

'The same applies. None — of — your — business.'

'What about Derek Oswin, then? What have you done with him?'

'Oswin?' Anger flared in Roger's eyes. He began to advance towards me. 'How many more times am I going to be asked to explain myself where that little shit's concerned? You've managed to plant some suspicion — some madness — in Jenny's mind. Don't try to persuade me that you believe any of it, though. *Just don't.*' He stopped about ten yards from me, the gun still rock-steady in his hand, still pointing straight at me. 'You aren't going to steal her from me, Toby. I'm not going to let you.'

'It's not up to you *or* me, Roger. It's up to her.'

'We'll see about that.'

'Yes. We — '

'*Shut up.*' His raised voice echoed in the passage. A muscle tightened in his cheek. I couldn't tell what his intentions were. I could only cling to the thought that killing me was about the surest way imaginable for him to lose Jenny. 'Take your mobile phone out of your pocket.'

'My phone?'

'*Just do it.*'

'OK, OK.' I slid the mobile out from inside my coat and held it up for him to see.

'Drop it on the floor.'

I bent forward, tossed the mobile aside and slowly straightened up.

'Now, open the door to your left.'

I stretched out my hand, turned the knob and pushed the door open. The light from the passage revealed nothing beyond a bare, linoleumed floor.

'Step inside.'

A couple of strides took me over the threshold. By the time I'd turned back round, Roger had moved to cover the doorway. We were closer than ever now. But I couldn't see the faintest trembling in his grip on the gun. Whether he could see the trembling I sensed in my own limbs was another matter.

'Turn on the light.'

There was no switch on the wall in the obvious place. I stared at where it should be, then noticed the cord hanging from the ceiling. I tugged at it and a fluorescent light flickered into life above and behind me.

'It's an old darkroom,' said Roger. 'My father was an enthusiastic photographer. He fitted this out to work in. No window. And a stout, lockable door.'

'You can't keep me here.'

'Close the door, Toby.'

'I'm due on stage this evening. The theatre management know where I am. They'll come looking for me.'

'Bullshit. You wouldn't have told anybody what you were planning. Close the door.'

'No.'

'I'm prepared to kill you, Toby. I'd almost be glad if you forced me into it, to be honest with you. It's your choice.'

We stared at each other for a long, slow second. I wasn't convinced he'd go ahead and shoot if I made a lunge at him. But Roger Colborn was capable of killing me. Of that I was convinced.

'Close the door.'

'You're making a big mistake.'

'I won't tell you again.' He raised his other hand to strengthen his grasp on the butt of the gun. I noticed the taut whiteness of his knuckle where his forefinger was curled round the trigger. His gaze was cold and intense.

'All right,' I said. 'Have it your way.' I closed the door.

A second later, I heard a key turn in the lock. Then nothing.

* * *

The room was about twelve feet square. There were work-benches round two sides and half of a third, with photographic equipment scattered across them — driers, trimmers, mounters, light boxes, processing trays and suchlike. A stool stood next to a sink set in one of the benches. There was a drying cabinet as well and an exhaust fan high on the far wall to provide ventilation. Sir Walter had done the thing properly. That much was obvious. And his thoroughness had extended to security. The door was solid. I've barged through a good few matchwood mock-ups in my time. Shoulder-charging the genuine article is a far cry from that. This door felt as if it wouldn't yield to anything short of a six-man battering-ram.

I opened the cabinet and checked the cupboards beneath the benches. Empty. What I could see was all there was. I sat down on the stool next to the sink and bleakly contemplated the folly of what I'd done. Jenny wasn't hiding *or* being held at Wickhurst Manor. I reckoned I believed Roger on that point. But *I* was being held, for how long and for what purpose I had no idea. The most disturbing reason that occurred to me was so that Roger could come back and deal with me after his staff had all gone home. Somewhat less disturbing, though depressing enough in its way, was the possibility that he meant to humiliate me by ensuring I missed tonight's performance of *Lodger in the Throat*. If so, his tactics were cruelly ironic. Only a few hours previously, Moira had urged me to avoid antagonizing Leo at all costs. Absenting myself from the theatre without explanation was, in the circumstances, just about the worst thing I could do. And Roger had it in his power to ensure that I did it.

I ran some water from the tap and douched my face, then massaged my forehead in the absurd hope that I could somehow force my brain to devise an escape route from the trap I'd fallen into. No bright idea, nor even a dullish one, came obligingly to mind. Roger was right: I was a bigger fool than he'd taken me for.

And then, quite suddenly, just as I'd abandoned the effort, perhaps *because* I'd abandoned it, an idea did present itself. *The sink*. My best chance of escape was while the staff were still on the premises. Roger couldn't afford to let them know he was holding me captive. But how could I take advantage of that fact? A flood was the answer, an emergency bound to attract the attention of everybody in the house.

I shoved the plug into the hole and turned both taps full on. The hot emitted nothing but a few dry-throated splutters, but no matter: the cold flowed healthily. The sink began to fill. I sat up on the bench opposite and awaited the inevitable.

Then the flow diminished. Within a few seconds, it had become a trickle. Within another few, it had stopped altogether. I stared at the tap in dismay. The water already in the sink was merely what the pipe this side of the stopcock had held. Roger had turned off the supply, guessing I might try just such a ploy. He was one step ahead of me yet again.

I held my head in my hands and uttered a mantra of curses. What was I to do? What in God's name was I to do?

Then the light went out.

* * *

It was 4.38 p.m., according to the luminous dial of my wrist-watch — the only source of light in the room — when I took my coat off, rolled it into a pillow and lay down on the floor. Being locked in a room you can't break out of is frightening, even if you're not prone to claustrophobia. There's the fear you can't reason away that you'll never be released, that this is the room you'll die in. I guess every prisoner must sometimes have the same nightmare: that the gaolers will vanish overnight, that the door will never reopen. Freedom isn't the greatest loss, I realized, there, alone in the darkness and the silence. It's the control of your own destiny, however partial, that you miss the most, suddenly and savagely.

Time, meanwhile, becomes an instrument of torture. You don't know how much of it you have. Your future is no longer yours to determine. And there's no way out, unless your captor deigns to provide one. There is no escape. Turn the problem over in your mind as long and hard as you like: there is no solution.

* * *

But there is sleep. I can't have appreciated just how tired I was. At some point, fatigue overcame anxiety. And I slept.

* * *

I was woken by the flashing of the fluorescent light before it fully engaged. Then I was bathed in cold, white brilliance, the faint hum of the tube confirming that power had been restored. I blinked and winced from the ache in my neck, rolled over onto my side and squinted at my watch. It was 9.43 p.m. I'd slept for five hours. *Lodger in the Throat* was into the second act of its Friday night run, *sans* Toby Flood.

'Shit,' I murmured, struggling to my feet. The panic and chaos my absence must have caused burst into my thoughts. Letting the others down again was bad enough. But there'd been no stand-in this time. I'd left them comprehensively in the lurch. 'Shit, shit, shit.'

Then I heard the key turn in the door-lock. I stared at the knob, expecting to see it revolve, to see the door open. But nothing happened. There wasn't so much as the creak of a floorboard from the passage.

I reached out, grasped the knob, turned and pulled. The door opened.

There was no-one waiting on the other side. I stepped into the passage and, in the same instant, the door at the far end, leading to the stairs, clicked shut.

'Colborn?' I shouted.

There was no answer, no response of any kind. I went back for my coat, then started walking along the passage, hesitantly at first, but faster with every stride.

There was no-one on the staircase. I headed down to the first floor and along the passage to the landing at the top of the main stairs. The door to the drawing room stood open. The fire had been lit within. I could hear the crackle of burning logs.

'In here, Toby,' came Roger Colborn's syrupy, summoning voice.

I stepped into the room. Roger was sitting in a fireside armchair, smiling in my direction. The chair opposite him was dwarfed by its occupant: a huge, broad-shouldered man dressed in black leathers, a mane of greying hair tied back in a ponytail to reveal a pitted face from which dark, deep-set eyes stared neutrally towards me. He tossed the cigarette he'd been smoking into the fire and stood up slowly, the leathers creaking faintly as he did so. He must have been six foot seven or eight and my immediate impression was that he'd have been able to break down the darkroom door without greatly exerting himself. He was Michael Sobotka, of course. But I wasn't supposed to know that.

Roger stood up too. 'Glad you could join us, Toby,' he said.

Sobotka was fast as well as big. He was next to me in two strides, grabbing my shoulders and hauling me across to the couch, where he plonked me unceremoniously down as if I were no more than a recalcitrant child.

'What do you want?' I demanded, trying not to sound as powerless as I felt.

'Just a little more of your time, Toby,' said Roger. 'That's all, I promise.'

'Who is this guy?'

'He's someone your late friend Denis Maple ran into earlier this week. Considering how Maple ended up, you'd be well advised to watch your step. My friend here is remarkably even-tempered, but brutal by nature. Isn't that so?'

This last question was directed at Sobotka, whose only reaction was to throw a fleeting glance at Roger while he busied himself with putting on a pair of tight leather gloves. The gloves worried me more than his sullen, menacing demeanour. A lot more.

'If you'd done your stuff Monday night and fallen for the honey-trap,' Roger continued, 'I wouldn't have had to dip deep into my well of generosity and offer to buy you out. But you didn't have the common sense to take advantage of your good fortune, or even to lay off Jenny, which as her future husband I was entitled to expect you to. You've inconvenienced me, Toby. You've strained my tolerance. In fact, you've forced me into this. Remember that. You've left me no choice. Here.' He tossed something to Sobotka, who caught it nimbly in a gloved hand. It was a wineglass, wrapped in a clear plastic bag.

'What the hell's going on?'

'You'll see soon enough.'

Sobotka took the glass out of the bag, grabbed my right hand with vicelike force and squeezed my fingers and thumb against the bowl of the glass, rotating it as he did so. The surface felt greasy to the touch. After several seconds or so of this, Sobotka held the glass up to the light, nodded with evident satisfaction, replaced it in the bag and tossed it back to Roger, who stood it on the mantelpiece.

'You entered this house covertly this afternoon,' said Roger. 'I have the CCTV footage to prove that. You hid until the staff had gone home. Then you emerged — and attacked me.'

'What?'

'You took me by surprise. It was a vicious and unprovoked assault.'

'You're mad. Nobody's going to believe that.'

'I think they are, actually.' He nodded to Sobotka. 'I'm ready.'

Sobotka moved back to where Colborn was standing and, to my astonishment, punched him in the face. The blow, landing near his left eyebrow, sent Colborn reeling, but he steadied himself and stood upright again. A second punch took him somewhere between the jaw and cheekbone. He yelped, staggered, shook his head, then held up his hand in a signal of surrender and sank slowly into his chair.

Blood was oozing from the side of his mouth. He dabbed at it with a handkerchief and raised his other hand to the already reddening and swelling mark above his eye, wincing as his fingertips made contact. 'I reckon a spectacular black eye's guaranteed,' he said, lisping slightly. 'And there's a tooth loose as well. The split lip should look very impressive. Jenny's going to think you've seriously lost it, Toby. And she'll be right. You *have* lost.'

I stared at him, unable for the moment to speak. The man was mad. He had to be. Mad and *very* dangerous. If he was willing to have this done to him, what was he prepared to do to me?

'Let me sketch out your evening for you, Toby. After leaving me here to nurse my wounds, you went back to Brighton and killed a few hours getting seriously stoned. You didn't show up at the theatre, or even bother to warn them you weren't going to. Then you hooked up with a prostitute and went back to her place. Something went badly wrong there. Maybe you couldn't get it up after all that booze. Anyway, you got angry and stuck a wineglass in her face. Nasty. Very nasty. And very stupid too. She'd recognized you from the poster outside the theatre. And you didn't take the broken glass with you when you left. Fingerprints all over it, I'm afraid. *Your* fingerprints.'

'You won't get away with this,' I protested.

'Jenny's going to want to have nothing to do with you after she learns what you're capable of, Toby. It's not going to do a lot for your career either, is it? They won't send you down for long. First offence, previous good character, etcetera, etcetera. You might even get away with a suspended sentence. But acting? Forget it. I've been in touch with your boss, Leo Gauntlett. I've offered to put some money into *Lodger in the*

Throat. Enough to give it a chance in the West End. I've suggested he recast James Elliott, though. Bring in someone more reliable. Maybe you got to hear about that. Maybe that's why you came here this afternoon. To have it out with me. If so, all you've done is make certain he'll take up my suggestion.'

'You bastard.' Anger finally won out over shock and fear. I launched myself at him. But Sobotka stepped between us and grabbed me, doubling one arm up behind my back, sending a lance of pain through my shoulder.

'Let's get him out of here,' said Colborn. 'We're done.'

Pinning both of my arms behind me with such ease that I sensed the slightest resistance on my part could lead to a dislocation or worse, Sobotka frogmarched me out of the room and down the stairs. He paused at the bottom long enough for Colborn to overtake and open the front door. Then Colborn led the way across the terrace to where a Ford Transit had been backed up in position at the edge of the drive. He swung one of the rear doors open and turned to face me.

'You'll be dropped on the edge of town. What you do then is up to you. It won't make any difference. You could try getting your story in with the police first, but they'll see through it fast enough. The evidence is all one way. Denials and counter-accusations will count against you in the long run. You could make a run for it, of course. That's another option. Gatwick's only half an hour away by train. You might be able to get on a plane bound for somewhere exotic before they raise the alarm. Or you could just sit tight at the Sea Air and wait for them to come for you. They're all losing bets, believe me. I've fixed the odds.'

'What if I offered to leave Brighton now, tonight, for good?' The plea must have sounded as desperate as it truly was. 'I could save you the bother of setting me up.'

Colborn chuckled. 'It's too late for that.'

'You don't need to do this.'

'Oh, but I do. You pushed me too far, Toby. It's as simple as that.'

'What about Derek Oswin? What are you going to do with him?'

'Don't worry about Oswin. Worry about yourself.' He nodded to Sobotka. 'Get going.'

Sobotka levered me backwards, raising my feet off the ground until they were above the level of the floor of the van, then rammed me in through the doorway, giving a final shove that sent me on a bruising roll against a boxed-in wheel arch. The door slammed shut behind me. The lock clunked into position.

I sat up and felt my way forwards until I reached the plywood screen blocking off the cab. The back of the van was empty. I was the only cargo.

The van sagged to one side as Sobotka climbed into the driving seat. He started the engine, then paused to light a cigarette. I heard the click of the lighter through the screen. There were two thumps on the side of the van — a signal from Colborn. Sobotka ground the engine into gear and started away.

⋆ ⋆ ⋆

Sobotka's priority clearly wasn't the comfort of his passenger. The journey into Brighton was a bone-jarring purgatory. All I could do was cling to one of the wheel-arch boxes and wait for it to end.

⋆ ⋆ ⋆

I had no idea where we were when the van slowed, bumped up onto a verge and came to a halt. The engine was still running as Sobotka climbed out of the cab. A few seconds later, one of the rear doors opened. Sobotka's gigantic shadow loomed before me.

'Out,' he said. It was the first word he'd spoken to me. And the last.

I made a stooping progress to the door. He stepped back as I clambered out. Then he moved swiftly past me, slamming the door as he went.

I heard the driver's door slam a few seconds later. The gearbox grated. The van lurched down onto the roadway and accelerated away. I stared after it as an awareness of my surroundings seeped into me. I was at the edge of an unlit single-carriageway road. Ahead of me was a roundabout, bathed in sodium light. The van crossed it, moving fast, as I watched.

Then a dark-blue saloon car completed a slow revolution of the roundabout and took the same exit as the van. There was no other traffic in any direction. It was a strange, hypnotic scene. The van. Then the car. I didn't know what to make of it. And my mind was too beset by other matters for me to dwell on it.

I started walking towards the roundabout.

* * *

Sobotka had dropped me just short of an interchange on the Brighton bypass. There was a roundabout either side of the dual-carriageway cutting. I glanced down at the surging traffic as I trudged across the bridge above it towards the amber dome of the city.

I was on Dyke Road Avenue, heading south through empty suburbia, destination uncertain, determination undone. The choices Colborn had so generously set before me were each as poisonous as the other. If I went to the police, I'd lose the small amount of room for manoeuvre I had left. It wasn't as if there was anything I could do to help the prostitute I was going to be framed for assaulting — Olga, presumably. The police were on to Sobotka, of course, which set me wondering again about the car on the roundabout. But that didn't mean they'd believe me, given that to have any hope of convincing them I'd have to admit to lying when Addis and Spooner questioned me this morning. Making a run for it was crazy, though undeniably tempting. Yet where would I run *to*? *What* would I run to? I had to prove to Jenny that I was telling the truth. But how could I convince her? And how was I to survive until I got the chance?

* * *

I walked for what must have been at least two miles past silent houses, to any one of which theatre-goers might soon be returning, complaining as they came about the last-minute change of cast in *Lodger in the Throat*.

It was well gone eleven o'clock by now. The Dyke Tavern was chucking out. I passed Dyke Road Park and the Sixth-Form College. I had my bearings in one sense, but in another not at all. I'd more or less come to the conclusion that going back to the Sea Air was about the best way to demonstrate my innocence. I might phone the police from there. I wasn't sure, though. I wasn't sure about anything.

At Seven Dials, I took a squint at the timetable displayed on one of the bus stops, according to which there was an 11.50 service to the Old Steine. Cold, footsore and limping on account of my strained thigh, I decided to wait there.

Fishing in my pocket for the pound fare, I winced as something sharp pricked my finger. I pulled out the offending article: Derek Oswin's Captain Haddock brooch. I'd jabbed myself with the pin.

I stared at the enamel face of the cartoon captain in the amber light of the nearby street lamp. I'd forgotten till then that I'd picked it up from the doormat at 77 Viaduct Road on Wednesday night. I must have dropped it into my pocket without thinking.

Another memory floated back to me then, of Derek confiding in me that he'd nicknamed Wickhurst Manor Marlinspike Hall. He'd made a point of telling me that though Tintin lived at Marlinspike in Hergé's books, Captain Haddock was the owner of the house. And there was some kind of coincidental connection with Roger Colborn's ownership of Wickhurst Manor. I couldn't remember exactly what it was — couldn't be sure Derek had even told me — but he'd certainly mentioned one. Emphasized its existence, indeed.

I imagined the scene as Derek was dragged down the stairs and out through the door of number 77, presumably by Sobotka. How had the Haddock brooch ended up on the floor? Had it simply been ripped off as they passed? Or had Derek deliberately torn it from his coat . . . and dropped it there . . . in the hope that I would find it? Was Captain Haddock his typically bizarre choice of messenger to me?

The idea was absurd, yet irresistible. I was clutching at a straw. But, as a drowning man, what else was I to do? I had Derek's keys. I could go to Viaduct Road easily enough and check whether there really was something I'd missed, some clue Derek had contrived to point me towards that would unlock the mystery. Besides, no-one would guess I'd gone there. As a hiding-place, it would take some beating. And, arguably, I did need a hiding-place.

I left the bus stop and headed north-east from

Seven Dials, downhill towards Preston Circus and . . . Derek Oswin's home.

* * *

Nothing had changed at 77 Viaduct Road, except for the arrival of an electricity bill. I moved it off the doormat and pinned the Haddock brooch back onto Derek's abandoned duffel-coat, covering the tear. Then I went into the kitchen, hoping against hope that I might find something alcoholic to drink. I certainly needed something a lot stronger than cocoa.

A search of the cupboards turned up a half-empty bottle of sweet sherry. Valerie Oswin's tipple, perhaps. Or maybe Derek was a trifle addict. But I couldn't afford to be choosy. I poured some into a tumbler and took it with me into the sitting room.

The Secret of the Unicorn was the book in which his heroes finally moved to Marlinspike Hall. I dug it out of the slew of Tintin books on the floor and sat down to look at it. The blurb on the back referred to a sequel, *Red Rackham's Treasure*. I dug that one out as well.

The Tintin characters were vaguely familiar to me, but the stories hadn't left the faintest trace in my memory, though I'd read a good few in my childhood. I began to flick through *The Secret of the Unicorn*, gleaning the plot that underpinned the visual game-playing as I went. It didn't take long. Soon, I was able to move on to *Red Rackham's Treasure*. The story, as the titles imply, amounts to a treasure hunt, at the end of which Tintin and Captain Haddock are able to move from their humble lodgings to Haddock's ancestral home, Marlinspike Hall. A voyage to the Caribbean in search of the buried riches of the pirate Red Rackham draws a blank and Haddock is actually only able to buy Marlinspike thanks to some money his friend Professor Calculus comes into by selling a valuable patent. Not until after taking possession of the house do Tintin and Haddock finally discover the treasure, hidden in a marble globe in the cellars.

I sat back and took several sips of sherry, though, like Haddock, I'd much have preferred whisky. A sense of futility, and, worse, stupidity, swept over me. What in the name of reason and sanity was I doing poring over Derek Oswin's childhood reading matter while my life was unravelling around me? Poor Olga had probably already had her cheek slashed to bolster the case against me, while Leo had doubtless decided to sack me from the production of *Lodger in the Throat* and never employ me again. I was staring scandal and disgrace none too steadily in the face. Maybe I should have taken Colborn's offer when it was on the table. I didn't like to think what had happened to Derek because of my refusal. I liked even less to think what was going to happen to *me*.

The worst was that there was nothing I could do to prevent it. The idea that the Haddock brooch was some kind of message from Derek had been born of sheer bloody desperation. There was no message, no clue, no key, no hope, no globe waiting to spring open to my touch, revealing —

'Bugger me,' I said aloud, sitting suddenly upright. 'The globe.'

* * *

It stood on the desk in Derek's bedroom, in front of the window: a one-foot-diameter mounted globe, presumably given to him by his parents during his schooldays. Certainly the USSR hadn't yet dissolved into its constituent republics in this representation. I revolved the globe slowly, wondering whether I really was on to something, or had just been suckered by meaningless coincidence.

The Oswins hadn't stinted their son. That was clear. The globe was an illuminated version. I noticed the wire trailing down to the plug behind the desk. I stooped to the socket and switched it on, but nothing happened. Then I spotted the rocker switch on the wire itself and tried that. Still nothing. The bulb inside the globe must have blown. Derek hadn't bothered to replace it.

But that, I knew, wasn't Derek's style. He bothered. He would have replaced it. Unless, of course, it hadn't blown. Unless, that is, he'd removed it. For a reason. For a very good reason. Red Rackham's treasure had been hidden inside a globe.

I picked the globe up and shook it gently. Something inside was sliding to and fro. I noticed a catch of some kind on the spindle at the north pole. I prised at it, releasing a pin inside the spindle and allowing the globe to be lifted off its base. As I manoeuvred the globe out of its sickle-shaped mount, something fell through the hole at the south pole and landed on the desk.

It was a microcassette, identical to those I've been using. But on this one there was a small paper label stuck to the front, with a date written on it in spidery ballpoint: *7/10/95*. Whatever was on the tape had been recorded a month or so before the death of Sir Walter Colborn in the autumn of 1995.

Where there was a cassette, there had to be a machine to play it on. That stood to reason. I checked the drawers of the desk. And there it was, at the back of the bottom drawer: a machine somewhat larger and probably a good few years older than the one I'd left at the Sea Air, but doubtless still working. The take-up spindle whizzed into action when I pressed the play button. There was plenty of charge left in the batteries.

I loaded the cassette, stood the machine on the bedside cabinet and sat down on the bed. Then I pressed the play button again.

There were two voices: a man and woman talking to each other. The man sounded old, gruff and querulous, the woman younger, softer-toned, more distant. At first, I couldn't tell who they were. Then, as their identities became apparent, ignorance turned to disbelief. These two people couldn't be conversing in October 1995. It just wasn't possible, and yet they were. I could hear them. I could hear every word.

MAN: *Ann?*

WOMAN: *Yes?*

MAN: *Is that really you, Ann?*

ANN: *Yes, Walter. It's really me.*

WALTER: *It doesn't . . . sound like you.*

ANN: *I'm speaking through another. Besides, it's been a long time for me as well as you. Well, not time exactly. But long. Yes, it's been that. And I've changed. I'm Ann. But not the Ann you remember. Not quite. Although, of course . . .*

WALTER: *What?*

ANN: *I never was. Not really. Not the Ann you chose to believe I was. You know that, if you're honest with yourself. As I hope you are. As I hope . . . contacting me like this . . . proves you are.*

WALTER: *How can I be sure it's you?*

ANN (chuckling): *Still one for certainty, aren't you, Walter? Plain and unvarnished facts. You can live by them. But you can't die by them.*

WALTER: *I just want . . . to be absolutely —*

ANN: *I remember the look on your face when you came into my room at the maternity hospital and saw Roger bundled up in my arms. I remember it exactly. Do you?*

WALTER (after a pause): *Yes. Of course.*

ANN: *What do you want of me, Walter?*

WALTER (after another pause): *The truth, I . . . suppose.*

ANN: *The truth?*

WALTER: *Yes.*

ANN: *But you already know it.*

WALTER: *No. I don't.*

ANN: *You mean you don't wish to.*

WALTER: *You left no note. No . . . explanation.*

ANN: *A note would have become . . . public property. Studied by the coroner. Entered on the record. Would you really have preferred that?*

WALTER: *All these years, I've wondered.*

ANN: *What have you wondered?*

WALTER: Why?

ANN: *I couldn't stand the pretence any longer, Walter. It's as simple as that. It became . . . unendurable. It didn't have to be. You made it so.*

WALTER: Me?

ANN: *It doesn't matter. I forgive you. I forgave you even as I drove the car over the edge. It wasn't all your fault. I was partly to blame.* You could say I started it. Yes, you could, Walter. In fact, why don't you? Why don't you call me some of the names you used to, when you were drunk and . . . burning with the shame of it?

WALTER: *I didn't really mean . . . any of that.*

ANN: *Yes, you did. I don't blame you. It was a hard blow for a proud man to bear. And you've always been . . . so very proud.*

WALTER: *Not any more.*

ANN: *When did you change?*

WALTER: *It started . . . when you left. And lately, as I've grown older . . .*

ANN: *You've thought about death.*

WALTER: *Yes.*

ANN: *Face it with a clear conscience, Walter. I advise you, I implore you, free yourself of guilt. I ran away from my guilt. Don't make the same mistake.*

WALTER: *You didn't have so very much to feel guilty about, Ann.*

ANN: *Oh, but I did. I helped make you an unkinder man than you might have been.*

WALTER: (after a bitter laugh): *Roger's taken after me in so many ways. There's irony for you. You made him . . . a likeness of me. You have no idea how unkind we've both been. A lot of people . . . have suffered.*

ANN: *I'm here for you only, Walter. It's impossible to explain. I feel nothing. But I understand everything. Whatever wrongs you've done, it's not too late to put them right.*

WALTER: *I'm afraid it is. In most cases, far too late.*

ANN: *But not in all cases?*

WALTER: *No. Not all.*

ANN: *Then attend to those. Without delay.*

WALTER: *Like you always urged me to?*

ANN: *You weren't listening then.*

WALTER: *I'm listening now.*

ANN: *I loved you once. But you drove love out. And all the ills of my life and yours rushed in to take its place.*

WALTER: *What am I to do?*

ANN: *Love again. That's all. Make peace with the world.*

WALTER: *I'll try. I truly will. But . . . there's something else. Roger. Oh God.* (A cough.) *Did you tell him, Ann? Did you . . . before you . . . ? Does he know? We've never spoken of it, he and I. And I've always wondered . . . whether he might have guessed, or . . . I just need to be certain, Ann?*

ANN (in a whisper): *He knows.*

The recording ended there, with the last word cut off so abruptly that it was easy to believe there was more to be heard in some other, fuller version of this strangest of exchanges. Sir Walter Colborn, talking to his dead wife, barely a month before his own death. It had to be a séance of some kind. Sir Walter had said Ann didn't sound like herself. That was because she'd spoken through a medium. He'd gone to someone who could call up her ghost, her spirit, her . . . whatever he believed it was. I'd have said Sir Walter Colborn was the last person to fall for that sort of thing. But what would I really know about him? Or about his relationship with Ann? Or about Ann herself, come to that?

I listened to the recording again. If the medium was a charlatan, as I had every spiritualist down as, she was a smart one, no question. Sir Walter was convinced he was talking to Ann for the first time in thirteen years. You could hear the certainty of that growing in his voice. The reference to something no-one but she would be able to remember clinched it for him. And it lured him into discussion of some secret they'd long shared, about . . . Roger. '*Did you tell him, Ann? Does he know?*' Yes. Ultimately, he had her word for that. And so did I. '*He knows*.'

But what does he know? What is it that he and his father never spoke of, but both knew, without knowing that the other knew? And did anyone else know? Was anyone else in on the secret?

'What about you, Derek?' I said aloud. 'Is this what you've been getting at all along?'

I lay down across the bed, my head resting against the wall, and stared up at the shadow-vaulted ceiling. A dog was barking somewhere not far off, the sound echoing in some backyard similar to the ones I'd see if I opened the window and looked out. Then a police or ambulance siren challenged the noise and swamped it as it drew closer.

I sat up, suddenly and irrationally certain that they were coming for me. But no. They were taking some other route, bound for some other destination. The wail of the siren receded. The dog continued to bark. I was safe here, for the moment. But that was all. *For the moment*. The rest of tonight. Part of tomorrow. That was as much of a chance as I could carve out for myself of bringing Roger Colborn's world tumbling down around him. And the tape, hidden by Derek Oswin in a place where just about nobody — except me — might find it, was my only hope of doing so.

But what did it tell me? What was its *real* message? What was the secret?

If Derek knew, how, I asked myself, could he

have come into possession of such knowledge? What connected him with the late Ann Colborn? Colbonite, obviously, if indirectly. But that applied to the whole workforce. And I had no reason to suppose Ann ever went near the place anyway. There had to be something else. There had to be something *more*.

Ann had lived far from the tight, dull little circles Derek moved in. There was no point of intersection between their lives apart from the factory owned by *her* husband and *his* employer. And even that only applied to the six years between Derek going to work there in 1976 and Ann's suicide in 1982. There was nothing else. I thought of the Colbonite site in Hollingdean Lane, squeezed between the railway line and the municipal abattoir. Then I thought of the high white cliff top of Beachy Head, the blue of the sea below, the green of the turf above. And then —

I fell to my knees and grabbed the photograph album from where I'd left it yesterday, amidst the scattered contents of the wooden chest in the middle of the room. I flicked hurriedly through the pages, looking for the pictures I remembered. 1955. 1958. 1965. *Yes*.

Beachy Head, July 1968. There were two photographs of Derek as a ten-year-old, in striped T-shirt and short trousers with turn-ups, sitting on a picnic rug in one, taking guard with a cricket bat in another. Only the caption confirmed the location. The background could have been any fold of Sussex downland. There was no way to tell how close to the cliff the

Oswins had chosen to picnic. I flicked on through the pages and soon came to another Beachy Head shot. August, 1976. The year, quite possibly the month, Derek had started at Colbonite. He was standing with his father in this picture. They were posed and smiling. Behind them, the ground fell, then rose again, exposing a white flank of cliff to the camera and the candy-striped lighthouse out to sea that fixed their location as exactly as a grid reference. The road described a long curve towards and then away from the edge of the cliff behind them. There were two or three cars parked in a lay-by just beyond the road's closest approach to the edge. Was one of them the Oswins'? I wondered. No. It couldn't be. Surely Derek had said his father had bought the car in which he killed Sir Walter only after he'd become ill, as if, prior to that, they'd had no car at all. I imagined they could easily have travelled to Beachy Head by bus. They wouldn't have needed —

My thoughts froze as my eye seized on the distinctive profile of one of the cars in the lay-by. The sleek line of boot and roof and bonnet, sunlight gleaming on polished paintwork. It was a Jaguar 2.4. And I had absolutely no doubt who it belonged to. Nor, come to that, as my mind dwelt for a second on the implications of what I was seeing, who had taken the photograph, who Kenneth and Derek Oswin were smiling at so warmly in the summer sunshine all those years ago, *who* I was *really* meant to see.

SATURDAY

Circumstances are subtler conspirators than humans. They decree stranger alignments and juxtapositions than any we can devise. I spent last night lying on Derek Oswin's bed in the house he was born in forty-four years ago, staring into a darkness familiar and congenial to him, but novel and threatening to me. I'd used *his* dictation machine to record *my* experiences. My own machine was out of bounds at the Sea Air, where I couldn't safely return. The police would be on my trail, I felt sure, chasing the dangerous man Roger Colborn had arranged for them to believe I was. That made my inexcusably unexplained no-show at the Theatre Royal a trivial problem by comparison. But it was made to seem trivial in its turn by my discovery of the truth about the Oswins' connection with the Colborns; the truth — and all the other truths it beckoned me towards.

But so far those truths were only suspicions. What I needed — what I had to lay my hands on before the police laid hands on me — was proof.

* * *

It was barely light when I left 77 Viaduct Road, unobserved, as far as I could tell, by Mrs Lumb at number 76. The morning was chill and damp, a fine drizzle fuzzying the still glowing street lamps. I headed down Ditchling Road to The Level, then cut across to St Bart's, following in the long-ago footsteps of Derek Oswin's grandfather, on his way home from a ten-hour shift at Colbonite. His day would have been ending. Mine was only beginning.

⋆ ⋆ ⋆

I got into a taxi at the railway station and asked to be taken to Ray Braddock's address in Peacehaven: 9 Buttermere Avenue. The driver gave a couple of meaningful glances in the rear-view mirror as he started away and my heart jolted in alarm. Maybe the police had told the local radio station they were looking for me. But, when he spoke, he only did so along the 'Don't I know you from somewhere?' line I'd heard hundreds of times before.

'No,' I replied, forcing a smile. 'I just have one of those faces.'

⋆ ⋆ ⋆

Buttermere Avenue, Peacehaven, a long, straight road of cloned semi-detached pebble-dash bungalows, was as silent as the grave many of its residents were no doubt close to. Number 9 had an immaculately kept garden that made the house itself look shabbier than it really was. The sunburst gate creaked so loudly when I opened it that I seriously wondered if Braddock deliberately refrained from oiling it in order to be forewarned of visitors. The NO HAWKERS, NO

CIRCULARS sign certainly didn't suggest he welcomed casual callers.

There was a light showing through the dimpled glass of the front door and I could hear the faint burble of a radio within. I pressed the bell, long and hard. There was no way to go about this but head-on. The burble was cut off at once.

A blurred and growing shape disclosed itself through the glass and the door was pulled abruptly open. Braddock, unshaven and swaddled in threadbare sweater *and* cardigan, glared out at me. Then, seeing who his visitor was, he softened his expression.

'Mr Flood. Have you heard from Derek?'

'No. But I've heard news of him.'

'You'd best come in.'

He led me down a narrow hall into a kitchen at the back of the house. The scent of fried bacon hung in the air. An egg-smeared plate and a breadboard thick with crumbs stood beside the sink. On the table in the middle of the room was a teapot and a half-filled mug, steam whorling up from the rim. Plonked next to it was an open copy of the weekend edition of the *Argus*. I could only hope it had gone to press too early to report the mysterious absence of the star of the show from last night's performance of *Lodger in the Throat*.

'There's tea in the pot if you want some,' said Braddock.

'No thanks,' I responded.

'What's this about Derek, then?'

I took the photograph I'd brought with me out

of my pocket and laid it on the table.

Braddock sat down, fumbled in his cardigan for a pair of heavy-framed glasses, put them on and squinted at the picture. After a moment's scrutiny, he frowned suspiciously up at me. 'Where'd you get this?'

'It was in the album at Viaduct Road.'

'Yeah, but — '

'I have a key.'

His frown deepened. 'You never told me that.'

'There are things you never told me, either.'

'I don't know what you mean.'

'Look at the picture.'

'I have done.'

'What do you see?'

'Ken and Derek at Beachy Head. A good long while ago.'

'Twenty-six years ago, to be precise. August, nineteen seventy-six.'

'If you say so.'

'What else do you see, apart from your old friend and your godson?'

He made a show of re-examining the photograph, then shrugged. 'Nothing.'

'There are cars in the lay-by.'

'Be odd if there weren't.'

'One of them's a Jaguar two point four.'

'Maybe.'

'Ann Colborn's car.'

'It could be anybody's.'

'No. It's hers. You know that.'

'I don't.'

'She took the photograph.'

'*What?*'

I sat down beside him. 'There's no point acting dumb, Ray. I've worked it out. With a little help from Derek. Your friend Ken Oswin and your boss's wife, Ann Colborn, were lovers, weren't they?'

He looked as if the suggestion had angered him. But shocked? No. He didn't look that. 'Are you trying to make fun of me, Mr Flood?'

'Certainly not. I'm just asking you to confirm what I'm sure you've known for many years. Roger Colborn is Ann's son by Ken, not Walter. Which makes him Derek's half-brother. He knows too. They both do.'

Braddock rubbed his chin thoughtfully, patently debating with himself whether to opt for denial or admission. His instinct was to damn me for a liar. But in the end his anxiety about what had happened to Derek swung the contest. 'How did you find out?' he said eventually.

'Does it matter?'

'There's no proof. There can't be.'

'There can be these days, actually. But Roger's hardly likely to submit to a DNA test, so we're left with strong suspicions and firm beliefs. Ann, Walter and Ken were in no doubt. Nor are you. Are you?'

'Ken never . . . came out and said it to me in so many words.'

'But . . . '

'Look, only Ann Colborn would know for sure, wouldn't she? Maybe not even her. And what difference does it make, anyway? There was something between her and Ken once, that's true. Maybe he was Roger Colborn's natural father. *Maybe*. But Roger's still Walter's boy in the eyes of the law. What the hell does it matter now, when all three of them are dead and gone?' He glared at me defiantly, but we both recognized the hollowness of his words. It mattered. It definitely mattered. 'Are you sure Derek knows?' he murmured.

'Yes.'

'And Roger knows and all?'

I nodded in answer.

'Dear Christ.'

'What about Derek's mother? Was she in on it?'

'No. I'm sure of that. Val wasn't . . . the inquisitive type. It happened before they were married. And it didn't last long.'

'It lasted till she died, Ray. The photograph proves as much.'

'I meant . . . ' Braddock chewed his lip. 'I meant . . . they weren't lovers for long. But I don't suppose they forgot in a hurry, not if Roger . . . ' He gave a helpless shrug.

'Beachy Head a regular rendezvous, was it?'

'How should I know?'

'Are you saying you don't?'

'Well . . . ' He cleared his throat. 'Val never went there. She couldn't abide heights. But Ken and Derek liked a walk. Summer Sundays, they often used to take the train to Seaford, walk round the cliffs to Eastbourne and catch another train back from there. I suppose Ann Colborn . . . might have known that.'

'All this sheds new light on Sir Walter Colborn's death, don't you think?'

He bridled. 'I don't see how.'

'Maybe Ken blamed Sir Walter for Ann's suicide.'

'If he did, he never said so to me. And he waited a hell of a time to do something about it, didn't he?'

'He waited until he was dying. Until he no longer had anything to lose.'

'I don't believe it.'

'That's your prerogative. Anyway, it doesn't matter. What matters is whether Derek believes it.'

'If he's gone and stirred all that up . . . ' Braddock shook his head. 'Whoever told him about it has a lot to answer for.'

'Maybe no-one told him. Maybe he just worked it out.'

'Did he put this in his damn book, do you think?'

'Reckon so. Along with the explanation for the high death-toll among Colbonite workers. Not a palatable combination if you're Roger Colborn.'

'What's this man done to Derek?'

'I don't know. Let's hope nothing.' I was holding out on the old man, of course, shamelessly so. But I knew if I played him Derek's message he'd urge me to comply with Colborn's demands and go quietly — which I was no longer in any position to do. For me, it was all or nothing. And though Braddock had confirmed what I suspected, he hadn't given me what I needed: proof. Indeed, he'd made it clear he didn't believe any proof existed. But I didn't go along with that. I couldn't afford to. 'Who else knew about this, Ray? Who else knew for a fact?'

'No-one. Like I said, how could they, anyway? For a fact, I mean.'

'Think, man, think.' I'd grabbed his forearm without realizing it, I suddenly noticed. He seemed to have been as unaware of this as I was. Sheepishly, I let go. 'I have to nail this down.'

'Why?'

'For Derek's sake.'

'You reckon the boy's in danger?'

'I do, yes.'

'Well . . . ' He licked his lips hesitantly.

'What?'

'There's Delia Sheringham, I suppose.'

'Delia?'

'Walter's sister.'

'I know who she is,' I snapped, realizing as I did so that Braddock might well have supposed I didn't. In the same instant, I remembered how close Syd Porteous had said the two of them were. 'What about her?'

'I bumped into her at the hospital once when I was visiting Ken. It was only a couple of weeks before he died. They'd let him out of prison on bail by then, knowing the state he was in. Delia was coming out of the ward as I went in. She didn't recognize me. Well, I wouldn't have expected her to. But *I* recognized *her*. Pulled me up short, seeing her there. Why was she paying a call on the bloke supposed to have done her brother in?'

'Did you ask him?'

'No need. Ken told me straight off. He

seemed to think it was funny. I mean, he was chuckling about it when I got to his bed. 'What do you reckon, Ray?' he said. 'Sir Walter died without leaving a will. His sister's just been in to tell me. Reckoned I ought to know.' That seemed to tickle him. Which was some achievement, seeing how much pain he was in. I pretended not to understand, but it was plain as the nose on your face what he meant. Sir Walter didn't make a will because he no more had a wife living to leave his money to than he had — '

'A son.'

Braddock stared at me, then slowly nodded. 'That's how I read it.'

'And Delia wanted to make sure Ken knew about Sir Walter's intestacy?'

'Apparently. I don't know why. After all, it made no difference, did it? Roger inherited the lot, will or no will.'

'But it proves she knew.'

'That it does.'

I thought for a moment, then said, 'Can I use your phone? I need a taxi.'

'Where do you want to go?'

'Back into Brighton. In a hurry.'

'Going to see Delia, are you?'

'Yes.'

'I'll take you in my car, if you like.'

'All right. Thanks.'

* * *

Ten minutes later, we were heading west along the south coast road towards Brighton in

Braddock's patched-up old Metro. The first couple of miles passed in silence. We both had plenty to think about, complicated in Braddock's case by a continual struggle to keep the windscreen clear of condensation.

By the time we were out of Saltdean and into the open country between there and Black Rock, the significance of Sir Walter Colborn's intestacy had begun to expand in my mind. It went beyond underlining his awareness that Roger wasn't his biological son, well beyond. Braddock had set the ball rolling for me by saying it made no difference. But it did. Potentially, it made all the difference in the world.

'That's it,' I suddenly said aloud.

'That's what?' asked Braddock, glancing round at me.

'Don't you see? Roger inherited as Sir Walter's son under the rules of intestacy. If it had been shown at the time that he wasn't his son, he wouldn't have inherited. The estate would have gone . . . to Gavin and Delia, presumably. Still would now, come to that. Gavin would press his claim even if Delia refrained. He'd have Roger by the short and curlies.'

'Are you sure about this?'

'I'm no lawyer. Maybe Gavin would have a case, maybe not. What I am sure of is that Roger wouldn't want to be tied up in the courts for years finding out.'

'You mean Derek's been a bigger threat to him than we reckoned?'

'Looks like it.'

'Then what do we do?'

'*You* do nothing. Leave it to me. I think I see a way to cut the ground from beneath Roger Colborn's feet. And it's going to be a pleasure.'

★ ★ ★

I had Braddock drop me in Clifton Terrace, just round the corner from Powis Villas. He was clearly still struggling to catch up with my thinking, preoccupied as he was with a question other concerns kept pushing to the back of my mind: where was his godson?

'I don't care if Roger Colborn comes out of this smelling of roses or horse manure, Mr Flood, just so long as Derek comes to no harm.'

'I reckon Derek's lying low,' I lied. 'Waiting — wisely — for the trouble he's caused to blow over.'

'And when will it blow over?'

'If I have anything to do with it . . . ' I gave him what I intended to be a reassuring smile. 'Today.'

★ ★ ★

It wasn't till I reached the door of 15 Powis Villas that I realized just how hollow that reassurance was. I couldn't force Delia to tell me anything. Her husband was an unknown quantity. And they might both simply be out.

That last was my dismal conclusion when several lengthy prods at the doorbell went unanswered. I stepped back for a view of the drawing room through the front bay window.

The room was empty.

Suddenly, I was aware of a movement behind me, dimly reflected in the window. I turned to find Delia Sheringham regarding me quizzically from the pavement. She was dressed for the weather, in raincoat, gloves, scarf and hat. The well-stuffed Waitrose carrier bags in either hand made it unnecessary to wonder where she'd been.

'Toby,' she said. 'This is a surprise.' She marched up the drive to where I was standing. 'And a relief.'

'In what way a relief?'

'I overheard two women in the queue for the checkout talking about *Lodger in the Throat*. One of them went last night.'

'Unlike me.'

'Exactly. But I see you've recovered from . . . whatever was wrong.'

'Hardly.'

'You'll be on tonight, though, I'm sure. Did I mention that John and I have tickets?'

'You did. But I wouldn't count on seeing me on stage. Or of feeling in the mood for a night at the theatre.'

'Why on earth not?'

'I've something to tell you.'

'Do you want to come inside?'

'I should think you'd want me to. It's the sort of thing best discussed behind closed doors.'

'You're being very mysterious, Toby.'

'Case of having to be.'

She sighed and bustled past me to the door.

* * *

Once we were inside, she led the way down the hall past the dining room to a large kitchen at the rear, instructing me over her shoulder to bring along the post that was lying on the mat. The kitchen windows looked out over a small, high-walled garden. I dropped the post onto the table as she stowed a few perishables in the wardrobe-sized fridge. Then she took off her coat, hat and scarf and filled the kettle.

'Coffee?'

'Thanks.'

'John's playing golf. It's something of a Saturday morning ritual, come rain or shine. He'll be sorry to have missed you.'

'I doubt it.'

She looked at me sharply. 'Why do you say that?'

'Because I doubt you'll tell him I've been here.'

She went on looking at me, saying nothing. I held her gaze. Then the kettle came to the boil. She spooned coffee into cups. 'How do you like it?'

'Black. No sugar.'

'Same as me.' She handed me my cup, took a sip from hers and flicked through the post.

Suddenly impatient, I took the photograph out of my pocket and dropped it onto the sheaf of letters. She stopped flicking.

'What's this?'

'I found it in an album at the Oswins' house. That's Derek. And his father. At Beachy Head, in the summer of nineteen seventy-six.'

'Really? I don't quite see — '

'And that's your sister-in-law's car.' I stabbed at the image of the Jaguar in the lay-by. 'She took the picture.'

'That seems singularly improbable.' Delia sat down at the table and sipped some more coffee. 'I don't believe Ann knew the family.'

'She and Kenneth Oswin were lovers.'

'Don't be absurd.' She glanced reprovingly up at me.

'I won't if you won't.' I sat down opposite her. 'I've worked it out, Delia. I understand. I *know*.'

'What do you know?'

'That Roger is Kenneth Oswin's son, not Walter's.'

'This is utterly preposterous.' She took yet another sip of coffee. 'I think it might be best if you left.'

'I can prove it.'

She frowned at me. 'I don't think so.'

I took out Derek's pocket dictation machine and stood it on the table. 'I have a tape I want you to listen to. When you've heard it, you'll have to change your tune. You may as well do so now.' The only response I got to that was a toss of her head. 'You know it's true, Delia. You've always known. Ann confided in you. Gavin doesn't know obviously, otherwise — ' I broke off. 'Why don't I just play it?'

'If you feel you must.'

'Oh yes. I do feel I must.' I pressed the PLAY button. And leant back in the chair.

Delia recognized Walter's voice at once. Her

considerable powers of self-control couldn't suppress a flinch of surprise. She looked at me with a mixture of outrage and amazement, in which there was also a trace of fascination. Then, as the exchanges between her long-dead brother and her still-longer-dead sister-in-law proceeded, her gaze shifted to the machine itself and stayed there, fixed and focused, as if the tape inside was more than just a recording device, as if it held the souls and secrets of those two dead people she still loved.

The recording ended with Ann's whispered words, '*He knows*.' I leant forward, pressed STOP, then REWIND. 'You want to hear it again?'

Delia licked her lips. 'No.'

'There's a date on the label. Seventh October, nineteen ninety-five.'

'May I see?'

'Sure.' I ejected the cassette and showed it to her.

'I don't recognize the writing.'

'Nor do I. The medium's, perhaps.'

'You think what we've heard . . . was a séance?'

'Nothing else it could have been. And hardly shock news to you, Delia. I could tell from your expression that you understood the context straight off. My guess is Walter told you he was going to a psychic in the hope of contacting Ann.'

'Very well.' She drew herself up. 'As far as that's concerned, you're correct. Walter became interested in spiritualism in the last year or so of his life. He told me of his intention to consult a medium who'd been recommended to him and he asked my opinion.'

'Which was?'

'That such people are charlatans trading on the gullibility of grieving people.'

'You evidently didn't convince him.'

'That was clear to me at the time. Where did this tape come from?'

'Same place as the photograph.'

'How can Derek Oswin have come by it?'

'He's been preparing his case against Roger for years. Presumably, the tape originated with the medium. How Derek got hold of it I don't know. I'd be happy to ask him. *If* I could find him.'

'I fail to see how this . . . recording of a con trick . . . damages Roger.' She looked as if she believed her own words. But I knew she didn't. She *couldn't*.

'The medium mentions the look on Walter's face at the maternity hospital. That's what convinced Walter he was really talking to Ann. Doesn't it convince you?'

Delia shrugged and said nothing. Her mouth tightened.

'They as good as come out and admit it. Roger wasn't their child. It's implied in more or less everything that's said.'

'Is it?'

'You know it is. Even if the medium is just acting a part, Walter isn't. '*Does Roger know?*' he asks. '*Did you tell him?*' What's he referring to, Delia? What's he so anxious about?'

'I really can't — '

'Yes, you can, God damn it.' I thumped the table as I spoke, rattling the cups in their saucers. Delia started back in her chair. 'Walter died intestate. He made no provision for Roger. He left no will naming him as his son. Irresponsible bordering on incomprehensible for a well-organized businessman with a large estate, wouldn't you say?'

'It was . . . an unfortunate oversight.'

'Bullshit. It was a tacit acknowledgement of the truth. Unlike your visit to Kenneth Oswin in hospital to tell him about Walter's intestacy. There was nothing remotely tacit about that.'

I'd wrong-footed her at last. She looked confused, weakened by a surfeit of contradictions and evasions. Braddock was right. She hadn't recognized him.

'You were seen, by an old friend of Ken's from Colbonite.'

'They must have . . . made a mistake.'

'Ken told him why you'd been there. He laughed about it.'

Delia closed her eyes for a moment and drew a long breath. Then she looked at me with much of her placidity and deliberation restored. 'Why are you doing all this, Toby?'

'Does it matter?'

'I believe it does. Your motive is actually transparent. To win back Jenny. As simple as that.'

'And pretty reasonable, given the kind of man — the kind of family — she's got herself mixed up with.'

'And what kind is that?'

'You tell me, Delia.'

'There have been tensions. Difficulties. I don't deny it. Since you insist upon pressing the point, I'll admit you're correct about Roger's parentage. Ann formed an attachment with Kenneth Oswin the summer before Roger was born. Walter was often away on business. Kenneth was shop steward at Colbonite and Ann fancied herself as some kind of socialist. She and Walter were going through a rough patch. He was . . . neglecting her, I suppose. And she was always . . . attracted to risk. Her pregnancy was a slap in the face for Walter. The doctors had already told him by then, you see, that he couldn't father children of his own. So . . . ' Delia spread her hands eloquently. 'You may judge for yourself the anguish it caused. Ann told me the whole sordid story. She seemed in some strange way proud of herself. She delivered the son Walter craved. Our parents were delighted. They had no idea the baby wasn't really their grandson at all.'

'What about Gavin? He definitely didn't know?'

'I was the only member of the family in on the secret. Walter was deeply hurt, of course, but he doted on Ann quite pitifully. He couldn't bear the thought of losing her. He even agreed not to sack Kenneth Oswin because Ann threatened to leave him if he did. And he raised Roger as a loving father would. He never took out on him any of the pain he must have felt. In a sense . . . ' Her voice drifted into silence. She smiled weakly. Then she resumed. 'I think that was his revenge.

To make Roger so much like himself. To steal him from Ann. And he became more ruthless, of course. The Colbonite workforce — including Kenneth Oswin — suffered for that.'

'Why did Ann kill herself?'

'Self-destructiveness was part of her nature. As for the immediate cause, I can only guess. Shortly before her death, she confided in me that she'd decided to tell Roger the truth. He may not have reacted as she'd expected.'

'Meaning?'

'I think she wanted him to forgive her for betraying Walter. I think she wanted to . . . reclaim him. To have his blessing, as it were.'

'Which wasn't forthcoming?'

'Perhaps not. I don't know. Roger and I have never discussed it. I don't even know for a fact that she went ahead and told him.'

'You heard the tape.'

'And you heard my opinion of mediums.'

'Is that why you visited Kenneth Oswin in hospital? To find out if Roger had told him he knew he was his son?'

There came another weak smile and a faint nod of her head. 'How very perceptive of you, Toby. Yes. It had long troubled me. With Walter gone, I felt I could safely ask the question.'

'What answer did you get?'

'An unsatisfactory one. Kenneth told me Roger had said nothing to him on the subject. Ever. And yet . . . I wasn't sure I believed him.'

'Why should he lie?'

'Ah. Clearly there are limits to your perceptiveness. But, as I said earlier, your motive is a narrow one. You seek only a reconciliation with Jenny. Have the decency to admit it, since you've obliged me to be so painfully honest. If she walked into this room now and said she wanted to revive your marriage, you'd happily forget Derek Oswin and Roger's alleged character flaws.'

'They're more than character flaws. Do you know why I missed the performance last night? Because *your nephew* held me prisoner and set in motion a plan to have me arrested for assaulting a prostitute.' The outburst had carried me too far. But it was too late to back out. 'Roger's scared, Delia. Do you know why? Not because he's afraid I'll steal Jenny from him. But because he's afraid Gavin will steal his inherited wealth from him, along with Wickhurst Manor, if he can prove Walter *wasn't* Roger's father and Roger therefore *wasn't* his rightful heir.'

'Nonsense.'

'You know it isn't.'

'On the contrary. I know it *is*. Listen to me carefully, Toby. You clearly have no understanding of the law. Even if Gavin could prove Kenneth Oswin fathered Roger, which would be next to impossible, he'd have no hope of persuading a court to overturn the settlement of Walter's estate on him, since Roger was born in wedlock and acknowledged by Walter as his son.'

Now *she* had wrong-footed *me*. 'Are you certain?' I mumbled.

'I made it my business to find out. As I'm sure Roger has. He has nothing to fear on that score.'

'But — '

'Which means he has no reason to engage in risky and illegal actions designed to prevent either you or Derek Oswin publicizing matters that can at worst merely embarrass him.'

'He held me in a locked room at Wickhurst Manor last night. And he instructed a drug dealer he knows called Sobotka to set me up on an assault charge. The police are probably already looking for me.'

'Really?' Her expression was suitably sceptical.

'Really. And truly.'

'It doesn't seem very likely.'

'But it happened.'

'So you say. But — ' The ring of the wall-mounted telephone, modulated by the burbles and rings of various extensions elsewhere in the house, silenced Delia. She frowned, then rose smartly from her chair, marched across to it and picked up the receiver. 'Hello? . . . Oh, hello, darling. Still at the club?' The caller was clearly her husband. My attention drifted.

If Delia was right about the legal position, as I didn't seriously doubt she was, the tape and the photograph amounted to nothing but proof of a long-ago infidelity that posed no threat to Roger Colborn. But something did. That much I knew for certain. Something more than my love for Jenny and any affection she still harboured for me. But what could it be? What —

'Are you sure about this?' A note of urgency had entered Delia's voice.

When I looked towards her, I saw concern and puzzlement etched on her forehead. 'What can they possibly have been looking for? . . . Surely not. It's unthinkable . . . I've heard nothing from him . . . Of course . . . All right, darling . . . Yes . . . See you then. 'Bye.'

She put the telephone back on the hook and stared at me, her frown fading only slowly. She raised a hand to her mouth.

'What's wrong?' I prompted.

'The strangest thing,' she murmured.

'*What?*'

'John met somebody at the golf club this morning who lives at Fulking. Just down the road from Wickhurst Manor. He mentioned . . . well, it seems . . . ' She moved slowly back across the room, but didn't sit down. She stood beside her chair, gazing out into the garden, collecting her thoughts, composing her words. 'It seems the police were at Wickhurst Manor last night. In force. It was described . . . as a raid.'

I remembered the dark-blue saloon car following Sobotka's van into Brighton after he dropped me near the bypass and felt a surge of relief. Maybe the police had picked up Sobotka before he could do his worst. Maybe I was in the clear after all. And maybe Roger wasn't. 'Did they make any arrests?'

'Apparently not. But they were there for some hours. John wondered if I'd heard from Roger. Or from our solicitor. He's Roger's solicitor too.'

'They're trying to link him with Sobotka, Delia. They were looking for drugs and any other evidence they could unearth.'

'I don't believe it.'

'I think you'll have to.'

'No. There has to be — '

The peremptory buzz of the doorbell cut her off. She glanced round, then down at me. The frown was back, in earnest.

'That could be them now,' I said softly. And it *was* a distinct possibility, one I faintly welcomed, whereas, before the phone call — The bell rang again. 'Are you going to answer it?'

'Wait here,' came the tight-lipped instruction. Then she was off down the hall, out of my sight, heels clacking on the wood-block floor. She reached the door just as the bell rang for a third time. It stopped in the instant that she turned the handle and pulled the door open.

It wasn't the police. I knew that before Delia said a word. I knew it by the nature of the brief silence that followed. 'Roger,' she said in quiet surprise. 'What brings you here?'

'Can I come in?'

'Of course. Please.'

I heard the door close and Roger clear his throat. There was another silence, as telling as it was fleeting. I didn't move a muscle. I may even have held my breath.

'Goodness,' said Delia. 'What happened to your eye?'

'I was attacked,' Roger replied, lisping slightly. 'By Toby Flood.'

'That's dreadful. Why would — '

'Jealousy. Pure and simple. The man's out of control. Which is why I have to contact Jenny. Urgently.'

'Don't you know where she is?'

'She went away for the weekend. To think, she said. She didn't want to be disturbed. After all the lies and innuendo Flood's filled her head with, I didn't blame her. But things have changed. Her mobile's switched off, so I have to find out where she's gone. I've tried her parents and her sister. No luck.'

'I don't see how I can help.'

'I thought she might have told you where she was going. In case of emergencies.'

'Well, I . . . '

'I'm right, aren't I? You do know where she is.'

'It's difficult. I . . . promised not to put you or Toby Flood in touch with her unless . . . well, unless . . . '

'Where is she?'

'I'm not sure I can — '

'*Where is she?*'

'Roger, let go. You're hurting me.'

'*Colborn,*' I shouted, jumping from my chair and striding to the door into the hall.

They were at the far end, near the foot of the stairs. Colborn had grabbed Delia by the wrist. He held on as he turned and looked towards me. He was gaunt and unshaven, dressed in black, his left eye haloed by a purple bruise.

'Let your aunt go,' I said, emphasizing each word. Slowly, with a half-smile, he released her. 'Of course,' I went on, suddenly eager to goad him, 'I use the word *aunt* advisedly. You're no blood relation to each other. Are you?'

'There's no need for this,' said Delia, flashing a look of irritation at me.

'What have you told him?' Roger demanded.

'Nothing,' I answered in her place. 'I'd already worked it out.'

'The hell you had.'

'Toby brought me a tape he wanted me to hear,' said Delia. 'Maybe you should hear it too.'

'What tape?' Colborn strode towards me along the hall and Delia followed him. I moved back to the table and, as they entered the room, pressed the PLAY button on the dictaphone.

The voices of Sir Walter and the medium Sir Walter clearly believed had contacted the spirit of his dead wife stopped Roger Colborn in his tracks. But only for a minute or so. Halfway through Ann's recollection of the expression on her husband's face at the maternity hospital, Roger moved to the table and stabbed the STOP button. He looked at me, then round at Delia. His thoughts were unreadable, his intentions unguessable. Did he have the gun on him? I wondered. It was hard to say if there was anything that heavy weighing down a pocket of his long, loose overcoat.

'I don't need to hear it again,' he said quietly.

'Did Derek send you a copy?' I asked, backing a sudden hunch.

'Somebody did,' Colborn answered levelly.

'You sent Sobotka to find the original at Viaduct Road, didn't you? But he didn't search thoroughly enough.'

'I don't know anyone called Sobotka.'

'I'm sure that's what you told the police, but the line's wasted on us. Probably on them too. They must have arrested Sobotka last night, before he could fit me up. Lucky for me. Unlucky for you. They'd already followed him to and from Wickhurst, I'm afraid, tying you in with his cache of drugs out at Fishersgate. Did they find anything incriminating when they turned the house over? We know about that as well, you see. Gossip on the nineteenth hole.'

'It's true,' said Delia, catching Roger's glance. 'John phoned from the clubhouse a few minutes ago. Alan Richards mentioned to him that the police . . . had been to see you.'

'Sorry I didn't tell you they had Sobotka's number, Roger,' I said. 'It must have slipped my mind.'

He pressed the EJECT button on the machine and took out the cassette.

'My guess would be that Derek made several copies. He's a belt-and-braces sort of guy. Whatever he may have told you, that's almost certainly not the original.'

'He's told me nothing.'

'You *have* spoken to him, then?'

'I didn't say that.'

'Where are you holding him?'

'I don't know what you're talking about.'

'Maybe you've released him now the police have started breathing down your neck. That would have been the sensible thing to do. But being sensible isn't always easy, is it?'

'Did you prevent Toby appearing at the theatre last night, Roger?'

Roger looked round at her. 'Is that what he's told you?'

'*Did you?*'

'Of course not.'

'But you do know this man . . . Sobotka?'

Roger sighed synthetically. 'All right. Yes. I

know Sobotka. I used him for some . . . building work at Wickhurst. He's a bit of a rough diamond. I suppose it shouldn't come as a total surprise to learn he peddles drugs on the side. He was at the house yesterday. The police were obviously tailing him. They seemed to think — wrongly — that I'm the Mr Big in his operation. It may take me a little time to convince them I have nothing to do with it. In some ways, I'm sorry they didn't show up at the house earlier. They might have stopped Flood giving me a black eye.'

Looking at Delia, it was possible to conclude she actually believed Roger's version of events. I spread my hands. 'For God's sake.'

'Do you have anything to do with Derek Oswin's disappearance?' Delia persisted.

'I don't know where he is and I don't care,' Roger replied with studied weariness. 'He's nothing to me.'

'He's your half-brother,' I corrected him.

Roger glared at me. 'Congratulations on digging up that nugget of dirt on my family, Flood. Yes. Kenneth Oswin was my natural father. Delia's known that a lot longer than I have, so bringing it to her hasn't got you very far. As for the tape, if my father — the man I always regarded and still do regard as my father — was credulous enough to pay some tea-leaf reader to fake a *conversazione* with the spirit world, well, you know what they say, don't you? There's no fool like an old fool.' He tossed the cassette onto the table. 'It gets you nowhere. Absolutely nowhere.'

He was right. The thought hit me like a blow to the face. My ignorance of the finer points of intestacy had left me where I was now: swaying in the wind.

'I need to speak to Jenny, Delia,' said Roger. 'I think this has to count as an emergency, don't you?'

'I . . . suppose so.'

'I take it you *don't* believe any of Flood's allegations?'

'Well, I — '

'She visited Ken Oswin in hospital shortly before he died,' I interrupted, grabbing the only chance I seemed to have left of coming between them. 'I bet she's never told you that.'

Roger frowned. 'Is that true?'

'Yes.' Delia sat down in her chair between us. I read the move as an attempt to win some allowance for her age and sex. But she certainly had good reason to feel unsteady on her feet. 'I couldn't ask you if you knew he was your real father in case you didn't. I thought it likely, however, that if you did know you'd have spoken to him about it at some point. So, I . . . went to him and asked.'

'I knew. Thanks to Mother,' said Roger. 'But I never spoke to Ken Oswin about it.'

Delia nodded. 'That's what he said.'

'But you didn't believe him,' I put in.

'I had . . . some doubts, it's true.'

'Why?' asked Roger.

'I'm not sure. Clearly, I misjudged him. His . . . evasiveness . . . may have had more to do with his responsibility for Walter's death than anything else. Meeting the sister of the man he'd killed . . . may have unnerved him.'

'I suppose that accounts for it,' said Roger.

'I believe it must.'

'He never breathed a word to me about his relationship with Mother.' Roger picked up the snapshot of the Oswins, father and son, and stared at it for a moment. 'In all the years. Not a single word.'

'It must have been difficult for you,' said Delia softly. 'I'm sorry I — '

'Forget it.' Roger dropped the photograph. 'Toby here isn't interested in hearing about *my* problems.'

'You're still hiding something,' I said, determined to show him mere lack of proof couldn't shut me up. 'And I mean to find out what it is.'

'Of course you do.' He cast me a weary glance. 'I'd expect nothing less.' With a swirl of his coat, he moved past me and sat down in my chair, facing Delia. 'I have to speak to Jenny. Will you tell me where she is?'

'The Spa Hotel, in Tunbridge Wells.'

'Not so very far away, then.'

'She just needed . . . a chance to think.'

'Thanks to Toby and me messing her about.' Incredibly, Roger sounded genuinely remorseful. 'Poor Jenny.'

'If I leave a message on her mobile, she'll phone me back.'

'No need. I have a better idea.' He looked up at me. 'It's not much more than thirty miles to Tunbridge Wells. We could be there in less than an hour. That's we as in 'you and me', Toby.

What about it? You can say your piece to Jenny and I can say mine. You can tell her all about my shady parentage and apparently criminal associations. You can pull out all the stops. Subject to my right of reply. And when we're done, you and I, we'll see which of us she trusts the more. Which of us she really loves.'

'I'm not sure that's wise,' Delia began. 'If — '

'Leave this to us.' Roger's voice was raised now, his tone dismissive. He hadn't taken his eyes off me. 'What do you say, Toby? It's a fair offer.'

So it was, in a way. The very fact that he was making it smacked of desperation, or of deviousness. He had some trick up his sleeve, I felt certain. But he was daring me to believe I could trump it.

'Let's get it all out in the open. Give Jenny the choice. You or me. Or neither, I suppose. I'll stand by her decision. Will you?'

I could hardly reject the challenge, as Roger had surely calculated. In a sense, I'd been pressing for something of the kind all week. I had to accept. He knew that.

Which meant he was confident of the outcome. It wasn't a fair offer. It couldn't be. In fact, it was bound to be anything but. Nevertheless . . . 'All right,' I said. 'I'll go with you.'

'Good.' Roger stood up. 'Let's get going.' He moved past me to the door, then stopped and looked back. 'Don't forget to bring the cassette and the player, Toby. I'm sure you'll want Jenny to hear what's on the tape.'

His sarcasm made it certain that whatever happened in Tunbridge Wells he'd devised some way of coming out on top. All I could do now was cling to the hope that Jenny would see through him at the last. I loaded the cassette back into the machine and put it in my pocket, along with the Beachy Head photograph. Delia glanced at me anxiously, but said nothing. I held her gaze for a moment, then murmured, 'We'll speak later,' and headed after Roger.

'Don't worry, Delia,' he called, as he led the way down the hall. 'This is for the best, believe me.'

She made no reply and Roger didn't seem to expect one. We reached the front door. He held it open for me and I stepped out. His Porsche was parked on the drive. The house door slammed behind me and Roger fired his remote at the car, which unlocked and flashed a welcome. He walked past me and round to the driver's side, opened the door and slid into the car. He made no comment as I climbed into the passenger seat, merely started the engine and reversed out into the street.

And there, unexpectedly, he stopped. The Porsche idled throatily at the kerbside for several seconds. Then he said, 'Hold on,' threw the door open and jumped out.

'Where are you — ' The slam of the door cut me short. And the answer to my question was soon apparent. He marched back up the drive of number 15 and rang the bell. He didn't glance once in my direction as he waited for Delia to respond. Then I saw the door open. He stepped inside.

I sat where I was, staring ahead at the wedge of sea visible between the houses. What was he up to? What could I do to outmanoeuvre him? I bludgeoned my mind for answers.

* * *

Several minutes passed. It suddenly occurred to me that Roger must have wanted to say something to Delia in my absence, something that would swing her sympathies away from me and towards him. Foolishly, I'd left the field open for him. There was no time to lose. I had to intervene.

Too late. He was already hurrying back down the drive. 'What's going on?' I snapped as he flung himself in.

'I just wanted to make sure Delia will keep this morning's events to herself.'

'Worried about the trouble Gavin might give you if he found out you're not his brother's son, are you?'

'Not worried. Keen to avoid it. There's a difference.'

'And did Delia promise to help you out?'

'Her lips are sealed.' He slipped the car into gear and started away in a burst of acceleration that carried us round the corner and along Clifton Terrace to the junction with Dyke Road, where he turned left and headed north.

By the time we'd reached Seven Dials and turned east towards Preston Circus, the silence between us had become heavy with tension. I broke it as defiantly as I could. 'However you spin it, Jenny isn't going to believe you, Roger. Do you realize that?'

'You reckon not?'

'I've known her a lot longer than you have.'

'True. But have you known her better?'

'I love her. I've always loved her.'

'Tell me why.'

'What?'

'Tell me why you love her.' The traffic was moving slowly ahead of us, through the lights under the railway bridges behind Brighton station. 'I'd really like to know.'

'I . . . er . . . '

'Not a fluent start, is it, Toby? 'I, er.' I suppose you actors need lines to be written for you before you sound convincing. You see, I don't think you do love her. Not in the way I do. I think you only want her back to prove you haven't ruined the most important relationship in your life.'

'A man like you is incapable of understanding love,' I fired back at him. '*That's* why I can't explain it to you.'

'I preferred the umming and erring. At least they were honest. I told you when we first met that I love Jenny because she makes me a better person than I can ever be without her. I told you that because it's true.'

'This 'better person' is the man who held me captive last night and tried to frame me for assault.'

'You forced me into that.'

'Did I really? No doubt I forced you into

hounding Denis Maple to his death as well.'

'I wasn't to know he had a heart condition. His death was unfortunate.'

'Unfortunate? Is that the best you can come up with?'

'It was Sobotka's doing, not mine.'

'But Sobotka was working for you.'

'He's been useful to me, certainly.'

'Like when he kidnapped Derek Oswin, you mean?' The traffic had eased and we were speeding along Viaduct Road now, past the very door of number 77.

'You're wrong about that, Toby. I called Sobotka off after Maple died. He didn't go near Oswin. Nor did I.'

'You'll be telling me next he didn't break into the Sea Air and steal my tapes.'

'I would, if I thought it'd do any good. I've no idea what tapes you're talking about.'

'You met Sobotka at Devil's Dyke car park Thursday morning. You were seen there by Ian Maple. So much for calling Sobotka off the day before.'

'*Ian* Maple? Who's he?'

'You can drop the pretence with me, Roger. It's pointless.'

'Sobotka's under arrest, Toby. He's facing a lengthy prison sentence for drugs trafficking. Doubtless he's doing everything he can to chalk up some points in his favour. Pinning something on me would win him a whole load of points. So, if he could lead the police to where you seem to think I'm holding Derek Oswin, he would. But he can't. Because I have no more idea where

Oswin is than you have.'

We'd joined the Lewes Road and passed the turning that formerly led to Colbonite. Roger was driving faster as the traffic thinned on the dual carriageway out through the suburbs.

'You're the one who's been cosying up to Oswin this past week, not me,' he continued. 'You're the one who knows how his picky little mind works. So, it shouldn't really be beyond you to figure out why he's done a runner. Or where to.'

Could it be true? Had Derek vanished of his own accord? Had he faked his own abduction? I began to think about the scene at his house: the evidence of a struggle; the carefully scattered clues. It could have been stage-managed. Even the 'commotion' the neighbour had heard on Wednesday night could have been the work of one clever, calculating, painstaking man.

'Want to know what I think, Toby? I think Oswin's been pulling your strings all week. A twitch here, a twitch there. And off you've gone, causing me more trouble than he ever could.'

'No. It's his manuscript you're worried about. It's what he says in it about Colbonite. That's why you removed the original from Viaduct Road and stole the copy I'd sent to my agent.'

'Run past me how I managed that last bit, given that I didn't know you had it to send. I don't even know who your agent is. Or care.'

'Jenny could have told you.'

'Well, we can check that with her, can't we?'

'Derek can't have . . . done it all himself.' The words died in my throat as the implications of such a possibility ramified in my mind. There was more to consider than his apparent abduction. There were the stolen tapes, returned with a threatening message in which only his voice featured. And there was the missing manuscript, the damage it might do Colborn rendered tantalizingly unquantifiable. I hated Colborn because Jenny preferred him to me. It was as simple as that. And Derek knew it. The question was: had he exploited my hatred to serve his own?

'Do you know what the biggest irony is in all this, Toby? It's the fact that none of the digging for dirt you've done would have mattered if Sobotka hadn't gone and got his collar felt. He's been useful. But not useful enough to justify the risk he's exposed me to. I can't afford to have the police sniffing round my business affairs. They might catch a few iffy aromas. Chances are I can fend them off. But not if you feed your suspicions into the works. I have a horrible feeling that would give their investigation more momentum than I can soak up.'

'I'm surprised you think you have anything to worry about,' I said bitterly. And it was true. I *was* surprised.

'That's because you don't know what's likely to emerge. Maybe Oswin does. I'm not sure. Either way, it's time I put *you* in the picture.'

'What do you mean?'

'I mean it's time I told you the truth.'

'You must be joking. *You* tell *me* the truth?'

'It's up to you whether you believe it, of course. But I think you will.'

'I doubt it.'

'Wait and see.'

He paused for a moment, concentrating on the flow of traffic as he joined the A27, eased the Porsche into the outside lane and took her swiftly up beyond the speed limit as we headed east towards Lewes. Then he resumed, his tone of voice bizarrely relaxed.

'You and Jenny would still be together if you hadn't lost your son. Let's be honest, now. You would be. Peter's death was too big a blow for you to bear. You blamed yourselves and each other. And the blame drove you apart. Most of all, though, the loss did that. The grief. The pain. The having him and then the not having him.'

'If you're expecting me to thank you for your six penn'orth of psychological platitudes, then . . . '

'I'm making a point, Toby. Bear with me. If I'd died aged four and a half, do you think my parents would have parted? I don't. In fact, I suspect they'd have drawn closer together. *Back* together. Because I wasn't theirs. Not wholly. I *wasn't* their son. I was twenty-eight when Mother told me who my real father was. *Twenty-eight*. I thought I knew exactly who and what I was. Then she took it away from me. She had some idea that I needed to understand her. She was egotistical to the last. Suicide's a pretty selfish act, don't you think?'

'Depends what leads to it.'

'In my mother's case, the realization that I wasn't going to forgive her. Driving off Beachy Head, where she'd staged so many calculatedly indiscreet assignations with Kenneth Oswin, was her way of making me feel guilty for not stopping her. It was her last mistake. I didn't blame myself for what she'd done. I blamed her.'

'But you never told your father that you knew the truth.'

'My legal father, you mean? No.'

'So there was never any chance *he* might blame you.'

'Ha. You reckon that's why I said nothing to him, do you? Nice try, Toby. But wide of the mark. I said nothing because he said nothing. I wanted to be as real a son to him as I could be. And I believed he wanted the same.'

'Didn't he?'

'Not strongly enough, as it transpired. He hankered after Mother. More and more as he aged. I didn't know about the medium until I was sent the tape. If I had, I'd have put a stop to it. As it was, I had to deal with the consequences as best I could.'

'What consequences?'

'His abrupt change of heart. His U-turn on the question of compensation for Colbonite workers suffering from cancers supposedly caused by exposure to a chloro-aniline curing agent we used in the dyeing shop. Suddenly, he was all for giving them every penny he had. And every penny I stood to inherit from him. The séance was a set-up. I'm sure of it. The medium was probably one of our former employees, or the relative of one. 'Whatever wrongs you've done, it's not too late to put them right.' Remember that line? Money's what she was talking about. A commodity that doesn't count for much in the spirit world.'

'You don't believe the medium was in touch with your mother, then?'

'Of course I don't. It was a scam. But a clever one, I admit. Father swallowed it whole. He suddenly saw a way to assuage the guilt he felt for not saving Mother from herself by throwing money around in a fit of late-life generosity. I tried to talk him out of it, but his mind was made up.'

'Some would say he simply saw the error of his ways.'

'Only people with soft hearts and simple minds. We've got a National Health Service to look after the sick and dying. None of the so-called victims had any claim on my birthright.'

'Even though one of them was your real father?'

'What had Kenneth Oswin ever done for me? I owed him nothing. The debt was all the other way.' Roger sniggered. 'Though I suppose you could say he paid it off in the end.'

'What do you mean?' I asked, even as his meaning began to dawn on me.

'I couldn't let Father squander the capital the sale of Colbonite had left him with. I'd been loyal to him. I'd done his dirty work. And I wasn't about to be cheated out of my reward. I couldn't make him see reason. He was determined to go ahead. So, I had to stop him.'

'You're saying — '

'Oswin killed him at my bidding, Toby. Yes. You've got it.'

'But . . . why would he . . . '

'I promised to look after Derek. Financially, I mean. Oswin was dying. And he was worried his son wouldn't be able to cope without him. As we've seen, I think he underestimated the resourcefulness of my half-brother, as you kindly defined him. So, the deal was that I'd featherbed Derek for the rest of his life . . . provided Oswin made sure I had the means to do so.'

'You . . . played one father off . . . against the other.'

'That's one way to put it. And I'll tell you what, Toby. They both deserved it.'

'You welched on the deal, didn't you?'

'No. Valerie Oswin did that. I'd made an initial payment to her husband, without which he'd never have gone ahead, and another afterwards. But the cheques were never cashed. After he died, she sent them back to me. Exactly how much she knew, I have no idea.'

'And Derek, what does he know?'

'Nothing, I suspect. His father had every incentive to keep our agreement to himself. And that's where it could — and should — have stayed. Our secret. Mine and a dead man's. But now, of course, I've been forced to share it with you.'

'I haven't forced you.' That was surely true. Indeed, I couldn't understand why he'd revealed so much to me, glad though I was that he had — for more reasons than he needed to know. My puzzlement on the point made little impact on me at that moment, however, amidst my astonishment at discovering how coolly and almost casually, by his own admission, he'd arranged his father's murder.

'Blame circumstances, then. Perhaps it's fairer to,' he went on. 'They've conspired against both of us, I'm afraid. Have you noticed, by the way, that we're not on the right road for Tunbridge Wells?'

'What?'

He braked heavily and flicked on the indicator. 'We should have taken a left at the last roundabout but one.' The car slowed sharply to a crawl. Roger steered it up over the grass verge and we came to a juddering halt by an overgrown five-bar gate. 'This is the Eastbourne road.'

I was still trying to absorb all the implications of what he'd confessed to and, come to that, why he'd confessed. The sudden switch of subjects to the banalities of route-finding barely registered. As far as that went, I took him at his word, realizing I'd been unaware myself of our surroundings for several miles. I assumed he was about to turn round and head back, although there hardly seemed room for the manoeuvre. But he didn't attempt to. Instead, he jumped out of the car, strode round to my side and pulled the door open.

As he did so, I saw the gun in his hand, held low, where no passing driver would glimpse it, displayed for my benefit alone. 'Move over, Toby.'

'What the hell's going on?'

‘*Move over to the driver’s seat.*’

‘Why?’

‘Just do it. Or, believe me, I *will* shoot.’

I looked into his eyes and read there only deadly seriousness. The fear of imminent death jagged into me. ‘All right,’ I said. ‘*All right.*’ I released the seat belt, then cautiously levered myself over the gearshift and handbrake and settled behind the steering wheel.

‘Belt up,’ said Roger. I obeyed. Then he slipped into the seat I’d just vacated and slammed the door, shutting out the rush of traffic. He pushed himself well back and away from me, the gun still held in his hand, still pointing straight at me.

‘I thought we had an agreement,’ I said, my voice unsteady.

‘We do. I just didn’t mention all the caveats. But then, neither did you. Like taping our conversation.’

‘I don’t know what you mean.’ I did, of course, and can’t have sounded genuinely uncomprehending. But I had to mount some kind of pretence.

‘You ran the tape to the end of the séance when I went in to see Delia, then started recording when I came back out. I saw you reach into your pocket to press the button as I came down the drive. I probably wouldn’t have noticed, but I was looking out for it, you see. I was expecting it.’

‘Why didn’t you stop me?’

‘No need. What can be recorded can just as easily be erased.’

'You want the tape?'

'Not yet. And there's no need to switch the machine off. Let's just carry on as we are. Start driving.'

'Where to?'

'Straight ahead.'

'To Eastbourne?'

'Just drive. I'll handle the navigation.'

I put the car into gear, edged out into the traffic and took her up to fifty.

'Give her a bit more. She likes to cruise.'

I accelerated. We flashed past a sign: EASTBOURNE 10, HASTINGS 22. The road ahead was a ribbon of drizzle-glossed black between dun-green fields. Low grey cloud had camped on the downs to our right. The chilling thought struck me that I might never see the sun again. This could be it: a dull winter's day my last on Earth.

'Nothing to say, Toby? Perhaps you should stop recording after all.'

'Why don't you do the talking?' I cast him a quick glance. 'You've done most of it so far.'

'Why do you think I've told you the truth?'

'I don't know.'

'Think about it.'

'*I don't know*.'

'I'm serious. Think, Toby. What possible purpose could it have served? Take your time. Mull it over. We've a few miles to go yet.'

'I could never prove you conspired with Kenneth Oswin to murder your father.'

'Without the tape, you mean? No. I don't suppose you could. But you could tell Jenny what I've told you. If you could convince her it was true, she and I would be finished.'

'She wouldn't believe me.'

'Maybe she would. Maybe she wouldn't. Who can say? If someone else corroborated the story, of course, she'd have to believe it. She'd have no choice.'

'No-one else knows. You said so yourself.'

'Did I? I must have forgotten Delia.'

'*Delia?*'

'She prevaricated when you challenged her about her hospital visit to Oswin. I noticed the way she avoided my eye when she said she had a few 'doubts' about Oswin's truthfulness. I could see it was more than that. She knew he'd lied when he denied I'd spoken to him about my parentage. And she knew why he'd lied.'

It was suddenly as clear to me as it was to Roger. '*Why should he lie?*' I'd asked her. '*Ah,*' she'd replied. '*Clearly there are limits to your perceptiveness.*' Yes. There were limits to my perceptiveness. But not, apparently, to hers.

'When did she rumble me, I wonder?' said Roger, musingly. 'There and then in the hospital with Oswin? Or later? Well, it doesn't matter now. It doesn't matter at all. Because I've devised a solution to all my problems. And you're it, Toby.'

'What?'

'I'll explain when we reach our destination. Speaking of which, I need to set up our rendezvous there with Jenny.' He plucked a mobile phone out of his pocket with his free hand.

'Don't drag her into whatever you're planning, Roger.' I glanced pleadingly at him. 'For God's sake.'

'Don't worry. At least' — he gave me a lopsided grin — 'don't worry about Jenny. She's going to be fine. I'll make sure of that. Now, keep your mouth shut.' He extended his arm until the barrel of the gun was jabbing into my ribs, then punched in some numbers on the phone and held it to his ear. A few seconds later, he got an answer. 'Good morning. I need to speak to one of your guests urgently. Her name's Jennifer Flood. My name's Roger Colborn. Yes, I'll hold.' A few more seconds passed. 'Thanks.' Then a few more. When he next spoke, it was in a tone I hardly recognized as his. 'Hello, my sweet . . . Look, I'm sorry, but I persuaded Delia to tell me where you were staying . . . I know, but . . . Well, this *is* an emergency, I'm afraid. It's Toby. He's become completely unreasonable . . . None of my doing, I promise . . . I'm on my way to meet him now . . . I had to agree for Delia's sake . . . Well, naturally that's a worry, especially after what happened yesterday . . . He came to the house . . . Not pleasant, no . . . Look, I can't see this ending well unless you're there to talk him round . . . You will come, won't you? . . . It's for the best. We need to put a stop to this . . . Beachy Head.' So. Our destination was the place where Ann Colborn had gone to kill herself twenty years ago. My heart was racing now, sweat beading on my upper lip. Most of what Roger was telling Jenny he seemed to be making up as he went. But his prediction was spot-on. I couldn't see this ending well either. 'I don't know,' he continued. 'It makes no sense. But then he *isn't* making sense . . . Yes . . . The lay-by closest to the lighthouse . . . Right . . . You'll see the car . . . OK . . . Yes, I will be . . . See you soon . . . Love you . . . 'Bye.' He rang off and dropped the phone back into his pocket.

A minute or so of silence followed. Then I asked a question I wasn't sure I wanted answering. 'Why are we going to Beachy Head?'

'I'll explain when we get there.'

'But we're not just going to talk to Jenny, are we? We could have done that in Tunbridge Wells.'

'No, Toby. We're not just going to talk.'

'You said that if I could convince her you'd paid Kenneth Oswin to murder your father, she and you would be finished. You must realize the same certainly applies if you kill me.'

'That's true. So, maybe I won't kill you. *Maybe*. You'll find out soon enough. Until then, I'm not sure we have anything more to say to each other. Just drive. I'll give you directions when you need them.'

'But — '

'*Shut up*,' he shouted so loudly that I flinched. 'Question time's over.'

* * *

Aside from telling me which turnings to take and when, Roger Colborn didn't say another word as we skirted Eastbourne and headed south across the empty, rolling downs towards the end of the land and the end of our journey.

My fear didn't diminish as we went on. If anything, it increased. But I began, slowly and slightly, to control it, to calm my mind just enough to think about what he might be planning.

Little good it did me. If he meant to kill me, he surely wouldn't have told Jenny where we were going. But, if he meant to let me live, how could he guarantee I wouldn't, sooner or later, tell her what he'd confessed to me and play her the tape to prove it? How, come to that, could he be sure Jenny wouldn't phone Delia and be given a version of events wildly inconsistent with the one he'd just presented?

It made no sense. And yet it had to. Colborn was calm and confident. He knew exactly what he was doing. He'd thought of everything. He had a plan. And I was central to it.

* * *

The next words I spoke were, 'Is this where your mother came?' We were in a lay-by on a sharp curve in the road along Beachy Head. Beyond a low bank, the ground sloped up ahead of us for less than a hundred yards to the cliff top. It was cold and grey and drizzly, cloud drifting like gunsmoke across the hummocked turf and wind-sculpted patches of gorse, the disused lighthouse on the bluff to the east blurred by the misting fret. There wasn't another car — another human — in sight.

'Yes,' said Colborn, in laggardly answer to my

question. 'Witnesses reported that she sat here in the Jag, engine running, for several minutes, then drove straight up the slope — and over.'

'If you're planning some kind of double suicide . . . '

'No. Turn the engine off if it'll reassure you.'

It did, though not a lot. Silence wrapped itself around us, broken by the mournful wail of the foghorn on the new lighthouse out of our sight at the foot of the cliff.

'There was no bank round the lay-by when Mother killed herself,' Colborn resumed. 'But then it's only really intended to prevent accidents. You could get over easily enough with a few runs at it. Then it's a straight drive to a sheer drop of more than five hundred feet. Death guaranteed. It's a popular spot for suicide. Twenty or so every year. And the number's climbing. It draws them. The closeness to the road. The certainty. The symbolism. End of land. End of life.'

'Why are we here?'

'For you to make a choice, Toby. For you to decide what happens to us — you, me and Jenny.'

'What choice do I really have? You're holding the gun.'

'It'll be another half an hour at least before Jenny arrives. We have some time. Just enough, in fact.' He stretched forward, opened the glove compartment, took out a pair of thin leather driving gloves and tossed them into my lap. 'Put those on.'

'Why?'

'Do it. Then I'll explain.'

'All right.' I pulled them on. 'Now, why?'

'Because there has to be some way to account for your fingerprints not being on the gun. *If* it's ever recovered.'

'What are you talking about?'

'It may have struck you that if Jenny phones Delia — as she well might — she'll realize I've lied to her.'

'It's struck me.'

'Not actually a problem, however, because if Jenny does phone Delia, she won't be able to speak to her.'

'Why not?'

'Delia's dead, Toby. That's why not.'

I looked round at him. 'You . . . ' The horror of what he was saying burst into my mind. 'You . . . killed her . . . when you went back . . . into the house?'

'I had to. She knew what I'd done. I mean, she probably knew a long time ago. But this morning she knew without a shadow of a doubt. And with you as an ally, she wouldn't have let it lie. Believe me. I had no choice. It was her or me. I asked her for the phone number of the Spa Hotel. She'd written it on a post-it note stuck to a cupboard door in the kitchen. I shot her through the back of the head as she reached up for it. There was a lot of blood. More than I'd expected.' He took something out of his pocket — a small, crumpled piece of bright-red paper — and stuck it to the dashboard: it was the post-it note; as it curled up, I saw that the back was still the original yellow. 'Lucky I was standing out in the hall. I didn't get a speck on me.'

'My God.'

'I left the car engine running so you wouldn't hear the shot.'

'You're mad. You must be. To . . . murder your aunt.'

'I don't feel mad. And it was you who reminded me that she wasn't really my aunt at all. Besides, I didn't do it. You did, Toby. You went back in and shot her, then forced me to drive here at gunpoint, phoning Jenny on the way.'

'No-one will believe that.'

'I think they will. You intended to kill us both and have Jenny arrive to be confronted by the tragic consequences of rejecting you. But the enormity of what you'd done to Delia got the better of you. You decided at the last moment to spare my life. You let me get out of the car. Then you drove it off the cliff.'

'I won't do it.'

'I can't force you to. But if you don't, when Jenny arrives . . . I'll kill you both.'

'*What?*'

'I won't let you have her, Toby. There's no way in this world I'll allow that. If you try to drag me down, I'll take us all down.'

'You said . . . you love her.'

'I do. More than life itself.'

'You *are* mad.'

'That's your opinion. And this is your choice. Prove *you* love her. By sacrificing yourself to save her. I'll look after her. I'll help her get over it. I'll make her happy. Happier than you ever could.

I'll even keep the tape in a safe and secure place so that one day, after my death, the truth will be uncovered. You'll be a hero. A posthumous one, it's true. But a hero none the less.'

I stared at him, sick with the certainty that he wasn't bluffing. He'd already killed once. Twice, if you counted his father. He had nothing to lose. If I didn't take the blame for what he'd done, he'd destroy us all. The offer to salvage my reputation one day was so unlikely it might even be genuine. But we'd both be dead by then, in my case long dead, though probably not forgotten. Abandoning Jenny to a man I knew to be a murderer was a strange way to prove my love for her. Yet the alternative was worse. Only one question mattered. Would he do it? Would he kill her if I refused to co-operate? *Would he?*

'What's it to be, Toby? Death and glory? Or just death?'

'You said I had a choice.'

'So you do.'

'It doesn't feel like it.'

'Should I take that as a yes to death and glory?'

'Maybe.' It was a yes to something. But to neither of the options he'd presented. I could see only one way out. And it was by no means certain.

'I'll leave you to it, then,' he said. 'Hand over the tape.'

'I'll swap it for the gun.'

'Nice try, Toby. But the gun stays with me. You might reckon killing me is a smarter choice than suicide. Or you might bottle out at the last moment and try to drive away. I can't risk that.'

'The police won't buy your story unless the gun's found on me.'

'I'll drop it over the cliff after you. They'll conclude it was thrown out on impact.'

My escape was barred. It had been a frail hope that in truth was no hope at all. 'Don't do this, Roger. Please.'

'Too late for appeals to my better nature, Toby. Far too late. My mind's made up. Is yours?'

'Hold on. Let's — '

'No. Let's nothing. You give me your answer. Now.'

'All right. I . . . ' His gaze was fixed and unblinking. I took a deep breath. 'I'll do it.'

'Good. I knew you'd see it my way.'

'You mean you knew I'd have to.'

'Exactly. Stop recording now and give me the tape.' He held out his left hand. 'The rest . . . will be silence.'

Flood, Toby (1953–2002)
Bland English character actor. Started on the stage, then broke into TV as *Hereward the Wake*. A few film appearances, but Hollywood did not take to him. He returned to the stage, without his former success. Committed suicide at Beachy Head after murdering a woman in Brighton, where he was performing in a play.

Some such form of words, from a future edition of *Halliwell's Who's Who in the Movies*, recited itself in my head as I sat at the wheel of Roger

Colborn's Porsche and he climbed slowly out of the passenger seat, closing the door behind him with perfectly judged force. I saw him move away, then stop and look back at me.

I felt sick. My hand trembled as I reached for the ignition key. My breathing was shallow, my pulse racing. My palms were moist with sweat. I cursed Colborn and fate and my own stupidity for finding myself seemingly only a few minutes away from the death he'd arranged for me. I was going to end my life on Colborn's terms. I had to. Because every alternative was worse. That, apparently, was to be Toby Flood's quietus.

I started the engine, clunked the gearstick into reverse and edged back from the bank bounding the lay-by. Tears were fogging my vision now, tears of anger and fear and utter despair. I blinked them away and looked up the slope to the broken, dipping edge of the cliff. Beyond it, I knew, was thin air and the sea far below — a plummet to certain death. 'Dear Christ,' I murmured. 'What a bloody awful way to go.' I slipped the gearstick into neutral.

Then I saw movement ahead of me. A figure had emerged from behind one of the clumps of gorse and thorn dotting the slope and was hurrying towards me across the grass. It was a mop-haired man, dressed in duffel-coat, jeans and desert boots. It was Derek Oswin.

I glanced at Colborn and realized he hadn't yet seen the approaching figure. I couldn't even guess what would happen when he did. And I had only a few seconds in which to forestall him. I yanked on the brake and jumped out.

'What the hell are you doing?' shouted Colborn. 'Get back in the car.'

'We have company, Roger,' I responded as I rounded the bonnet. 'You'd better put the gun out of sight.'

Colborn glanced round and saw at once what I meant. He drew his right arm in close to his side, shielding the gun from Derek's view. A spasm of cold fury crossed his face and he shot me a glare that implied I was somehow responsible for this apparition.

'Mr Flood,' Derek called. 'And . . . Mr Colborn.' He reached the top of the bank and stood there, looking down at us. He was breathing hard, his cheeks flushed from exertion. 'I th-th-thought . . . I'd f-find you here.'

'Where have you been these past few days, Derek?' I asked. 'I've missed you.'

'A . . . guesthouse in Bognor Regis. Very . . . r-reasonably p-priced . . . at this time of the year. I'm . . . sorry if I . . . caused you any . . . anxiety.'

'You trashed your house yourself, didn't you?'

'I . . . m-messed it up a little, it's . . . true.'

'Stole my tapes.'

'B-borrowed them . . . Mr Flood.'

'And stole the manuscript from my agent.'

'R-reclaimed.'

'I told you,' said Colborn, in a steely undertone.

'Why?' I asked softly, the anger I should have felt at being manipulated by Derek Oswin supplanted by a steadily growing hope that his intervention might somehow save the day.

'To . . . see what would happen.'

'*'See what would happen*'?'

'But I . . . think I went too far.'

'That, Derek, is the understatement of the century.'

'It's a b-bit early to say, d-don't you think . . . Mr Flood? W-with . . . ninety-eight years st-still to go . . . I mean.'

'How did you know we'd be here?'

'I d-didn't. Not for certain. It was just . . . a hunch. I've been ch-checking the house each day . . . to see if you'd discovered the t-tape in the globe. I must . . . have just missed you this morning. When I found the tape was gone, I knew you were on the last lap. Thanks for pinning Captain Haddock back on my coat, Mr Flood.' He was talking more confidently now, the stutters and hesitations fading. 'I went to see Uncle Ray, to find out if you'd spoken to him . . . about Dad . . . and Mrs Colborn.' Slowly, as Derek continued, Roger Colborn turned to look at him, crooking his arm behind his back to obscure the gun. 'He told me you'd gone to see Mrs Sheringham, so I got him to drive me round there. P-Powis Villas was cordoned off by the police. There'd been a m-murder. Of Mrs Sheringham . . . one of the neighbours said. She'd seen Mr Sheringham, looking . . . very upset. And a P-Porsche had been spotted . . . driving away. Well, I knew what that meant. I g-guessed . . . Mr Colborn . . . would bring you here . . . b-because of his mother. I left Uncle Ray . . . in the car park . . . at the Visitor Centre.' He nodded in the direction of the building whose roof I could just make out through the murk on the eastern skyline. 'I . . . suppose, logically, I shouldn't have come. I mean, you could argue my plan's . . . worked out b-better than I could ever have hoped.'

'Go on, then,' said Roger. 'Argue that.'

'Well, you're . . . finished, aren't you . . . Mr Colborn?' For the first time, Derek was addressing his half-brother directly. 'I've b-brought you down.'

'It wouldn't have worked if you'd stayed away, Derek,' I said, edging closer to Colborn. 'He'd devised a way to pin the murder on me. After I'd conveniently driven off the cliff.'

Derek blinked at me in surprise. And then at Colborn. 'R-really?'

'Yes,' said Roger. 'Really.'

'That's t-terrible. I'd . . . ' Derek looked back at me. 'I'd n-never . . . have let him . . . get away with that . . . Mr Flood.'

'No,' said Roger. 'I don't suppose you would. Which makes your arrival here . . . quite fortuitous.'

I saw the decision taking shape in the sudden tensing of Colborn's face. He could still pull it off, by blaming a second murder on me, one that only increased his chances of laying the first at my door as well. He swivelled to face Derek, swinging the gun out from behind him and taking his eyes off me as he did so.

I slammed into his midriff in a stooping charge, capitalizing on the only advantage I had: weight. I caught him off balance and he fell. The gun went off with a deafening crack close to my left ear. We hit the tarmac hard. For the moment, I could hear even less than I could see. I looked up in desperate search of Derek. And there he was in front of me, hopping down the bank and bending to grab the gun which had slipped from Colborn's grasp as we fell.

'Run,' I shouted. And Derek did run, back up the bank and away across the grass towards the cliff, the gun clutched by the barrel in his right hand.

Then Colborn's elbow struck me hard under the chin, hurling me sideways with my tongue viced agonizingly between my teeth. I rolled onto my back, then struggled up to see Colborn already over the bank, racing in pursuit of Derek. I scrambled to my feet and headed after them.

They were about ten yards apart and stayed that way, fear offsetting for Derek any edge Colborn's greater athleticism should have given him. They were running hard across the wet turf, following a beeline to the edge of the cliff. My lungs strained as I followed them, my chest tightening, my left ear ringing. I could hear nothing except my own panting breaths, could see nothing but the two figures ahead of me, one in black, one in brown, moving like fleet ghosts in the thickening fret.

Derek came to a stumbling halt a few feet short of the edge and tossed the gun over. Then he turned to face Colborn, who'd stopped in the same instant, those vital ten yards behind. But I kept running.

Derek was smiling. He opened his mouth

and spoke, but I couldn't catch the words. Whether Roger said anything in reply I had no way of telling. He glanced back over his shoulder at me, judging my distance, measuring his moment. Then he turned and ran straight at Derek.

Derek's only chance was to run away from the edge, towards Roger. But he shrank back, if anything closer to the edge. Maybe he hadn't realized what Roger's final way out of all his problems was to be. Or maybe he *had* realized. Maybe that was why he didn't try to evade his brother's embrace.

They went over together, Roger's arms wrapped round Derek's waist, the momentum of his charge carrying them out a yard or so into the grey void before they began to fall.

They were still together when I reached the edge. I dropped, gasping, to my knees and watched the few remaining seconds of their descent.

They struck the foot of the cliff and rolled apart down the beach. The sea lapped in around them. And retreated, foaming red.

⋆ ⋆ ⋆

That was then. This is now. Late. Very late. Too late, for Derek Oswin and Delia Sheringham. And for Roger Colborn too. Three deaths. And every one of them could have been mine.

⋆ ⋆ ⋆

Late, like I said. But still too early to impose a strict order on the events that followed that double fall from the cliff. I remember the lighthouse offshore, banded the colours of blood and chalk; the cliff face, pale as bleached bone; the seagulls, muted by my deafness, gliding wraithlike in and out of the mist; and Derek's strange, triumphant smile. I remember all those things. Their clarity seems to grow, indeed, as much else fades.

I flagged down a car and the driver called the police on his mobile. He ferried me the short distance to the Visitor Centre, where I found Ray Braddock waiting patiently for his godson to return. I can't recall how I broke the news to him, nor how he reacted. He was sitting in his car, hunched at the wheel, staring straight ahead, when I walked away.

I returned to the lay-by and waited by the Porsche for Jenny. Maybe it was just as well, in the circumstances, that the police arrived before she did.

Initially, it was just one patrol car. The two policemen in it got the message in the end that this was no routine suicide and contacted Brighton CID. A coastguard crew followed and surveyed the scene down on the beach from the cliff top. They started to set up some sort of derrick preparatory to winching down with stretchers to recover the bodies.

Then Jenny did arrive. Exactly what the police told her I couldn't catch. Whatever it was, she clearly couldn't take it all in at first. The officers tried to keep us apart. I remember the look on her face as she stared at me between their broad shoulders across the lay-by. She probably still thought Roger had been telling the truth when he phoned her from the car. She probably thought I was mad. She started shouting. '*What have you done?*' And crying. '*What have you done?*'

Two more police cars arrived. I was bundled into one of them and driven to Eastbourne General Hospital. On the way, I noticed that my ear had been bleeding. I was fast-tracked through Casualty and into a cubicle, burly policeman in attendance. A young doctor looked me over. He pronounced the eardrum intact and said my hearing would slowly recover over the next twenty-four hours. It already was recovering, in fact, though shock prevented the improvement doing much for my coherence.

Then a familiar face showed up: Sergeant Spooner. I was loaded into another police car and driven to CID headquarters on the northern outskirts of Brighton. There I was put in a blank-walled interview room, given a mug of tea and a ham sandwich and left alone for more than an hour. What they were waiting for I didn't know. Most probably they were listening to the tape I'd told them they'd find in Roger Colborn's pocket and trying to decide for themselves what had happened that morning at Powis Villas and Beachy Head — and why.

Eventually, Spooner came in with Inspector Addis and the questioning began. They knew now that I'd lied to them yesterday when they'd asked me about Ian Maple. But, thanks to the tape, they also knew I'd stopped lying. We went through everything, step by step. At least, I suppose we did. I can't recall more than a fraction of what was said. I should probably have asked for a lawyer to be present. They may even have encouraged me to. But I couldn't see the point. There was only one story to tell now: the truth.

In the end, Addis couldn't seem to decide whether to reprimand me or sympathize. The gist of what he said was that Ian Maple and I should have come to him with our suspicions on Thursday. Then none of this need have happened. Three people who were now dead would still be alive, Ian wouldn't be in hospital with a smashed leg and I wouldn't be . . . I think he left me to sum up my condition for myself. I didn't argue. I didn't have the strength, let alone the will.

'You can go now, sir,' he said at some point, after I'd signed a statement and drunk some more tea. 'When will you be returning to London?'

'Tomorrow, I expect.'

'I dare say we'll be in touch with you there. The press will be on to you for certain, you being a bit of a celebrity and all. Tell them nothing. If I hear you've sold your story to one of the tabloids, I may have to take a serious look at whether you should be charged with breaking and entering, or wasting police time, or . . . whatever. Catch my drift?'

'You seriously think I want this splashed over the papers?'

'I don't know, sir. You might decide it'd be helpful to your career.'

'Talking of which, sir,' put in Spooner, 'we spoke to a Mr Sallis at the theatre and explained the situation. As best we could.'

'Thanks.'

'Will you be wanting to be dropped somewhere? We can arrange a car.'

'I'd like to . . . see my wife.'

'Not sure I'd recommend that, sir. I gather she insisted on remaining at the scene until they'd brought up the bodies. Wanted to be certain Mr Colborn really was one of them, I suppose. That was pretty upsetting, as you can imagine, given the state they were in and the fact that Mr Braddock was there as well. A WPC's with her out at Wickhurst Manor as we speak, waiting for Mrs Flood's sister to arrive. A Mrs Butler. I presume you're acquainted with the lady.'

'Yes. We're acquainted.' It was natural enough for Jenny to turn to Fiona in a crisis.

'We'll be seeing Mrs Flood later to report our preliminary conclusions. It might be best if you postponed a visit until after that.'

'Perhaps I could . . . phone her.'

'Be our guest.'

'And those . . . preliminary conclusions. What are they?'

'You already know, sir,' said Addis. 'You knew before we did.'

* * *

Spooner brought in a phone for me to use, then I was left alone. I stared at the thing for several minutes, struggling to form some words into a sentence that might somehow measure up to the bloody havoc I'd played no small part in inflicting on Jenny's life that morning. I still hadn't succeeded when I picked the phone up and rang her mobile. It was switched off and I didn't leave a message. I tried the house number instead.

The WPC answered and seemed reluctant even to ask Jenny if she wanted to speak to me. She came back to say that Jenny was too upset to come to the phone. I sensed a wall was being thrown up between us. But for the moment there was nothing I could do to break it down.

⋆ ⋆ ⋆

In the end, I declined the offer of a lift and left the police station on foot. Business was frenzied at the nearby superstore. I walked past the jam-packed car park and looked up at the shoppers wheeling out their laden trolleys. It was a normal pre-Christmas Saturday evening for them. The murder at Powis Villas and the deaths at Beachy Head were minor news items. Their futures were unaltered, their lives unaffected. The world went on its way. As it always does.

⋆ ⋆ ⋆

I can't remember how far I was intending to walk. I doubt in fact if I had much in the way of intentions at all. Somewhere in the seemingly endless sprawl of housing I found myself wandering through, I boarded a bus to the Old Steine. I sat at the back and kept my head down. No-one noticed me.

I felt numb, disconnected, overwhelmed by events. My hearing had recovered, but my thinking hadn't. I slunk into a crowded pub in St James's Street and downed several whiskies. Probably more than several. Then I headed for the Sea Air.

* * *

Eunice's greeting was double-edged. She was relieved to see me in one piece, alive and relatively well. But she was also angry over my failure to keep in touch.

'It's only thanks to Brian Sallis and the police that I haven't been worried sick about you. Though what they told me didn't exactly stop me worrying. Seems you've been through the mill, Toby, and no mistake, so I suppose I'd better not be as hard on you as I'm tempted to be. Come downstairs and I'll rustle you up something to eat.'

Protesting that I wasn't hungry did me no good and I was soon perched blearily at the breakfast bar in her kitchen, picking at cauliflower cheese and admitting to myself that, of all the various ends to the day that had seemed possible to me in the course of it, this had certainly not featured.

'What did Brian say?' I wincingly enquired.

‘That you’d got mixed up in some dreadful goings-on and been taken hostage by a murderer. Is that really true, Toby?’

‘Oh yes. It’s true.’

‘But the murderer threw himself off Beachy Head?’

‘Yes.’

‘And you were there at the time?’

‘Yes. I was.’

‘It’s mortifying just to think about it.’

‘So it is.’

‘The things that happen while we law-abiding folk are going about our daily lives.’

‘I’ll tell you all about it . . . when it’s not so raw in my mind.’

‘But the murderer . . . was your wife’s . . . ’

‘Can we leave it, Eunice? I honestly can’t — ’

‘Sorry.’ She gave me a sudden and genuinely affectionate hug. ‘You don’t want me rabbiting on.’

‘It’s all right. I . . . What did Brian say . . . about the play?’

‘Nothing. Except that . . . well . . . ’

‘What?’

‘They’re coping without you.’

I managed a rueful half-smile. ‘No doubt he meant that to be reassuring.’

‘You could always . . . phone him.’

‘I don’t think so.’

‘Are you still planning to go back to London tomorrow?’

‘I suppose so. It’s probably best, after all. Look at what’s happened in the six days I’ve been here.’ I thought about that for a protracted moment, as a forkful of cauliflower cheese congealed on the plate in front of me. 'Yes. It's probably best.'

* * *

That was not so long ago. This is now. Late. Very late. Too late, for Derek Oswin and Delia Sheringham. And for Roger Colborn too. But for Jenny and me? I don't know. She should be grateful to me for discovering Colborn's true nature before she married him. But I doubt she feels grateful. I doubt that very much.

I should give her a chance for the shock to fade, of course, for the grief to give way to an understanding of what he was and what he did. I should go back to London and bide my time. I should let my own wounds heal as well as hers.

Yes. That's what I should do. That's definitely what I should do. It's for the best.

Probably.

SUNDAY

I have no memory of lying awake until the small hours last night, struggling to accommodate in my mind everything that had happened. I would have expected sleep to be as hard to come by as hope and consolation, but, strangely, it wasn't. Exhaustion asserted its imperative. I plunged into a deep, absolving unconsciousness.

* * *

I hadn't closed the curtains of my room and was woken by the stealthy grey onset of dawn. A few seconds later, I realized that, no, I hadn't dreamt the events of yesterday. Only in a fast-fading dream, in fact, could I walk along a railway viaduct with Derek Oswin high above Brighton and pull him back from the parapet when he seemed about to fall. In the real world, where I dwelt and had to go on dwelling, he was beyond saving. Nor was he alone in that.

I showered and shaved hurriedly, then dressed and packed for my departure, sensing it might be best if, when I returned later, I could just grab my bag and go. Whatever logic and calculation had suggested was my wisest course of action, it wasn't what I meant to do. I had to speak to Jenny. I had to *see* her. Without delay.

* * *

But someone else had decided to see *me*, also without delay. As I closed the door of the Sea Air quietly behind me and stepped out into the dank, chill, silent morning, there was a beep on the horn of one of the cars parked on the other side of the street.

It was a battered old Metro. The driver's window had been wound down. And Ray Braddock was staring out at me.

I walked slowly across to speak to him, wondering what I'd find to say and remembering Colborn's taunt about actors needing lines to be written for them before they could sound convincing.

'Sneaking off back to London?' Braddock asked. He was unshaven, his eyes red-rimmed, his manner bleak.

'I'm sorry about Derek, Ray,' I said, holding his gaze determinedly. 'Truly I am.'

'You said you'd look after the boy.'

'I don't think I — '

'You said it would all blow over.'

I let his accusing glare seep into me. 'I was wrong.'

'I tried to stop him going round the cliff to find you and Colborn. I told him to think of himself. But he wouldn't have it. 'I got Mr Flood into this,' he said. 'I've got to get him out.' '

'He said that?'

'He did.'

'Well, he was as good as his word, Ray. He got me out.'

'He saved your life.'

'Yes.'

'At the cost of his own.'

'No doubt you wish it was the other way about.'

'I do.'

'But you can be proud of him. You really can. Isn't that something?'

'When you're old and poor and lonely . . . it's sod all.'

'I'm sorry.' It was true. I *was* sorry. But it was also true that my sorrow wasn't enough. For either of us.

'I don't think Derek got you into anything,' said Braddock. 'I think you got yourself in. And I wish to God you hadn't.'

'You may be right. In which case . . . ' I shrugged. 'I wish the same.'

'Do you now?' Braddock's anger suddenly ebbed. His expression softened marginally. He shook his head dolefully. 'Fool to himself, that boy. Just like his father.'

'There are worse things to be.'

'So there are.' He sighed. 'If you want to . . . show your respect . . . for what he did . . . '

I suddenly noticed that he was proffering something to me through the window: a small white card. I took it and found myself looking at the name, address and telephone number of a local undertaker.

'They'll be able to tell you when the funeral is.'

'Thanks. I . . . '

'It's up to you.' Braddock started the car. 'I'd best be off. Looks like someone else wants to speak to you.'

'What?' I turned and saw Brian Sallis standing on the pavement outside the Sea Air in his jogging kit.

'Good morning, Toby,' he said solemnly.

'Brian. I . . . ' I walked across to him, glancing round as I heard the Metro draw away.

'Who was that?'

'Derek Oswin's godfather.'

'I see.' Brian gave me what was meant to be a sympathetic pat on the shoulder. 'This has been a bad business.'

I nodded. 'You can say that again.'

'I've been trying to raise you on your mobile.'

'I . . . mislaid it.'

'Where are you off to now?'

'The taxi rank in East Street.'

'Can I walk with you?'

'Sure.'

We set off and reached the end of Madeira Place before another word was spoken, the right thing to say proving equally elusive for both of us.

'I'm sorry . . . not to have been in touch,' I said as we rounded the corner into St James's Street.

'Don't worry about that. At the time, we were all pretty narked, but . . . well, from what the police tell me, the circumstances were about as extenuating as they come.'

'I gather you coped without me.'

'I went on for you.'

'Yes.' I winced at the thought of Brian stumbling through my part, script in hand. 'I suppose you had to.'

'It's been a while since I did any acting, I know, but . . . I quite enjoyed it, as a matter of fact.'

'I've never experienced someone going on with the book. I can't believe it's enjoyable, though.'

'Well, actually . . . '

'What?'

'By last night, I was word perfect. I'd already boned up on the part, you see. With Denis gone and you . . . behaving erratically . . . I . . . '

We were crossing the Old Steine as Brian mentioned Denis, no more than fifteen yards from the fountain where I'd found him dead on Tuesday night. I kept my eyes fixed on the middle distance, straight ahead. 'You saw it coming, did you, Brian?'

'Not . . . what happened. Of course not. I mean . . . '

'It's all right. I understand. How did Leo react to news of my absence?'

'Ballistically. But he doesn't know the reason yet. When he does . . . '

'He'll soften. But not enough to hire me again in a hurry.'

'I wouldn't say that.'

'You don't need to.'

'Look, Toby, you've been through a terrible experience. I don't want to add to your woes. I'll make sure Leo appreciates that you missed the last three performances through no fault of your own.'

'Thanks.'

'When are you going back to London?'

‘Later today.’

‘Probably wise. I haven’t heard from the press, local *or* national, so I’m guessing they haven’t tied you in with yesterday’s events yet. But they will. It’ll be easier to lie low in London than here. Unless you’re going on somewhere else, of course.’

‘I haven’t thought that far ahead.’

‘Most of us are catching the eleven fifty up to Victoria, if you want to — ’

‘There are things I have to do first, Brian.’ I stopped at the corner of East Street and signalled to the driver of the only taxi on the rank. ‘I doubt you’ll see me on the eleven fifty.’

‘How’s Jenny taken all this?’

‘I don’t know. That’s one of the things I have to do.’

* * *

There was no sign of the press out at Wickhurst Manor either, which was a blessing. I had the taxi driver, a mercifully tight-lipped bloke, drop me at the end of the lane leading to Stonestaples Wood as an additional precaution and approached the firmly closed gates on foot.

At first, there was no response to the intercom button. But I persisted, reckoning there was close to no chance that Jenny would be anywhere but at home. If Wickhurst Manor could properly be regarded as her home any more, that is.

Eventually, there *was* a response. I recognized the voice as Fiona’s. ‘Yes?’ She was probably expecting the press. She sounded as if she meant to see off whoever it might be in short order.

'It's me, Fiona. Toby.'

There was a brief silence. I thought I heard a sigh. 'You shouldn't have come here, Toby.'

'I have to see Jenny.'

'That's really not a good idea.'

'Let me in, Fiona. Please.'

'I . . . don't think I can.'

'For God's sake . . . '

'You should have phoned first.'

'I'll go into Fulking if you like and phone from the call box for an appointment.'

'Don't be ridiculous.'

'Then, let me in.'

'No.'

'Fiona — '

'Sorry, Toby. I have to put Jenny first. Phone later. Maybe tonight. Or tomorrow. But not now.'

She switched off the intercom and I was left staring at the grille, rooks cawing around me in the trees, a fine drizzle filming the steel plate set in the pillar in front of me. I pushed the button again. There was no answer.

I stepped back and surveyed the gates. It looked as if someone younger and fitter than me could climb them.

But they weren't about to try. I was.

* * *

Fiona opened the front door of Wickhurst Manor five minutes or so later with the weary look of someone who knows what they're going to see. A sororial resemblance to Jenny has never extended in her case to a fondness for me. She's always regarded actors as suspect by definition — unstable, unreliable and essentially undesirable.

'Couldn't you just for once have taken my advice?' she snapped, pursing her lips irritably.

'It didn't sound like advice.'

'That's because you weren't listening properly.'

'Can I come in?'

'What have you done to your leg?' She glanced down at my left ankle. There was a V-shaped tear just above the hem of my trousers where I'd snagged them on the spike at the top of one of the gate pales. When I looked down myself, I saw there was blood seeping through the hole. Fiona gave a heavy sigh. 'Come into the kitchen. And keep your voice down. Jenny's asleep. I'd like her to stay that way.'

I followed her into the hall and round to the large north-facing kitchen at the back of the house. Its windows looked out onto the lawn I'd crossed under cover of dusk on Friday afternoon. My last visit to Wickhurst Manor felt far more distant to me than it really was, almost from a different age.

'Sit down there,' said Fiona, pointing to a chair by the kitchen table as she closed the door behind us. 'And roll up your trouser leg.'

For the next few minutes, she busied herself with soap, water, Dettol and sticking plaster in a fashion I guessed her two sons would easily recognize, repeating phrases like 'Such a very stupid thing to do' under her breath as she cleaned me up. The dog wandered in from the scullery, regarded us mournfully, and wandered back out. Then Fiona pronounced the job done and turned briskly to more serious matters.

'You shouldn't have come, Toby, you really shouldn't. Have you any idea how big a shock this has been to Jenny?'

'Yesterday didn't exactly pan out as I'd expected either.'

'But you haven't lost a fiancé, have you? Or a close friend. Delia's death seems to have affected her almost as deeply as Roger's. And it's hard for her at the moment not to blame you for both.'

'*Me?*'

'She loved Roger, Toby. Learning he was capable of murder doesn't alter that overnight.'

'More than capable. Guilty.'

'Yes. I know. He was a monster. A bigger one than I ever suspected. But, let's face it, if you hadn't — '

The door sprang open and Jenny walked into the room. She was in a dressing-gown and slippers, her hair scraped back, her face pale, almost grey, but for the moist redness round her bloodshot eyes. She'd been crying and was clearly still on the verge of tears. And she was trembling, her fingers shaking as she smoothed the collar of her robe, her lips quivering as she looked at me and tried to speak.

Fiona and I both stood up. Fiona moved towards her. But Jenny held up a hand, signalling that she needed a little distance, a little space in which to compose herself.

'I thought you were sleeping,' said Fiona.

'I heard the door,' Jenny responded after a few seconds' delay, like someone communicating via an interpreter. 'And Toby's voice.'

'I had to come,' I said, willing Jenny to hold my gaze over her sister's shoulder.

'I suppose you did.'

'Can we talk?'

'Would you be able . . . to drive Toby back into Brighton, Fiona?'

'Of course,' Fiona replied.

'Good. Just . . . give us a few minutes . . . would you?'

'OK. I . . . ' Fiona glanced round at me, then back at Jenny. 'OK.'

She slipped out of the room then, closing the door gently behind her. I heard myself swallow nervously in the silence that followed. Then the dog pattered back into the room and ambled to Jenny's side, where he nosed at her hand.

'He misses his master,' she said neutrally, almost observationally.

'How are you — '

'*Don't*. Please don't.' Her voice cracked. She took a deep breath. Then another. 'Just listen to me, Toby. Please. The police told me everything. I know it all. What Roger did to his father. Both his fathers. And to Delia. And to Derek Oswin. What he *tried* to do to you as well. I never . . . saw that side of him. It seems I never . . . grasped his true nature. I've been a fool. An utter fool. Maybe I should thank you for forcing me to understand that.'

'I never meant it to turn out like this.'

'Of course not. Who would? But if you'd waited till I got back . . . If you'd only . . . bided your time . . . nobody need have died yesterday, need they? That's what I can't help thinking, you see. Delia, Derek Oswin, Roger. They'd all be alive. With plenty to face up to, it's true. With a great deal to answer for, in Roger's case. But they'd be *alive*. Living and breathing. However dreadful it would be, at least we could talk about it, Roger and I. At least — ' She stifled a sob. 'I blame myself. For involving you. For letting you . . . back into my life. I should have known better. I really should. You kill everything you touch.'

Grief and anger and a measure of shame were mixed in what she'd said. I knew that. The one victim she hadn't mentioned — our son — had been added implicitly to the list. Fiona was right. I'd come too soon. And Jenny was right too. I hadn't known when to bide my time. I never had. There was nothing I could say in answer to the charge. I stared at her with a tenderness I couldn't express. I forgave her. For not forgiving me.

'I can't think about the future now,' she went on. 'There's just . . . too much to contemplate. John — Delia's husband — is distraught. The police will be back. And the press will be onto the case. It's all . . . horrible. Too horrible for words. That's why I can't bear there to be any between us, Toby. Words, I mean. I just . . . can't do it.' She pressed the heel of her hand to her eyes and looked at me. 'Please go. We'll talk. Of course we will. We'll have to. But not here. Not now. Not . . . any time soon. You understand?'

I didn't speak. I didn't even nod. But she took some fractional narrowing of my gaze as a kind of confirmation. I didn't agree. I didn't accept. Yet, nevertheless . . . I understood.

'Please go.'

* * *

Nothing was said during the drive into Brighton. Fiona, never one to waste her words, didn't bother to point out how big a mistake my visit to Wickhurst Manor had been. It was as she'd tried to warn me it would be. It was too soon. And it was probably too late as well.

'Shall I wait outside while you pick up your luggage, then run you up to the station?' Fiona asked as we headed down Grand Parade towards the Sea Air. She'd broken her lengthy silence, I noticed, only for the most practical of reasons.

'Thanks,' I replied. Then I remembered what the numbing anguish of my parting from Jenny had blotted out. I wasn't yet free to go — even if I wanted to. 'Actually, no. Drop me at the hospital. There's someone I have to see.'

* * *

Ian Maple was in a room of his own, off a ward deep in the rabbit warren of the Royal Sussex. His right leg wasn't in a plaster cast, as I'd expected. Instead, the section between the knee and the ankle was held fast in an armature of wires and pins. That apart — which was a lot to disregard — he looked well. And his greeting was somewhat warmer than I'd expected.

'I wondered if I'd see you before you left,' he said by way of lightly ironic opener.

'I must have caused you a lot of anxiety by holding out on the police,' I responded, lowering myself onto a bedside chair. 'I *am* sorry.'

'I guessed you had good reason.'

'I thought I did, certainly.'

'I'm not sure they ever seriously thought I was in business with Sobotka, anyway. They just couldn't see the big picture, that's all.'

'They see it now.'

'Yeah. Three dead, including Roger Colborn.' Ian shook his head. 'I wanted to make someone pay for what happened to Denis. But this . . . is too much.'

'Jenny blames me for the way it's turned out.'

'You didn't force Colborn to murder his aunt. Or Derek Oswin. You couldn't have predicted how the guy would react under pressure.'

'No. But I'll tell you something, Ian. I was determined to find out.'

'And now you have.'

'Yes.' I looked past him. 'Now I have.' My gaze wandered to his braced and cradled leg. 'What do the doctors say about that?'

'That it'll mend. Slowly. I might need another operation. I'll definitely need a lot of physiotherapy. I'll be off work . . . for months.' What was his work? I realized I'd never bothered to ask. 'I'll have to go to Denis's funeral in a wheelchair.'

'When will it be?'

'Thursday. Golders Green Crematorium.'

'I'll see you there.'

'Yeah. Time enough to worry about the future after that, hey?'

'Oh yes.' I nodded. 'Plenty of time.'

* * *

I headed down to Marine Parade after leaving the hospital and walked slowly west towards Madeira Place through the cold, dank morning. The sea and the sky were two merged planes of grey, the horizon as murkily indefinable as the future. The pier, where I met Jenny a week ago, loomed ahead of me, just as our meeting, and the foolish hopes I'd vested in it, faded behind me into the past. It was time to leave. But I had nowhere to go.

* * *

It was nearly noon when I reached the Sea Air. Brian and most of the cast and crew of *Lodger in the Throat* would be on the train to London by now. It was safe to make my own exit from Brighton, to beat my solitary retreat. I went straight down to the basement to say goodbye to Eunice and settle up. That would be it, I reckoned. I'd be on my own then.

How wrong can you be? Eunice had a visitor. More accurately, *I* had a visitor.

He was perched at the breakfast bar in her

kitchen, a mug of tea cradled in one hand, a grin plastered across his face. Blazered, cavalry-twilled and cravatted, Sydney Porteous was lurking in wait for me.

'There you are, Tobe,' he said, winking. 'Eunice had me half-believing you were going to stand me up.'

'What are you doing here, Syd?'

'Our lunch date. Don't you remember?'

Sunday lunch at Audrey's, with Syd. Yes, I did remember, albeit hazily, though why I'd agreed I certainly couldn't recall. 'I'm sorry. I'm going to have to cry off.'

'On account of these desperate goings-on Eunice has been telling me about? Understandable reaction, Tobe, entirely understandable. But let me urge you to reconsider. Not only because of Aud's legendary roast spuds, but because I reckon a spot of company could be just the ticket, given the doleful circs. You need taking out of yourself. And you can trust me to do the taking out.'

'I don't think so.'

'Syd's right, Toby,' Eunice put in. 'Go and have lunch.'

'Do you two know each other?' I asked, the conviviality of the atmosphere finally registering with me.

'Syd and I were in the same year at Elm Grove Primary,' Eunice trilled.

'Until the old man hit the jackpot and enrolled me at Brighton College,' said Syd. 'Who knows what might have happened if we hadn't been split up?' He rolled his eyes.

'Sorry, Syd. It's still no go. I've got to get back to London.'

'Why the big hurry?'

'It's . . . complicated. I just . . . have to go.'

'You won't regret staying on for a few hours, believe me.'

'Even so . . . '

'Truth is, Tobe, you *have* to stay.'

'Sorry?'

'You can't leave. Not yet.'

'What?'

'You see . . . ' Syd cleared his throat and grew suddenly serious. 'There's something I need to tell you. And you *do* need to hear it.'

* * *

I couldn't decide whether Syd was bluffing or not. In the end, it seemed easier to let him reveal the answer in his own good time. We loaded ourselves into his undersized and underpowered Fiat and set off towards Woodingdean, where I was given to understand Audrey Spencer lived and was even then labouring for our benefit over a hot stove.

'Bloody awful what happened yesterday, Tobe,' Syd said, much of his *bonhomie* gone now we'd left the Sea Air. 'Worse for you than anyone, of course, but a real choker for anyone who knew the people involved, even so.'

'How did you hear about it?'

'Gav was on to me last night with the gory details. Cold-blooded bastard, that bloke. No love lost between him and Roger, it's true, but you'd think Delia's death would knock him back. It certainly knocked me back. Not Gav, though. All he seemed bothered about was his inheritance.'

'Inheritance?'

'Roger's estate. Gav is sole surviving heir. Unless Roger bequeathed the lot to Battersea Dogs' Home. Which I doubt, worse luck. You'd have thought Gav had won the Lottery the way he was going on.'

'As you say. Cold-blooded. Like his nephew.'

'You ought to know I had a chinwag with Ray Braddock this morning. He told me what happened out at Beachy Head. I had a word with a copper I know as well. Seems you're a lucky man, Tobe.'

'I don't feel lucky.'

'Derek saved your life.' Syd glanced round at me. 'That's how I read it.'

'You read it right.' Something in the tone of Syd's voice and the look on his face when he mentioned Derek was strange, familiar, almost . . . affectionate. 'You talk as if you knew him.'

'I did.'

Syd slowed abruptly. We were driving along the open northern side of the Racecourse now. He flicked the indicator, pulled into a gateway and stopped. The passing traffic rocked the car as it sped by. Drizzle began to mist the windscreen. I said nothing.

'I've got you out here under false pretences, Tobe. There's no lunch waiting for us at Aud's. She's too upset to eat, let alone cook.'

'Why is she upset?'

'Because she knew Derek too.'

'How come?'

'She's a psychic, Tobe. A medium.'

'Audrey Spencer is a medium?'

'Yup.'

'A *practising* medium?'

'Now. *And* seven years ago. When Sir Walter Colborn consulted her.'

'My God.'

'Not sure if God comes into it, Tobe. Heaven. Hell. Purgatory. That's all down to your choice of religion, if you want to choose one. I'm strictly Church of Agnostics myself. But the spirit world? It's out there somewhere. Aud's convinced me of that. Her . . . powers . . . don't brook many quibbles, take my word for it.'

'You're saying she really put Sir Walter in touch with his dead wife?'

'I didn't know Aud then. But she's no con artist, that's for quite sure and absolutely certain. She believed it. Wally believed it. Well, you know that, don't you? You've heard the tape.'

'Yes. I've heard it. But I didn't recognize the woman's voice on it as Audrey's.'

'You wouldn't. She sounds different . . . in her trances. Halfway between herself and . . . whoever she's contacted.'

'Hold on.' A thought had struck me. 'You must have known about the tape hidden at Viaduct Road all along.'

'I gave Derek my word I'd keep out of his . . . campaign. Bumping into you at the Cricketers was a pure-as-the-driven-snow coincidence. Seeing where it might lead didn't mean

I'd broken my promise — as long as I didn't blow the whistle on Derek.'

'Audrey gave him the tape?'

'Wally left her in no doubt that he meant to do right by the Colbonite workers who were ill and the families of those who'd already died, as per Ann's urgings from beyond the grave. When he went to his own grave so soon after, Aud smelt a rat. She didn't do anything about it at first. But as the cancer cases kept mounting and Roger aren't-I-a-smart-arse Colborn kept popping up in *Sussex Life* society spreads, she . . . decided to act. She contacted Derek Oswin and told him what she knew. She records all her séances. Once Derek had listened to the tape of the one she'd held for Wally, there was no holding him. He went after Roger . . . in his surprisingly effective way.'

'You should have told me.'

'I'm a man of my word, Tobe. Hard though you may find that to believe. My hands were tied.'

'You should have stepped in. Before everything . . . got out of control.'

'I would have done, if I'd known what was going to happen. Just as you would have done, I guess.'

'Don't Audrey's powers extend to foreseeing the consequences of interfering in people's lives, then?'

'No.' Syd smiled at me ruefully. 'Since you ask, they don't.'

We sat in silence for a moment. Such anger as I felt faded as quickly as it had flared. It seemed we both had regrets aplenty.

'How's Jenny?' Syd asked eventually.

'Much as you'd expect.'

'Taken it hard, has she?'

'What do you think?'

'I think she's taken it hard. Aud's pretty cut up too. You ought to be prepared for that.'

'I thought lunch was off.'

'It is. But meeting isn't. She wants to see you.'

'Any particular reason?'

'Oh yes.' Syd started the car and squinted into the wing mirror. 'A very particular reason.'

* * *

A modern semi-detached house in a Woodingdean cul-de-sac isn't exactly the *locus operandi* I'd have imagined for a medium, genuine or otherwise. There were certainly no occupational trappings on view when Syd and I arrived. Audrey Spencer was waiting for us in her neatly decorated home, the sparkle in her eyes I remembered from our previous meeting replaced by welling tears, some of which she transferred to my cheek in the course of a welcoming hug.

'There are no words to describe how I feel, Toby,' she said, leading me into the lounge. 'Nor you either, I dare say. What a terrible, terrible thing to have happened.'

'Tobe reckons we should have levelled with him sooner, darling,' said Syd.

'It's useless to think such things,' Audrey responded, sinking into a sofa. 'Yet it's impossible not to.' She waved me into an armchair on the other side of the fireplace and gazed across at me. 'You can be no harder on me than I've been on myself, Toby. Blame me if you like. I don't mind.'

'I blame all of us,' I said, truly enough.

'Well, there's sense in that,' said Syd, settling on the sofa beside Audrey and closing his sausage-fingered paw round her clutched hands and the damp tissue squeezed between them. 'But blaming isn't undoing, if you know what I mean.'

'I wanted to punish Roger Colborn for thwarting the good intentions Ann had inspired in Walter,' said Audrey. 'It's not often my calling has such an obviously beneficial effect. To see it frustrated as it was rankled with me. Through Derek I saw a way to do something about it.'

'You succeeded,' I said. 'Roger was certainly punished.'

'Yes. But for Derek to die as well . . . and poor Mrs Sheringham . . . ' Sobs overcame her. Syd released her hands so that she could staunch her tears with the tissue while he wrapped an arm round her shoulders and whispered some soothing endearment in her ear. 'I'm sorry, Toby. Please forgive me. I feel things . . . perhaps a little more deeply than I should.'

'Don't worry. It's all right.'

'You should tell him now, darling,' Syd prompted. 'About the tape.'

We'd come, then, to Audrey's *very particular reason*. Syd swivelled round to pluck some replacement tissues for her from a box on a shelf behind the sofa. She dried her eyes and blew her nose.

'Well, Toby, the thing is this. None of us may have foreseen these dreadful events. But it seems . . . Derek had some inkling . . . that it might all go terribly wrong.'

'How do you know that?'

'I . . . sense certain things, Toby. It's part of my calling. Or my curse, depending how you look at it. Anyway, this morning I . . . played the tape of the séance I conducted for Walter. Derek copied the original and returned it to me several months ago. Something made me . . . play it to the end. And there I found . . . waiting for me . . . for us . . . a message . . . from Derek.'

'What did it say?'

'Hear for yourself.' She picked up a remote that had been lying, unnoticed by me, on the arm of the sofa, aimed it at a hi-fi stack in the corner of the room and pressed a button.

There was a click from the tape player, followed, after a pause of a few seconds, by Derek's voice.

'I don't know whether you'll ever hear this. Perhaps I'm being too clever by half. Dad often said I was. And Dad was right about most things. Not everything, though. He shouldn't have accepted Roger Colborn's offer. He shouldn't have agreed to kill Sir Walter. The fact that he did it for my sake only makes it worse. But he was ill. He wasn't thinking straight. I forgive him. Roger Colborn wasn't ill, though. He knew exactly

what he was doing. I don't forgive him. And I won't, until he's paid for what he did. I've thought of a way to make him pay now. It involves Toby Flood, the actor. He's coming to Brighton in December to perform in a play. His estranged wife, Jennifer, lives with Roger Colborn. That's the connection I propose to exploit. I'll tell you about it soon. But not all about it. There are risks, you see. More than I'll let you know of. They'll be worth running, though. I hope to do more than punish Roger Colborn. I hope to make him see the error of his ways. And to atone for them. I also hope to persuade him to acknowledge me as his brother. Because that's what we are. Brothers. And brothers shouldn't be apart. They should be together. Which is what I think Roger and I can be, at the end of this, if all goes well. But if it doesn't go well, I want you to know that it's my fault. Not yours, Mrs Spencer, or Mr Porteous's, or even Mr Flood's. But mine. I accept full responsibility for the consequences of my actions. Dad would have said that's what growing up is all about. Thanks for helping me understand what I have to do, Mrs Spencer. And just in case I need to say it: goodbye.'

'Derek exonerates us, Toby,' said Audrey, after the tape had run to the end and clicked off. 'One and all.'

I looked across at her. 'But can we exonerate ourselves?'

'I don't know. I only know he'd want us to. And therefore . . . perhaps we should.'

* * *

'Will you try to contact him?' I asked Audrey a little while later, as I stood in the open doorway of her house. Syd was already sitting in his car, waiting for me, with the engine running. I'd left the obvious question late. But not too late.

'Of course,' she replied. 'But the dead speak — or not — as they please. I don't contact them. *They* contact *me*. I'll try. But the question is: will he? He may have said . . . all he has to say.'

'Do you think he really knew what was going to happen?'

'Yes. But without necessarily knowing that he knew. They died together, didn't they, he and Roger? Together. Not apart.'

It was true. I'd seen them fall. I knew. Derek had been acknowledged by his brother. In the end.

* * *

Neither Syd nor I felt the need to say much as we drove back to the Sea Air. Syd's loquacity had reached its limit long since. And my thoughts could no longer be expressed in words.

It was a relief in a way to find that Eunice wasn't at home. I fetched my bag from my room, left the key, a farewell note and a cheque on the hall table, then let myself out.

'That was quick,' said Syd as I climbed back into his car.

'Eunice wasn't there,' I explained.

'We can wait, if you like.'

'No need.'

'Had a bellyful of goodbyes, have you, Tobe?'

'Yes. I think I have.'

'Understood.' He started away. 'I'll keep ours short and sweet.'

'Thanks. In return, I won't take you to task for playing fast and loose with the facts during our sessions at the Cricketers.'

'I never told you any out-and-out porkies, Tobe.'

'Didn't you?'

'Well, maybe just the one. And it didn't amount to anything.'

'Which one was that?'

'When we first bumped into each other in the Cricketers last Sunday, I told you I'd met Joe Orton there on a Sunday night in the summer of 'sixty-seven. Not strictly true, I have to admit. In fact, not true at all.'

'You made it up?'

' 'Fraid so.'

'Why?'

'Sensed our chance encounter was slipping through my fingers. Needed something to get your attention. Keep us talking. Simple as that.'

'But how did you know you could get away with it? I've read Orton's diaries. He was in Brighton the last weekend of July, nineteen sixty-seven. And he was out on the town, alone, on the Sunday night. So, theoretically, you could have met him. I can't believe you just got lucky with your choice of day.'

'Ah, well . . . ' Syd treated me to a sly, sidelong grimace. 'Truth is, there was this dwarf lodging in the same house as me back then. Used to perform on the pier. Made up in personality what he lacked in height. After Orton's murder was splashed all over the papers, he told me he'd — '

'It's OK,' I interrupted, recalling Orton's matter-of-fact account of oral sex in a Brighton public convenience on Sunday, 30 July 1967. 'I get the picture.'

'You do?'

'In Cinemascope. Besides . . . ' We'd passed the Royal Pavilion by now. It wasn't much further to the station. 'You don't have time to do justice to the story, Syd. Leave me to imagine the details.'

* * *

Fifteen minutes later, I was sitting alone at a table outside Bonaparte's Bar at the edge of the station concourse, sipping a whisky to while away the half-hour I had to wait for the next train to London. I'd pulled my copy of *The Orton Diaries* out of my bag to double-check Syd's story. Orton's encounter with Syd's neighbour, the cottaging dwarf, was much as I remembered it.

What I'd forgotten, though, was that afterwards Orton had gone into the station for a cup of tea. The café he'd used had presumably transmogrified itself since into Bonaparte's Bar. Selling whisky on a Sunday afternoon back then would have been inconceivable as well as illegal, of course. But that and most of the other changes were largely superficial. Thirty-five years, four months and one week ago, Orton could have been sitting exactly where I was sitting today.

'I had a cup of tea at the station,' he wrote. *'I thought a lot about* Prick Up Your Ears.' (The next play he was planning to write, but, in the event, never did.) *'And things in general.'*

Ah yes. Things in general. 'They can be a bugger, can't they, Joe?' I murmured.

⋆ ⋆ ⋆

The train was announced. I went through the barrier and boarded one of the front carriages, hoping that would mean no-one would sit next to me. I'd bought an *Observer* to hide behind if I needed to.

I looked out of the window. There was a view across the platforms of the station car park, washed with rain, and, beyond that, the soaring flank of St Bartholomew's Church. I checked my watch. We'd be under way in a few minutes. I was taking my leave of Brighton. My week was over. My time was up. In so many more ways than one.

⋆ ⋆ ⋆

Then I saw something I couldn't quite believe. A woman was hurrying across the car park towards the station: a woman in jeans and a short waterproof; a woman I recognized very well.

I watched, transfixed, as she moved out of the rain into the shelter of the station canopy and headed along the far platform towards the concourse, her pace quickening as she went.

Then I too started moving.

* * *

I forced a passage to the barrier through a ruck of London-bound passengers. Jenny was standing beyond them on the concourse, staring at me between their shoulders and hoisted bags. They were there, jostling past me. But, in another sense, they weren't there at all.

My ticket wouldn't operate the exit gate. I kept looking at Jenny as I moved to the manned barrier, mumbled a request to be let out and was ushered through.

'I didn't expect to see you,' was all I could manage to say when I finally reached her.

'I didn't expect you would either,' she said softly.

'How did you know which train I was catching?'

'I didn't. I went to the Sea Air first. Eunice had just got back and found your note. She hadn't been out long, though, so we reckoned it was worth me coming on here. I very much wanted . . . not to leave things as they were.'

'How do you want to leave them, then?'

She shrugged. 'I'm not really sure.'

* * *

I went back to Bonaparte's Bar. This time, I wasn't alone. I bought Jenny a cup of coffee. And myself another whisky. We sat at the table I'd only recently vacated. The London train pulled out. The hubbub it had generated died. The concourse grew quiet enough for me to hear the cooing of a pigeon from some perch above us in the station roof.

'I don't know what to say,' I admitted.

'Neither do I,' said Jenny.

'Shall we just sit here, then?' I suggested. 'Until we think of something.'

We looked at each other. Several seconds passed. Then Jenny smiled hesitantly. 'Yes,' she said. 'Let's do that.'

And we did.

End of transcription

LATER DAYS

Lodger in the Throat by Joe Orton ran for five months on the London stage. The part of James Elliott was played throughout the run by Toby Flood. He never missed a performance.

* * *

The High Court upheld a claim by a group of twelve former employees of Colbonite Ltd to the estate of Roger Colborn, who was found to have died intestate. Under the rules of intestacy, his estate devolved upon his half-brother, Derek Oswin, who had died with him, but, being the younger of the two, was deemed to have died second. Derek Oswin had on the other hand made a will, the terms of which were therefore held to apply to Roger Colborn's estate. Derek Oswin's property was left to be shared among any former employees of Colbonite Ltd in need of financial assistance. Gavin Colborn, Roger Colborn's uncle and only surviving blood relative, appealed against this decision, but died before the appeal could be heard. An inquest subsequently found that he had suffered a fatal head injury in a fall down a steep flight of stairs at his home in Brighton while under the influence of alcohol.

* * *

Jennifer Flood never made the necessary application to the High Court for her divorce from Toby Flood to be declared final and absolute. The couple remain married.

Acknowledgements

I am indebted to the following for the help they generously gave me in the writing of this book. My dear friend Georgina James plied me with invaluable information about Brighton as well as various nuggets of legal advice. Peter Wilkins, David Bownes and the great man himself, Duncan Weldon, ensured my portrait of an actor did not stray too far from the reality with which they are so familiar. Veronica Hamilton-Deeley provided a diligent coroner's perspective on events. And Renée-Jean and Tim Wilkin ensured that those fictional events took place in genuine Brighton weather. Thank you, all.

Other titles published by
The House of Ulverscroft:

SIGHT UNSEEN

Robert Goddard

1981. The peace of a summer's day at the ancient stone circle of Avebury is shattered by the abduction of two-year-old Tamsin Hall and the violent death of her sister Miranda. One of the witnesses, Ph.D. student David Umber, was waiting at the nearby pub to meet a man called Griffin who claimed he could help him with his researches into the identity of Junius, pen-name of the famous and mysterious eighteenth-century letter-writer. But Griffin never showed up. Nine years later, notorious paedophile Brian Radd confessed to Tamsin's murder and the case was closed. However, in 2004, retired Chief Inspector George Sharp seeks Umber's help in reopening his inquiry. He has never believed Radd to be guilty. And he has received a letter reproaching him for botching the original investigation — signed Junius.

PAST CARING

Robert Goddard

Martin Radford, history graduate, disaffected and unemployed, jumps at the chance to visit Madeira at the invitation of an old university friend who is running the local English language newspaper. Luck continues to run for him when he is offered a lucrative commission to research the mysterious resignation and subsequent obscure retirement on Madeira of Edwardian cabinet minister Edwin Strafford. However, his investigation triggers a bizarre and inevitably violent train of events which remorselessly entangles him and those who believed they had escaped the spectre of crimes long past but never paid for.